Wives & Sweethearts

Wives & Sweethearts

LILIAN HARRY

LONDON NEW YORK SYDNEY TORONTO

This edition published 1999
by BCA
by arrangement with Macmillan
an imprint of Orion Books Ltd
CN 1782

Typeset at The Spartan Press Ltd,
Lymington, Hants

Printed and bound in Germany by
Graphischer Grossbetrieb Pössneck GmbH

To Rosemary de Courcy
With many thanks for all her encouragement and support

'To wives and sweethearts . . . may they never meet.'

Traditional Naval Toast

Chapter One

The shrill of the bell sliced through the quiet murmur of the ward, signifying the end of visiting time. Clare, lying on her back in the high hospital bed and holding her husband's hand tightly in her own, felt as if it had sliced her life in two.

In a few moments, Martyn would walk out of her life, leaving her to face alone the reality of childbirth, the unknown of a baby, a new person for whom she – and only she – would be responsible. For her, within hours, life would change for ever, while for him it would be just as he had planned and expected it to be. And it would be a year before he could even begin to catch up. A year before she would see him again.

The bell rang for a second time. They stared at each other, agonised.

'I've got to go,' Martyn said miserably. 'Oh, *Clare* . . .'

'It's all right.' She gazed at him, her brown eyes almost black with misery, trying to memorise every detail of his face, trying to ignore the slow tightening of her stomach. 'I know.' Her mouth quivered suddenly and she turned her head away slightly, feeling the hard lump in her throat. The tightening sensation had eased. She reached out her hand and touched his face, letting her fingertips move slowly over cheeks, chin, eyebrows, nose, as if trying to learn his features that way. It'll be a year before I can do this again, she thought despairingly, a whole year. We won't be together again till 1960. Nineteen-*sixty*. And we'll be different people then. We'll be parents. Her stomach tightened again.

'I'm sure it's starting. I'm sure it is.' Her hand shook. 'If it's born before five o'clock in the morning, you'll be able to see it. Just for a few minutes. Oh, Martyn, you will ring up, won't you? Just in case.'

'Of course I will, but I won't be able to come for long. The ship sails at seven o'clock.' He laid his face beside hers on the pillow and kissed her lips. 'It's you I want to see most. I don't know how I'm going to get through it. A year. A whole year.' He rubbed his nose gently against her cheek and stroked her long fair hair, lifting it in his hand and winding it round his fingers. 'At least you'll have your family and Kathy to keep you company.'

Kathy Stubbs was Clare's best friend. They had known each other for years – since they were five years old and had sat nervously at the same desk in infants' class on their first day at school. Kathy's fiancé Brian and Martyn had been friends for years too, and had been apprentices together at HMS Collingwood. Now they were serving on the same ship. The four of them had met at a Collingwood dance and had gone about together a lot, sometimes swimming at Stokes Bay or going to a summer show at South Parade Pier in Southsea. They'd got engaged at about the same time, but when they found that the ship would be away for a year, Clare and Martyn had brought their wedding forward while Kathy and Brian had decided to wait.

When the boys were away, the two girls would meet at least once a week, and Kathy had been into the maternity home once already, in the week before the ship came into Portsmouth harbour. She was almost as excited about the baby as Clare.

The bell rang again, insistently, warning the stragglers. The other husbands were straightening up, moving away from their wives' beds. Nobody glanced towards the corner where Clare and Martyn struggled with their goodbyes. They all knew that he was going away for a whole year, and that Clare's baby was due almost any minute. They kept their faces averted, to give the couple as much privacy as they could. It was such a shame that they couldn't have spent their last night together in their own home, the new bungalow they had scraped together the money to buy, instead of in this public place.

'I don't know why they can't let you have your curtains drawn,' Marge in the next bed had said as the women sat up in bed, brushed and combed and made-up, waiting for visiting time to start. 'It's cruel, making you say goodbye in front of everyone.'

'It's so that no one thinks there's something wrong.' Clare had asked the staff nurse already and been refused. 'Someone might get scared.' But they would soon have been reassured, she thought. Everyone in the ward knew about her and Martyn. Not that it had mattered all that much anyway. She and Martyn were too absorbed in each other to worry that others might be watching them. Nothing mattered on this night, in their last few moments together for a whole long year.

It was their last kiss. She felt his lips, hungry and despairing. She clung to him, wanting to pour all her love into this last anguished caress. For just a few moments more, he was here in her arms, warm and solid, smelling of that curious smell that was his alone, a mixture of coaltar soap and sweat and fresh white shirt and navy-blue doeskin uniform. She drew in her breath, wanting to hold his warmth, his scent, in her memory and in her heart.

'Goodbye, Clare, my darling,' he whispered, and she closed her eyes as he drew away.

'Goodbye, Martyn.' Determinedly, she held on to her voice, willing it not to shake. 'Take – take care of yourself. Write as often as you can.'

'I'll write every day.'

He was standing up. He was moving away. She watched him turn from her, walk down the ward. At the door, he paused and looked back and lifted his hand. She touched her fingers to her lips, and then he was gone. The space where he had stood was empty.

She caught one more glimpse of him, walking past the window, lagging a little behind the other husbands, his head bent as if he was trying to hide his tears. A tall, slender young man, not quite twenty-three years old, soon to be a father. Perhaps tonight. Perhaps after all this wasn't their goodbye and he would be back in the morning, arriving with the first trill of the blackbird, to catch a glimpse of their baby almost as soon as it was born. But she didn't think it was likely. The contractions, if that was what they were, were too faint, too far apart. The nurses had told her that first babies usually took longer to arrive. There wasn't much chance that this one would be born before morning.

Now he was truly gone, and the ward was beginning its late-night bustle. The flowers had to be taken out to a side room by the mothers who were up and about, the cocoa and biscuits handed round, the babies brought in for their last feed. Clare, who was not allowed out of bed except to go to the toilet, and who had no baby to feed, lay back on her pillows. She stared for a minute or two at the sketch she had once made of Martyn and had framed beside her bed, but it made her want to cry and she looked round for the first time and caught Marge's eye.

'You all right?' the other girl said, and Clare nodded. 'I think you're ever so brave. I couldn't let my chap go off like that, knowing I'd not see him again for a year. I'd be in floods.'

'It wouldn't help him, would it?' Clare said. 'It'd just make us both feel worse.' She knew that if she started to cry now she wouldn't be able to stop. The lump in her throat was so hard she could barely swallow the cocoa, and the biscuit was as dry as sand.

She watched the babies come in, the nurses carrying two at a time, one on each arm, and she felt her stomach tighten again, but that was all it was: just a tight feeling. It wasn't a pain. The baby wasn't going to be born this side of tomorrow.

'I think I'll go to sleep,' she said, and lay down, turning on her side away from the other women, looking at the drawing again. He'd be on the bus now, she thought, going down to Portsmouth harbour. He'd get on the little ferryboat and chug across to Pompey, and then walk up the Hard on the other side and in at the dockyard gate and through the yard, past HMS *Victory* in her dry dock and so to the Southern Railway jetty where his own ship was moored. And then he'd get undressed, folding all his clothes neatly and putting them in his locker, perhaps looking for a minute or two at the picture of the Isle of Wight she had drawn for him. Then he'd get into his bunk and lie there like her, maybe sleeping, maybe just lying awake, dreading the long, empty year that stretched ahead.

Except that it wouldn't be empty. By the time they met again, Martyn would have been all round the world. He would have been to the Far East, to Australia, to the Caribbean. And Clare would have had her first baby. The baby would be a year old.

You knew it would be like this, she told herself. You knew if you married a sailor you'd have to be separated a lot. But she hadn't known that she'd have to let him go the night before their baby was born. She hadn't known that the pain of letting him go was going to be like this.

Her stomach tightened again, slowly, softly, like the tender squeeze of a lover, but it still couldn't really be called a pain, and it wasn't enough to keep her awake. Worn out by bitten-back misery, she closed her eyes and slept.

When she woke next morning, it was half-past seven and Martyn's ship had been at sea for thirty minutes.

Martyn was on deck as it steamed slowly out of the harbour, passing the masts of HMS *Victory* in her dry dock, and the semaphore tower to the port side, and the jostling yachts at Camper & Nicholson's, and the ferry pontoon at Gosport to starboard. He gazed longingly up the little creeks in the direction of Elson, where Clare was lying in her bed at the maternity home. He'd telephoned at five, as he'd promised, but there was no news and he'd been half disappointed and half relieved, knowing that there would have been barely time for him to get there and back in time for the sailing, and such a brief time together, even seeing the baby, would have been almost too painful to bear.

It had never occurred to him, when he'd signed up for twelve years' service, that he would fall so deeply in love, or that leaving would tear him apart like this. Going to sea had been his ambition ever since he'd first been taken to Plymouth as a small boy and gone aboard one of the naval ships in Devonport. Although it hadn't quite fulfilled his romantic, boyish dreams – the life was harder than he'd expected – it was also much more demanding and satisfying. And he liked the companionship of the other men, and the runs ashore in foreign ports.

All the same, he had never foreseen the dreadful ache of having to leave the woman he loved, and the thought of her giving birth to his baby – perhaps at this very moment – and then being on her own for a whole year, stabbed him with anguish. A whole year before he saw her again, a year before he saw his child for the first time. It wouldn't be a baby by then, it would be a toddler, crawling, perhaps even walking, starting to talk. Would Clare teach it to say 'Daddy'? Would she show it his photograph, and would the baby understand?

Suppose it didn't like him . . .

'Come on, Martyn,' Brian said as they made their way down to the mess. 'A year's not so long, really. And babies aren't much cop for the first few months. It'll just be getting interesting when you go home.'

'Well, it's all part of the deal, I know,' Martyn said, casting a last look at the Gosport shoreline as the ship passed out of the harbour into the Solent. 'And Clare understands that too. But it still tears you to bits.' He glanced at his friend. 'Don't you feel that too? Aren't you missing Kathy already?'

'Yes. Yes, I am.' Brian, too, gave a last swift look at the ferry gardens. Kathy had promised to be there to wave goodbye and he was sure he could see her, leaning on the rails. 'But I'm not going to let it stop me enjoying this. A year at sea, Martyn! Think of it – and think of all the places we're going to see. It's what we always wanted. We're going to have a whale of a time.'

He clattered swiftly down the gangway and Martyn followed more slowly. The smell of frying bacon was wafting up from the mess and he was aware of sudden hunger. He still ached for Clare, but he knew Brian was right. They'd dreamed of this for years. There was no point in not making the most of it.

Sixteen, that's all Clare Whiting had been when she'd first met Martyn Perry, and he'd been nineteen. He was an apprentice at HMS Collingwood, the Naval shore training station between Gosport and Fareham. He'd just got a motorbike and joined the local motorcycle club. Clare's brother Ian belonged to the club too, and Clare often went with him to watch the trials or scrambles that the club organised. She'd met Martyn at one of them.

Ian was in the Navy too. He was in the Fleet Air Arm, servicing aircraft. He'd been away a lot when Clare was younger, serving his own apprenticeship in Scotland, and then spending time at sea on aircraft carriers. At the time when Clare had met Martyn, he was stationed at HMS *Siskin*, in Gosport, and able to live at home with her and Mum and Dad. He'd been specially active in the motorcycle club then, and had encouraged Martyn to join in the activities.

'Not many Collingwood boys join local things,' he'd said when he was telling the family about the young apprentice who'd turned up with a little 197cc motorbike. 'They go to dances and that sort of thing, but that's about all. He'd make a nice boyfriend for Clare.' He winked at his sister.

'Clare doesn't need a boyfriend,' their father said at once. 'She's only just turned sixteen. Plenty of time for her to be thinking about that sort of thing. We've got enough trouble with our Val.'

Valerie was their elder daughter. She was two years older than Clare and the two sisters had always been good friends. Now Valerie was talking about getting engaged to Maurice Hutchins across the road, whom she'd been going out with for the past eighteen months, and the subject seemed to occupy every conversation. Bill Whiting didn't have any objection to Maurice himself – he'd known the Hutchins family ever since they moved into Abbeville Avenue before the war – but he didn't approve of young girls getting serious about boys too soon. On the other hand, he still expected them to get married and have children rather than jobs, and as Valerie remarked, you couldn't have it both ways.

'He just likes to assert his authority,' she said unworriedly. 'He'll come round, once he's convinced himself it's his decision.'

'Like Mum, when she wants the living-room wallpapered,' Clare said, giggling. 'She puts the idea into his head and then waits for him to come out with it as if it was his in the first place.'

Valerie and Maurice wanted to get engaged on Valerie's birthday in July. Valerie, who worked in Portsmouth, spent all her lunchtimes wandering down Commercial Road, gazing into the windows of the jewellers' shops, choosing her ring. Clare had gone over on the ferry with her one Saturday afternoon and had a look for herself. She wondered what ring she would choose when her time came.

Not that that would be for years yet, if Dad didn't even think she was ready for a boyfriend at sixteen.

The next Sunday, Clare went to the club trial at Browndown with Ian and looked out for the young naval apprentice. He was there with his little blue bike, looking out of place in his uniform: apprentices weren't supposed to wear civvies when they came out of Collingwood. He wasn't taking part in the trial but he was standing by one of the sections, watching as the riders came through.

Browndown was a large area of rough ground between Gosport and Lee-on-the-Solent. It had been used by the military during the war and was still nominally under their control, but it was open now for people to go and wander its paths and little woods, and pick blackberries. There were numerous little hummocks and hollows amongst the bracken, left by the explosions of military exercises, and children used these to make dens or play games. It was ideal terrain for the rough scrambling or trials-riding so beloved by the motorcycle club.

Clare went out on her pushbike, riding down the long, straight Military Road, past *Siskin*. She left the main road and cycled along the rough track till she came to the part they were using for the trial. They had marked out a number of sections which would make tricky little tests for the motorcyclists – narrow, twisting paths through the trees, along ditches and in and out of the steep little hollows. You were supposed to get through in a certain time, without having to put your feet down for balance. Most of the riders fell off at some point and landed in deep, soft mud, to the delight of the onlookers. There was a watersplash too, which they all went through as fast as they could, sending up clouds of mucky spray.

When they had all gone through one section, the little crowd moved off together to the next. Clare found herself next to the tall young sailor.

'Hullo,' she said, catching his eye. 'You must be the chap my brother was telling me about. You're at Collingwood.'

'That's right,' he said, looking surprised that anyone would have bothered to discuss him. 'Is your brother in the motorcycle club?'

'Yes, he's Ian Whiting. That's him, coming through now.' They watched as Ian approached the steep hummock above the watersplash. His bike gathered speed as it came down the slope and it hit the deep puddle at the bottom with a shower of liquid mud. Everyone squealed and ducked out of the way, and Ian emerged from the deluge with his teeth grinning white through the grime plastered on his face.

'Mum'll never let him in the house,' Clare said with a giggle. 'He has to hose his bike down every Sunday afternoon before Dad will even let it in the garden. He'll have to hose himself down as well this afternoon.'

'I don't think I'd better stand too near,' the young apprentice said, looking down at his uniform. 'I wish they'd let us wear civvies when we come out. It's a darned nuisance having to worry about your clothes all the time. Number eights would be better for this job.'

Clare knew all about the numbered grades of uniform that the artificers wore. Standing somewhere between the matelots in square rig and the officers with scrambled egg and gold rings, the 'tiffies', as artificers were known, wore suits and peaked caps. Number ones were their best uniforms, kept for special occasions, and from there you went on down to number eights, the overalls that could get as dirty as necessary.

'You ought to bring them out with you,' she said. 'Or put your number eights over the top.'

'I would, if I had anywhere to change. I'd be in trouble if anyone saw me, all the same. Your brother could shop me if he wanted to.'

'Ian wouldn't do that. He's been through it all himself.'

She hesitated. Dad didn't want her to have a boyfriend yet, but this was Ian's friend, not hers. And she'd often heard Mum say what a shame it was that all these young boys were away from home and how nice it would be to invite one of them to tea some time, just for the friendliness of it. She'd hoped someone would do the same for Ian when he'd been far away in Scotland.

'Would you like to come back to tea with us?' she asked. 'Mum wouldn't mind, and you can talk motorbikes with Ian.'

Martyn looked at her. He was quite good-looking, she thought. He must be at least six feet tall, a bit thin, but that was better than being fat, and he had nice blue eyes. Clare's were brown, very dark, and she'd often wished they could have been blue, which would have gone better with her pale blonde hair. All the Whiting family had eyes of some shade of brown. He had a nice smile too, she noticed.

'Thanks. I'd like that. If you're sure it'll be all right.' He paused. 'I'll take you on the back of my bike, if you like. Or will you be going with Ian?'

'On that mucky thing? No thanks! I came on my pushbike. It's not all that far.'

They watched the rest of the trial together. At the end, everyone's points were added up and a small silver cup presented to the winner. Ian came second. He received an even smaller cup, which he accepted with great pride. It was about big enough to put a robin's egg in, Clare thought, but it would look nice on the mantelpiece alongside the other bits and pieces that had been acquired over the years.

As Clare had promised, Iris Whiting wasn't in the least put out by the unexpected visitor. She opened another tin of pilchards, set another place at the table and put an extra teaspoon of tea into the pot, taking it for granted that Ian had invited the young apprentice back. They all sat round the table together and Bill Whiting asked the boy what his job was, and seemed impressed when Martyn said he was training to be a radio and electrical artificer.

'That's good. You'll have a decent trade at your fingertips when you come out. Say what you like, the Services give a chap a good grounding. Get a job anywhere. Mind you, if you've got any sense you'll stay in, you'll never get the same security anywhere else. I keep telling our Ian that.'

'I haven't decided yet,' Martyn said. 'I'm in till I'm thirty, anyway. If I still like it then, I might have a go at getting promoted above deck.'

'Above deck!' Clare said. 'You mean be an officer?'

'That's right. Chaps do, sometimes. You can get quite high these days.'

'Catch me doing that,' Ian said, helping himself to salad to go with an extra pilchard. 'I'm coming out as soon as my twelve years are up. The Navy might give you a good grounding, but they want to own you. Civvy Street's the place to be.'

'Ian!' his mother said. 'You've only been in the Navy five minutes.'

'Five years,' Ian corrected her, 'and it feels like a lifetime. I'll be glad when I can thumb my nose at 'em, I'll tell you that.'

Bill looked down his nose. 'Don't know when you're well off, that's your trouble. Why, when I was a boy it was considered a privilege to serve in the Royal Navy. And there was plenty would have liked your job, during the Depression.'

'And what about during the war?' Ian said. 'Was it a privilege to get killed?'

Bill flushed an angry red. He had been in the Navy himself until 1930, when he'd come out and gone to work in Portsmouth dockyard. He'd gone back into the Navy during the Second World War and narrowly escaped drowning when his ship had been sunk. He was back in the dockyard now, a big solid man doing a hard day's work and proud of it.

'Listen,' he said, 'I've *seen* blokes getting killed during the war. Good blokes, better than you're ever likely to be. And, yes, as a matter of fact, I think they *were* proud to die. They died for their country, and their names are up on that war memorial to prove it. And they're entitled to a bit of respect.'

'All right, Bill,' his wife said. 'No need to get all aerated.' She was small and round, with a smiling face and white hair, and seldom got flustered. She turned to Martyn. 'Would you like a bit of fruit cake?'

'Yes, please, Mrs Whiting,' he said, and she cut him a generous slice. 'It's good to have a real tea. I miss my mum's fruit cake.'

'Where d'you come from?' she asked him. 'You sound a bit West Country.'

He nodded. 'I'm from Devon. Little place called Ivybridge. It's not far from Plymouth – near Dartmoor. My mum and dad keep a shop there – electrical stuff, mostly – and Dad does electrical repairs.'

'Dartmoor!' Bill said. 'I went there once. Gloomy sort of place, I thought it was – all fist and mog.' The family laughed and Martyn looked bewildered. Clare took pity on him.

'Dad's always doing that – swapping round words and letters. They're called spoonerisms, Dad,' she told her father. 'I heard about it the other day on the radio. There was this man at Oxford called Dr Spooner, he was a lecturer in one of the colleges, and he did it all the time. He told one of his students once that he had tasted two whole worms, hissed all his mystery lectures and been caught fighting a liar – see, Dad? – in the quad, and he told him to leave Oxford by the next town drain.'

'He did what?' It took Bill a few minutes and at least two repetitions to figure all this out, but at last he laughed and slapped his knee. 'Well, d'you hear that, Iris? If an Oxford don can do it too, I'm in good company. I must be brighter than I thought.'

'I reckon you could pass exams in it,' Iris commented dryly, knowing that her husband would be worse than ever now that he had, as it were, official permission.

Bill loved to play with words, using the wrong ones deliberately and making puns. He drove small children mad by referring solemnly to herds of sheep and flocks of cows, and he swapped about the first letters of words or even whole words themselves, so that his conversation was peppered with phrases like 'roaring with pain' to describe a wet day, or 'let's fight the liar' on a cold one. Sometimes the phrases turned out rather rude and Iris scolded him, but all the children could see that she was trying not to laugh.

'If you say that thing about darting about among the fishes once more . . .' she warned him, but he gazed back at her with an innocent look on his face.

'I can't help it, Iris, you know I can't. It's like stammering – a peach insediment.' And she had to laugh despite herself.

Martyn stayed till nine o'clock, helping Ian to wash down his bike and look it over for any repairs that might need doing after its rough afternoon, and then coming in to listen to *Variety Bandbox* on the wireless with the rest of them. Iris made cocoa and he drank a cup before standing up to go.

'Thanks a lot,' he said. 'It's been really nice. I hope I see you again.'

'Well, so do I,' Iris said. 'Any friend of Ian's is welcome here. Come to tea any Sunday. We'll be pleased to see you.'

He thanked her and then looked suddenly awkward, as if he didn't know quite how to get out of the door. He glanced at Clare.

Clare stood up. 'I'll see you out.' She went past him and opened the door to the little passage leading to the front door. Out in the cool evening air, she looked at him and giggled. 'They think Ian asked you back!'

'I know.' He grinned. 'Does it matter?'

Clare considered. 'I don't think so. So long as you come again. You will, won't you?'

'I'd like to,' he said. 'Look, there's a scramble on next Sunday, up at Trafalgar Farm. Will you and Ian be going to that?'

'I expect Ian will,' she said. 'I hadn't thought about it yet. But I could.'

'I could come and fetch you,' he said. 'Save you riding your pushbike up Portsdown Hill.'

Clare had ridden up Portsdown Hill plenty of times. But she nodded and smiled at him.

'All right. Come round after dinner, and then you can come back to tea afterwards.'

They both grinned with sudden excitement. Then he got on his bike, kicked it into noisy life, and roared off up the street. Clare watched him out of sight before turning to go back indoors.

I reckon I've got a boyfriend, she thought with a shiver of delight.

Chapter Two

The rest of the women came and gathered round Clare's bed, sitting there with her all morning, knitting and chatting. Some of them had husbands in the Royal Navy too, and knew what it was like to be separated for long periods. They understood the loneliness, the hours spent writing letters, the eagerness with which their husbands' letters were awaited. They all felt sorry for Clare, having to say goodbye only hours before her baby was born.

'She's such a kid, too,' one of them commented later when Clare was in the bathroom. They hadn't realised the door was slightly ajar and she might hear as they talked about her. Listeners never hear good of themselves, she thought as she stood before the mirror, her hands freezing in the middle of brushing her long hair. All the same, she didn't move away or pull the door shut.

'Not twenty till July, she told me. It's too young to be married and expecting, if you ask me. Her mum and dad ought to have known better.' Jean Baker was the oldest mother in the ward, thirty-six years old and having her fourth. She was a nice enough woman but had great faith in her own opinions. 'They ought to have made her wait till he came back. Now she's tied to a baby and a house, and she's not even out of her teens.'

'Seems older, though,' Marge said fairly. 'I mean, she's not a flibbertigibbet. She's got her head screwed on.'

'I'm not saying she hasn't. What I'm saying is, she's being left with a lot of responsibility, and it ain't fair on a youngster. She ought to have been let to have a bit more of her own life before getting saddled with a baby. And going in for a mortgage at their age! Daft, I call it.'

Clare decided she had heard enough. She gave her hair one last fierce brush, ran water noisily into the washbasin and then pushed open the door. The other women were talking about something else by the time she came through it, some of them sitting in their beds, others in the small armchairs that were gathered in a circle in the middle of the ward. They looked up as she came in, smiling sympathetically. She tried to smile back, knowing they meant well but feeling annoyed about the way they'd criticised her parents. Mum and Dad had understood, she thought indignantly; they knew how much she and Martyn loved each other, they knew how much they'd wanted to be married before he went away . . . Her smile started out well and then twisted a little as her stomach tightened more painfully than before.

'A pain?' Marge asked at once. 'Here, get back on your bed. I'll call Sister.'

'It's all right. It's gone now. It wasn't that bad – just took me by surprise.' She heaved herself on to her bed and looked at them, forgetting her annoyance. 'Do you think it's really starting?'

'I reckon it must be. Your waters have been broken for days now. It's got to start soon.' Marge surveyed her. She had had her baby boy three days earlier and was allowed out of bed now. 'You know, that doctor could've started you off by now. They can't let you go much longer, you'll be dry as a bone.'

'I asked him on Thursday. I asked if he could bring it on, so Martyn could see it.' Clare paused as the contraction began again. It started in the small of her back and slowly drew itself around her body, around the swelling of her abdomen, like a broad belt being too tightly fastened. 'He said no. He said we still have to leave some things to the Almighty.'

Marge sniffed. 'It's not him having the baby, though, is it? They'd induce you fast enough if it suited them.'

'He said they'd think about it if I hadn't had the baby by Monday.'

'Well, there's one thing certain,' another of the women observed. 'It won't stay there much longer. They all do get born in the end, even if it seems like they never will.'

The next time the sister came into the ward Clare told her that the contractions were coming more strongly now. 'About every fifteen minutes. There should be one any second.' She held her breath, then nodded. 'It's starting . . .'

The sister put her hand on Clare's abdomen and concentrated. 'Yes.

13

I think that's it.' She smiled at Clare. 'I think you're on your way at last.'

'Oh, thank goodness.' But her throat ached suddenly. It doesn't really matter now, she thought sadly, there's no hurry any more. Martyn won't be back for a year. The baby can wait as long as it likes, it'll make no difference to him.

She lay back on her pillows, thinking of Martyn already at sea, absorbed in his part in keeping the ship afloat. He was a petty officer, a radio electrical artificer, and it was his job not to operate the radar system but to maintain it, making sure that it worked efficiently all the time. Clare had imagined that it would hardly ever go wrong, but apparently these systems were breaking down all the time. It could be the vibration of the ship, he said, or any number of things, but there was always plenty of work. Sometimes he had to climb the mast and make repairs to the aerials, even during a storm or at night.

Clare preferred not to think about that. Instead, she let her mind drift back over the times they'd spent together – their days out on his motorbike, exploring the New Forest or the downs of Sussex, the walks they'd had, the spots where they'd stopped to kiss under a canopy of leaves. The picnics and the little cottages where they'd sometimes had tea. The day they'd parked the bike in Lymington and caught the ferry to the Isle of Wight, sharing a huge bar of chocolate as they watched the green hills draw nearer, and then wandering the little streets of Yarmouth before catching the ferry back. The youth hostelling holiday they'd had on the Island just after they'd got engaged.

All those times, all that happiness, leading inevitably to this moment when she lay alone in a hospital bed, waiting for the birth of their first baby – and feeling the ache of loneliness even more strongly than the pain of her contractions.

The contractions went on until lunchtime, getting slowly stronger. They couldn't be called pains, not at first, but by the time the ward orderlies started to bring in the cutlery and lay the table in the middle of the ward, Clare was feeling decidedly uncomfortable. After a bit, the sister came in and laid her hand on Clare's abdomen again and felt the strength. She nodded, but said she thought it would be quite a long time yet. 'First babies are never in a hurry.'

'You mean it's going to go on like this for ages?' Clare asked as the worst period pain she had ever had gripped her.

The Sister smiled and said no, not like this. 'It'll get worse before it gets better,' she added, turning to go. 'Don't worry. Most women survive and think it's worth it. I'll pop back again in a little while.'

Clare gazed after her. She looked around at the other women, who had all had their babies and survived it. 'How bad does it get?'

'Depends,' Marge said. 'Some people have babies like shelling peas. Others . . .' She shrugged.

'I don't know if I can stand it getting worse than this.' Clare said. The contraction started again, and there was no mistaking it now as pain. It started low in her back, spreading around until it gripped her like a tightening iron band. She gave herself up to it, feeling the sweat break out on her forehead. The band loosened slowly and the pain faded away.

'You don't have no choice, I'm afraid,' Jean Baker said. 'You had that nine months ago.'

They all laughed, and someone said, 'It's knowing which time you're going to fall that's the problem!'

Clare knew exactly when she had fallen for this baby. It was on the second morning of her honeymoon. She and Martyn were in a small country hotel in the Cotswolds and in their innocence they hadn't got enough Durex with them. Martyn had thought two packets of three would be enough, but they'd used two the first night and another one on the Sunday morning. They'd gone out for a walk then and come back in the afternoon, and gone to bed again. That was another one. Then there was one that night, and the one Martyn had split when he was trying to get it on, and then they were all gone. And on the Monday morning they'd wanted to make love again, wanted it so badly, and they'd looked at each other with desperate eyes and decided to take a chance.

'We've been so careful,' Clare whispered. 'It won't matter, just once.'

But it had mattered, and one morning six weeks later she woke up feeling sick and took the day off work, staying at home in the tiny flat they'd found. By teatime she was better and Martyn came home to the little furnished flat they were renting to find her making chips for their supper. 'It must have been something I ate yesterday,' she said cheerfully. 'I'm fine now.'

Next morning she was sick again and it was only after a week of this that they began to wonder if she might be pregnant.

'You'd better go to the doctor,' Martyn said, and they went together. The doctor confirmed that Clare was pregnant and told them they ought to be very happy. 'It happened on your honeymoon,' he said. 'The best time of all to start your family.'

Clare and Martyn didn't know to begin with whether they were happy or not. They came out of the surgery feeling dazed, holding each other's hand tightly. They hadn't meant this to happen for another two years, to give them time to save up for their own house, and they already knew that Martyn was likely to be away for much of that time on his new ship.

'You'll be all on your own,' he said. 'How will you manage?'

'I'll be all right. I know how to look after babies.' By that time, her sister Valerie had been married for two years and had a baby son, Johnny. Clare was always going over to Portsmouth, where Valerie and Maurice lived, and helping to look after the baby. The thought of having her own filled her with excitement as well as apprehension. 'It's going to be lovely,' she said. 'We'll be a real family.'

They paused at the edge of the pavement and dithered. Going back to the flat seemed a bit dull after such momentous news.

Martyn glanced at her uncertainly. 'Shall we walk out to Stokes Bay? Is it all right for you to go that far?'

Clare laughed. 'I don't see why not. I'm not ill. Not till tomorrow morning, anyway. Let's do that.'

Stokes Bay had always been important to them. Wherever they'd been, they always tried to leave time before going home for a few minutes out at the bay, looking at the Isle of Wight. It was this view that Clare had sketched once and given to Martyn to take to sea, to remind him of their favourite place.

Tonight, as they passed Alverstoke church and came within sight of the bay and the Island beyond, Clare was still trying to grasp the fact that she was having a baby. That somewhere deep inside her a new life was beginning, a tiny body already forming. Not much more than a tadpole at the moment, so the book had said, but already beginning to take shape, to look vaguely human.

'Can *you* believe it?' she asked Martyn as they sat down in one of the shelters, looking out at the sea. 'A baby of our very own. A baby *we've* made.' She sat silent for a moment, then asked a little tentatively, 'Do you mind?'

'Mind?' He turned and looked down at her. He was still holding her hand but he let go now and put his arm round her shoulders, pulling her close. 'Mind? I think it's smashing!'

'Oh . . .' She relaxed against him. 'Oh, that's good. So do I.' She wasn't totally sure of this, but she didn't know how else she was supposed to react, couldn't quite identify the other feeling that fluttered somewhere inside. 'I think it's smashing too. It just shows – it really can happen after only one time.' She giggled a little hysterically. 'Just as well we never misbehaved ourselves before! Oh, Martyn, I can't wait to tell Kathy!'

Kathy was more surprised than pleased when Clare told her the news. She'd been sure that they'd wait until Martyn came home before starting a family. She looked at Clare, not knowing what to say, and Clare grinned self-consciously.

'We didn't really mean it to be so quick,' she admitted. 'We just – well, we took a chance once, and that was it. Anyway, I'm thrilled and so's Martyn. We'll be a proper family.'

'What do your mum and dad think?'

Clare made a face, remembering her mother's reaction. She hadn't been exactly disapproving, but she'd obviously thought it was a pity. However, she'd soon recovered and started to look out knitting patterns from when Valerie had been expecting, and when Bill had been told he'd just shrugged and said that since he was now married to a grandmother, whether he liked it or not, he might as well make the best of it.

'They think we should have waited a bit longer. But we wouldn't have got married if we hadn't been prepared to have children. Anyway, it's done now and they'll be just as pleased when they've got a new grandchild. You will come and see me as often as you can, won't you, Kathy? And we want you to be a godmother.'

'Of course I will.' Kathy looked at her friend, trying to see if there was any difference in her. She was a married woman, expecting a baby. She ought to be different, somehow. Kathy felt suddenly young and ignorant. She didn't even know what it was like to make love, not properly, going all the way. Brian would have liked to, she knew, but she was too scared of the consequences, and seeing how easily Clare had fallen convinced her she was right.

Kathy still couldn't quite believe that someone like Brian Bennett could be in love with her. He was big and confident, as good-looking as a film star, with dark, wavy hair and dark blue eyes. Kathy, who was small and fair, with straight hair that was too fine and silky to do anything more with than cut short, couldn't believe that he could find her attractive. However, he seemed to like her smallness. He said he could pick her up and put her in his pocket. He seemed to like looking after her, walking on the outside of the pavement and standing aside so that she could go first through doorways. She rather enjoyed it. As eldest of her family, she'd always been expected to take care of the others, and nobody had ever treated her as though she needed protection, as though she was worth it.

It wasn't long before they were talking about getting engaged.

'I don't want to get married yet,' she said to him as they sat in the front room at home, holding hands. It was Sunday evening and Brian had to leave soon to catch the bus to Fareham for the coach back to Plymouth. His home was in Bristol, so he was a West Country rating, based in Plymouth, like Martyn, and when he'd left Collingwood he'd been drafted to the Plymouth-based aircraft carrier, HMS *Pacific*. 'I'd rather wait till you come home and we can start properly together.'

They knew the *Pacific* was going to be away for a year. Already, it was going off for shorter trips – six weeks up to Scotland and over to Scandinavia and then Hamburg, three weeks to France and Spain – before sailing for the Far East and Australia. After that Brian would probably be drafted again, hopefully to a shore base.

The ship had been in Plymouth, preparing for its long voyage, but to their delight it was going to come to Portsmouth for a week before it sailed for the Far East. Brian was round at Kathy's house almost before it docked, and Kathy's mother said he could stay the nights, sleeping on the sofa in the front room, so that they could have as much time as possible together. Kathy had taken a few days' leave as well. It meant less holiday later on, but what use was holiday to her when Brian was thousands of miles away?

'I wish we could go away together,' Brian said as they went out for a walk along Stokes Bay. 'We could be properly on our own. Not have to come in for meals at the right time. Not have to be in by half past ten. Just imagine it.' He squeezed her hand. 'We could pretend we were married.'

'Oh, no we couldn't,' Kathy said, but she knew he didn't really mean anything by it and she softened and smiled at him. 'I know what you mean, Bri. It would be lovely, but Mum and Dad would never let us.'

'Not even though we're engaged?' He lifted her hand and looked at the little diamond ring, giving it a kiss. 'Martyn and Clare went off for a week, walking round the Isle of Wight, just after they got engaged. Her mum and dad didn't seem too worried.'

'I know, but they went youth hostelling, you see. That's respectable.'

He made a face. 'Bit energetic, though. All that hiking! I suppose they thought Martyn and Clare wouldn't have the strength to get up to anything they shouldn't, after they'd walked twenty miles. It's daft really, though, isn't it? I mean, a couple could come out for an hour in the afternoon and do all the things they shouldn't. It doesn't have to be at night.' He stopped and put his arms round Kathy's shoulders. 'Sometimes, I wish we'd got married before I went away, like them. I love you so much, Kath.'

'I know.' She laid her head against his chest. 'But I think we were right to wait, Brian. I'd hate to be like Clare now, expecting her baby any time and knowing she's going to be on her own with it all the next year. And she hasn't even had Martyn with her much while she's been carrying it. It's almost as if she didn't really have a husband.'

'Well, you know what they say . . .'

'If you marry a sailor, you've got to expect it. I know. We'll be separated a lot of the time too, I know that, but at least when you come home, we'll be able to look forward to a couple of years together, to start us off. I want that, Brian.'

'So do I.' He nibbled her ear. 'And you know what else they say. Being married to a sailor is like being on honeymoon whenever he comes home. It's got its advantages, Kath.'

Kathy thought that being married and living an ordinary, everyday life was better than being on honeymoon for a few weeks every year and on your own the rest, but she didn't say so. Chaps like Brian and Martyn had joined the Navy because they loved the idea of being at sea and going to places all over the world, and you couldn't complain because they'd joined before they knew you. And as Brian had just said, if you didn't like it you just didn't marry a sailor. You had to make your own choice over that.

Except that to her, there didn't seem to have been much choice. She'd fallen in love with Brian and that was that. Choice didn't really come into it.

'We can save up while you're gone,' she said, 'and have enough to put a deposit on a house and buy some nice furniture. That'll be better than going into married quarters.'

'You've been talking to Clare,' he said. 'Martyn says she doesn't want to go into married quarters either.'

'Well, they can be so snobbish, and the other wives can be so catty. And you never see anyone who isn't Navy. I'd rather go on seeing the sort of people I know already, people who've got all sorts of jobs and different lives. And have our own home. Wouldn't you rather have that, Brian?'

Brian considered. He didn't come from a naval family himself. He had grown up partly in Bristol and partly in Devon where he had been evacuated during the war. That was when he'd met Martyn, and they'd stayed friends ever since. When he went home again after the war, his mother was living with a man who wasn't his father, and Brian had been there when his soldier father came home and found them. He tried not to think about the row that had happened before his dad disappeared for good, and although Brian had stayed, he had never felt welcome and had gone into the Navy when he was sixteen, as much to get away from home as for any other reason.

'Yes, I would,' he said. 'People know too much about you on a naval estate. And there are too many rules and regulations. You're never free.'

'That's settled, then,' she said contentedly. 'We'll get engaged and then save up for our own house, and I'll wait for you.'

'You better had!' he said, putting his arms round her and kissing her. 'I don't want any of these "Dear John" letters coming while I'm away.'

Kathy looked at him, puzzled. 'What's a "Dear John" letter?'

'It's what a girl writes to her bloke when she wants to finish with him. I've seen a few of my mates getting them. It's rotten when you're away. You can't do anything about it – can't go round and have it out with her or find out what's wrong – and by the time you get home it's too late. Chances are she's married some other chap. That's why a lot of blokes get married before they go away, to make sure of the girl. It's probably why old Martyn's so keen.'

'Oh, I'm sure it's not. Clare wouldn't ever do a thing like that. And neither would I.' She kissed him back. 'I'll stay in every night, writing you letters, and they won't start, "Dear John"!'

'Well, just make sure they don't.' His arms were very tight around her and there was a tight, white ridge around his mouth. 'You're my girl, Kathy, and no other bloke's going to have you, so don't you forget it.'

Kathy stroked his head tenderly. She knew about his mum, and knew that he hardly ever wrote to her or went home now, and she felt sorry that he'd been so hurt. But it was nice, all the same, to feel that he loved her so much.

'I'll be true to you, Brian,' she whispered, laying her cheek against his. 'You don't have to worry. I'll stay faithful.'

Brian didn't worry too much about Kathy when he went to sea. He was well aware that she didn't think of herself as a girl boys would chase after, and she was too much in love with him to stray. As long as he wrote regularly she'd stop at home by the fire and be waiting for him with open arms when he got back.

20

It was different for him. Sailors couldn't be expected to spend weeks at sea and then not enjoy a run ashore when they got the chance. He and Martyn were always ready for the liberty boat, and explored the foreign ports eagerly, calling at the first bar they saw for a quick beer before penetrating further. The area around the dock was always well provided with bars, and there were plenty of girls too, ready and willing to link arms with a sailor and spend the evening with him. Brian eyed them as he and Martyn strolled along.

'I wonder if these little French popsies are all they're cracked up to be,' he remarked. They were in Le Havre, only a few hours across the Channel, so they hadn't exactly had weeks at sea, but it felt just as exciting. 'I like the look of that little dark one.'

'Don't be daft,' Martyn said. 'We've got our own girls back home and my Clare could knock spots off any one of these.'

'Oh, sure. So could Kathy. All the same – you can't help wondering, can you?'

Martyn looked and grinned. Brian was right, you couldn't help wondering, but that was as far as it would go. 'Think she fancies you too?' he said. 'She's giving you the eye. Know any French?'

'I know all I need to. *Voulez-vous coucher avec moi – ce soir?* That means—'

'I know what it means, and you're not going to say it. They're probably riddled with VD. D'you want to be lined up in front of the doc in a few days' time? It's self-inflicted injury, you know – you get put on a charge as well as having to have some nasty treatment. They don't have much sympathy for blokes that get caught.'

Brian laughed. 'Don't worry, I'm not going to waste my money on tarts. If ever I do, it'll be someone with a bit of class, not one of these doxies. And I've got Kathy's photo in my wallet to keep me on the straight and narrow. But that doesn't mean we can't have a bit of fun, does it? Let's go in here and have a jar or two and then see what else this place has got to offer.'

They turned into a small tavern packed with sailors and girls. The sound of concertina music floated above the hubbub of voices, and the air was thick with cigarette smoke and the fumes of alcohol. Brian and Martyn grinned at each other happily and elbowed their way to the bar.

'This is what it's all about,' Brian said, fishing for some francs. 'This is why we joined the Andrew, Martyn, my old mate. Let me stand you a snifter of the local brew.'

*

While the ship was away, Kathy spent a lot of time with Clare, helping her get ready for the baby, and for her new home. Clare was full of enthusiasm, as if domesticity was all she had ever wanted. Her sketchbook lay untouched. All she drew now were plans of rooms.

'Mum and Dad are giving us money for a few bits of furniture. It's ever so good of them, when you think they paid for the wedding only a few months ago. And Mum says she'll make a loose cover for one of their old armchairs, and we can have that. I thought of a nice bright red, to look contemporary. And our Val's giving me an old kitchen table, so we can eat our meals in the kitchen, but we'll need some chairs. Two kitchen chairs will do, or maybe stools. And I thought in the living-room – the *lounge* – we could have this long coffee-table, see, and when we've got people to tea we can have it in there, not bothering about sitting up. I think we'll be able to afford another armchair too, a new one. It's going to be smashing, Kath.'

Kathy thought of her own savings, slowly gathering in her bank account. Was it all going to be spent on furniture and houses like Clare's? She'd seen a really nice skirt in the little shop opposite the office a couple of days ago, and she wanted to buy it, but she wondered whether she ought to. Perhaps she should be like Clare and think about her home instead.

No. I'm glad we're not getting married yet, Kathy thought. Clare's going to be so tied down. She won't have any life of her own.

Brian thought so too, but his sympathy was for Martyn. 'The poor bloke can't even afford to go ashore for a drink of an evening,' he complained the next time he was in Gosport. 'He says Clare wants money for nappies or vests or bootees. For Christ's sake, he's only twenty-two and he talks like an old man.'

'Well, it's his baby. He's got to take responsibility.'

'That's what he says,' Brian admitted. 'I mean, he doesn't seem all that bothered by it, he's still like a dog with two tails. You wouldn't think anyone had ever had a baby before. But I reckon a bloke needs a bit of fun when he's away from home.'

Kathy looked at him doubtfully. 'Fun?'

'Just going out for a drink,' he said. 'That's all. You've got to get off the ship some time, and what else is there to do?'

It was much the same for the girls left at home, Kathy thought. She didn't go out much herself, and she listened enviously to the other girls at work talking about the dances they'd been to, the boys they'd picked up, the evenings in the pub. Kathy didn't want to pick up boys but she was bored and restless at home. It didn't take long to write to Brian each evening, and she was fed up with the wireless, and even the new television set didn't hold her attention for long.

'There's a new community centre starting up in town,' her mother said one day. 'Why don't you go along to that? They're doing different activities, like a youth club, and I don't see anything wrong in an engaged girl going to that sort of thing.'

Kathy thought she might as well. You could go on your own, you didn't have to have a partner, and people didn't pair off – it was just groups. She looked at the prospectus and thought she'd like to join the music group and the debating circle, and go to the social evenings.

There were quite a few people there she knew from school, but many of them were strangers – either older, or a bit younger, from different parts of the town, or who had been to other schools. It was pleasant and friendly, and you could get coffee and biscuits and sit about in low armchairs and talk, as well as joining groups. Kathy started to go every evening, except for the nights when she went to see Clare, and she soon began to make new friends.

'It's nice because it doesn't have to mean anything,' she told Clare. 'Everyone knows I'm engaged, so the boys I talk to aren't expecting me to flirt with them or anything like that, it's just ordinary. It's a shame you can't come along too.'

She looked at Clare's swollen body and thought of her own getting like that, misshapen and fat. Suppose it never went properly back to normal? And it wasn't just that. Clare had had all sorts of things wrong with her. Morning sickness, when she'd looked as pale as a wraith, and then indigestion and backache, and a horrible pain like toothache, all down her side and leg, that she said came from the baby pressing on the sciatic nerve. And then she'd had heartburn after meals, from carrying the baby high, and then there was the high blood pressure that meant she had to rest a lot and would have to go into the Blake before the baby was due, so that she could be properly looked after. And on top of that, she'd had a varicose vein starting. A varicose vein, and she was only nineteen!

It's like being old, Kathy thought. Old and ill. I don't want all that. I'm not ready for that.

She went to the Thorngate next evening with some relief, knowing that nobody there was going to talk about babies or being pregnant, or even about buying furniture. Instead, they discussed Fidel Castro's new regime in Cuba, the latest space rocket sent up by the Russians to orbit the moon, and Buddy Holly's death, along with Big Bopper and Richie

Valens, in a plane crash. And then they put on some records and danced to the latest hits, and Kathy talked and laughed and, for a little while, forgot to be lonely.

Chapter Three

'I think it's time to take you to the labour ward,' the sister said, coming to look at Clare as she lay sweating and clutching the iron bars behind her head. 'Now, remember what Matron told you in the antenatal classes. Deep breaths, right down into your tummy. That's right.' Her cool hand rested on Clare's wrist, fingers lightly pressing on her pulse. 'That's right. Easing off now, is it? That's a good girl. No, you don't have to walk. I'll get Audrey to bring the trolley. Just rest for a minute or two. It's going to be all right. Everything's going to be all right.' She smiled reassuringly down at Clare's suddenly panic-stricken face. 'This time tomorrow, it'll all be over. You'll be a mum, with a baby all of your own.'

'His name's Christopher,' Clare said weakly when the baby was born at last. He was big – over eight and a half pounds – and lusty, with just enough fuzz on his head to know that he was blond, and a face that was already round, with crumpled jowls like Winston Churchill. Clare looked at him with some amazement as he lay swathed in towels in the crook of her arm. After all the long months, the waiting and the preparation, it didn't seem possible that he was here at last. A baby. A little boy. Christopher. Christopher Michael.

'It's nice it's a boy,' the pupil midwife, who had helped the sister deliver him, said to Clare as she busied herself around the small labour ward. 'You won't have all that expense of a wedding later on.'

Clare opened her mouth to say that she was already married, but then realised what the girl meant. If she hadn't been so tired, she would have giggled. Fancy thinking ahead that far, when the baby was only half an hour old! 'I expect he'll want other things,' she said, stroking the soft cheek. It still seemed impossible. A real, living human being, out of *her* body, made on a Monday morning nine months ago just because she and Martyn had run out of french letters . . . No, because she and Martyn loved each other. It was beyond understanding. It was a miracle.

'He looks like his dad, doesn't he?' the midwife said, coming close to look down at the sleeping face. 'I can see him there, can't you?'

Clare turned her head and examined the baby's face more closely. 'Yes,' she said, in some surprise, 'I think he does. He *does*.' She smiled, feeling a flood of warmth. It was like having a bit of Martyn still with her. That's what the baby was; a bit of Martyn and a bit of her. Made up to be someone who would turn out quite different from both of them, someone all his own. Christopher. Christopher Michael. Christopher . . .

When she woke again, she was back in the ward and the baby had been put into a cot in a separate nursery with the others. She would only see him now when he was brought in for feeds. It gave the mothers a rest – the last one they'd get until they came in again for the next baby, someone observed wryly. By the time they left the maternity home, a fortnight after the birth, they were on their feet again, full of life and energy and ready to cope.

Once the baby was born, Clare discovered, all the problems that went with pregnancy disappeared. This might have seemed obvious, but somehow she hadn't expected it. Without actually thinking about it, she'd assumed they would go slowly, like in a convalescence. Instead, the sickness that had plagued her all the way through vanished overnight like the huge bump she'd carried around for the past few months. Her blood pressure came down, and when Christopher was three days old she was allowed to get out of bed, have a bath and go to the toilet. She hadn't needed stitches, so she was spared their discomfort, and she felt well enough to go home straight away.

'I want to get back to the bungalow,' she told her mother, who came to see her almost every evening. 'I want to take Christopher out in his pram.'

'Plenty of time for that,' Iris said. She thought Clare was looking pale and thin. Once the baby was born, it was obvious that the girl had lost a lot of her own weight during her difficult pregnancy, and although she seemed tickled pink at being slimmer than she'd ever been before, it wasn't right in a new mother. 'The rest'll do you good. You're allowed to be up and about more than I ever was, as it is. I wasn't allowed to put a foot to the floor for a fortnight.'

'I feel I could walk ten miles.' Clare grinned. 'I'll be able to walk down to see you when I'm out.'

'That's something I wanted to talk to you about.' Iris hesitated. Clare was an independent girl, always had been, but there was no getting away from it: she wasn't twenty yet and apart from a few months in that flat she'd never even had a home to look after, let alone a baby. 'Your dad and me have been thinking. Why don't you come back home for a couple of weeks first? You'll have a lot on your plate, and you'll be all by yourself. I can help you, show you how to go about things . . .'

Clare stared at her. All this time, she'd been looking forward to taking her baby back to her own home, to the new bungalow. And now her mum was suggesting she shouldn't go back there at all. Instead, she was to take Christopher back to her parents' house, to be shown how to look after him, to be told how to bath him, dress him, when and how to feed him . . . He won't be my baby, she thought. I know Mum means well, but he won't be my baby, and I'll have lost that first fortnight for ever.

'Thanks, Mum,' she said, 'but I want to start off in my own place. By the time I get out of here, I'll have been away for a month. And they show us how to look after the babies in here, how to bath them and all that. I'll be all right. It's not as if I have to look after a husband as well,' she added with wry smile. 'I won't have anything else to do.'

Iris looked as if she might argue, but thought better of it. Clare was a married woman now, even if she was still under twenty-one, and you couldn't tell her what to do. She just said, 'Well, you know you can change your mind if you want to,' and then went on to say that Kathy had been round to see her and ask if she could come in and visit one evening. 'I told her she could come tomorrow, if that's all right with you. Then I can go to the Fireside Club meeting.'

'Oh, yes,' Clare said, relieved that there was to be no argument. 'Yes, that'll be lovely. She can tell me about going to see the ship sail.'

Kathy arrived next evening with a small box of chocolates for Clare and a cot blanket for the baby. It was cellular, in soft pink and blue checks. 'I know you wanted yellow, but they didn't have any and I thought this would do for a girl as well, if that's what you have next time,' she said with a grin.

Clare wasn't so sure now that there was going to be a next time. Giving birth hadn't been any fun at all, and she was inclined to think she might not let herself in for it again. However, when she held

Christopher in her arms and felt him nuzzling at her breast, she was overwhelmed with love, and knew that she would want to go through it again, if only for this enormous delight. And they all said second babies came much more easily.

'Tell me about the ship,' she said. 'You did go to see it sail, didn't you?'

Kathy nodded. 'I was down on the Hard by half past six. There were quite a few of us there, even though she's really a Plymouth ship. I suppose there are quite a few Gosport wives and girlfriends. It was lovely watching her go, but ever so sad. The sailors were all lined up round the flight deck and you could hear the bosun's whistle as they went past the *Victory*. I watched till I couldn't see her any more and then I just went and had a cup of tea in the Dive and got to work early. There wasn't really time to go home again.'

'I couldn't bear to think about it,' Clare said. 'I thought the baby was going to come at any moment and I just sat in bed knitting all morning. The other girls were smashing, they all came and sat with me. And by dinner-time I wasn't thinking about anything much, except getting it over with.'

'I'm dying to see the baby,' Kathy said. Only new fathers or, in cases like Clare's where the husband was away, grandmothers were allowed to visit the nursery. 'I'll come round and see you the minute you get home, though.'

'Yes, it seems a waste no one else seeing him while he's so tiny and new. Come the day after I get home.' Clare smiled. 'I got Mum to bring my camera in. I'm going to get one of the others to take pictures of me with Christopher.' It still seemed funny, talking about the baby by name. 'He looks just like Winston Churchill!'

'All babies look like Winston Churchill,' Kathy said. 'Or maybe it's just that he never grew out of looking like a baby.' She sighed, and Clare realised suddenly that Kathy too must be feeling lonely. The year stretched ahead of them all, but for Kathy it must have seemed even emptier than for Clare. I've got Christopher to think about, Clare thought. I can watch him growing and learning – to sit up, to crawl, maybe even to walk, to smile and laugh and play and say a few words. For Kathy, nothing's going to change during this year; she'll be just the same when Brian comes back as she is now.

It seemed horribly dull.

'Are you going to start going to the community club again?' she asked, and Kathy nodded.

'I might as well. Not for a week or two, perhaps, but there's nothing much else to do. I'm going to join the hockey club too, next autumn. I've got to do something.'

'Of course you have, but you'll come and see me at least once a week, won't you?'

'Try stopping me,' Kathy said, and they smiled at each other.

By the time Clare was finally allowed out of the maternity home, she had been in there for a month and felt as if she'd been let out of prison. It was strange and wonderful to walk out with her own baby in her arms and get into a taxi with her mother, waving goodbye to all the nurses and other women as it swept along the drive. Even stranger to arrive at the new bungalow, looking much the same as it had when she'd left it, except that someone had dug up the front garden and raked it flat, and planted grass seed to make a lawn. That must have been Dad. The taxi stopped and she got out and stood looking at her home.

There hadn't been many new houses built yet after the war. The government had been too busy getting people rehoused after the bombing, first with prefabs and then with proper council houses, but at last they'd got nearly everyone sorted out and now builders could turn their attention to their own developments. The little cul-de-sac of bungalows that Clare and Martyn had found was one of these.

'It's just right for us,' Clare had told Kathy excitedly. 'I know we didn't mean to go in for our own place so soon, but Mrs Spooner won't let the flat to anyone with children, so we've got to move out. And we might as well be paying a mortgage as rent.' She showed Kathy the plans. 'See, it'll have two bedrooms and a nice big lounge – eighteen feet long, it'll be, with a picture window at the end. I think that's much better than a front room and back room, don't you? I mean, look at my mum and dad, they hardly ever use the front room, and it's got all the best furniture but we all have to squash into the back room with the old stuff. I don't see any point in that. And it's got a nice bathroom too, and we can choose the colour. White, blue or pink. I've decided on blue, with black tiles, I think that'll look really smart.'

'It's handy for Collingwood, too,' Kathy had said, studying the street plan. 'See, if Martyn gets drafted there, he'll be able to get home for dinner.'

Clare thought of this now, standing with her baby in her arms. Martyn, coming home for dinner – he'd have to get a bike – and then again for tea, being there all evening, all night, *every* night. It seemed like a fantasy, but perhaps it would really come true.

*

'You're sure you don't want to come down to us?' Iris said, thinking that now the moment had come her daughter might be feeling a bit daunted at the idea of being on her own.

Clare shook her head firmly. 'I want to start off in my own place, just as if Martyn was here.' She walked up the short path and stopped, wishing she had her own key to open the front door, but Iris had it, and Clare had to wait while her mother opened the door and walked in ahead of her. It ought to have been me, she thought, and then swept the brief resentment aside. Her mother just wanted to help, and was almost as excited as Clare was to have a new baby in the family. And she'd done a lot already, and would do more.

Evidence of what Iris had done was already apparent. In the living-room, the carrycot they'd bought from one of Iris's friends stood on the studio couch, made up with soft new sheets and blankets. Clare laid the baby inside and they stood and gazed down at the tiny, sleeping face.

'They said he's ever such a good baby,' Clare said. 'Sleeps all through the night, never needs feeding.'

'I dare say he'll want something. It's a long time for a tiny baby, ten o'clock till six. I should just give him a small feed if he wakes, and some water.' Iris bent over the cot and touched the peach-bloom cheek. 'He's lovely. I can't wait to have a proper cuddle.'

'Well, he'll be waking up pretty soon. Let's have a cup of coffee.' Clare went out of the room and began to wander round the bungalow, reminding herself what it was like. It didn't take long. Two bedrooms, one completely empty, one with the big cot and the whitewood furniture. A shining new bathroom with its blue bath and the black tiles everyone had raised their eyebrows at when Clare had chosen them, and which did look just as smart as she had thought they would. The kitchen, with its fitted cupboards and Formica worktops and the brand-new electric cooker which had been hardly used before Clare went into hospital.

'I can't believe it,' she said, filling the kettle. 'I've got all this! I just wish Martyn could be here too.'

'I know, but the time will soon go, especially now you've got the baby. You'll have to send him lots of photos.'

Clare had already had photographs taken in the nursing home, showing Christopher propped like a miniature grumpy old man on her lap. She intended to take new ones every week, so that Martyn could see just how he grew over the year. And she would write every day, as she'd always done. There would be lots to tell him now.

From the living-room, they heard a stirring of bedclothes and a mewing cry. They went back and Clare lifted the baby out and gave him to her mother. 'There you are. Another grandson for you.'

Iris held him close and looked down at the blue, unfocused eyes. Her own eyes were filled with tears. 'He's lovely, Clare. He's really, really lovely.'

Christopher waved small, clenched fists no bigger than furled roses, and kicked his legs. He's strong, Clare thought, still overwhelmed by the miracle of his being. He's strong and healthy, and it's up to me to look after him now. Wherever I go, he'll have to come with me; he'll be with me every minute of the day and night, and if he isn't I'll have to make sure there's someone I trust looking after him. He's my responsibility.

She felt a pang of uncertainty. Maybe she should have gone home with Mum, after all. But then she reminded herself that she'd been taught all she needed to know in the Blake, and that women had been having and looking after babies ever since the world began. All you had to do, after all, was feed them and keep them clean. The rest would just happen naturally.

She could feel the milk tingling in her full breasts. She sat down and unbuttoned her blouse and held out her arms for her baby.

Keeping them clean and fed wasn't all you had to do for babies, Clare discovered, or if it was, they had their own ideas about how and when you should do it. Christopher, exhausted by the changes in his routine on his first day at home, slept through the first night, and Clare woke next morning feeling rested and triumphant. There's nothing to it, she thought. He's a really good baby. It's all going to be fine.

She lay for a few minutes on the studio couch in the living-room, made up as a single bed, and watched the pattern of sunlight shining through the curtains on to the ceiling. Now, at last, she could cry for Martyn if she wanted to. She hadn't let herself shed so much as a tear during her time in the hospital, afraid that if she started she wouldn't be able to stop. Yesterday had been a flurry of visitors – her mother had stayed with her all day, Valerie had come in the afternoon with Johnny, her father had come straight from work, so they'd all had tea together, and her new neighbour Janet, who had two boys of nine and seven, had popped in. There hadn't been any time at all for her own private thoughts and feelings.

But there was no one to see now, no one to interrupt or try to offer useless comfort. If she wanted to, she could cry all day.

To her surprise, however, she didn't want to. It was as if somehow the moment had passed, as if it was too late. Even as she lay thinking about it, she heard a movement from the carrycot, which she had placed across two kitchen chairs; a stirring of bedclothes and a faint murmur, like the whimper of a very young kitten. Her heart leaped and she pushed back her own bedclothes and leaned over the cot, feeling the wonder spread its glow over her body all over again as she touched the downy cheek with her fingertip.

'Hello, baby,' she said softly. 'Hello, Christopher.'

Christopher stretched his arms and screwed his face up in a grimacing yawn, and Clare laughed. His eyes opened, and she gazed into them, convinced that he saw and knew her. They said babies couldn't focus properly, she thought, but how did they know? He was looking at her, she knew he was, and nobody could convince her otherwise.

The baby screwed his face up again and began to cry. Hastily, Clare unfastened the nursing bra she had been advised to wear – a huge, heavy thing, like a suit of armour – and lifted him out. She settled him against her and leaned against the back of the couch.

Martyn wasn't forgotten, but it wasn't the right moment to cry for him now, either, not with Christopher suckling at her breast. And after he'd fed, she would have to change him and then get washed and dressed and have her own breakfast before it was time for his daily bath, and then another feed . . . and then there would be the nappies to wash, and lunch to be got ready and eaten before his two o'clock feed, and then the afternoon walk that everyone seemed to think so necessary . . . And Kathy was coming this afternoon, she remembered, and staying to tea . . . and then there would be just Christopher's evening feed to think about before she went to bed . . .

It didn't seem as if she was ever going to have time to sit and weep for her husband.

By this time, Martyn's ship was in the Mediterranean. They had crossed the Bay of Biscay in fine, calm weather and called at Gibraltar. The ship lay moored under the great rock and all the sailors flooded ashore, eager to take trips up to the top to see the famous apes, or just to find the nearest bar.

Brian found Martyn in the mess, stretched out on his bunk in his underpants, staring at a handful of little black and white photographs.

'I just got these from Clare,' he said. 'They're of the baby.' He tried to say 'Christopher' but somehow the baby didn't seem real enough for that yet. He'd been lying there for an hour, gazing at the snaps, trying to convince himself that this funny little creature was really his son.

'Good God,' Brian said, taking one and staring at it. 'He looks like a cross between a coconut and a garden gnome.' He ducked, as if expecting Martyn to swing a punch at his head.

Martyn didn't punch him and he didn't laugh. He hardly seemed to hear the insult. 'Clare says everyone thinks he looks like me,' he said, taking the photograph back.

'I didn't say he didn't.' Brian looked at his watch. 'Come on, Martyn, get your skates on. I want to get ashore.'

'Go on, then.'

'What do you mean, *go on*? You're coming for a run, aren't you?'

'No. Don't think I'll bother. I haven't read this letter yet—'

'Christ, man, the letter won't go bad if you leave it for an hour or so! Or read it now and I'll wait, only don't take too long about it because I've got a thirst I wouldn't flog for a week's rations. Come *on*, Martyn.'

Martyn shook his head. 'You go on. I'll catch you up somewhere. You can't get lost in Gib. I'll find you.'

Brian stared at him, baffled, then shrugged and sauntered out of the mess. Most of the other men had gone too and Martyn was left alone to gaze at his photographs and read his letter. He unfolded the pages slowly, imagining Clare writing the words, trying to feel her hands on the paper, trying to feel her kiss and caress.

'It's like having a huge hole torn in me, being without you,' she had written. *'And I wish so much that you could be here to see Christopher while he's tiny. Oh, Martyn, I love you so much, so very very much . . .'*

I love you too, he thought. And it feels like a huge hole in me as well. I don't know how I'm going to get through a whole year like this . . .

True to her word, Kathy came at least once a week, straight from work, to spend the evening with Clare and the baby. She spent hours cuddling and playing with him, marvelling at his tiny fingers and toes, marvelling again as he grew. 'It's like seeing a different baby every week,' she said. 'I can't believe he can grow so fast without bursting out of his skin.'

'Well, it grows with him, I suppose,' Clare said. She enjoyed these visits as much as Kathy did. Cooking a meal for someone else made a pleasant change, and she didn't feel constricted as she sometimes did with her mother and father. Iris had her own very definite opinions on what should be served up at various meals, and disapproved of some of Clare's ideas – a constant bone of contention was the fact that Clare never bothered with potatoes, unless they were roasted or done as chips.

'I don't like boiled or mashed spuds,' she said, defending herself. 'They're boring, so why should I bother with them?'

'You'll have to bother with them when your husband comes home,' Iris told her. 'He'll want something a bit more substantial to fill up on. And mashed potato will be good for the baby when he starts to eat solids.'

Clare thought that there were plenty of other things he'd like just as much, and if he did want potatoes she could always cook him one. But when Kathy came to tea there were no such worries, and they experimented happily together. Tonight, they were having Clare's latest invention, egg and cheese pie – alternate layers of hardboiled eggs and cheese, baked in flaky pastry. She made some salad to go with it, and opened a couple of bags of crisps.

Christopher was four months old now. He was struggling to sit up, and Clare propped him against a pillow in the armchair. He surveyed them from this throne, his eyes watching as they ate. There was a tiny crease across his brow as if he were trying to solve a difficult problem.

'He's wondering what we're eating,' Kathy said, laughing at him.

'He knows what food is,' Clare said. 'Wait till he sees his bowl and spoon.' She had started him on solids now and he had three or four spoonfuls at every mealtime. She made up thick Farex, like a porridge, for breakfast, and gave him mashed vegetables – carrots, peas or swede, but not potatoes – at dinner-time. For tea, he usually had banana or Farex again, and she sometimes gave him a rusk like a thick biscuit, to hold in his fist and gnaw.

He was fat and cheerful, a happy baby who seemed to smile on command, as if he couldn't help it. He laughed and chuckled uproariously when tickled, and spent hours sitting in his pram just outside the kitchen window, watching his mother working inside. Soon it would be too cold, and he'd have to come indoors, but the summer of 1959 had been gloriously and continuously hot, and Clare had been able to put him outside almost all day. His skin had turned a light golden brown, just from being in the open air under his canopy. In the hottest weather, she had taken off all his clothes and let him lie naked on a nappy, kicking his fat little legs.

Clare had settled quite happily into being a mother and staying at home. It was what was expected of a girl, after all – that, after a few years at work, she would get married, have a family and stay at home in the traditional manner. Kathy would do it once Brian was home again, and because she'd had this extra year at work they would probably be able to afford a bigger house, one with three bedrooms.

She was surprised to find how much there was to do. What with feeding, bathing and playing with Christopher, and then washing and cleaning and shopping, the days just flew by. At least once a week she either caught the bus down to Gosport to visit her mother, or walked if the day was fine, and sometimes she stayed the night so that she could see her father in the evening. Now and then she invited them to the bungalow for Sunday tea, and as often as not Bill brought some tools and did a few small jobs about the place. Valerie and Maurice came too and it was like a family party, especially when Ian managed to get home as well.

'You need that garden dug over and planted,' Bill told her, looking at the lumpy ground left by the builders. 'You've got room for a nice little vegetable plot there.'

'I'd never have time to look after it,' Clare objected. 'I'd rather have a bit of lawn for Chris to play on.'

Bill pulled down the corners of his mouth. In his opinion, lawns were for people with really big gardens, and a waste of space for ordinary folk who ought to be growing their own food. However, Iris had impressed on him that Clare's life was her own now, so all he said was, 'Well it still wants digging over. I'll bring up my fade and spork next time I come.'

'Thanks, Dad,' Clare said with a grin, and gave his arm a squeeze before going indoors to put the kettle on. She'd made a batch of scones and a fruit cake for tea, and Iris was already in the kitchen getting a sponge out of a tin and putting it on a plate. She never came without some offering and to her Sunday tea wasn't Sunday tea without at least two sorts of cake.

'That baby's looking a picture,' she said as Valerie came in with Christopher in her arms. 'I must say, Clare, you're turning out to be a good little mother. I don't mind telling you, that first couple of weeks I was on tenterhooks the whole time, thinking you'd be at the door saying you'd dropped him or something.'

'Mum! Whatever d'you think I am? Did you think I wouldn't take care of my own baby?' Clare rubbed his peachskin cheek with her finger. 'Why, he's the best thing that ever happened to me – after Martyn, of course. I'd never let anything happen to him.' She wasn't too annoyed, though. She knew that her mother only meant it for the best, but she was glad that she hadn't gone to stay for that first fortnight, as Iris had suggested. I've proved myself, she thought, and felt a twinge of satisfaction as she carried the scones into the front room and looked around at her home, and at the family who had come to visit her. I've proved I'm grown-up and independent!

She'd made friends with some of the neighbours too – Janet, who lived next door with her husband Stan and the two boys, and Hazel and Mike, who lived on the other side and had a baby only a couple of weeks older than Christopher. Clare and Hazel went to the baby clinic together every Thursday to have the babies weighed and buy the dried milk that Hazel used all the time and Clare occasionally. They often went shopping together at the local co-op, and had a cup of tea in one or another's house afterwards.

As the evenings began to draw in, Hazel had started to invite Clare in on Saturday evenings, to watch television, which Clare and Martyn couldn't afford yet, and have a bit of supper. Clare had taken her egg and cheese pie in once and they'd been very impressed.

Kathy came up every Tuesday straight from work. She listened to Clare's account of how the days flew and wondered if she would ever be able to settle down like this.

'You must get lonely, though,' she said. 'I mean, having to do everything yourself, without Martyn here to help you.'

'I miss him all the time, but I don't know that it's any harder this way. I've got Chris for company, and I don't have to think about getting meals for anyone else or doing more washing. I'm not tied to being home at any particular time – I can stay out all night if I want!' She grinned. 'I already do – sometimes I walk down to see Mum and Dad and stay the night. I keep a few nappies down there and a change of clothes, and it's no trouble to put a few things in the pram.'

'I know, but even so . . .'

'It's only what you've got to expect,' Clare said. 'It's no use moaning about being lonely when you're a sailor's wife. You know you're going to be on your own a lot of the time.'

Kathy walked back to the bus stop later, thinking over what Clare had said. It was true that a sailor's wife had to expect long periods of loneliness. The ships were often away for a year at a time, and if a man had a foreign draft ashore, in Singapore, for instance, or Malta or Hong Kong, it could be over two years. Often they would take their wives with them on these drafts, but not everyone did, and not all wives wanted to go. If you wanted to marry a sailor, you had to go into it with your eyes open.

The bus came along, and Kathy got on and sat staring out of the window into the darkness. Clare seems happy enough, she thought. It must seem endless to her, this year, but she stays cheerful. She writes to Martyn every day, and she loves being at home with Christopher. I dare say they'll have another baby quite soon, once Martyn gets home. She said once she didn't want her children too far apart. And she'll just stop at home, looking after them all, being a perfect wife and mother, without ever wishing that things could be different . . .

So what's wrong with me? Why is it that, although I can see Clare's happy with what she's got, it just doesn't seem enough? Why do I feel more and more as if I'm in some kind of a trap?

And what on earth am I going to do about it?

Chapter Four

Kathy went to the community centre at least three times a week. There was always something interesting going on – a debate, or a quiz, or dancing to records. You could usually find someone to play table tennis with, or you could just make a cup of coffee and sit and talk. It was better than staying at home listening to the wireless or watching the television with Mum and Dad.

One Wednesday evening she recognised a boy who had been about three years ahead of her at school. He came over while she was drinking coffee and sat down in the next chair. 'I haven't seen you here before,' he said. He had dark, curly hair and a shy smile. He was thinner than Brian, but about the same height.

Kathy raised her eyebrows at him. 'You haven't been looking, then. I've been coming for ages.'

'On Wednesday evenings?' he asked doubtfully, and she relented.

'No, I don't usually come on a Wednesday, but I got fed up sitting at home so I thought I'd come down and see what was on. There aren't many people I know here tonight, though.'

'Well, you could get to know me,' he offered a little diffidently. He glanced at her hands. 'Are you engaged?'

Kathy nodded. 'My fiancé's in the Navy. He's away.' She remembered the boy's name. 'You're Terry Carter. I remember you at school. You were in the sixth form when I was in the third.'

'No!' he said, pretending to be amazed. 'Don't tell me you were that skinny little brat with pigtails who was always getting into trouble.'

'I never got into trouble,' Kathy said with dignity, 'and I wasn't skinny either. And I *never* had pigtails.' They both laughed and he looked at her cup.

'D'you want another coffee?' He went and fetched them both fresh coffee and they sat for a while, exchanging reminiscences about school and discovering mutual friends and acquaintances. Then he said, 'What are you doing now?'

'I'm in the civil service. I work at Cambridge Barracks, doing service pay. What do you do?'

'I work in Portsmouth too,' he said. 'I'm an accountant. I've just finished my articles.'

Kathy was impressed. She looked at him again. He had a pleasant face, quite ordinary but with a nice smile and warm brown eyes. She felt a little sorry that they couldn't get to know each other better. If I weren't engaged, she thought, we could meet at lunchtimes, or go across on the ferry together, but of course she was engaged and Brian wouldn't like her meeting another chap, even just as a friend. Coming to the community centre was all right, but going out alone with someone would be quite different.

'I thought about the civil service too,' he said, 'but one of my friends was going to be an accountant so we decided to do it together. I'm glad now. D'you like your job?'

'It's all right. I like the people there and the job's okay. I don't suppose I'll stay there for ever, though. I mean, when Brian comes home next year we'll be getting married, and I suppose we'll start a family. I won't be able to go on working then. I'm not an established civil servant, so I expect I'll have to leave anyway. They don't always let married women stay on if they're not established.'

'Sounds a bit daft,' he said. 'Why don't you get established? What d'you have to do?'

Kathy was a bit vague about this. 'It's to do with pensions and gratuities and things,' she said. 'If you're going to leave, it's better not to get established, and then you can get a lump sum. It's all a bit complicated.'

'Well, if they chuck you out, you come to me,' he said with a grin. 'I'm sure we can find an ex-civil servant a job in our office.'

Kathy laughed. Terry Carter was nice, she decided, and it was nice too to be able to sit and chat with a boy like this. She went home, wondering if Terry Carter had a girlfriend and what time he went to work in the mornings. Quite likely, they'd been going on the same boat for months and never noticed each other. Next morning, she looked out for him but he didn't appear and she decided that he must catch a later boat. Civil servants started work at eight thirty, but he probably didn't have to be at work till nine.

That evening, she stayed at home and wrote a long letter to Brian. Now that autumn was setting in, the time seemed to drag even more. The evenings grew dark too quickly to go for walks and the sea was too cold for swimming. There was nothing much to do but go to the pictures or to the centre, and going to the pictures on your own wasn't much fun.

'Everyone seems to have someone to go with,' she remarked one evening to Terry. 'There's a good picture on next week, with Ian Carmichael in it, but I don't want to play gooseberry.'

'Well,' he said, 'you could come with me.' When she started to shake her head, he added, 'Why not? What's the difference between sitting here drinking coffee and sitting in the Forum watching a film? It doesn't have to mean anything.'

Kathy looked doubtful. She thought Brian would be able to see a difference, but Terry was right. And Brian went ashore and into pubs or whatever they had abroad, and had drinks with the other lads. It wasn't as if he was sitting aboard ship, not enjoying himself.

'I don't know . . .'

'Look,' Terry said, 'I'm not going to make a pass at you. We're just friends, all right? We can pass the time together without making something of it.'

Kathy knew he hadn't got a girlfriend. He was rather shy and serious, and didn't seem to know how to flirt. She believed him when she said he wouldn't make a pass at her. You could feel safe with Terry, she thought.

'All right. We'll go together.' She smiled at him. 'We go Dutch, mind. I'm not asking you to pay for me.'

'We'll see about that—' he began, but Kathy shook her head firmly.

'No. It wouldn't be right. It's not like going out on a date. If I were going with a girl, we'd pay separately.'

He agreed, but unwillingly, and when they met in the Forum foyer the following Wednesday he looked embarrassed as she proffered the money. 'I don't like this. It looks bad, a bloke not paying for the girl.'

'I'll give it to you later, then.' Kathy put her purse away. But he seemed just as uncomfortable afterwards, when she tried to give him the money in private. 'Look, you don't have to feel awkward. We just went as friends, that's all. I'm not your girlfriend.'

He gave her an odd look. 'It still doesn't seem right. I mean, it's like telling lies – I pretended to pay for you but it wasn't really true. Honestly, Kathy, I can't see what the fuss is about. I've got a good job and I don't have anything else to spend my money on. Why not let me pay when we go to the pictures?'

'Oh, so we're going again, are we?' Kathy teased him, and he grinned.

'I don't see why not, do you? I know you're engaged, but that doesn't mean you've got to sit at home knitting all the time. You'll have fifty or sixty years to do that after you're married. We can go about together till Brian comes back.'

'I suppose we could.' Kathy had enjoyed going to the pictures with Terry. It was nice to sit there in the dark with a man beside her, even if he didn't hold her hand or put his arm round her shoulders. She'd been once or twice on her own and felt uncomfortable by herself, especially during the interval when everyone else had someone to chat to.

Fifty or sixty years! she thought now. Fifty or sixty years of being married to one man, not able to go out with anyone else at all, *ever*, or have any other male friends except those who were married to her own friends, like Martyn and Clare. Terry was right. She was only nineteen years old, and this year was her last chance to have some fun. And she wouldn't be doing anything that Brian could really object to.

'All right, but I still think I ought to pay—'

'Listen,' he said, with mock sternness, 'I've got a say in this too. If you want to come out with me, you've got to put up with me paying. It'll make me feel a lot better. You don't want me feeling miserable all the time, do you?'

Kathy laughed and gave in. She knew that he earned a good deal more than she did, and they wouldn't be going anywhere expensive, after all. Just to the pictures now and then. And she knew that men were funny about girls paying for themselves; they didn't really like it, just as her dad had objected when Mum wanted to get a part-time job once. He'd acted as though she was insulting him, as if she was saying he couldn't provide for his family, and it had caused such bad feeling Mum had had to give up the idea.

'That's settled, then,' Terry said. 'So are we going to see next week's picture? It's another Ian Carmichael, and that chap Peter Sellers is in it too.'

Kathy made a face. 'I don't know. It's about trades unions and that, isn't it? *I'm All Right, Jack*. It sounds a bit boring to me.'

'It won't be with those two in it,' Terry said. 'Come on, Kathy, say yes. And I'll let you win a game of table tennis at the club tomorrow night.'

'*Let* me win! Chance would be a fine thing. Okay, Terry, we'll go to the pictures again *and* you can pay, but I'll bring the sweets, all right?'

After that, they went to the cinema most weeks and started to go for walks on Sundays as well, when it was fine. They strolled along Stokes Bay and out to Lee-on-the-Solent, and had tea in the tower snackbar. They went to the top of the tower and looked at the view of the Isle of Wight and the long shingle beach that stretched from Hillhead to Gomer.

'It's getting scruffy now, this tower,' Terry remarked. 'They're not looking after it properly.'

The tower had been built in the 1930s and had a ballroom with a very good dancefloor, and a cinema. It had been a popular meeting-place but now it looked old-fashioned and shabby. Perhaps they'd do it up, Kathy thought, and make it smart and popular again.

She and Terry didn't go to dances. Terry wasn't a dancer, so the question never arose, but she wouldn't have wanted to do that with another man. Dancing was her and Brian's special thing, and she wouldn't have felt right, letting another boy hold her like that.

Kathy was already feeling a bit guilty. She hadn't told Brian much about Terry in her letters, and she certainly hadn't mentioned that they were going around together. She'd referred to him once or twice when talking about the club, but even that had resulted in a grumpy tone in Brian's next letter. He was 'glad she was going out and enjoying herself', but he hoped she wasn't 'forgetting to wear her ring'. It was plain that he didn't really relish the idea of her meeting other boys, and she was pretty sure he wouldn't take kindly to descriptions of evenings in the cinema or walks along Stokes Bay.

All the same, I've got to do something with myself while he's away, she told herself. I don't see why I should stay in every night, when he's off seeing the world and having a good time ashore.

Terry invited Kathy to his own home a couple of times, but the atmosphere wasn't easy there. His mother and father had parted a few years earlier, and she'd married again. Terry and his stepfather didn't get on, and after one or two visits Kathy was glad he didn't suggest going there again.

'Why don't you leave and get somewhere of your own?' she asked once, when Terry was telling her about an argument he and his stepfather had just had. 'You could afford a flat or something, couldn't you?'

'I'm not living in someone else's house. I'd rather wait and save up to buy my own.' As yet, though, there weren't many houses to buy, and it wasn't usual for a young man on his own to get a mortgage and live by himself. Most people lived with their parents till they got married, and then started off in rooms or a flat. Clare and Martyn had done that, till she'd found herself pregnant and they'd scraped together the deposit on the bungalow.

Kathy had told Clare about Terry and she started taking him on her usual Tuesday visits. She would arrive after work, play with Christopher and have tea with Clare, and then Terry would come just before Christopher went to bed. The three of them would sit and chat and play Scrabble until it was time for Kathy and Terry to go. Clare told Kathy that she liked Terry, and Kathy got the impression that she preferred him to Brian.

It wasn't long after that when Kathy began to wonder whether she didn't, too.

I'll stay in every night, writing you letters, she'd said. *And they won't start 'Dear John'.*

Just make sure they don't, Brian had answered, and Kathy had felt a little thrill of pity mixed with something almost like fear as she heard the intensity in his voice and saw the whiteness around his mouth.

I meant to stay faithful, she thought. I really did mean to. I never thought I'd even be *able* to fall in love with anyone else. I know I never meant to fall in love with Terry . . .

Terry's first kiss had been tentative but sweet. For weeks, as they sat in the cinema together, arms only an inch or two apart, and walked decorously side by side along the beach, he'd never touched her unless it was to help her scramble up the bank or get on a bus. But one night, as they said goodbye at her front gate after an evening at the club, he suddenly bent his head and touched her lips with his.

Kathy had been startled, yet at the same time felt that she'd been waiting for it. Fleetingly, she thought she ought to draw away, but she didn't. The feel of his lips on hers was like a sip of fresh, cool water to someone lost in a desert. She closed her eyes and swayed a little, and he laid his hands on her shoulders and then pulled her closer.

The kiss was over, swift and gentle as the brush of a butterfly's wing.

Terry let her go and stepped back, rubbing one hand over his face. In the light of the streetlamp, he looked confused and upset. 'I'm sorry – I shouldn't have done that.'

'It's all right.' Without thinking, Kathy laid her hand on his arm. 'Terry, it's all right. I – I liked it.'

'You're engaged. I promised I wouldn't . . .'

'You promised you wouldn't make a pass at me. That didn't feel like

43

a pass. It felt like a nice, friendly kiss. Between friends,' she added as if he might not have understood.

He looked down at her. 'It wasn't meant to happen, honestly. I just – wanted to kiss you.'

'Well, that's all right.' Kathy smiled at him. 'I wanted to kiss you too.' He had turned his face away slightly so that it was half in shadow. She reached up and laid one hand on his cheek, turning his face back to her. 'Look, it's nothing to worry about. We're friends, that's all. We can give each other a goodnight kiss without turning it into a world crisis.'

Terry laughed, and she felt better. 'All right, then. So long as you don't get the wrong idea.'

'I won't,' Kathy said, and to prove it she stood on her toes and kissed him again, very lightly.

After that, they'd always kissed goodnight and, almost without their noticing it, the kisses had become more lingering and tender, until one night, holding her close in his arms, Terry had whispered, 'I knew this wasn't a good idea.'

They weren't saying goodnight. It was a brilliant, moonlit night and they'd walked out to Alverstoke and were sitting on a bench at the top of the beach, looking out across the darkly twinkling sea. A silver path of moonlight lay across the water, as if someone had tossed down a glittering scarf, and the lights of Ryde were like star clusters on the dark mass of the Island.

The late October night was sharp with frost and Terry had slipped his arm around Kathy's shoulders. It seemed natural to her to turn her face to his, and she closed her eyes as he kissed her.

'What d'you mean?' she murmured. 'What isn't a good idea?'

'I shouldn't ever have started this,' he said, resting his face against her hair. 'I shouldn't ever have kissed you that first time.'

Kathy was silent. She wanted to say she didn't know what he meant, she wanted to tell him again that their kisses were just friendly, they didn't mean a thing, but it wouldn't have been true. She knew very well what he meant, and their kisses weren't just friendly any more.

'You know what's happened, don't you?' Terry raised his head and looked down into her eyes. 'I've fallen in love with you, Kathy.'

'Yes,' she said quietly. 'I know. And I think I've fallen in love with you too, Terry.'

There was a pause. They sat very still, loosely encircled in each other's arms, looking into each other's eyes. Kathy felt an odd mixture of emotions: dismay because this had never been meant to happen; remorse because of what she was doing to Brian; and a creeping, guilty

44

delight because she was in the arms of the man she loved, and he'd just told her he loved her too.

'*Kathy*,' he said, and drew her hard against him.

There was nothing tentative about his kiss now. He didn't almost devour her, like Brian did sometimes, but she could feel the desire in his lips and her own leaped to respond to it. She tightened her arms around his neck and let herself melt against his body, her senses whirling. Terry, she thought, Terry . . . This couldn't be happening, it mustn't be happening; but it was and she didn't want it to stop.

I ought to stop it, she thought, dazed. I'm engaged to another boy. But Brian seemed very far away, thousands of miles away across that dark sea, and the time until he returned seemed endless. And Terry was here, and kissing her, and she wanted him to go on. She loved him . . .

They were both breathless when their kisses stopped at last. They sat close together, holding each other tightly, shaken by the sudden surge of passion. It seemed an amazing thing that nothing else had changed. Even the pathway of the moon had not moved.

'You ought to slap my face,' he said remorsefully. 'You won't want to see me again.'

'Who won't? Of course I will. And I dare say a lot of people would say it's me who ought to have my face slapped.'

He smiled suddenly and tapped her cheek lightly with his palm. 'There. Consider yourself slapped.'

Kathy giggled, feeling a release of tension. 'You dope! Oh, Terry . . .' She snuggled closer against him. 'I've been wanting you to kiss me like that for so long.'

'Have you?' He sounded surprised.

'Well, I don't think I actually realised it,' she said honestly, 'but now I come to think about it – yes, I think I have. Am I awful?'

'I don't think you're awful at all. I think you're wonderful.' His palm was still against her cheek, stroking it softly. 'I've been in love with you all along, but I honestly never meant this to happen. I thought I'd just enjoy being with you for a while, and then when Brian came home I'd just have to forget you.'

'Oh.' Kathy felt blank. When Brian came home . . . 'But you will, won't you?' she said miserably. 'We both will. I can't let Brian down.'

There was a moment of silence, before Terry said, 'You mean, this isn't going to make any difference?'

'It can't, can it? I'm engaged. I've promised—'

'Engagements can be broken. You're in love with me. You just said so.'

'I know, but there's Brian. I love him too. At least, I think I do. I *do*.' She listened to her own voice, trying to gauge the truth of her words. 'Oh, I don't know, I feel muddled – I love you both. But he was first . . .' She twisted her hands together, feeling the roughness of Brian's diamonds on her finger. 'Terry, what am I going to do?'

'I don't know, do I?' The euphoria, the delight of their kisses, had evaporated. A small cloud came from nowhere and drifted across the face of the moon and the night seemed darker and colder. 'It seems pretty simple to me. First come, first served. That's what you're saying, isn't it?'

'*No!*' But it was, she thought. It was certainly what it sounded like, anyway. 'I've promised him. We're engaged. I said I wouldn't – wouldn't—' Tears suddenly choked her and she laid her face against his chest. 'Oh, *Terry*.'

'Wouldn't what?' he asked after a moment.

'I said I wouldn't write him a "Dear John" letter,' she wept. 'I *promised* him I wouldn't. I said I'd be faithful to him.'

Terry was silent for a long while. He kept his arm around Kathy's shoulders, stroking her hair with his fingers as he stared out across the Solent. There was a ship passing between Stokes Bay and the Island, a tanker probably, with lights all along its deck and strung between its masts. A lot of big ships used the Solent, on their way to Southampton. You could see the big 'Queens' – the *Queen Mary* and the *Queen Elizabeth* – on their way to New York, yet just as frequently this stretch of water was alive with sailing dinghies and yachts from local sailing clubs. In the summer, during the Cowes Regatta week, you could almost walk from one shore to the other across their decks.

'Well, I never did really think you could want an ordinary bloke like me when you could have someone like him,' he said at last. 'I mean, I've never even done National Service. My eyesight wasn't good enough.'

Kathy lifted her head and stared at him. 'What's that got to do with it? I don't fall in love with people because they've got good eyesight!'

'No, but a chap like your Brian is bound to be more interesting than someone like me. I mean, look at all the places he's been. I've never been further than Bognor Regis.'

Kathy started to laugh. 'At least you're around to take a girl to the pictures! Terry, none of that matters. It's other things that are important. Things like – well, the way you are. The way you look after me and take notice of me. How nice it is just being with you. That's what makes me love you. You're so *nice*.'

'And isn't Brian nice as well?' he asked.

Kathy sighed. 'Yes, of course he is. That's just the trouble. You're both nice, and I love you both and I *don't know what to do.*'

'It's all my fault. If I'd just never kissed you goodnight in the first place—'

'Well, you did, and we can't change that,' Kathy said, but her briskness quickly disappeared. 'Anyway, I'm glad you did. I like you kissing me, Terry.'

He looked down at her and then groaned and bent his head to lay his mouth once more upon hers. They clung together, oblivious to the increasing chill in the air. Their passion grew until at last Terry broke away.

'Kathy, we've got to stop. I'd better take you home. It's getting late.'

She wanted to say she didn't care, but she knew that he was right. Things were bad enough without her father coming out to look for her, as he was quite capable of doing. 'Half past ten's your time, my girl,' he would say, 'engaged or not.' And since the man she was out with wasn't the one she was engaged to . . . Yes, Terry was right. She had to go home.

'You won't want to see me again, I suppose,' he said as they walked along Jellicoe Avenue, holding hands.

'Terry, of course I will! More than ever.' She knew she ought to be agreeing with him. She shouldn't go on seeing him, now that this had happened. 'I can't give you up that easily,' she added in a low voice. 'It's been so nice, going about with you. And there's the club . . . we're bound to see each other there.'

'So what do you want? Just to go on being friends?'

'It's all we can do, isn't it?' she said, not looking at him. 'It's been nice, hasn't it, being friends? It can go on being nice like that.'

He didn't answer for a moment, then he said quietly, 'But no kissing.'

'None at all?' she asked wistfully. 'Not even a little goodnight kiss?'

'Look, I want it just as much as you do.' His hand gripped hers tightly, and then, quite deliberately, he let it go. 'But I won't be able to bear just a little goodnight kiss. And it wouldn't stop there anyway. No, if we're going to go on as just friends, that's all it's got to be. Just friends. Nothing more, *nothing at all.*'

They said no more until they came to Kathy's gate. For a moment they stood silent, awkward, not knowing how to part. Then Kathy, feeling near to tears, unlatched the gate with shaking fingers and pushed it open.

''Night, then. See you at the club tomorrow?'

47

'I don't know.' His voice was strained. 'I might give it a miss this week.'

'All right.' Her own voice was high and unnatural. 'Next week, maybe.'

'Yes. Maybe. Yes, I expect so.' For a moment, he hesitated and she stared at him, thinking he was about to say more. Then he turned away. ''Night, then, Kathy.'

'Goodnight, Terry,' she whispered, and walked the few steps to the front door. In the shelter of the little porch, she paused, still half hoping that he would turn back. But all that she could hear was the sound of his footsteps, growing fainter along the dark, quiet road.

Chapter Five

The visits to the cinema stopped. Nothing was said about them; there just didn't seem to be a film worth seeing for a week or two, and neither Kathy nor Terry suggested going again. There were no more walks on Sunday afternoons either, and Terry didn't come to Clare's on Tuesday evenings any more.

'Have you had a row?' Clare enquired, but Kathy shrugged and picked up Christopher, hugging him and hiding her face in his tummy so that he chuckled and kicked with delight.

Clare said no more, but she was sorry not to be seeing Terry again and surprised when he turned up on her doorstep one Wednesday evening, looking embarrassed and uncertain.

'Terry! Come in.' It was raining and his mackintosh dripped on the hall floor. 'Take off your coat. D'you want a cup of coffee?'

He nodded and followed her into the tiny kitchen. Clare bustled about, putting on the kettle and getting out cups. She opened the door of the small larder and took out a bottle of milk and a tin of biscuits. Terry stood watching her without speaking.

'You do know it's Wednesday?' she asked him doubtfully. He looked thin and miserable, his hair dark with rain. She gave him a towel and he rubbed his head with it dejectedly. 'Kathy was here yesterday.'

'I know. It's you I wanted to see.'

Clare gave him an even more doubtful glance and put the mugs of coffee on a tray with some biscuits on a plate. She carried them through to the lounge and Terry followed her. Like a little dog, she thought, and began to have some inkling of why he was here.

'I've missed you lately,' she said, setting the tray down on the coffee-table in front of the fire. 'I think Kathy has too.'

'I've missed her. You know we're not seeing each other any more.'

Clare nodded. 'Well, I realised it. Kathy hasn't actually said anything. Did you have an argument?'

He grimaced. 'Not really. Only about whether she was going to write Brian a "Dear John" letter, if you know what that is, and we didn't even argue about that. There didn't seem any point.'

Clare stared at him. 'A "Dear John"?'

'That's what she called it. You know what it is, I suppose.'

'Oh, yes,' Clare said faintly, 'I know what it is, but I didn't know she – I mean, I thought you were just friends. I didn't think there was anything . . .'

'Nor did I. Nor did she. It just happened. We – well, we got too fond of each other, I suppose. Inevitable, really. Well, inevitable that I'd get fond of *her* – I never thought she'd look at me, that sort of way. I didn't think I had a chance.'

'Oh, Terry,' Clare said. She felt inadequate, helpless. She stared at him and then said, 'I know she liked you a lot.'

'It was more than that, but not enough. It's still Brian really.' He gazed at Clare and she saw the misery, the uncertainty, in his eyes. 'At least – oh, *hell*, Clare, I wish I knew for certain. I don't think *she* knows, not really. It's just that she says she's promised him, she's engaged to him, and she can't back out of it. But why not? That's what I want to know. What's the point of staying engaged to him if she doesn't really love him? What's the point of getting married?'

'Are you sure she doesn't love him?'

'I don't know. I told you, I don't think she knows herself. But I know one thing: she thinks a lot more of me than an engaged girl ought to think about another chap. She's in love with me, Clare, and I'm in love with her. She ought at least to give me a chance.'

Clare picked up her mug of coffee and sipped it. She felt at a total loss. Such a situation had never come her way before and she didn't know how to handle it. It was true that she liked Terry better than Brian, but that didn't mean Kathy ought to break off her engagement. Perhaps she just needed some time to herself to sort out her feelings.

'I'm really sorry,' she said, 'but people don't break off engagements just like that. I mean, it's a serious thing—'

'It's a serious thing to fall in love with someone else,' he broke in. 'You can't get married like that. It's not fair on anyone.'

Clare looked at him helplessly. 'Well, what d'you want me to do about it?'

'I don't know if I want you to do anything. I just needed to talk to someone who knows us both, and there isn't anyone but you. I can't talk to anyone at the club. You're Kathy's friend. Maybe you could talk to her about it. Make her see—'

'I can't do that. Not unless she wants to talk to me, and she hasn't said anything at all yet. I think she wants to work it out for herself.'

'I'm not asking you to persuade her. Just – well, let her know that you know about it. Then if she does want to talk . . . Clare, it's not just that I want her myself – I don't want her to marry a chap she doesn't really love. I don't want her to be unhappy. Can you understand that?' He leaned forward, dark eyes intense in his thin face. 'It doesn't matter about me. If she never speaks to me again, I'll survive, somehow. But I can't watch her marry that bloke, knowing that she doesn't really love him, and just not do anything about it. I can't.'

'You don't *know* she doesn't love him,' Clare said, outraged. 'Just because she – *you* and she – well, I don't know what's happened between you, but I know Kathy, and I know she'd never do anything wrong. And I don't think you would, either,' she added fairly. 'So what was it – just a few kisses? *That's* not enough to jump to the conclusion that she doesn't love Brian any more.'

'She's not sure,' he repeated obstinately. 'She doesn't know her own mind. That's all I'm saying.'

'Look,' Clare said, and she leaned forward as well. 'Brian's been away for nearly seven months. She's lonely. You've been going to the pictures, going for walks – you're good friends. I'm sorry, Terry, but it was asking for trouble really. You were bound to get hurt.'

'You mean it's just an infatuation,' he said quietly. 'Once Brian comes back, she'll forget all about me.'

Clare sighed unhappily. 'I'm sorry, Terry, but it's more than likely.'

There was a long silence. She glanced at his cup. 'You haven't touched your coffee,' she said gently.

'I don't think I want it.'

'Please. Just a sip.' She felt as if she were talking to Christopher, coaxing him to try a new food. 'It'll make you feel better.'

Terry's mouth twisted but he picked up the mug and sipped. He put it down again. 'No. I don't believe it. I don't believe it's no more than an infatuation. She does love me, Clare, I know she does. I can't let her go – not just like that.'

'Well, I still don't see what you expect me to do about it,' Clare exclaimed. She was exasperated and frightened. The idea of Kathy breaking her engagement was appalling. An engagement was a promise, almost as big a promise as marriage. You didn't break off engagements

51

just like that, especially when your fiancé was at sea for a year and couldn't do anything about it.

'You don't have to do anything.' Terry stood up. He sounded weary and disheartened. 'I don't suppose there's anything anyone can do. It's up to Kathy to make up her own mind.' He walked out to the tiny hallway and took his raincoat off the hook. 'Just tell her I came, will you?'

He paused for a moment and Clare stood in the doorway, watching him. He looked haggard and unhappy, and she felt sorry for him. But that's what you get when you go out with someone who's already engaged, she thought sadly.

'I'm sorry,' he said. 'Sorry to have landed on you like this. And now I suppose you won't want to see me again either.'

'Of course I will,' she said. 'You're always welcome here, Terry. Come whenever you like.'

He gave her a wry smile. 'Aren't you afraid I'll do the same to you?'

Clare shook her head. 'I'm married and I've got a baby. Nobody's going to come between me and Martyn and Christopher.'

'Well,' he said, 'I'll drop in some time. Give Chris my love, won't you? He's a smashing baby.' He turned and opened the front door. A gust of cold, wet air blew in and he drew his coat closer around him and turned up the collar.

He shut the door behind him and Clare heard his footsteps move rapidly away. She sighed and went back into the lounge. The fire had died down a little, so she put on some more coal and poked it into life and then sat before it, gazing thoughtfully into the flames.

Poor Terry. And poor Kathy. And – though he didn't know it – poor Brian as well. What was going to happen to them all?

By now, HMS *Pacific* was in Singapore. She had steamed through the Mediterranean and through the Suez Canal, calling at Malta and Aden, and then down the coast of Africa and across the Indian Ocean. On the way she had taken part in a number of exercises with the smaller ships accompanying her, and the men's letters home had been full of technical terms that their wives skimmed over in the search for more human pieces of news. But there wasn't much happening at sea to interest families at home, and the sailors were all too busy to write at any length. They wrote instead of their love and longing for the day when they would steam back into Plymouth Sound.

The men looked forward to their letters even more than their wives. Sometimes, when they were at sea, a week or two would pass with nothing, then there would be a mail drop or a transfer from another ship, and they would fall on the bundles of letters, sorting them into order and retreating to their bunks to indulge in an orgy of reading.

When they reached Singapore, there were the usual sacks of mail awaiting them. Martyn grabbed his bundle and opened the first one. It contained photographs of Christopher, now propped up against pillows in his pram, smiling a broad, toothless grin. He looked less like a coconut now and more like a human being – rather a jolly little human being, Martyn realised suddenly, with that merry smile. He stared at the picture of his son, feeling an odd movement somewhere under his heart. I bet he laughs if you tickle him, he thought, and felt a great yearning to be able to hold the round, cuddly little body and poke his fingertips into the yielding flesh and hear the baby chuckle. He wanted to be able to look into those twinkling eyes and see them respond to him, to know that Christopher knew him for his daddy. Oh, God, he thought, another seven months . . . He'll be different again by then. He'll never be like this again. I'm missing it all . . .

Brian was reading his letters on the opposite bunk. He had a small frown on his face and after a while he stuffed the paper back into the envelope and leaned across to shake Martyn by the shoulder.

'Come on, mate. Let's go ashore. Keep the rest till later.'

Martyn looked up from the third letter in his bundle. Clare had told him all about how her father had offered to dig over the garden and sow grass seed. He'd much rather plant cabbages, she said, but she wanted lawn for the children to play on. The children . . . I haven't even seen this one yet, he thought, and she's talking as if we're going to have more. Well, I suppose we will some time, but I'd like to get to know Chris first. And have Clare to myself a bit too, without her being pregnant.

'Come on,' Brian urged. 'We've been at sea for weeks. I need to feel a bit of solid land under my feet. I need to see what a real woman looks like, instead of a pin-up.'

All the men kept pin-up pictures inside their locker doors. It was a sort of competition to see who could find the most pneumatic blonde. Martyn had a picture of Marilyn Monroe, while Brian favoured Jayne Mansfield. They were good to look at, and seemed to lessen the craving for a real female body in your arms, but, as Brian said, there was really nothing to replace the real thing. After weeks at sea, you needed to know that such women actually existed outside photographs.

It was something the girls found difficult to understand. Even Clare would have wondered why he needed a busty picture to look at instead of her own photograph. He had pictures of Clare as well, of course, and looked at them every day, but looking at Marilyn Monroe was different. She wasn't real, she was a fantasy, and deep down there was a part of him that yearned for fantasy.

Brian was ready to go. He gave Martyn an impatient push, and Martyn folded his letters and swung his legs off his bunk. They were wearing tropical gear now, white shorts and shirts, and the air outside was hot and steamy, like a bathroom. They clattered down the gangplank and made their way through the dockyard and into the town, sniffing the strange, exotic scents and staring about them at the crowded streets.

'Blimey, there are more bikes here than people,' Brian exclaimed. 'Hey, we'll have to get a ride in a rickshaw . . . And look at those food stalls. What the hell are they eating?'

'Dunno, and I don't think I want to find out. The chief told me they eat dogs. It smells all right, mind. Let's find a bar and see what the beer's like.'

As usual, all the bars were filled with girls and sailors. The girls here were different, though – they were Chinese or Malayan, with tiny, curvy bodies encased in silk cheongsams slit to the thigh. They had smooth black hair, shiny as coal, and black doe eyes that glanced at you and flirted. They looked like porcelain figurines and you couldn't help wanting to touch them, just to see if they were real.

As soon as Martyn and Brian entered the bar, two of the girls appeared from nowhere and linked arms with them. They had high, twittering voices, like starlings, and at first Martyn found it difficult to understand what they were saying. It was plain enough, however, that they were suggesting drinks, and they pushed the two sailors into a seat in the corner and went to the bar to fetch them. Martyn gave Brian a glance.

'We'd better be careful. This could cost us.'

'It's all right. They're just like waitresses.'

'A bit friendly for waitresses,' Martyn commented, but he knew Brian was right. You could almost certainly buy whatever favours you wanted from the girls, but if you didn't want they would just sit with you for a while and then go in search of more promising game. Meanwhile, it was rather pleasant to be waited on by a pretty little Chinese girl in a cheongsam.

'How's Kathy?' he asked. Brian had said nothing about his letters and Martyn had caught him looking a bit thoughtful once or twice. 'She's okay, isn't she?'

'Sounds like it,' Brian said, but not as if the fact pleased him. 'Keeps on about this club she's joined, down at the community centre. She goes there two or three times a week. They do things like have debates and quizzes.' He scowled.

Martyn looked at him in amusement. 'So what's wrong with that? Sounds all right to me. Keeps her out of mischief, doesn't it?'

'I dunno. Does it? She's meeting blokes there, isn't she? Spending time with them. And she's going to the pictures a lot too, and she doesn't say who with.'

'Well, I suppose she goes with one of her mates,' Martyn said. 'You can't expect her to stay in knitting every night, Bri. She's not like Clare, with a baby to look after.'

'No. Sometimes I think it's a pity. Maybe we should have got married, like you did, and I could have made sure she had something else to think about. Debates!' he said in disgust. 'Quizzes! That's not the sort of thing a girl does when she's engaged and getting ready for her wedding.'

'Well, she can't get ready for a while, can she?' Martyn pointed out. 'She's got to pass the time somehow.'

Brian shook his head. 'I don't like it. She's changed. I can tell by her letters. I tell you what, Martyn, it just makes me feel so bloody helpless. I mean, stuck out here on the ship – there's nothing I can do, is there? She could be out with some bloke now, at this very minute, and there's bugger-all I can do about it.'

The girls came back with their drinks and snuggled on to the men's laps. Martyn felt the little body wriggle against him and knew that he couldn't help responding. He felt the small, firm curves under his hands and closed his eyes. Clare, he thought, Clare. It's you I want. Not this little Chinese tart. Not anyone else. Just you and me and our baby in our own home. He felt a great surge of loneliness wash over him.

He drank his beer and pushed the girl off his lap. Brian was laughing and nuzzling at his girl's neck. Martyn stood up, ignoring the twittering voice of the little Chinese, and said abruptly, 'Let's go somewhere else.'

'Sure.' Brian stood up too. 'The night is young. There's plenty more where these two came from.' He pinched his girl's bottom and she squealed and pouted, clinging to his arm to try to prevent him leaving. 'All right, sweetheart, you can let go now. There'll be another liberty boat through in a few minutes. We're out for some serious drinking, okay?'

He elbowed his way out of the bar and they found themselves on the crowded street again. The night sky was like black velvet and the air was as warm as an eiderdown. They wandered on, stopping to gaze at the stalls, shrugging away the girls who offered their favours, shaking off the children who darted round their feet begging for money. The confinement of weeks at sea was forgotten and they felt free and easy, thousands of miles from home in this exotic city, with nobody to see what they did. They looked at each other and grinned, and then guffawed with laughter.

'This is the life!' Brian said, and punched Martyn on the arm. '*This* is the life!'

Martyn and Brian had become friends as boys, when Brian was evacuated to Ivybridge. Sent to stay with an elderly spinster aunt, he had been like a square peg in a round hole and yearned for the streets of Bristol rather than the narrow lanes and open moors of Devon. Martyn had found him mooching along by the river one day, throwing stones at the ducks, and after a brief, suspicious encounter and a few punches to establish the relationship, they had become inseparable. Like chalk and cheese, they had each found something attractive about the other. Martyn had been intrigued by Brian's brash city cockiness, and Brian had been reluctantly dependent on Martyn's country skills. The two had roamed for miles, playing soldiers amongst the rocks and bracken, and keeping a lookout for spies. They had stood outside their homes in April 1941, listening to the German bombers and watching the sky glow red as Plymouth burned, and they had gone later to stare at the devastation and pick their way through the ruined streets that had brought death to the city and then become an adventure playground for small boys.

By the time Brian returned to Bristol, they had agreed to join the Navy together. Their first idea had been to become boy sailors at HMS Ganges or St Vincent, but their schoolmasters had persuaded them to look higher and become artificers. Square rig uniform was replaced by the suit of the petty officer apprentice, and they went to Collingwood to learn about radar and electronics.

Being together on their first ship was what they had dreamed of. It wouldn't last – they knew that they were unlikely to get another draft together – but for now, they could enjoy all the new experiences. Their relationship was, as always, a tug of war, with Brian pulling Martyn further than he really wanted to go, and Martyn holding Brian back. Their friendship was so old that they had forgotten why they were friends. It was a habit that had begun years ago and would never die.

They knew each other as well as brothers. And as they wandered the streets of Singapore together, Martyn knew that there was something wrong with his friend. He knew it from Brian's unaccustomed silence as they left the ship, and from his sudden excitable behaviour now. He knew it from his outburst over Kathy and, although he did not tell Brian this, he knew it from a certain vague restraint, something he couldn't quite pin down, in Clare's letters to himself.

Well, there was nothing he could do about it but stick close to his friend and make sure he didn't get into any trouble. For Brian had a fierce and sometimes violent temper, and when he was upset about something, he was liable to lose control of it. And Martyn didn't want him to end up in a Singapore jail.

Clare did not have to tell Kathy about Terry's visit when she came on her usual Tuesday evening visit the next week. Kathy had evidently made up her mind. All through tea she was quieter than usual, and as soon as Christopher had been put to bed she took a deep breath and faced her friend.

'I've got something to tell you.'

Clare had been just about to use the very same words. She closed her mouth and waited, hardly daring to breathe.

'I've decided,' Kathy said, 'that I don't deserve to be engaged to Brian any more.'

Clare found she had been holding her breath. She let it out on a sigh. 'Oh, *Kathy*. Whyever not?'

Kathy gave her a sideways glance. 'You know why not. Terry came round here last week, didn't he? He told you about us.'

'He told me he was in love with you,' Clare said cautiously. 'He didn't seem to know how you felt about it.'

'Well, he knows now,' Kathy said with an attempt at lightness. 'We talked about it all day Sunday. I saw him at the club on Friday. We've been avoiding each other, going on different evenings, but I made up my mind I had to see him. I just couldn't stand it any longer,' she said half pleadingly. 'I missed him.'

'But you miss Brian too. Don't you?'

Kathy turned her face away and answered in a muffled voice. 'Not as much as I missed Terry.'

There was a silence, before Clare said, 'Have you written to tell him? A "Dear John"?'

'Yes.'

'Oh, Kathy.'

'I didn't want to,' Kathy said with sudden desperation. 'I've been trying for weeks to put Terry out of my mind, to tell myself it was just an infatuation, it didn't mean anything, but I can't. And it's no use going on with an engagement I don't believe in any more. I thought of waiting till he came home and telling him then. Or at least waiting till after Christmas. But that wouldn't make it any better. He'd already started to talk about the wedding. How could I go on writing letters like that, knowing I was going to finish it when he came home?'

'You couldn't.' Clare moved to sit beside her friend. She laid her arm across Kathy's shoulders. 'Oh, Kathy, I'm so sorry.'

Kathy bowed her head and covered her face with her hands. Her shoulders trembled and she began to cry. 'I really did love him. I never meant to let him down. I couldn't bear to think of writing that letter – him reading it, on the ship, thousands of miles away, and with Christmas coming. Why did it have to be like that, Clare, why? I never wanted to hurt him. I promised I wouldn't.'

Clare hugged her. 'I know. I know. It isn't your fault, Kathy.'

'It is. It is my fault. I shouldn't ever have gone to the club. I should have stayed at home and – and knitted things. I shouldn't ever have gone to the pictures with Terry, I should have known what it would lead to.'

'I don't see how you could have known.'

'Of course I should have known,' Kathy said with weary exasperation. 'What do you *think* is going to happen when a chap and a girl go out together? Sitting there in the pictures in the dark, going for walks along Stokes Bay on Sunday afternoons. It was daft. Plain, stupid *daft*.'

Clare said nothing. In a way, Kathy was right, it had been asking for trouble, but it was a poor thing if a girl couldn't have friends and go out and enjoy herself with them when her man was away. 'I suppose it's best to stay in a group,' she said, thinking aloud. 'Then there's not the temptation.'

'Don't fool yourself,' Kathy said bitterly. 'We were in a group at the club. But people pair off, don't they? It's nature.' She fished in her cardigan pocket for a hanky and blew her nose. 'Well, no use crying over spilt milk. Or broken dreams.' Her mouth quivered and for a moment she seemed about to break down again, then she pulled herself together and gave Clare a brave, albeit rather watery, smile. 'I've done it now. I can't go back.'

'When do you think he'll get the letter?' Clare asked.

'Some time this week, I suppose. Or the beginning of next week. And then I dare say he'll write back.' She grimaced. 'Can't say I'm looking forward to that much, but I guess whatever he says, I'll deserve it.'

'Kathy, it's no good blaming yourself. It's happened, and there's nothing more to be done. I'm sure you told Brian you were sorry.'

'Oh, I did! But me being *sorry* isn't going to be much comfort to him, is it? He's going to be livid, Clare.' Kathy shivered. 'I don't know what he'll do.'

'He won't do anything. There isn't anything he can do. You're entitled to break off your engagement if that's the way you feel. It's not a crime.'

'I don't know. You hear about these breach-of-promise cases. People get taken to court.'

'Not people like us. That's just upper-class people with a lot of money. Brian won't do anything like that. It costs hundreds to go to court, and what good would it do? You can't be forced to marry him.' Clare looked closely at her friend. 'You're not scared of him, are you?'

'No, of course not.' Kathy gave a little laugh. 'I'm just being silly. Oh, Clare, it's been awful these last few weeks. I missed Terry so much and I kept telling myself it was Brian I was missing. But it wasn't. I'm still fond of him, of course, I still care about him. He hasn't done anything to me, after all, but I just don't love him the way I did, and it's no good pretending I do.'

'No,' Clare said, 'it isn't.' She took her arm away from Kathy's shoulders. 'I'm going to make us a cup of coffee. I think you need one.'

She returned a few minutes later to find Kathy somewhat recovered, her tears wiped away and her short, pixie hair brushed and smooth. She gave Clare a wavering grin as she accepted the coffee and said, 'I do feel better now I've made up my mind. It was the not knowing what to do that was so awful.'

'So what are you going to do?' Clare sat down in the old armchair that her mother had covered in plain, bright red. 'Will you and Terry get engaged?'

Kathy shook her head. 'Oh, no. Not yet. It doesn't seem decent, somehow. Anyway, we haven't really got to that stage yet. I haven't, anyway. I don't even know if we will. I just didn't think it was right to go on being engaged to Brian while I could be so interested in someone else.' She paused to drink some of her coffee. 'I don't even know if I'm really ready to get engaged at all. I know I don't want to get married yet! And it's the same thing, really, isn't it? I mean, if you get engaged, it's because you want to get married.'

'Yes, it is.' Clare glanced at Kathy's left hand, wondering why she hadn't noticed earlier that it was bare. 'Well, you'll know when you are ready, I suppose. Is Terry coming round tonight?'

Kathy blushed. 'We hoped you wouldn't mind. He said you were really nice to him last week.'

'Of course I was. You know I've always liked him. And he seemed so miserable.' Clare grinned at her. 'I'd better get another cup ready, hadn't I? Oh, lor' – I've just thought. I'd better say something to Martyn next time I write. Brian's bound to tell him, isn't he?'

'I should think so, but perhaps you'd better wait till Martyn mentions it, just in case he doesn't. Oh, I don't know . . .' Kathy began to look woebegone again. 'He'll have to know, won't he? He was going to be Brian's best man. They've been planning it all.'

'Don't start crying again,' Clare said hastily. 'Terry'll be here any minute. He won't want to find you weeping all over the place. He'll think you've changed your mind again. Look, I won't say anything to Martyn until next week. By that time, he'll probably have mentioned it to me anyway. I suppose he'll take Brian's part.' She sighed. 'It's probably just as well they won't be back for another five months – it'll give time for the dust to settle.'

There was a knock at the door and they looked at each other. 'That'll be Terry,' Clare said. 'You go and let him in and I'll make some more coffee. And don't worry, Kathy. I'm sure you've done the right thing. You can't marry someone you don't love, and you couldn't have let him go on thinking everything was all right. You'd have been telling lies in every letter you wrote.'

'I know. Thanks.' Kathy gave her a quick smile and went to open the door.

Clare went back to the kitchen and filled the kettle noisily, not wanting to eavesdrop on their first few words. She was sad about what had happened, and sorry for Brian. All the same, she didn't really see what else Kathy could have done. It was surely better to find out now that they weren't suited, rather than go on with an engagement and even a marriage that just wasn't right.

I'm glad it's not happening to me, she thought with a shiver. Not that it ever could. Martyn and I really love each other. There'll never be anyone else for us.

'It's a "Dear John".' Brian stared blankly at the sheet of paper in his hand. 'It's a fucking "Dear John".'

Martyn's head jerked round. The latest bundle of letters had arrived half an hour ago and he'd taken his to his bunk and started to read immediately. They came more frequently when the ship was in port, but Clare wrote and posted her letters so often – almost every day – that they were bound to come in batches. He'd noticed as he picked his up that Brian's batch was smaller than usual, but he hadn't thought anything of it. Now he stared at his friend in dismay.

'A "Dear John"? You're not serious.'

'Would I joke about it?' Brian asked bitterly, and thrust the sheet of paper towards him. 'Here – read it for yourself.'

Martyn took the letter reluctantly. He scanned it quickly, noting the phrases. *'Don't deserve to be enaged to you any more . . . can't go on writing lies . . . so sorry . . . never wanted to hurt you . . . sorry, sorry, sorry . . .'* He looked up at Brian's face. 'Oh, God, Bri. God, I'm sorry . . .'

'That's what *she* says. Over and over again. Sorry! As if *sorry* can make it better!' Brian snatched the letter back and stared at it again as if hoping the words might have changed. 'I knew there was something wrong, I knew it. All that talk about debates and stuff. And going to the pictures or out for walks and never saying who with. It's another bloke, isn't it? She's found another bloke.'

'She doesn't say that.'

'She doesn't have to. It's all there. You only have to read between the lines. Why else would she break off our engagement? Not just so she can go to some damned youth club and play Twenty Questions. There's another bloke, Martyn. She's chucked me for another bloke.'

Martyn didn't answer. He thought Brian was probably right but he didn't think it would do much good to say so. He looked at his friend in some alarm. Brian's face was white, the skin taut and hard, and his eyes were glittering feverishly. He paced up and down the narrow space between the bunks, the letter crumpled in his fist. He looked as if he would start smashing things up at any moment, and Martyn remembered times when they'd been boys and Brian had lost his temper over some incident. He'd chucked a stone through a window once, and almost killed an old woman sitting just inside, and another time he'd thrown all his old aunt's best cups and saucers on the floor.

'Cool it off a bit, Bri,' he said. 'It's no good getting worked up about it.'

'So what else should I do?' Brian demanded. 'Send her a telegram congratulating her? Write her a pretty little note saying, it doesn't matter, all I want is for her to be happy and let's keep in touch and be friends?' He waved the letter in Martyn's face. 'That's what she says! Let's stay friends. How the hell can a bloke stay friends with a girl that does this to him? Stay friends? I'd like to strangle her, that's what I'd like to do. I'd like to put my hands round her neck and *strangle* her.'

'You don't mean that. You know you don't. You've got every right to be upset, but—'

'Upset? I'm bloody furious!'

'All right, you've got every right to be furious. But you'd never hurt her. You know you wouldn't.'

Brian stopped pacing and looked at him. His face was bone-white against his dark hair, and his eyes were like hollows. His mouth looked tight and stiff, and his voice was hard, like cold iron.

'Don't you be too sure about that, Martyn. Don't you be too sure.'

Martyn stared helplessly at him. He had seen Brian suddenly lose control before, when they were ashore, and get into fights, but it had always been with people who were able to take care of themselves, and the occasional brawls had resulted in no more than a bloody nose or black eye. Surely he didn't really mean his threats against Kathy.

All the same, Martyn could well understand his friend's rage. He tried to imagine how he would feel if Clare had done such a thing to him, and knew he too would feel this dreadful, impotent fury. They were so far away, that was the trouble, and it would be months before anything could be done about it. If you were at home, you could go round and have it out with the girl, but stuck like this thousands of miles away . . .

'She's not worth it,' he said. 'Look at it that way. You're well out of it. Let's go ashore and have a few pints.'

'Bitch,' Brian said bitterly. 'You're right, Martyn, she's not worth it. And I suppose she's round with your Clare now, weeping on her shoulder and saying what a bastard I am. Little bitch.'

'Well, that's something we can do something about,' Martyn declared. 'I'll write to Clare and say she's not to have Kathy in the house again. I'm not having my best mate treated like this.'

'We should have got married before I came away,' Brian said. 'I should have got her pregnant, like you did with Clare. That would have put paid to all this.' He unfolded the letter again and stared at it, then screwed it up and threw it in a corner of the mess. 'Bloody, two-timing *bitch*! I reckon she's been taking me for a real fool all this time – all this time I've been going ashore and passing up all those girls, keeping faith, thinking she was doing the same, and she's been laughing behind my back, been having it off with some other bloke, letting him do things she never let me . . . Well, at least there's nothing now to stop me making the most of all those other girls, is there? Okay, Martyn, let's go ashore. Let's go ashore and have ourselves a really good time.'

Martyn followed him. He was still afraid that Brian would get into trouble if he went ashore on his own. In this mood, he was capable of almost anything. Someone had to keep an eye on him.

He felt his own anger rise again. Brian was right. It shouldn't have been hard for Kathy to stay faithful. *She* wasn't spending weeks at sea, far away from home. All she had to do was go on living and wait, like Clare was waiting for him.

They just didn't know what it did to a bloke, to receive a 'Dear John'.

Martyn's letter came on the following Tuesday, and as soon as Kathy came in and took off her duffel-coat Clare knew that Brian had written as well. The two girls gave each other a rueful look.

'Is he very upset?' Clare asked, thinking what a silly question that was. Of course he was upset.

Kathy nodded. 'Upset and furious. I knew he would be. You were right, Clare, it's just as well they can't come back till the end of April. I think if he could get hold of Terry now, he'd kill him.'

'Oh, Kathy, I am sorry.'

'Well, it's the way he is. I always knew he had a bit of a temper. I dare say he'll calm down, though. I hope he does,' she added. 'I get the feeling he'd kill me too, if he could.'

'Kathy!'

'Well, maybe he wouldn't go quite that far, but he really is mad about it all. I don't really blame him. It must be awful, getting a letter like that when you're on the other side of the world. He must feel so helpless.'

Clare nodded. 'I know. That's what Martyn said. I had a letter from him this morning. He's angry too. I can understand it – he's Brian's best mate, he's bound to take his side.' She didn't tell Kathy all that Martyn had said: that she wasn't to have Kathy round any more, that he didn't want her and her new boyfriend in his house. Kathy's my friend, she thought rebelliously, and this is my house as much as his. He can't tell me who to have here when he's away. And she can bring Terry too. He's my friend as well now.

She didn't know what would happen when Martyn came home, but it was best not to worry about that for the moment. By then, he too would have calmed down.

'Well, there's nothing else you can do about it,' she said to Kathy. 'I suppose you won't go on writing to him?'

'There's no point, is there? What would I say? No, it's over and finished with. I'm sorry, but there it is.' Kathy walked into the lounge, where Christopher was sitting on the floor, playing with a big soft ball that had a tinkling bell hidden inside it. 'And how's my best boy, then? I wonder how many hearts you're going to break, with those big blue eyes of yours.'

Christopher looked up and his round, fair face broke into a huge grin. He gave a crow of delight and stretched up his arms, an irresistible invitation to be picked up.

Kathy bent and swooped him up in her arms. 'You're gorgeous,' she said, burying her face in his soft, warm neck. 'You're just the most gorgeous baby there ever was.'

She stood in the middle of the floor, cuddling him close. Maybe Clare had got it right after all, she thought. At the same time, though, she knew that she had never been more glad of anything in her life than that she and Brian hadn't got married before he went away.

Chapter Six

Christmas came soon after Kathy had broken off her engagement. Clare spent it with the family. There had been some talk of everyone going over to Valerie's and Maurice's house in Portsmouth, but the ferry didn't run on Christmas Day, which meant they'd all have to stay at least two nights, so in the end Valerie and Maurice with little Johnny came over to stay with Clare.

It was odd waking up on Christmas morning in her own home, without Martyn beside her. Lying in bed cuddling Christopher, she shed a few tears of longing for him and thought of last Christmas, when they'd been together, even though she hadn't been feeling up to much. Well, we're seven months nearer to being together again than we were when the baby was born, she thought philosophically, and gave him her breast, feeling the familiar warm contentment spread through her as he began to suckle.

Johnny was old enough to appreciate a stocking, and just as Christopher finished his feed Clare heard his excited cries coming from the front room, where Valerie and Maurice were sleeping on the studio couch. She hastily wiped the baby's mouth and pulled her dressing-gown around her to go and join them.

'A trumpet!' Johnny squealed, waving an armful of toys. 'Look, Auntie Clare, a *trumpet*!' He gave it a lusty blow and Christopher jumped in Clare's arms.

'I think your Auntie Clare knows you've got a trumpet,' Valerie said a trifle grimly. 'I've got an idea she slipped it into Santa's sack herself. Just you wait,' she added to her sister, 'I'll get back at you next year and give Chris a drum.'

'I shan't mind, so long as you don't give him the sticks as well.' Clare

65

sat down on the carpet and unwrapped a present marked for Christopher. It was a coloured wooden clown with a round bottom, and when she placed it on the floor and pushed it with her finger it rocked back and forth. Christopher squealed with delight and sat in front of it, waving his arms and kicking his feet, his smile as broad as the clown's.

'That'll keep him amused for hours,' Clare said. 'I don't think we need to unwrap any more of his presents. Let's see what else you've got, Johnny.'

They ate a cheerful breakfast together and then walked down to Iris's and Bill's. It was a good two miles, but the day was bright and clear and they arrived with good appetites for the Christmas dinner.

'It's a shame his daddy can't see him for Christmas,' Iris said, lifting Christopher out of his pram. 'His first one, as well. I bet those men would love to be at home with their families.' She looked sad and Clare knew she was thinking of Ian as well, on board his ship in the Med.

Most of them would, Clare thought, but she guessed that less fortunate ones like Brian, with no sweetheart to return to, were just as happy out in Australia, where the ship was spending Christmas. Or just as unhappy, whichever way you looked at it. She felt a lump in her throat again and hastily turned to shake off her coat and get the presents out of the pram. The smell of turkey and stuffing, and the aroma of Christmas pudding, filled the air, and Bill came into the room with a bottle of sherry.

'Let's all have a drop of Christmas spirit while we open our presents. I'll probably need it to appreciate the tie your mother's knitted me this year.' This was a perennial joke. Years ago, Iris had indeed knitted Bill a tie and when he'd put it round his neck it had stretched and reached almost to his knees. He'd never thrown it away, and he'd never found a use for it either, but every Christmas it surfaced again to haunt her. This year, it was draped like a garland around the tree.

Iris's knitting had improved now and this year she presented her husband with a very nice Fair Isle pullover which she'd made during the afternoons so that he wouldn't know about it. He gave her a necklace which she knew about very well, since she'd gone into Pickett's & Purser's herself to choose it, but she behaved as if it were a great surprise and the nicest present she'd ever received.

'It's lovely, Bill. I'll be able to wear it with all my best things.'

'The stones are real, straight off Stokes Bay beach,' he told her. 'I collected them myself.'

'You never stop talking rubbish, do you?' she said. 'Now go and get that special present you've got for Johnny.'

Valerie looked at her son, who was making Christopher's clown rock to and fro. 'Hear that? Grandad's got a special present for you. Good heavens,' she exclaimed as her father staggered in with a large, strangely wrapped parcel. 'What on earth is it?'

'You said he liked cowboys and Indians, so I thought I'd make him a fort.' Bill dumped the present on the floor and helped his grandson tear off the paper. 'There you are, Johnny, and they've got real ows and barrows as well.'

Everybody immediately got down on the floor to examine and play with the fort. Bill was clever with his hands and liked making things. He had made Ian a wooden engine he could ride on when he was little, and Valerie still had the doll's house she and Clare had played with for years. The two girls watched now as the men of the family began a game of cowboys and Indians, and then got up to go and help their mother in the kitchen.

When Christmas dinner was over, the turkey a pile of bones with enough leftover meat to last till New Year's Day and the pudding a warm, spicy memory, Bill poured them all a glass of port.

'A toast,' he said, holding his glass to the light. 'A toast to absent friends. Martyn and our Ian. Let's hope they'll both be here with us next Christmas.' As they all raised the glasses, murmuring through the sudden lumps in their throats, he added with a smile towards his own armchair, where Christopher was propped up with pillows to watch the feast, 'And here's a toast to someone who wasn't here last year. Our little Christopher. May he have many, many more Crappy Histmases . . .'

Kathy had asked her mother if she could invite Terry for Christmas Day, explaining that he didn't get on with his stepfather. He arrived at twelve o'clock, bringing a bottle of sherry for her mother, whisky for her father and a small box, wrapped in gold paper, for Kathy.

She looked at it a little nervously, feeling her heartbeat quicken. 'What is it?'

'Open it and see,' he told her. He'd waited until they could be alone in the front room before giving it to her. 'Go on, Kathy, don't take all day.'

She took a deep breath and began to unwrap the little parcel. Since she had formally broken her engagement, there had been no reason for either of them to hold back their feelings, and they were gloriously in love. Nevertheless, the thought that this might be an engagement ring and that Terry might be about to propose frightened her. I'm not ready, she thought. Not yet.

However, to her relief the box didn't appear to be the right size or shape for a ring and she opened it to find a thin gold chain nestling on the satin. She drew it out with a little cry of pleasure.

'Oh, Terry! It's lovely. *Thank* you.' She threw her arms round his neck and kissed him. 'And here's my present for you.'

His was a small box too, containing cuff links. He smiled broadly and kissed her with equal enthusiasm. 'They're exactly what I wanted. I wish I had my other shirt on, I'd have worn them straight away.'

'Wear them tomorrow. And I'll put my chain on now.' It was long enough to loop over her head. She got up and looked in the mirror, lifting the thin golden links across her hands. 'It really is beautiful, Terry. You shouldn't have spent so much.'

'It's my first present to you,' he said seriously. 'I wanted it to be something special.'

They went to join the rest of the family, showing off their gifts. The family had already opened their presents and were now busy with the dinner preparations. Kathy's grandmother was there too and she patted the seat beside her and commanded Terry to sit down. Kathy smiled at the little pile of romantic novels beside her chair. Gran hadn't lost her taste for a touch of romance.

It was going to be a really happy Christmas, she thought. All the same, she couldn't help feeling a little sad for Brian, so lonely out there on the ship. I'm sorry, love, she whispered to him in her mind. I'm really sorry. But it wouldn't have worked. How could it, when I couldn't even stay faithful for a few months?

On HMS *Pacific*, now in Sydney Harbour, Christmas was very different. They did all the right things – decorated the mess, had turkey and Christmas pudding – but without their own homes and families it could never be the same. And the blistering heat and brilliant sunshine seemed strange and unnatural.

During the morning there was a service, broadcast over the ship's radio, and then a programme of record requests. The families had been sent invitations to make these requests for their menfolk, and the men all listened in the hope of hearing a message from their own wives or sweethearts. Martyn was eating his pudding when he heard his own name mentioned. Clare had asked for their favourite record – 'Unchained Melody', sung by Jimmy Young – and sent him all love from herself and Christopher. Martyn felt a sudden lump in his throat that was nothing to do with the pudding, and stopped chewing for a minute. He thought of little Chris, seeing his first Christmas tree, and his eyes stung. I ought to be there, he thought, I ought to be with him. I ought to be with Clare. It's all I want, just the three of us to be together.

Brian was sitting beside him. 'Kathy used to like that record, too.'

'Well, it's sort of appropriate, isn't it? Hungering for your touch and all that.' He stopped and wished he hadn't said that. 'Well, you know what I mean.'

'Oh, yes. But there isn't anyone hungering for my touch, is there? Not any more.' Brian's voice was bitter, as it so often was these days. His cocky brashness had gone sour and when he went ashore now it was to drink heavily and look for a woman. He came back late and with a sore head.

Martyn was glad when they'd left Singapore and gone back to sea. At least Brian was out of harm's way aboard the ship and would have time to settle down and come to terms with losing Kathy. But Brian didn't seem to want to settle down. He brooded sullenly over the crumpled 'Dear John', which he had retrieved from the corner where he'd thrown it, and resented Martyn's attempts to cheer him up. His attitude to women changed too. In place of his former rather suave polish he treated them with a chilly contempt. Not that it seemed to lessen his attraction, Martyn noticed. They seemed to fall over themselves to be the one to melt the ice and discover the soft centre they believed must lurk deep inside.

Martyn wasn't sure that there was a soft centre any more. Brian had been betrayed once too often – first by his mother, when she'd brought her lover into the house to be discovered by Brian's father, and now by Kathy. It was as if he had decided to take out his pain on all women. He used them, then tossed them aside as if they were worthless.

'So they are,' he said when Martyn remonstrated with him. 'Whores and tarts, the lot of them. What other sort of woman comes on board a ship to entertain the sailors? What else do you think they mean by entertainment?'

'They're decent girls, the ones who come to mess parties.' There were always a few such events in naval ports, where a visiting ship would entertain and be entertained by shore-based personnel. 'They're not like the ones who hang around the dockyard gates.'

'Don't kid yourself. They're all the same. All I'm doing is giving them what they're panting for. And if it's a bit more than they bargained for, well, they'll know better next time, won't they?'

Martyn said no more. He knew that Brian was acting out of his own pain and misery, and there was nothing he could do about it. On Christmas Day, with loving messages being broadcast over the ship's radio, there was even less.

Everything will be better when we get back to England, he thought, forgetting how much they'd looked forward to this voyage. Brian will settle down and find himself another girlfriend. And I'll be with Clare again.

The trip was over halfway through. It was all downhill from now on.

For Clare, the waiting seemed endless as she counted the months, the weeks and days before Martyn came home again. At the same time, the days seemed to fly by, with Christopher reaching a new milestone every day. At ten months he was crawling, and he could already say a few words – 'Mum', 'Gamma', which served for both Grandma and Grandpa, and half a dozen others that only Clare could understand.

Next door, Hazel's baby Kevin was even more forward, crawling at seven months and walking at ten. The two babies scrambled about on the floor together like puppies and appeared to hold long, solemn conversations, as serious as two old men, as they were wheeled side by side in their prams to the shops and clinic. Hazel still invited Clare in for Saturday evenings in front of the television. Hazel and Mike were different from Clare's other friends; they were several years older and had lived for three years in Hong Kong. Hazel seemed very worldly wise and sophisticated. She was a Liverpudlian and had different attitudes from those Clare was used to.

'Bloody hell, look at that silly sod,' she would say, startling Clare, who wasn't used to swearing. She was never actually annoyed about something, she just said it. She painted her fingernails bright red too, and one day even dyed her dark hair a rich golden blonde. All things that Clare's parents would have disapproved of, yet it didn't take Clare long to discover that Hazel was lively company, and as good-hearted as any Gosport person. She was religious too, a devout Roman Catholic, though it didn't seem to have much effect on her swearing.

'Us Scousers don't mean it like you southerners do,' Hazel explained. 'It's just our way. We don't see that much wrong with it.'

Even Hazel, however, decided that she ought to moderate her language a bit when she heard Kevin, at nine months, come out with his first word. 'Bugger!' he cried jubilantly, banging his little rubber hammer down on his peg-board. 'Bugger, bugger, *bugger*.'

'I never thought he'd pick it up so quick,' Hazel confessed, half amused, half appalled. 'Mike says I'll have to try to get him to say bucket instead.'

Clare couldn't help laughing, though she shuddered to think what her mother would say if she heard Christopher swearing like a tiny trooper in his pram.

January and February were dark and dismal. Clare tried to take Christopher out most days, but sometimes it was just too wet or cold and they stayed indoors by the fire. Sometimes she caught the bus round the top of the harbour to Portsmouth, to see Valerie, and sometimes Valerie came to her, but by now Valerie was expecting her second baby and didn't feel up to the journey. Iris came up once a week, and there were Kathy's visits to look forward to. Apart from that, Christopher kept her pretty busy and she didn't seem to have much time for anything else.

Even Ian was away again, and his motorbike stood idle in the shed at home. Martyn had sold his soon after they were married. It seemed as though those days were gone.

'I don't think spring will ever come,' she said to Kathy one Tuesday evening. It was the middle of February and a cold wind was blowing rain almost horizontal outside. Clare had.built up the fire and they drew up the armchairs and stretched themselves out to the blaze. 'Sometimes I think we're just stuck here for ever, and it'll go on being the same always.'

'April will come,' Kathy said.

Kathy could afford to relax, Clare thought a little enviously. She wasn't waiting for the ship any more. She'd finished with the Navy. Her boy was here in Gosport and not likely to go away. She could look forward to a lifetime of seeing him every day, being with him every night – if that was what she wanted.

'Are you and Terry thinking of getting engaged yet?' Clare asked curiously. 'You've been going out together a few months now.'

'We haven't talked about it.' Kathy sounded offhand. 'I'm not that keen to settle down anyway. I'm happy enough as we are. Why saddle ourselves with rent and mortgages and furniture and insurance and all that when we don't have to?'

'And babies,' Clare said. 'Like me and Martyn.'

Kathy turned her head and looked at her. 'Oh, lor'! Talk about putting your feet right in it.'

Clare laughed. 'It doesn't matter. You know we never meant to start

71

so soon. But once you get married, you have to accept the fact that babies will come along. Well –' she blushed and grinned '– you don't *have* to, but anyone can make a mistake.'

'There ought to be a pill,' Kathy said. 'Something you can take so that you just don't fall. Maybe there will be one day.' She looked into the fire. 'It's not that I don't *want* to get married and have babies – some day. I just don't feel ready for it now. And I don't want to get engaged again for a while. I don't want to feel tied down.'

'What about Terry? What does he think?'

'Oh, he'd walk up the aisle tomorrow. Not that men do, do they? They're already there, waiting at the altar when the bride arrives.'

'They must walk up the aisle to get there,' Clare pointed out, and they laughed. 'He really wants you to get married, then?'

'I think so. Well, yes, he does.' Kathy frowned. 'But I'm not going to be pushed into anything, Clare. I think that's what happened with me and Brian. He sort of swept me along with him. You know what he's like: large as life and twice as noisy. I never had time to think until he went away.'

'Terry's not like that. Terry's just the opposite.'

'I know, but I still want time. I want to be sure.'

Watching them together when Terry arrived, Clare thought they seemed very sure. They sat on the studio couch together, holding hands, looking contented and happy. There was no tension between them, no impatience to be sensed in Terry's thin, clever face. He'd been very intense that night when he had come to see Clare alone, but now he seemed relaxed, as if he had no doubts and was happy to let things take their course.

He had taken to calling Kathy 'Pixie' because of her short hair and small figure. She pretended to be indignant but Clare could see she enjoyed having a nickname. It went with his new, protective attitude, as if she were something fragile and precious to be cherished and looked after. Clare, who had seen her on the hockey pitch at school, racing up the field with her stick a peril to anyone who dared come near, couldn't quite believe in Kathy's fragility, but it was nice to see the way Terry took care of her.

'Come on, Pix,' he said now. 'Time you were home, tucked up in your little bed.'

'For heaven's sake, Terry,' Kathy said. 'You talk like an Enid Blyton book. I don't live in a toadstool, you know.'

'Just as well,' he retorted. 'I can't stand toads. Mind you, it's just the weather for them outside, it's raining bats and frogs.'

He went and fetched their coats and helped Kathy into hers. There was a bit more banter and some arrangements made for the following week, and then Terry opened the front door and they went out, leaning into the wind. Clare watched them to the corner, hugging herself against the cold, and then closed the door again and went back to the fire.

At this time every evening, before she went to bed, she always added something to the ongoing letter she wrote to Martyn, a sort of serial that was posted off three or four times a week, keeping him up to date with all the tiny events of her life and with Christopher's progress. Tonight, however, she didn't feel like writing. For once, there didn't seem to be anything to tell him.

It's because I can't say anything about Kathy and Terry, she thought. Martyn still hadn't forgiven Kathy for what she'd done to his best oppo, and Clare hardly dared think what he would say if he knew she had Terry round every week as well. But they're my friends, she thought defensively, and it's so lonely, being here without my own man.

It was all very well to say you had to accept the loneliness if you married a sailor. That didn't, in the end, make it any easier to bear. You still had to go to bed alone, get up alone, do everything around the house and for the baby, alone. Nobody ever cooked you a meal or brought in a scuttleful of coal. You never·even got a cup of tea if you didn't make it yourself.

I wonder if you know what it's like, she thought, trying to make out the shape of Martyn's face amongst the glowing coals. I wonder if you've got any idea what it's like, being at home on my own, while you're on a ship with a hundred other men, seeing the world.

Kathy and Terry struggled to the bus stop against the driving rain. They could time it now so that they had only half a minute to wait until the bus came, but they were soaked through even so. They climbed up to the top deck, wiping their wet faces, and sat on seats that were already damp from other people's raincoats. There was nobody else there and they had the front seat.

'I'm thinking of getting a car,' Terry observed, looking at the black, streaming windows. 'On nights like this I think about it even harder.'

'Oh, wouldn't that be lovely,' Kathy said, rubbing her handkerchief over her short hair so that it stood up in spikes. 'Just think of getting in

73

straight from one front door, and not getting out till we reached the next. Luxury!'

Terry would go home with Kathy and then have to walk back to her nearest bus stop and catch another bus to take him to his own home at Elson, on the other side of Gosport. Often, he walked, but the idea of walking any farther than he had to on a night like this was distinctly unappealing. 'It's expensive, though. I don't want to lay out that sort of money if it might be needed for other things.'

'What other things?' Kathy caught a glimpse of her reflection in the window and groaned. She looked even more like a pixie with her fair hair standing up like that. Straight out of a Rupert book, she thought. How on earth could any man take her seriously when she looked so ridiculous?

'Well – a house. Furniture.' He glanced at her and felt his heart twist: she looked so enchanting with her huge brown eyes, her spiky hair and her face glittering with rain. 'A wedding ring.'

Kathy turned her head and stared at him. 'A *wedding* ring? But we're not even engaged.'

'All right, then, an engagement ring. And then all those other things. But we wouldn't be able to afford a car as well, not to start with.'

Kathy looked down at her hands, folded together in her lap, thinking of Brian's ring which she had only taken off a little while ago. 'I don't know that I want to think about getting married yet,' she said in a low voice. 'I've already told you that, Terry.'

He took one of her hands and held it in his. 'I know, and I don't want to push you, but if I buy a car, the money will be spent and it'll take me a long time to save up that much again. Longer, because I'll have to run the car as well, you see.'

Kathy didn't answer. She felt confused and uncertain. Terry might not think he was pushing her, but he was, all the same. He wanted an answer from her – he wanted her to say that he shouldn't buy the car now, he should wait, because some time – perhaps in the next month, perhaps in the next year – she would say yes, she was ready, and they would get engaged and then married, and they'd need the money for all the things he'd talked about. Rings. A house. Furniture.

'I don't know,' she said miserably. 'I don't want to decide now.'

'You don't have to. I just want—'

'But I do have to!' she cried. 'That's just what you're asking me to do. You're asking me to say I'll marry you. You can't pretend you're not by covering it up with a lot of stuff about a car.'

Terry stared at her. 'Well, and what if I am? Most girls would be thrilled to get a proposal.'

'On top of a bus?'

The conductor appeared beside them, and Kathy felt her face burn. She looked away quickly, biting her lip, as Terry paid their fares. The man clattered back downstairs and she turned back, furious.

'You see? He must have heard every word, he was bursting to laugh. I expect he's down there now, almost hysterical. Probably everyone can hear us. Oh, Terry, you're so *stupid* at times!'

'I don't know what I've done wrong. All I did was say I was thinking about getting a car. What's so terrible about that?'

'It's not that. It's – oh, I give up.' Kathy turned and stared out of the side window, but her own reflection stared back like something from a fairy story. Irritated and impatient, she looked ahead and found the same face peering at her from the front window. 'Oh, it's like being in a *goldfish* bowl up here!'

Terry's lips twitched. He took her hand again, which she had snatched away, and stroked it comfortingly. He knew that she was still upset over breaking her engagement to Brian, and she'd told him plainly enough that she didn't want to be tied down again for a while. He hadn't meant the conversation to go this far.

'I'm sorry,' he said. 'I didn't mean to upset you. Let's forget it for now.'

'So you're not going to get a car?' she asked, unable to let it rest immediately.

'I don't know. I might look round for a cheap one, but I'm not really sure I want the expense anyway. You have to pay for insurance and tax as well as petrol, and then there's getting it fixed when it goes wrong. I couldn't do that myself, I'm no good with engines. I'd need to learn to drive too. I think I'll have to stick with buses for a while.'

Kathy looked out of the window again. She felt irritated and aggrieved. It wasn't that having a car meant all that much to her – although it would be lovely, not just for bad weather but for going out into the country at weekends, being able to thumb your nose at public transport – but she felt as if she'd been manoeuvred into a situation she didn't want. Terry had somehow shifted the responsibility to her, and whatever she said took on a meaning she didn't intend.

'Well, it's up to you,' she said, knowing she sounded huffy and further annoyed because of that. 'It's nothing to do with me really.' She knew from his expression that she had hurt him, and felt even more exasperated. 'I'm sorry. I'm *sorry*. I don't know what's the matter with me tonight.'

Terry said nothing. He kept hold of her hand, still stroking the fingers gently, but for the rest of the ride they sat in silence, just watching the rain stream down the windows, and when they got off they walked to Kathy's house without speaking. He shook his head when she asked him in for a cup of cocoa, saying he was too wet, he'd better just go straight home. His kiss, before he turned to leave her, was brief and unsatisfactory.

Kathy went indoors slowly, thinking of him trudging through the rain and the wind, getting on to the other bus – which would probably not come for at least ten minutes – and sitting wet and uncomfortable until he finally arrived home. By the time he went in through his own front door, she would probably be tucked up in a warm bed. In a car, he could do the whole thing in less than ten minutes and stay dry.

Why doesn't he just buy one? she thought impatiently, shrugging off her raincoat in the hall. Why can't he stop thinking so far ahead and just do what he wants to do now, and then see what happens next?

But she knew why. What Terry really wanted to do was get engaged and then married. He wanted his own home, with her as his wife, and beside that a car came a very poor second.

Easter came. Clare read newspapers and listened to the wireless, keeping up with the world news. There had been a terrible massacre in America, at a place called Sharpeville, while at home excitement was mounting over Princess Margaret's forthcoming marriage to Antony Armstrong Jones, a photographer. Clare was pleased for her. She could remember the furore a few years earlier when the Princess had fallen in love with the divorced Peter Townsend, and how she'd finally given him up because of her position. It was unthinkable for a member of the Royal Family, and the Queen's sister in particular, to marry a divorced man. Now, it looked as if Margaret was going to find happiness at last.

Even news like this couldn't keep Clare's mind from her own excitement for long, however. The ship was coming home at the end of April – exactly a week before Christopher's first birthday. The Navy wouldn't keep them away for a whole year, Martyn wrote, because they had to pay the men more if they did. They were getting their pound of flesh, though, Clare thought, folding the letter away, keeping them at sea till almost the last minute.

The ship was due to come back to Plymouth, so Clare planned to go there to meet her. She had been to stay in Ivybridge with Martyn's parents for a couple of weeks, back in October, and they invited her again, saying she could leave Christopher with them while she went out to meet the ship, and they hoped she and Martyn would stay on for a few days after he arrived. However, Clare and Martyn agreed that they wanted to come straight back to their own home for the whole of his leave, and Clare wrote to her mother-in-law saying that they would come back to Ivybridge together afterwards and stay while he was back on board, during the second leave.

'And I'll take Chris out to the ship with me,' she added. 'I want his daddy to see him the first possible minute. He's waited almost a year already.'

Mrs Perry had to be satisfied with that, although she liked to have control of the family, and she disapproved of Clare taking the baby out on the boat that was going to ferry families out to the ship as it arrived in Plymouth Sound. She had never really been in favour of the marriage anyway, saying that both Clare and Martyn were too young, and believing that Martyn was marrying beneath him. Clare's father was only a workman, whereas she and her husband kept a shop. That was really why she hadn't attended the wedding, using the excuse that there was no one else to take care of the shop.

The visit in October had done a lot to mend matters, for little Christopher, then six months old, had won everyone's hearts. His face was always beaming with smiles and he hardly ever cried. He didn't mind who picked him up and cuddled him, and when his grandmother took him into the shop and propped him up in his carrycot behind the counter all her friends and neighbours came in specially to see him and congratulate her on her beautiful grandchild.

Clare hoped that Martyn would like the things she'd done to the bungalow. She had done some decorating while he was away, painting the walls of the narrow little hall pale grey and every door a different colour – daffodil yellow into the lounge and kitchen, pillar-box red into the bedrooms, sky blue into the bathroom. The ceiling was blue too, a lighter shade like the Cambridge boat-race colours, and the skirting boards and doorframes were ice-blue. The effect was bright and cheerful, and just as good as any in the magazines Clare read for inspiration. Contemporary, they called it.

As the time drew nearer, she became more and more excited and nervous. A whole year had passed, and when Martyn had last seen her she'd been the size of a house, wearing a hospital nightie and just starting labour. It was eighteen months since he'd seen her anything like normal, and even then she'd been suffering from 'morning' sickness which had gone on for most of the day. Things had never really been the same for them since a month after their wedding.

We used to have so much fun before we were married, she thought wistfully, thinking of afternoons spent on the motorbike, exploring the New Forest. Now the motorbike had gone and they had a house and a baby. Would Martyn be able to adjust to what was, for him, a sudden change?

He had been away for a year, living the life of a sailor, on a ship where his only responsibilities were those of his job. He hadn't had to think about electricity bills or rates or the mortgage, or anything like that. He hadn't had to get up in the night to a crying baby, or decide when it was time to put Christopher on the bottle or start him on solids. Or help with the household chores. Most of those were women's jobs, Clare knew that, but a few husbands did help out. Mike next door often washed the windows, and Hazel had said he always cleaned the oven, and did it better than she ever would. He took it all to pieces and cleaned each bit, so that it was like new. He did the gardening too.

True to his promise, Bill had dug over the back garden and seeded it with grass. It was coming through now, a mist of fresh green. She hoped that by summer it would be strong enough for Christopher to play on, but that would bring a new chore – regular mowing. Perhaps Martyn would see to it when he came home.

Meanwhile, she went into a frenzy of spring-cleaning. The house must look just as new and shining as when he'd gone away – only better. Then, it had been just a shell: now, it was a home.

Martyn too was conscious of a growing nervousness as his excitement over his homecoming increased. Everything was going to be so different. They'd only moved into the bungalow a few days before Clare had gone into hospital, and now she'd been living in it a year. It wouldn't be so new any more. There would be things he didn't recognise, and more than anything else there would be Christopher. Martyn had never known a baby or a toddler before and he didn't know what to expect. Would he need changing every couple of hours, or would he be out of nappies by then? Was he still drinking from a bottle? It was a strange new world, and yet Martyn was expected to feel at home in it.

Suppose his son didn't even like him? Some kids were frightened of strangers, especially strange men. Suppose they never took to each other?

And Clare – she'd be different too. When they'd got married she'd been a girl, still in her teens, full of life and laughter. Then as her pregnancy advanced she'd been pale and wan, always feeling sick and tired, her sense of fun gone. That last night she'd been really brave, determined not to cry, but he'd known how miserable she was as he left the maternity ward. And now she was a mother, she'd been living on her own for a year, doing what she liked when she felt like it. Martyn had a horrible feeling that she just wouldn't need him any more.

Her letters didn't say that, of course. Like his to her, they were full of love and longing, always looking forward to the day when they could be together again. But that didn't mean they'd click when they actually met. People didn't always. He'd heard other men say so, older men who were disillusioned with their home life and glad to go back to sea again.

It was even going to be different just living in a house instead of on board. There'd be more room to move about, comfortable carpet under his feet, nice chairs to sit in. And he'd be his own man – free to go in and out as he pleased, able to walk out of the door without having to let someone know or sign a book, come back when he liked without having a patrol looking for him. It was almost like being let out of prison!

At the same time, he wouldn't be so free as when he was at sea. He wouldn't be able to go for a run with his mates and stay out till all hours drinking. He was a family man, a husband and father, and those days were gone.

Brian too was restless as the ship steamed towards home. He went up on the flight deck and paced about, staring out across the broad, green expanse of the sea. His first wild reaction to the 'Dear John' had calmed down at last, but he was still deeply hurt and smoulderingly angry, and he didn't really know now how he felt about Kathy.

'Sometimes I still want to strangle her,' he told Martyn as they walked round and round the flight deck. 'And sometimes I just want to take her to bed and kiss her to death. It's as if I'd got this huge beast inside me – like a tiger, wanting to get out – but I don't know what it wants to do. I don't know if I hate her or if I still love her.'

'Will you go and see her again?'

'I dunno. I don't know what I might do if I see her. But I'm not sure I'll be able to keep away. I tell you what, though, I'd like to see that Terry Carter bloke. I'd know what to do with him, all right!'

Clare had told Martyn about Terry, and Martyn, after some debate, had told Brian. He'd thought it might help Brian to get over Kathy if he knew there was no chance for him now. He still wasn't sure if it had been wise, but Brian was bound to find out eventually, with the two girls being such friends.

'Maybe it'd be better if you didn't go to see her,' he said. 'It might do more harm than good.'

'That depends, doesn't it? It can't do me any more harm than it already has, and I don't much care what harm it does him.' Brian paced restlessly about and stared down at the waves far below. 'You know, there were a couple of times I nearly chucked myself into the oggin, but I couldn't bear to give him the satisfaction.'

'That's daft,' Martyn said. 'Plenty of blokes have had "Dear Johns" and got over it. There's plenty of other fish in the sea.'

'Yeah, well, maybe I was going to see if I could find them,' Brian said with a grin, 'but I decided I'd rather have a nice little Chinese tart in a cheongsam. Tell you what, Martyn, some of them were right little scorchers. You ought to have taken the chance while you had it.'

Martyn shook his head. 'Not interested. I'd sooner wait till I get back to Clare.'

He turned away, thinking of those nights in Singapore, Malta and Australia. There'd been temptations, he couldn't deny it. But when you had a smashing little wife at home, and a new baby as well, you just didn't go messing about. All the same, he knew that the frustrations had been almost impossible to bear at times.

It would be a good thing when these last weeks were over and they were back in Plymouth at last.

The day finally came. It was warm and sunny, the air fresh with yesterday's April showers, and people's gardens were full of tulips and the last of the narcissi. Clare caught the train at Fareham, and as it ran through the cuttings she saw the embankments starred with clusters of primroses. She sat in a carriage with two other women who turned out also to be going to Plymouth to meet the ship, and the three of them chatted. They were sympathetic when she told them that Christopher had been born the day Martyn went away, and had not yet seen his daddy. He sat on her knee, dressed in a little white coat that Iris had made for him, and beamed, and they smiled back and took turns in holding him.

'He's gorgeous,' Thelma said. 'His daddy's going to love him. Does he walk yet?'

Clare shook her head. 'He goes round the furniture but he can't really stand on his own yet. I'm glad – I want Martyn to be there when he takes his first steps. He's missed so much already.'

'It'll be a bit different for him, having a baby to think about,' Pam observed. 'You reckon he'll settle down all right? He won't be jealous?'

'Oh, no,' Clare said. 'I've made sure of that – he gets passed round to everyone. And he's such a friendly little boy, he'll be no trouble.'

The other woman grinned. 'I meant your husband! Men can be like babies themselves, you know. He might be jealous of you giving so much attention to Christopher.'

Clare shook her head again. 'He won't be. I've decided the best thing is to include him in everything – feeding and bathing, taking him out in the pram – and then he won't feel left out. And Christopher still sleeps a lot – we'll get plenty of time to ourselves,' she added with a smile.

The other two were staying that night at the NAAFI Club, a big square building in Notte Street. Clare was getting off the train at Ivybridge to go to her mother-in-law's, and she and Martyn would spend one night there, then go straight back to Fareham. She would see Thelma and Pam next morning in the dockyard. They were being taken out on a launch to board the carrier moored out in the Sound and then all sail in together.

The train arrived at Ivybridge and Clare gathered her things together to get out. She scrambled out of the train with her suitcase and Pam handed Christopher down to her. She looked around and saw Martyn's mother approaching along the platform.

'There you are! I thought the train was going to be late.' It wasn't, but she made it sound as if the mere possibility could be Clare's fault. 'And how's my best boy, then? My, haven't you grown!'

She took Christopher from Clare's arms and sat him in the pushchair which Clare unfolded. The train steamed on its way, taking Thelma and Pam with it. Next morning, Clare would be back for the short journey to Plymouth and the last hour or two of the year since Martyn had gone away. Somehow, it still seemed an eternity away.

They walked down into the village. Ivybridge was a small place on the main road to Plymouth from Exeter, and its main street was narrow and noisy, but once you got away from that it was quiet enough. The river Erme flowed under the little bridge in a series of dramatic cascades and waterfalls, breaking over the boulders scattered between the tree-lined banks. Christopher gazed down at it, entranced.

'I'll take him for a walk after tea,' Clare said. 'He loves waterfalls. It's one of his favourite words, isn't it Chris?'

'Waterfall,' he said, enunciating each syllable. '*Water*fall.'

Clare laughed. 'You'll see better than that tomorrow,' she told him. 'You'll see waves – proper waves. We're going to sea, just like Daddy!'

The launch churned its way through the choppy water. The sun had disappeared today behind a thin, high cloud and the sea was grey, but nobody cared about that. The women and children on board the launch were tense with anticipation. None of them had seen their man for a year, and the launch itself seemed to quiver with their excitement.

The aircraft carrier loomed large as they drew nearer. They came in under its overhanging flight deck, and everyone looked up in awe. Like most of them, Clare had seen it before and had been on similar carriers during Navy days, when the ships were open to the public. This was special, though. As well as the ship, they could see the men, lined up around its deck, and people were beginning to wave and call out.

'There's my Bill! There he is – look. The one with the beard . . .' '*There's* Daddy – there he is. Wave. Wave to your daddy . . .' 'I can see him. I can *see* him . . .'

In a few moments all these women and children would be wrapped in arms they hadn't felt for twelve long, lonely months. In a few moments, this long separation would be over, and although everyone knew there would be many others to come, just at that minute they wouldn't care at all. They would be together again.

Clare was first up the gangplank. She had lost sight of Pam and Thelma. She held Christopher close against her and ran up the sloping wood, jumping breathless and flushed on to the steel deck. She looked around her and suddenly she was enveloped in a pair of strong arms and pulled close against a chest she knew, her mouth almost crushed in a kiss she had only dreamed of for such a long, long time.

'Martyn . . . Oh, *Martyn* . . .'

'All right,' another voice said good-humouredly, 'move along now – there's another hundred blokes wanting to do what you're doing.'

Martyn lifted his head and grinned, and guided her along the deck. 'We'll go to the radar office. We're not supposed to, but who's going to know or care?' He looked down at her, and she gazed at him, trying to assimilate the slight differences that had been wrought by the past year – the deep tan, a faint crinkle or two in the corner of his eyes. His glance shifted to the baby in her arms. 'So this is Christopher,' he said, and put out a tentative hand to stroke the little boy's cheek. 'Hello, Chris. I'm your daddy.'

The tears were suddenly streaming down Clare's face. She stopped and pulled Martyn against her, burying her face in his sleeve. The well-remembered smell of him filled her nostrils and the past year suddenly seemed a very long time indeed.

I don't know if I can cope with this, she thought. All these separations – months at a time, a year . . . It doesn't seem right. It doesn't seem right at all.

Chapter Seven

A t last they were back in their own home, in the little bungalow they had moved into only days before Clare went into hospital and Martyn sailed away. They stood inside the little hallway, their front door closed behind them, and looked at each other.

'Oh, Martyn,' Clare said, her voice shaking, 'it's been such a long time.'

He put his arm round her shoulders. He felt pretty emotional himself, but he hoped that Clare wasn't going to start crying again. She'd cried rather a lot in the two days that they'd been together so far – first, that moment on the ship when she ought to have been smiling and happy like all the other wives and sweethearts, and then again in the bedroom in his parents' house later that night when they'd made love for the first time in over a year. She'd apologised, of course, and he'd held her tenderly and tried to comfort her, but it was as if she couldn't stop.

'It's all the crying I didn't do while you were away,' she'd said with a tremulous grin, and he couldn't help thinking it was a pity she hadn't done it then, while she was on her own and had plenty of time.

'I'm here now,' he said comfortingly. 'And you know what I want most? A cup of tea made in our own kitchen.'

'Oh, yes!' Clare reached up to give him a quick kiss, then pulled away and went through the yellow door.

Martyn stood blinking for a minute. She'd told him about the painting and decorating she'd done and he'd wondered what it would look like – so many colours sounded a bit gaudy, and very different from the steel-grey surroundings he was accustomed to. However, he was relieved to find that he rather liked it. The colours were clear and bright, and their difference made them especially appealing. We couldn't have done this in married quarters, he thought: the Navy tells you what you can do and can't do even in your own home. They can't control us here.

He followed Clare into the kitchen. She had wheeled Christopher's folding pushchair in there and it stood alongside the cupboards. Clare had painted their doors too, all different colours like in the hall. It was bright and cheerful, not like the stark white he remembered.

'I'll have to make Christopher's bottle first,' Clare said, filling the kettle. 'He's due for his supper. I won't bother with his bath tonight, though, he'll be too tired. You can get him out and take his coat off if you like. Take him in the lounge, and I'll bring his bottle in to you.'

Martyn hesitated, then bent and unclipped Christopher's harness. He lifted the baby out and held him awkwardly in his arms. 'He's wet.'

'I'm not surprised,' Clare said cheerfully. 'It's a while since he was changed. Clean nappies are in the airing-cupboard.'

Martyn stared at her. 'But . . .'

'Used ones go in this bucket,' she continued, indicating with her foot. 'If they're dirty, just hold them in the toilet and flush the stuff off first – but don't let go, whatever you do! I shouldn't think he's dirty now, though, he's very good on his potty.'

'Look,' Martyn said, watching her helplessly as she bustled about, 'I don't think I can manage this. Can't you do it? I don't want to hurt him.'

'Oh, he's pretty tough.' Clare grinned at him. 'All right, I'll do it, but you watch carefully, so that you know just what to do. Oh, and when the kettle boils, make up his milk in this jug, all right? Then you can put it on again for tea.'

Wordlessly, Martyn handed the baby over and Clare balanced him on one hip while she went to the airing-cupboard in the main bedroom and fished out a clean terry-towel nappy. She came back into the kitchen and sat down on one of the chairs. Martyn was pouring hot water doubtfully into the Pyrex jug, stirring with a teaspoon.

'Make sure there aren't any lumps, won't you,' Clare said, laying Christopher on his back over her knees. She unbuttoned his blue romper suit and pulled away the knickers, revealing waterproof pants and a bundle of sodden terry-towel. The nappy was fastened across the baby's stomach with a large curved safety-pin. 'Now, watch what I do . . . There. Only takes a couple of minutes. All comfy and dry again, aren't you, my sweetheart?' She nuzzled her face into Christopher's neck and he chuckled and grabbed her hair. 'Now go to Daddy, and he'll give you your bottle as soon as it's cooled down.'

'I'll make the tea,' Martyn said hastily, but she shook her head at him.

'No, you won't. I've been looking forward to making our first cup of tea in our own home. You take him through and I'll be in as soon as the kettle boils.' She poured the made-up milk into a clean bottle, ran cold water into the sink and stood the warm bottle in it.

'Isn't it nice that we've got a bed now and don't have to sleep on the studio couch,' she said, carrying the tea-tray into the lounge. Martyn was sitting in the new armchair. He had set Christopher down on the floor and the baby had pulled himself to his feet by the big window and was gazing out. 'I thought you might make one the same for Christopher when he gets big enough. I watched how Dad had made the bedbase, it looked quite easy – just a frame and a piece of hardboard nailed across it. And the legs, of course.' She settled herself on the couch and drew her legs up beneath her. 'You look smashing in that chair. The man of the house. Oh, Martyn, it *is* nice to have you back.'

'It's great to be here.' He took a cup of tea and leaned back, letting his gaze travel round the room. 'You don't know what it's like, being in a house again after a year on board a ship. And when it's my own house . . . I've never had a place of my own before.'

'Nor had I. I've got used to it now, of course.' She grinned. 'You *are* allowed to use the saucer as well!'

Martyn glanced down and gave a little snort of laughter. 'That's what being on a ship does for you. We don't use saucers on board.'

'I suppose you thought they were little plates,' Clare said, gently teasing. 'Martyn, you're miles away. Why don't you come over here? Or shall I come and sit on your lap?'

'I'll come over there.' He got up and crossed the room, but before he reached her Christopher turned from the window, his face screwing up in sudden tears, and crawled rapidly across the room to grab his mother's knees. She jumped up at once.

'His bottle! Oh, you poor little thing. Did Mummy forget all about it, then? I'll go and fetch it.' She went quickly back to the kitchen and reappeared a moment later. She held the bottle out to Martyn. 'Would you like to give it to him?'

Martyn opened his mouth to speak, but Clare was already turning away to pick up the baby. She held him out and Martyn sat down again in the armchair, the bottle in one hand. Clare set Christopher on his knee and laid him back against the crook of Martyn's arm.

'That's right. Just put the teat in his mouth. He'll hold it himself, but he likes you to hold it too. There, my love,' she said to the baby, 'isn't that nice? Daddy's giving you your bottle.' She bent and rubbed her face against Martyn's hair. 'Oh, isn't it lovely. We're a real family at last. You, me and our baby. You know, sometimes during this last year I've thought it was never going to happen.'

'I know.' Martyn reached up one hand to hold her head against his. 'I did too. I felt as if I'd never get back. But that's what the Navy's like. We knew it would happen.'

'Oh, I'm not complaining. I'm just happy to have you here now. The three of us together.' She stood up straight. 'Here, finish your tea and while Christopher has his bottle I'll start getting a meal ready. Mum said she'd put some chops in the larder for us, and Dad was going to give us some vegetables from the garden. Oh, it's so lovely to be getting you a meal. Do you realise, we've been married nearly two years and we've hardly had any proper married life? I'm going to make the absolute *most* of this fortnight's leave.'

She hurried out to the kitchen, and Martyn sat still, the baby on his lap, listening to the clicking of doors opening and closing, to the clatter of pans, to the soft sound of his wife's voice humming a tune. He looked around the room which he had known for only a few days before going away last year, trying to accept the fact that this was his home, that this baby was his son, that this was where he lived. That he was no longer a sailor on shore leave, roaming some exotic port looking for a place to have a drink, but a respectable married man, settling down to ordinary married life.

That's what I want, he told himself. That's what I got married for. And anyway, it's only for a fortnight.

He looked down at Christopher. The baby had emptied his bottle and fallen asleep. Carefully, Martyn slipped his arms under the warm body and lifted him, standing up with his son still cradled against him. He carried him into the smaller of the two bedrooms and laid him in the white-painted cot, then he went out to the kitchen where Clare was busy stringing beans.

'Leave that,' he said, coming behind her to slip his arms around her body, his hands on her breasts. 'Christopher's asleep. Let's try out this bed your dad took all that trouble to build for us.'

The fortnight slipped by all too quickly. As well as settling down to the 'proper married life' that neither of them knew quite how to achieve, there were people to see and things to do. Clare's parents had a family

Sunday for them the first weekend, with Valerie and Maurice over. Ian was home on leave too, and Clare wanted him to come to tea separately, as well as with her parents and sister when she invited everyone back for her own party – a housewarming, she said, as well as a welcome-home for Martyn and to celebrate Christopher's first birthday.

Clare spent several days preparing for this party, making cakes, biscuits and cheese straws as well as plates of sandwiches and salad on the day itself. She set Martyn to slicing up ham, and boiled half a dozen eggs which she smothered with mayonnaise.

What with all this and attending to Christopher's routine, there didn't seem to be much time left over for the sort of things they'd enjoyed in the past. They lived too far from Stokes Bay now to be able to get there easily; two bus journeys and a walk were too much to manage with the baby, and a quick trip last thing at night to watch the lights was out of the question. Martyn missed his motorbike sorely and thought wistfully of days spent roaming the New Forest, taking whichever turning caught their fancy. He thought of hiring a car for a couple of days, but Clare shook her head.

'We were going to buy bedroom furniture. I saw a lovely wardrobe and dressing-table in Courts the other day. It would be nice to get our bedroom properly furnished, and you need somewhere to hang your suits too.' At present, all their clothes were stowed in a whitewood chest of drawers that Clare had bought and painted, and a child-sized wardrobe. Being a sailor and trained to be tidy in a small space, Martyn could see that they needed more storage so he gave up the idea of a car and they went over to Southsea one afternoon and ordered the bedroom suite.

Kathy came round to tea one afternoon. Martyn was in the lounge reading the evening paper when she arrived, and she followed Clare through from the kitchen a little cautiously.

He got up and shook hands. 'Hullo, Kathy.'

'Hullo, Martyn.' There was a small silence. 'I expect you're glad to be home.'

'Yes,' he said. 'Soon be going away again, though.'

'I know. Is the ship in Plymouth for long?'

'Not long. A month for leave and a couple of weeks for a bit of a refit, then we're going up to Scotland.'

'Oh, yes.'

They looked at each other uneasily.

Clare said brightly, 'Martyn's hoping for a new draft after that. He thinks he might get to Collingwood as an instructor.'

'That'll be good. You can live at home then.'

'That's right,' Martyn said.

Another silence fell, then Clare muttered a few words about going out to do something about tea, and Kathy followed her. They shut the kitchen door and spoke in whispers.

'He doesn't want me here. I knew I shouldn't have come.'

'Don't be silly,' Clare hissed. 'He just doesn't know what to say. He'll be all right in a little while.'

'Brian's his best friend. I bet he hates me . . .'

'And you're *my* best friend. I've known you since we were five years old – I'm not having you stopping coming to see me. What will we do when he's at Collingwood?'

'What's he said about it?' Kathy asked miserably. 'Has he told you what happened when Brian got the letter?'

'He hasn't even mentioned it. Honestly, Kath. He knows we're friends, and he'll get used to it. He'll have to. Look, they can't have it all their own way – going off for months on end and leaving us on our own, and then complaining about the way we spend our time! We've got lives too, and we've got to be able to have our own friends. You haven't done anything to Martyn. If I want you to come round here to tea, then you *come* to tea, and he's just got to like it or lump it.'

Kathy looked doubtful, but just at that moment they heard Christopher call out from his cot and she went to fetch him. Martyn was still in his chair as she passed the open lounge door, and didn't glance up. She went back into the kitchen.

'Clare, wouldn't it be better if I just slipped away?'

'Don't you dare! Look, I told you, he just feels awkward. He'll be all right in a minute. Look, I'll make a cup of tea and we'll take Chris in and play with him. He can show you his new toy. You'll show Kathy your Kolly, won't you, Chris? Shall we go and fetch him?'

Holding both Christopher's hands, she walked slowly along the short passage to the bedroom, the baby toddling unsteadily in front of her. Kathy watched, entranced. 'Clare, he's walking!'

'Not on his own, but he won't be long, will you, Christopher? He lets go of the furniture now and just stands there. He's a clever boy, isn't he?' she added, speaking half to the baby and half to Kathy. 'Who's his mummy's clever, clever boy?'

Kolly was a toy koala bear that Martyn had brought from Australia. It was covered in thick, soft fur – not koala fur, Martyn had explained, that wasn't allowed, but kangaroo fur. It was said to be the softest fur in the world. Chris greeted the appearance of his bear with cries of joy, as if he had been parted from it for at least a month rather than about three minutes, and clutched it against his chest. They all went back into the lounge and Christopher plonked himself down in the middle of a pile of toys.

'So how's things?' Martyn asked, having evidently made up his mind to be friendly to Kathy.

'Oh, all right.' She sat down on the couch and hesitated. 'How – how's Brian?'

Martyn gave her an odd look. 'I wouldn't have thought you'd be interested in him.'

'Of course I am. Just because I broke off our engagement doesn't mean to say I don't like him. I still care about him.'

Martyn muttered something that sounded like 'funny way of showing it' and shook out his newspaper in exactly the way Clare's father did when he was annoyed about something.

Clare sighed. She was annoyed with both of them – Kathy for bringing the subject up and Martyn for reacting as he had. She said sharply, 'Kathy's asked you a civil question, Martyn.'

He looked at her. 'All right, I'll give a civil answer. He's fed up. He's fed up with the Navy and being on board ship, he's got nothing to come home for and he's fed up with women. Does that make you feel any better?'

Kathy was scarlet. She looked as if she might burst into tears. Clare bit her lip. The afternoon wasn't going at all as she'd hoped. 'Martyn—' she began, but Kathy broke in, her voice trembling.

'I never wanted to hurt him, never. I just didn't think it was right to go on being engaged to him when I wasn't sure any more. What else was I to do? Let him go on thinking we'd be getting married when he came home? Let him go on making plans? You don't know what it's like – knowing you've done the wrong thing, and knowing it's going to be a whole year before you can talk properly about it. You—'

'No, and *you* don't know what it's like being away at sea for that year,' Martyn snapped, throwing down his newspaper. 'Surrounded by a lot of blokes, waiting for letters that don't come, wondering what's going on back at home. And then getting a "Dear John" and not being able to do a bloody thing about it. How do you think he felt about that? One minute everything's fine, the next it's all over, smashed to pieces, and you know it's going to be another six months before you can get home and punch the bastard's nose. And it might be too late even for that. For all he knew, you could have been married by the time he got back.'

'Martyn!' Clare cried, outraged. 'D'you mind not swearing in my living-room? And in front of my baby?'

'*My* living-room,' he corrected her. 'And *my* baby. Just because you've had it all your own way for the past year, you needn't think it's exclusively yours.'

'*Martyn!*'

They stared at each other, appalled. Kathy, still crimson, looked from one to the other, her eyes filled with tears. On the floor, Christopher stopped playing and gazed around at the angry faces. His mouth quivered, opened and turned square as he began to cry.

'Now look what you've done!' Clare snatched him up and cradled him against her, glaring at Martyn.

Kathy looked helpless. She lifted her hands and let them drop, then she began to get up. 'I'd better go.'

'No,' Clare said above Christopher's bawls. 'No. Please don't go. Let's sort this out.' She looked at Martyn. 'Kathy was really upset when she wrote that letter. She didn't want to hurt Brian at all, but what's the use? Like she said, you can't go on pretending, not for months on end. And you know what you all say about us wives and girlfriends – if we can't take a joke, we shouldn't have joined? Well, that applies to you too.'

'What d'you mean?' he said sullenly.

'We've got to put up with you going off and leaving us behind,' she said quietly, 'but you've got to put up with things too. Not just being away from home – you chose that. You've got to put up with the chance that things will go wrong and you can't be there to put them right. It's like all the rest of it – it goes with the job.'

There was a longer silence. Christopher's sobs diminished and he started to play with Clare's necklace. She put him back on the floor and he crawled over to Kathy and dragged himself up to stand by her knees. She bent her head and gave him a kiss, and then he turned back to look across the room at Martyn.

'Dad,' he said. 'Dadda. *Dad.*' He let go of Kathy's knees and took a tentative, unsteady step, and then another, before walking the rest of the short distance between them, laying his hands firmly on Martyn's knees and looking up into his face.

'Dadda.'

After that, somehow, it was all right. The tension was released as though a bubble had been pricked, as they all laughed and exclaimed and congratulated the baby. They tried to get him to do it again, calling him across the room from one to another, and for a few minutes he co-operated, crowing his delight at his own prowess, before he tired of the game and reverted to crawling. Martyn looked disappointed, but Clare laughed and shook her head.

'Now he's got the idea, there'll be no stopping him. He'll be running down the road to meet you next week, Kathy. Oh – no, he won't, we'll be in Devon. We're going to stay with Martyn's mum and dad in Ivybridge for the second leave. But you'll come as soon as we're back, won't you?'

Kathy glanced at Martyn, who made a wry face and said, 'It's all right, Kath, I won't be here then. We'll be on our way to Scotland. But Clare's right – it's daft, us not being friends. And maybe you're right, too, about Brian. I mean, if you didn't want to go on with the engagement, there wasn't much else you could do, I can see that.'

Clare breathed a sigh of relief. 'I'll get tea ready,' she said, scrambling to her feet. 'It's egg and cheese pie. Martyn hasn't had it yet. I've been saving it till you came.' She gave the briefest hesitation and asked, 'Is – is Terry coming round?'

Kathy glanced at Martyn again. 'He's coming to call for me later on. About eight. He doesn't have to come in. I can just go then. I didn't know what you would want . . .' Again, her eyes strayed to Martyn's face.

'Oh, let him come,' Martyn said impatiently. 'I'll be interested to see him anyway. And you needn't worry,' he added to Clare. 'I won't punch his nose or start an argument.'

Clare had to admit, when Terry arrived, that Martyn did nothing to make their visitor feel uncomfortable. He invited him in, offered him a chair and a glass of beer, tried to talk, but it was clear from the start that the two were never going to be friends. Not the way Martyn and Brian were friends.

'We've just got nothing in common,' Martyn said to Clare when the other two had left. He sat on the side of the bed and pulled off his socks. 'I mean, he's never been in the Services, he's never been on a ship bigger than the Isle of Wight ferry, he doesn't know any of the slang. He's like a bloke of about forty. I don't know what Kathy sees in him, to be honest.'

'I think she just likes him because he likes her,' Clare said slowly. She too had seen Terry in a different light this evening – ill at ease, too serious, out of touch with the subjects Martyn talked about with such breeziness. 'And because he's *here*. He's not going to go away and leave her on her own.'

'And that's what matters most, is it? Being at home all the time?'

Clare turned from the dressing-table where she was brushing her hair and stared at him. 'No! I didn't mean that at all. Not for me, anyway. You know I'd want you even if you were away twice as much. I'll always wait for you, Martyn.'

'I hope you will,' he said, looking back at her. 'I hope you will, because if you ever did to me what Kathy did to Brian – well, I don't know what I'd do. I don't think I'd want to go on living at all.' He thought of Brian, saying how he'd felt like jumping off the side of the ship, and understood the bleakness of his despair. 'You won't do that, will you?' he said with sudden urgency.

'*No!*' She was by his side, her arms around him. 'No, I'll never do that, never. We're not like Brian and Kathy, Martyn, we're *us*. We're different. Nothing's ever going to come between us.'

'Oh, Clare.' He held her tightly and laid his head on her shoulder. 'Clare, you don't know what it's like being away all that time, not knowing what's happening at home. And the last few weeks – it's almost unbearable, because you don't know what it'll be like *being* at home either. You want to get back, yet somehow you're scared of it. Scared in case it's not as good as you expect – scared in case people have changed and things go wrong. And you think you'll have forgotten how to live in a house – like me with the saucers – and people will think you've gone nuts or something.'

He paused and added, 'I'm sorry if it hasn't all been easy, Clare. It's my fault – I'm just not used to babies, and somehow I hadn't realised Christopher would be *around* so much. I mean, I knew he would, of course, but I didn't know what it would be like, I couldn't quite imagine it . . .'

'But you do love him, don't you?' she said anxiously. 'You don't wish we hadn't had him?'

'No, of course not. He's a smashing kid and I wouldn't swop him for the world. It's just that it takes a bit of getting used to.' He lifted his head and looked down at her. 'I'm sorry about blowing my top earlier on. It's just that – well, I thought maybe you were getting fed up with me. You and Chris – you seem to have settled down so well together and I felt a bit like an intruder. I felt as if I didn't really fit in.'

'Oh, Martyn,' she said in dismay, 'of course you fit in! You're his daddy. And you're my husband,' she added softly, 'and when we're together, nothing else matters. Nothing at all.'

He looked at her and grinned suddenly. 'That's what I want to hear. That we're still just you and me.' He leaned back and grabbed Clare round the waist, pulling her down on top of him. 'You're my wife and you're never going to send me a "Dear John", and you're *never* going to get fed up with waiting till I come home. Because *you* –' he began to punctuate his words with kisses '– know *I'm* – worth – *waiting* – for. *Don't* – you?'

Clare lay in his arms. The familiar heat was already coursing through her veins. She sighed and stretched against him like a cat, revelling in the feel of his skin, the warmth of his body, the sharp, unique smell of him. 'And I'm worth coming back to,' she whispered. 'Oh, Martyn . . . I love you so much . . .'

Chapter Eight

A month later, the ship sailed again, this time for a shorter trip. The crew had all had their fortnight's leave and there were three more months until decommissioning, when they would all go to new drafts and a different ship's company would take over the aircraft carrier.

Brian spent his leave aimlessly. He went home to Bristol to see his mother, but he still couldn't get on with his stepfather and left after a couple of days. Martyn invited him to come to supper one evening but the atmosphere was strained, with Clare feeling embarrassed and expecting him to ask about Kathy at any minute. Most of the time he stayed on board, going ashore in the evenings to drink in Portsmouth's pubs. He found a girl who was willing to meet him most nights, but after a few dates she bored him and he didn't bother to turn up again.

Wherever he went, he found memories of Kathy. He stood on the flight deck, looking at the harbour and watching the little ferry chug across from Gosport to Portsmouth. She would be on that every morning, coming over to work, and going back in the evening. If he wandered down the pontoon at the right moment, he'd see her amongst the hurrying crowds. He waited till later and went over to Gosport, walking out to Haslar and along the sea-wall where she liked to go swimming. He went out to Stokes Bay and stared across the Solent at the Isle of Wight. They'd gone over for the day once, walking along Ryde pier and round to Sandown. He even walked down the road where she lived and stared at the windows.

He was still torn between bitterness and yearning. He longed to see her face, but didn't know how he'd react if they met. He didn't know whether he would go weak at the knees or just want to slap her face.

He was thankful when the leave ended and the ship sailed out of Portsmouth again.

They spent the last few weeks of the draft visiting British ports and then the ship's company was disbanded. To Clare's delight, Martyn's new draft was to HMS Collingwood, the shore station only two miles away from the bungalow.

'You can get a bike, then you'll be able to come home for *dinner*,' she said, her eyes glowing. 'Oh, Martyn, that's marvellous. And you're going to be an instructor! Sounds really posh. They must think a lot of you.'

'I reckon we all get a turn.' But he was pleased too, she could see that. He picked up Christopher and swung him in the air. 'You'll have your daddy home all the time – for a while, at any rate.'

Christopher squealed and Clare watched them, smiling. Martyn had got used to the baby now and could do anything for him. There had been a few times during that first leave when she'd been scared that it wasn't going to work – she'd tried so hard to involve him, and make sure he wasn't jealous, that she'd gone too far the other way. Eventually, however, they'd managed to achieve a better balance and now when Martyn came home Christopher staggered to meet him and lifted his arms to be swung up to his father's shoulder.

'We'll be a proper family,' she said. 'How long will you be at Collingwood?'

'A year, probably. Maybe a bit longer – eighteen months if we're lucky.' He held Christopher against him. 'He'll be nearly three before I go away again.'

'There'll be time to have another one,' Clare said. 'Two years is a good gap, don't you think?'

Martyn looked at her. 'D'you really want to? You weren't too well last time, with all that sickness.'

'The doctor said it probably wouldn't happen again, but if it does, I'd rather have you here with me. I couldn't cope on my own. Let's think about it, Martyn. I don't want Chris to be an only child. You know we said we'd like three.'

'I know. I've only just got used to having one, though.' He thought of another pregnancy, with Clare feeling off-colour and getting big and cumbersome again, and another baby wanting her attention. He thought of life changing yet again.

'But you never saw him as a baby. You'd see the next, if we started it soon.' She gazed at him, standing there with his son in his arms. 'It might be a girl next time. Or another boy.' She realised what she'd said and laughed at herself, and Martyn grinned.

'I should think it's pretty likely to be one or the other. Let's leave it for a while, though – just have some time like this together first.' He glanced around the lounge. 'You never decorated this room.'

'I know. I wanted to leave it till you came home; I thought we could do it together. And the kitchen too, it looks grubby. The cupboards are all right but I'd like to do the walls and maybe the ceiling. What d'you think about a coloured ceiling? Pale blue, like the sky.'

'Sounds all right. How about the walls?'

'I thought yellow, to make it light and sunny. A nice wallpaper for three of the walls and plain yellow paint for the one with the cooker on. It'd be lovely.'

Martyn considered. 'Okay. We'll do it soon, shall we? We'll go to that wallpaper shop in West Street and we could have a look at papers for the lounge at the same time.' He wasn't mad about decorating – another new skill he was going to have to learn – but at least it seemed to have taken her mind off having another baby. And it might be fun, slapping paint on the walls and putting up fresh paper.

Clare sat back in her chair, feeling warmly content. This was what she'd been looking forward to – the cosy domesticity of ordinary married life. Looking after the baby, talking about the house, having Martyn at home every day and every night just like an ordinary married couple, like her mum and dad. It wouldn't last, she knew that. One day he would get another draft and have to go back to sea, away for months on end, perhaps a whole year again. For the moment, however, she could forget that. It was too far in the future to bother about.

She thought of Kathy, who would have been planning her wedding now if she hadn't broken off her engagement to Brian, and wondered if she wasn't really sorry, deep down. She and Terry didn't seem to be talking about getting engaged. They were still going out together regularly, to the club or the pictures, or for walks on Sundays. They'd been to London a couple of times to see the sights and go to the theatre. Probably Terry would propose before long. He had a good job, after all, and ought to be able to afford a house. And at least she wouldn't have the constant separations that she'd have had to endure if she'd married Brian.

'Again, Mummy.'

Clare laughed and lifted Christopher out of the bath. 'I've already sung it half a dozen times. It's time to come out now.'

'Again,' he insisted, and she wrapped him in a big fluffy towel, hugging him against her. He smelt fresh and clean.

Obligingly, Clare began to sing again. Cliff Richard's 'Living Doll' was Christopher's favourite song and had become their traditional bathtime entertainment, along with 'Itsy-bitsy, Teeny-weeny, Yellow Polka-dot Bikini', which was good for drying because it could also be accompanied by lots of tickling. Bathtime was generally pretty noisy.

As Clare finished and snuggled Christopher into the dressing-gown Iris had made him from an old winter dress, she heard footsteps on the path outside. The doorbell rang and she lifted Christopher in her arms and went to answer it. She stared in surprise at the tall young man in naval uniform.

'Brian!'

'Hullo, Clare. How're you?'

'I'm all right.' Unable to think of anything else to say, she added, 'Martyn's on duty tonight. D'you want to come round tomorrow and see him?'

'It's you I want to see.' He made a slight movement and she stepped back so that he could come inside. He closed the door behind him and they stood in the narrow hall. Clare felt stupid and awkward. She hadn't seen Brian since he'd come to supper soon after *Pacific* had come home. She'd never been alone with him before, and she didn't know what to say. And why had he come to see her, and not Martyn?

Brian looked around the hallway with its coloured doors. 'You've been busy. Did you put a paintbrush in old Martyn's hand the minute he came off the ship?'

Clare felt annoyed, as if he'd accused her of treating Martyn like a labourer. 'I did this myself. But we're going to do the kitchen and the lounge soon.' She turned away from him. 'You'd better come in and sit down. D'you want a cup of coffee?'

'Not really.' He followed her into the lounge and stood looking around. 'It's nice here. I like the big room. Better than two little rooms, like in older houses. It's only two bedrooms, though, isn't it?'

'That's all we need now. We can move into a bigger place later, if we want to.' She felt defensive, as if he were criticising her, and he gave her a quick look.

'I'm not saying anything against it, Clare. I think you're lucky. I'd like a place like this of my own.' He glanced at Christopher, still held in her arms, and added in a low voice, 'I wouldn't mind a kid like that, either.'

Clare immediately felt sorry. She put Christopher down on the floor

98

and said, 'Sit down, Brian. I'll make a cup of coffee. It's nice to see you again.'

Brian followed her out to the kitchen and stood watching as she bustled about. She got the biscuit tin out and put some gingernuts on a plate. The coffee went into two large mugs and she carried it all into the lounge on the wooden tray someone had given them for a wedding present.

'You're a real little housewife,' he observed, sitting down in the big armchair. 'D'you like being at home all day? Don't you miss going to work?'

'Not really. Chris keeps me busy, and now that Martyn's home as well I've got plenty to do. I missed the friends I had there at first, but I've got nice people next door, and Kathy comes up every week—' She stopped abruptly, colouring, and turned away to pick up the plate of biscuits. 'Have – have a gingernut. And your coffee, it's in the blue mug. D'you take sugar? I forgot a spoon – I'll go and get one—' She half rose and he put out a hand to stop her.

'It's all right. I don't take sugar. Clare, it's Kathy I came to talk to you about. How is she?'

Clare felt her colour rise further. She stared at him dumbly.

'I'm only asking how she is,' he said quietly. 'I'm not asking anything secret.'

Clare found her voice. 'She – she's all right.'

'And what about this other bloke? This Terry? Is she still going round with him?'

Clare looked down at her mug of coffee. Christopher was playing with his wooden bricks and providing no distraction at all. She nodded.

'Look, I'm not blaming *you*,' Brian said. 'I know she brings him here, but it's not your fault she met him in the first place. I just want to know how she is, that's all.'

'But why?' Clare asked. 'Why d'you want to know? You're not engaged to her any more.'

'Aren't I?' he said. 'And suppose I don't agree with that?'

Clare stared at him. 'What do you mean? Of course you've got to agree. She's broken it off. She wrote to you—'

'I know that. A "Dear John". You don't have to remind me.' In the bleakness of his voice she heard all the pain and frustration of a man receiving a letter like that when he was thousands of miles from home, helpless to do anything about it. 'Do you know what it feels like to get one of those, Clare? You feel like jumping over the side. Some blokes do it, too.'

She stared at him, appalled. 'But you – *you* didn't feel like that, did you?'

'I just told you. Anyone would. I didn't do it, though, because I felt more like getting home to punch this Terry bloke on the nose. I still might,' he added, looking at his cup.

'Brian, you mustn't. It wasn't Terry's fault. They were just friends.' She lifted her shoulders helplessly. 'It wasn't anyone's fault. Kathy just realised she wasn't ready to be married, that's all.'

'So why couldn't she just have said that? Why write and break it all off? We could have gone on being engaged – I'd have waited till she was ready. She must have been interested in this Terry bloke, whatever she said about them being just friends.'

'Well, yes, I suppose she was,' Clare said, 'And that's why she didn't want to go on being engaged. She didn't think it was fair to anyone.'

Brian looked at her. 'So it was more fair to me to write me a "Dear John".'

'Oh, I don't *know*,' Clare said. She felt hemmed in by his questions, and uneasy about the look in his eyes. She remembered what he'd said about punching Terry on the nose. He's capable of that, she thought, he's capable of going after him now and starting a fight. And he's bigger and stronger than Terry, and didn't Kathy tell me once he'd been keen on boxing? 'Look, it's no use asking me all this. I don't think it's any use asking Kathy either. It's over, Brian. That's why she wrote to you, so that you'd know before you came home—'

'So that she wouldn't have to face me,' he said grimly. 'What was she scared of, Clare – did she think I'd beat her up or something?'

'No! Of course not.' But, again, she felt disturbed by the look in his eyes. 'She just didn't want to raise false hopes, that's all.'

'So she shot 'em down in flames instead.' Brian put down his mug and got up. He had filled out in the year he'd been away and looked tall and powerful, looming over her. Clare got up too, but she still only came to his shoulder, and she realised suddenly how much smaller Kathy would look beside him. I wouldn't like him angry with me, she thought with fresh unease.

'Brian, don't go looking for Terry. There's no point. It wouldn't make Kathy come back to you. She's made her decision – there's nothing you can do about it now.'

'Isn't there?' He looked down into her eyes. His own were very blue. 'So you don't agree that I've a right to ask for an explanation, and put my own side of the story?'

'But you haven't *got* a side!' She saw his face change and added hurriedly, 'I didn't mean that – of course you've got a side, but it's not as if you had a row that can be sorted out. It's about how Kathy feels, and there really isn't anything you can do to change that.'

Brian smiled a little and moved away towards the door. 'Isn't there? I wouldn't be too sure about that if I were you, Clare. I just wouldn't be too sure . . . Thanks for the coffee. Be seeing you.'

He was gone. She heard the front door close behind him and went to the window to watch him stride away down the road. His back looked straight and determined. He's going to do it, she thought. He's going to find Terry and punch him. And I can't even warn them.

A sudden crash and a scream made her turn quickly. Christopher had made a huge pile of bricks and knocked them over, and some of them had hit him on the legs as they fell. He sat in the middle of the carpet, sobbing and holding up his arms.

'Oh, silly boy.' She picked him up and sat down, cuddling him against her and crooning. 'There, then, there, let Mummy kiss it better. Poor little legs. Poor little boy. But that's what happens when you knock things over, you see – you get hurt when they fall.'

Like Brian had been hurt, she thought, and Kathy too. She just hoped it would stop there.

Kathy was at home when Brian knocked on the door. She had just washed her hair and it clung like a smooth cap to her head, darkened to deep gold by the water.

Nobody else was in, so she slung a towel round her neck and went to the door. For a moment, she stood blinking, unable to take in immediately who it was who stood there, blocking out the sunlight.

'Can I come in, Kath?'

His voice was quiet but there was a note in it that told her he wouldn't take no for an answer. Without speaking, she stepped back and he came into the hall.

'Where shall we go? In the front room?'

Kathy found her voice. 'It doesn't matter. Everyone's out.' She opened the door to the front room anyway. It was where they'd always sat when they'd wanted some privacy – where she and Terry often sat of an evening now. She wished suddenly that she'd taken Brian through to the back, but it was too late now.

Brian made no comment on the fact that they were alone in the house but sat in his accustomed place on the sofa. Kathy hesitated and then took one of the armchairs, not missing the look on his face as she did so.

'Not even friends any more?' he asked. 'I didn't realise I was that repugnant to you.'

'Oh, Brian, it's not that – I told you, I just didn't feel I had the *right* to be engaged to you any more. It wasn't anything you did.'

'I just wasn't good enough. Or was it because I was in the Navy? I've got a right to know, Kath.'

'I *told* you,' she said again, a little desperately. 'It wasn't you at all. It was me.'

'And you don't even want me as a friend.'

'I didn't say that. I said I hoped we'd stay friends.'

'And just how were we supposed to do that?' he demanded. 'Did you write to me again? Did you ask me round when the ship came to Pompey? Did you even bother to ask Clare if she'd seen me? How were we supposed to stay friends, when you did your best to pretend I didn't exist?'

Kathy stared at the floor, her eyes smarting with tears. There was a rug in front of the fireplace, a rug her mother had spent all the winter evenings making. It was dark red with a big golden rose in the middle of it. Kathy had been going to make a rug too, but instead she'd spent her evenings at the club, and then going out with Terry.

'I suppose I meant, I hoped we wouldn't hate each other,' she said in a low, trembling voice. 'Or that you wouldn't hate me – I didn't hate you, Brian.'

'No, you made that clear, writing to me like that.' He asked the same question he had asked Clare. 'D'you realise what it does to a bloke to get a "Dear John" when he's miles away and has got months to get through before he comes home?'

'Brian, I'm *sorry*. I *said* I was sorry. There isn't anything more I can do.'

'Isn't there?' He reached across suddenly and caught hold of her left wrist. Kathy gasped and tried to pull away, but his grip was firm and it tightened as she resisted. He stared at her hand. 'You're not wearing a ring. Aren't you engaged to this bloke?'

'No. I'm not engaged to anyone.' She looked at him, trying to make him understand. 'I don't want to be engaged yet. I want more time before I think about that again.' She got up, her legs trembling. 'I'll give you your ring back. I'll go and get it now.'

'Never mind rings. I want to hear more about this Terry. So you're not engaged to him. Just going out with him. Just friends – is that it?'

'Well, a bit more than friends.'

'How much more?' He snapped the question at her. 'Are you sleeping with him?'

'*No!* Of course not. Look, Brian, I think you'd better go—'

'Not till I've got this straight. So you're just friends with this Terry – or a bit more than friends – but not as much as you were with me. You're not engaged and you don't want to be. You're not tied to him.'

'No, I'm not. But I don't want—'

'And if you're not tied to him, or to anyone else, that means you're free to go out with whoever else you like. Is that right?'

Kathy watched him. She could see what he was driving at but she couldn't see how to divert him. Better to let him steamroller on and get it over with, she thought with a sigh. 'Yes, that's right. Except that I don't—'

'You don't want to go out with anyone else. Not even your best friend of all – the bloke you thought you wanted to marry, the bloke whose ring you were wearing when you first started going about with Terry. The bloke you wrote to and said, *specifically*, that you wanted to stay friends with. Didn't you? *Didn't* you?'

'Brian! You're hurting my wrist . . . Yes, I did say that, I know I did, because it wasn't anything you did, it was me. But that doesn't mean—'

'Doesn't mean you were telling the truth?' he said grimly. 'Because that's all I can think of now, Kathy. Because if you'd been telling the truth, if you'd really wanted to stay friends, if it really wasn't anything I'd done, you'd be only too pleased to see me, wouldn't you? You'd be only too pleased to come out with me. As friends. *Wouldn't* you?'

Kathy gazed at him helplessly. 'Brian . . .'

He dropped her hand suddenly and his voice softened. 'Kath, don't let's quarrel. I didn't come here for that. I just felt – well, that you'd been stringing me along. I know you wouldn't do that, not really. Tell you what – your hair's dry now, let's just walk out to the bay, shall we, and have a drink in the village pub? Just for old times' sake. And after that, if you really don't want me around, I'll stay away. It was just that I thought you meant it when you said you wanted to stay friends, you see.'

'I did.' She looked at him, wanting to say no but unable to think of a good reason. All that he said was true. How could she say she wanted to stay friends and then treat him like a stranger? They'd loved each other. Perhaps he really did still love her. In any case, there was no reason for them to quarrel.

And yet going out together, even just for a walk, seemed somehow dangerous.

Brian was smiling. 'Come on, Kath. I'm not asking you to elope to Gretna Green with me!'

She laughed and felt better. He was right really. There couldn't be any harm in a walk – it was the least she could do. She could give him back his ring, and then they'd say goodbye, and perhaps he would find himself another girl.

'All right. I'll just go and get a jacket. Only a walk, mind – I don't want to be late.'

'A walk and a drink,' he confirmed. 'I'll have you back by ten, like a good girl. Or does Daddy let you stay out later now?'

'He's starting to get round to it,' she replied with a grin, 'but tonight it's me who's saying I've got to be in by ten. This isn't a date, Brian.'

'I know. Just two friends, spending an hour or two together, catching up on the news.' He gave her his familiar, boyish grin, and her heart skipped a little at the way his eyes crinkled at the corners, making them seem bluer than ever. His teeth were very white and strong and even, and she felt an odd sense of *déjà vu* at seeing these things that had once been as well known to her as her own reflection.

As they walked along the road together and she turned her head to look at him, she realised that her head tilted at just the right angle to accommodate his height. It had taken ages to get used to Terry's shorter stature . . .

Brian gave her a warm smile, a friendly smile with no hint of anything more intimate in it. He's right, she thought, we ought to be able to go on being friends. And friends ought to be able to spend time together. That's what being friends means.

The sense of danger persisted, all the same. Just this one walk, she thought, and then – goodbye.

Chapter Nine

Having decided that she would like to try for another baby, Clare found herself longing to be pregnant again. She had read an article about how to plan the best time for conception. There were three nights which would be the most likely, she told Martyn.

'Only three in the whole month? How come we struck so lucky last time, then?'

'Well, I suppose it just happened to be that time. It's in the middle of the month, you see, and when we fixed the wedding date I made sure it wouldn't be a time when I had my period. I suppose that's why it's always been traditional for the bride to choose the date, when you come to think about it.'

'Are you really sure it's just that three nights?' Martyn asked, not very interested in tradition. 'I mean, if you can only fall then, why do people bother so much with French letters and things, and why do so many people get caught?'

'I don't think it's the only time. It's just that it's more likely then. But Roman Catholics use it, don't they? They call it the rhythm method or something.'

'Is that what they mean?' Martyn said, astonished. 'I thought it was doing it to music.'

'Ha ha,' Clare said. 'Very funny. Anyway, I've worked out that it's next Tuesday, Wednesday and Thursday, so . . .'

'I'm on duty next Wednesday.'

Clare put down her calendar and stared at him in dismay. 'On duty? That means you'll be at Collingwood all night. And—'

'Asleep all Thursday. Well, I should be fit by Thursday night, and Tuesday'll be okay. There's no problem.'

'Yes, but Wednesday would be the best night of all. Oh, Martyn, can't you change it?'

'Don't be daft. What do you want me to do, go to the officer of the watch and say I'm sorry, sir, I can't come in tonight because my wife wants me to—'

'Martyn! Don't be coarse,' Clare said, giggling.

'I'm not being. Look, you know I can't change my duty, Clare, not without a good reason, and whatever you might think, that isn't a good reason. Not as far as the Navy's concerned.' He reached over and took her hand. 'Look, we'll have both the other nights, and even if we don't make it this time we'll have all the fun of trying next month. It won't be the end of the world if we don't start a new baby straight away.'

'No, I suppose it doesn't. It's just that I do want us to have our family when we're together – we're going to be separated so much after this draft. But the main thing is that you and I are together, Martyn. And it *is* fun, trying!'

Martyn grinned and kissed her. Truth to tell, he wasn't bothered if they didn't start another baby just yet. Life was good enough as it was, with the three of them in their own home, and he still didn't fancy having nine months of Clare being sick and miserable as she'd been last time. He'd been worried about her then, but knowing she was at home with her mother had meant he needn't worry too much. If she was as sick this time, he'd have to look after her himself, as well as do his job, and it would certainly mess up the short time they had together.

Clare pulled a wry face. 'Yes, but the longer we take to start, the less time we'll all have together afterwards. I want us to be a proper family, Martyn. I want this baby to know who her daddy is.'

'So it's going to be a girl, is it?' he said, grinning. 'As far as I know, it's not even a twinkle in my eye yet.'

Clare looked at him and grinned back. 'It is. Your eyes are twinkling already. They always are.'

'Well, then.' He still had hold of her hand and he stood up, drawing her to her feet. 'Why don't we have a try now? You said that next week is just the most likely time – it can still happen at other times. Why don't we see if this is one of 'em?'

'I don't think it will,' she said seriously. 'According to this article—'

'Oh, flip the article! We don't have to do everything by the book, do we? Let's call it a rehearsal.' He pulled her against him and kissed her. 'Or shall we just call it making love, and never mind the consequences!'

Clare nestled in his arms. This was what she had longed for during all those lonely months. The kind of relaxed life where she and Martyn could make love just whenever they felt like it, without the pressure of knowing there were only a few more chances – perhaps none at all – before he had to leave her and go back to sea.

'Making love,' she agreed, reaching up to nuzzle his neck. 'That's what it is. But all the same, it would be nice if there were consequences!'

There were consequences too for Kathy, after she had been for the walk with Brian. He had set out to be the young sailor she had fallen in love with – as fresh and breezy as the sea air that brushed their faces as they walked along Stokes Bay, with not even the slightest touch of bitterness or reproach. Kathy, who had been expecting further recriminations and sour remarks directed at Terry, relaxed and began to remember why she'd agreed to marry him. The long separation was a thing of the past now, the loneliness something she could barely remember, and she felt sorry that she had hurt him when he was so far from home.

'Remember how we used to come out here and swim on summer evenings? Or just look at the lights in winter?'

Practically every courting couple in Gosport must have done that, Kathy thought. It was a job sometimes to find an empty seat in the shelters. She nodded, gazing out at the shimmering golden path laid on the sea by the sunset. The fiery colours lit the sky behind the Island and threw it into sharp relief. It was so clear and so quiet that she could hear the deep tolling of a bell somewhere across the water.

'That's Quarr Abbey,' she said. 'You can only hear the bells occasionally. It's a monastery down near the shore – I went to see it once.'

'You mean they let you in, with all those monks? I thought they weren't supposed to look at women. It must drive them mad, being cooped up together with a lot of other men all the time.'

'I don't know. We didn't see many of them. Perhaps the others were all locked away.' She grinned at him. 'I don't suppose it's all that different from being on board a ship with other men. You go weeks without seeing women.'

'Yes, but we make up for it when we go ashore.' He stopped suddenly, realising what he'd said. 'Well, some of the blokes do. Not engaged ones like me.' Again, he seemed to realise what he'd said and stopped, biting his lip. 'I mean – like I used to be.'

An awkward silence fell. Kathy found herself examining his words, wondering what they meant. Had he gone ashore looking for women, after she'd written the 'Dear John' letter? A picture rose in her mind of sailors pouring down the ship's gangway in some exotic foreign port, and all going off arm-in-arm with the girls who were always hanging around the dockyard gates. She knew it must happen, she'd seen it happening in Portsmouth itself, but she'd never thought of Brian as being one of that roistering crew.

'You mean, after I wrote you that letter, you—?'

'Would you have cared if I did?' he asked, and she bit her lip. It was none of her business, that was what he was saying. And he hadn't really answered her question.

'I don't know. I mean, whatever you did – whatever happened after – well, you don't have to tell me anything.' But she couldn't stop the visions of Brian strolling off into the foreign port with his arm round some girl's waist, and to her dismay she couldn't stop the feelings that rose in her breast at the thought of what might have happened. It's almost as if I was *jealous*, she thought in amazement, but how could I be?

'I don't think a bloke's really responsible for what he does then,' Brian said. 'You don't know what it's like, Kath. It's like having a knife stuck into your gut and twisted round and round.'

Kathy turned her head towards him. He was standing quite still, looking down at her. His eyes were dark and very serious. She felt an odd movement inside her, as if her heart had really turned over, or at least twisted a little. She wanted to look away, but his eyes held hers and she felt for a moment as if she were spinning. A tremor shook her body.

'Kathy,' he said, and laid his hands on her arms. 'Kathy, we're not going to let it end, are we? You still love me, I can see you do. I'm not going to let you go. I can't.'

Kathy stared at him. This was what she had dreaded. She knew she ought to pull away, tell him to stop, to leave her alone. She ought to walk away from him and never see him again, but when she looked into his eyes, so intent, so desperate, she couldn't do it.

She didn't want to do it.

'I know what you said,' Brian went on, 'but I don't think you meant it, Kath. I didn't think so even when I got your letter. You were lonely, you were fed up. There was Clare, with her house and her baby, and you didn't have anything except an engagement ring. I know what it was like.'

'You *don't* know!' Kathy found her voice but to her annoyance it was shrill and trembling. 'You don't know what it was like – how could you? You were at sea, doing what you want to do; you were going all over the world, seeing places like Australia and Japan and Singapore. How could you possibly know what it was like for me, cooped up in Gosport and not even supposed to go to the pictures or for a walk with someone else? And Clare and the baby had nothing to do with it. If you want to know, it was seeing Clare even more cooped up than I was that made me feel I didn't want to be engaged to *anyone*.'

Brian stared at her. 'You mean you don't want your own home? You don't want babies?'

'Yes, of course I do – some time. But not yet. I'm not ready for all that.'

'You don't want to get *married*?' he asked, as if she had just announced she was giving up eating.

Kathy sighed. 'That's just what I've been trying to tell you, Brian. I don't want to be married or engaged *yet*. I just want to enjoy my life as it is.'

'But that's not normal. *All* girls want to get married and have babies.'

'Well, thanks very much. I didn't realise I was actually abnormal.' Kathy moved away from him. 'I didn't say I *never* wanted those things. I just don't want them yet, that's all. What's so abnormal about that?'

Brian shook his head. He looked baffled and angry. 'But couldn't you have just said that, instead of writing me a "Dear John" and breaking it off? I wouldn't have minded if you'd said you wanted to wait a bit longer. At least I could have come home and talked to you about it. Didn't I have a right to expect that?'

Kathy looked at him. It didn't seem as if he was ever going to understand. She tried to speak gently but firmly, like Miss Millington, the senior mistress at school. 'Brian, I didn't want to wait a bit longer. I didn't want to be engaged at all. Didn't you hear me say that? I didn't want to be tied to *anyone*.'

'No, but you're still going out with this other bloke, this Terry. You're tying yourself to him.'

'I'm not. I'm not tied to him. We're just going out together.'

'It's more than that,' he said positively. 'You're going steady. You used him as an excuse for not coming out with me.'

Kathy was silent. Brian was right: she and Terry were more than friends. They weren't sleeping together, but they kissed and caressed with increasing intimacy and she was aware of a growing warmth in her feelings towards him. They had started out casually enough, sharing a walk or a trip to the cinema, but the casualness had gone and she didn't know how far they might progress.

She did know that she had felt mildly guilty at coming out with Brian this evening, and that Terry would be anxious and probably a bit jealous if he knew.

'Don't keep on at me, Brian,' she said. 'I did the best I could. It wasn't fair to go on being engaged to you and letting you go on thinking everything was all right when I didn't feel that way any more. How could I write to you about wedding arrangements when I knew there wasn't going to be a wedding? What else could I do but write and tell you?'

'You shouldn't have let us get engaged in the first place. Not if you weren't really in love with me.'

'I *was*. I *was* in love with you.'

'Well, it didn't last long, did it?' he said, and there was no mistaking his anger now. Kathy's heart sank. This was what she'd dreaded. 'Easy come, easy go, that's you, Kathy. I wonder if this Terry bloke knows that. Perhaps I ought to tell him.'

'No!' she cried. 'You're not to tell him anything. Just leave him alone – leave us both alone. And stop calling him "this Terry bloke". It sounds stupid.'

She turned and began to walk quickly away, but she had gone no more than a few yards when Brian caught her arm and swung her roughly round to face him.

'Don't you walk away from me like that, Kath. Don't you dare. I haven't finished what I wanted to say—'

'Don't I *dare*?' she retorted, as furious now as he. 'Just who do you think you are, Brian Bennett, talking to me like that? You're not my fiancé now, remember – and you never would have been if I'd known what you were like!'

'And what the hell d'you mean by that?' he demanded, keeping a tight grip on her wrist and dragging her towards him. 'You knew what I was like, Kath, and you liked it. Maybe it's you who ought to be doing some remembering – and maybe this will remind you.'

He gave her wrist a sudden jerk so that she stumbled and fell against him. In an instant, his arms were around her, gripping her to his body. She felt a sudden spasm of terror. Although she had never seen Brian in a real fury, she had always known his temper was there, held in check but smouldering beneath the surface. She could feel it in him now, quivering throughout his body, hardening his muscles, etching his face with bitter lines. And she could feel the heat of his excitement too, the tautness of his desire. She looked up into eyes that were almost black, rimmed with only a thin bright circle of blue, and knew that she was helpless.

The kiss was rough and demanding. She could feel all his frustration and anger, all his hurt and miserable disappointment, pouring through his body and into the lips that crushed hers. His teeth grazed her mouth, his arms were like iron bands around her body, his fingers bit cruelly into her flesh. She struggled, aware that he could be in a mood really to hurt her, and then stopped, knowing that she could only wait for him to release his hold. And then, slowly, she became conscious of a change between them.

She could never be sure whether it had begun in him or in herself. She knew only that the kiss became gradually more tender, that the cruelty in his fingers had turned to a caress. The angry hardness of his body softened against her; she could still feel the power in him, still feel the muscular strength of his hold, but the fury had gone and was replaced by a tenderness and passion that she remembered from their earlier days. The memory flooded back, taking her by surprise so that she was astonished to feel the heat of tears in her eyes; and at the same time, her own body softened and melted against him, and she knew that he was no longer holding her against her will. Instead, she had wound her arms about his neck and let her mouth open to his, and the kiss was no longer an assault but something shared and lovely.

At last they drew their heads apart and stared at each other. Their bodies still stood close and trembling, and Kathy felt Brian take a breath before he spoke, his voice shaky.

'You do remember, don't you, Kath? It's the same as it ever was, isn't it? Oh, *Kath* . . .'

'Brian—' she whispered, dazed. 'Brian, don't—' But he was kissing her again, with a fervour she could not deny, and then he rubbed his cheek against hers and laid his lips in the hollow of her neck, and held her face between his hands and kissed her lips, again and again, until she was gasping. '*Brian* . . .'

'Kath, I love you. I still love you. And you love me, I know you do, I can feel it . . .' He held her away from him a little, his eyes searching hers. She could see his dilated pupils, and the expression in them caught at her heart. I do still love him, she thought, her mind spinning, I do . . .

'He never kissed you like that, did he? Tell me he didn't. He couldn't. And you never kissed him – not that way – you didn't, did you, Kath? That's ours – *ours*.'

She shook her head, still dazed. It was true. Terry's kisses were not like that. They were soft and gentle, undemanding yet tremulous, with a sweet tenderness that had caught in a different way at the strings of her heart. Oh, what am I going to do? she thought with sudden frantic despair. Why did this have to happen?

With a swift movement that took even her by surprise, she twisted out of Brian's arms and turned away from him. Once again, she ran a few steps before he caught her, and this time she faced him and raised both hands, pressing them against his chest so that he couldn't pull her close.

'No, Brian. No. Don't kiss me again. *Please*.' She hadn't meant to sound as if she were begging him, but to her dismay her voice broke and she felt tears in her eyes again. 'Let me go. Just let me go.'

'But why? Why should I?' He sounded half angry, half bewildered. 'Kath, it isn't over between us, you can't tell me it is. Not after the way you kissed me then.'

'*You* kissed *me*.'

'And you kissed me back. You know you did. You wanted it as much as me. You can't pretend with me, Kath, we were *engaged*, remember?'

'Well, we're not now. I've told you, Brian, it *is* over. I broke it off and now I'm going out with Terry. Oh, I *knew* I shouldn't have come out with you, I knew it!'

'Well, I think it's a good job you did,' he retorted. 'You're obviously still in love with me, and it's no good pretending you're not. That's what you've been doing, Kath, pretending, pretending to *yourself*, and now you can't do that any longer. You won't be able to kiss this Terry without thinking about me, without comparing us, and I reckon I know who you'd rather be kissing!'

Kathy stared at him, baffled and dismayed. He's right, she thought, I did want him to kiss me. I wanted to see – I wanted to know. And now I do . . . and I wish I didn't . . .

Oh, Terry, what have I done?

She turned away again, but this time there was no point in trying to run away. Brian fell in beside her and together they walked slowly along the quiet promenade and back towards Jellicoe Avenue. For a few minutes there was silence, and then Brian spoke more quietly. 'You know it's true, don't you, Kath? You do still love me.'

She shook her head and tears flowed glittering from her lashes. 'I don't know. I don't seem to know anything any more. I'll have to think about it.'

'But the way you kissed me—'

'I told you, Brian, I want to *think* about it,' she flared. 'Don't keep on at me – *please*. Surely I've got a right to be left alone if I want to be.'

'All right, but you're not the only one round here with rights,' he muttered. 'It's my life you're playing with too, you know, and I'm getting fed up with it. I want to know where I stand. Don't *I* have a right to that? Don't I?'

'I don't know – I suppose so. But I can't think straight at the moment, Brian. I'm all upset. I shouldn't have come out with you, then none of this would have happened.'

'And you'd never have known. You'd have married this Terry – or maybe someone else – and you'd never have known why it didn't work. Because you'd never have known you were still in love with me. If you ask me, I've done you a good turn.'

'Who says I'm still in love with you? Only you! You can't go by one kiss. It didn't mean a thing.'

'It did,' he stated. 'It meant a hell of a lot. You know that as well as I do.' He studied her averted face. 'All right, Kath, have it your own way. Think about it. Think for as long as you like, but I'm not giving up now. You're mine, you always have been, and you're going to be mine again. I've got that ring now, Kathy.' He patted his pocket, where he had put it when she'd handed it to him only an hour before. 'And I'm ready to put it back on your finger, where it belongs, the minute you say the word.'

She turned her head and stared at him. Her eyes went to his hand, still resting against his pocket. She started to speak, stopped and bit her lips, then said at last, 'I won't be saying the word, Brian. I won't.'

'Oh, yes, you will, Kathy,' he said, and she shivered a little at the look in his eyes. 'Oh, yes, you will.'

Chapter Ten

Now that Christopher could walk, he was on his feet all the time, his gait still rather unsteady and liable to let him down at unexpected moments. He fell so often that he sported two permanent bruises on his forehead, as if he were growing horns, and Clare was afraid people might think she was hitting him. But her mother laughed and said that anyone who knew anything at all about babies could see what was happening.

Clare was in seventh heaven now, with Martyn coming home each evening and the family all close enough to visit. Iris came up on the bus to see her one afternoon a week, always careful to leave for home before Martyn cycled round the corner, because she believed that a man wanted his home to himself when he got back from work. Sometimes they invited her and Bill up to tea on a Sunday, or went down to them, and sometimes they all went over to Valerie in Stubbington Avenue. Clare would have liked to go over during the week, on her own, to have a 'sisters' afternoon', but it was a long journey, involving either two bus rides and the Gosport ferry or a long bus trip from Fareham and through Portchester. It was too much with a toddler to cope with, and worse for Valerie, whose baby was due quite soon.

'Wish I was you,' Clare said one Sunday when they were all down at Abbeville Avenue with their parents. They were spending the whole day there, so in the afternoon they took a picnic out to Stokes Bay and the sisters grasped the chance of a private chat. 'Don't tell anyone, but me and Martyn are trying too.'

'You're not!' Valerie stopped for a minute and pressed her hand against her back. 'I thought you'd be happy just to let it go for a while.'

'What's the point? If we wait till Martyn goes away again, I'll have to cope all on my own. Or else wait till he comes back, and that'd mean Chris could be four or five years old before we had our second. I want them close together, like yours, so that they're companions.'

'I know, but suppose you're poorly again?'

'All the more reason for making sure Martyn's home to help.' Clare glanced at Valerie's outline. 'You're not sorry you're having another one, are you?'

'No, of course not. I'm like you, I want them close together, but I've got Maurice at home all the time. I just think you're going to miss a lot if you spend this next few months being half-dead like you were last time.'

'Well, thanks a lot!' Clare laughed. 'Now I know what a bundle of laughs I must have been.'

'Well, let's face it, you were pretty miserable most of the time. Not that any of us blamed you, what with being sick at all hours right through, and hardly seeing Martyn. I'm amazed you're willing to risk it at all, to be honest.'

'Well, I don't reckon I'll get that trouble again, and if I do the doctor'll know how to treat me. He gave me those vitamin B6 injections towards the end last time, and they really seemed to work. This time, he'll probably give them to me straight away.'

Valerie looked at her. 'D'you reckon you are already? Expecting?'

'No. I worked out the best dates last month but we must have just missed them. So we're going to try again.' Clare gave her sister a mischievous glance. 'It's tonight, as a matter of fact!'

'Ohhh. *I* see.' Valerie returned her look and they both giggled. 'So you won't be wanting to stay at Mum and Dad's too late, will you?'

Iris, who was pushing Johnny's pushchair just in front of them, turned at the sound of their laughter. 'What are you two tittering about? Honestly, you're just like a pair of silly schoolgirls when you get together.'

'They always have been,' Bill remarked. 'Specially Clare. Laugh to see a pudding crawl, that one would.'

'Well, wouldn't you?' Clare enquired. 'I mean, you've got to admit you'd be surprised if one of Mum's spotted dicks suddenly started crawling round the table.'

'Dotted spick!' he said. 'Now that's what I call a real pudding. Beats celly and justard any day.'

The others groaned. They walked on through Stanley Park, the big garden given to Gosport by the Sloan-Stanley family who had owned a lot of land in the area. It wasn't a garden in the sense that Bill's and

Iris's backyard was a garden, a narrow strip of ground with a path running down one side and just enough room to grow a patch of tomatoes and a few flowers. Stanley Park was huge, with a vast area of grass, and shrubberies with big, old trees and sprawling bushes. Johnny and Christopher were set free from their pushchairs and rushed about squealing after a ball that Martyn and Maurice kept kicking just out of their reach. The rest of them sat down on the grass and Bill set down the picnic basket he had been carrying.

'Why don't we just stop here and have our tea?' he suggested. 'I'd rather be on the grass under a few trees than on the beach, sitting on shingle.'

It was just this sort of phrase that had everyone holding their breaths and then sighing with relief when the danger had passed – if it did. This time, Bill made no spoonerism but their relief didn't mean that the others agreed with him.

'Oh, no! Of course we want to go to the beach. We've brought our bathers, and we promised Christopher he could paddle. He and Johnny will love playing in the waves and building sandcastles.'

'So would I, if I thought we'd be able to find any sand to build them with.' Stokes Bay beach was notoriously shingly, with only a few patches of sand dotted here and there, and these patches were invariably grabbed by earlier arrivals. 'Well, they can be bar-tabies instead.'

'*Tar*-babies,' Clare corrected him with a grin, and then pulled a face. 'Honestly, you'd think they'd have got all the tar cleared away by now – it's years since the war was over.'

Stokes Bay had been one of the beaches used for the D-Day invasion of France in 1944. For almost two years before that it had been barred to civilians, who couldn't get through the festoons of barbed wire even if they'd wanted to, and huge concrete slipways had been built there, as well as some of the great Mulberry Harbour docks that had been towed across the Channel to form an artificial harbour. All that was left of this activity were broken slabs of concrete and patches of tar and oil that persisted year after year, surfacing from beneath the shingle as if an oil-well had been struck.

'I reckon a lot of it comes from ships going up and down the Solent,' Iris said. 'Wherever it's from, it's mucky stuff and it takes ages to get it off your clothes. I think your father's right, Clare, we ought to have our tea here and then just have a walk along the beach. The kiddies are enjoying themselves all right, look at them.'

'I suppose so.' Clare had to admit that it was pleasant sitting here in the big park, and there was nothing to stop them having a bathe and a paddle when they did reach the shore. 'So long as they can play in the water as well. I want Christopher to get used to it and learn to swim as soon as possible.'

Iris began to unpack the picnic baskets and bags, and the men came back as soon as they noticed the food being laid out, bringing the toddlers with them. They all sprawled around the big blanket and Iris set out plates of sandwiches and sausage rolls.

'There's a good big fruit cake as well, and a couple of Thermos flasks of tea.' Everyone had brought something to the feast and they all tried each other's contributions. Clare had made her special egg and cheese pie, and a batch of flapjacks, and Valerie had brought a bag of homemade doughnuts, with crunchy brown outsides. There were fresh tomatoes grown in Bill's back garden, and a big cucumber.

'I don't suppose we'll get many more days like this,' Iris remarked, cutting a slice of pie. 'The trees are already starting to turn, look.'

'The horse-chestnuts always go first,' Clare agreed. 'And there'll be some good conkers soon. You can see how fat the shells are getting.'

She sat with her arms around her knees, pretending that the park was her own garden. The school grounds had been part of this park once, and the fence between them ran near by. She thought how nice it had been to come to a place like this to school, and hoped her own children would come here too.

Her children . . . People seemed surprised that at only twenty-one she had settled down into marriage and motherhood, but to Clare, it seemed right and natural. Working in an office had never suited her, and she loved the freedom of not having to go out to a job each day. But most of all, she loved being with Martyn in their own home, and having her baby to look after.

Looking after babies is the best thing a girl can do, she thought. Bringing them up to be good citizens. It's the mother who has most to do with how children grow up. It must be just about the most important job in the world.

Hazel, next door, had missed going out to work. She looked after her baby just as well as Clare did, but she fretted for the companionship and independence she had given up. When Kevin was about nine months old, she had tried leaving him in a day-nursery and had got a job in the office of one of the big chemical factories along the Fareham Road. Kevin hadn't settled in the nursery, though, and he'd cried so much at night that Hazel, exhausted, had decided to give up the experiment after only one week.

Clare hadn't been able to understand why she'd wanted to go in the first place. Why trap yourself in a nine-to-five routine, letting other people boss you about for eight hours a day – forty hours a week! – when you could be at home and decide your own life? Obviously the extra money would be useful, but was it worth giving up all that time with your baby? They grew so fast, and you'd miss such a lot. And if it made the baby miserable . . .

'I don't think it did really,' Hazel said, justifying her actions. 'He just had a bit of a cold that week, that's all. I didn't really like the job anyway.'

Clare didn't think that was true, but she didn't argue. She was pleased to have Hazel back next door all day, and to be able to pop in for a coffee or walk down to the shops together. She looked forward to telling her she was pregnant again. Hazel, who had decided to have only one baby, would think she was mad, but Clare didn't mind that. She thought of the coming night and wondered if she and Martyn would click this time. She leaned her cheek against her knees and hugged herself, feeling the stirring excitement within her, and when she looked at Martyn she could see that he knew what she was thinking and felt it too.

Later, when they were in bed at last, they turned to each other and smiled.

'That was a good day,' Martyn said, stroking her cheek with one fingertip. 'Chris really liked the sea, didn't he?'

'Mm. I think Mum thinks I push him too hard, but it really is true that babies can learn to swim if you start them soon enough. And he nearly did, didn't he? I reckon he'd be a real water-baby if we kept up with it.'

'Trouble is, I don't think there's much chance of that,' Martyn said. 'It'll be too cold for swimming in the sea soon, and the baths will be closing too. It's a pity this town hasn't got an indoor swimming bath.'

'Well, we'll just have to take whatever chances we can and hope he'll remember next year. And now,' Clare said, lying back in Martyn's arms and moving slowly against him, 'how about taking a different sort of chance?'

'You know,' he said, moving his lips over her face and neck and down to her breasts, 'sometimes you're just too sexy for your own good, did you know that?'

'No,' she whispered, feeling the delicious tingle spiral through her stomach, 'I didn't know that. And I don't believe it either. I think it's very good for both of us. Oh, Martyn . . .' Her voice ended on a tiny squeak as his lips moved further still. 'It could even be for three of us. I'm sure it's going to work tonight, I'm *sure* of it.'

'We'll make sure of it,' he murmured, his hands caressing her shivering body with an increasing urgency. 'We'll *make* it work, Clare, my darling, darling sweetheart.'

Martyn was on duty again on Tuesday evening, and Clare looked forward to a cosy evening gossiping with Kathy. Somehow, with Martyn around, it wasn't so easy to share their confidences and Clare felt out of touch with her friend's life. She didn't even know for sure if Kathy was still seeing Terry.

'He hasn't come to pick you up lately,' she said as they sat eating their meal from the low coffee-table, with Christopher in his low chair spooning up banana custard from a bowl. 'You haven't had a row, have you?'

Kathy shook her head and looked embarrassed. 'No, not exactly. It's just – well, it's a bit awkward, with Martyn here. Being Brian's friend, I mean. Terry feels he's not really welcome.'

Clare put down her fork and stared at her. 'That's daft! Of course he's welcome. When have I ever said anything—?'

'It's not you. And Martyn hasn't *said* anything. It's just the way he looks sometimes. Terry doesn't blame him, nor do I. And – well, there's something else.' Kathy dropped her eyes and fiddled with her knife. 'Look, I've been wanting to tell you – I'm surprised you don't know already. Hasn't Martyn said anything? About me and Brian?'

'No. What should he say?' Clare looked at her again and felt the dawning of sudden realisation. 'Kathy, you're not going out with Brian again, are you?'

'No! Not exactly. Well, we've been for a couple of walks together, but that's all.' Kathy raised her eyes and gave Clare a pleading glance. 'What was I supposed to do, tell him to get lost? He just wanted to talk things over, that's all, I couldn't refuse him that, could I? I mean, we were engaged, after all. He's got a right . . .'

'You're thinking of going back to him,' Clare said slowly. 'You are, aren't you?'

Kathy sighed. 'I don't know. I don't know what I'm thinking any more. It's all such a muddle.'

'But why is it? You knew what you wanted before. You wanted to be free. You wanted some time to yourself, to make other friends. Why is it a muddle now?'

'It just is. Seeing Brian again – well, it's stirred up all my feelings. I still care about him, Clare. I never stopped. When I wrote to him, I was really upset about it. I didn't want to hurt him. It wasn't as if I'd stopped liking him, after all. It wasn't as if we'd had a row.'

Clare gazed at her. Kathy was clearly upset and, as she had said, muddled. She'd broken off her engagement for what seemed at the time like good reasons, and now she wasn't sure any more. Brian had come back and refused to take no for an answer, and someone was bound to get hurt.

'So who is it going to be?' she asked at last. 'Brian or Terry?'

'I don't know! I don't know why it's got to be either of them. Why can't I be allowed just to be friends with someone without everyone thinking I'm swearing eternal love? D'you know, Clare, I've a good mind to just go away and leave them both. I could, you know. I could apply for a transfer somewhere. London. They're always looking for people to work in London. I think I could enjoy that for a while.'

'You don't mean it! You'd hate being in London all on your own. You wouldn't really go away, would you? It wouldn't solve anything.'

'No, I don't think it would,' Kathy agreed gloomily. 'Brian would just follow me there. He won't give up, Clare.'

'And what about Terry? Will he give up?'

'I don't really know what he wants. We've never talked about it.'

'Not at *all*? But I thought—'

'Well, I suppose we have, in a way. I told him I didn't want to go serious. And he said he'd just wait.' Kathy gave Clare a rueful look. 'It's not exactly talking.'

'No, but it's pretty near it. I mean, if he says he'll wait, it means he does want to be serious, doesn't it? And he thinks you are too, really. He's just giving you time.' Clare paused. 'Does he know you've been out with Brian?'

'I haven't been *out* with him. I mean, we haven't had any proper dates – he's just come round a couple of times and we've gone for a walk, that's all. You can't call that going out together.'

Clare thought you could, but all she said, patiently repeating herself, was, 'Well, does Terry know?'

'Sort of. I mean, I didn't tell him the first time, but after the second time I thought I ought to. Someone might have seen us, and told him – and, anyway, it didn't seem fair to keep it a secret.'

'What did he say?'

'Nothing much. Only that he supposed that since we weren't engaged I was free to go out with anyone I liked.' Kathy looked at Clare with real misery in her eyes. 'I felt awful. I didn't know what to say. In the end, I said . . .' She looked down and fiddled with her knife and fork again. 'I said there wasn't anything for him to worry about, I wasn't going back to Brian.'

'Oh.' There was a small silence. Clare took hold of Christopher's hands, which were now covered with custard, and wiped them with the flannel that was as much a part of mealtimes as salt and pepper. 'Into the bath with you, my boy, before you go *any*where,' she told him as he wriggled to be set free from the chair. She looked back at Kathy. 'But you don't know if that's really true, do you? About not going back to Brian.'

Kathy shook her head. 'No,' she whispered.

There was another small silence. 'Oh, lord,' Clare said at last, 'you really are in a muddle, aren't you?' She got up and lifted Christopher into her arms. 'I'll have to clean this little monkey up. D'you want to come too?'

Kathy usually loved helping to bath Christopher, but this time she shook her head and said, 'No, I'll clear away the tea-things. I'm sorry, Clare, I'm a misery tonight. Perhaps I'd better go home early.'

'Don't you dare,' Clare told her. 'What are friends for if you can't be a misery with them sometimes? Don't take too much notice of the screams, I've got to get this mess out of his hair.'

She returned half an hour later, Christopher fresh and pink in clean pyjamas, still drawing in the occasional sobbing breath but smiling and sleepy nevertheless. He climbed on to Kathy's lap and she cuddled him, burying her face in the creases of his neck. He still had a bottle of milk at bedtime and she gave it to him and then carried him in to bed. When she came back, there were tears on her cheeks.

'He's so gorgeous, Clare. You don't ever regret getting married and having him so quickly, do you?'

Clare shook her head. 'No, how could I? Especially now Martyn's at Collingwood. I just wish he could be home like this all the time.' She glanced at her friend. 'Are you feeling sorry you broke it off with Brian?'

Kathy sank down in the red armchair. 'Oh, I don't know. Sometimes I wish I'd never done it and sometimes I think I was absolutely right – and sometimes I just wish I'd never got engaged in the first place! I wonder why I did. It's sort of expected, isn't it? You leave school, get a job in an office or something, and after three or four years you get engaged and then married and start a family. It's what everyone does and what everyone expects, but – I don't know, it seems to me more like the end of life than the beginning.'

Clare stared at her. 'Whatever do you mean?'

'Well, it's like a pattern, isn't it? You follow it whether you want to or not. Once you're married, that's it. House, kids, no money, and nothing else till they're all grown up and you're too old to do anything else even if you want to. I just think sometimes there ought to be more than that.'

'Like what? Working in an office all your life?' Clare shuddered. 'Not me! I hated it – all those bits of paper, and half the time you know very well they don't mean anything. I used to think if I didn't come in nobody would ever notice, except that no one would make the tea. I don't call that much of a life.'

'No, but there are other things people can do. I could get promotion. I could get up to executive officer and be in charge of a department. Or I could go abroad.' Kathy leaned forward. 'There was a girl in our office once, she'd been to Canada. She saved up her money and bought a ticket and got a job there. She did all sorts of things – canoeing and skiing and climbing – she had a smashing time.'

'So why did she come back, if it was so good?'

'Well, she only went for two years. She didn't want to live there. But she *did* it, that's the point, she's done something really interesting and she's got something to look back on. And people can emigrate to Australia. It's like a new country, they want young people to go out and help build it up. There are heaps of things to do.'

'Australia! I've always dreamed of going to Australia. Or Singapore, if Martyn got an accompanied draft so that we could all go with him.' Clare's eyes shone. 'I'd love to live in a different country for a while. But what would your mum and dad say if you went on your own? And Terry? And Brian?'

'They'd go mad, the lot of them, but it's my life, Clare. Why should I let them live it for me? I'm twenty-one, I can do as I please. I don't want to be tied down to a job in the civil service all my life, or a house and a baby and a husband who's never at home—' She stopped suddenly, flushing. 'I mean—'

'You mean Brian. You're still thinking of him being the one you'll marry. You know what you're doing, Kathy? You're trying to run away from him. You're trying to run away from yourself.'

There was a long silence. Kathy bit her lip and Clare was dismayed to see fresh tears redden her eyes. Then she said shakily, 'So what am I supposed to do? Tell him I'm sorry, he was right all along? Tell Terry I don't want to see him any more? I don't think I can do it, Clare. Terry doesn't deserve that. He's too nice. And I think I do love him, in a way. I can't bear to think of hurting him.'

'But you can't marry a man just because of that,' Clare said. 'You're talking about a *lifetime*, Kathy. Fifty or sixty years. You've got to be sure.'

'I know. And that's just the trouble – I'm not sure. I'm not sure of anything any more.'

Clare gazed at her. It upset her to see her friend so troubled but she didn't know what she could do to help. Talking and listening might help a bit, she supposed, but in the end only Kathy could make the decision and it might be years before she knew if it had been the right one.

'Well, as far as I can see, all you can do is wait,' she said at last. 'Don't let anyone push you into anything. Just wait until you are sure, and then do whatever seems right to you, and right for you. It's no good worrying about people getting hurt – someone *is* going to get hurt. I don't see how you can prevent that now.'

'No,' Kathy said miserably, 'neither do I.'

They talked for a little longer but Kathy was obviously tired and unhappy, and when she got up to go early, Clare didn't try to stop her. She watched sadly as her friend put on her duffel-coat and walked away down the street, then she went back indoors and thought that she too might as well have an early night.

The bed seemed big and lonely without Martyn, but it was only for this one night, for his monthly night-duty. Tomorrow he would be home again, and eager to make love after their brief separation. Clare lay still, her hands covering her flat stomach. Perhaps there was a new life beginning in there now, after Sunday night. Daring to tempt fate, she started to think of names. Shaun was popular for boys just now. Or Stephen. And Julie and Kim were both used a lot for girls.

She thought of Kathy, rejecting the idea of a husband and family. Was she really keen to emigrate, or was it just that she was scared of being tied down? The thought of seeing the world was exciting, but Clare knew that she wouldn't swop Martyn or Christopher – or the new baby, who might even now be a part of her – for the sake of living abroad.

I don't suppose she'll go in the end, she thought. She'll make up her mind between Brian and Terry, or maybe she'll fall in love with someone quite different. But whatever happens, there's not much I can do, except be here to support her whenever she needs me.

She sighed, feeling sad at the thought of her friend's unhappiness. There was nothing fickle about Kathy – she was genuinely confused, and upset by the knowledge that her own confusion was hurting others. Perhaps it would be better after all if she went away for a while. Perhaps it would give them all time to think.

Chapter Eleven

Brian had been drafted to a new ship, based in Portsmouth, and Kathy breathed a sigh of relief when it went to sea towards the end of September. At least, that's what she told Clare and even tried to believe herself. She didn't mention the nights when she lay awake going over their last evening together, or the strange sense of something missing that accompanied her days.

She went out for a walk with Terry on the Sunday after Brian had gone. They caught a bus out to Titchfield and wandered round the old village, then had a sandwich in one of the pubs before taking the footpath beside the river to the tiny harbour at Titchfield Haven.

'It's such a pretty walk,' Kathy said as they paused to lean over a small bridge. 'We don't have many rivers around this way, only the Meon. There's the Test, of course, and the Hamble, but they're too far away to go for a walk. I'd love to live in a place that had a river running through it.'

'I wouldn't call this a river, really,' Terry said, looking down into the shallow water. 'It's not much more than a stream. You ought to see some of the rivers in the rest of the country – the Severn and the Tamar, and the rivers of Yorkshire. Mind you, they've got the countryside for rivers – hills and moors and rocks to make falls and pools and rapids. Hampshire's too flat for rivers.'

Kathy turned and looked at him in surprise. 'You're sounding quite poetic! Have you seen all those rivers?'

'Some of them. I went to stay with my gran and auntie in Devon during the war, and then I had other relatives in Yorkshire to go and visit later on. My dad used to take me in an old canoe he'd made himself – a folding one, he called it a Rob Roy.' He fell silent, frowning a little.

Kathy waited, not sure what to say. Terry seldom mentioned his father. She knew only that his parents had parted a few years ago and must have got divorced, because his mother had married again. Terry didn't seem to have seen his father since.

'What happened to your dad?' she asked tentatively. 'You never talk about him. Does he still live in Gosport?'

Terry's frown deepened and she wished she hadn't asked, but he answered readily enough. 'No. He went to Australia. He got fed up with this country after the war. He said it wasn't pulling itself together, everything was dark and dismal, it was all a mess after the bombing and everything, there was even more rationing than when the war had been on – he just wanted to make a new start. He wanted us to go with him, but Mum wouldn't go, and I was only twelve, so I didn't have a choice. They argued about it more and more and in the end she just told him to go, and he did.'

'Oh, Terry.' Kathy could tell from the tightness in his voice that the memory still hurt. 'Did you really want to go?'

'Well, what do you think? I'd hardly seen my dad all through the war – he was in the Army, out in India – then he came home for a year or two and then he was gone again. They never seemed to get on, but I was fed up with rationing too, and Australia sounded like paradise to me. But kids don't get asked, and I had to stay with Mum. And then she got friendly with Fred Smith and that was that.'

Kathy was silent for a moment or two, then she said carefully, 'I still don't understand why you don't move out if you hate being with them so much.'

'I've told you why,' he said abruptly. 'It's my home. She made me stay when I didn't want to, and I'm damned if I'm going to move out to suit *him*.'

'But if it's making you miserable—'

'Look, Kathy,' Terry said, 'there's only one thing that'll stop me being miserable. And that's knowing I really matter to someone. That *someone* is going to put me first. Then I'll move out and start my life properly.'

Kathy glanced at him and then looked away, disturbed by the intensity of his gaze. So far she had managed to keep their relationship under control. She had known it was developing, but she didn't want it to move too fast. She wanted time to be herself, but men like Terry and

Brian didn't seem to understand that. They wanted her attention focused on them.

'Didn't you ever think of going to Australia too, once you were grown up? Didn't you think of going to join your father?'

'What's the point? He's married again too. They've got a couple of kids. They wouldn't want me.'

Kathy turned back and stared at him. 'How do you know that? Surely he'd want to see you. You don't have to go and live with him. You could go and start a new life – you could do anything.'

'I couldn't. I'm an accountant. Everything would be different out there, I'd have to start again.'

'Well, so does anyone who emigrates. It's a challenge. It's exciting. *I'd* go, if it was me.'

Terry gripped her hand as it lay on the parapet of the little bridge. 'Would you? Would you really?'

'Yes. As a matter of fact, I've been thinking of doing something like that anyway. There's this girl at work, she's been to Canada and she's thinking of going to Australia. I'd like to do that. I've been making enquiries—'

'Making enquiries? You were thinking of going to Australia, and you never said a word to me about it?' His fingers tightened. 'Suppose we went together?' he said. 'Suppose I said I'd go with you?'

'*You'd* go to Australia with me?' She felt dizzy, shaken by his sudden passion.

'Yes. Or Canada. Anywhere. I'd do it if you were with me, Kathy. It would make all the difference, having you.' His face was alight with eagerness. 'Let's do it! Let's go away together, away from everyone we know, and start again.'

Kathy stared at him. His fingers were crushing hers against the stone of the parapet. She wanted to draw back, but his dark eyes burned and she could not look away. She felt her heart jerk and beat unevenly.

'Say you will, Kathy,' he urged, but she shook her head slowly, as if it were too heavy to move.

'Terry, I can't – not just like that. I need to think about it. I don't know . . .'

The light died from his face. 'You don't want to.'

'I've never thought about it.'

'You have. You just told me you'd thought about it. You said there was this girl at work, and you'd like to do what she'd done.'

'Yes, but she did it by herself – she didn't go with someone else.'

'You mean you don't want to go with *me*.'

Kathy turned away, staring across the reedy meadows towards the Solent. 'It's not that. I don't *know*. I've never thought about going with you, or anyone else. I haven't thought all that seriously about it at all – it was just an idea. I was just finding out a bit about it, that's all. I probably wouldn't have gone in the end—'

'You'd have gone abroad with Brian if he'd been drafted to somewhere like Malta or Singapore,' Terry stated.

'Yes, but we'd have been married. Wives do go with their husbands.'

'So suppose we were married?' he said. 'Would you come with me then?'

'But we're not even engaged—'

'Because I wanted to give you time to get over Brian. I didn't want to take advantage of you, on the rebound, and I didn't think you wanted to get serious just yet.'

'I didn't.'

'And because I thought you might change your mind when you saw him again,' he went on. 'But he's been back, and you've seen him again, and you haven't gone back to him, so there's hope for me, isn't there? And if you're thinking about emigrating—'

'I'm not *thinking* about it! I just mentioned it.' Kathy cast about in her mind, trying to remember how the subject had come up in the first place. 'It was you, talking about your dad in Australia—'

'It's an idea, though, isn't it?' He gripped her hand again. 'Think of it, Kathy, the two of us together, setting sail on one of those big liners – setting off to start a new life, in a new country, together. It's a wonderful country, Australia, it's got everything a young couple needs. Opportunities – space – freedom. Sunshine. And they want people like us to help build it up. It doesn't even cost much to go. You can get a passage for only ten pounds. *Ten pounds.* It's only half a week's salary. That shows how much they want people.'

'Let's get this straight,' Kathy said. 'Are you asking me to marry you?'

Terry opened his mouth, then closed it again. Then he said, 'Yes. I must be. I *am*. Of course I am.'

'And did you intend to ask me this afternoon?' she asked. 'Did you think this would be a nice, romantic place to propose? Is that why you started to talk about Australia?'

'No. I didn't know we were going to talk about anything like that, but it's the obvious solution.'

'Solution to what? I didn't know there was a problem, Terry.'

He looked at her. He was frowning again, a puzzled frown this time. 'What do you mean?'

'There's nothing to stop us getting married and staying in Gosport,' she said. 'We could have our own home. You could stop living with your mother and stepfather. If that's what you want.'

'Well, it's not *all* I want,' he said, a little defensively. 'You know that, Kathy. I want us to get married. I've said so.'

'But we've never really talked about it,' she pointed out, 'and now it seems to be just a sort of afterthought to this idea of going to Australia. As if I'm just someone to keep you company. Had you even thought of emigrating before this afternoon?' she persisted, and saw him drop his eyes.

'Not exactly, no.'

'So it's a sudden idea.'

'Well, that's what ideas *are*,' he burst out. 'Sudden. You don't get them gradually. Well, maybe you do, but *some* of them are sudden. It doesn't mean they're any the worse for it.'

'No,' Kathy said, 'but it means you've got to think about them carefully before you rush into making a decision.' She withdrew her hand from his. 'Look, I'm not saying yes, but I'm not saying no either. Not definitely. Let's just think about it for a while. It's a big step. We can't just decide all in a few minutes.'

Terry pursed his lips and then nodded. He gave her a wry grin. 'I suppose you're right. It's not like me to rush into things anyway. I always take my time to make a decision. It's just that – well, I don't mind telling you I've been worried these past few weeks. Knowing you were seeing Brian again, wondering if you might go back to him after all. Look, it's you I really want, Kathy. Cars, Australia – you're right, they're not important. It's you that's important, you and me together.'

They stood close for a few minutes, then began to walk on alongside the little river. Kathy felt confused and uncertain. Terry could not have declared his feelings more plainly, yet to her surprise she could not quite respond. It seemed too big a step. I'm not ready, she thought. I need a bit more time . . .

Soon, the river ran through a little wood and then twisted away through the reed-beds, spreading out into shallow pools and marshes. The path kept to firmer ground and emerged on the road not far from the little harbour. It was low tide and the stream was little more than a trickle running from the marsh through the mud.

'It's really pretty – like a little bit of Devon or Cornwall,' Kathy said as they paused to look at the scatter of dinghies and small motor-boats heeling on their sides. 'You know, I've hardly ever been here before.'

They walked back along the shore and the low cliffs to Hillhead and on to Lee-on-the-Solent. The seabed was very flat at Hillhead and at every low tide people stood hundreds of yards out at the edge of the water, digging in the mud for bait or cockles. At Lee, the shore sloped more steeply and the tide was not so far away, but you'd still have to paddle a long way before you could swim. They stopped for a cup of tea in the little café opposite the Tower, and then strolled across Brown-down and the Warren to emerge on the Military Road. From here, it wasn't far to Kathy's home, where they were to have tea before going to the pictures.

Kathy felt tired and a bit depressed. It had been a good walk and she felt she ought to have enjoyed it, but somehow it had turned faintly sour. She had been proposed to – in a way – but she felt uneasy and unhappy about the way it had happened. There was none of the romantic joy she'd felt when Brian had asked her to marry him, none of the secret excitement and the anticipation of buying the ring.

I wish we weren't going out tonight, she thought miserably.

They turned along the road leading to the house. Kathy's parents lived at the end. Her father had recently bought a car, and it stood outside, signifying that they were at home. She sighed, wondering how to suggest to Terry that they might cancel their evening out and, if they did, that he should go on to his own home. Knowing how he felt about it, he was unlikely to take readily to such an idea.

'Look,' she began uncertainly as they drew near the front gate, 'I've got a bit of a headache. D'you mind if we don't—?'

She paused suddenly. The front door had opened and a tall figure stood framed there, watching their progress along the street. Kathy caught her breath and felt Terry tense beside her.

'It can't be,' she whispered, and turned her head to look up at Terry's face. One look told her that she wasn't imagining things. She stopped, feeling her heart kick and begin to pound. 'It *can't* be Brian. They've gone to sea . . .'

'They've come back, by the look of it,' Terry said grimly. He stopped and put his arm very deliberately around Kathy's waist. 'And he hasn't popped in just to say hello. If I'm not much mistaken, this is where you make up your mind, Kathy, my darling.'

Dimly, she registered that this was the first time he had ever used such an endearment. Dimly, her mind protested that she didn't have to make any decisions at all – that nobody had the right to exert such pressure on her – but more clearly than either of these thoughts came the flood of joy and pleasure at the sight of Brian's face – the joy and pleasure that came from knowing he had come back, so unexpectedly, that he had come straight to her, that he had waited for her to come home.

'*Brian* . . .' she said, and ran towards him.

The ship had developed a fault twelve hours out at sea. The engineers hadn't been able to repair it without further equipment and so it had been ordered back into Portsmouth. They would be in dock at least a fortnight, Brian told her as they sat close on the sofa in the front room later that evening. Time to get engaged all over again. Time to start again planning their wedding.

Terry had left as soon as Kathy had pulled away from him to run those last few yards. He'd stood at the gate, watching her, and when she'd turned back, her face filled with distress at the hurt she must have caused him, he'd shrugged and told her not to worry.

'I always knew this could happen. I never really believed you'd give him up.' He gave Brian a brief nod. 'I guess the best man's won after all.'

'Terry!' Kathy had cried out, but Brian held her hard against him and returned Terry's nod without any noticeable sign of friendliness.

'That's right, mate. Better be on your way. She won't be wanting you any more.'

'Brian, don't talk like that! Wait, Terry—' But Terry had already turned away and was walking rapidly back along the street. She watched helplessly, wanting to cry, but Brian was pulling her back into his arms and at his kiss her distress receded and she felt only the delight of seeing him again. 'Oh, Brian . . . Brian, I've missed you so *much*!'

There was no more arguing, no more torment. The engagement was on again. True to his word, Brian had the ring ready in his pocket and when he fitted it on her finger Kathy felt as if it had never been gone. She gazed at it through her tears and then pressed her cheek against his breast.

'Brian, I'm sorry. I don't know what happened to me. I must have gone mad for a while.'

'You were lonely. We ought to have got married before I went away.' He tightened his arm about her. 'We'll start planning that wedding again straight away. I'm not taking any more chances.'

'There aren't any more to take.' Thoughts of travelling to Canada or

Australia, with or without Terry, seemed as outlandish as going to the moon. 'But you'll be going away again as soon as the ship's ready.'

'Only till Christmas. We'll be back then. How do you fancy a Christmas wedding? And if I take first leave, we'll have a fortnight in our own home before the ship sails again.'

Kathy shuddered. 'I don't want to think of you going away again.'

'You know I'll have to, but it won't be for so long as last time. This ship's not going out East. It'll just be a few weeks at a time, in European waters. And after that I ought to get a shoreside draft. By the time that's over I'll only have a couple of years left to serve. It's not going to be so bad.'

'You really do mean to come out at thirty?' Kathy asked, and he nodded.

'Definitely. They're not turning me anchor-faced. Coming out at thirty will give me a better chance of a decent job. Leave it till forty and you're too old. Anyway, I want to be at home with my wife and kids. Now I've got you back, I'm not letting you go again.'

'A Christmas wedding,' Kathy said dreamily. 'It sounds wonderful. A bit chilly for lace dresses, though – perhaps I'll have velvet. White velvet for me and a colour for the bridesmaids . . . oh, Brian, it all sounds so lovely. And to think I nearly threw it all away. I don't know what got into me. I really am sorry. I never wanted to hurt you.'

'Let's forget it now,' he said, and nuzzled his lips against her neck. 'Let's put it all in the past. Let's just make plans for the future.'

It was late before Kathy went upstairs and collected the spare pillows and blankets for Brian to make up his bed on the sofa. They kissed their final goodnight and then she went to her own bed, where she lay wakeful for a while, reliving every moment of the evening. Before she went to sleep, however, she thought of Terry and felt a pang of sadness at the way their friendship had ended.

It didn't seem right, though, she thought. The way he seemed to depend on me to help him break away from his mother and stepfather – the way he jumped at the idea of going to Australia, so long as I went too. And the way he proposed to me – if you could call it a proposal – just to make it possible. You can't get married like that.

Clare was right. You had to think hard before you committed yourself to another person for the rest of your life. But she hadn't had to think hard about Brian, because she'd done all that thinking months ago, before she'd lost track, and now all she had to think about was how lovely it was to be together again, to have all her problems safely behind her. And how nearly she had lost her chance.

She fell asleep, seeing her life stretch before her like the shimmering pathway that the moon made across the sea at night. Nothing could go wrong now, she thought contentedly. Nothing.

Chapter Twelve

The wedding, everyone agreed, was the most romantic they had ever attended.

Perhaps it was the fact that the engagement had been broken off that made it all the more sentimental. Like Romeo and Juliet, Clare heard a couple of old aunts telling each other, and although she knew it wasn't a bit like that really, she understood what they meant. There was an added piquancy to an on-off romance, and she could almost hear the clash of pistols at dawn when she thought of Brian coming home (he should have been riding on a white charger) to claim his errant bride.

She still felt sorry for Terry, though. She believed he was really in love with Kathy. He was so totally different from Brian, so shy and diffident, and so sensitive. He had seemed to be always aware of Kathy's mood, always ready to meet her needs. He was more serious than Brian, with none of Brian's breezy, blustering sailor's attitude to life, but he had appealed to Kathy nevertheless and it was her decision. Clare could only accept it and hope that it was the right one.

'You don't think you're rushing back into it a bit too quickly?' she asked a little doubtfully, when Kathy had told her the news. 'I mean, it's only a week or so since you were saying you didn't want to be tied to anyone – you wanted your life to yourself for a while.'

'I think I was trying to convince myself as much as anyone else,' Kathy said. 'I don't feel like it now, anyway! I just want to be married and know all the indecision is over. I feel so much better, Clare – it must be the right thing.'

'And what about Terry?' Clare asked quietly. 'How does he feel?'

Kathy sighed. 'I know you think I've been rotten to Terry, but I haven't really, Clare. Honestly. He's a bit upset, of course – we had some nice times together. But there was never anything serious, you know that. We weren't engaged.' She flushed slightly, remembering the evening when Terry had begged her to go to Australia with him. 'It wouldn't have worked out between Terry and me,' she finished a little defiantly. 'We didn't even expect it to – we were only friends.'

Clare wasn't so sure, but she saw that Kathy had convinced herself of this too. She thought of the previous week, when Terry had turned up on the doorstep one evening. Martyn had been on duty and Clare had asked Terry in and made him coffee and, finding that he hadn't eaten, poached egg on toast. He'd sat in the red armchair, talking about Kathy, and her heart had gone out to him. He had seemed so sad. He'd fully accepted the fact that Kathy had gone back to Brian, he even said it was no more than he'd expected, but the unhappiness had darkened his eyes and Clare could see that he had lost confidence in himself.

'I knew she wouldn't stay with a bloke like me for long,' he said. 'What have I got to offer? I'm not glamorous like Brian, going all over the world to places like Singapore and South America. I'm just ordinary, in a nine-to-five job – I haven't even got a car to take her about in. I'm not good-looking and I don't even like sport.'

'Don't be silly,' Clare said sharply. 'You've got a lot to offer. And I thought Kathy *wanted* someone with an ordinary job, who'd be at home with her instead of on the other side of the world. To tell you the truth, I'm not sure she knows what she does want.'

'Oh, yes, she does,' Terry said, pushing aside his half-eaten egg. 'She wants Brian. I reckon she always did.'

Perhaps she had, Clare thought as she watched Kathy and Brian make their vows in Alverstoke church. She certainly looked happy enough now, standing beside her bridegroom in her long, white velvet gown with its trimming of soft white fur. She no longer looked like a pixie; instead, she was a winter princess, a snow queen, enveloped in a mantle of ermine, with a hood of heavy lace and a tiara that glittered like ice framing her small, glowing face.

Brian was in naval uniform and looked tall and confident. He had chosen Martyn as best man, and Clare was to have been chief bridesmaid – matron of honour really, Kathy had said when she asked her, since Clare was married and therefore no longer a 'maid'. Clare had been forced to withdraw, however: her second pregnancy was now well under way and she was suffering again from morning sickness.

So although she did feel well on the day of the wedding, Clare stood instead in the second pew, behind Kathy's parents and family, and watched as Martyn handed the rector the two gold rings.

Christopher stood on the seat beside her, dressed in a pageboy suit that Iris had made him – black velvet trousers and a little velvet waistcoat over a white shirt. He gazed, round-eyed, at the ceremony.

The reception was held at a small hotel in Lee-on-the-Solent. The wedding breakfast was a buffet and there were small tables placed all about the room. Clare and Martyn found one with a highchair already set beside it for Christopher, and Clare sat down while Martyn fetched plates of food for them all.

'What a gorgeous little boy,' a woman at the next table commented, admiring Christopher's velvet outfit. 'I'm surprised Kathy didn't have him as a pageboy.'

'She did think of it, but we didn't dare let him loose in the aisle,' Clare confessed. 'There's no knowing what he might have done. Or said,' she added feelingly.

The woman laughed. 'Oh, I thought he behaved perfectly. I'm Kathy's Auntie Joan, by the way. Are you her friend Clare? I've heard her talk about you.'

'Yes, we were at school together. There are a few more of us here too.' She looked around the room, smiling at various familiar faces. 'Kathy's been better at keeping in touch with people than I have.'

'Perhaps she's had more time.' Auntie Joan glanced at Clare's loose dress. 'Do you have another one on the way?'

Clare blushed and nodded. 'In June.' She looked up as Martyn returned, bearing two plates piled with sandwiches and sausage rolls. 'This is my husband, Martyn.'

'Ah, the best man. Of course. You're Brian's friend in the Navy, aren't you? I can see you two girls will be a great support to each other when the men are away at sea.'

'They better had,' Martyn said cheerfully. 'Too late now for "Dear Johns".'

Auntie Joan looked baffled, while Clare felt herself flush scarlet. She gave Martyn a glowering look and turned away to choose a sandwich for Christopher. Auntie Joan's own plate had arrived, brought by a man whom Clare supposed to be Kathy's Uncle Percy, and she too turned away, with a final smile at Christopher.

'What's the matter?' Martyn asked, sitting down and taking a swig at his glass of wine. 'What have I said?'

'Well, fancy talking about "Dear Johns"!' Clare hissed, glancing over her shoulder to make sure that Kathy's aunt couldn't overhear. 'They must all know what happened.'

'So why not mention it? I can't see the problem.'

'You wouldn't.' Clare cut Christopher's sandwich into small triangles and put them on a plate on his tray. 'It was a lovely service, wasn't it? Doesn't Kathy look gorgeous!'

'Bit like an eskimo, if you ask me, with all that fur. I bet she's finding it hot now.' They both looked across the room to where Kathy and Brian and the immediate families were sitting at the table which had been laid for them. Kathy's heavy lace veil had been flung back and her tiara pinned over it. Her short fair hair framed her small face like the petals of an opening flower. A Christmas rose, Clare thought, opening in the snow.

'I hope she'll be happy,' she said. 'I really do hope she'll be happy. It's been very hard for her, this past year.'

'It's been a bit rough on poor old Brian too,' Martyn remarked. 'I mean, he never actually did anything to deserve all that grief, did he? Just went away to sea, and couldn't do a thing about it. If you ask me, Kathy's been a damned sight luckier than she deserves.'

Clare said nothing. She couldn't blame Martyn for taking Brian's side and feeling that way, but she knew how tormented by doubts Kathy had been.

'Well, I think they've put all that behind them now,' she said, 'so we'd better do the same. Have one of these sausage rolls while they're hot.'

Kathy and Brian were buying a new house in Fareham but until it was finished they had to go into married quarters a couple of miles from the bungalow. While Brian's ship was still in Portsmouth they came round on Tuesdays as usual to spend the evening together. It wasn't the same, though, and Clare looked back with some nostalgia to the days before Martyn had come home, when she and Kathy had been able to spend the whole evening chatting.

'We never seem to get much time on our own,' she remarked. 'It's nice being a foursome, I'm not saying it's not, but the men aren't interested in the same things as we are.'

'And they don't want to listen while we talk about them,' Kathy laughed. 'I know. But Brian'll be away again before we know where we are, and we'll have all the time in the world then. And now that we've finally got together – well, I want to make the most of it.'

The evenings followed a recognised pattern. Clare spent part of the afternoon resting, then Martyn arrived home and helped get the tea ready. Brian and Kathy met at the harbour bus stop and came up together. They all played with Christopher, and after he had gone to bed, settled down to a game of Scrabble.

It wasn't long before Brian's ship was sailing out of the harbour. Kathy came on the following Tuesday, subdued and inclined to go off in a dream. The game of Scrabble didn't go as well as usual and after a bit Martyn said he thought he might go out for a drink.

'It'll give you two time for a chinwag,' he said, and bent to kiss Clare. He grinned at Kathy. 'You can look after her, can't you?'

The door closed behind him and Kathy gave Clare a grin. 'He thinks the world of you, doesn't he? Do you still get breakfast in bed and that sort of thing?'

Clare nodded. 'I feel so tired all the time. It's being pregnant, Kathy, I'm just not very good at it. I get weepy over nothing and poor Martyn has to bear the brunt of it all. And he's only home for a year or two. He's so good and he never complains but I feel guilty about it. It's not fair on him.'

'Well, it's his baby too,' Kathy said. 'It'll be all right when it's born. Just think, by the summer you'll have two gorgeous kids, and all this will just be a memory. You won't even bother to think about it!'

Clare agreed that she was right. They went on to talk about Kathy's and Brian's new house, and the long voyage that the ship would make later in the year. Clare felt guilty at having bemoaned her own problems when Kathy was so soon to be left alone, but Kathy laughed and advised her to forget it. Brian and she weren't looking forward to the separation, but they had set their sights on the long term. In a few years, he would be out of the Navy and they would be able to be together all the time.

By the time Martyn returned, Clare was feeling much more cheerful – so much so that she told him he could go to the pub every Tuesday evening when Kathy was there, and Brian could go too when they came together. She took her last pills for the day and went to bed, and when Martyn joined her they made gentle love and then lay peacefully together, their arms wrapped about each other's bodies.

It wouldn't be too long before Martyn was thirty too, Clare thought as she listened to his even breathing, and then he could leave the Navy and they could have a proper, ordinary married life like her parents had had, with the children growing up knowing that their father would be home every night and every weekend.

The children . . . Christopher and his little sister. Or brother. She smiled to herself and drifted into sleep.

*

Gradually, Clare's sickness disappeared and she began to feel more like her normal self. She made herself a new dress – more like a marquee, she remarked wryly – patterned all over with big yellow sunflowers. It would do as a housecoat after the birth. She looked out all Christopher's baby clothes and the yellow quilt that had covered the pram.

'Two years is a good gap,' Iris said, bringing her a pile of newly knitted jackets. 'They'll grow up nice little companions. Have you thought of any names yet?'

'Hundreds,' Clare said. 'Martyn's mother wants us to call the baby Elizabeth if it's a girl. She's convinced it will be – I don't know what she'll say to me if it's another boy!'

Mr and Mrs Perry were coming to stay the next week. They seldom managed to get away from the shop, but they had recently decided to get an assistant, and the woman they employed was so useful that they felt able to leave the place in her hands for a few days. They arrived the following Tuesday, and were going to go home again on Saturday.

'I wish we could stay longer,' Mrs Perry said, cuddling Christopher on her knee. 'This little chap's growing so fast. He's different every time we see him, aren't you, my pet?'

Christopher leaned against her, holding a corner of his blanket against his cheek. He would be two and a bit when the new baby was born and he was more like a little boy now than a toddler. He wore blue shorts and a white blouse and had recently had his first haircut. He copied every word he heard and was beginning to put sentences together, and Clare and Martyn took a wicked delight in teaching him long words. 'Rhinoceros,' he said now for no reason at all. 'Hipper-otumas.'

'He'll be as bad as your father,' Mrs Perry said. 'Getting all his words backwards.'

'Gosh, I hope not,' Clare said. 'Dad nearly drives us mad at times. I never know if he's doing it deliberately or not.'

'Deliberately,' Christopher said, and they all laughed. Clare lay back in her chair, feeling warm and contented. She'd always been wary of her mother-in-law, thinking that she wanted to interfere with their life and their marriage, but this time Mrs Perry seemed more relaxed, as if she had accepted Clare as a suitable wife for her son. It was Christopher who had done it, she thought, smiling. Nobody could be with him for long without falling for his sunny charm, and nobody could complain that he was a badly behaved little boy. She just hoped the new baby would be as easy.

The Perrys went out to Stokes Bay and looked at the sea, and then went to tea with Clare's parents. The two couples got on well, and the next day Clare and her mother took them over to Portsmouth to see Valerie. Bill and Maurice came in together from work, and the three men disappeared to inspect the second-hand Austin Seven that Maurice and Valerie had just bought. Before the women knew what was happening, the men were all inside and the car was chugging away up the street.

'Well, how do you like that!' Iris exclaimed. 'Gone off gallivanting without a word. I suppose they never thought we might have liked a bit of a ride.'

'There's not room for us all, Mum,' Valerie said, laughing. 'Anyway, it's like a new toy to Maurice, he can't resist showing it off. He'll take you for a ride too when they come back.'

'If they don't find themselves in some pub till closing time,' Iris said darkly. 'Well, we might as well put the kettle on. No use waiting for them.'

Clare waved her in-laws goodbye on Saturday morning, feeling quite sad to see them go. She had promised to go down to see them just as soon as the new baby was old enough to travel, and of course they'd be coming up for the christening. She turned away from the station and decided to walk round to see Kathy.

Kathy's and Brian's house was finished by now and they'd moved in. It was on a new estate and had three bedrooms and a large living-room, big enough for a three-piece suite at one end and a dining-table and chairs at the other, with a serving-hatch through to the kitchen. They bought G-Plan furniture in dark mahogany and a Kosset carpet in flecked oatmeal. None of their furniture was secondhand or passed on by family members, such as Clare and Martyn had had to begin with, and as Kathy didn't fall pregnant she was able to keep her job and save money. They had a car, not new but in good condition, and Kathy was talking about learning to drive.

They had been married for a while now, and Kathy had settled down. She tried not to think of Terry, and told herself she was thankful only that Brian had refused to take no for an answer. His positive, breezy assurance and the way he took charge of her life convinced her that he'd been right. Her father had been the same, and although she'd often resented his authority and bossiness, she felt secure with it. Brian would look after her, just as her father had always looked after her mother and the family. She would be safe.

She had forgotten her dreams of seeing the world, living her own life, having adventures. Clare had been right, she thought, she was just trying to run away from responsibility. But she would have had to be even more responsible then, responsible for herself, with nobody else to turn to. Now, cocooned in marriage, she could let Brian take charge.

To her own astonishment, after all her attempts to resist it, she found that domesticity was just as much an adventure after all. She laughed at herself sometimes, when she found herself gazing at dining suites and armchairs instead of clothes and jewellery. She couldn't wait for the house to be finished so that they could move into it, and she occupied her lunch hours with visits to furniture shops and spent her evenings making curtains.

By the time Brain had come back for Easter leave, the house was ready to move into, and they had spent the fortnight revelling in their new domain. There was little to be done: the kitchen was fitted with cupboards, everything was new, and once the furniture was in place and their wedding presents and other possessions unpacked, they were free. Kathy had a week's leave as well as the long Easter weekend, and they stayed in bed late every morning, ate their meals when they felt like it and made a game of such chores as shopping and washing. In the evenings they went for walks or to the pictures to see the latest films – *West Side Story, Breakfast At Tiffany's* for Kathy, *The Guns of Navarone* for Brian – or stayed indoors to cuddle on the sofa while listening to records.

On the morning that Clare walked round after waving goodbye to her parents-in-law, Brian was back at sea and Kathy was polishing the furniture. Clare smiled, amused to see how houseproud her friend had become.

'It's lovely,' she said, settling Christopher on the floor and sitting down thankfully in one of the armchairs. 'It all looks gorgeous.'

There was no envy in her tone as she looked around the living-room, furnished with its fitted oatmeal carpet and soft armchairs and sofa upholstered in rich cream. The curtains that Kathy had made were of a heavy, darker oatmeal tweed, reaching to the floor, with a fine net across the big picture window for privacy. The cool, pale effect was brightened by a tall orange floor lamp standing in one corner, and a huge arrangement of dried bronze chrysanthemums in the fireplace.

'My place wouldn't look like this for five minutes, with Chris about,' she remarked with a grin. 'You're obviously not planning a family, Kath!'

Kathy coloured a little. 'Well, not yet anyway. We want to get our home together first, and I'd like to wait till Brian comes out of the Navy. It won't be so very long, after all.'

'Five years. You'll be twenty-seven.'

'That's not too old to have a baby. I know you wouldn't have had it any other way now, Clare, but you didn't really mean to start so quickly, did you? And it has made things harder, as far as money goes.'

Clare admitted this was true. 'We hadn't bargained on losing my wages so soon. But apart from that, no, I wouldn't change a thing. And it'll be perfect when the baby's born.' She rubbed her back and grimaced. 'I'm beginning to feel like a ship in full sail!'

After Clare had gone, Kathy wandered round the house, as she often did when she was alone. It was quiet and tidy, its rooms rarely disarranged. Brian was, like all sailors, trained to be orderly, and Kathy was by nature neat. She knew that to Clare it had seemed a little empty, but Clare was accustomed to toys scattered about and Christopher's clothes and nappies forever drying or airing in front of the fire. It was difficult to imagine such cheerful disorder here.

It'll be all right when we're ready, she thought. I won't mind the mess then. But just for a while, I want to enjoy it as it is.

'She's beautiful. She's really beautiful.'

Clare lay back in her bed, smiling. The baby had been born only four hours after Martyn had left her at the maternity home, and although it had been four hours that Clare didn't care to remember, the only important thing was that she had been presented with a perfect baby girl, looking faintly suntanned – that was a touch of jaundice, the sister said, because she was a couple of weeks early – and with a quiff of dark, curly hair and long black eyelashes.

'She's so different from Chris,' Clare told Martyn when he came in to see her, first through the door at visiting time that evening. 'He was fair and bald and had no eyelashes at all, and she looks as if she's wearing mascara! And her eyes are huge, and a lovely dark blue. She's gorgeous.'

'I really didn't think you'd have her so soon,' he said, stroking her hand. 'I thought you'd be back home by teatime. And here you are with our daughter. I'm dying to see her.'

'You'll be able to in a minute.' Fathers were allowed to go to the nursery and look at their babies, though not to pick them up. It was so different from last time, Clare thought, watching Martyn disappear with the other men. Poor Chris hadn't seen his daddy till he was a year old, but Laura would know him right from the start.

Martyn came back a few minutes later, looking bemused, and Clare realised that he'd never seen so small a baby before. 'She's so tiny,' he kept saying, 'and sort of crumpled. Is she all right?'

'Of course she is,' Clare said, nettled. 'They all look like that at first. I told you, she's beautiful.'

Martyn didn't look as if he thought beautiful was quite the right word, but he didn't argue. He glanced at the box of chocolates he'd brought Clare, and she laughed and told him to open it. 'We'll have some now, to celebrate. It ought to be champagne really, but I don't think they'd let me have it in here.'

'We'll have it when you come home,' he promised, tearing the Cellophane off the box. 'How long did you say you'll be in?'

'Nine days. It's ten really, but today counts as day one, since Laura was born before noon. Better than when I had Chris – it was a fortnight then.' Clare sighed. 'I don't know how I'm going to bear not seeing him for all that time. I know he's all right with Mum, but I'm going to miss him terribly. You will go to see him every day, won't you?'

'Well, I said I'd go out with one or two of the blokes tomorrow night, after coming here. To wet the baby's head, you know. But I'll go and see him first.'

'You mean you're going drinking.' She shook her head at him. 'Well, so long as you come and see me first, and see Chris most days.'

'I will. Of course I will. I'm not going out on the razzle every night.' The bell sounded and he bent to kiss her. 'You get a good night's rest now. You deserve it. And I'll bring you some fruit and stuff in tomorrow.'

'And tell everyone we've got a gorgeous daughter,' Clare said, smiling again. 'Tell Kathy, won't you? She didn't even know I was going in this morning. Oh, and she'll be coming round for tea – you'd better ring her up at work, first thing. Or go and see her now. Could you do that?'

'Stop panicking,' he said with a grin. 'I've already told Brian, at Collingwood. Who do you think I'm going out with tomorrow?' He kissed her and walked off down the ward.

A few minutes later, the double doors swung open and the nurses started to come in, a baby on each arm. Clare sat up eagerly, her weariness forgotten. The dark quiff of her daughter's hair stood out from the crook of the nurse's elbow and she reached out to take the tiny bundle.

'Hello,' she said, smiling down at the sleeping face. 'Hello, my sweetheart. Hello, Laura.'

The baby opened her eyes and stared up into her mother's face. The eyes were dark and fringed with the sooty lashes that Clare had already marvelled at. The skin was smooth, still with its faint hint of gold, and the tiny, furled lips were already beginning to work in a sucking motion.

Crumpled indeed! Clare thought, and put the baby to her breast.

Chapter Thirteen

Laura was very different from her brother. Bright and quick and full of deep, chuckling laughter, she was a more demanding baby than he had been, not at all content to be laid in her cot or pram and left to watch the sky, and insisting on being with the family, part of all that was going on. Christopher adored her and almost choked her to death when she was three weeks old by filling her mouth with Smarties when Clare was busy unbuttoning her blouse for the morning feed. He'd said he was sorry for her, never getting anything to eat.

For a few months, Clare felt she was living her dream of ordinary family life. Martyn was home every day for lunch and back again by teatime. He helped with both children, often giving Laura her bottle when Clare reluctantly gave up breast-feeding, and changing her nappies. He went out for a drink with his mates once a week, and Clare decided to have an evening out too so joined a badminton club with Kathy. The rest of the time they spent together.

They knew, of course, that it couldn't last, and sure enough Martyn's new draft came through just after Christmas. They'd been expecting it – he had been at Collingwood for eighteen months and a new posting was due – but the news that his next ship would be Plymouth based had come as a disappointment to Clare, who was hoping he would be in and out of Portsmouth. Martyn, itching to be back at sea after a long time ashore, hadn't seemed to feel the same sense of loss, but during the first week on the new ship he had been desperately lonely.

'This isn't going to be very amusing,' he said as they lay in bed that night. 'I never knew I'd miss you so much. And the mess is just that – a mess. It's squalid. A cramped little space with only just room for a locker and to sling a hammock, and all squashed up together with the other blokes with only inches in between us . . . I must have got used to being shoreside.'

'Well, we'd better move down there with you,' Clare said. She had missed him too, worse than ever before. The last eighteen months had gone all too quickly, half of them used up by her pregnancy. 'Christopher can't understand why you've gone away. At least if we were near by you could get home at night.'

The idea gripped them both. They talked about it far into the night and planned for Clare to come down to Plymouth for a weekend as soon as possible to look for a house. 'We could sell the bungalow and get something bigger. We'll need three bedrooms some time anyway. It'll be lovely, Martyn. I always did want to live in Devon.'

'My mum'd be pleased,' he said, thinking of his mother and father in Ivybridge. 'I don't know so much about yours, though.'

Clare refused to worry about it. Valerie would still be near by with her two children. Her second baby had been a girl too, a rosy little beauty called Stephanie. And Ian was getting married soon, to a girl called Carol who seemed happy to stay in Gosport. 'They can come and stay. It'll be fun, showing them round the area.'

They stayed awake for hours, planning where they would like to live and when Clare could come down to Plymouth for house-hunting. By the time Martyn left on Sunday evening to go back to the ship, they had agreed that he would stay down there next weekend and go to some estate agents, and Clare would come down the following week.

'I'll tell Mum and Dad straight away,' she said. 'I'll ask them to look after Laura and bring Chris with me. It'll be like a holiday!'

The idea of breaking the news made her feel nervous, but she was so excited that she gave little thought to her mother's reaction. She was surprised at the expression that crossed Iris's face.

'Devon?' her mother echoed, as though Clare had announced she was moving to the moon. 'But that's miles away!'

'It's not that far, Mum.' Belatedly, Clare realised she could have broken the news more tactfully. 'And we'll be able to be together much more. You know I don't like the idea of trailing round the country with the kids. I think they ought to have a settled life, go to the same schools from start to finish. Not that we wouldn't take an accompanied draft if one came up, but as long as Martyn's at sea I want to be in a proper home.'

'But *Devon* . . .'

'It's a lovely place, Mum. You'll be able to come and see us for your holidays. It's only a few hours on the train. And it'll be so much better

146

for the children to be able to see their daddy more often.' She looked at her mother's face again and tried to find some words of comfort. 'You can come as often as you like, Mum. And I'll write to you all the time.'

'I hope so. I don't want to lose touch with you.' Iris looked as if she might be about to cry and Clare reached out, horrified, to touch her hand.

'You won't lose touch! I promise you won't. I'll write every week and we'll come back here too, to stay with you. You'll probably see more of us than you do now.' She looked at her father for help. 'And you've still got Valerie and Ian close by. We'll never lose touch.'

'Of course they won't,' Bill said. 'We'll track 'em down, wherever they go. They won't be able to get away that easily. Besides, Martyn's still got that screwdriver I lent him.'

Iris gave a wry smile. 'I know. I know you've got to live your own life, and if it means you and the children can see more of Martyn . . . When are you thinking of moving? It won't be for a while yet, I suppose.'

'Well, as soon as we can. We thought we might go house-hunting next weekend.' Clare hesitated. 'I wondered if you'd have Laura for the weekend. I'll take Chris with me.'

'Well, you know I'm glad to look after the children any time. Of course I'll have her.' Iris was always delighted to be entrusted with her grandchildren, especially the babies. She had looked after Laura several times for a day to give Clare and Martyn a chance to go somewhere together, and sometimes she'd had both children. 'I'll have Christopher as well if you like.'

'No, I'll take him. He's missed his daddy so much, I couldn't leave him behind. Martyn's going to get details of some houses and we'll stay at the NAAFI Club together. It's like a big hotel – we went there for a snack once when I was in Plymouth before. We're going to hire a car for two days so that we can get round easily.'

'You seem to have got it all worked out,' her father remarked.

Clare nodded. 'We talked about it all weekend. We just wished we'd thought of it before. I don't think Martyn realised how much he'd miss his home and family.'

In fact, she had been rather hurt by Martyn's obvious eagerness to go back to sea. She'd known, of course, that that was why he'd joined the Navy in the first place, that the idea of being at sea on a ship had always excited him. There was something that she couldn't understand or share in his feelings about the Navy. It was like a club to which only the men could belong, another life set apart from that of ordinary people. It was more than a job, it was a way of life. The Navy demanded a huge

147

commitment, a loyalty that wives and families couldn't compete with. All they could do was follow, to get as close as they could so that they would be there when the ship came home and the Navy relaxed its hold for a while.

While he was at Collingwood, there had been some social life for the wives too. One of the officers' wives had set up a luncheon club and Clare had gone along, feeling very shy, and enjoyed meeting some of the other women. One had invited her round in the afternoons and she'd gradually got to know some of the others. Most of them lived in married quarters and knew each other well. There were dances too and social evenings at Collingwood, but once Martyn had been drafted these were more or less closed to Clare. She could only go if one of the other wives invited her, and she didn't want to be there on her own.

Perhaps there would be more social life in Devon, but for now it would be enough to be with her husband again. She had felt comforted by knowing that Martyn had missed her more than he'd expected, and wanted her to move to Plymouth to be near him. The idea had come at just the right time. The bungalow was already beginning to feel small, with only two bedrooms. When Laura began to be mobile it would seem smaller still. And moving now, two years before Christopher started school, would give him a chance to settle into new surroundings and perhaps make a few friends. Clare knew it was easy to meet people when you had small children.

'I suppose you'll look for somewhere in Plymouth,' Iris said, but Clare shook her head.

'I'd rather be in the country. I've always wanted to live where there are fields and woods. Maybe even on the edge of Dartmoor!' Her eyes sparkled. 'Or in Cornwall. We're going to look at all sorts of places.'

Her excitement overrode any objections her parents might have, and it carried her through until she found herself getting off the train in Plymouth the following Friday afternoon. The last time she'd come here had been to meet Martyn, when Christopher was barely a year old and hadn't taken his first steps. She remembered her first view of the Devon countryside on that teenage holiday, when she'd been travelling down with her parents to spend a week in a caravan at Brixham. The sight of the sweeping bay of Torquay and the long, jutting cliffs of Berry Head had caught at her heart and she'd felt as if she were coming home.

Now, she was doing just that. She was coming to her favourite county, to find the home that she had dreamed of.

Martyn was waiting at North Road station. He came towards her, grinning broadly, and swung Christopher in his arms before taking the suitcase. They walked out of the station and waited at the bus stop.

'Remember when we came off the ship last time you came? I couldn't believe we had to carry Chris all the time – I thought we could stand him down on the pavement, but we couldn't. Now you're a big boy, aren't you?' he said to his son. 'You could walk all the way to the NAAFI if you wanted to, couldn't you?'

The bus came along and they climbed aboard. It was a short journey and soon they were in their room at the NAAFI Club. Christopher explored while Martyn and Clare hugged each other, and then Martyn spread on the bed the details of the houses he'd found.

'There's one at Calstock. There's a railway line to Plymouth, so I could get in all right in the mornings. And there's Bere Alston, and a couple of places at Tavistock. That's a bit further out, but it's only half an hour by train and there are two lines.'

'Two railway lines?' Clare thought for a moment. 'Didn't I come through Tavistock?'

Martyn nodded. 'You came on the main line. The other one goes to Launceston, so we could live anywhere along either of those lines. And there's a good bus service to Tavistock as well, but that takes longer.'

'It's right on the edge of the moor,' Clare said, looking at the map. 'What sort of place is it?'

'Oh, quite a nice town, but not very big. It has a market and a big fair every year – the Goosey Fair, they call it. The river Tavy runs through it.'

'It's got a river?' Clare gazed at him. 'What are these two houses like, then? Can we go and see them tomorrow?'

Martyn laughed. 'That's why you're here! We're picking up the car at nine, so that we can get out really early. We can see both those in the morning and then go on to Bere Alston and Calstock in the afternoon. We'll get something for lunch in Tavistock and have a look round the town.'

They went down to the dining-hall for tea and then took Christopher up on to the Hoe for a walk. He ran ahead, shouting at the seagulls, and then stood staring at the Smeaton tower.

'Lighthouse!'

'There's one in a new book Mum gave him,' Clare explained. 'I told him we might see one.'

'There's another one out at sea,' Martyn told him. 'You can just see it, like a tiny pencil right out on the edge of the sea. That's where this one used to be.'

Christopher gave him a disbelieving look and ran off again after another gull. They walked down to the railings that lined the edge of the low cliffs and gazed at the rock pools and the big semicircular swimming-bath. Out in the Sound, a few sailing dinghies were tacking to and fro against the April breeze, and the green heights of Mount Edgcumbe bordered the western banks of the Tamar estuary.

'It's lovely here,' Clare said contentedly. 'I'm going to like living in Devon.'

The car Martyn had hired was a Ford Classic, a sleek car with its back window cut away stylishly. Christopher clambered into the back and sat commenting on everything he could see as they bowled along the road across the moor to Tavistock next morning.

Clare studied the map. 'We're at Yelverton now. What an odd place. It's so flat and that row of shops looks like a shanty-town.'

'There used to be an airfield here,' Martyn told her, turning left at the large roundabout. 'It was used during the war. I suppose the shops were put up then too. The houses on the other side are much older, though.'

They went through another village and then over a narrow bridge before climbing a twisting road through tall trees and emerging on a high ridge. Clare looked about her eagerly. 'The first house is in Whitchurch. That must be it over there, with that little church. Take the next right turn, Martyn.'

There was no village green at Whitchurch, but the church itself stood at the top of the village close to the moor. Martyn drove past it and over the cattle grid, and they gazed at the open spaces before them. Ponies grazed quietly in little clusters, and a few early lambs skipped about on the hummocky ground. The sky was a soft blue, hazed over by drifting muslin clouds, and when Martyn switched off the engine the silence was broken only by the twittering of birds in the trees bordering the moor.

Clare felt for his hand. Ever since she was a child, she'd dreamed of living somewhere like this. Somewhere with wild, open spaces where you could walk without needing permission, without being afraid that someone would turn you away. Somewhere with grass growing and rocks scattered about, and gorse and stone walls, and streams running free. Somewhere with a river.

'I hope one of these houses will be the right one,' she said softly. 'I want to live here, Martyn. I want to be able to walk in a place like this every day. I want my children to be able to play on grass instead of in a street. I want us to live in the same house for years and years, and always be happy there.'

He squeezed her fingers. 'So do I, Clare. So do I.' He glanced at his watch and switched on the engine again. 'Come on, let's go and start looking. We'll find the right place. I just know we will.'

Less than ten minutes later, they were there, and Clare knew that they need look no further. This was the house she wanted to make her home.

Dale View stood halfway up one of the narrow lanes leading to the moor from the road between Whitchurch and Tavistock, slightly back from the lane and looking down the hill and across the valley towards Cornwall. From its windows, they could see the distant heights of what the owners told them were Kit Hill and Caradon Hill. Below, in the garden, were half a dozen apple trees and a curving lawn with wide flower borders beside the path.

'*Martyn* . . .' Clare whispered as they followed the owners around, but he squeezed her hand, warning her not to look too enthusiastic. She bit her lip and kept silent, but she was afraid she would find it impossible to keep the light of excitement out of her eyes.

Apart from the garden at the front, leading down to the short hedged driveway from the lane that served only this house and the one next door, there was a square patch at the side, bordered by hedges and, by the back door, a bank with a rowan tree growing on it. From here, there was another way leading out through a somewhat ramshackle garage on to the lane, higher up than the front driveway. The garden was scattered with primroses, and the grassy bank was sprinkled with violets.

Even before they went inside and saw the spacious rooms downstairs and the three big bedrooms with that wonderful view, Clare knew that this was the house she wanted. It was hers already; she felt almost offended by the sight of strange furniture and wished she could clear the cupboards of their clutter. She and Martyn would have the front bedroom, she thought, gazing out towards Cornwall, and Christopher could have the middle one, which was almost as big, and Laura the end one which had a pretty cottagey window that looked out at the rowan and was just right for a little girl . . . Or maybe they'd both be in the middle one at first, to make it easier to go to them in the night . . . There was a bathroom too, not as smart as the one in the bungalow but it would do, and a separate toilet at the top of the stairs. And because they didn't have enough furniture yet to furnish the two living-rooms downstairs, the children could have one as a playroom.

'Well, thanks for showing us round,' Martyn said to the owner, a rather stocky man in his fifties, with a red face and grey hair. 'We'll think about it and let you know. We've got a few other places to see as well.'

Clare looked at him, agonised. She had no desire at all to look at other places. Suppose someone else came and made an offer for this one while they were gone? 'Can we come and look again later, if we want to?' she asked. 'Tomorrow, perhaps? Will you be in?'

The man nodded. 'I'd only be going up to watch the cricket. The pitch is just up there on the moor. Give me a ring and one of us will be here.' He showed them out and they walked back down the lane to the car, parked on the main road.

'Martyn, that's *it*! We must live there. It's lovely. All that space – and only a few yards from the moor. We'll never find anything better than that. And it's the same price as we're asking for the bungalow. I can't believe it.'

'I know. I like it too. But we'd better go and look at these other places as well. You never know, one of them might be even better.'

'It won't be,' Clare said, but she agreed that they couldn't let the other people down, and it was a chance to look around the area as well. They went into Tavistock and found a café where they could get a cup of coffee and some squash for Christopher.

'It looks a nice town,' Clare said, gazing at the wide square, dominated by the big church and the handsome stone buildings. 'Let's have a look round.'

They walked back across the square to the bridge they had crossed on the way down from Whitchurch. Clare lifted Christopher up so that he could look down into the clear, shallow water as it ran over the weir. A footpath ran beside the water and they went down the steps to walk along it, gazing at the rocks that broke the singing water into a series of cascades, and laughing at the ducks which sat on them preening their feathers.

'It leads to a park,' Clare said in delight. 'Oh, Martyn, it's lovely! Look, there's another stream or something on the other side, by the children's playground. It's a canal – I wonder where it goes.'

They walked back under the great trees and found the car again. The second house they were to see in Tavistock was a cottage by the river itself, which had attracted Clare when she saw the details, but when they entered it they knew at once it wouldn't do.

'It's nice and cosy, but it's too small,' she said as they came out. 'The rooms are tiny and the garden isn't very big either. I'd really love to be close to the river, and it's near the park, but you want your own bit of garden for children to play in. And suppose Chris climbed the wall and fell in! He'd be halfway to Plymouth before I even knew he'd gone. Where next? Calstock, isn't it?'

Calstock proved to be a quaint village on the banks of the Tamar, just over the border into Cornwall. It was as hilly and tumbled as any fishing village, with cottages crammed together in the narrow, twisting streets. There was a high viaduct where the railway ran above the little town, and a broad quay by the river, which was tidal and therefore wide and murky, not clear and merry like the Tavy.

Martyn parked the car on the quay and they went in search of the house they were to see, but they were all tired now and Christopher began to grizzle as they climbed up the steep, twisting streets. 'Home,' he said plaintively.

'In a little while, sweetheart,' Clare said. 'Martyn, I don't think I want to live here. It's too crowded.'

Martyn looked at her in surprise. 'There's hardly a soul about.'

'I don't mean that. It's the way all the houses are crammed together. I'd get claustrophobia in a place like this.'

'Well, we'd better look now we're here.' He paused. 'This must be it – this gate in the wall. The house is through here.' They stepped through the gateway into a tiny courtyard. 'I suppose this is the garden.'

'I told you it wouldn't do,' Clare said as they returned to the quay half an hour later. 'I mean, it's quaint and interesting, but it's no good for a family. All those tiny rooms, and that little yard for a garden. And it's surrounded by other houses – they're practically looking down each other's chimneys. Let's go and look at Dale View again. That's the one we ought to have.' She stopped and looked at Martyn, her expression a mixture of excitement and longing. 'Let's live there. Please – let's live there.'

Chapter Fourteen

L ife was changing for them all. The whole world was changing. The Space Race had brought science fiction into the realms of fact, with John Glenn becoming the first American to orbit the Earth. He said that he had never seen anything so beautiful as the Earth from space, and the people of Perth, Australia, turned on all their lights so that he could see the city from his spacecraft.

President Kennedy and his Russian counterpart Nikita Kruschev were constantly in the news, and now the figure of Fidel Castro was making headlines as well. To Clare, places like Cuba seemed too far away to have much effect on her own life, but she was uneasily aware that Martyn was in a fighting Service and could be sent anywhere in the world, and she was old enough now to understand what had been going on during the Second World War. A baby then, she had barely known enough to be frightened of the air raids that had raged over Gosport and Portsmouth, but the thought of another war now turned her blood cold.

The dread of a nuclear war was never far away during those days. She read articles in the newspapers about fallout shelters, and how to make yourself a safe room in your own home. It needed to be somewhere without windows or doors to the outside, and you were supposed to stock it with tins of food. How many houses had rooms like that? And how much food would you need? How would you manage about the toilet and getting fresh water? Those questions never seemed to be answered.

She got a book out of the library one day, written by Nevil Shute, who was one of her favourite authors. It was called *On The Beach*, and it was about people in Australia, waiting for a cloud of radiation that was travelling all across the world to reach them after a nuclear war. They were the last people alive, and when it finally came, the whole of the human race would be wiped out, along with all the rest of the animals, birds and plants. Nothing would be left.

It was too immense, too horrifying, to contemplate. Like most other people, Clare turned her thoughts away from it and back to everyday life, to her own concerns and those of her friends.

Kathy had settled into a routine of going to work each day, doing her housework at weekends and spending a lot of time waiting for Brian to come home. It wasn't so very different from being single, she reflected as she crossed the harbour on her way to work. She was a married woman with her own home, yet she still seemed to be spending her life alone. And now she couldn't even go to the community centre as she'd done before.

After all the excitement of the wedding and moving into a new house, she was feeling a bit flat. It was nice to be able to go home each evening and know that it was her very own, and she didn't have to live under her parents' rules any more, but she missed the cheerful family meals and banter; she even missed the race for the bathroom in the mornings. When Brian was home, taking charge, it was lovely, and she adored the attention he paid her and his insistence on knowing where she was and what she was doing all the time – but once he was away she felt like a piece of driftwood floating on the tide, waiting for a current to take her in the direction she should go.

Fortunately, her job was safe now – once she had decided to marry Brian and not to emigrate, she had set about becoming an established civil servant, so that she couldn't be dismissed. It meant she didn't get her gratuity but she was earning a good salary as a clerical officer, and since she expected to work for at least another two or three years she would soon recoup the loss. She thought again about trying for promotion – it wasn't that she was especially keen to have a career, for she knew that she would eventually settle down to being a mother and housewife, but the work would be more interesting and the money even better.

Clare's news about the move dismayed her almost as much as it had Iris.

'I'm going to miss you terribly,' she said. 'And the children. What am I going to do on Tuesday evenings?'

'Oh, dear,' Clare said. 'Nobody seems pleased about it but me and Martyn.'

'Well, you can't expect us to be. We like having you here. Still, I can see why you want to go – it's miserable being on your own. But will you see that much more of each other? I mean, the ship will be going to sea before long and then you'll be even more lonely.'

'Oh, I'll soon get to know people. And we'll be coming back quite often, and I hope you'll all come to see us too. But the main thing is that we can be together when the ship comes in, like you and Brian. It's hardly ever going to come to Pompey.'

'Sometimes,' Kathy said, 'I just hate the Navy.'

Clare laughed. 'Well, let's hope they both come out when they're thirty. Then we can settle down properly. Maybe you'll move down to Devon too. Brian likes it there, doesn't he?'

'He seemed to enjoy being evacuated there,' Kathy admitted, 'but it really depends on where he can get a job . . . Anyway, that's years away yet. Well, I'll just have to drive down and see you at weekends, that's all.'

'Oh, yes, you must,' Clare said enthusiastically. 'That'll be lovely.'

Kathy went home feeling flatter than ever. A half-written letter to Brian lay on the table and she looked at it apathetically and heaved a sigh. There was nothing much to write about, except for Clare's news. Nothing of her own. Got up, went to work, came home, went to bed, she thought dejectedly. On Tuesdays she went to see Clare, on Thursdays they played badminton, at the weekends she did the vacuuming, the washing and the ironing. He was going to be really riveted by that, wasn't he? He was going to really look forward to coming home to this exciting livewire of a wife.

But how could anyone be exciting and alive when they couldn't go anywhere or do anything interesting?

Brian had no reason to complain that his own life wasn't interesting. His ship was touring Europe and had called at Stockholm, Copenhagen and Oslo. Now it was in Hamburg and as usual he was off the ship at the earliest possible moment with some of his mates.

'Let's go to a nightclub,' Knocker White suggested. 'There's a place I went to last time I was here – it's got this British rock band. Kids from Liverpool. They're good.'

'Scousers!' Brian said. 'Scum of the earth.'

Knocker, who was from Liverpool himself, took a swing at his head. 'Say that again and I'll relieve you of all your teeth.'

'You and whose army?' Brian jeered, and, laughing and joking, they swung along the streets, looking – as Knocker said – for good bars and bad girls. Hamburg, it seemed, was rich in both.

The nightclub was underground, a dive of smoke and the smell of German beer. The Liverpool group was performing as they came in, a quartet of long-haired youths with guitars who leaped about the stage, thrusting their instruments out like phalluses, and belting out a music that was raw with energy. Brian watched them in amazement.

'They're good. They're really good. What are they called?'

'I dunno. Some fancy name. Sounds like an insect. Spiders?'

'Beatles,' one of the other artificers said. 'That's what they call themselves.'

'Well, I think they're good,' Brian said. 'I reckon they ought to try making a few records.'

They sat at a table and ordered drinks. Before long, several German girls had drifted over to join them and Knocker ordered drinks for them too. They sipped and eyed the men, and one of them came and sat on Brian's lap.

He took a breath. She had long black hair, curling down to her bare shoulders, and a deep cleft between her full breasts. She leaned against him, giving him the full benefit of her curves, and smiled into his eyes.

Brian shook his head. 'Sorry, sweetheart. I'm a married man. Got a nice little wife waiting for me at home.'

She shrugged and pouted. 'Ach, home, what is that? This is your home tonight.'

He laughed. 'Well, that's one way of looking at it, I suppose. But I don't think my Kathy would see it that way.'

She stroked his lapel, letting her fingertips stray against his neck. 'How will she ever know? You're not going to tell her, huh?'

'There's not going to be anything to tell,' Brian said firmly.

The move took place at the beginning of May. The bungalow had sold quickly and the purchase of Dale View had gone through without a hitch. Clare had organised the removal herself, preferring to have Martyn on hand when they were settling into the new house, and he had spent only the last night or two at the bungalow before returning to Devon to be there when the furniture arrived.

Iris had offered to come down with Clare to help with the children on the journey. They saw the furniture out and then Clare said goodbye to Kathy, Hazel and Kevin and went back to her parents' home for the night. They were to leave early next morning and arrive at Tavistock in the afternoon, by which time the furniture should be in and only the unpacking left to do.

'I know you'll like it,' Clare said, feeling more and more excited as they drew nearer to Devon. 'So will Dad. You will try to come down and stay soon, won't you?'

'Well, I'm coming now,' Iris pointed out, smiling. 'Yes, of course we will. We've always liked Devon. It'll be nice to spend our holidays with you.'

Martyn was at the station to meet them, with a taxi waiting. It drove through the town, and Clare pointed out the square and the church and the statue of the Duke of Bedford, who had been responsible for so many of Tavistock's buildings.

'There's a statue of Francis Drake as well, at the other end of that long road – they stare at each other. Drake was born here, you can see the place from our windows, but there's nothing there now. He bought a big house later on, Buckland Abbey, a few miles away.' She chattered on as the taxi swept up Whitchurch Road and then turned up the narrow lane. 'This is it. We're halfway up. Oh, I can't *wait* to see our own furniture inside!'

They got out of the taxi and looked over the garden gate. The lawn hadn't been mown and was speckled with daisies, like stars amongst the lush grass. The apple trees were in blossom and there were bluebells against the hedges. Several shrubs, which had been bare twigs when Clare had seen them last, were now in full leaf and some had flowers already appearing. ·

Clare gave a sigh of pure bliss and looked at her mother. 'Isn't it *lovely*?'

Iris nodded slowly. Her eyes took in the house, with its bay windows upstairs and down, its conservatory running along the front, its flower borders and curving lawn. She turned and gazed back across the neighbouring hedges at the view, over the little town and far beyond to the Cornish hills. From the top of the lawn, from the windows of the house, you would be able to see even further. It was just the sort of house she would have liked to live in herself.

'It is,' she said, and smiled at her daughter. 'It's lovely.'

Settling into a new area, far from everything familiar, was both exciting and daunting. Once all the furniture was unpacked and one or two shopping trips made to Plymouth, Iris went back to Gosport. She had been up on the moor with the children and had looked around Tavistock, finding the Meadows where Christopher could feed the ducks on the canal as well as play on the swings and the old steamroller that someone had painted in bright colours and left there. She knew that she and Bill would enjoy coming here for holidays, but she felt sad when she said goodbye at the railway station.

'You will write every week, won't you? And I'll ring you up.' Dale View had a telephone installed, and Iris could use the public phone box at the top of the street. She hugged Christopher, feeling the tears smart in her eyes, and bent to give Laura a last kiss.

'Of course I'll write. I'll tell you everything we do. And you'll come and stay as soon as you can.' Now that the time had come for parting, Clare felt unexpectedly bereft. She realised suddenly that there would be no more casual visits, with her mother dropping in for a morning coffee, no more walks down to her parents' house for tea. Of course, she had known that these visits would no longer be possible, but she hadn't felt the loss so keenly as she did now. She clung to her mother for a moment, then stepped back as the train puffed alongside the platform. Iris climbed aboard and dragged her suitcase after her, and they stared at each other through the billowing steam. They both wanted to say something more, but neither could find the words.

'Look after yourself,' Iris said at last, as the train began to move again. 'Look after the children.'

'I'll write,' Clare promised again. 'I'll write every week. Goodbye, Mum.'

They stood on the platform, a lonely little group, until the train was out of sight, and then Clare sighed and turned to leave the little station and walk back down the hill to the town.

Christopher slid his hand into hers and she looked down at him. Her eyes were blurred with tears. I didn't know it would feel like this, she thought miserably. I didn't know I'd feel so lonely when she'd gone.

She wheeled the pushchair back through the town to the bus stop outside St Eustachius' church. How could she possibly be lonely, she thought, with Christopher and Laura to keep her company? And maybe they could get a kitten too – perhaps even a dog to take walking on the moors. There was plenty of room at Dale View.

Even though it wouldn't be long before Martyn went away again, there would be lots to keep them happy and occupied.

Making acquaintances was easy – you simply walked down the road with the children, and people stopped you to say hello and peer into the pram to coo at Laura. Making proper friends took more time. Laura was past the age of being taken to the baby clinic, and Christopher wasn't old enough for school. After a few weeks, feeling increasingly lonely with Martyn away again, Clare stopped as she passed a garden where a young woman was playing with a little boy about Christopher's age.

'Hello,' the young woman said, smiling. She had shining fair hair, falling like silk to her shoulders, and very blue eyes. She was slim and delicately built, and her smile was wide and friendly. 'I've seen you walk past a few times. Have you just come to live here?'

'Yes. My name's Clare Perry. I live up the lane.' Clare hesitated, then said before she could change her mind, 'I wondered if you'd like to bring your little boy to play with mine one day. We – we don't know anyone here yet and he needs someone to play with.' And I need someone too, she added silently. I need a friend.

The other girl laughed. 'I'm sorry – this isn't my little boy. Andrew lives next door – I'm just looking after him for the morning. I don't have any children.' Her blue eyes studied Clare for a moment. 'But why don't you come in and have a coffee? Then the children can play together and I'll introduce you to Sue when she comes back.'

A few minutes later, Clare was installed on a garden seat with a mug of coffee in her hand, while Christopher and his new playmate started to fill a large plastic truck with wooden bricks. Laura was taken out of her pram and set on a rug on the grass where she was given a smaller plastic vehicle to examine, and Clare explained where she had come from and why she and Martyn had chosen Tavistock to live.

'My name's Veronica Challoner,' the other girl said. 'My father was in the Navy too. He was a commander.'

'Oh.' Clare was disconcerted by this news. Officers and ratings didn't mix socially and she wondered if Veronica had been disappointed to learn that Martyn was only an artificer. But the blue eyes laughed at her.

'He's not in the Navy now. And I never have been! My husband's father was, though, and he and Daddy knew each other quite well. They served on the same ship once. That's how Alex and I met – because our fathers were friends.'

'Is your husband in the Navy too?' If he was also an officer, Clare knew there would be no chance of a friendship between them, but Veronica shook her fair head.

'He's a teacher at a boys' prep school near here.' She wrinkled her nose a little. 'They wanted him to live in a flat at the school but we wanted our own place. I had enough of living over the shop when I was little – Mummy and Daddy always had an officer's house, and you couldn't do a thing without the entire Navy knowing all about it!'

Clare laughed. 'I know. That's why we didn't want married quarters. It's a bit more of a struggle, having a mortgage, but I think it's better.'

'Well, I think you're very brave,' Veronica said. 'I mean, it must be very lonely moving to a new place when you don't have your husband home every night.'

'It is rather,' Clare admitted. 'That's why I stopped and spoke to you just now.'

They watched the two little boys playing with the truck. They had emptied out all the bricks and were examining the wheels, looking for all the world like a couple of mechanics trying to puzzle out a problem. Laura had dropped her toy and was watching something small walk across the grass.

'Creature,' she announced, and Veronica's eyebrows rose.

'She's very advanced, isn't she?'

'Not really. It's just her favourite word at the moment. Anything that moves is a creature. If you can eat it, it's a sausage, and if you can drink it, it's beer.' Clare gave Veronica an apologetic look. 'Martyn taught her that. He said she wouldn't remember it, but she has.'

'Let's hope he doesn't teach her anything more naval than that,' Veronica said. 'She's sweet.'

Clare thought of Kevin next door, back in Gosport, and their efforts to get him to change his first word from 'bugger' to 'bucket'. 'They're just little parrots at that age,' she said. 'They don't understand what they're saying.'

'So why doesn't she call spiders "beer" and milk "sausages"?' Veronica said. 'I bet they understand a lot more than we think. You know, you don't look old enough to have a child Christopher's age. How old were you when he was born?'

'Nearly twenty,' Clare said, blushing. 'He was born exactly nine months after we were married.'

'Good heavens,' Veronica said. 'So you're twenty-three now. I'm twenty-two and I don't feel anything like ready to have children. Alex wouldn't mind – he's older than me – but I want to have some fun first.'

Clare didn't reply. Once the pregnancies were over and the babies born, she thought having children was quite good fun. There was a lot of hard work involved, of course, but life would be very boring without them, especially if you didn't go out to work.

'Do you have a job?' she asked, and Veronica shook her head.

'I trained as a florist after I left school, but only because Mummy thought it would be nice to be able to arrange flowers. I did work for a while in a shop in Exeter, but when Alex and I got married and came here there didn't seem to be much point.'

Clare gazed at her. 'What do you do all day? Don't you get bored?'

Veronica laughed. Her laugh was as pretty as her face, silvery and tinkling, like a chime of bells. 'Bored? Why should I? There's loads to do. I've got quite a lot of friends around here and in Plymouth – people I've known for donkey's years, a lot of them naval – and there's always Dartmouth, of course. I can always find someone to go and have coffee with – I've got my own little car, Daddy gave it to me for my twenty-first. And there are things going on at the school. They like the masters' wives to be involved.' She got up suddenly. 'Come and see the house. I have a lot of fun finding bits and pieces for it. The boys will be all right there.'

Clare picked up Laura and followed her inside. The house was detached, standing in a garden that was mostly lawn with various shrubs and two or three large trees. It looked as if it had been there for quite a long time, unlike the modern estate that had been built close by, but wasn't as old as Dale View.

'It's lovely,' Clare said, standing in the spacious square hallway with Laura in her arms. The floor was tiled in black and white and the stairs rose from one corner, with balustrades of dark, polished wood, with deep red carpeting. The walls were papered in red and cream Regency stripes and there was a chair with a curved mahogany back and a deep red upholstered seat beside a narrow side table with a scalloped edge.

Dale View could look like this, she thought. I wonder what this sort of paper costs. I suppose teachers get good wages, though – better than artificers in the Navy.

Veronica took her all over the house. It was furnished in what to Clare's eyes looked an old-fashioned way, but she recognised that the furniture was good and suited the rooms. The only room that looked really modern was the kitchen, which had units all around the walls, faced with sunny yellow Formica, and – Clare noted enviously – all the latest appliances, including a brand new Hoovermatic washing-machine and a refrigerator.

'It's lovely,' she said again when the tour was over. She had been keeping an eye on Christopher from the windows and now she set Laura on the floor and went to the back door to let him know where she was. 'I'm here, Chris. Are you having a nice time?'

'Busy, Mummy,' he replied without looking up, and she shrugged and laughed and came back into the kitchen.

Veronica was putting the kettle on. 'I'll make another cup of coffee. I'm glad you like the house. Mummy and Daddy gave us quite a lot of the furniture and Alex's people helped too, of course. We could never have had all this on the pittance he gets as a teacher!'

'Oh.' Clare was slightly embarrassed by this revelation. She looked around again and thought that probably Veronica's idea of a pittance and her own were two rather different things. Even if the two sets of parents had chipped in quite a lot, you wouldn't have a place like this if you couldn't afford to keep it up. Papering the walls alone must cost a fortune.

'Alex's coming home for lunch today, so you'll be able to meet him,' Veronica prattled on. 'He doesn't have any classes on Wednesday afternoon but he has to go back for prep at five. That's the boring thing about boarding schools – they all have prep after tea. Or even more lessons. It's to keep the little dears occupied so that all they can do when they get back to their dorms is clean their teeth and fall asleep. They're on the run the whole day – it comes as a real shock to the ones who were brought up on Enid Blyton and expect to have midnight feasts.'

Clare jumped up in alarm. 'I ought to be going,' she said, remembering her mother's edict that a man likes his home to himself when he comes in from work. 'You must have a million things to do.'

'Oh, no. I've just made a few sandwiches. You could stay and have some with us.'

Clare shook her head, but before she could speak the back door opened and closed and a tall, rather spare man strode into the kitchen. He carried a battered briefcase which he dropped on the floor and had already bent to kiss Veronica when he caught sight of Clare. He finished what he had set out to do, giving her a wink as he did so, and then straightened up.

'Hello. Have we met before?'

'No, you haven't,' Veronica said, rubbing her face against his sleeve like an affectionate kitten. 'Nobody's met Clare because she's only just come. She's moved into the Warburtons' house up the lane. Her husband's a sailor.'

'A sailor, eh? Well, he'll be able to swap old salt's tales with my old man when he comes to visit. I wonder if they've ever come across each other? No – probably not, come to think of it, unless your chap's a lot older than you.'

Clare shook her head. 'He's three years older than me. And he's an artificer.' There was no point in beating about the bush, but she hoped that he would be as dismissive of rank as his wife. She didn't want to lose this chance of a friendship.

'An artificer? They're the ones who know how to work all the gubbins, aren't they? God, what a mess today's Navy would be in without them. Which branch?'

'Radar,' she said with shy pride, and he pursed his lips in a silent whistle.

'Really clever stuff. At sea now?'

Clare nodded. 'But he'll be home again in a few weeks. They're just doing short trips at the moment.'

'Followed by a long one. I know. Well, you know where to come when you're lonely. Ronnie and I are always glad to see people. That your little chap out in the garden? He looks a real smasher. And this is your little girl – looks just like you. Those eyes are going to break a few hearts, I can see!'

Clare laughed and blushed. She didn't think Laura was in the least like her, and she'd certainly never had such beautiful eyes. Alex was just being friendly, she knew. She smiled at him across the kitchen table.

He caught her glance and held it. His eyes were very dark brown, the colour of burnt amber, and his hair was a deep chestnut. His face was rather thin and angular, but when he smiled it lit up with great charm. His arms and legs were long and sprawling, with the gawky, yet appealing grace of a newborn colt. He wasn't at all handsome in the accepted sense, and yet . . .

Clare caught her breath. In all the years since she had first met Martyn, there had never been another man she had felt that she fancied. Yet now, staring at Alex Challoner, she was conscious of a tiny movement somewhere under her heart. For a brief moment, her gaze was held and then, aware that her blush had deepened, she turned quickly away and was heartily thankful when the back door opened again and another young woman burst into the kitchen.

'Is that coffee brewing? You're an angel, Ronnie. Hello, Alex. Hello—' She stopped, realising that she hadn't met Clare before. She was small and quick, with dark auburn hair cut short like a cap, reminding Clare of Kathy. She had sparkling hazel eyes that took in Clare at a glance, and a three-cornered grin that lit up her freckled face with mischief. She looked even younger than Veronica, but she couldn't be really, unless she'd had Andrew when she was about seventeen.

'Hallo. Is that your little boy out there being led astray by my monkey? Oh!' Her eyes lit upon Laura, now sitting in the middle of the blue-tiled floor rolling a tin of beans back and forth. 'You've got a little *girl*! Oh, isn't she *gorgeous*! May I pick her up?'

'I should have told you,' Veronica said to Clare, 'Sue's a dead sucker for babies. She'd breed all the time if Don would let her. Luckily, he's got more sense.'

'I *must* have a little girl,' Sue declared, cuddling Laura against her. 'She's perfectly adorable. Couldn't you just *eat* her? She's so *delicious*.'

'I'll remember that next time we run out of food,' Clare remarked. 'But she's more likely to eat you, I'm afraid. She's got an appetite like a donkey.'

'Sausages,' Laura announced.

Veronica said, 'There you are. She does understand what we say.'

'No, I really have got some sausages,' Sue told them. 'Mind you, I don't know how she can tell, they're buried at the bottom of my bag. They'll be as flat as pancakes . . . So where do you live? What's your little boy's name? Have you known Veronica and Alex long?'

'About half an hour,' Clare said, laughing. 'I was just passing and I asked if she'd bring her little boy to play with mine, and she invited me in.'

'But Veronica hasn't got a little – oh, I see what you mean. You thought Andrew was *hers*. Oh, if *only* . . . You can have him to play any time you like, Clare. I won't charge a penny. What did you say yours was called?'

Clare laughed again. 'His name's Christopher and we live up the lane on to the moor. We've only been there a few weeks. My husband's in the Navy and he's away a lot so I'm glad to be able to make friends.'

'Oh, you poor *thing*. I don't know how I'd manage if Don went away a lot. Don't you know *anyone* round here? Where are your family?'

'Near Portsmouth.' Not many people had heard of Gosport, she'd found, but most knew where Portsmouth was. 'But my in-laws live at Ivybridge.'

Sue wrinkled her nose and the freckles ran together in a mass of golden-brown. 'Is that good or bad? Mine live in Exeter, and that's too close for me. It's too easy to get here by train. I never know when they're going to turn up on the doorstep.'

'Well, mine run a shop so they can't surprise us too much.' So far, they had been twice. Mrs Perry had looked around rather critically, remarking that it would take a lot of decorating and warning Clare of the expense of using the telephone too much and the dangers of letting the children go on the moor alone. She'd added that Tavistock was very cold in winter, suggested warm dressing-gowns for the children's next Christmas presents and then departed, telling Clare to be sure and ring up regularly. (Apparently this was an admissible expense.) Mr Perry had examined the electrical wiring, bringing an instrument with him specially, and declared it 'not too bad, considering its age'. By the time they left, Clare had felt partly depressed and partly defensive, and wishing that her own parents lived nearer.

She was saved from answering Sue's question by Sue herself, who had finished her coffee and was gathering up her shopping. 'I'll *have* to go now, Veronica, thanks for having the pest. Don'll be home for his lunch in half an hour . . . Come in and see me sometime, Clare. I live about a *mile* away by road, down the estate road and round the corner, but our garden backs on to Veronica's so I can just hop over the hedge. And I'd love to have Christopher to play with Andrew, but only as long as you let me have that *gorgeous* Laura as well. Come in tomorrow afternoon, if you like.'

'Thanks,' Clare said, feeling bemused by the sudden expansion of her social life. 'Thanks, I'd like to very much.'

Christopher trundled in, deprived of his new playmate, and Clare set down her own cup. She glanced swiftly at Alex Challoner, who had picked up Laura and was playing round-and-round-the-garden-like-a-teddy-bear on one of her fat palms, and said again that she'd have to go. Veronica made another attempt to get her to stay and have lunch with them, but Alex didn't look up and Clare, feeling slightly rebuffed, refused.

A few minutes later, she was on her way back up the lane, having quite forgotten that she had originally set out to walk into town for some shopping. I can do that this afternoon, she thought, remembering as she unlatched the gate. The important thing is that I've started to meet people and make friends.

For a while, since Martyn had gone away again, she had been lonelier than she had ever known it possible to be, and had begun to wonder why they had moved to Devon at all, and to wish that she could be back in Gosport again, with her mother and father only a walk away, her sister over the water in Portsmouth, and Kathy coming to see her on Tuesday evenings. Now, things were looking brighter, and she hummed a tune as she got lunch ready for the three of them.

'We're going to be all right here,' she told the children as she settled Laura in her highchair and Christopher on his cushion. 'We're really going to be all right.'

She made herself a sandwich, thinking of Veronica and Alex eating theirs in that immaculate and up-to-date kitchen. The kitchen at Dale View was shabby and untidy – the only furniture they had was a Formica-topped table and chairs, and a kitchen cabinet they had bought after they'd moved here – but she liked it better than Veronica's. It was more homely.

The strange sensation she had experienced when she had first seen Alex Challoner had disappeared. She tried, experimentally, to see if she could feel it again by conjuring up his face, and she couldn't.

Relieved, she wiped Christopher's face and fed Laura her last spoonful of mashed carrots.

Chapter Fifteen

Alex and Veronica had chosen the following weekend to go to North Cornwall. The tide would be just right for surfing at Polzeath, their favourite beach, and the forecast was for a good breeze, which meant that the waves would be high. Alex got the surfboards out on Friday evening and put them by the car. He was already beginning to feel the tingle of excitement that always came to him before a day's surfing.

He heard the telephone ring inside the house but took little notice. The phone was always ringing for Veronica. After a few minutes, she came out into the garden and he looked up at her with a smile.

'We'll make an early start. It's going to be hot, and we'll need to get a good place on the beach. Everyone will be heading there tomorrow.'

Veronica sat down on the garden bench. She was looking very pretty, in a floral sundress, her hair falling like a shimmering curtain to her bare shoulders. She had a light golden tan and her skin was smooth and satiny.

'Darling, that was Mummy on the phone. She wants us to go over to spend the weekend. Aunt Esme and Uncle John have come down from London.'

Alex looked regretful. 'That's a shame. We'll miss them. How long are they staying? Perhaps we could pop over one evening during the week.'

'Oh, no, there'll be no need for that – I said of course we'd go. We're to be there for lunch tomorrow.'

Alex put down the surfboard he had been holding. 'But we've arranged to go to Polzeath.'

'I know, darling, but you don't really mind, do you? We can go there any weekend, after all. You've only met Aunt Esme and Uncle John at our wedding, and it's ages since I saw them. We can't be rude and not go.'

'Why would it be rude? They must realise we might have made other arrangements.'

'Well, of course they do, darling, but we can unmake them, can't we? Anyway, I told them we were only going surfing, and they'd be terribly hurt if we put that first.' She gave him her enchanting smile and laid her hand on his arm. 'You don't really mind, do you? We'll be together, and that's the main thing, isn't it?'

Alex looked at her. He struggled with the idea of saying, no, it wasn't, the main thing was to do what they'd arranged to do, what he'd been looking forward to all week. But he couldn't take that delicious smile from her face; he couldn't be the cause of those lovely blue eyes filling with tears. He couldn't let her think he'd rather be surfing than with her at her parents' house – and it wasn't true, anyway. He did want to be with her.

Being with Veronica was like being with a flower perpetually in bloom, with a butterfly whose jewelled colours always shimmered with sunlight. Alex was as enraptured by her as he had been the first time he'd set eyes on her as a blossoming young woman. The rather spoiled, petted little girl he had known had grown into a fairy creature, as ethereal as gossamer and as elusive as a dream, and he had been enthralled by her ever since.

'Yes, of course that's the main thing,' he said. 'We'll go surfing another time.' However, the tide would be wrong next week, and the weekend after that was the last weekend of term, with speech day and parties for boys and parents. And then the school holidays would have started and Cornwall would be invaded by holidaymakers, and the peace gone.

He put the surfboards away and came indoors to decide which clothes to take for a weekend with his parents-in-law and an aunt and uncle he had met only once. John Curtis, his father-in-law's brother, was a retired captain, so the naval influence would be strong. Alex felt a premonition of the puzzled reception he would receive. The son of a naval commander, marrying the daughter of another, would be expected to have gone into the Navy himself, to be at least a lieutenant-commander by now. Instead, he had set his face against a naval career, gone into the Army to do his national service and then come back into Civvy Street and taken up his university training to become a schoolmaster.

'We'll probably dress in the evening,' Veronica said, taking his dinner-jacket out of the wardrobe. 'It's a good thing I had this dry-cleaned last time. And you'll need casual for the daytime. That new shirt and pullover would do. And your grey slacks and blazer.'

In that outfit, he would look as near naval as possible, and the others could forget he was a civilian teacher. He watched gloomily as she picked out suitable ties, and thought of the weekend he'd planned, messing about in old shorts and swimming-trunks.

Veronica didn't surf much. She came in a few times, for the look of it and just to say she had, and then spent the day lying on the sand with a tube of suncream and a magazine or book, baking herself a deeper gold. She had several different beach outfits – two bikinis and a one-piece swimsuit, a couple of pairs of brief shorts and some shirts – and she draped herself about in these, apparently perfectly happy to just lie in the sun and watch Alex trudging out with his surfboard again and again, to come riding in on the foam-topped waves.

When the tide had turned and the waves began to decrease, Alex would come in, salty and burned even darker by the sun, and gulp down tea from the Thermos flask before drying himself. Then they would saunter back across the sand to the cottage where they always put up overnight, and wash off the sand before going to bed. It was always good then, with the heat of the sun still on their bodies, Alex filled with the exhilaration of the surf and Veronica warm and sleepy as a cat after her day's sunbathing. And later, still sleek with wellbeing, they would drift into the village and have supper at a local restaurant or in an inn, before wandering back in starlight to make love again and look forward to another blissful day on the beach.

Alex had been anticipating this all through the week. And now, instead, he would have to dress in smart clothes, with a *tie* round his neck, and make polite conversation to people who would look at him and, however politely they tried to disguise it, wonder what could be wrong with him, that he didn't want to go into the Navy.

Veronica's parents lived near Ashburton, on the eastern fringe of Dartmoor. When Keith Curtis had retired from the Navy, he had moved away from the temptations of Plymouth and Dartmouth, where he had spent most of his working life, and devoted himself to the moor and to his garden. 'I don't want to end up as one of those anchor-faced old salts you see wandering on the Hoe, wishing they were still in command at sea, and then drowning their sorrows in pink gin,' he said.

'The Navy's had all it's going to get of me. I'm going to work at being a landlubber.'

It was all talk, of course. He still played an active part in naval associations and kept up with all his old cronies, but he was able now to give rein to the parts of his personality that had been forced to remain dormant for so many years – the gardener and countryman, the birdwatcher and hillwalker. He gave up the tie for the open-necked shirt or, if pushed, the cravat, and was usually to be found clad in old wellingtons and baggy trousers, with his sweaters torn by his tussles with thorns and shrubs.

Elizabeth Curtis had taken less readily to life ashore. She missed the glory of being a captain's wife, and she missed the companionship of the other wives with their coffee mornings, cocktail parties and endless gossip. There had been a special hierarchy among the women, and she missed being at the head of it. However, she had been too pleased to have her own home, instead of a succession of naval quarters, to object, and once settled in she had turned her formidable energies to organising the village.

Here, she was entirely successful. Like many villages not too far from a small city, this one had enough inhabitants to sustain a reasonable social life – a Women's Institute, a flower club, a tennis club and a golf course. From these sprang a number of private groups who played bridge together, gave lunches and dinner parties and sometimes went to the theatre or a concert together. And all of these things had to be organised by someone.

Elizabeth Curtis was eager to be that someone. Accustomed to being in charge, she took command of anything that needed a mastermind, and villages being what they were, the locals allowed her to take the reins, while muttering beneath their breath about incomers who wanted to take over and change everything.

By the time Alex had come along and married Veronica, Elizabeth and the village had settled down to a working relationship and she had made friends amongst the others who, like her, enjoyed being on committees and making decisions about jumble sales and country fairs. Under her firm guidance, the village had already won two best-kept village awards, and she was now working on an idea for opening a dozen or so village gardens to visitors one day the following summer.

Elizabeth was never seen in muddy wellingtons or torn sweaters. If she went for a walk, she put on proper, stout walking shoes and a tweed suit, and carried a stick to swish down nettles. Most of the time, she looked as if dressed to meet friends for lunch in town, and often that was just what she was on her way to do.

'Veronica! Sweetheart!' she cried, coming out of the house as Alex drew the car to a halt in front of the door. 'How lovely to see you! Take the car round to the back, Alex, there's a dear. We're having drinks on the terrace.'

Veronica got out of the car and her mother embraced her. Elizabeth was an older, more statuesque version of her daughter. Fair, fat and forty, she'd once laughingly described herself, but by now she must be well on the way to fifty. Her hair was carefully waved and her figure was shown off in a dark blue dress fitted closely to its rich curves. She linked her arm with Veronica's and led her round the side of the house to the terrace.

Alex drove round the other side, to the old stables that had now been converted to garages and a workshop. Keith Curtis spent a good deal of time in the workshop, for one of his many interests was carving wood, and he was experimenting with making animal and bird figures. However, there was nobody here now and Alex left the car and made his way round to the terrace.

The Grange was a long, low house, its roof thatched and overhanging small cottage windows. It had undergone much renovation over the years and was now as comfortable and well equipped as any modern house. Along the back, extending the kitchen and dining-room, was a long conservatory filled with plants, and at the side the terrace overlooked the main part of the garden. When Alex arrived, the whole party was gathered there for drinks.

'*There* you are!' Elizabeth cried, as if he'd been gone for hours. 'Esme, John – you remember Alex, don't you? He's the one who took our darling daughter away from us.'

Alex shook hands, wishing his mother-in-law wouldn't make jokes like that. He was never entirely sure that they were intended as jokes, and he wondered if other people noticed the barb as well.

Perhaps John Curtis did, for he gave Elizabeth a reproving look and said, 'Now then, Liz, you wouldn't have wanted Veronica to become an old maid, would you?'

Liz! Alex glanced sideways at Elizabeth to see how she took this. Presumably she was used to it, for she just laughed and said, 'Of course not. You take me up too quickly, John. It's just another way of saying that Alex is Veronica's husband. And of course we're very happy about it, we couldn't wish for a nicer son-in-law. Look at the way he's given up his weekend, just to be with a set of old fogies like us.'

Yes, just look at it, Alex thought, wondering what the surf was like down at Polzeath.

'Old fogies?' John Curtis said gallantly. 'You'll never be an old fogey, Liz.' He sat back in his Lloyd Loom chair.

Alex thought he was just how you would expect a retired naval captain to be – big and bluff and hearty, with piercingly blue eyes and a ruddy face under a fluff of white hair. As if even civilian clothes must form a kind of uniform, he was dressed exactly like Alex, in a navy blazer with gold buttons, a white shirt and grey slacks. Instead of a tie, he wore a cravat in dark red Paisley silk. He looked as if he would be in command wherever he went.

The terrace was wide and paved with flagstones, looking over a lawn of such perfection that Alex was tempted to wonder if it had been laid by carpet-fitters. Borders were filled with flowers of blazing yellow, deep scarlet and burnt orange, and at the far end was a small arboretum and a honeysuckle-covered archway leading, he knew, to the vegetable garden.

Keith Curtis spent a lot of time in his garden, but he could not have achieved this perfection alone. During the week, he had a gardener who came in two or three mornings, just as Elizabeth had a cleaning woman who came in several times to keep the house in order. It was an idyllic lifestyle, but one that Alex knew he could never aspire to on his teacher's salary, although he was sometimes uneasily aware that Veronica regarded it as her natural birthright.

It'll be different when we start a family, he thought. She'll realise then that there are more important things than a perfect garden or immaculate house. She wasn't ready yet – in a strange way, she wasn't yet quite grown up – but soon she would be, and then their life together would truly begin. It was as if this was a kind of playtime, a preparation for real life, a halcyon period between childhood and maturity. A period that couldn't go on for ever, but was here to be enjoyed now – though not, he hoped, for too long.

He let his mind play pleasantly with the idea of two or three small children – rather like those who had been there when he had arrived home for lunch the other day – scampering about the house and garden, scattering their toys everywhere and filling the quiet rooms with laughter.

They'd been engaging little scraps, he thought. He already knew Andrew, of course, but the other two, belonging to that young woman who had recently moved to the area, had especially attracted him: the boy with his fair hair and sunny smile; the baby girl with her enormous eyes and long, dark lashes. And their mother was an attractive girl too, only a year or two older than Veronica at a guess, and appealingly shy. He remembered the way she'd glanced at him across the kitchen table, and the way her look had suddenly held, as if she'd been unable to turn her eyes away. And the odd, tingling sensation he'd felt as he'd stared back . . .

'Aren't we, darling?' he heard Veronica say, and he snapped guiltily out of his thoughts and back to the present.

'I'm sorry – I was miles away.'

Veronica laughed, but there was a brittle edge to her laughter. 'And I can guess where, too! You were busy surfing down at Polzeath, weren't you? Sometimes,' she said to the others, 'he's just like a little boy whose favourite toy has been taken away. I told you, darling, we can go next week.'

'And *I* told *you*, the tide'll be wrong then,' Alex pointed out, realising too late that he must be sounding exactly like the disgruntled child she had portrayed. 'Anyway, I wasn't thinking about surfing at all. I was just admiring your father's garden and wondering how he gets the weeds to stop growing.'

They all laughed and Keith said, 'They don't. I just keep hoeing them out. And even then, sometimes I find some huge brute growing where I hadn't noticed it.'

'Weeds!' Esme said, lifting her hands. 'I don't even know which is which.'

'That's easy,' her husband said. 'They're the ones that are hard to pull up.'

Alex thought about this and decided it was really rather witty. He warmed to Keith's brother. In fact, he liked Keith as well, and he could easily tolerate his mother-in-law, whose heart was in the right place even if she was bossy and effusive. It was really rather pleasant sitting here on this terrace, looking out at the sunny garden, with a glass of gin and tonic in his hand. If you couldn't be surfing in Cornwall, there were a great many worse places to be than this.

'I was just saying,' Veronica said, with an edge to her voice that told him she was irritated at having been ignored for too long, 'that we're thinking of going abroad for our holiday next year. Aren't we?'

He stared at her. 'Are we?'

'Darling, you *know* we are. We talked about it the other day. We thought France, perhaps. I'd like to see the Riviera.'

'The Riviera?' Alex searched his mind for any memory of such a conversation, but could find none. Probably Veronica had been talking about it one morning over breakfast, when he was never at his best. 'Well, we'll have to see what we can afford. It's not cheap, going abroad for holidays.'

'Darling, don't be so boring. There's lots of time before then. Birthdays and Christmas. I'm sure we'll be able to save up enough money.' She smiled at her father. 'After all, we were *very* economical with our honeymoon.'

Alex drew in a breath. This was no place to start an argument, but he really could not allow Veronica to beg so shamelessly from her parents, who had already given them far too much help. He knew that she was the apple of their eye and they found it difficult to refuse her anything, but she was his responsibility now, and he must cut his coat according to the cloth. He was already aware that their home reflected an income much above his salary, and he often felt uncomfortable when people came to visit them, believing that his home gave a false impression of the people he and Veronica really were. Or perhaps it would be truer to say the person *he* really was. Perhaps it was the home Veronica ought to have, and it was his inadequacy that made him feel uncomfortable.

Before he could speak, Elizabeth stood up. 'I must just go and see to the lunch. Come and give me a hand, Veronica darling, and we can have a good old chinwag while the others set the world to rights out here.'

'I'll come too,' Esme offered, and the three women went into the house together.

Left with the two older men, Alex felt slightly uncomfortable. Their world was so very different from his. They would want to discuss naval acquaintances, he thought, and the kind of gossip in which he could have no part. He got up from his chair.

'D'you mind if I have a look round the garden? I'd like to stretch my legs a bit after the drive.'

'Of course not,' Keith said. 'Go where you please, my boy. Here, let me top up your glass and you can take it with you.'

Alex wandered away down the path beside one of the borders, hearing the two older men already deep in a conversation that sounded as if it had started some hours earlier. They were happy, he thought, and warmed towards them for not trying to make polite pretence for his sake. Slowly, enjoying the feel of sunshine on his bare head, he sauntered along the path and through the honeysuckle arch into the vegetable garden.

Here, he was out of sight of the house. He sat down on a bench, sipping his drink and contemplating the neat rows of vegetables. Did Keith and Elizabeth really eat all these crops? he wondered.

His mind drifted back to the young woman with the two children. Clare, her name had been. Her husband was in the Navy too. He was an artificer, a rank that came between the officers and the seamen. Artificers wore the same navy blue suit as the officers, rather than the 'square rig' worn by seamen, and they wore the same peaked cap, but without the 'scrambled egg' gold on the cap, or the rings round the sleeves that denoted the rank of an officer. They were like qualified tradesmen, who had completed an apprenticeship. Some of them went through the ranks of petty officer and chief petty officer and then aspired to make the jump to sub-lieutenant, coming into the wardroom with officers who had been to Dartmouth and, in theory, able to rise as far as lieutenant-commander. Higher than that wasn't likely, mainly because of the time needed to climb so high on the ladder; by then, they would probably be too near retirement to make another rung.

Alex knew that officers generally had a great deal of respect for their artificers, even though they would not usually 'know' them socially. There was still a very definite line of demarcation between the decks.

Alex had, like Veronica, grown up in the Navy. Ever since he was a small boy, he had listened to naval talk and moved within an atmosphere of naval life. He had gone to a prep school attended mostly by the sons of naval officers, and a large number of them had departed to go to Dartmouth, where they were virtually in the Navy already. Alex had been subjected to a certain amount of pressure to do the same, and had suffered a good deal of incredulity when he had refused.

'I don't want to be a sailor. I don't want to go to sea.'

'But your father and your grandfather were both in the Navy. Your great-grandfather served with Nelson. You can't break the tradition now.'

'Why not?' The pressure hadn't come from his father, or his mother, but from an uncle who had no children of his own and had stood godfather for Alex at his christening. He had been retired early through ill-health, and even at the tender age of twelve, Alex had understood that he bore the brunt of his uncle's disappointed hopes.

'I'm sorry, Uncle Ted. I really don't want to go in the Navy.'

His uncle had stared at him, disbelieving. 'Well, what *do* you want to do, then?'

Alex hadn't known. All he knew was that he didn't want to go to sea for months on end, didn't want to be away from home as his father had been, didn't want to be in a Navy that demanded to come first, before the home and family, before all else. He knew that it had to be so, for the Service to work at all; he just didn't want to be part of it.

'Alex! *Alex!*'

Once again, Veronica's voice startled him from his reverie. He got to his feet but before he could move, she was coming round the corner of the hedge. She was dressed in white, her shoulders bare, and the breeze was lifting her hair into a swirling cloud. Her blue eyes laughed at him and he felt a surge of love.

'There you are! Alex, what on earth are you doing, skulking off down here by yourself, hiding behind the hedge? Everyone wants to talk to you.' She came close and linked her arm through his, snuggling her head against his shoulder like an affectionate kitten.

'They don't,' he said, smiling at her. 'They're far too interested in their reminiscences and golfing stories. They don't want a dull old chemistry teacher.'

'Don't be ridiculous. You're not dull – and you're not old, either.' She rubbed her face against his sleeve. 'What's the matter really, Alex? You're not frightened of Uncle John, are you?'

Alex laughed 'No, not at all. I like him. I just feel that he and your father have got their own interests and their own catching up to do. And I like walking round the gardens.'

Veronica glanced about her. 'They're nice, aren't they? Daddy does far too much work in them, of course. Mummy was telling me she's been trying to get him to rest more, but he just won't . . . You're not sorry we came, are you, Alex? I know you wanted to go surfing. But they really do love to see us.'

'No,' he said, looking down at her face and thinking again just how much he loved her. 'I'm not sorry we came. We'll go surfing another time.'

They walked back to the house, arms about each other's waists. As they walked through the immaculate garden with its close-cropped lawn and weedless flowerbeds, Alex thought of the pleasure it gave his parents-in-law to see their only child. A pleasure he could only imagine, and one that still seemed as far away as on the day he and Veronica had married.

And he couldn't help conjuring up a picture of another garden, scattered with toys, its grass rough and trodden by playing feet, its quietness broken by shrill voices and childish laughter.

Running towards him across the grass, he seemed to see two figures.

A small boy with a fair, laughing face, and a stumbling little girl, scarcely more than a baby, with curly dark hair and huge, black-lashed eyes.

Chapter Sixteen

ew regular visitors came to the front door of Dale View. They
usually walked round the side of the house to the back, where an
old horseshoe nailed to the door served as a knocker. A ring on
the front doorbell, therefore, signified a stranger or a more official
visitor.

It came just as Clare was pouring a cup of tea in the kitchen after
putting both children down for an afternoon sleep. I won't be able to do
this for much longer, she thought. At three, Christopher was getting too
old, and Laura, although only just past her first birthday, had already
begun to protest and often awoke grumpy and miserable for the rest of
the day. However, Clare valued this oasis of peace after lunch, and used
it as a chance to put her feet up and read for half an hour without
interruption.

The shrill sound of the bell was a jagged irritation, but she couldn't
refuse to answer it. Sighing, she put down her cup and went along the
passage.

Most visitors waited at the door of the conservatory after ringing the
bell. This one, however, had come right in and was standing outside the
front door as she opened it. Startled, Clare stepped back a little, and
then her eyes widened in astonishment.

'Brian!'

'Hi there.' He grinned, sketching a salute. 'Surprise, surprise.'

'But what are you doing here? Is Kathy with you?'

He shook his head. 'Of course not. She's at home. Well, she's
probably at work right now.' He gestured at his uniform. 'The ship's in
Plymouth for a couple of days so I thought I'd drop in and see you.
Aren't you going to ask me in?'

'In Plymouth? Kathy never said . . .' She stepped back again to lead him through to the kitchen. 'Did she know you were coming? Why didn't you ring me up? I might have been out and you'd have had a wasted journey.'

Brian shrugged. He looked tall and broad in the kitchen, and Clare remembered the smart, newly furnished house in Fareham and was suddenly conscious of the shabbiness of her own home. She indicated the cup she had just put down.

'Would you like a cup of tea? I've just made one.'

'Thanks. It's not a bad place you've got here, Clare.'

Clare immediately felt defensive. 'It's not smart, but we've got plenty of room. And when we can afford to redecorate . . .'

'No, I mean it. It's nice. A good, solid house. Those houses on our estate are made of cardboard – dead flimsy. I'd sooner have a place like this any day, but you know what Kathy's like, she wanted everything new.' He glanced around the big kitchen with its scuffed cupboards and Rayburn. 'I bet this'll be really cosy in winter when you've got that going.'

'I'm not using it yet,' Clare said. 'I'm not really sure how you work them.'

'Oh, I can show you that. We had one where I was evacuated in Ivybridge.' Clare remembered that that was where he and Martyn had met. After the war, Brian had gone back to his home in Bristol, but he had never talked much about his family there and even Kathy didn't seem to know much. She had been to visit them once or twice, briefly, but none of them had come to the wedding.

'Look,' he was saying, squatting down in front of the Rayburn, 'this is the firebox and this thing is the riddler. You just work it backwards and forwards so that the ashes and cinders fall through. Then you can just pull out the tray and empty them away, see?'

Clare crouched beside him. 'There's something in there now. A big lump.'

'That's clinker. You get it from burning things like coke. It forms a lump, like a heavy piece of metal, and it won't go through the grid. You have to get it out with your hands.' He stripped off his jacket and rolled up his shirtsleeves, then reached in and worked at the lump of clinker until he could lift it out through the firebox. Clare fetched a piece of newspaper and spread it on the floor and Brian laid the clinker on it. His arms were smeared with ash and soot. He grinned at her.

'I don't know, I've only been here five minutes and you've got me doing dirty jobs! I shall expect payment for this, you know.'

'Payment?' Clare stared at him, feeling suddenly uncomfortable, but he only laughed.

'It's all right. A cup of tea will be enough. Tea and sympathy, that's what a bloke needs when he's away from home.' He brushed ash from his hands. 'I'll just finish the lesson before I wash this lot off. All you do is lay your fire in here, you see, and open up this airway so that it gets a bit of draught. Close it down later or you'll have the fire roaring up the chimney, and your oven and hotplates will start to get hot. And that's all there is to it. Stoke it up at night before you go to bed, close down the damper so that it won't all burn away in the night, and you'll have a lovely warm kitchen to come down to in the morning.'

'It sounds easy,' Clare said, standing up. 'Thanks, Brian. D'you want to wash in the scullery?' The scullery was a tiny lean-to on the side of the kitchen, holding only the sink unit, which had been one of the things Clare and Martyn had put in when they'd arrived, to replace an old, chipped sink and wooden draining board. In some ways, it was convenient to have the sink outside the kitchen, in others it was a nuisance, and Clare suspected that in winter it would be cold and uncomfortable.

She gave Brian a towel and he washed off the soot, then followed her into the garden for the promised cup of tea. He didn't put his jacket on again or roll down his sleeves, and she noticed the muscular strength of his arms.

'Where are the kids?' he asked, as if he'd only just noticed their absence, and Clare told him they were both asleep.

'They'll be awake pretty soon, though. I usually take them out for a walk then. We go up on the moor, they can run about and play there.'

'Sounds good. Have they got a ball we can take?' He seemed to take it for granted that he would be coming too, and Clare found she rather liked the idea. It wasn't often she had company, and Martyn had been away for nearly a month now. It would be nice for the children to have a man about the house for a few hours.

'Stay to supper,' she said. 'It won't be anything much – just sausages – but there's plenty. The buses run back to Plymouth all evening.'

Brian smiled at her, and she felt a twinge of sensation. Do I really want him to stay? she wondered. What would Martyn say if he knew? But Martyn wouldn't mind at all – why should he? Brian and he were old friends, and Martyn knew that he could always trust Clare. Brian was attractive, with his dark, film-star looks, but he was her husband's best 'oppo' and the husband of her own best friend. And anyway, there wasn't anyone for her but Martyn.

She was safe with Brian, She smiled at him again.

'It's nice to have you here. I'm glad you came to see me.'

Brian came twice more while his ship was in Plymouth, although his next visits were confined to the evening. He played with the children and gave them presents – a new red ball for Christopher, a soft toy for Laura, a bag of sweets. After the children were in bed, Clare made coffee and she and Brian sat and watched television, or talked. They discussed impersonal things, such as space exploration – both the Americans and the Russians had put men into orbit by now – and the death of Marilyn Monroe. On his last visit, Brian brought Clare a large box of chocolates and handed it to her just before leaving.

'Brian, you shouldn't. You've spent too much on us already.'

'Kathy'd want me to do it,' he said. 'She misses seeing you all. She used to really enjoy Tuesday evenings at your place.'

'Well, you must both come to see us on your next leave,' Clare said. 'I miss Kathy too, but I'm making friends here now.' She told him about Veronica and Alex. 'They live down on the main road, in that rather nice house with the big tree in the garden. And Sue lives behind them, on the estate. She's been up here several times now, with her little boy, Andrew. He and Chris have a great time.'

'That's good. I'm glad you're settling in.' He gave her a wicked grin. 'And it's very convenient for me to have a nice girlfriend handy for Plymouth. You know what they say about sailors, don't you?'

Clare blushed a little. 'Every nice girl loves one.'

'I wasn't thinking about that. I was thinking about the one that says a wife in every port.'

Clare's blush deepened and she turned away quickly. 'You shouldn't say things like that.'

'Come on, Clare, it's only a joke. You know I'd never do anything to hurt you or Martyn.' He paused. 'Not that I haven't been tempted to make a pass once or twice, the past few days. It's a crime, a girl like you being left all by herself.'

'Brian! Please don't talk like that.' She turned and looked up into his eyes. They were narrowed as he gazed back at her, and a smile flickered about his mouth. She felt her heart thud a little, and then he laughed and shook his head.

'Look, I told you, there's nothing to worry about. I'm not going to try anything on. But you've got to face facts – we're both on our own, both a bit lonely. These things can happen.'

'Not with me,' Clare said firmly. 'I'm not interested in anyone but Martyn.'

'I know that. That's why I'm telling you, you've got nothing to worry about. But you do need to watch it, Clare. Not too many visits from lonely sailors, hm?'

'I don't know what you mean. I don't have any other visitors. I don't even know any other sailors.'

'Keep it that way,' Brian said lightly. 'They're not all as gentlemanly as me.' He shrugged into his jacket and reached out to touch her face. 'Don't look so worried, little brown eyes. Nobody's going to hurt you. Now, I'd better be going or I'll miss that bus, and you'd have to put me up overnight. And I don't think that would do at all.'

Neither did Clare, and after he had gone she waited anxiously for a while, half afraid that he would come back, saying that the bus had already gone. However, he didn't arrive and after a while she went to bed and lay wakeful, staring into the darkness and wondering why she felt so restless. It was as if Brian had woken something in her, something she didn't fully understand and would rather had stayed asleep.

It was only at that moment that she realised that she had missed writing her daily letter.

The friendship between Clare, Veronica and Sue flourished, and the three girls spent at least two afternoons a week together, sitting in one or the other's house or garden, drinking tea and gossiping while the children played. Logically, Clare thought, she and Sue were the ones who had most in common and ought to have been the closest friends, but somehow Veronica, the childless one, seemed to be the pivotal member of the three. It was at her house that they met most often and she who suggested their occasional outings.

'Let's go down to Magpie Corner,' she said one morning, ringing them up before lunch. 'We can catch the bus by the oak tree at two and take a picnic tea. The children will love it.'

Magpie Corner was on the Plymouth road, between Whitchurch and Horrabridge. The river Walkham ran under a stone bridge and then through thick woods until it met the Tavy at Double Waters. You could walk all the way along from the road, and even back to Tavistock, although this was much too far for the children.

It was a popular picnic spot, with plenty of space for families along the banks of the shallow river, and safe for paddling and bathing; there were also a few pools a short distance from the river, but these were stagnant and nobody played in them. They found a spot on the grass and sat down, spreading out their rugs and stripping Christopher and Andrew down to bathing trunks. Even Laura was undressed down to her nappy and frilly waterproof pants, and sat on her rug almost enveloped by a huge sunhat, waving the squashy rabbit Brian had given her. It had become her favourite toy and she wouldn't be parted from it.

Veronica leaped to her feet and took the boys down to the water. They shrieked as they felt the chill on their toes, and clung to her, and she laughed and splashed their faces. Christopher looked alarmed, but Andrew splashed back and after a moment or two they were all at it, soaking themselves in the fresh, cold water.

'Veronica's in her element,' Clare remarked, sitting up and hugging her knees. 'I wonder why she doesn't have any children of her own. She always seems to like playing with ours.'

'Veronica will have kids when she's ready for them,' Sue said. 'And Alex has got too much sense to push her. He must want some, though. He's a lot older than she is, you know. Ten years, I think. Quite a big gap, really.'

The little boys had settled down with buckets and spades. They couldn't build sandcastles here, but they could excavate holes which the river immediately filled with water, and they soon got the idea of building a network of shallow waterways at the edge of the little shingle beach. They worked on happily and Veronica came back to the rugs, laughing and shaking water off herself.

'They're a couple of thugs,' she said, flinging herself down beside Clare. 'I shall have little girls like Laura, and dress them in pretty frocks which they will never get dirty.'

'Don't kid yourself,' Clare said. 'Laura can get as dirty as Chris any day she likes. You should see her with a bar of chocolate.'

'Oh, yes,' Sue agreed. 'We gave Andrew one when he was about nine months old and then took photos! He got it everywhere. We're going to hold the pictures over him as blackmail when he starts going out with girls.'

A few more families arrived and the children began to play together in a group. Most of them were under school age and equipped similarly to Christopher and Andrew, with spades and buckets and balls which they threw randomly about on the grass.

'Let's have some tea,' Veronica suggested, and they turned to their baskets and began to unpack. They had all brought sandwiches and a few cakes which, set out on plates, looked quite a feast. Clare got out

Laura's beaker and filled it with milk, while Veronica unscrewed a Thermos of tea and Sue poured lemonade for the older children.

A loud crying made them look up. A large woman was walking towards the bank, holding a small boy by the hand. He was smothered from head to foot in green slime, his eyes tightly shut against the murky water that streamed from his hair, and his mouth formed a wide, square opening in his scarlet face.

'It's Christopher!' Clare exclaimed, and jumped to her feet. 'Chris! *Chris!*'

'But he's down by the river—' Veronica began, and then saw that he wasn't. Only Andrew was still playing with the other children, and by now everyone had stopped to look at the cause of all the noise.

Clare dashed over to the fat woman, who handed over her charge with evident relief. Christopher lunged for his mother and grabbed her legs with his slime-covered arms, burying his wet, crimson face in her skirt. She bent and scooped him into her arms.

'Thank you,' she said to the woman. 'Oh, thank you so much. I thought he was down by the river. He *was*, a moment ago. I was unpacking our tea, I never saw him wander off. I only took my eyes off him for a minute. He could have *drowned* . . . Oh, Chris, *Chris* . . .'

''Tis all right, maid,' the woman said. 'I was just settin' over there when I heard the poor little toad cry out. Don't 'ee blame yourself, now, 'tis easy for them to wander off, and with all these here pools around they'm certain to fall in some time or other. He'll be all right – smell you out of the house, but that won't worry he!'

She waddled off to her own family and Clare led Christopher back to the rugs. His screams were diminishing now to a series of snorts, chokes and sniffles, and, contrary to what his rescuer said, he quite obviously did not like the smell.

'I *stink*, Mummy,' he said. 'I smell like *pooh*.'

'He does, a bit,' Veronica said. 'You'd better wash him off in the river, Clare.'

Even after a sluice-down with river-water, which did nothing to restore his equanimity, Christopher still smelt, as Veronica said, distinctive. Clare dried him and dressed him in his dry clothes, and Sue gave him a sandwich. He shook his head dolefully and she offered him a cake instead.

'Poor little scrap. He must have been terrified.'

'So was I, when I saw him.' Clare was beginning to recover, but she still felt her heart lurch whenever she thought of what might have happened. Suppose the fat woman hadn't seen him . . . Suppose *nobody* had seen him, and he'd lain there, face down in the stagnant water . . . She shuddered and felt sick.

'Have some tea,' Sue said practically, handing her a steaming plastic cup. 'Don't worry about it, Clare. He's all right. Nothing awful's happened, he's just had a fright, that's all. He won't go near those puddles again, that's for sure.'

He won't, Clare thought, because we won't come here again. I'm not taking any more risks with my children. There might not be a fat woman about next time.

She was quiet for the rest of the afternoon, and reluctant to let Christopher go near the water again. When the sky clouded over and they decided to pack up and go home early, she agreed with relief. All she wanted to do was get Christopher home and into a bath, to wash off the smell of the river and the memories of the moment when she'd realised that the little boy walking across the grass, screaming and covered with green slime, had been her own son.

Later, with both children bathed and fed and tucked up in bed, she sat on the sofa and thought about it again. Her initial panic had disappeared, but she had realised today, more sharply than ever before, just what it meant to be a naval wife and a mother. It meant responsibility – full responsibility – for everything that happened. It meant being grown up, at whatever age you were when you took on the job.

Having children was an awesome responsibility.

Chapter Seventeen

The destroyer was in the Mediterranean with a small convoy of other ships. They had joined up with some French and Norwegian ships for an exercise, and Martyn was kept busy on the radar. The ship's company was much smaller than the one on board *Pacific*, and he found himself in close contact with the radar officers, and even the captain.

'You've done well, PO,' the head of the department said to him when the main exercise was over. 'The old man wants to congratulate you. You had a tough time last week, keeping the equipment in working order.'

'It was that storm that did it.' Martyn had spent almost all of one night working up the mast, feeling the ship roll beneath him and glad he couldn't see the direct fall below, one minute to the steel deck, the next to the heaving black waves. 'We'd have been all right if the weather had been better.'

'Well, you can feel proud of yourself.' The lieutenant paused for a moment, then said, 'Ever thought of taking a commission?'

'Becoming an officer?' Martyn looked at him. 'Well, I did think I might, at one time. But then I got married and you know how it is . . .'

'Do I?' Lieutenant Jeffreys looked amused. 'I'm married, and it hasn't stopped me.'

'Well, I know, sir, but – we've got a couple of kids, you see, and I hardly know them. I had some time at Collingwood, instructing, but that's all. They change so quickly. And my wife gets lonely.'

'So do all naval wives. They learn to cope.'

'Oh, I know,' Martyn said hastily. 'She doesn't grumble, sir – she never has. But I know she'd rather I was home all the time. And I have sort of promised her I'd come out at thirty.'

'*Sort* of promised?'

Martyn felt uncomfortable. 'She's expecting me to. I wouldn't like to go back on it.'

'Judge' Jeffreys gave him a straight look. 'This is your life we're talking about, Perry. Your career. Your wife knew you were in the Navy when she married you. She accepted it then – couldn't she accept it again? Especially if you came up to the upper deck. The money's better – you'll qualify for a good pension . . .'

A good pension seemed very far away to Martyn. He knew the pay was better, of course, and it was certainly something to think about. And with a higher rank he'd have more responsibility. More interesting work. And he wouldn't have to spend cold, stormy nights clinging to a mast!

'Think about it,' Jeffreys advised him. 'You'd get a good recommendation from the captain, and from me. You could go a long way, Perry.' He clapped Martyn on the shoulder and went off to the wardroom.

Martyn leaned thoughtfully over the rail. He'd always intended to make the Navy his career, and to become an officer if he could, but since marrying Clare he'd shelved the idea. Now it pushed itself forward again, demanding to be considered, and he found it surprisingly attractive.

Of course he didn't like being away from Clare and the children. But he was surviving it, and so were they. And apart from that, he liked the Navy. He liked the work and he liked being at sea, with other men. He liked the wide space of sky and water that was never empty, never the same. The huge upturned bowl of the sky, covered with scudding pink clouds at dawn, flawless blue during the day, thickly speckled with the shimmering frost of stars at night. Or heavy with clouds, bellying like grey canvas hammocks, the wind scouring them into torn rags as it whipped the sea into a maelstrom of towering, crashing, splintering waves. The ship rolled ferociously then, the water pouring over the deck and along the gangways, the spray rising high above them. It was exhilarating and frightening, and all too often it made you sick – more than once, Martyn had had to work with a bucket beside him. But when it was over and the sea was calm again and the ship steady, you felt a satisfaction that could compare with nothing else on earth. Except, maybe, sex.

That was what you missed most, he thought. Sex. Making love to your wife or your sweetheart – no wonder so many men found girls in every port. He'd been tempted himself often enough, but the thought of Clare and the children had kept him steady, so far. As he had said once to Brian, why have hamburger when you're out when you've got best steak waiting for you at home?

'The only trouble with that,' Brian had retorted, 'is that you can starve to death while you wait to get back to the steak.'

If I stay in the Navy, Martyn thought, I'll have at least another ten years' waiting for best steak. Do I really want that? What is Clare going to say?

No. He wouldn't do it. He wouldn't disappoint her. He wanted to be at home with his family, living an ordinary life, going to work in the mornings, coming home at night.

He gazed out over the broad expanse of dark green water and thought about it. The sameness. The predictability. The same walls round him every day. He thought of the suffocation he'd felt during those last few weeks at Collingwood, the rising excitement as he'd travelled to Plymouth to join a real ship again. He'd missed Clare and the children horribly, of course he had, but then they'd all moved to Tavistock and he had the best of both worlds. What would it feel like to know that he was never going back to sea again, that his life was going to be the same every day, till he was old, till he retired?

It was going to be like that one day, he knew. He'd have to leave the Andrew eventually. But maybe not yet. And if he did decide to stay in, he might as well have a bit of scrambled egg on his cap.

Martyn sighed and shook his head. No. Clare needed him at home. Dammit, he *wanted* to be at home.

By the time Iris and Bill came on their first visit, Clare felt she had settled in at Dale View. She had developed a routine – washing and housework in the mornings, sketching or painting in the afternoons while the children slept, then a walk or visit to Sue or Veronica. On Friday mornings she pushed the big pram down to Tavistock and shopped in the pannier market. Most of the groceries were delivered: a man from Underwoods in Tavistock came to the house on Monday mornings to collect the printed list that Clare had filled in, and the box of groceries arrived on Tuesday. Monday mornings were always an event for Christopher, who liked Mr Williams and was allowed to stick two weekly stamps into the Christmas club book.

She had also acquired two kittens, a ball of marmalade fur with big orange eyes, whom she named Bartholomew ('because he mews,' she explained to Christopher) and a coal-black female called Liquorice ('because she licks herself'). They chased each other all over the house and regularly found new hiding places in which to disappear, so that Christopher seemed to spend all his time hunting them and Laura yelled with frustration because she couldn't follow.

The weather was fine for the whole of Iris's and Bill's visit. Now that Bill was retired, they could stay as long as they liked, and they decided to make it three weeks. Being on holiday for that length of time was a strange experience for them, and Bill brought a few tools with him so that he could do some gardening and work about the house.

'Nothing but lave slabour, that's what I am,' he said, pruning away at the shrubs. 'This retirement lark's hard work – your mother's got me at it all the time, painting and papering, mending this, making that. And when I'm not slaving away round the house I'm over the allotment, growing vegetables for half the street.'

'Well, we can't eat all those things ourselves,' Iris said. 'Not now the family's all gone.' She sighed. 'The house seems proper empty now. Valerie comes over once a week same as ever, but with our Ian away and you down here I don't know how to fill my time up.'

'I bet you do,' Clare said, trying not to feel guilty. 'Look at all those clothes you brought for the children. They didn't make themselves. Anyway, you've done your stint, it's time you had a rest.'

'Rest!' Bill said, gathering together a pile of prunings. 'Chance would be a fine thing. I don't know how I ever had time to go to work.'

They slipped quickly into Clare's routine and went out for walks in the afternoon, and sometimes had a day out in Plymouth or Exeter, catching the little train at Whitchurch Halt or on the main line overlooking Tavistock. On Sunday afternoons, Bill walked up the lane to the Ring, where the Tavistock cricket club had their pitch and you could sit in the sunshine, watching the game and gazing out over the town. Clare and her mother took the children further, to the Pimple, a triangular building on a grassy knoll that covered a small reservoir. A seat ran round the little building and they could sit and gaze out as far as Cornwall in one direction and Princetown in the other, while Christopher clambered up the slope of the knoll and rolled to the bottom again. Clare took out her sketchpad and filled it with quick drawings of his round bottom sticking into the air, or his face peering backwards between his legs.

'You seem to have settled in all right,' Iris said after a while on one occasion.

'Yes. It was a bit lonely at first, but I'm making friends now, and I'm

joining the badminton club. Sue plays and she says it's a good club –
they go in for quite a lot of competitions.'

'Well, that'll be nice. I suppose you'll get a babysitter all right.'

'Oh, yes, there's a girl just across the lane. She's about sixteen and
she wants to earn a bit of money. I can't afford to have her more than
once a week, but it'll be so good to get out now and then without the
children.' Clare added a few lines to her sketch and stared at it critically.
'D'you think that looks like Chris?'

Iris took it from her. 'It's just like him. I don't know how you do it,
with just a few lines. I mean, it's not a portrait, exactly, it's just a sort of
a sketch, but anyone could see it's him.'

'I don't know. His nose isn't quite right . . .' Clare took it back and
sighed. 'I wish I'd had lessons in doing this. I'd join a class if there was
one, but all the art things seem to be on in the afternoons.'

'What do you want to do that for? You can draw already.'

'I'd like to be able to do it better, though,' Clare said restlessly. 'We
hardly learned anything at school. I'd like to know about different sorts
of paints, and about some of the really good artists. I got a book out of
the library last week, about oil painting. It looks really interesting, but
the paints and canvases are so expensive.'

'Well, maybe you'll be able to do it a bit later on, when Martyn's
money goes up a bit,' Iris said. 'You'd be better off doing a bit of sewing
or knitting while the children are little – save yourself some money.'

Clare pushed down a spasm of irritation. She hated sewing, and
although she didn't mind knitting she knew it could never give her the
satisfaction that drawing and painting would. However, she knew also
that her mother would never be able to understand this desire for a
'useless' hobby when she could be filling her time so much more
productively. 'People like us,' she would say, 'don't do that sort of
thing.' Clare had given up asking why not. It was just the way her
parents' generation thought. It was no use getting annoyed over it.

'Well, it's your fault I'm so keen on it,' she said with a smile. 'You
used to buy me all those sheets of paper to scribble on when I was little
and you wanted to keep me quiet while you sewed.'

They got up and strolled back down to the cricket pitch, where the
players were drawing their stumps and walking back to the little
pavilion. Bill wandered up to meet them, catching Christopher in his
arms to swing him round. Below the little plateau, the town of
Tavistock lay dreaming in the late afternoon sunlight, and beyond that
rose the hills of Cornwall and the shadowy outline of Bodmin moor.
Clare paused for a moment, feeling a spreading contentment as warm as

the sunset, and then thought of Martyn, far away at sea, and felt a cold stab of loneliness.

I want you at home, she thought, sending her thoughts across the skies to reach him. I want you here with me. I want us to be a *family*.

Kathy and Brian came in the summer too, when Brian had his leave. They drove down in the car and took Clare and Martyn and the children out to places they wouldn't normally be able to get to – to Dartmeet, to have tea at the Badger's Holt, or to walk along the twisting crevices of Lydford Gorge. Kathy looked happy, but there was a slight reserve at the back of her eyes and when Clare asked her if everything was all right, she shrugged the question aside.

'Of course it is. What could be wrong?'

'Do you ever hear anything of Terry these days?' Clare enquired one day as they sat on rugs in the garden, watching the children play and the kittens stalk butterflies. Kathy shook her head.

'Haven't seen him since before Brian and I got married. Whenever is Laura going to start walking? She'll wear out her knees at this rate.' She reached out and pulled the little girl to her, hugging and tickling her so that Laura squealed and roared with laughter.

Clare laughed. 'She is late, isn't she? She seems perfectly happy just crawling but I don't think she'll be long now. She's pulling herself up on the furniture.'

'Christopher's gorgeous,' Kathy remarked, watching him kicking the ball Brian had brought him. 'He's a real little boy now, isn't he? And his hair's a lovely colour. Real corn-gold.'

'It'll probably go darker as he gets older. Martyn's did. His mother showed me some photos of him as a little boy, and he was just as fair as Chris. It's funny that Laura's hair is so dark.'

'She takes after a different side of the family, I expect.' Kathy let Laura go and stretched herself. 'It's lovely to be here. I think your house is really nice.'

'It's not all smart and new like yours,' Clare said a little apologetically, but Kathy shook her head.

'It doesn't have to be. It's big and comfortable and it's got a friendly feel. I think it's a happy house. You can imagine families living here for years and years, all happy. Nobody's ever lived in ours before. It looks too new, somehow – it hasn't got any character, like yours has.'

Clare had thought that was what Kathy had liked about it. 'Well, it's up to you to give it some, then,' she said lightly. 'Fill it up with kids. That'll soon give it character.'

Kathy laughed, but there was a tiny edge to her laughter. 'What, and spoil all that lovely paintwork?'

'Don't you want any children?' Clare asked after a moment.

'Yes, of course I do, but not while Brian's going away so much. I just don't think it's fair.' She glanced at Clare. 'I saw the way you had to manage all by yourself that first year. I don't want to be left on my own like that, having the baby with no husband to be with me or be there when it's small. I don't think I could cope with it.'

'It's not so bad,' Clare protested, feeling defensive in spite of Kathy's words. 'It's what you have to expect if you marry a sailor.'

'No, it isn't. Not if he's going to come out of the Navy when he's thirty. We can wait till then and have a normal life. And we'll have more money too.'

Clare was silent. It was true that money had always been tight for Martyn and herself. The move to Devon had actually given them a few hundred pounds spare, but it had soon gone on beds for the children's rooms and a dining-table and chairs. There seemed to be no end to the things the children needed – winter coats, new shoes, socks, vests, gloves. Even though Iris made a good many things, the material still had to be bought, and she couldn't make shoes or wellington boots.

'Well, it's no good having a baby if you're not ready for it,' she said, knowing that despite all their difficulties she would still rather have the children than the extra money.

'Listen,' Kathy said, sitting up again, 'let's go out this afternoon. Let's go to a beach somewhere and build sandcastles. Where can we go?'

The subject had been changed again. Clare felt disappointed and slightly let down. She and Kathy had always shared so many confidences, and now there was a distance between them. Perhaps it was because they saw so much less of each other these days, but Clare didn't think it could really be that. No, there was something else wrong, something that was troubling her friend.

I wish she'd tell me, Clare thought, but if she doesn't want to, there's nothing I can do about it. I can't force her.

As she waved Kathy and Brian off a day or two later, she did so sadly, feeling that something more than a hundred miles or so had come between them.

Brian drove across the moor in silence for a few miles, then glanced sideways at Kathy and said casually, 'Well, did you enjoy that? Seeing Clare again – having a good old natter – sharing your girlish secrets?'

'Of course I enjoyed it,' Kathy said. 'Clare and I have always been good friends, you know that. It was lovely to see her and the children again.'

'Well, you certainly seemed to find plenty to talk about.'

'Yes, we usually do.'

There was a short pause, then he said, 'And the secrets?'

'I don't think Clare told me anything secret,' Kathy said, knowing that wasn't what he meant.

Brian's lips tightened. 'Come on, Kathy. Don't play games. I know you told her all about us. How badly I treat you – all that sort of thing. All women do when they're together, it's standard practice.'

'I didn't! I didn't say anything at all about us. Anyway, you don't treat me badly. I don't know what you mean.'

'You mean you never mentioned how I stay late at the mess on Saturdays? How I go to the pub two nights a week with my oppos? How I never wash up or walk round with the vacuum cleaner? How—?'

'Oh, stop it, Brian,' Kathy said wearily. 'Don't start another row. You know I don't expect you to do those things, not when you're hardly ever at home.'

'No, and that's the big complaint, isn't it? I'm away all the time, leaving you on your own. You never did like it, did you, and you don't like it any better now.' He slowed down to pass a huddle of sheep. 'You've got what you wanted – a smashing house and nice furniture – and you'd still rather be out enjoying yourself.'

'No! I do get lonely, all naval wives do, but that doesn't mean I want to be single again. I love you, Brian. I just miss you when you're away.' Her voice shook and she turned her head and stared out of the window. 'Would you rather I didn't?'

Brian said nothing for a minute or two, then he laid his hand on her knee and said, 'No. Of course I wouldn't. I'm sorry, Kath. It's just that sometimes, well, I get scared. Thinking about being away and – and what happened last time. Sometimes I wonder if you're still thinking about *him*. I wonder if you're seeing him again. Imagining I'm him.' He shrugged and laughed without amusement. 'Daft, I suppose.'

'Yes, it is,' Kathy said, turning swiftly back. 'It *is* daft, Brian. I've told you, time and time again, all that's *over*. I haven't seen Terry since before we were married. I don't want to see him. It was a big mistake and it's finished.' She laid her hand over his and squeezed his fingers. 'Don't keep thinking about it. Don't.'

He glanced sideways again and gave her a small grin. 'All right. If you say so.'

'I do say so. I do.'

Brian sighed and slid his hand out from under hers, laying it on the wheel. They were just running into Princetown, the grey moorland village which seemed to have been built solely because of the prison that lay to one side. Kathy glanced at it as they passed, imagining the men inside that grim barracks, perhaps staring hopelessly out of the windows at the car driving past with people who were free to go where they chose. What must it be like – to be trapped for years, perhaps the rest of your life?

They came out of Princetown and took the Moretonhampstead road. Once again, Brian drove in silence, and Kathy looked out of the window at the rolling moorland, wondering if he knew she hadn't been telling the truth. Because she did think about Terry, often. She thought of his gentleness, his tender touch, his care. She thought of the pain she had given him, and felt the bitter taste of regret.

Yet she could not truly say that she was sorry. As soon as she had seen Brian again, the first time when he'd come to the door when she was washing her hair, she'd known that the attraction was still there between them, powerful, overwhelming. She'd wanted to be held in his arms, she'd wanted him to love her. She'd wanted his loving to wipe away all her doubts, all her uncertainties.

It hadn't quite happened. Brian had the power to sweep her away, to storm all her defences, to lift her high on a wave of delight and excitement and desire. Yet when it was all over, when she lay beside him in bed, listening to his deep, satisfied breathing, she was aware of a small ache of something unfulfilled. Something that craved a gentler touch, a closer communion. And it was then that she thought of Terry.

There had been talk of Martyn and Clare going back to Gosport for Christmas, or of Iris and Bill coming to Devon, but in the end everyone had decided to stay in their own homes. With Martyn's leave so short, they were reluctant to leave Dale View, and it gave Martyn's parents the chance to come across and spend a few days with the family.

'They don't see much of the children, even though we're not all that far apart,' Clare wrote to her mother. 'The shop ties them down so much, and it's a difficult journey for me with two little ones.'

Getting to Ivybridge meant catching either the 'little' train at Whitchurch Halt, or going all the way across Tavistock for the mainline train, then changing at Plymouth. If you were only going to Plymouth, Whitchurch was ideal, being only ten minutes' walk away, but the trains were less frequent. Clare had used it a lot since coming to live at Dale View, and it made travelling to Plymouth much easier for Martyn, but to their dismay the line was soon to be closed, along with a huge number of other small branch lines all over the country.

'It's that Dr Beeching,' Clare said when she heard. 'He must have something against trains. Can't he see how useful they are? And it's such a lovely line too – it's so pretty, I'd go on it just for the ride.'

The Launceston to Plymouth line ran through beautiful countryside, along the side of Lydford Gorge, across the moor and beside the cascading river at Shaugh Prior where you could often see a heron standing at the water's edge. It ran over high viaducts and through tunnels. At one place it was single-track, and the engine-drivers could only proceed if they were in possession of a metal loop which they handed to each other at the next station. There was a friendly, family atmosphere which made it fun to use the line, and everyone was sorry it was going to be closed.

They all enjoyed Christmas. Laura was too young to remember her first and stared wide-eyed at all the decorations, the tree and the presents. She fastened on to the first one she opened, a soft furry panda made by Martyn's mother, and hugged it close, refusing to put it down or to open any of the other parcels. Christopher's favourite was a wooden train set which he could put together and play with by himself. He tried all kinds of different arrangements – circles, loops, elongated ovals – and when Clare put him to bed he insisted on taking it with him, stoutly denying that it was at all uncomfortable to share his mattress and pillow with an assortment of engines and carriages.

Clare gave Martyn a new watch and, to her amazement and delight, received a set of oil paints and a palette in return. She gazed at it with rapture, stroking the tubes tenderly.

'I'll paint you the most gorgeous picture you ever saw.'

'It'll have to be a self-portrait, then,' Martyn said, giving her a kiss. 'Just enjoy it. That's all I ask.'

The Perrys had to leave soon after Boxing Day to reopen the shop. The weather was bitter. There had been some snow just before Christmas and it had thawed and then frozen again so that the pavements were covered with hard masses of ice. Next morning snow began to fall again in earnest. They stood at the windows, staring out.

'It's a white-out,' Martyn said, awed. 'You can hardly see to the bottom of the garden.'

The view across the valley had disappeared in a thick, yellowy-grey curtain of falling snow. It swirled in the air, so that if you looked up all you could see were millions of black specks against the bruised and lowering sky. Already, the grass and paths of the garden had disappeared under an inch-deep blanket of white, and as the day wore on so the blanket grew thicker. By evening, it was ten inches deep and the wind was piling it up against the house.

'It's the last night for the railway line tonight,' Martyn said as they drew the curtains. 'They say the trains are going to be full of trainspotters, coming for the last ride.'

'It'll never get through. The lines will be blocked, surely.'

He shrugged. 'You know what these railway enthusiasts are like – the trains will be packed. They'll get out and pull if they have to.'

He had brought in plenty of fuel and banked up the Rayburn and the fire in the living-room. They turned out the lights and sat on the rug, wrapped in each other's arms and gazing into the flames. Outside, the wind howled and the snow rattled against the windows. The cats curled up beside them, oblivious to the weather.

'We'll be snowed up,' Clare said dreamily. 'I've never been snowed up before. I've always thought it would be rather romantic.'

'So it is,' he said, squeezing her against him. 'Just you and me and a log fire, surrounded by snow. By morning it'll be too deep to go out and nobody will be able to get to us. We can stay in bed all day and no one will know.'

'Except the children,' she said ruefully. 'You don't imagine they're going to let us get away with that, do you?'

'Well,' he said, nuzzling her neck, 'we've got quite a few hours before they wake up. We can be romantic for a while, can't we?'

'Mm.' She turned in his arms and reached up to kiss him. 'Oh, Martyn, it is lovely to be here together, just the two of us, all cosy and warm with the children safe upstairs. I wish it could be like this all the time.'

'It's like it now,' he said, and lay back on the rug, pulling her down with him. 'Forget about the rest, Clare. Just enjoy being here – with me.' His hands moved over her body, sliding underneath her jumper, touching her skin with cool tenderness. 'Let's pretend there's nowhere else in the world but this room, with you and me and the snow outside. Let's pretend this is for ever. It'll go on and on always, just the two of us together, being happy for the rest of eternity.' He drew her head down with both hands and kissed her on the lips. 'Let's make love, Clare, my darling Clare, let's make wonderful, wild, passionate love.'

Clare rolled on to her back and brought him with her so that he rested on his elbows above her, his face half in shadow, half lit by the dancing firelight. She gazed up at him and felt a tremor deep within.

'Oh, Martyn,' she whispered. 'Martyn, I love you so much. So very, very much.'

The wind had risen to a howl. They could almost feel the house shake as it buffeted the walls and snow rattled against the windows. As Martyn began again to caress her, Clare fancied she could hear the distant sound of a train's whistle passing along the railway below them, and she imagined the people on board. It must be like travelling through Russia, she thought. Like one of those books she had read, where people sat in carriages like guards' vans for thousands of miles as they crossed the vast, frozen wastes, wrapped in furs and boiling up samovars of tea in corners. When the train stopped at stations that seemed hundreds of miles from anywhere, they slid back the doors to find a sheet of ice encasing the carriage itself.

Then she forgot the train and its passengers, forgot the snow, forgot the wind, as the pulsing of her blood took over and the surge of desire swept her away in a storm of her and Martyn's own making, a storm that buffeted and tossed them as if on wild seas, and left them at last, exhausted and dizzy, before a fire that had almost died down and had left them in smouldering darkness.

When Clare woke in the morning from a dream of the Siberian winter, she wondered for a moment if it had been a dream at all. Martyn was standing at the window, and as Clare opened her eyes it appeared that he was outlined against a huge drift of solid and densely packed snow that pressed against the windows as if it reached to the roof. Outside, the howling of the wind sounded like wolves.

'How deep is it?'

Martyn turned, two mugs of tea steaming in his hands. 'Not up to the roof, at any rate. That's just where the snow's stuck to the windows. It's the same downstairs, you can't see a thing. But I've looked out of the back door and it's up to the windowsills – getting on for three feet. It looks fantastic.'

'Three feet deep!' Clare sat up, shivering, and pulled a cardigan round her shoulders. The bedroom was icy. 'We'll never be able to get out. How's the Rayburn?'

'Still alight. I've stoked it up, and it's nice and warm in the kitchen. I'll light the fire in the other room after breakfast and we'll keep the oil stove going upstairs.' He laughed. 'You should have seen the cats! They looked out of the door and their jaws just dropped. Liquorice couldn't get back by the Rayburn fast enough, but Barty started to tunnel his way through the snow like an escaping prisoner of war.'

'Poor things. They'll have to have a litter-tray if they can't go out,' Clare said, resting against him as he climbed back into bed. 'Thank goodness you're here. It would be awful to be here on my own in this weather. I wonder what happened to the train.'

'I shouldn't think it got back to Plymouth. The way it was snowing last night, they'd never have made it across those high viaducts. They'd have been blown off the top.'

They sat drinking their tea. It was still snowing hard, and even if the windows had been clear there would have been nothing to see. There was obviously no chance of going out, and there was little to do but bring in fuel for the fire and Rayburn, and make sure the house was snug.

'It's quite romantic really, isn't it?' Clare observed. 'We're lucky we didn't get any burst pipes. It was so cold last week, we could have had. Veronica told me that somebody she knew had water flooding all over the house during that thaw.'

'I don't reckon we ought to take any chances, all the same. If it freezes hard again we'll drain the system down every night, just in case.'

'Drain it down?' Clare repeated in dismay. 'You mean empty out the whole house?'

'That's right. It just means turning off the stopcock and running the water off the taps, that's all. It'll fill up in the morning as soon as we open it up again. Better than having burst pipes – we'd have to turn it off then, anyway, and we'd have it draining itself down all over the house instead, like Veronica's friend.'

Clare made a face. Being snowed up began to seem a little less romantic.

As the house grew warmer, the snow melted from the windows and they could see out again. The blizzard had eased slightly and although it was still not possible to see across the valley, they could see as far as the end of the garden. As Martyn had said, the snow was level with the windowsills all around the house, and the gate was marked only by a row of green tips along the top of the snow. All the hedges were capped by towering eiderdowns and the roofs of neighbouring houses were thatched with white. The silence was almost overpowering.

'I've never seen anything like this,' Clare whispered in awe. 'Well, I remember the winter of nineteen forty-seven, of course, there was a huge snowfall then, but it wasn't quite the same in Gosport. You couldn't see it in the same way, not in the streets.'

'I remember that too, but we didn't get it as bad in Ivybridge.' Martyn grinned. 'Mum was right about that! I'd better give her a ring in a minute or she'll be imagining us buried alive in an avalanche.'

After breakfast, he went out to dig a path through to the coalhouse. The snow was piled up against the back door and a great lump fell in as they opened it. Convulsed with giggles, Clare pushed it out again and Martyn floundered through to the shed.

'We ought to have brought a spade in last night. This coal shovel's useless. Shut the door again quick, Clare, it's still blowing a hooley out here.'

The snow swirled in as she slammed the door behind him, and she came back into the kitchen where the children were sitting on a rug in front of the Rayburn. They looked up at her and Christopher said, 'When will it stop snowing, Mummy?'

'I don't know. Soon, I expect, or it'll be up to the chimneys.'

'Can we build a snowman then?'

Clare laughed. 'He'll have to be a giant! But I expect we will. With one of Daddy's caps on?'

Christopher giggled. 'A snow sailor!'

'That's right. We could make him a snowship as well. But we can't go out in it yet, it's still snowing too hard. And there's lots to do to keep the house warm, so you be a good boy and play with Laura while I get the breakfast things cleared away.'

It continued to snow all that day and again into the night. When they woke next morning, it had stopped and the sky was lighter. They gazed out again, fascinated.

'I've just *got* to go for a walk,' Clare said later. 'I want to see what it's like up on the moor.'

'I don't think you'll be able to take the children,' Martyn said doubtfully. 'It'd be over Christopher's head.'

'I wouldn't even try. You don't mind looking after them for an hour, do you? You can go when I come back.'

She pulled on an extra sweater and her gloves, scarf and boots, and then set off up the lane. It was harder work than she'd expected, tramping through the snow. It was almost thigh deep, and she had to lift each foot high above the surface and then plonk it down in front of her before lifting the other one. I shan't get far in this, she thought, swinging her arms to keep her balance, and she wondered how the sheep and the ponies were getting on. She had heard that sheep clustered together in the lee of a wall or hedge and let the snow form a steamy igloo around them, but the poor ponies could do nothing but stand there, in whatever meagre shelter they could find, and let it pile up around them.

Just above the house, the lane was blocked by an enormous snowdrift. Clare tried to push her way through it but gave up and followed the footsteps of some previous pioneer who had managed to make a narrow passage at one side. She stayed in their tracks to the gate, where the snow seemed to have been piled less deeply, and climbed over and on to Whitchurch Down.

The scene was more like the wastes of Siberia than the green, rolling moorland she had become accustomed to. She stayed on top of the gate for a few moments, gazing out across the endless stretches of white. The sky was clearing now and she could see as far as the little hilltop church of Brentor, like a miniature volcano in the distance. Everything was clad in the same thick blanket of white.

'Quite fantastic, isn't it?'

Clare jumped and turned, startled. Alex Challoner was standing on top of the snow, about two yards away, watching her with a grin on his thin, dark face.

'Oh, I didn't see you there.' She smiled at him. 'Yes, it is. What are you standing on?'

'The snow. It's so hard, you can walk on top. Come on over.'

Clare stepped off the gate and moved forward gingerly, surprised to find that he was right. You could actually walk on top of the deep snow without your feet sinking in more than two or three inches. She looked at him and laughed. 'It's weird!'

'It is, rather. I'm not sure I'd want to strike out into the middle, but it seems to be all right close to the banks and hedges.' He stretched out a hand. 'Come on, if one of us sinks we'll save each other.'

'More likely sink together,' Clare giggled. She put her wool-clad hand into his, feeling the strength of his fingers. 'It's years and years since I saw snow like this, and I was only a little girl then.'

They struggled on together, hand in hand. Clare had expected to feel cold, but the walking was so strenuous that she soon found herself warm and glowing. They paused to look back to where Tavistock lay in the valley, its roofs a patchwork of white, the church towers shimmering as if they had been iced. There was no colour to be seen at all, only a dazzling white, broken by the stark outlines of winter trees or dark roofs from which the snow had been scoured clear by the wind. Hedges ruled black lines across the fields beyond the town, and even the distant hills of Cornwall and Bodmin Moor were white.

She turned to Alex and smiled, her face radiant with warmth and pleasure. 'Isn't this wonderful?'

His eyes dwelled on her face, darkening a little. 'Yes. It is. Wonderful.' For a moment, disconcerted by his terseness, she wondered if she had annoyed him. She tried to pull her hand away, as if she could not keep up with his longer strides, but he gripped her fingers more tightly and slowed down, smiling down at her, and she realised with a small shock just how warm he could look. Until now, she'd always thought him rather remote.

'Didn't Veronica want to come out in the snow?'

Alex smiled again. 'She was in the garden all morning, building a snowman with Andrew, but after lunch she said she was just going to stay by the fire with a book and a box of chocolates. I couldn't bear the thought of missing it all, so I came on my own. I'm glad I did. It's nice to have company, though.'

'Yes, it is,' Clare said on a note of discovery. 'Of course, I'm used to being on my own, so I don't think much about it. But you're right, it is more fun with someone else.'

He looked at her. 'Isn't Martyn home now?'

'Oh, yes, but we couldn't both come out because of the children. It's too cold and too deep for them. So we're taking turns. We do that a lot.'

'Don't you ever go out together?'

'When we can take the children too, otherwise we just stay at home. We only do things like going for walks on our own. I mean, we don't go to the pictures much, or the pub.'

'What about when he's away? How do you manage then?'

'Well, I just take the children for walks in the afternoons. Things like that. It'll be easier once Laura's walking, but even then we won't be able to go too far. It doesn't matter, though; we'll be able to do things when they're older, and we'll still be young enough to enjoy it.'

'Don't you miss being able to go out with your friends? Meeting them for lunch and that sort of thing? Or going shopping?'

'No, not really. I can see Sue and Veronica a couple of times a week, and I'm making other friends. Mostly, they've got children too, so they're in the same boat. I get a bit fed up sometimes, but who doesn't? I love living here and I love my kids, so what else matters?'

Alex stared at her. 'What indeed?'

They paused. Trudging along on the top of the hard-packed snow was easier than floundering through the softer parts, but it was still hard work and now the wind was rising again. Clare shivered and used her free hand to pull her scarf more closely around her neck.

'I thought I was warm, but now I'm not so sure. I think I'll go back, or it'll be too dark for Martyn to come out.'

Alex turned to walk back with her. They made their way to the gate in silence and he helped her over. 'So you bring the children up on the moor most days, do you?'

'When I'm not doing anything else. It's so lovely for them, they can run about and play just as they please. Next summer, I'm going to bring picnics and see if we can go a bit further. We'll be able to take the pushchair to give Laura a rest. It'll be fun.' She glanced at the wasteland around them and laughed. 'Not that it looks like it just at the moment!'

'Oh, summer will come again.' They tramped down the lane, retracing the tracks they had made coming up. 'I'm glad I met you, Clare. It was good, sharing the snow with you.'

She smiled at him. They were level with the back entrance to Dale View now and she paused, not quite certain what to say. She couldn't kiss him, and shaking hands would have been ridiculous, but somehow she felt that their parting ought to be marked in some way. In the end, she just smiled again and turned towards the house.

'Goodbye, Alex. Give my love to Veronica.'

'Thanks. And regards to Martyn.'

They both hesitated again, then Alex walked off down the lane, following the deep footprints he had made earlier. Clare stood for a moment watching him go and then went on into the house.

Martyn had lit the fire and made some tea. He was ensconced in the armchair and looked too comfortable to think of going out into the cold. In any case, he said, glancing out of the window, it was starting to get dark and looked as if the snow was going to begin again.

Clare poured herself a cup of tea and gave Laura and Christopher some milk. She quite forgot to mention that she'd met Alex on the moor.

Chapter Eighteen

The severe weather continued. After the first week, there was little more snow, but the temperatures dropped to well below freezing and stayed there. On some nights, the thermometer sank as low as minus eighteen degrees, and Clare and Martyn turned off the water and drained the system to prevent the pipes freezing. The snow froze into walls of solid ice, so that shifting it became a task for bulldozers rather than shovels, and in many country lanes the drifts seemed almost permanent and the houses behind them were cut off from all normal traffic.

Water falling over the weir below the bridge in Tavistock froze into a suspended arch of ice, and as more water ran over it, that too froze, so that the arch became gradually thicker and higher, forming a dam behind which the river began to rise. It came round the side, down the salmon leap instead, and council workmen kept it clear by breaking the ice. The canal through the Meadows froze solid and people skated on it, looking like figures from a Dutch painting. Snowmen appeared in gardens and stood there like sentinels, and up on the moors the snow lay in drifts so deep that old countrymen recalled the great blizzards of the past and prophesied that there would still be snow lying about in June.

Clare went out with her sketchbook whenever she could, and pinned her drawings up on the kitchen wall. The frozen weir, the skaters, the snowmen, Liquorice and Bartholomew going mad as they careered across the garden and, above all, Christopher and Laura bundled up like fat little cushions, staggering and laughing in the drifts. There was one in particular, her favourite, of Martyn and both the children building their own snowman in the garden, and she decided to try to make an oil painting of it one day, when she had more time.

'I'm so glad you're on leave,' she said as they came in from the garden, stamping the snow from their boots and stripping off wet gloves and scarves. 'It's lovely to have this time together. Let's get snowed up every winter.'

'I'll see what I can do,' he promised, kneeling down to help Laura with her boots. 'I can't think of anything better myself. Though I don't think every winter's like this one, even on Dartmoor.'

The television news showed pictures every day of the blocked roads and frozen fields, for the weather was the same over all the country, but most interest was centred on Dartmoor and the bitterly cold weather endured by the sheep and ponies which had been caught by the snowstorms on the moor. Many had been brought lower down, but nobody had expected such severity and there were animals which could not be reached by any way except air, and helicopters were used to drop feed to them. Clare watched the pictures of ponies gathering as the helicopters hovered overhead and wondered if they would survive.

Out in the garden, the birds flocked in search of food. Clare threw out all the scraps and bought seed to scatter, yet still she found dead birds on the ground every day. Redwings, which in normal winters were shy, came right to the back door and she found their bodies in the morning, huddled against the wall. Finches, redpolls and bramblings came to the table she had made from a few bits of wood balanced on a couple of logs, and several times she saw woodpeckers there too. The air was like ice, freezing your lungs as you breathed it.

After the Christmas leave was over, Martyn went away again, leaving Clare to cope alone. Thank goodness, she thought, the house seemed to be secure against the weather. The children spent the morning in the warm kitchen while Clare did her work about the house. It was too cold for the children to play outside, and when she had to go to town, Clare wrapped them both up warmly and took them down to spend the afternoon with Sue. Laura could not yet walk as far as Tavistock and it was too cold either to keep her in the pushchair or make Christopher walk beside the big pram. Their only other outings during those bitter weeks were to Veronica or one or two other women Clare had become friendly with, and she thanked her stars that she had made friends with people who lived so near.

Before darkness fell, she would clear out the Rayburn's ashes, and bring in enough coal and coke to last them until next day, and then the curtains would be drawn against the bitter cold.

Upstairs, she kept an oil stove burning on the landing, to keep the chill off the bedrooms, but it could never be said to be warm, and all the beds were filled with hot-water bottles before anyone dared get into them. The children wore thick pyjamas made by Iris, and Clare wrapped herself in socks, a sweater and a woolly hat. She wrote to Martyn that she put on more clothes to go to bed than she did to go outside.

'You wouldn't be interested in going to bed with me now!' she wrote wryly, but he replied that he would, he missed her more than anything in the world, and he'd rather go to bed with her in a suit of armour than have to sleep alone as he was doing now. The ship had crossed the Bay of Biscay and was now in the warmer waters of the Mediterranean but he'd rather be snowed up at home than basking in the sunshine.

While he'd been at home, Martyn had pushed thoughts of promotion out of his mind. The Christmas leave had been so full, with Christmas itself and the visit from his parents, and then the snow, that there'd hardly been time to think of anything else. However, once they were at sea Lieutenant Jeffreys had raised the subject again, and although Martyn shook his head and said he wasn't interested, he couldn't entirely dismiss the idea.

'I thought it was what you'd intended,' 'Judge' said. 'Didn't you once say you'd have liked to go to Dartmouth? You've obviously considered becoming an officer.'

'I was just a kid then. I didn't know what was involved.'

Judge shot him an amused look. 'What do you mean? It's just like the job you're doing now, only with a bit more responsibility, more pay and a bit more comfort in the wardroom.'

'And more time in the Navy,' Martyn said.

'Look, you could stay in just as long as a CPO. Why not take advantage of it? I wouldn't be saying this to you, Perry, if I didn't think you had it in you. I'm not on a recruiting drive.'

'No, sir, I know. I'm sorry – I appreciate the fact that you're taking an interest, but, well, I don't know. I'd just like more time to think about it.'

He went up on deck and stood for a long time watching the sea. It was blue and calm and the bow wave frothed gently along the ship's side. There was nothing quite like being at sea, he thought, and he'd miss it desperately if he left the Navy. He'd miss the freedom, the life amongst the other men, the sense of being your own person. He'd miss swinging off ashore in a strange port, exploring the streets, listening to the foreign voices. He'd miss the *space*.

But he missed being at home too. He missed Clare and the children. He didn't much miss the journey into Plymouth and back home on the train, and it would be even worse now that the branch line had closed and he'd have to go all the way across the town, or catch the bus. Neither did he miss all the things that needed to be done at home – the garden, the repairs and mending, the decorating Clare thought was necessary – but he did miss the warmth of being there, of having meals cooked especially for him, of having a big, comfortable bed to go to with his wife beside him.

I don't know what to do, he thought, watching the small blue waves break against the steel hull. I don't know how to decide.

Only a few people struggled up the lane to visit Clare during those bitter months. Sue brought Andrew once or twice a week, and either stayed for a cup of tea or took the opportunity to go to Tavistock to do her own shopping. Veronica stamped cheerfully up through the snow dressed in a jacket, made from a deep golden fur, that could never have been bought out of Alex's salary, and once or twice she and Alex came to spend an evening playing Scrabble by the fire.

'You must get so *tired* of it,' Veronica said, shaking the bag in the hope of finding a blank tile. 'Being here all by yourself so much. You must feel totally hemmed in. Like a *prisoner*.'

'Not really,' Clare said, smiling. 'I think it's all rather exciting. It's so lovely to look at, for one thing, and when the wind blows and changes all the drifts it's as if a sculptor had been out there, carving out the shapes. Of course, it's all right for me to say that, I don't have to work outside – I feel sorry for people who do, but I still can't help enjoying it myself!'

Veronica wrinkled her nose. 'Well, I'm fed up with it myself. I mean, you can't *go* anywhere or *do* anything. It's weeks since I've been able to see some of my friends. The roads are still too bad to go to Dartmouth, and we can't get across the moor to see Mummy and Daddy. At least, *Alex* says we can't.' She cast her husband a reproachful glance. 'I think we could *try*.'

'We'll be able to go soon enough,' he said, as if this was an argument they'd had many times, and one which Veronica didn't even expect to win. 'The snow won't last for ever.'

'Well, it seems like it,' she muttered, but Clare could see they were just repeating the words for form's sake. They weren't really arguing.

She sighed, envying them their companionship and wishing Martyn could be here so that she too could enjoy this easy, loving friendship. That's what marriage really is, what it should be, she thought – a loving friendship, only deeper and more loving than any other friendship. And with Martyn away so much, we're wasting so much time, so much *life*. She frowned at the letters on her board and suddenly saw where she could place a word.

'*Quiet*,' she said. 'That's seventy-two for the triple word score and another five for turning *one* into *tone*.'

'Oh, that's *disgusting*,' Veronica said bitterly. 'I shall never catch up with you now.'

Alex clicked his letters back and forth, his eyes narrowed in concentration. 'Have you been able to go walking on the moor much, Clare?' he asked, gathering up a handful.

Clare watched, wondering what he was going to do. She was beginning to know that look of secret delight on his dark face. It meant he was going to claim a huge score. She shook her head. 'I can't get up there much because of the children. It's too cold for them to go far. We go up for a quick walk most days, but I don't go any further.'

'Oh, you should. It'll all be gone soon and you'll have missed it.' He looked at her, still holding the tiles. 'Why don't I babysit for you tomorrow afternoon, and you and Ronnie go for a good tramp? It'd do her good to get out as well, she spends far too much time in front of the fire.'

'And that's where I mean to stay, thanks very much,' Veronica retorted. 'If anyone's going to go for a tramp in the snow with Clare, it'll be you, Alex. *I'll* do the babysitting.'

'All right,' he said, putting down his tiles. 'I will. I'll take Clare for a good long walk and you can look after the kids and have tea ready for us when we come back. All right?' He set his tiles out and sat back, triumphantly pleased. 'And how about that? *Disquieting*. Sixty-six points.'

'Oh, for heaven's *sake*!' Veronica exclaimed in mock exasperation. 'It's just not *fair*.'

'It's fair enough,' Clare said, laughing. But there was a tremor of unease beneath her laughter.

Fair, it certainly was. But it was also unnervingly appropriate.

'It's how I imagine Siberia,' Clare said, pausing at the top of the Pimple. 'All white, with patches of dark grey and black. No colour at all.'

Alex glanced at her bright red jacket. 'You're the colour. A spot of brightness in the black and white. I bet you can be seen for miles.'

Clare laughed. 'Useful if we get lost.' She drew in a deep breath. 'Oh, it's so good to be out like this. I sometimes feel I'm chained to the kids – much as I love them,' she added hastily. 'It's just that I can never go anywhere without them, so I can only go to places they can go. Things like long walks are right out – for years, I suppose.'

'I never thought of it like that,' Alex said thoughtfully. 'It really is hard for someone like you, isn't it? Without anyone else to help out.'

'Well, it can be, but it's not that bad. I mean, when you think of someone with a handicapped child, for instance. At least I know my kids are going to grow up strong enough to walk and run and play games. And meanwhile, we do other things. All the same, it's lovely to be able to just walk away and leave them for a few hours and do what *I* want to do.'

'I'm glad you wanted to do this,' Alex said quietly. He turned away and began to descend the short, steep bank of the Pimple. 'It's good for me too, to have some company. Ronnie's not much of a one for walking.'

Clare followed him, uncertain of what to say. She believed that Alex and Veronica were happy together, but once or twice she had detected a slight undercurrent, so tenuous that she wasn't sure it really existed. She didn't want to encourage Alex to look on her as a confidante.

'How far d'you want to go?' she asked. 'Shall we walk over to Pennycomequick and then back along the stream?'

'Sounds good.' They set off in the direction of the valley between Whitchurch Down and the Princetown road. To their left, the tumbled granite rocks of Cox Tor made a rugged silhouette against the pale afternoon sky and straight ahead the television mast at North Hessary Tor rose like a beacon. The cricket ring was deserted, except for a few ponies looking for the hay that was left for them each day during this bitter weather, but there were a few hardy golfers on the tees near the end of Down Road.

'You'd think they'd be frozen,' Clare said, and Alex smiled.

'They're a tough breed. Ronnie's father plays, and he's out almost every day, unless it's actually blowing a hurricane with rain and snow to match. Luckily, the wind seems to have scoured most of the snow off the course and piled it neatly in the bunkers.'

Clare giggled. 'It must be difficult when they hit a ball into one. They wouldn't even be able to see it against the snow.'

'It concentrates the mind,' he said solemnly. 'Improves their game no end.'

They walked on in companionable silence. I must savour every moment of this, Clare thought. It's a treat, being out with someone like this, striding out at my own pace, knowing the children are all right at home, feeling easy and comfortable, not having to make conversation, knowing it will just come naturally . . . Knowing it will have to come to an end.

She was wearing an old pair of fur boots, soft as a pair of slippers, and thick socks. Her skirt wrapped around her like a blanket and her red jacket, made by her mother, was buttoned to the neck. With her hands encased in mittens she had knitted during those long evenings by the fire, she was as warm as toast and ready to walk for miles.

Alex, still slightly ahead, turned to look at her and almost stopped, transfixed by the look on her face. He stared, his gaze caught as if by an invisible thread, and Clare, meeting his eyes, opened her mouth to ask him what was the matter.

She could not speak. There was something almost palpable in his expression, something that took the words from her mouth before they were formed and stilled them on her lips. She felt the pierce of it in her heart, and the heat of it spread through her body and into her limbs.

'Alex?'

'I'm sorry,' he said in a rush. 'I'm sorry, Clare. I didn't mean to stare, it's just that you look so – so perfect, somehow, standing there in the snow in that bright red coat with the sun behind you and the sky like a backdrop. Like a painting. That's what I'd like to do – paint you. If I were a painter,' he added, and grinned suddenly. 'I'm talking rubbish, aren't I? You're the artist – I can't draw a straight line.'

Clare looked down at her jacket. 'It's this colour. It makes me look like a robin!'

Alex laughed, as if released from an unexpected tension. 'You'd make a wonderful Christmas card.'

'Well, and why not? I can't think of anything better than being propped up on thousands of people's mantelpieces all over Christmas.' She smiled at him and he put out his hand.

'Come on. Let's get moving again – we'll freeze if we stand here too long, nattering about robins and Christmas cards. Let's see how fast we can walk to Pennycomequick.' He took her hand and tucked it into his arm. 'Veronica's brought crumpets for tea. I'm looking forward to them already.'

'Crumpets! So am I.' Clare felt the warmth of his arm, holding her hand firmly against his body. He kept her close as they walked quickly down the slope of the moor and into the little valley, where snow lay piled in huge, billowing drifts and icicles glittered in the half-frozen stream, tinkling together like chimes of crystal bells as the water flowed between chunks and floes of broken ice.

'It's like sculpture,' Clare said, kneeling on the bank to gaze in fascination at the smoothly moulded curves and the jagged spikes. 'Ice sculpture. Or diamonds, flashing in the sunlight. I don't think I've ever seen anything so beautiful.'

'Neither have I,' Alex said quietly, but when she glanced up at him he shifted his gaze quickly from her face to the ice. 'It's unforgettable.'

'We should have brought a camera. We'll never see it quite like this again. And I'd love to get it on to canvas.' She scrambled to her feet. 'Oh, Alex, I'm so glad we came. I just haven't had a chance to get out like this. I'd have hated to miss it.'

'Me too.' There was something strange in his tone, a remoteness that she couldn't understand. She took a swift look at his face and then tucked her hand into his arm once more.

'You must wish Veronica would come out for walks like this. I wish she would too. She's missing so much. But if she doesn't enjoy it, there's nothing to be done about it. It's just the way she is. You've got plenty of other things to enjoy together.'

'Yes,' he said, still looking at the ice, 'we have.'

'And if you ever want to come out for a walk again,' Clare said, squeezing his arm against her, 'you know just where to come.'

Alex removed his gaze from the ice and looked her full in the face. She felt again that strange tremor, and pushed it away. She thought, quickly and firmly, about Martyn.

'I may hold you to that,' Alex said.

The thaw came suddenly on a fine afternoon in March. Until then, the snow had been slowly and steadily growing thinner – 'sublimating off', Alex said – but the icy cold had prevented it from melting. Today, however, there was a sudden rise in temperature.

Clare, on her way to spend the afternoon with Sue, was just coming down the garden path, arguing with Christopher about whether he needed a scarf. 'I know it's not so cold today, but you could still get a cold. It isn't summer, not by a long way.'

'Spring,' Christopher said. 'It's spring.' He jumped up into the air. 'That's spring as well. Andrew told me.' He paused and frowned. 'Andrew's mummy doesn't make him wear a scarf.'

'Andrew's got a nice warm duffel-coat.' Clare became aware of a rushing sound, like water overflowing, and looked back towards the house. 'Have we left a tap running somewhere?'

Christopher shook his head. 'It's a river.'

'Don't be silly. You know there's no river here.' She hesitated, frowning, but the sound didn't seem to be coming from the house. 'It's in the lane. I wonder if a main's burst.' She hurried down the path and out into the short driveway that led from the lane to the gate of Dale View. As the children caught up with her, she put out her hands to stop them going further.

'It *is* a river!' Christopher cried, enraptured. 'Mummy, we've got our own river! We'll have to get a boat. Oh, *look* at it! Will there be fishes in it? Will we be able to *catch* fishes?'

'Of course we won't.' Clare stared at the water, as fascinated by it as he was. It filled the lane, at least six inches deep, thundering down the steep slope like a cataract. All the snow must have melted at once, she thought, and was running off the moor in all directions, taking the easiest routes – which were, in most cases, the straight, narrow lanes which led like the spokes of a wheel up to the hub of Whitchurch Down. It wouldn't stop until it reached the Tavy, far below in the valley, and swooped down to join the Tamar and so out to sea.

There was clearly no question of going anywhere until the water had subsided, and Clare went to fetch a ball, so that the children could at least have a game and some exercise in the fresh air. They stayed outside, listening to the rush of water for half an hour or so, and then went to investigate again.

'It's gone,' Christopher said, disappointed. 'Our river's gone.'

'And so has all the snow,' Clare said, gazing across Crowndale. 'Look, Chris, all the white's disappeared and you can see the green again. Well, the brown anyway. And soon it'll be all green again. Spring's coming,' she added, feeling a sudden lightheartedness. 'And do you know what's going to happen then?'

Christopher stared at her. Then his face broke into a wreath of smiles. 'Daddy's coming home!' he shouted. 'Daddy! *Daddy!*'

And Laura, scarcely knowing why, laughed and clapped her hands and joined in too.

'Daddy! Daddy! *Daddy* . . .'

Chapter Nineteen

K athy had been unable to visit Clare during the bitter winter of 1963. Although she had passed her driving test, she didn't feel confident enough to make the journey from Fareham to Tavistock alone, and Brian was once more away at sea. Instead, she fell back into her old routine of going to work at the office each morning, doing what housework was necessary in the evenings or at weekends, and spending the rest of her spare time watching television or writing to Brian.

There seemed to be an awful lot of spare time these days, though, she thought as she walked alone along the beach at Stokes Bay. And the winter had seemed dreadfully long, with all the snow and ice making the roads treacherous, so that often she dared not take the car out and caught the bus to work instead. She hadn't been able to drive down to her parents' house then either, and the bus journey from Fareham to their part of Gosport was too difficult to make in the evenings. TV and the radio had helped, but she'd felt very lonely in the tidy lounge with no one to share the pale, oatmeal-coloured three-piece suite.

I'd forgotten how lonely it was when Brian was away, she thought, remembering the long months when she had started to go to the community centre to try to pass the time. She couldn't do that now. There was a centre in Fareham, but she didn't feel like joining it. It was different when you were married. And she dared not go to the Gosport one, in case she met Terry.

Terry. Kathy stopped and stared across the cold water of the Solent towards the Isle of Wight. She'd told Clare the truth when she'd said she'd heard nothing of him, but that didn't mean he was out of her thoughts. Indeed, she was guiltily aware that he was all too often in them. She couldn't help wondering how he was, whether he'd found someone else, whether he was still living at home. Whether he was happy.

I'm sorry, Terry, she thought, thrusting her hands deep into her pockets. I never wanted to hurt you, but I didn't want to hurt Brian either. I didn't want to hurt anyone. It's as though it all got just too much for me.

She dared not think too much like that, dared not let her mind dwell on Terry, on what might have been. You're married to Brian now, she told herself sternly. You love him. You're lonely because you miss him, and *that's all there is to it.*

Once this long, cold winter was over, once Brian was back again and could take her in his arms and kiss away her depression, all would be well again.

'You're looking really peaky these days,' said one of the girls at work. 'Come down the pub with us on Friday evening. We have a lot of laughs.' Kathy shook her head. Brian wouldn't like her going to pubs, and she knew she would only feel all the more lonely, seeing the others all in couples and then having to go home alone. Besides, it was just too cold, and once she got home she was too tired to think about changing and going out again.

She knew no other young naval wives. On the estate where she and Brian had bought their house, there were no other naval couples at all. They were all busy young working couples, newly married like herself and Brian, going out to work early each morning, and coming home to spend the evenings together, decorating their homes, watching TV, going out to spend the evening in a pub or at the cinema.

Sometimes Kathy saw them going to each other's houses to admire the latest decorations or look at holiday slides or ciné. They always went in couples, though, and although they were all friendly enough when she encountered them in the street, they never invited her.

'You'll have to come round and see us when your husband comes home,' one or two had said, and Kathy had made up her mind that she wouldn't be dragged into their houses even in chains. If I'm not good enough on my own, she thought, I don't want to go at all.

The snow had vanished and the ice that had fringed the edge of the sea had melted away. Kathy had driven out to the bay and parked the car near the sailing club at the end of Jellicoe Avenue. She strode along, drawing fresh air deep into her lungs like a tonic. It wasn't really warm yet, but it certainly felt better than those months of cold, and the sun's rays touched her cheeks like a caress. Go on like this, she thought, and there'll be people in the sea, swimming.

'Kathy.'

The voice stopped her in her tracks. She'd been walking so fast, and so absorbed in her thoughts and in looking at the sea, that she hadn't noticed anyone walking towards her along the concrete strip at the head of the beach. Now, her heart thumping suddenly at the memory of a voice she'd once known so well, she found herself staring into a face she had not seen for nearly two years.

'*Terry!*'

'I didn't think it could be you at first. I didn't know whether to say anything or not.' He had stopped and she stopped too, so that they stood facing each other awkwardly. 'You haven't changed at all.'

Kathy felt her face flush. 'Is that a compliment or a criticism?' she said with an embarrassed laugh. 'Should I have grown taller, or something?'

He shook his head. 'No. You shouldn't have done anything.' There was a small pause, then he added quietly, 'I didn't want you to change at all, ever.'

Kathy's flush deepened and she bit her lip. 'Terry . . .'

'It's all right. I'm not going to say anything else.' His glance fell to her left hand, still buried in her coat pocket. 'I know you're a married woman now, but that doesn't mean we can't talk to each other.'

'No. No, I suppose it doesn't.'

There was another short silence. Kathy looked at her feet. She wanted to walk on, but didn't know how to say goodbye.

'You're all right, are you, Kath? Keeping well?' He hesitated, and went on in a voice that sounded as if he'd swallowed something, 'You're . . . happy?'

'Yes. Oh, yes.' Kathy's voice sounded too quick, too positive. 'Yes, I'm fine. And you?'

Immediately, she wished she hadn't asked. He shrugged. 'I'm okay. Bit fed-up with things at home. You know.'

She welcomed the exasperation his words brought, and her voice was sharp when she said, 'Well, you know what to do about that. Move out. Get somewhere of your own.'

Terry looked obstinate. 'I've told you—'

'And I've told you, I think you're daft,' she interrupted. She never had told him that, in fact, but she had nothing to lose now. He wasn't going to be hurt by anything she said, and she wasn't in a mood to mince her words. 'What's the point of wasting your life, living in a place

215

you don't want to be, with people you don't want to be with? You're cutting off your nose to spite your face. And what about your mum? Doesn't she warrant a bit of consideration? What d'you think it's like for her, having to look at your long face every day?'

Terry opened his mouth and then closed it again.

Kathy started to walk, quickly and crossly, and he fell in beside her. It didn't occur to her to tell him not to. They walked side by side, arguing as they'd never argued when they were together.

'It's my home too. I pay my keep.'

'That doesn't make it yours. You'd pay your keep in digs but it wouldn't mean the house was yours. D'you pay towards the wallpaper when they do a bit of decorating? D'you chip in with some hard cash when the roof needs repairs or the walls have to be repointed?' Both of these jobs needed doing at her parents' home and Kathy had heard a lot about the expense involved. And owning a house of her own had made her more aware, too. 'Well, do you?'

'I painted the front door only last week.'

'And who paid for the paint?'

Terry stopped. 'Look here, Kath, who gave you the right to harangue me like this? All I said was—'

'It was what you said that gave me the right,' Kathy said, facing him. 'Saying anything at all gave me the right. You can't expect to moan at people, especially when you've been moaning for years, and not get answered back once in a while. Maybe I should have done it a long time ago.'

'Maybe you should.' He was as angry as she. 'Maybe if you'd just said the right word at the right moment, I *would* have moved out. And we would have been together now, you and me, living in *our* own home.'

Kathy felt her anger drain away, as if it was running out of the soles of her shoes and into the hard concrete. She stared at him and felt a sudden wash of sadness. He looked thin and unhappy, his eyes set in dark hollows. Surely he couldn't still be carrying a torch for her. Surely there'd been another girl, or girls, in the past two years.

'Oh, Terry,' she said. 'I'm sorry. You're right. It isn't anything to do with me. It's your life.'

'But it could have been yours too,' he said doggedly, as if unwilling to let it go. 'It could have been everything to do with you.'

Kathy sighed and tried to find the right words. Gently, she said, 'Terry, that's all over. Whatever happened between us, it's almost two years ago now, it's in the past. You've got to forget about it and go on living.'

'Got to?' he said. 'Got to?' The dark intensity of his eyes disturbed her. 'Kathy, nobody can tell me what I've *got* to do about my own feelings.'

She looked away from him, towards the sea. 'No, I suppose not.'

He went on, quickly, a new eagerness in his tone. 'Kath, there's not a day goes by when I don't think about you and wish it had never happened. There's not a night when I don't lie awake, missing you, wishing we could be together. I wanted you so much, Kath. I *loved* you so much.' And, in a lower voice, so low that she barely heard it above the whisper of the waves, 'I still do.'

'Terry, you mustn't—'

'There you go again,' he said. 'Look, Kath, you can do what you like, you can make a bloke fall in love with you, you can make him think you love him back, you can go off and marry someone else, you can mess up as many lives as you like – but you can't tell anyone what they've *got* to feel or *mustn't* feel. I'm sorry, Kath, but you just can't.'

Kathy drew in a quick breath. After a moment, she said, 'No, I suppose I can't. I just wanted to help. I don't like seeing you unhappy. It makes me feel unhappy too.'

'Oh, in that case, I'll try to stop,' he said in a light, bitter tone. 'Can't have you feeling unhappy, can we?'

Kathy turned away. 'I think I'd better go on by myself. We shouldn't have started talking.'

'*Shouldn't*,' he said experimentally, as if he hadn't heard the word before. 'Sounds a bit like *got to* and *must*, doesn't it?'

'Oh, for goodness' sake!' she exclaimed, whipping back to face him. 'You know what your trouble is, Terry? You're just sorry for yourself! You're just wallowing in self-pity, that's what you're doing. Don't like living at home but won't move out. Can't get over me and won't try. You wouldn't know what to do if you didn't have things to feel miserable about, would you? You wouldn't know what to think about.'

He looked at her and then moved away in his turn, staring out towards the Island. It was very clear on this fresh, blue day. The bare trees stood out sharply against the skyline and the church spires pointed jabbing fingers towards the sky. A few early sailors had taken their dinghies down the beach and launched them, and their sails filled and bellied with the breeze like white wings, driving the little boats through the water.

'You make me sound a real moaner,' he said at last.

'Well,' Kathy answered, 'I'm sorry, Terry, but I'm afraid that's just what you are.'

217

They might have parted then, on a note of bitterness, but instead they fell quite naturally into step and walked on together without speaking. Terry seemed deep in thought and Kathy, feeling some regret for her harshness, was reluctant to hurt him any further. It doesn't hurt me to walk beside him, she thought, and there'd be no reason for Brian to feel jealous any more.

'Are you still living in Fareham?' he asked at last, and she nodded.

'We bought a house on the new Barratt estate. It's nice.'

'How did you get out to the bay, then? On the bus?'

She shook her head. 'We've got a car. I passed my test last October.'

He gave her an admiring glance. 'Good for you.' A slight pause. 'I bought a car too. After – after a while. It makes things easier.'

'Yes, it does. I haven't driven it much during the winter, though. I didn't like the ice.'

Their conversation was polite, almost stilted, and she tried to think of something to say that would sound more natural. 'Do you still go to the community centre?'

'Sometimes. Not much. Getting too old, I suppose.' His mouth twisted a little wryly. 'Most of the people there are younger than me. I feel a bit out of it.'

Terry, you were always out of it, she thought sadly. Shy, diffident, unable to let go with jokes and laughter; too awkward for dancing strict tempo and too self-conscious to let himself go in rock 'n' roll or the Twist. But it had been that shy quietness which had attracted her. He'd been so different from Brian . . .

'Maybe you ought to find something else.'

'Someone else,' he said. 'That's what I need. But it never seems to happen. And now I suppose you'll say I'm wallowing in self-pity again.'

Kathy stopped. 'Terry, I'm sorry I said that. It was unkind. It was cruel.'

'It wasn't. It was true. It's just what I have been doing. All this time, I haven't even tried to forget you, I've thought about you deliberately, I've *made* myself think about you. I've gone to all the places we used to go to, done all the things we did . . . Maybe I kidded myself it was a way of getting over you, but it wasn't. It was like a drug and I couldn't give it up. I couldn't give *you* up. I *wouldn't* give you up.' He stood before her, his face grave, and held out his hand. 'Let's start again, shall we? Oh, not that way –' as she began to protest '– but as friends. At least, let's part friends, and then maybe I'll be able to start again and live my own life. How about it?'

Hesitantly, not quite sure of his words, Kathy drew her hand out of her pocket and put it into his. It seemed little enough to do. If he'd really been so unhappy, even if she'd been right and he had been overcome by self-pity, it was still partly her fault. She had led him on, she had let him fall in love with her, she had left him. If she hadn't done those things, he wouldn't be standing here now, asking – *begging* – her to release him.

His hand felt cold in hers, but the shape of his fingers and the curve of his palm were unexpectedly familiar. She felt a small tremor and wondered if he felt it too. For a moment, she was alarmed, then she reassured herself. It was only natural that she would feel something, touching his hand for the first time in a year.

'I honestly think you ought to move out,' she said, letting her fingers rest in his. 'You'll feel better away from all that. Get a flat. Or a house. It'll give you something to do, buying furniture and redecorating and all that. You'll enjoy it.' And then, before she could stop herself, before she even knew she was going to say it, 'I'll help you.'

His face lit up. 'Would you? Would you really? Oh, Kathy, if only you would. I've thought about it over and over again, I really have, but the thought of actually doing anything about it – well, I just didn't have the heart for it. But if you were there—'

'Only as a friend,' she broke in, already wondering what had possessed her to make such an offer. 'And I couldn't do much – I have to go to work, and I've got my own things to do at home. And Brian will be home for Easter.'

'I know, but if you'd just look at one or two places with me – tell me what you thought – and help me choose a few bits of furniture, just to start me off. I've got the money saved up. I haven't had much to spend it on, so it's just been sitting there in the bank . . . I wouldn't expect you to do anything when Brian's home. I'd keep out of the way then. I wouldn't pester you, I promise.'

'Well, I don't know . . .'

'Please, Kathy,' he begged. 'If I find somewhere, will you just come and look at it, and give me your advice? That's all I ask. Please.'

'All right,' she said. It would help pass the time until Easter, and if it helped Terry to feel better and get his life on track again . . . 'All right.'

They walked back to her car and she got in and turned the ignition key. Terry stood beside her window, smiling a goodbye. He looked better already, more cheerful, more positive. Perhaps this was really all he'd needed, someone to take a proper interest in him, someone to care.

But you can't care, Kathy, she told herself as she drove away. Not really. He's in the past.

And that's where he ought to stay. You can't afford to care about him.

Chapter Twenty

Terry had not contacted Kathy by the time Brian came home at Easter, and she hoped that he had decided not to take her advice on house-hunting after all. All the same, she dreaded his arrival while Brian was on leave, and was relieved when Brian suggested a trip down to Devon to visit Clare and Martyn.

'He'll be on Easter leave too, so it'll be a good time. We can go out for a few jars and you girls can have a good natter at home.'

'And suppose we want to go out too?' Kathy asked. 'You'll be pleased to take a turn at babysitting, I suppose.'

'Not my responsibility,' Brian declared breezily. 'If old Martyn wants to go and get himself tied down with kids, it's up to him to see that his wife knows how to look after them.'

Kathy was doing her ironing, while Brian sprawled on the sofa, reading the evening paper with a glass of beer beside him. She stopped, her iron held up so that it steamed and spluttered into the air, and stared at him. 'Clare does know how to look after them! She's a wonderful mother.'

'I didn't say she wasn't. I just think it's a woman's place to stay at home and take care of the kids, that's all. She can't expect to unload 'em off on to poor old Martyn the minute he comes back for a bit of home life.'

'But Clare has them all the time,' Kathy said. 'Twenty-four hours a day. She needs a break sometimes, and Martyn's the one to give it to her.'

'Listen,' Brian said. 'Clare wanted to get married. She must have wanted those kids. She can't complain now she's got 'em. She knew the score, she knew he'd be away most of the time.'

'I don't think anyone really knows what it's like till it happens,' Kathy said slowly. 'You don't know how lonely it is for a woman, Brian. I saw what Clare went through when she was pregnant, and that first year with Christopher. She never complained, but I know she was lonely.'

'Is that what put you off getting married?' Brian asked, suddenly quiet.

Kathy looked at him. 'Yes, I think it was, partly. I mean, everything seemed so hard for her. They hadn't had time to save up any money and when she did have some it all had to go on the baby or something for the house. I mean, she was only just twenty! And she was living like a – like a middle-aged woman. A *mum*.'

'Well, so she is a mum. Twice, now.'

'I know, but, well, she didn't seem to me to have had any life. Of her own, I mean. Three years out of school and there she was tied down with a house and a baby. I mean, I thought Clare would *go* somewhere. Do something with her drawing and painting. She's good, Brian, she was the best in the class, one of the best in the school. She could have made a career of it.'

'So why didn't she? Why did she go into the civil service?'

'Well, that was her parents, wasn't it? They couldn't imagine anyone making a career out of art, least of all a girl. They're nice people, but it's the way their generation thinks. Girls don't need careers, they'll get married and have children, so why—'

'Well, that's just what she did,' Brian pointed out. 'So they were right, weren't they? And it's not just their generation that thinks that way. Ours does too. *I* do.'

Kathy stopped ironing and looked at him.

'You think I ought to stop working and have children, so I can stay at home and look after them?'

'Well, you will eventually, won't you? Once we've got all we want in the house and a bit saved up. You don't want to make a career out of working. You're not that mad about your job.'

'No, I'm not,' Kathy admitted, 'but that doesn't mean I just want to stay at home. I want children eventually, I suppose. But for now – oh, I don't know *what* I want.' She put down the iron in sudden frustration. 'And I don't suppose it would make any difference if I did. Look at me! Standing here ironing your shirts, while you sit around reading the paper and drinking beer. I'm the little woman already, staying at home like a good little girl waiting for hubby to come home. What difference does it make if I have half a dozen kids to look after as well?'

Brian tossed the paper aside and stood up. He was wearing a blue crew-necked jumper that Kathy had knitted him during the winter. It set off the tan he had acquired during the weeks out in the Mediterranean and Kathy thought he looked almost devastatingly handsome, as handsome as a film star. Clark Gable, perhaps, in *Gone With The Wind*. And as dangerous.

'Brian—' she said anxiously. 'Brian, don't let's quarrel . . .'

'Quarrel? Who's quarrelling?' He smiled at her and held out his arms. 'Come on, Kath. You're right, you shouldn't be wasting time ironing. Not when we've got so little time together. I'll send my shirts to the laundry. And in the meantime . . .' he drew her close and dropped his lips to the curve of her breast ' . . . we've got only ourselves to think about. Ourselves and our home, and the fun we can have . . . mm?' He ran one hand down her back, so that she shivered. 'What's so wrong with being a little woman, anyway? *My* little woman . . .'

Kathy sighed and melted against him. She had never been able to resist Brian in his seductive mood, never been able to prevent herself from being swept away by his persuasive passion. Her own desire rose to meet his and she forgot the times when she had found herself lying awake in the darkness afterwards, listening to his breathing, forgot the tiny ache of longing and regret that haunted her dreams.

She was *glad* she had married Brian. They were happy. *Happy*.

Clare was delighted to see Kathy again and quite willing to let the men go off for a drink round at the Whitchurch Inn to give the two friends an evening to themselves. 'It suits me fine,' she said, 'so long as we get a turn too.'

'I wouldn't bank on it,' Kathy said. 'Brian doesn't think it's a man's place to look after the kids.'

'Well, Martyn'll soon put him right there,' Clare said with a grin. 'He's a dab hand now at babysitting. Not that he has to do much of it, of course, but he never minds me going off shopping and leaving him with the children, and he'll always get up to them if they cry in the night. Especially Laura – she's a real daddy's girl.' She smiled. 'Don't worry about Brian, Kathy. He'll be just the same once you have your own.'

'Yes. I expect he will.'

But Kathy's tone was unsure and Clare looked at her curiously. 'Is everything all right, Kath? You look a bit sad sometimes. You're not sorry you married Brian, are you?'

'No! No, of course I'm not. It's just – well, you never really get to know anyone properly until you're married, do you, and with him being away so much . . . Don't you find it difficult sometimes, Clare?'

'I hate Martyn being away,' Clare said honestly, 'but we can't say we weren't warned, can we? It's hard at times, when there's so much to do for the children, and looking after the house and everything – but then again, I can do it all in my own time, with no one going to work in the morning and coming home for meals. I can't pretend I wouldn't rather he was home all the time, but I'd rather have it this way than not be married to him at all.'

'Don't you find it a bit awkward when he does come back?' Kathy asked. 'The first day or so – getting used to having a man in the house again? I mean, I know it's lovely, but – sometimes I find it difficult to adjust.'

'Yes, it is.' Clare looked thoughtful. 'You're strangers, yet you've got to go to bed together! Actually, that's the best way to get over it – go to bed and make mad, passionate love. It's all right after that.' She smiled. 'I think it's harder for the men really, you know. They've got to adjust from living on a ship with a lot of other men to being in a house with a wife and children. It must be a huge difference.'

'Yes, it must. And when they go ashore, they've got all that freedom. They're single again.'

'Not too single, I hope,' Clare said with a grin, but Kathy didn't return her smile. She looked away and didn't speak for a moment, and when she did her voice was low and a little sad.

'We don't know that, do we? We don't know what they get up to.'

Clare stared at her. 'Oh, surely – you don't doubt Brian, do you? He loves you – anyone can see that. And I certainly don't doubt Martyn.'

'No, I don't – not really. Only he used to tell me things, things about what the men did when they were abroad. Going into bars and clubs, that sort of thing. I mean, there are always women about where there are sailors. And they've been at sea a long time. It must be hard to resist.'

Clare shook her head. 'They don't all give in. I know Martyn doesn't. And Brian, well, he might have had a fling or two after you wrote to him that time, but I'm sure he doesn't now. You don't really worry about that, do you, Kathy?'

'No,' Kathy said. 'No, I don't.' She lifted her head and smiled. 'I'm just being silly, that's all.'

Clare hesitated, then asked, 'Do you ever see Terry these days?'

She was startled by her friend's reaction. Scarlet colour ran up Kathy's neck and into her cheeks and she turned away swiftly as if to hide it, bending to pick up one of Laura's toys that had rolled under the sofa. When she answered, her voice was strained and a little high-pitched. 'Terry? Why d'you ask that? I thought you'd have forgotten all about him by now.'

Clare paused a moment before speaking. She didn't want to pry or to upset her friend, but Kathy's response made it obvious that there was something she wasn't being told, something that perhaps Kathy needed to be able to tell someone. 'No, I haven't forgotten him, Kathy, and I don't suppose you have, either. It wouldn't be surprising if you saw him, after all, both living in the same area.'

There was a short silence. Kathy sat up again, playing with the toy in her hands. It was a somewhat misshapen purple rabbit, made of soft fur fabric. She stared down at it, biting her lips, and when she looked up Clare was astonished to see that her eyes were filled with tears.

'Yes, I have seen him. I met him one day out at Stokes Bay – not by arrangement, I'd just gone out for a walk and we bumped into each other.' She stopped abruptly, looking down at her hands again.

'Did you speak to him?' Clare asked gently. Kathy could tell her to mind her own business or she could say she just didn't want to talk about it, but she might just need a question or two to help her talk. 'Did he say anything to you?'

'Yes. We stopped and talked. We walked along for a little way together. Oh, Clare,' Kathy burst out, 'he's so *miserable*. He's so unhappy. He looks thin and sad and as if nobody loves him. I don't think anyone does love him, except perhaps his mother, and she must be torn in two between him and his stepfather. He's still living at home and he hates it, hates his stepdad, it must be awful for all of them.'

'Then why doesn't he move out?' Clare asked, as Kathy herself had done. 'Why doesn't he get a place of his own?'

'I know. I asked him that. He just said what he always did say, it was his home first – I mean, he's just like a silly, spoilt *kid*, Clare, and it drives me crazy, but at the same time I can't help feeling sorry for him. I didn't tell him that, though, I tore him off a real strip. Told him he was wallowing in self-pity. Told him it was about time he cut himself free from his mother's apron strings, or words to that effect.'

'And how did he take that?'

'Oh, he agreed with me. He said he would do it – find himself a place of his own.' Kathy paused for a brief moment. 'If – if I'd help him.'

'If *you'd* help him?' Clare echoed. 'Kathy! You didn't agree?'

Kathy bent her head and nodded very slightly.

Clare stared at her in dismay. 'Oh, *Kathy*.'

'It's not so very much,' she said defensively. 'He only wants me to look at one or two places and say what I think. It won't be any more than that – well, and giving him a bit of advice about furniture and that sort of thing. That's all.'

'That's all? Kathy, you're out of your mind. Brian will go mad. Have you told him about this?'

'No, of course not. Look, I don't suppose it'll even happen. It was weeks ago when we met and he hasn't done a thing about it, I haven't heard a word. He's probably forgotten all about it.'

'He probably hasn't,' Clare said grimly. 'Look, he knows enough about the Navy to know that Brian's probably on Easter leave now and will be away again in a few weeks. I bet he even knows what ship Brian's on. The minute he thinks it's safe, he'll be knocking on your door, and what are you going to do then? Go trotting off house-hunting with him? Go round Courts to choose bedroom furniture? Suppose someone sees you and kindly tells Brian? What are you going to say?'

'Nobody will see us.'

'Oh, you know that, do you? You've got power over these things? Kathy, have some sense. Even if you get away with it, can't you see it's a dangerous situation? You'll be with Terry again – while Brian's away. Don't you see?'

Kathy stared at her stonily. 'No. No, I don't see. I don't see what you're making a fuss about. Things are different now. I'm married.'

'Kathy, you've just been telling me what Brian might get up to when he's away, and now you're talking about doing the same thing—'

'It isn't a bit the same! It's perfectly innocent. Look, all I'm going to do is look at a couple of houses. We're not going on dates. What could possibly happen?

'What happened before?' Clare asked, and then drew in a sharp breath. 'Kathy, I'm sorry. Forget I said that. I didn't mean—'

'You did.' Kathy dropped the rabbit and stood up. 'You meant I can't stay faithful to my own husband. You meant that I'll let him down again, just like I did before.'

'No! I didn't, I really didn't. I know you'd never do anything like that. Kathy, don't let's quarrel over this, please.' Clare was on her feet too, distressed and angry with herself. 'I just meant it's a dangerous situation, but if you think you can handle it . . . Look, don't take any notice of me. Let's talk about something else.'

Kathy hesitated and then sat down again. She gave Clare a wry glance and grinned a little, then picked up the rabbit again. 'This really is the most awful soft toy I've ever seen. I mean, whoever thought of making a rabbit this colour? Its ears are lopsided too. And it's got a sort of sneer on its face.'

Clare laughed, thankful to be able to ease the tension. 'Veronica made it. She had a phase of doing things like that during the winter. All the children got an animal of some sort. You should have seen her first effort, it was even worse. At least you can see that's a rabbit.'

'Veronica? Is she the girl who lives down on the main road?'

'Yes. She and Alex have been really good friends. And Sue, and her husband Don. I've asked them all up, for a bit of a party.' She gave Kathy a smile. 'I want to see all my friends together.'

Kathy smiled back. Their disagreement was pushed aside, and with it her anxiety about Terry. Time enough to worry about that later.

'Let's hope it's a success, then. People's friends don't always get on well together, you know.'

'Oh, you will,' Clare said confidently. 'I just know you will.'

'So how's life as a father?' Brian asked, carrying his pint to a corner table. 'Or do I really want to know?'

Martyn sat down opposite. 'It's great. The kids are smashing. They change a hell of a lot when I'm away at sea, though – takes me all my time to get to know them again.'

'Don't you find it a bit of a restriction?' Brian asked curiously. 'I mean, you're tied right down at home, you and Clare. You can't even go out for a drink together without getting a babysitter. You practically have to get permission to go out on your own.'

'No, I don't. Clare would never stop me going out if I wanted to. I just don't do it. It doesn't seem fair, not when she's at home on her own all the time I'm away.'

'But don't you get fed up?'

Martyn eyed him and sipped his beer. 'What's the matter, Bri? You're not having second thoughts about married life yourself, are you?'

'No. I like being at home with Kath, I like having our own place and all that. But it's different for us, we haven't got kids. We can go out and enjoy ourselves or we can stay in bed all day if we feel like it. I just wonder what it would be like if we couldn't do that, if we had kids. I mean, your life's over then, isn't it? You've got to settle down.'

'I wouldn't say my life was over,' Martyn said, grinning. 'It's just different, that's all. It's not as if it was all the time – I'm away more than I'm at home. It doesn't make much difference when you're at sea.'

'Makes a difference when you're in port, though,' Brian said, taking a long swallow.

'Not to me, mate. I never went in for a girl in every port, you know that. I had Clare at home before I ever went to sea. Besides, you never know what you're going to catch. I don't want my plates and mugs marked with a red X, thanks very much.'

'They're not all poxed.'

'No, but how d'you tell the difference? Anyway, I didn't think that was your scene either.'

'No, it's not, really,' Brian admitted. 'I'd sooner have a proper girlfriend – only not *too* proper. But, like you say, it's different when you've got someone at home. For short trips, anyway. I can manage a few weeks all right. It's when it gets to months – to a year or more – and you don't know what they're getting up to at home. And you get all these gorgeous young females swarming round the ship. When you go to places like Bali or the West Indies . . .' He pursed his lips in a silent whistle. 'Well, it takes a bit of willpower, that's all. I mean, grass skirts and nothing up top . . . We're only human, Martyn.'

'Well, take my advice and keep away,' Martyn said. 'Anyway, what do you mean about what they're getting up to at home? You don't think Kathy's going to two-time you again, do you?'

'She did it once.'

'Yes, but that's over. She's married you. She thinks the world of you, anyone can see that. You trust her, don't you?'

'Yes. Yes, I think so.' Brian took another drink, frowning, then set his glass down hard. 'Oh, I dunno, Martyn. How can a bloke be sure? When it's already happened once . . . And she acts funny sometimes. As if she's not quite with me. I tell you, I wonder sometimes if she's thinking of him. If she's pretending *I'm* him.'

'Don't talk daft,' Martyn said uneasily. 'Of course she doesn't.'

'How can you be sure? How can *I* be sure?' Brian lifted his glass again and finished his drink with one gulp. 'I tell you what, if I ever find that bloke's sniffing round after her again, I'll screw his neck for him. I will, straight.'

'He's not. Kathy wouldn't let him. She's mad about you.' Martyn stood up and picked up the two empty glasses. 'Let's have the other half and talk about something else. Have you ever seen anything of old Nobby Clarke? And Lofty, what happened to him? I heard he was going with a Wren officer. You'd think a girl like that'd have more taste, wouldn't you?'

He went to the bar, uneasy about their conversation. Brian was pretty steady most of the time, but he had a hot temper, and when it was roused he took a bit of restraining. Martyn had seen it happen a few times when they were boys, and it had happened once at Collingwood when they were both apprentices. One of the instructors had sneered at Brian's accent, a mixture of Bristol and South Devon, and it had caught Brian on the raw. The instructor was staggering back with a bloody nose before anyone realised what was happening, and Brian had been put on a charge, given a month's punishment, and told to consider himself lucky. Since then, he'd kept clear of trouble but there had been a note in his voice and a hard look in his eyes which warned Martyn that he was still simmering with anger over the man who had almost taken Kathy away from him.

It'll come to nothing, Martyn told himself, carrying the drinks back to their table. Carter will stay away from Kathy and she won't have anything to do with him anyway. She knows better than to make that mistake twice.

For the next few days, Clare and Kathy kept busy preparing for the party.

Veronica arrived looking enchanting, her small figure clad in a dress of cornflower blue that exactly matched her eyes. Her hair gleamed as if it had been polished, falling in a luxuriant bell shape to her shoulders. Clare caught Kathy's eyes on it, and saw her unconsciously lift her fingers to her own smooth cap. Kathy had never been able to grow her hair long.

'Martyn!' Veronica exclaimed, shrugging gracefully out of a short fur cape. 'What a treat – you're hardly ever here. No wonder Clare wanted to give a party, to prove she really has got a husband. And is this your friend, Brian? Are you a sailor too?' She moved close to Brian and laid her hand on his sleeve, gazing up at him through long, darkened lashes.

She made it sound as if being a sailor was something really special, like an astronaut or a prince, Clare thought with amusement, and there was no doubt that it had an effect. Brian was looking at her as if he'd never seen a pretty woman before. Don't take it seriously, she told him silently. Veronica always talks like this. It doesn't mean a thing.

The house was suddenly full of people. They settled down round the fire and Martyn poured drinks – beer for the men, Babycham for the girls. They didn't have the right glasses for Babycham, only ordinary wineglasses that he and Clare had been given for a wedding present, but Clare had got cherries and little sticks to decorate them and had also put out little dishes of nuts and crisps. It all seemed very sophisicated.

Brian set himself to be the life and soul of the party, telling jokes, getting just ahead of Martyn in offering to refill glasses, and recounting tales of his travels overseas. Martyn had been to all those places too, Clare thought, but he didn't have the same gift of story telling, and soon all attention had shifted to Brian and his stories. Not that Martyn seemed to mind. He was looking as proud as if Brian were his own creation, and Veronica was hanging on every word. Brian had made sure she was next to him on the settee and she snuggled against him, looking up into his face as he talked.

Kathy sat quietly on a small stool in the corner. She had refused Martyn's offer of an armchair, and had little to say as her husband talked. Clare saw her watching him and wanted to tell her not to worry, Veronica was deeply in love with her own husband, and although she might flirt with Brian there would be no more to it than that. However, she was uncomfortably aware of a tension between Kathy and Brian, an undercurrent of feeling that had been present all through their visit, and she knew that Kathy was feeling extra sensitive. She does feel guilty about seeing Terry, whatever she might say, she thought.

'Didn't we, Kath?' Brian asked, and Clare switched her attention back to what was happening. Everyone was looking at Kathy, amused smiles on their faces, but Kathy was silent on her stool, her face flushed.

'I don't think anyone's interested in that, Brian,' she began, but he laughed loudly and shook his head.

'She doesn't like being reminded. Anyway, it was nothing serious in the end, was it, Kath? Just got into a bit of a muddle, didn't you? All over and forgotten now.' He smiled at her kindly.

Kathy flushed an even deeper red. She glanced around the room. The others had fallen silent, clearly embarrassed, and she got up suddenly. 'Excuse me. The bathroom is at the top of the stairs, isn't it, Clare?' An odd question, since she was staying in the house, but it got her out of the room.

Clare watched her, feeling sorry, and followed, murmuring something about the kitchen. As she left the room, she heard Brian say with mock remorse, 'Whoops! Sounds like I've said the wrong thing again. But that's me all over – open my mouth and put my foot right in it!'

The others laughed, though their laughter was strained. Kathy, at the top of the stairs, paused and Clare saw her hand tighten on the banister before she went on into the bathroom.

Oh, dear, Clare thought. I hoped there wouldn't be trouble between those two.

*

'Everyone thinks he's the life and soul of the party,' Kathy said to her in the kitchen, after the others had departed. 'He makes it look as though I'm the one who's sulking – but I can't make jokes and pretend everything's fine when it's not.'

Clare looked at her. It was the first time Kathy had actually admitted that there was something wrong. 'Kathy, what is it? Yesterday, you said—'

'I know what I said. I said I wasn't sorry I'd married Brian. And it's true. I'm not. I love him, Clare, and he loves me. You can see that. He can hardly bear me out of his sight, and if another man talks to me, he nearly goes mad with jealousy. Look at tonight, when Don and I were chatting – Brian had to come over and join in. He doesn't *look* jealous, but he is.'

'But he can't go on like that,' Clare said. 'You're bound to talk to other men sometimes. What about when he's away? He has to trust you then.'

'I didn't say he doesn't trust me!' Kathy's response was swift, almost indignant. 'And of course he knows I'd never be unfaithful to him. Not again.' She bit her lip, flushing. 'Not that I ever was, not really. I just didn't know my own mind for a while . . . Now that we're married, it's different. It'll be better when he comes out of the Navy and we can be together all the time.'

'I suppose it will.' Clare counted the years until that could happen. It seemed a long time to be walking a knife-edge, as she sensed Kathy and Brian were doing. She hesitated, then said, 'Don't you think, Kathy, that it's all the more risky for you to start seeing Terry again? I mean, if you still have any feeling for him . . .'

'Look, the only feeling I have for Terry is guilt. I didn't treat him fairly: I let him believe we could have a future and I knew all the time, if I'd thought about it properly, that we didn't. That's why I would never get engaged. I never felt ready. And now that I'm married, he knows there's no future, so it's quite safe. Anyway,' she added, 'I'm not *seeing* him. I'm just giving him a bit of a hand getting away from his mother and set up in his own place. Once he's settled, he won't need my help any more.'

Clare gave her a doubtful look, but at that moment the kitchen door opened and Martyn came breezing in. 'We've finished putting the room straight, and there's still half an hour before closing time, so Bri and me are going down to the Cattle Market for a last pint. You girls'll be okay, won't you?'

'I suppose so,' Clare said, feeling a touch of annoyance, 'but I thought we could all sit down and have a drink together.'

'No beer left. No, we'll just stroll down for a jar on our own and you can natter about clothes or whatever it is you talk about when you're on your own.' He gave her a quick hug and planted a kiss on the side of her head. 'See you later. Don't wait up.'

'Don't wait up?' Clare said, as their footsteps died away. 'How long does it take to have a last pint?' She gave Kathy a wry glance. 'Well, we little women had better do as our lords and masters tell us, hadn't we? Let's go and talk about clothes. I'll tell you all about my old winter skirt that got scorched when I stood too near the fire, and you can tell me about that new cardigan you bought in Marks & Spencers. Or we can go on talking about whatever else it is we talk about when we're on our own, with no men to make the conversation interesting.'

Kathy laughed, but there was a brittle edge to her laughter. 'On the other hand,' she said, 'we could just play your new Beatles records and forget there are such things as men. And football. And cars. And beer.'

'And the *Navy*,' Clare added, and this time they laughed together.

Any summer would have been a relief after the long, cold winter, but the summer of 1963 seemed in retrospect to have been nothing but a succession of warm, sunny days. Clare and the children spent almost all their time on the moor, or in the garden where she had put a paddling pool on the lawn. During the week she saw Sue and Veronica, but at weekends her friends all went down to the Cornish beaches to surf and swim, and with Martyn at sea again she was alone once more.

Most Sundays she walked round to Whitchurch to take the children to morning service. They always arrived early enough to be able to watch the bellringers at the back of the church. There was a team of enthusiastic teenage boys who practised regularly, and Christopher was fascinated and declared that he too would be a bellringer when he was big. Laura loved the colourful sallies on the ropes and was delighted when the team captain gave her one of her own, from an old rope. Clare washed it until it regained all its original fluffiness, and Laura took it everywhere, cuddling it as if it were a doll.

It was a year for big news. The newspapers were full of the Profumo scandal. It dominated the front pages all through June and July, displaced only by a terrible earthquake in Yugoslavia at the end of the month. In the middle of August the talk was all of the Great Train Robbery, and then of Martin Luther King's great speech in which he declared, 'I have a dream . . .' It was a dream, Clare thought, of a world that ought to be, but perhaps never would, because so many people just wouldn't let it. And then, as she sat in the kitchen watching television on the evening of 22 November, an announcer interrupted the programme with the most dreadful news yet.

The announcer was Richard Baker, and the news was of the shooting of President Kennedy.

Clare sat stunned in her chair. After a moment or two, during which only brief details could be given of the scene in Dallas, the programme continued. She kept it on, but could not concentrate on it, and when at last the camera cut back to Richard Baker she sat forward, as anxious as if the President had been one of her own relatives.

The news was bald. There was no way of delivering it gently. There was no way of softening the shock that ran through every person who heard it, that ran through the entire world.

'President Kennedy is dead.'

The announcer's mouth twisted a little as he said the words, as if he were as shocked as everyone else – and of course, he was, Clare thought, switching off the set. There was nothing more to wait for; there would be nothing to see, no photographs as yet from Dallas. Whatever was happening now would be reported soon enough; for the moment, she needed time to assimilate the news, to try to believe in it.

She was surprised by her own reaction, by her tears. Jack Kennedy, with his energy and good looks, had become a figurehead, a symbol of good, of forward-looking. He was going to make the world a better place, she thought, and he didn't have the chance. He'd hardly started. And now some crazy fool, some mad criminal, had gunned him down. It didn't make sense.

At nine o'clock, she switched on the TV again. All the news was of the assassination; it was as if nothing else had happened. They'd brought in politicians and 'experts' (experts in what? she wondered) who discussed it endlessly, trying to predict what would happen next. Who had carried out the crime? Nobody seemed to know. Security men had rushed into every building in the vicinity, searching for the culprit. Whoever it was hadn't a chance of getting away – all of Dallas would be after him, all of America. There would be nowhere in the world that such a murderer could hide.

The next day both radio and television were full of the news of Kennedy's assassination. There were pictures on the front pages of all the newspapers too. Someone in the crowd had been filming the President's cavalcade as it drove slowly through the streets. The moment of the shooting had been captured, and the pictures, blurred as they were, showed Jackie Kennedy leaning over her husband, cradling his head, her face filled with grief and terror. Although she hadn't been shot, she couldn't have known whether she too was in danger, yet she made no attempt to hide herself. Her concern was all for her dying husband.

Clare couldn't imagine anything more terrible than to be sitting beside the man you loved and see him killed. Unless, of course, it was one of your children. That, she thought, would be even worse.

For once, she was glad that there was nobody with her that weekend. She was surprised and a little embarrassed by the tears that kept welling to her eyes and pouring down her cheeks. It was almost as if she had lost a member of her own family, yet she had never met President Kennedy, never seen him in the flesh, would never have been likely to. It didn't seem to make any difference. She wept for him on and off all day Saturday, all day Sunday, so that both the children were alarmed and she had to try to explain to them that a good man a long way away had died, and the world was a poorer place because of it.

They'd caught the murderer, though. Clare, cuddling Bartholomew for comfort, saw the pictures on the screen – Lee Harvey Oswald, a thin, dark young man no older than she was herself. Why had he done it? Was he a Communist, or one of Castro's men? Or was he just crazy, his distorted mind driving him to gun down one of the world's most powerful men, just for the hell of it? It would all come out at his trial, she thought, and then felt as let down as the rest of the world when Oswald himself was shot dead as he was being transferred to the county jail. This time it was an older man, his face contorted with fury. Jack Ruby, a nightclub owner, said to be mad with grief, yet also suspected to be an accomplice, shooting Oswald to prevent him from talking . . . Clare, stunned by it all, wondered if the truth would ever be known.

Finally, there was the funeral, a solemn procession through Washington to the cathedral, and then to the burial place at Arlington. And then it was over, and the world had to pick up the shattered pieces and move on.

Clare went back to her normal routine. Soon Martyn would be home again for Christmas, and then his ship was due for a three-month refit before going out to the Far East, which meant he would be coming home from Devonport each evening until after Easter.

We can have a proper married life for a while, Clare thought, washing Laura's face. We can sit by our own fire together all through the winter, and take the children for walks on the moor at the weekends. Perhaps we can redecorate the kitchen and buy some new units to replace those old ones that the last people left behind. And we could go to Gosport for Christmas and stay with Mum and Dad and see all the family, and go to see Kathy and Brian as well.

Her heart lifted. Life went on, and life was once again feeling good.

Chapter Twenty-One

After her talk with Clare in the spring, Kathy hadn't mentioned Terry again. She knew that her friend would assume that this meant she hadn't heard any more from him, and although it felt like telling lies, she let her go on thinking so. It's not really lying, because I'd tell her if she asked, Kathy told herself, but she still felt uncomfortable about it. She and Clare had never kept secrets from each other, ever since they'd met at the age of five. All the same, she was pretty sure she knew what Clare would say if she knew the truth, and Kathy didn't want to hear it.

There's no harm in it, she thought defensively. Terry's just a friend. He's like a brother to me now. There isn't any harm in it at all.

For a while, like Clare, she'd thought she wasn't going to hear from him again after all. Leaving his home, even though he was unhappy there, seemed to be too big a step for him to take. It was like admitting defeat, like conceding that his stepfather had more right there than he did. It was something he could only do if he had a good reason to offer – such as marriage, or emigration.

Pretty drastic reasons for leaving home, Kathy thought, but that was what Terry seemed to need. So she was surprised when, some time after Brian had gone back to sea, he telephoned her one evening.

'Terry! How – how are you?' Even though she was alone, she felt the colour flood her cheeks as she stumbled over the words. His light, pleasant voice was so familiar, yet so unexpected – and equally unexpected was the sudden jump of her heart when she heard it.

'I'm fine.' He hesitated, then said, 'Kathy, you said you'd help me find a place of my own. Is that still on? I mean, will you? Will you come and look at somewhere with me?'

'Well – yes, I suppose so.' All Clare's warnings sounded in her mind like a clang of bells. 'If you really want me to, but *you've* got to decide, Terry.'

'I know. I know that. I just want someone to look with me. It's only a couple of places,' he went on, in a rush. 'I'm not asking you to traipse round a lot. I've been doing that already.'

'Oh.' She felt pleased. So he had taken her words seriously, and he was actually doing something about it. Well, she had a sort of responsibility to help him, didn't she? And if it was only a couple . . . 'When d'you want me to come?'

'Well, as soon as possible. Whenever suits you. We could go to one on Friday evening, and the other on Saturday. We can't do both on Saturday; I tried but the people are out. Could you do that?'

'Yes, that would be all right.' Friday evenings and weekends were lonely for Kathy. Most of her friends were in couples now and went out together then. If she wanted company to go to the pictures it had to be during the week, and even then it was only if someone's boyfriend or husband didn't want to see the film himself. Most of her social life was conducted at work.

'Where are these places?' she asked.

'One's a bungalow at Hillhead, and the other's a house in Old Portsmouth. Pretty far apart,' he added, 'so it wouldn't have been too easy to do them both on the same day anyway. We can go to the one at Hillhead on Friday. Shall I pick you up?'

'No – no, don't do that.' There were too many eyes around here, Kathy thought. Someone was bound to see if a young man came and collected her by car. 'I'll meet you at Hillhead. Tell me where and what time.'

The tide was out when Kathy parked her car next evening by the low cliff at Hillhead, leaving a broad stretch of soft, muddy sand, and there were, as always, a few men digging for bait for the weekend's fishing. As a child, Kathy had often come here with her parents to collect a bucketful of cockles, which they had had for tea a day or two later. Kathy could remember looking at the bucket of shells, watching to see them open and blow out their last minute bubbles of air before her mother declared they were safe to cook.

Terry was waiting. He came forward to greet her, smiling anxiously. Kathy too felt awkward. She had spent most of the day worrying about whether she should ring him up and cancel their meeting, but there had been no chance to make a private call at work, and she hadn't been able to summon up the determination during her lunch hour. Well, I'll go tonight but I won't go tomorrow, she thought. I'll tell him he's got to make up his own mind where he wants to live.

'Thanks for coming,' Terry said, stopping. He took her hand and looked down into her eyes. 'Look, I don't want you to get the wrong idea about this, only I really do need someone else to look at these places, and you're the only one I felt I could ask. There isn't anyone else who knows as much about me as you do.'

Kathy stared at him. It seemed an almost indecent amount to know about someone she wasn't married to, didn't even see any more. 'Terry, that's really sad,' she said. 'There ought to be someone for you. Haven't you met anyone else at all?'

He shook his head. 'I haven't even looked. I don't think there is anyone else for me.'

'Oh, Terry,' Kathy said helplessly. 'I really am sorry.'

He shrugged. 'Water under the bridge now, Kathy. So long as you're happy. That's all that really matters.'

They walked along the road together. Hillhead was a small hamlet a mile or so further along the shore from Lee-on-the-Solent, and it had its own distinct character. It consisted of little more than a straggle of houses and a public house, scattered along the road only yards from the beach, with a few shops and a post office. You could get there by bus, but most people got off at Lee, where there were more facilities and a better beach, with low tide 'still in walking distance', so it was always quieter at Hillhead.

The bungalow Terry was interested in stood near the post office. It had a low wall and a front garden which was mostly lawn, with a paved path leading from the gate to the green front door. Kathy followed Terry up the path and waited as he lifted the brass knocker. A small, stout woman with curly white hair opened the door.

'Mr Carter. Come in. And you've brought your young lady, too. Come in, my dear. It's a pleasure to meet you.'

Kathy opened her mouth to speak, and then closed it again.

Terry said, 'I'm afraid it's not my young lady, Mrs Jennings. This is Mrs Bennett. She's a friend – she's come along to give me some advice.'

'Oh. Oh, I see. Well, never mind.' The old lady turned away. 'Well, you know your way about, so I'll leave you to look round by yourselves. Just come into the kitchen if you want anything. My hubby's in the garden, if you want to ask him about the plumbing and such. I'll call him in.' She looked at Kathy. 'Would you like a cup of tea, my dear? It will be ready in the kitchen when you've finished looking round.'

Kathy felt disconcerted. 'Well, I had one not long ago—'

'A cup of tea would be very welcome,' Terry said. 'I've come straight from work. Thank you, Mrs Jennings.'

'It's our daughter, you see,' Mrs Jennings explained later, as she got out the cups. 'She's moved up to Winchester, bless her, and she wants us to go too, to be near her. Well, we've lived all our lives round here so we're not that keen, to be truthful, but you want to be where your family are, don't you? When you're getting on, you do. I mean, we're not going to live for ever, and one of us is bound to go first – we've faced that, you have to, don't you – so it seems only sense to be near our Muriel. And her hubby's been ever so good to us, bless him, so we know we wouldn't be in the way, and what with her being our only one, and the grandchildren getting bigger, well, we thought perhaps this was the best time. No good waiting till you're too old, is it, now?'

Kathy, who could not imagine ever being as old as this couple, shook her head and sipped her tea. Mrs Jennings turned to her husband, a thin, gangling man who could have been taken for a scarecrow as he worked in the garden.

'You'll never guess what I did, Father. I took this young lady to be Mr Carter's sweetheart! Well, it was a natural enough mistake to make, what with her coming to view the house with him, but no, she's just a friend come to give him the benefit of her advice. But when I saw them walking along the road together I was sure she was his young lady, bless her. They looked so right together, if you know what I mean. Like our Muriel when she brought her Frederick home to meet us that first time. Sort of shy and proud and excited, all at once.'

Kathy stared at her cup. She didn't want to meet Terry's eyes. Proud and excited, indeed! Was that how they'd looked? Was it how *he'd* looked?

'I think I'll have to be going soon,' she said, with a glance at her watch.

'Oh, but you haven't seen the garden yet,' Mrs Jennings said at once. 'My Albert's pride and joy, that is. You can't go without seeing his vegetable patch and my bit of a flower border. Take them out there now, Albert, before it gets dark, and I'll make another pot of tea.'

By the time they had been shown the tiny patch of lawn, the flowerbed with its cluster of daffodils and primroses, and the vegetable patch, neatly tilled and with tightly stretched garden twine to indicate where later there would be broad beans and peas and cabbages, it was dusk. The two men went into the shed so that Terry could be shown where tools were kept on nails and how the bench had been made specially strong enough for a bit of woodwork, while Kathy waited outside. She felt hemmed in and constricted. The garden, like the house, seemed too crammed and full, almost stuffy. If I lived here, she thought, I'd spend all my time in that upstairs room. It's the only place that's got any air.

It was eight thirty before they finally got away, and the moon was already up and sending a shimmering path over the rising tide.

Kathy lifted her head and took a deep breath. 'I thought I'd suffocate in there! Don't they ever open any windows?'

'Well, I suppose he gets his fresh air in the garden,' Terry said, and added wickedly, 'Bless him.'

Kathy laughed. 'Terry, you mustn't make fun. She's sweet really. Lots of old people are like her, they don't know when to stop talking. And I don't suppose she meets all that many young people.'

'She's got "our Muriel". And the grandchildren – bless them.' They had reached the cars and Terry paused awkwardly. 'Would you like to come in the pub and have a drink before you go home, Kath?'

'A drink? I'm awash with tea already.'

'I mean a real drink. Somewhere we can sit and talk for a while. Please, Kath.'

Kathy hesitated. Going to a pub hadn't been on the agenda, but to go home now would seem an anti-climax. She'd be in by nine, and in Kathy's view that was almost the worst time to get home, especially on a Friday evening when most people would be just beginning to enjoy themselves. And she still hadn't got around to telling Terry she wouldn't be going with him tomorrow.

'All right,' she said. 'Just one, then.'

They settled themselves in a seat by the window. It was fully dark now and the lights of the Island twinkled across the gently rippling water. Terry went to the bar and came back carrying a pint of beer for himself and a shandy for Kathy. He sat down opposite her and smiled. 'This is nice. Like old times.'

'Terry . . .'

'It's all right,' he said. 'I'm not going to pester you. Wouldn't be much point, would there, with that ring on your finger? Tell me what you thought of the house.'

'You know what I thought. It's stifling.'

'That's only with the Jenningses in it. Think about it with none of their furniture in, and some different wallpaper.'

'You don't mean you'd get rid of those blue cabbages!'

'And the upstairs room turned into a sitting-room, like you suggested. You'd only need to go into the downstairs rooms to sleep

240

then. And suppose we knocked down the wall between the dining-room and kitchen, and made it into one big room – that would be better, wouldn't it? And then we could—'

'Hang on a minute,' Kathy interrupted. 'What's all this "we"?'

Terry stopped abruptly. The excitement died from his eyes and his shoulders sagged. He picked up his glass and buried his face in it. 'I'm sorry, Kath. I wasn't thinking. I didn't even realise I'd said it.'

There was a short, uncomfortable silence, then Kathy said brightly, 'I think it could be nice, the way you'd do it, Terry. It would make all the difference. And with different furniture – something modern and bright – it could look really good. And it's in a lovely position, with the sea on the doorstep.'

'Yes,' he said, 'that's what I thought.'

His pleasure seemed to have evaporated, though. Kathy bit her lip. She didn't really need to have bitten his head off like that. He hadn't meant to say 'we' – it was just that he still hadn't got used to her being married to Brian. And he hadn't asked her out so that he could make a pass at her, Terry wasn't like that. She hated herself suddenly for making him miserable.

'Let's wait till we've seen the one in Portsmouth,' she said, thrusting away her determination not to go with him the next day. 'Then we'll have something to compare it with. And if there are any others you're interested in . . .'

Now you've done it, Kathy Bennett, she thought, seeing the light come back into his eyes. You've not only promised to go tomorrow, you've as good as said you'll look at other places too. And it doesn't matter what you said to Clare, you know she's right really.

It was dangerous to go on seeing Terry Carter. *Dangerous.*

The house in Portsmouth was equally small, but pretty. Situated in the oldest part of the city, not far from the Camber Dock, it was one of a Georgian terrace, with a bow window at the front and a tiny courtyard of a garden at the back. The present occupier was an old man who had lived there all his life, staying doggedly through two world wars, but he had been widowed a few years previously and now he was going to live with his married daughter.

They stopped and looked at it for a few moments. There was no front garden, not even a little strip of yard; the door opened straight on to the street. However, people were starting to do up these little houses and some of them were quite pretty, with windowboxes and coloured front doors. Nothing had been done to the one Terry was looking at, but that wasn't surprising if it was occupied by an old man. He probably didn't even notice what colour the door was, and if he had repainted it he'd have chosen brown, Kathy thought. Not red or yellow or blue, like a young person would have picked.

'You could make this look nice,' she said. 'What's it like indoors?'

Terry knocked on the door. They heard a distant shuffling sound which came gradually nearer, allied to a series of wheezing grunts. Kathy looked at Terry in some alarm and he grinned back at her.

'It's all right. He's got a dog. A Cairn terrier, I think it is.'

'It sounds as old as he is.'

The door opened at last and the old man peered out at them. He had probably once been as tall as Terry, but age had shrunk and bowed his shoulders so that he was now bent almost double, like a hairpin, and his eyes were almost obscured by straggling grey hair. His face, when Kathy could see it, proved to be a mass of tiny seams and wrinkles, like a piece of thin, fine leather that had been squeezed tightly in a ball and then let go, so wrinkled that it was difficult to determine which crease was his mouth and which were his crinkled eyes. When he spoke, his voice was little more than an extension of his wheezing breath.

The dog not only sounded as old as he was, it looked it. Its stained rusty hair straggled around its face in almost exact parody of its master's, and its eyes were completely hidden. Its breath was stertorous and its bark, probably once a frenetic yap, no more now than a grumbling whine. It made a perfunctory attempt at jumping up, and then collapsed in a state of exhaustion at Kathy's feet.

'Get down, Queenie,' the old man ordered unnecessarily. 'Friends. Be quiet.'

He shuffled back into the dark passage and Terry and Kathy followed him into the room with the bow window.

'This is the parlour,' the old man wheezed. 'I sits in here and watches telly, and does all me bits and pieces. I mends clocks and watches for people.' He lifted a crumpled hand and indicated the strewn table while Kathy wondered if he even knew which bits belonged to which, and whether he would ever get them back together again. 'Mind, I don't get so much work these days,' he continued, unsurprisingly. 'Folk takes 'em to the shop these days. But I still got a few customers.' He turned and looked at Terry. 'Have to leave 'em with you if they've not come for them before I goes up to our Pearl's. Then you can send the money on to me, see.'

Kathy stole a glance at Terry and bit her lip. The old man shuffled past them and into the back room. This was obviously the kitchen and had probably been redecorated during the 'fifties, in the light green and cream so popular at that time. There was a table covered with green American cloth, cupboards with green doors, and cream distemper on the walls. At least, Kathy supposed it had once been cream, but it was now stained a dirty brownish colour, and the linoleum on the floor, which had once been green, was splotched with murky stains.

The only furniture was the table, a couple of wooden chairs, a kitchen cabinet and a small gas stove on ornate bent legs. Kathy's grandmother had had one like it, before she went to live in her flat. This place is like a museum, she thought, except that nobody would want to look at these old things.

There was a scullery next, with a chipped Belfast sink and a wooden draining board stained with green algae, and an outside lavatory. Hanging on the wall was a zinc bath, which the old man told them proudly was brought in 'every Friday night without fail, and me and Queenie has our baths then, in front of the fire'. Together? Kathy thought, having more and more difficulty in suppressing her giggles. And if not, who goes first?

Upstairs was little different. Two bedrooms, each large enough for a double bed, though only one was so furnished. The other was a depository for the hoard of a lifetime, with newspapers and magazines piled up in one corner and a jumble of boxes, ornaments and numerous household artefacts heaped all over the floor.

'*Whew!*' Kathy gasped when they were outside on the pavement at last. 'Terry, it's awful. It would need gutting and starting again. You can't seriously want to do all that.'

'Not really, but it seems a good bargain. It's so cheap, Kathy.'

'You'd have to count what you'd need to spend on it as well, though.' She shook her head. 'Why don't you go for a nice new place on an estate, like ours? There's no cleaning to do, no redecorating, you get a nice modern bathroom and proper electrical wiring with modern sockets. Honestly, Terry, that's what I'd do. It's much less trouble and you know what you're getting.'

'I don't know. I wanted a place with a bit of character. I don't want to live in a box.'

'Our house isn't a box,' she said defensively, 'and at least it's not going rotten. That house could have been really nice, but it's been let go. It's old, the walls and the roof are old. You don't know what sort of rot's festering away in there. And I bet there's woodworm.'

'Perhaps you're right.' He turned away. 'Let's go and have a drink before we go back.'

Kathy walked beside him, feeling rather guilty that she'd been so condemnatory. The house would look quite different without all the old man's junk, and without his smell. Given a lick of paint and with that pretty bow window cleaned so that some light could get in, it would probably be really nice.

'I'm sorry, Terry,' she said, slipping her arm through his. 'You shouldn't have asked me to come. I don't really know anything about houses. Brian and I didn't look at many, only the ones on the estate, and we only chose ours because it's on a corner. And I don't know what sort of furniture you're going to have, so I can't imagine these places any different.'

'No, you've been a help, really you have.' They reached the pub and went inside. The windows looked out across the narrow entrance to the harbour. An Isle of Wight ferryboat was passing, so close that you could almost have stepped aboard. Kathy watched it while Terry got the drinks.

'Look,' he went on, 'you're probably right about those two houses. Maybe I ought to look at a few more. The only trouble is –' he looked at her over the rim of his glass '– I really do need someone with me. I know I said I wouldn't ask you any more, but d'you think you could come again? Maybe if we had a look at some furniture too, so that you know what sort of stuff I'll be having – d'you think that would help?'

Kathy gazed at him and sighed. I never meant to do this, she thought. I shouldn't be saying yes, but he looks so miserable and so lonely, and he really is trying. And when you think of the way I treated him, it's the least I can do . . .

'All right,' she said. 'All right, Terry. I'll come with you.'

The warning bells of danger clanged again, deep in the recesses of her mind. But Kathy closed her ears and her heart against them.

Chapter Twenty-Two

In the end, they found the ideal place – a flat in a new block down by Gosport Hard. It was on the fourth floor and overlooked the harbour, and there was a balcony you could sit on in fine weather. Terry had only a two-minute walk to catch the ferry, and was only a short drive away from his friends and family in Gosport. It seemed ideal.

Kathy told herself that once Terry had found a place to live, she would be able to slip quietly out of his life again. But as they stood in the bare sitting-room with its plain white walls, looking across the harbour towards the round bastion of Sallyport and the square tower of the cathedral, he reminded her that she'd promised to help him choose furniture (had she?) and advise him about decorations. 'You know I don't have a clue about these things, Kathy.'

'Terry, I can't. Brian will be home soon for summer leave. They'll be in for six weeks. And then he'll be getting a new draft; he might be back in Pompey for any amount of time.'

'Well, it'll be September before I can move in. It takes that long for all the legal stuff to be done. We could have a look at some furniture now, and choose some colours for the walls. I'm not asking any more than that.'

'You'll need to know what colour the carpet is first,' Kathy pointed out. 'That's the most important thing. You can change wallpaper and chair covers, but the carpet's going to stay the same for a long time.'

'All right, then. We'll go and look at carpets on Saturday.' And, without knowing quite how, Kathy had found herself agreeing. After all, she thought, the sooner we get it all sorted out the better, and then Terry will have to start living his own life.

The trouble was that she enjoyed these outings. It had been fun looking at all the different houses and flats, exciting when they'd seen this one and realised what an ideal solution it was. No garden to worry about, the whole of Portsmouth harbour to gaze at in all its different aspects – filled with the white sails of dinghies going out into the Solent at weekends, always bustling with ships, both merchant and naval, the water sometimes blue and calm, sometimes grey and choppy. I'd like to live here myself, Kathy thought, wandering out on to the balcony. I'd have pots of bright flowers here and a table and a couple of chairs. I'd just about *live* out here . . .

Choosing carpets and furniture was fun, too. Terry had saved quite a lot of money and could afford more or less what he liked. He didn't have flamboyant tastes, but he liked good quality and chose plain blue carpeting right through, and Ercol chairs and tables. In the bedroom, he had a wardrobe and chest of drawers in teak, and he decided to put up his own bookshelves and paint the walls himself.

'I won't have wallpaper to start with,' he said. 'I like it plain. With that big window looking out at the harbour, you don't need any more decoration.'

'You ought to ask your mum what she thinks,' Kathy said. 'I bet she'd love to help you choose things like that.'

'Oh, yes? And have *him* looking down his nose and making sarcastic remarks? I'll ask them here, Kath, but not until it's all done. Then he won't be able to put me off.'

By the time all these choices had been made, Brian was due home and Kathy put Terry out of her mind and concentrated on her own home. At least, she tried to, but thoughts of the flat and the fun they'd had choosing it and finding the furniture kept on popping up in her mind. It seemed dull in Fareham now, somehow, and the house and estate too quiet. She sat in her lounge and looked at the pale cream walls and the oatmeal carpets and curtain and thought of blue, echoing the dancing waters of the harbour and the wide, cloud-chased sky. It's because I'm on my own, she thought. It'll be better when Brian's here.

Anticipation was like a cord, drawing them slowly closer. As the ship steamed towards England and the time grew less, Kathy found herself thinking more and more of Brian's homecoming. She felt a mixture of excitement and apprehension – the excitement of seeing him again, being able actually to touch him, to run her fingers through his hair, to kiss him and wrap her arms about him. And the apprehension of the unknown. Would he still be in love with her? Would he want her just as much as before? Would they be able to make love, to laugh and talk and enjoy just being together?

Would he be able to sense that she had been seeing Terry again?

I might be different, she thought. I might look different, or talk differently. I might say something to give myself away. And fear rose beside her excitement, fear and guilt and dread. The innocence of her meetings with Terry seemed to evaporate and she knew that she must not allow them to go on.

At sea, Brian too was feeling the usual mixture of excitement and nervousness. He had still not really recovered from the shock of Kathy's 'Dear John', and never opened a letter now without a faint twinge of anxiety. He stared at the sea, straining his eyes for the first glimpse of the English coastline, thinking of Kathy, dreaming of the moment when he would hold her once more in his arms, dreading to find that he had lost her once again.

It's daft, worrying like this, he told himself. Kathy'd never go off again. She loves me. She belongs to me. She'd never dare . . .

All the same, he knew he wouldn't be able to rest properly until he had looked once again into her eyes and knew that it was true.

At last the ship steamed into Portsmouth harbour, passing the Sallyport and the cathedral on the starboard side, HMS *Dolphin* and the tower of Gosport's Trinity church to port. There were other towers there too, he noticed for the first time, tall blocks of flats right down near the Hard. But he glanced at them for only a moment. His eyes were on the dockyard, the semaphore tower and the masts of HMS *Victory*. Soon the ship would be docking and Kathy would be waiting. Soon he would hold her in his arms again and know that she was his.

They saw each other at once – Brian on deck, Kathy waiting on the jetty. For a moment, their eyes met and locked, and even at this distance there was a flash of communication. It was there and gone in an instant – a moment of recognition, a flash of understanding. And then he was hurrying down the gangplank and Kathy was in his arms, hiding her face against his shoulder, feeling his warmth, breathing in the scent of him. His lips found hers and she clung to him, digging her fingers into his arms, her eyes tightly closed. Brian, Brian. Brian.

'Kathy,' he whispered, letting her lips go at last. 'Kathy, I've wanted you so much.'

'I've missed you. Oh, I've missed you . . .'

'Let's go home,' he said. He had come ashore with his bag already packed, ready to leave the ship. 'Let's go home.'

They drove round Portchester to Fareham. It seemed impossible to

247

get there soon enough. He whirled her up to bed within twenty minutes of coming through the front door. His lovemaking was like a storm and Kathy felt afterwards as if she had been swept up by a tidal wave, caught on the crest and then tossed down to a beach to recover. She rested against him, shattered by the onslaught of emotional and physical excitement, wanting to talk, to find a different sort of intimacy, but Brian was already asleep.

Kathy lay wakeful. Next time it would be better. Next time he wouldn't be in such a hurry.

'God, I've missed you so much,' Brian said later, sitting up in bed with his arm around Kathy's naked shoulders. 'You know, the worst thing about being married is that it makes you miss your wife so much. I don't know how I'm going to manage when I'm away for longer than this.'

'And how about me?' Kathy asked teasingly. 'How do you think I'll manage? I miss you too, you know.'

'It's different for women. They can switch off more. Men need regular sex.'

Kathy turned and stared at him. 'Is that all you're concerned about? Just the sex? I thought you were missing *me* – not just my body!'

'Well, you are your body. I'd have a job to find you if you didn't have it! And a very nice little body it is too,' he said approvingly, running his hand down her breast. 'What's wrong with me missing it?'

'Nothing. I miss yours too.' He was as tanned as ever, his chest and back broad and muscular. 'But it isn't just sex, is it? I mean, we do have other things too.'

'Oh, sure. Your cooking.' They both laughed. 'I'll never forget the time you gave me boiled lettuce. And then there was that sponge. I really did think you meant me to use it in the bath, you know.' He ducked sideways as she took a swing at him. 'No, seriously, of course there are other things. Being at home with you. Taking you out, showing you off. Everything. But it's *this* a bloke thinks about when he's away.' He slid down in the bed, pulling her under the sheet with him. 'This is what a bloke starves for – not boiled lettuce and sponge cakes. I tell you, it keeps me going to think about coming home to you – knowing you're mine. Knowing you belong to me.' His hands and lips were becoming urgent. 'My Kathy. My wife. *Mine.*'

Martyn was home too, and he and Clare came up to stay with her parents for a few days. They left the children with Bill and Iris and came and had supper with Kathy and Brian one evening, and the four of them took the children to Stokes Bay on the Saturday afternoon, but that was all they saw of each other. Clare wanted to spend time with her own family and see more of her sister Valerie in Portsmouth. The four cousins were near enough in age to play together now, and they took them out to Southsea for another day on the beach. The leave was soon over, and Kathy had barely any time alone with Clare. Even if she had, she didn't think she would have mentioned Terry.

Once again, her emotions were see-sawing. Brian's passionate delight in being home had swept her off her feet, just as his determination to win her back had swept her into marriage, and her mind and senses were intoxicated with him. It was almost like falling in love all over again. She thought of the old saying that being married to a sailor was like having a series of honeymoons. It was true. And yet, she thought, it was somehow not quite satisfactory. Like eating nothing but sweets and chocolate – after a while you longed for something more substantial.

'Why don't we spend the weekend decorating the spare bedroom?' she suggested as they lay in bed late yet again. 'I saw some lovely wallpaper the other day, it would look really pretty in there. Little yellow flowers—'

'Hang on a minute.' Brian raised himself on one elbow. 'Am I hearing things? Did you really suggest spending the last weekend of my leave painting and decorating?'

'Yes, why not? What else did you have in mind?'

'I didn't have anything in mind. Well, only this.' He pulled her against him. 'Kathy, it's my last weekend.'

'No, it's not. There's second leave to go yet. You'll still be here for another three weeks.'

'Not on leave. I'll be going on board every day.'

'I know, but you'll be home in the evenings. And the weekends. We'll still have lots of time together.'

'Yes, but I didn't anticipate spending it painting and decorating,' he said, beginning to sound like a petulant small boy.

'Don't you want to do things to our home? Don't you want to make it look nice?'

'It does look nice. All the bits I see, anyway. I mean to say, the *spare bedroom*. Why does that need decorating?'

'It never has been, that's all. And I thought it would be something we could do together. It would be fun.'

'I can think of a lot of things we could do together,' Brian said, drawing her close again. 'And they're a lot more fun than putting up wallpaper. Come here, sweetheart, and stop talking nonsense. Tell me you love me.'

Kathy closed her eyes. 'I love you.'

Brian moved his lips over her face and lowered his voice. 'Tell me you want me to make love to you.'

'Brian . . .'

'*Tell* me,' he whispered, and she gave in.

'I want you to make love to me,' she said obediently, and waited for his hands to begin their accustomed, practised caresses. 'Oh, Brian, yes – I *want* you to make love to me . . .'

Kathy didn't see Terry again until halfway through September, when Brian was back at sea. Terry could have seen the ship leaving harbour, she thought, if he'd moved into the flat by then.

He rang her one cool, wet evening.

'Are you in? Are you settled?'

She was surprised by the flutter of emotion she felt at hearing his voice. She'd tried very hard to put him out of her mind all through the summer, and even after Brian had gone back to sea she'd resisted the impulse to telephone him. Clare was right, she'd thought, it was too dangerous. She dared not think what Brian would do if he ever found out. Besides, she was in love with her husband. She didn't want any other man.

I ought to put the phone down, she thought, holding it against her cheek. I really ought to. But I can't hurt Terry like that. It isn't his fault. I don't have to be rude to him, just talk politely for a while and then say goodbye.

'Last week,' Terry told her, sounding pleased with himself. 'It's smashing, Kathy. Come and see it.'

'Oh, Terry. I don't think I should. I'm sorry.'

There was a slight pause. 'Why not?'

'You know why not. I'm married to Brian. I can't start meeting you again – it wouldn't be right.'

'Don't you trust me?' he asked, sounding injured. 'You know I'd never do anything to hurt you. I didn't make any passes at you while we were house-hunting. Kathy, all I want you to do is come and look at the flat. I promise I wouldn't do anything you didn't like.'

'I know. It isn't that. I just know that Brian wouldn't like it, and it's not right to do anything I can't tell him about. I'm sorry.' She stopped and waited miserably. Hearing his voice was affecting her more than she'd expected. She was suddenly flooded with a longing to see him again.

There was a long silence. Then he said in a tight voice, 'Are you saying you won't see me again?'

'Terry, we can't. I can't – I don't want – Terry, please don't keep on at me. You know I'm married now. You know I can't come and see you in your flat.'

'We're just friends,' he said in a low tone. 'That's all. I'm not asking any more than that.'

'I know.' She felt cold and miserable.

'We're not living in the Dark Ages,' he said. 'This is the swinging 'sixties, not Victorian times. Men and women are allowed to be friends now.'

'I know.'

'So won't you come and have tea with me?' he asked, like a little boy. 'Just a cup of tea and a biscuit? Maybe a scone or a fairy cake? I've got real bone china cups.'

Kathy laughed in spite of herself. 'Terry, you are a dope.'

'Only with you,' he said. 'Nobody else would believe it. Everyone else thinks I'm stodgy.'

'You're not stodgy,' she said quietly.

There was a brief silence and then he said again, 'Will you come? Please?'

Kathy sighed. 'Terry, I don't think I should. Honestly. Look, I've got to go. Let's just say goodbye now and—'

'No!' he broke in, suddenly urgent. 'Don't say goodbye. Please, Kathy, don't say goodbye to me.'

'I have to,' she said, feeling suddenly desolate. 'You know I have to.'

'You don't. Not now, not on the phone.' She heard him take in a deep breath. 'Look, if you've got to say it, say it here. Here in the flat. Come just this once. I promise you, nothing will happen. But I just want to see you once more. Once. Please. And then you can say goodbye.'

Kathy closed her eyes. She heard the desperation in his voice and knew it for the peril it was. She could feel her own despair and knew the danger in which it placed her. She knew that she must not go to see him – and she knew that she would.

Nothing will happen, she told herself, echoing his promise. Nothing will happen.

'All right,' she said into the telephone, and heard him release his breath. 'All right, Terry. I'll come. Just this once.'

The flat was amazing. There was no other word for it, Kathy thought.

She stood in the middle of the living-room, turning slowly around, taking it all in. Amazing.

Terry watched her from the doorway. He'd stood back to let her go in first, wanting her to see it empty, wanting to see the impact it had on her.

'What do you think?'

She looked at him with shining eyes. 'It's lovely, Terry. Gorgeous.' She shook her head. 'I just can't believe it.'

'I haven't really done anything to it,' he said. 'It's just the things we chose together.'

Kathy nodded. The blue carpet was what they'd chosen together, stretching into the room from the big window as if it were a continuation of the sea and sky outside. She'd suggested the pale blue walls, with the shadows of the clouds racing past like clouds themselves on an indoor sky. The dark blue curtains framed the window like the echo of a deeper sea, and the deep red of the cushions on the chairs and Ercol settee were splashes of warmth, like a fire lit on a sunny beach.

There wasn't much else in the room, apart from a cupboard unit with a record player on top, and records in a rack beneath, the usual assortment of old 78s and newer LPs. There were some bookshelves on one wall, filled with accountancy books and a few classic novels, and a television in one corner.

'It's lovely,' she said again, going to the window. 'And you were right – you don't need much decoration with a view like this.'

From the balcony, she could see right up the harbour, to the big white chalk-pits quarried into the side of Portsdown Hill. The hundreds of masts of the boats moored at Camper & Nicholson's swayed like a forest of saplings just beyond the ferry pontoon. Over the harbour she could see an aircraft carrier moored at the Southern Railway jetty, with the semaphore tower and HMS *Victory*'s masts in the background, and directly opposite, across the narrow entrance to the harbour, the Sallyport and cathedral. To her right were the Gosport creeks that crawled along the back of the streets off the High Street and Stoke Road and into Gosport Park, and the buildings of HMS *Dolphin* and the tall Davey Escape Tower where men who were going on submarines did their training.

'You can see everything from here,' she said, marvelling. 'You'll know everything that goes on.'

Terry grinned. 'I won't have time to watch all that much. It'd be smashing to have a telescope here, though, wouldn't it? One of those big ones, fixed at the window.'

'You'd probably get arrested for spying.' She came back into the room. 'Show me the rest.'

There wasn't much more to see. The flat had two bedrooms, one of which Terry was using as a study. He had built some shelves in here and a worktop which ran all along one side to use as a desk. More accountancy books filled the shelves, and he was obviously doing some sort of course, since the desk was strewn with papers and books.

The big bedroom looked out over the harbour too. It had the wardrobe and chest of drawers that Kathy had helped him choose, and a double bed with a candlewick bedspread on it, dark blue like the curtains which matched those in the living-room.

She stood just inside the doorway, feeling embarrassed. 'Obviously blue's your favourite colour,' she said with a little laugh, turning to go back to the living-room. She bumped into Terry, still standing in the doorway, and caught her breath. 'Oh, sorry. I didn't realise you were there.'

'That's all right, Kath.' He put out his hand to catch her arm and they stood close together. 'Look, don't think anything about that bed. It was mine at home. I always had it. Mum said I ought to have it here. It doesn't mean . . .' He flushed and dropped his hand from her arm, turning away. 'Let's go back in the other room. Let's have a drink before supper.'

'You haven't shown me the kitchen yet.' Kathy's voice was high. She followed him through the short hallway. 'Oh, this is nice.'

She would have said it even if the kitchen had been a dungeon, but it really was nice. Tiny, but clean and bright, with the walls and cupboards all a gleaming white and an open hatchway through to the dining end of the living-room, so that you could still get a glimpse of the harbour. There was a built-in electric cooker and a shining white sink. Terry was clearly very houseproud. There was none of the clutter or mess that Kathy would have expected from a man living on his own.

A savoury smell was coming from the cooker and she sniffed appreciatively.

'Chicken casserole,' Terry said. 'I'm a dab hand at stews and casseroles. They're so easy to make.'

'I like them too.' She smiled at him, at ease again now that they were out of the bedroom. 'How about that drink, then? Let's toast your happiness here.'

He opened the fridge door and took out a bottle of white wine. He poured a glass each and they held them up and touched rims, solemnly. Terry's eyes were very dark.

'I mean it, Terry,' Kathy said softly. 'I hope you'll be really happy here. I hope life will be better for you from now on.'

'Thanks, Kath.' He took a sip and then looked at her again. 'Thanks . . .'

The chicken casserole was delicious. There were jacket potatoes to go with it, and green beans. Afterwards, Terry brought an apple pie to the table and confessed that it had been his first attempt at making pastry. Kathy tried to imagine Brian even letting the thought cross his mind, and knew that he never would. If he ever invited a girl to supper at all, the most it would be was fish and chips, bought from the shop and kept warm and soggy in the oven.

'It's good,' she said, tasting the pie. 'You're a real cook, Terry.'

'Well, you asked me to show some of my hidden talents,' he said, and flushed a little. He lifted the bottle again. There was just enough left for a glass each. Kathy smiled and shook her head, but he took no notice and she drank the wine anyway. She was feeling relaxed and pleasantly warm.

'Let's pull the settee over to the window and watch the lights,' he said, and they sat side by side, their wineglasses in their hands, watching the dusk creep over the harbour and the lights of Portsmouth flicker into life. The harbour was quieter now, but the Gosport ferryboats continued to chug backwards and forwards, and an Isle of Wight boat was still tied up by the pontoon. As they watched, it moved away and turned slowly to set out through the entrance, and after a few minutes another one came in, lit by rows of sparkling lights, and tied up in its place.

'I'd never get tired of this,' Kathy said softly. 'It's going to seem terribly dull at home, with nothing but the neighbours to look at.'

'Well, you can come down here any time you like. There's nothing I'd like more.'

Kathy sighed. 'Terry, you know I can't do that. I'm married.'

'You've been married all this time,' he pointed out. 'It didn't stop you helping me look for a place of my own, and helping to choose the furniture.'

'I know, but I said at the beginning that that was all I would do. Now you've got settled, we'll have to stop seeing each other. You know that.'

There was a silence. Terry placed his glass on the low coffee-table that stood beside him. He turned to Kathy and took hers from her fingers and put it beside his. He put his hands on her shoulders and drew her closer.

'Kathy. Tell me something. Tell me the truth. Are you happy with Brian? Are you really and truly happy with him? Are you glad you married him and not me?'

Kathy stared into his eyes. She had forgotten how dark they could be, how intense. She had forgotten the quiver that her heart gave when she looked into them, the tremor that ran through her body.

'Tell me the truth, Kathy,' he said, and his fingers tightened on her arms.

'Yes,' she said quickly, looking away. 'Yes, of course I am. Of course I am.' She bit her lip. Her eyes felt unexpectedly hot and her throat ached suddenly. I *am* happy, she told herself furiously, I *am*. I just need him to be home with me so that we can live a proper married life. I'm lonely, that's all. But I *am* glad I married him. I am. I am . . .

'It's not true, is it?' Terry said quietly. 'There's something the matter. There's something wrong. Oh, Kathy, you can tell me.' He drew her closer and folded his arms around her so that her head rested against his shoulder and his face touched her hair. 'Kathy, we're friends, we're special. You can tell me anything.'

The hot tears broke free and she gave a long, shuddering sob and then gave way. He held her close as she cried, patting her shoulders, murmuring in her ear, kissing her hair. She turned in his arms and he kissed her face, her wet cheeks, her streaming eyes, her mouth. He held her face between his hands and kissed her again and again. And she responded with kisses of her own, meeting his lips with hers, touching him with her hands, holding him tightly, sobbing and quivering against him.

'Oh, Terry . . .'

'Kathy, I love you. I've always loved you. It broke my heart, watching you go to him . . .'

'I think it broke mine too,' she whispered, 'but I never realised it till now.'

'What is it?' he asked. 'What's wrong between you and Brian? Isn't he good to you?'

She shook her head, fumbling for a handkerchief. 'It isn't that. It's just – Terry, I made a terrible mistake. I can see it now. All this time I've been worrying, wondering what was wrong, wondering why I got infatuated with you when it was Brian I really loved—' She saw the spasm of pain that creased his face and quickly reached out to smooth the lines away. 'No. Don't look like that. Because I was wrong. It was the other way around. It was you I really loved, and Brian I was infatuated with. I tried not to realise it, but all this past leave while he's been at home, I've known it – I've known it deep down all along. It seemed as if he had some sort of power over me, something I couldn't resist – but the power came from inside myself. I thought I loved him, I tried to believe it, and I almost persuaded myself. I tried not to know that it should have been you. Because he was the first, I thought it had to be him.'

'Oh, Kathy,' Terry said in a shaking voice, and held her against him again.

'What are we going to do?' she asked. 'What are we going to do?'

'I'll tell you what I'd like to do,' he said, and drew away slightly, holding her hands in his and looking gravely into her eyes. 'I want to make love to you. I want to take you to bed and make love to you. I want to kiss you all over and hold you in my arms and lie with you beside me all night. I want to wake up tomorrow and find you still with me. Kathy, I want you so much . . .'

'I want you, too,' she whispered. 'I have for a long time. Take me to bed, Terry. Take me to bed now. Please . . .'

Chapter Twenty-Three

From September until Christmas, Kathy spent all the time she could with Terry. She seldom stayed all night, knowing that someone on the estate would be bound to notice if she began regularly to be absent in the mornings – they all went out to work at roughly the same time, waving to each other as they got into their cars – but she usually spent the entire evening with him, and once or twice she had fallen asleep in his arms and had to go to work in the clothes she had worn the previous evening.

'I don't know why you worry,' he said, stroking her back as they lay together in the double bed. 'Nobody knows you're here. There's nobody to worry.'

The thought of there being nobody to know or worry about where she was gave Kathy a cold, lonely feeling. 'Brian might ring up. *He'd* worry.'

'You mean he'd be jealous.' Terry had heard by now of Brian's possessiveness. The way he didn't like Kathy to go out without him when he was at home, the way he asked her about how she spent her time, who she spent it with. 'That's not worrying.'

'It is. He's jealous because he loves me.' She sighed. 'Oh Terry, what are we going to do?'

'I don't know.' She felt his chest lift as he too took a deep, sighing breath. 'I don't know what we're going to do, Kathy.'

Sometimes, when he was making love to her, he'd use his old name for her. 'Pixie. Oh, my *Pixie* . . .' But that was when they were thinking only of each other, when the world was lost to them in a haze of delight and problems seemed to disappear. Afterwards, for a while, there was the lovely warmth of lying together, talking softly, stroking each other's bodies. And sometimes the swift, unexpected rise of a new passion, sweeping them away in a second storm of loving. But in the end, reality would come prowling back like a cat looking for a kill, and their private world scattered like sunbeams in the rain.

Kathy knew that Terry would never be able to bring himself to ask her to divorce Brian – or, more likely, to ask him to divorce her. Besides, people like her and Brian just didn't get divorced. There had been only one divorce in her family, an aunt and uncle years ago when she'd been a little girl, and although nobody had talked to her about it, she'd overheard plenty of murmured conversations between the adults of the family, and she knew that it had been a scandal, something to be ashamed of. The thought of bringing such trouble on her family turned her hot and cold. Mum and Dad would never speak to me again, she thought. Especially if they knew it was all my fault.

Even amongst her friends and workmates, hardly anyone had been divorced. People were, of course – there were those lists in the newspaper every week – but she never knew the people involved, apart from one of the senior male clerks at the office two or three years ago, and he had left soon afterwards. The rumour was that he'd been asked to leave, because he was setting a bad example.

I might lose my job, she thought with a tremor of fear. Terry might lose his. And Brian would kill me . . .

He wouldn't, of course. He wouldn't kill Terry either, but he might give him a beating. Brian had never hit her but she knew that there was violence lurking beneath his breezy manner and that one day it might well erupt.

'Terry, I feel so scared. When I think of what might happen . . . We shouldn't have started this.'

'I know. I tell myself that every day. I don't know why it happened, I never meant it to. I honestly thought we could just go on being friends. I thought that was all I wanted.' He paused. 'Well, no, I knew I wanted more than that, but I never thought it would actually happen. Just to be able to see you was supposed to be enough. But that night – well, you seemed so sad. I just knew there was something wrong, and then . . . what happened next seemed so *right*.'

'It seemed right to me too,' Kathy said softly. 'I don't really know what was wrong. I wasn't unhappy – at least, I didn't think so. It was just – well, so different, being with you. I felt as if it was where I belonged. And when we made love that first time . . . that was different too, Terry.'

'Different?'

'Yes.' She hesitated, feeling disloyal. You shouldn't talk like this about your husband. She continued, all the same; it seemed a bit daft to worry about saying disloyal things when she was lying in another man's bed, in his arms, after an evening of lovemaking. 'When Brian makes love, it's all over so quickly. He doesn't touch me very much and he only kisses me a few times. He's not really bothered about that. All he wants is – well, you know.'

'Well, I want that, too,' Terry said. 'More than anything. But I want all the rest of it too. I want to touch you, Kathy, and I want to kiss you, and I want you to touch and kiss me. And I want it to go on a long time. It makes it all the better.' His voice grew husky and he slid his hand down between her breasts, over her belly, turning his head to kiss her as she drew in her breath. 'Pixie. Oh, my *Pixie* . . .'

It seemed to have been agreed that nothing would change. Kathy and Terry would go on seeing each other whenever possible, but when Brian was at home their meetings would have to be much less frequent, or maybe stop altogether. I can't make love to two men in the same day, Kathy thought miserably, and knew that her first loyalty lay with Brian, because it was he whom she had married, to him that she had made her vows. It was he who deserved her loyalty. If you could call it being loyal, she added, with a surge of self-disgust. Still, she knew that this could be nothing but a lovely interlude. When Brian came back, she would try her hardest to make her marriage work.

'I know it will have to end some day,' Terry said when they met for the last time before the Christmas leave. 'Brian will come out of the Navy and you'll start having babies, and that'll be the finish of it. But as long as nobody finds out, we're not hurting anyone at the moment. We're entitled to a bit of happiness, surely.'

He knew that they weren't, Kathy thought, not when it's taken this way. We both know it. But she wouldn't let thoughts like that stay in her mind for long. Their time together was so brief, and when it was over it would be over for always. All this would be no more than a memory.

Let it be a beautiful memory, Kathy begged silently, let us have something precious and lovely to remember for the rest of our lives.

She went home after that last meeting, feeling a strange mixture of deep contentment and exquisite sadness. Their lovemaking that night had been like a dream, an evening of tender romance with the bedroom curtains drawn back and the harbour lights glittering their reflections in the moonlit water. Terry's fingertips had been like liquid gold, melting her skin, each touch creating a tiny burning focus from which ripples of scorching fire radiated through her body.

He had taken a long time, arousing her to a peak of longing and then gently, tenderly, bringing her down from the crest so that she could take a breath and then be aroused again. And each time the peak was a little higher, the longing a little greater, as if together they climbed a mountain, thinking they had reached the top only to discover a greater, more shining height beyond. And because by now they had made love many times, Terry knew exactly how to bring Kathy to the peak and, finally and gloriously, how to make her reach it and stay there, poised with him between heaven and earth – but closer, she said, closer by far to heaven – until together they slid from the top and, clinging to each other and crying out, slipped back from the peak and into the valley of peace and tranquillity and warm, loving intimacy which was what they had sought all along.

'It's never been like that before,' Kathy said breathlessly, when she could speak again.

'Never.'

'Terry, I love you. I love you so much.'

'I love you, Kathy. I'll always love you.'

There had been a sadness in their voices even then, a recognition that this would be their last lovemaking for some time. For weeks, at least, and perhaps for longer. Perhaps, though they could not have said why they felt it, perhaps for ever.

It was that sadness that Kathy carried with her when she let herself into her own house a few hours later. A sadness, and a premonition.

Nothing was ever going to be the same again, and yet she could not say why.

It was the most painful Christmas Kathy had ever known. Her heart and body ached for Terry day and night, yet she had to put on a smiling face for her husband, had to behave as though nothing was any different. She felt as if she were walking on eggs, afraid to be herself unless Brian noticed something was wrong, amazed that he didn't.

Brian was in a restless mood too. He was leaving his ship, and would join another in January. To his delight, it was the ship that Martyn was serving aboard, and they would be together again for the rest of the commission.

'We'll be going to the Caribbean,' he told Kathy as they sat at the dinner table that first evening. 'Kath, you don't know how good it is to eat a decent steak again. They starve us on board . . . We'll be going to the West Indies. Jamaica and Trinidad. It's going to be fantastic.'

Kathy looked at his ruddy face, a little fleshier now than it had been on their wedding day. He didn't look starved, but, then, he probably got a lot of calories from beer on shore runs. 'You'll be away for months,' she said.

'Best part of a year.'

'You're looking forward to it.'

'Oh, come on, Kath. I don't want to be away from you, you know that.'

'You are. You're looking forward to it. You're excited about it.' She got up and started to clear away the plates. 'Well, I suppose you're bound to be. Anyone would be excited about going on a cruise to the West Indies.'

'Hang on, Kath. It's not exactly a pleasure cruise, you know. We'll be working.'

'It's still nice work, if you can get it,' she said. 'There must be a lot of chaps who wouldn't mind doing their jobs on board a ship cruising round the Caribbean. Plumbers and electricians, or chaps who work in garages or offices.'

Brian's heavy brows drew together in an angry line. 'Well, they know what they can do. They can spend five years doing an apprenticeship. They can have their lives taken over by the Navy. They can spend months at sea away from their wives and sweethearts, waiting for letters. Waiting,' he said, 'for a "Dear John".'

Kathy slammed the plates back on the table. 'Oh, so we're back to that again! You're never going to forget that, are you? You're never going to let it rest.'

'You started it,' he said. 'Look, you knew what it was going to be like when you married me, you knew you'd be on your own for months at a time. It's too late to start whingeing now.'

'I'm not whingeing. It was just that you seemed so pleased at the idea.' Tears came to her eyes. 'You've only been home five minutes and you're already looking forward to going away again.'

'Oh, for Christ's sake, Kathy, don't start crying.' He got up and came round the table to hold her in his arms. 'You know what's the matter with us, don't you?'

'What?' Her face was pressed against his jumper, her voice muffled by the thick wool.

'We need to go to bed,' he said. 'We never feel right until we've been to bed. It's the first thing we do, usually – we've never waited till after supper like this. We haven't made love since the summer and we're frustrated.'

Kathy heard his words with a stab of guilt. It was only three days since she'd made love, not three months. And Brian was right, they were normally in bed within an hour of his arrival. But tonight she'd wanted to put the moment off: she'd felt nervous and anxious, as if it were their first time and she might not know what to do.

'Come on,' he said, guiding her towards the door, 'let's go to bed now. We can have our pudding later.'

Kathy allowed him to lead her up the stairs. There didn't seem to be anything else she could do. She lay on the bed, trying to make the right responses, smiling, whispering, crying out. And afterwards she lay very still, and felt tears slip slowly down her cheeks.

Terry, she thought, listening to Brian's heavy breathing. Oh, Terry.

Afterwards, when Brian woke, he lifted himself on his elbow and looked down at her quizzically.

'You didn't seem as keen as usual, Kath. What's the matter?'

She shook her head. 'I don't know. I've been feeling awfully tired lately. We've had a lot of extra work at the office, I suppose that's it.' She turned her face aside but he laid his fingers against her cheek and turned it back to study her.

'You do look a bit washed out. Never mind, you can have a bit of rest now I'm home. A few late lie-ins are what you need.' He grinned and gave her a smacking kiss. 'Oh Kath, it's good to be back with you in our own comfortable bed. And I'll tell you what, we'll go out tomorrow and have a slap-up meal somewhere. The best place you know. What d'you reckon?'

'Yes,' she said, her heart sinking. 'Yes, Brian, that'll be lovely.'

'Tell me you love me,' he said, lowering his face to hers. 'Tell me you're mine. Tell me you're all, all mine . . .'

After that he seemed to accept that she was no more than tired, although when the tension grew too much for her and she snapped in irritation over small things he raised his eyebrows at her.

'Touchy, aren't we? Time of the month, is it?'

'You know it isn't,' Kathy said edgily. 'I just get fed up with seeing your things lying about all over the place. I thought sailors were supposed to be tidy.'

'We are, on board ship.' He gave her an odd look. 'This is my home, Kath, just in case you'd forgotten. I live here, remember? I'm the bloke you put on that long white frock for.'

'I know.' She bit her lip, flushing. 'I'm sorry, Brian. I don't know what's the matter with me these days.'

'You're tired and you've been working too hard.' He took her in his arms. 'Tell you what, why don't we have a party? Martyn and Clare are coming down to spend Christmas with her mum and dad, aren't they? Let's get a few of the neighbours in and some of the blokes off the shop and have a bit of a knees-up.'

'Yes,' she said. If nothing else, it would help to pass the time. 'Yes, all right. That'll be lovely.'

Apart from the party, Clare and Kathy barely saw each other during that leave. For one thing, Clare and Martyn stayed in Portsmouth with Valerie and Maurice, so that the family could spend Christmas together without any of the children having to make late-night journeys home. Ian was there too, with his fiancée, who was a Portsmouth girl so could go home each night, and Bill and Iris slept on the sofa-bed in the front room (the 'sed-bettee', Bill called it the first night, and the name stuck, as did so many of his spoonerisms).

Martyn and Clare still had no car of their own, but had hired one for the holiday and arrived loaded with the usual paraphernalia that seemed to accompany all couples with young children wherever they went. They drove round to Kathy's party, two nights after Christmas, and found half a dozen other couples, all about the same age, sitting round the tidy lounge with drinks in their hands and a few plates of crisps and nuts spaced neatly on the coffee-table.

Brian welcomed Martyn with a clap on the shoulder and a great shout of laughter. 'Welcome aboard, shipmate! This is my oppo, Martyn Perry,' he told the rest of the guests. 'We're going to sea together again in the New Year. Did our apprenticeships together, served on our first ship together, and now the old team's going into action together again. That's right, isn't it, Mart?'

Martyn grinned and accepted a glass of beer. Clare caught Kathy's eye. She thought her friend looked pale and tired, and as soon as she could she slipped out to the kitchen to give her a hand.

'I'm just doing sausage rolls and stuff like that,' Kathy said, her voice over-bright. 'I don't suppose anyone wants a lot to eat, you're probably all over-stuffed. I know Brian and I are.'

'Kathy,' Clare said, 'what's the matter?'

'What do you think's the matter?' Kathy was concentrating on a plate of cheese straws, arranging them in a neat criss-cross pattern on a plate. 'They're going away again, aren't they? For a year, or as near as dammit. Aren't you sick of it, Clare? Because I can tell you, I am.'

Clare was silent, watching her, then she said, 'We knew what it was going to be like. You even had the chance to find out before you got married.'

'Oh, don't you start on about that too!' Kathy rounded on her. Her face was pink now, and her eyes bright. 'I've already had it from Brian. Other boys! Dear John letters! He's never going to forget it, Clare, never.'

'Oh, Kathy. I'm sure he trusts you.'

'Are you? Why should he? Why should I trust him? Why should *anyone* trust anyone else at all? It's too much to expect. It's not fair. It's putting a huge burden on people, to trust them. People are human, Clare. You can't expect them to be anything else.'

Clare stared at her, bewildered. Kathy's words weren't making any sense, she thought. Unless . . . 'Kathy, has something happened?'

'What? What d'you mean? What could have happened?'

Clare gestured helplessly. 'I don't know. Something about Brian? You don't think he's – well, you know –'

'How should I know? I'm not saying he's done anything. I'm just fed up with him being away so much. And I'm fed up that he's looking forward to it. What about you, Clare? What about Martyn? Is *he* looking forward to it too? Is *he* so excited about it he can hardly wait?'

Clare looked rueful. 'Well, he is a bit, but I suppose that's something we have to get used to. And I'd rather he was happy in the Navy than feeling as if he was in prison. He's got to stay in for a few more years yet, I wouldn't want him miserable all that time.'

'No. No, I suppose not.' Kathy shrugged and gave her a half-grin. 'Don't take any notice of me, Clare. I'm just tired. We hardly seem to have stopped this leave, and we've had almost no time to ourselves. I had to work right up till Christmas Eve and I'm back again tomorrow morning . . . To tell you the truth, all I really want to do is go to bed and sleep for about three days.'

Clare gazed at her. She noted the white face, the dark circles under Kathy's eyes, the nervous tightening of her forehead every few minutes. She saw the shake of Kathy's hands as she placed the last cheese straw.

'Is there anything else, Kathy?' she asked quietly. 'Is there anything else the matter?'

Kathy paused and for a moment Clare thought she was going to tell her. And then the kitchen door opened and Brian poked his head round, his face a shade or two redder than before, the aroma of Strong's best bitter wafting around him like a perfume.

'Come on, you two. No skulking out there in the kitchen. We're starving to death in here.' He pushed the door fully open and came in, grabbing the plate so that the cheese straws almost slipped off. He caught them just in time, pushing them back into an untidy heap. 'I'll take these in, shall I? Aren't the sausage rolls hot yet?'

Kathy sighed and turned to the oven, opening the door so that the smell of sausage rolls drifted out in a savoury cloud. 'Anything else the matter?' she repeated. 'Of course not. What else could be the matter?'

There was no other chance for them to talk that evening, and the next day, Clare and Martyn packed up the hired car and drove back to Devon.

Well, Clare thought, at least the ship's based in Devonport. Brian will be down here again, and maybe Kathy will come too, for a weekend. They could stay with us and we'll have a chance to talk then.

There *was* something wrong, she thought, and it could be something serious. But unless Kathy chose to tell her, there was nothing she could do but wait.

She sighed, unconvinced by her friend's assurances, and turned her attention to spotting Christmas trees in people's windows, so that she could point them out to Christopher and Laura.

Chapter Twenty-Four

Christmas leave was over and Martyn and Brian were together on their new ship, the aircraft carrier *Dramatic*. It was 1964, the year of the Olympic Games, and Clare found herself switching on the television every afternoon to watch the ski-jumping.

She thought she had never seen anything so exciting. Ordinary sports – running, jumping, hockey or cricket – didn't interest her much, and she would rather play tennis herself than watch someone else, but the thrill of seeing someone poised at the top of a huge ski-jump, sliding down the steep slope and then launching into space to land far down on the snow, caught at her imagination.

There was other skiing too – slalom and downhill racing. Partly, she knew, it was the scenery that attracted her, the wild beauty of the great Alpine mountains around Innsbruck. Who won the races wasn't especially important; she just liked watching them coming down the steep slopes and the narrow valleys. I'd like to do that, she thought. I'd like to go skiing. I'd like to go up into those mountains and see that scenery, be a part of it. Draw and paint it.

She had spent quite a lot of time painting during the past year. The snows of 1963 had given her fresh subjects and she had completed two oil paintings, one of the frozen weir and another of the sweeping view of Crowndale from the front window. More and more, however, she had found herself drawn to sketches – the children playing in the garden, ponies on the moor, the crowded scenes of Goosey Fair in October. She picked out amusing items in the newspapers and illustrated them, and when she wrote to Martyn or her parents her letters were littered with tiny cartoons.

Dramatic was in Plymouth for a few weeks before she sailed, and

Brian became a frequent visitor, usually coming home with Martyn and staying the night before going back with him on the train next morning. The trudge down into Tavistock and up Kilworthy Hill to the railway station was a nuisance, but since Dr Beeching's railway cuts had closed the line through Whitchurch the only alternative was the bus, which took much longer and didn't go near Devonport. Sometimes, if the weather was bad, Martyn used it nonetheless, preferring a walk at the other end to having to sit on the train in wet clothes, but he had begun to question the wisdom of living at Tavistock when it gave him such a long journey in each day.

'I don't see the point of moving into Plymouth,' Clare said when he grumbled. 'Not when you're away so much. It's so much nicer here. And the children are settling down. Christopher will be starting school after Easter, and I don't want to keep moving them about. Perhaps we could think about getting a car next time you come home.'

She decided to have a party for Martyn before the ship sailed, and invited Veronica and Alex, Sue and Don, and two or three other couples. Brian came too, of course. He came home with Martyn, looking very debonair in a tweed jacket and fawn twill trousers. It was a shame Kathy wasn't here too, Clare thought, but she hadn't seemed keen to come down even for a weekend since Christmas, preferring Brian to go back to Fareham on the weekend coach. Once again, Clare had the uneasy feeling that something was wrong, but Brian didn't seem bothered and breezed in with his usual air of being slightly too big for any room that he happened to be in.

'You're looking a stunner as usual, Clare,' he declared, giving her a smacking kiss. 'I like that outfit.'

'It's nothing special.' Still, she felt she looked quite reasonable in her pleated tartan skirt and white blouse with a dark red cardigan on top. No doubt Veronica would look gorgeous, as usual. Veronica would look gorgeous wrapped in an old sack.

Veronica was not, however, wrapped in a sack, old or new. Her slender figure was snuggled into a white angora jumper with a roll collar which, when she and Alex arrived, was pulled up round her face like a hood, and slim black trousers. Her pale, silky hair was loose on her shoulders, like a veil of gossamer, and her cheeks were rosy and her cornflower eyes sparkling from the walk up the lane.

Clare saw Brian's glance sharpen as he looked at her.

'It's *bitter* out there,' Veronica declared, sliding out of her fur jacket. 'I nearly refused to come. It was only because Alex promised me that Brian would be here.' She turned her face up towards Brian and gave him her enchanting smile. 'It's lovely to see you again. Tell me everything you've been doing.' Her smile glimmered through her lashes. 'And I do mean *everything*.'

Brian grinned and took her arm to lead her to the sofa. They sat together, their heads close, talking quietly, and every now and then they laughed together, Veronica's silvery tinkle contrasting with Brian's deeper tones.

'How are the children?' Alex asked, coming to sit beside Clare. 'I haven't seen them for a while.'

'That's because you work too hard, darling,' Veronica told him from across the room. 'You never come home for lunch now, and you stay late in the evenings.'

'I have to put in the time and effort if I'm to get promotion. You know that.' He looked at Clare again. 'Isn't Christopher starting school soon?'

'Yes, he and Andrew are going together. They've already had an afternoon there. They loved it, didn't they, Sue?'

Sue, sitting beside a couple who ran one of the greengrocery shops in Tavistock, nodded. 'Andrew can't wait to start. Someone told him there's a school football team and he thinks he'll be in it straight away.'

'At five?' Alex laughed. 'He's got a hope!'

Sue's husband, Don, was standing by the wall, admiring Clare's painting of the weir. 'Did you do this?' he asked her.

Clare nodded. 'It's just a hobby. Martyn gave me some oils last Christmas. That was my first real attempt.'

'Your first?' He looked at it again. 'But it's really good. Have you had much training?'

'No. None. I just mess about. I've always liked drawing.'

'Show me some more,' he commanded, and Clare hesitated. 'Please. I'm interested.'

Clare glanced around the room, but everyone was engrossed in conversation. She gave Alex a quick, half-apologetic smile, and got up. 'I've got a folder with some sketches in, that's all. I don't have time to do much.'

'Show him,' Alex said encouragingly. 'Show him your cartoons.'

'Oh, no—'

'Cartoons?' Don echoed. 'Do you do cartoons as well?'

'They're just silly things. Bits I pick out of the newspaper. Honestly, they're nothing—'

'Show him.'

'*Show* me.'

Clare looked from one to the other, sighed and went to fetch her book and folder. She brought them back and left Don in a corner with them while she went to make coffee. When she came back, Don was passing round the sheets of paper and everyone was laughing.

'Oh, no! You haven't let everyone see them.' She stood with the tray in her hands, scarlet with embarrassment. 'Alex, how could you let him? Martyn?'

'But they're *good*,' Don said, wiping his eyes. 'They're really good. Clare, you've got a talent for this, a real talent. Didn't you realise? Didn't you, Martyn? Sue, didn't you? Why didn't you ever *tell* me?'

'I never even thought about it.'

Don looked at Clare. 'Could you do this every week? Could you come into the office and pick out something funny from the news to draw a cartoon about, for the front page? Could you do that?'

'A cartoon?' she said, dazed. 'For the front page of the newspaper? *Me*?'

She looked across the room at Martyn and thought of the lonely months that lay ahead. However much she told people she was used to it and didn't mind, the loneliness was sometimes almost more than she could bear, and the ache of it was already beginning, somewhere deep in her heart. But the thought of having something of her own to do, something like having her own cartoon on the front page of the local paper every week, trivial though it might seem, gave her heart a sudden lift.

'Oh, yes,' she said to Don, her face alight. 'Oh, yes, I'd *love* to!'

By the time Christopher started school, Clare had supplied half a dozen cartoons to the local newspaper and *Dramatic* was on its way to the Pacific. Clare and Sue walked down to Tavistock together with the boys on their first morning and saw them in through the school gates, just opposite the Meadows. Their teacher was a comfortable, middle-aged woman who ushered all the infants into the classroom like a mother hen.

'Isn't it silly?' Clare said as she and Sue came out. 'I feel quite tearful.'

'Well, it's a big step, isn't it? Their first into the big wide world. And they all look so tiny!'

Clare looked at Laura, jigging about on the pavement beside her. Laura was two now and never stood still. She had wanted to go to school too, but had been persuaded by the promise of being able to play on the swings in the Meadows on the way home.

'Mind you, it'll be rather nice to have this one to myself. And it does seem amazing that I can take Chris there every day and not have to pay for the babysitting!'

Amazing though it was, Clare discovered that it didn't really give her as much time to herself as she'd expected. At twelve o'clock she was back to take Christopher home on the bus for dinner. By the time that was over and she'd walked home again, it was nearly two, and she would have to leave again soon after three to walk back and collect him. I'm going to spend all my time walking to Tavistock and back, she thought, and wondered about school dinners. Well, perhaps after a few weeks. Best to give him time to settle in first.

Christopher was delighted with his new adventure. He came home with a picture he had drawn and told her about the other children in his class. 'There are two boys I'm really sorry for,' he said. 'They've only got one face.'

Clare stared at him. 'One face? Whatever do you mean?'

'One face,' he said a little impatiently. 'Me and Laura have got a face each. Michael and Peter have only got one. They look just the same.'

'Oh!' Clare said. 'You mean they're twins.' She tried not to smile as she explained to Christopher about identical twins. He was sensitive about being laughed at. 'Think of all the fun they'll have, pretending to be each other,' she said. 'I expect the teachers will want them to wear different pullovers or something, so they can tell them apart.'

He gave her a withering look. 'They do. Michael wears red and Peter wears blue. But they've still only got one face.'

Laura came out from the living-room, looking innocent. Clare knew immediately that she had been up to mischief and went in to see what had happened. At first, she could see nothing amiss, and then she noticed the bananas.

There had been half a dozen, arranged neatly on top of a pile of apples. There were still half a dozen, but they looked different. She touched the top one and smiled.

It was an empty skin. Laura, who had a passion for bananas, had eaten it and carefully replaced the skin so that it looked as if it had not been touched. Clare lifted it off and then looked at the rest and laughed aloud.

Each one was empty, and each had been carefully arranged to look untouched. She must be stuffed full of banana, Clare thought, suppressing her amusement and trying to look stern. It might be naughty, but it was certainly ingenious. And I was looking forward to having her to myself!

It was difficult to be depressed, with children to look after, but she

270

couldn't help thinking of Kathy, who had no one to share the lonely hours.

'I've got something to tell you.'

Kathy was on the balcony of Terry's flat, watching the ships in the harbour. It was a bright, blustery July afternoon and a flotilla of sailing dinghies were bunching together, their sails like butterflies' wings as they competed for the wind to drive them out into the Solent. The sun glittered on the water, and myriad white horses danced on the tops of the little waves.

She turned as Terry came out beside her, carrying two mugs of coffee. He handed her one and repeated his statement, and she smiled, her eyes still on the bustling scene below.

'Look at me, Kathy,' he said. 'Listen. It's important.'

Kathy set her coffee on the floor and removed her gaze from the harbour. He was looking serious, and she felt a small tremor of alarm. 'What? What's wrong?'

'Nothing's wrong,' he said. 'At least, I don't know . . . Kathy, I've been offered a better job.'

'A better job? But that's marvellous. Oh, you are clever! Well done.' She threw her arms around him and kissed him, almost spilling the coffee he was still holding. 'What is it?'

'Well, it's promotion really. More responsibility. I'll be dealing with business accounts. Quite big businesses.'

'Terry, I'm so pleased. When do you start?'

He looked at her, frowning slightly. 'There's another question you haven't asked yet.'

'Another question? What's that?'

'Where is it?' he said.

'Well, where is it, then?' she asked obediently. 'Won't you be in the same office? Have you got to move – to Fareham, or Southampton?' She knew that Terry's firm had a number of different branches. 'That wouldn't be too bad, would it? I know you'd have a longer journey, but you could drive, or go by train. It wouldn't be too difficult—'

'It's not Southampton,' he interrupted. 'Or Fareham.' He stopped for a moment, then said, not looking at her, 'It's London.'

'*London?*'

'Yes. To Head Office.' He looked at her again. 'It's quite a big jump, Kathy.'

'Yes,' she said slowly. 'Yes, it must be . . . Have you *got* to take it, Terry?'

He gave a short laugh. 'They wouldn't think much of me if I didn't.'

'No, but if you really didn't want to go . . . I mean, you could wait, couldn't you? Another chance might come up – in Portsmouth, or Southampton . . .'

'What are you saying?' he asked quietly.

Kathy met his eyes and then looked down at her hands. 'I suppose I'm saying I don't want you to go.'

'You want me to stay in Gosport.' It was half question, half statement.

'Well, of course I do!' she cried. 'I don't want to lose you. I love you, Terry. I want to be with you. I don't want you to go off to London so that we hardly ever see each other.'

'And what happens when Brian comes home? Would I be able to go then?'

Kathy stared at him, then bit her lip and turned away. Her eyes filled with tears. 'That's different. You know it is.'

'Why is it? Why is it different?'

'You *know* why. Brian and I are married. I've got to be with him when he comes home.'

'And just where,' he asked, 'does that leave me?'

Kathy shook her head and looked away again. 'I don't know. Terry, I'm sorry. I know it's unfair. But I just don't know.'

'You want to stay with Brian, but you want me to be around as well, so that when he goes away, I'm here for you. Do you ever think what it's like for me when he's home?'

Kathy took both his hands in hers. 'Of course I do, Terry. I know how hard it is. I miss you too, but you know I can't see you very often then. If he ever suspected . . .'

'Sometimes,' Terry said, 'I think that would be the best thing that could happen.'

Kathy drew back, staring at him. 'Terry, you wouldn't . . . If Brian had any idea, he'd kill you. He'd kill me. He *would*!'

'He wouldn't do any such thing. He'd be livid, obviously, and I wouldn't blame him, but he wouldn't kill anyone. He'd just blow his top and probably turn you out.'

'Well, that's what I mean. He'd divorce me, and you'd be named. You know you don't want that. You could lose your job.'

'Could I? If I was working in London? It's different there, Kathy. People aren't so bothered. They needn't even know. We could get married. We could be together properly.' He took her hands again and gripped them tightly. 'It's what we really want. It's what we always wanted, it's what ought to have happened in the first place. We were *meant* to be together, Kathy.'

They stared into each other's eyes. Kathy saw the intensity, the dark fire that had always attracted her. Terry was so quiet, so easygoing, and yet deep within him burned these fires, and she knew that it was to these depths that she had always responded. Brian had the same passion in his nature, but with him it was closer to the surface and concerned more with himself and his own desires. Terry's right, she thought, we ought to have been together. I ought to have been loyal to him when Brian came home that first time, and not felt so guilty over the 'Dear John'.

'Come to London with me, Kathy,' he urged. 'Let Brian divorce you, and marry me instead.'

She stared at him, then pulled her hands away and turned aside. 'I can't. You know what your firm's like. They want all their employees to be as pure as the driven snow. Look at that man who left his wife and married his secretary – he was given a month's notice. And he was senior to you, a lot senior. How can you be sure they wouldn't do the same to you? I don't believe it would be any different in London.'

'I'd get another job,' he said. 'There are plenty of accountants.'

'And they all feel the same way.'

Terry sighed and ran his fingers through his hair. He gripped her shoulders and turned her to face him. 'Kathy. This is 1964. The Swinging Sixties. It really is different now.'

She almost laughed at him. The Swinging Sixties. Hippies all the rage, with bells round their necks and flowers in their hair. California the place to be, with San Francisco the culture capital of the world. Peter Sellers, reducing people to hysterics in *The Pink Panther* and everybody buying Motown records, made by the Supremes, Stevie Wonder and Marvin Gaye.

Only it wasn't like that, not in Gosport or Portsmouth, or any of the other places she knew.

'Where Did Our Love Go?' The song drifted into her mind. Where does love go, and why, when you thought it would be yours for ever?

Terry was giving her no time to think, no time to make a decision. It was as if the years of loving her and waiting for her had taken their toll, as if they had used up all his capacity for waiting and loving. It was as if making that first bid for independence in buying his own home had started a machine that couldn't be stopped.

'What will you do if I say no?' she asked in a low voice.

'I'll go anyway. I've had enough of it here. My life's stood still long enough. It's time to move, Kathy. I'm not going to be a yesterday man any longer.'

'But what about your flat? You're surely not just going to leave it. You haven't been in it a year yet.'

'It'll sell.' He hardly seemed to care. 'It's time to start a new life, Kathy. Either with you, or on my own. I can't live like this any longer.'

'Like what? I thought you were happy here.'

'Happy? Living like a shadow? Spending my life waiting till you can spare me some of your precious time? Sorry, Terry, Brian's coming home and I can't see you for six weeks. Sorry, Brian's coming home for good and I shan't be able to meet you again *ever*. You think that makes me happy?'

'Terry, I've never said that. Brian won't be coming home for good for another four years.'

'And won't you say it then?' he demanded. 'Won't you? Can you look me in the eye, Kathy, and tell me you won't say it then?'

Kathy stared at him and then turned her head away.

'You see,' he said flatly, 'you can't. You know you'll say it. And where will I be then, with my safe little job in Pompey, or perhaps Southampton? The man who wouldn't take promotion when it was offered and won't be given a second chance. The man who never looked for a girl who loved him enough to share her life with him, because he was too tied to a girl who didn't.'

She cried out in sudden anguish, 'Terry, no! It isn't like that. I *do* love you . . .'

'But not enough,' he said brutally. 'And tell me why I shouldn't talk like that. Because it upsets you, doesn't it? And whatever else happens, we mustn't let poor Kathy be upset. Never mind what hell she puts the rest of us through.'

Was that what it was like? Kathy wondered. Did she put them through hell – Terry and Brian? A cold feeling around her heart told her that it was true. She had sent Brian a 'Dear John', and given him months of misery at sea. She had abandoned Terry for him when he came back. And now she was betraying Brian all over again, and driving the knife even deeper into Terry's heart.

I don't even know how it happened, she thought miserably, staring out of the window at the harbour, alive with sailing boats and tugs. I never meant it to be like this. I never meant to hurt either of them.

Terry came up behind her. 'You've got to decide. Either you come to London with me or I go by myself. And that will be the end for us.'

'Terry, I need time to think—'

'You *don't* need time to think. You've had it. You've had four years to think. If you need time to think,' he said cruelly, 'it's because the answer is no, and you know it.'

She knew that he was right: thinking and logic played no part in this. If she truly loved him enough to want to be with him, no matter what, she would say yes. Without a moment's hesitation, she would say yes.

'Well?' he said. 'What's it to be? Do you love me enough – or don't you? Tell me now, Kathy.'

She faced him bravely. It was tearing at her heart to hurt him yet again, but this time she knew that she was doing it through courage rather than fear. This time she knew what path she must take.

'I do love you enough,' she said quietly, her voice shaking. 'And I'm not coming with you.'

Terry stared at her. His brow furrowed, his eyes narrowed and his mouth grew hard. His body tensed and for a moment she thought he was about to strike her, but instead he said in a harsh tone, quite unlike any she had heard before, 'And just what is that supposed to mean?'

'I won't ruin your life,' she said. 'I know what will happen if I leave Brian and come to you. Even in London. Your firm will sack you – all right, they're old-fashioned, but they're not the only ones. What sort of a position will you get with any other firm, with that hanging over your head? And it'll be the same for me. The Civil Service won't like it any more than your people. We shall both be out of a job, and what use will it be being in London then? Or anywhere else?'

'We'd manage. We could emigrate. We've talked about it before—'

'It'll be the same whatever we do,' Kathy said. 'I *know* we'd manage, Terry. I know we'd find jobs of a sort, we'd scrape a home together, we'd get by. We'd be happy – for a while. But how long could it last? Someday you'd think of what you could be doing, the position you could have risen to, and you'd regret it. If you stay with your firm, you could be a partner some day. I can't let you give all that up.'

'Kathy, that's not important. It wouldn't mean a thing without you—'

'It would. And, anyway, that's not the only reason. There's another one, and it's probably even more important.'

'And what's that?'

'Your principles,' she said. 'Look at the way you feel about your own parents. Your father, going off and leaving you and your mother. Your stepfather. You hate the whole situation. What would be so very different about ours, if we did what you want?'

Terry turned away sharply. 'It's not the same at all!'

'It's not so very different,' she said. 'You're asking me to leave Brian. I'm already your mistress and sometimes I wonder how your conscience feels about that. I know mine pricks me, whenever we're not together. Oh,' she said quickly before he could interrupt, 'I know it *feels* right between us – but it isn't really, is it? I've promised to be faithful to Brian, promised it in church, and I'm breaking that promise every minute of the day. And I know you hate it too, really. How do I know that one day you won't look at me and despise me? How do I know you'll ever really trust me – knowing what I am?'

Terry whipped round and pulled her roughly into his arms. 'Don't say such things! I'll never despise you, never. I love you. I *love* you.' He was kissing her, rough, biting kisses that left her skin and mouth sore and throbbing yet brought a searing flame of excitement leaping through her body. Half crying, she clung to him, holding him hard against her, returning his kisses, opening her mouth to his as if she wanted to devour and be devoured by the anguish of her love. Together, they staggered, half fell against a chair, then sank to the floor, moaning and sobbing as they tore at their clothes, and when they came together it was as if the sky were exploding around them and the world was in chaos about their heads.

The frenzy of their lovemaking was something that neither had ever experienced before. It took them to the heights and plunged them deep before sweeping them up again to a summit that was soaring and clear, somewhere beyond space. Yet when it was over, when they lay closer, more intimate, than they had ever done before, they each knew that this was the last time. There was nothing further to say.

This was their last goodbye.

Chapter Twenty-Five

Christopher was halfway through his second term at school when Kathy rang to ask if she could come down to Dale View to stay for a few days. Clare, delighted at the thought of seeing her friend again, spent the time cleaning the house and shopping. She went to Creber's, the speciality shop on the corner in Brook Street, where she could seldom afford to shop, and bought freshly ground coffee, hot roasted cashew nuts and three different kinds of cheese.

'We'll have roast chicken the first night,' she said to Laura, who was gazing round-eyed at the array of jars containing herbs and spices and other exotic foods in the window. 'And then we can have it cold next day. I'll buy a piece of gammon too, to go with it. It'll be lovely to have Auntie Kathy here, won't it?'

Laura nodded, a little doubtfully. She didn't know Kathy that well, Clare realised. Somehow, during the past year or so they hadn't seen so much of each other, and there had always been other people about. Martyn and Brian, of course, but other people too, people they didn't know, at parties. We won't have any parties this time, she decided. I want Kathy to myself for a change.

Kathy drove herself down, arriving soon after Christopher had come home from school. He was writing down lists of numbers at the kitchen table when Clare heard the car come up the lane and turn into the top driveway. She ran out and through the garage to meet her friend.

'Kathy! You're here! Come in and have a cup of tea. Did you have a good drive? Oh, it's so good to have you here!'

Kathy came in and put her suitcase on the floor. She smiled at the children and then lifted Bartholomew from the armchair Clare kept by the Rayburn, sinking into it with him on her lap.

Clare looked at her properly and frowned. 'Are you all right? You look a bit pale. Are you tired after the drive?'

'A bit. I just need a rest.' Kathy leaned her head back and closed her eyes. Clare gave her a doubtful glance and went to put the kettle on. A four-hour drive might be rather a lot to do all on your own, but it surely wasn't enough to make anyone look as worn out as Kathy did. There were big dark circles under her eyes, too, like bruises.

'You've lost weight,' she said, giving Kathy a cup of tea. 'Kathy, what's wrong? Are you missing Brian badly?'

Kathy gave her an odd look. 'If only that were all,' she said, and sipped the tea. 'Oh, *Clare* . . .'

'What? What is it?'

Kathy shook her head and glanced at the children. 'Not now. I'll tell you later.' She eased the big marmalade cat off her lap and stood up. 'Look, d'you mind if I just go and have a rest now? I'll take my tea upstairs. I really do feel knocked out.'

'No, of course I don't mind. I'll bring your case. You're in the back bedroom.' Clare led the way upstairs and watched anxiously as Kathy slipped off her shoes and lay down on the bed. 'Is there anything else you'd like?'

'No. I'll be all right now. Don't worry. I'll come down in an hour or so and we'll have a good old chinwag this evening, after the kids have gone to bed.' The bruised eyelids drooped. 'God, I feel so *tired* . . .'

Clare went downstairs, slowly and thoughtfully. When Kathy had telephoned, she had thought nothing of it other than that they could have a few days together to renew their old friendship, a few days filled with talk and laughter just as in the old days. Now, she saw that the visit was not just a social one. Kathy had come for a purpose. She had come because she was in trouble.

What is it this time? she wondered. What has Brian been doing? She racked her brains for any clues from Martyn's letters, but could find none. They were just as usual, a mixture of love and longing, together with grumbles about the ship and tales (probably bowdlerised) of runs ashore.

So if Brian hadn't been doing anything, it must be Kathy herself. And Clare, smearing the chicken with fat and sliding it into the Rayburn, had a sinking feeling that she knew what was coming next.

She had not, however, been at all prepared for what Kathy had to tell her.

It started when Kathy came downstairs. Clare had heard her moving about for some time, unpacking her case and then having a bath. When she finally descended, she had washed her short blonde hair and changed into a dark red skirt and jumper. She had a little more colour in her cheeks, but as she paused in the doorway it disappeared, leaving her whiter than ever.

'You're cooking chicken.'

'Yes. I thought it would be nice to have a proper celebration on your first night. I know it's your favourite. Why? What's the matter?'

Kathy shook her head. 'I'm sorry. I just can't bear the smell of chicken at the moment. D'you mind if I just have an egg?'

Clare stared at her. 'You can't bear the smell? Oh, *Kathy* . . .'

Kathy gave her a rueful look. 'I know. I didn't mean it to come out quite like that. Look, I'll go in the other room. It'll be all right once it's cooked but it really is making me feel sick. I'm sorry . . .'

Clare followed her into the living-room. She had lit the fire in there and it was warm and tidy. Laura and Christopher were watching *Pussy Cat Willum*, with Wally Whyton, on television and took no notice.

'You don't have to ask what's the matter now, do you?' Kathy said with a wry glance at Clare.

'I don't think I do. But Brian's been away since Easter. That's six months.'

'And I'm not six months pregnant. No. It's about ten weeks. They say this sickness wears off at three months, but it didn't with you, did it? I hope to God I'm not going to go on feeling like this till next April. It's bad enough as it is. In fact,' she said with an attempt at briskness, 'it couldn't really be any worse.'

Clare scarcely knew what to say. There were questions that must be asked, yet now was hardly the time, with the children sitting in the same room. Not that they'd understand what was being said, but they would know by the tone of their voices that there was something badly wrong. Kathy looked close to tears. She needs to cry, Clare thought, and she can't do that with the children here.

'Look,' she said, 'the chicken will be another half-hour. I'll have to finish cooking it now, but once that's done we'll have some supper and then Chris and Laura will be going to bed. Then we can talk.' She looked at Kathy. 'You want to talk, don't you? You want to tell me?'

'Oh, yes,' Kathy said. 'That's why I've come. I've just got to tell somebody . . .'

It was Terry's baby, of course. Clare had already guessed that, even though Kathy hadn't told her about the meetings, the house-hunting or the flat overlooking Portsmouth harbour. She had always had a feeling that there were things Kathy was holding back, secrets she wasn't giving away, and now they all came out.

'I didn't mean it to happen. I don't think Terry did, either. We both thought we could handle it. I thought being married made me *safe*.' Kathy creased up her mouth at the thought of her naïvety. 'I know, it's crazy, but it's like people taking drugs, they think they can do it a few times and not get hooked. Only you can't.'

'So you did it a few times. Kathy, even *once*—'

'I know. Once is all it takes to commit adultery, isn't it? What a horrible word that is, and yet when you think of it, *adult* isn't a horrible word, it's about being grown-up and responsible. It's only when you add *Terry* – that's a joke, isn't it?' Kathy's laughter was more like a sob. 'Oh, Clare, what have I done?'

'Tell me what happened,' Clare said, taking her friend's hands in her own. 'Just tell me whatever you want to. Let it out, Kathy.'

She listened quietly, hearing about the bungalow at Hillhead, about the old man in Old Portsmouth, about the flat overlooking the harbour. She heard how they had chosen furniture and carpets together, how they hadn't seen each other at all when Brian was home, so the first time Kathy had gone to the flat again it was furnished and Terry had moved in. She heard about the yachts sailing in and out of the harbour, the ships steaming through the narrow entrance, the masts of HMS *Victory*, the semaphore tower, the twinkling lights.

'It was then that we really started,' Kathy said in a low voice. 'In the flat. It felt like home, somehow. Our home – the home we ought to have had together.'

'But, Kathy—'

'I know. I chose Brian, and I told you I was glad I had. I really thought I was. I tried to believe I was, but I wasn't really. It was never really right.' She paused for so long that Clare thought she wasn't going to say any more, and then she added in a voice almost too soft to hear, 'I'm scared of him, Clare. He frightens me.'

'*Frightens* you?'

'Yes. I don't mean he's ever done anything – he's never hit me, or anything. It's just that he seems to have this sort of power over me. I can't resist him. And I can't bear him to be angry with me. It's as though I think he *might* hurt me, even though he never has. As if it's there, waiting for him to be angry enough.'

'And you think he will be, if he finds out?' Clare's glance fell involuntarily to Kathy's stomach. '*When* he finds out. Kathy, you're going to have to tell him!'

'I know. I *know*.' Kathy raised terrified eyes to her face. 'Clare, what am I going to do? Whatever am I going to do?'

Clare stared at her helplessly. This can't be happening, she thought. This sort of thing doesn't happen to people like us. We're like our parents: we live ordinary, decent lives and we don't get into this sort of mess . . . But Kathy had got into this mess, and Clare must do what she could to help her.

'What does Terry say about it?' she asked.

To her dismay, Kathy shook her head. 'He doesn't know. He's gone away. He went to London before I knew about this. It – it must have been the last time . . .' Her voice trailed away into despair.

'Terry's gone to London?' Clare was beginning to feel like a parrot, repeating everything Kathy said, but it seemed to be the only way she could even begin to understand the words. 'But why?'

Kathy drew in a deep, ragged sigh and spoke in a flat, monotonous voice. 'He's got a new job. Promotion. He's at Head Office. He asked me to go with him and I wouldn't.'

There was a short silence while Clare tried to assimilate this new information. Then, scarcely believing she was asking such a question, she said, 'Why wouldn't you go with him?'

'Why d'you think? Because he'd probably lose his job, and I can't do that to him. It would ruin his career – his life. And because I'm married to Brian.' Kathy looked at her with tormented eyes. 'You know what would happen if I ran away with Terry. Nobody would ever speak to me again. My mum and dad – they'd go mad. I'd never be allowed home again. And all my friends . . .'

'I would,' Clare said stoutly, even a touch indignantly. 'I'd stand by you.'

'Would you? Would Martyn let you?'

Clare was silent, unable to answer the challenge. Martyn was Brian's friend. It had been difficult enough the first time Kathy had let him down, but at least they hadn't been married then. This time, it would be impossible.

'Martyn doesn't tell me who I can have as my friends,' she said at last, but her voice didn't sound convincing and Kathy gave her a bitter look.

'None of them has ever done anything like this, though, have they? And none of them was married to *his* best friend.'

Clare sighed and tried another tack. 'Look, it's no use going over all that. The point is, what are you going to do now? What do you want to do?'

'What I want to do doesn't seem to come into it. I don't even *know* what I want to do.' Kathy buried her face in her hands. 'I just want it never to have happened.'

Well, that wasn't going to get them anywhere either. Clare put her arm around Kathy's shoulders. They were shaking with sobs and pity welled up in her – pity for her friend, for Brian, for Terry, and for the baby who was not yet more than an inch or two long, unformed, but whose presence was already a problem of giant proportions.

'Kathy,' she said at last, when the sobs seemed to be lessening, 'we've got to think of something.'

'What? It's too late to do anything about it. I can't take castor oil or jump off chairs now. I can't fall downstairs – I'd be too scared anyway. And in a few weeks it's going to start to show, and everyone will know. They'll know it's not Brian's.' Kathy looked up at last, her eyes terrified. 'Clare, I don't know what to do. I don't think I can go through with it. I'm so *frightened*.'

'I know. I know.' Clare tried to make her voice soothing, but inside she was almost as scared as her friend. There was a lot of talk these days about free love, but that meant other people, not people like herself and Kathy. There was still a stigma attached to illegitimate babies, and young girls still went into homes for unmarried mothers. Perhaps that was the answer for Kathy, although as soon as she'd formed the thought, Clare knew it was no answer. Those places were for *unmarried* mothers, and Kathy had a husband.

'When is the baby due?' she asked tentatively. 'Could you go away somewhere and have it so that no one would know, and then give it up for adoption?'

Kathy gave her a scornful look. 'How could I do that? I've got a job. I've got a house. Where would I go? What would I tell people? What would I tell Brian? Anyway, it's due in April – just when the ship's due home.'

Clare was silent. She kept her arm around Kathy's shoulders, needing the contact herself. She had never had to solve such a problem before and didn't know where to start. Her mind went back to Terry.

'Don't you think you should tell him? Terry, I mean. He's got a right to know. He'd want to help.'

'And what could he do? Look, I could go to London and tell him and he'd stand by me while – while Brian divorced me, and then we could get married. But *this* – you know what could happen, Clare. It's the same problem, only worse. He could lose his job over it. Immoral behaviour. They don't like it, those firms. They're in a position of trust.

Anyway, what do you think he's going to say if I turn up now? I wouldn't go with him before, but now I'm in trouble—'

'It's his trouble too.'

'Is it?' Kathy said bitterly. 'He doesn't have to believe it, does he?'

'I don't believe Terry would do that, Kathy. He wouldn't pretend it wasn't his.'

'No, he wouldn't. He'd want to help. But I'm not going to do it to him.' Kathy raised her eyes. 'Anyway, he didn't give me his address. He left his flat and went away, and I don't know where he is.'

'You could find out. His firm – his mother—'

'*No*,' Kathy said, and Clare could see she meant it. 'This is my problem. I won't involve Terry.'

Clare could hear the pain in her voice, see it in her eyes. What a mess, she thought, what a terrible mess. And what a waste as well – a waste of love, between the three of them. Kathy could probably have been happy with either man. Her tragedy was that she had met them both.

'Well, whether you tell Terry or not,' she said, 'you're going to have to tell Brian.'

'I know.'

'Look,' Clare said, 'why don't you go to the Naval Welfare people? They're supposed to help when there's trouble at home, aren't they? I've got their telephone number somewhere. We could ring them up first thing in the morning. Have you been to the doctor yet?'

Kathy shook her head vehemently. 'I can't! He knows me, he's known me since I was a baby. He knows my parents. I can't go to him.'

'Well, you're going to have to see a doctor some time,' Clare pointed out. 'I – I suppose you really are sure?' But she remembered Kathy's reaction to the smell of chicken. There was morning sickness too. And all the other signs of early pregnancy. There really wasn't any doubt about it.

'Let's go to bed now,' she said. 'You look worn out. We'll ring the welfare people first thing and see what they suggest. I'm sure they'll be able to help.'

'Nobody can help,' Kathy said drearily, but she allowed Clare to make her a mug of Ovaltine, and she took it upstairs with her while Clare put a guard round the living-room fire and stoked up the Rayburn. Clare heard her using the bathroom, and then her bedroom door closed and there was silence.

Clare finished tidying up and took her own drink to bed. She sat in bed, sipping thoughtfully, and then put out the light and lay down, knowing that she would not sleep.

Along the passage, she could hear the faint, muffled sound of Kathy weeping into her pillow.

The welfare officer who came to interview Kathy at Clare's home was a Wren, quite a bit older than Kathy and Clare, probably in her late thirties. She was smart, efficient and, in a brisk way, quite sympathetic. 'Well, you are in a pickle, aren't you?' she said when she had written down all the details in a folder. 'Obviously, your husband will have to be told, and the sooner the better, I should say.' She noticed Kathy's recoil. 'How do you think he will react?'

'Well, what do *you* think?' Kathy asked. 'He's going to go mad.'

'He'll be very upset, naturally,' the Wren officer said, 'but do you think he will stand by you? Of course, nobody can really predict how another person will react in extreme circumstances, but only you know your husband's character.'

'I don't know what he'll do,' Kathy said in a tight voice. 'I just don't know.'

The Wren looked at her speculatively. 'Are you afraid of what he'll do?'

'I told you. He'll go mad. He – he can be quite jealous. Especially of Terry Carter,' she added in a low voice.

'He knows the other man?'

Kathy nodded miserably. 'I – I was friendly with him before.' She sighed, glanced at Clare, and then said baldly, 'I broke off our engagement because of him. I sent Brian a "Dear John".'

'I see.' The Wren sat for a few moments without speaking, then she closed her folder and spoke briskly. 'Well, as I said, none of us can predict another person's reactions, and your husband is going to have to know. I suggest that I send a signal to his commanding officer, so that the news can be broken in a proper way. It wouldn't do at all for it to come in an ordinary letter, but of course you must write to him as well. If you'd like to do that and let me have the letter, I can send that as well, then we'll consider what to do next. It may be a good idea to bring him home for a spot of compassionate leave, so that you and he can sort things out a bit.'

'Bring him home?' Kathy looked as if she didn't know whether to be glad or terrified. 'But how could you do that?'

'We'd fly him home, of course.' The officer stood up. 'It rather depends on where *Dramatic* is now, but it can probably be done quite soon. Let me see, you live in Fareham, don't you? You'd probably rather he went there than came here.'

'Yes. Yes, I suppose so.' Kathy didn't look as if she wanted Brian to come anywhere. 'What shall I do now?'

'Stay here for the moment. I'll talk to the commander. He may ask you to come in to Devonport to see him. You'll also have to have a medical, to confirm your pregnancy. I can arrange that today with a naval doctor. I'll ring you later today with an appointment. Then we'll contact your husband's commanding officer and take it from there.' She nodded to Clare. 'Thank you for the coffee. Goodbye.'

Clare saw her out and then came back to the living-room. Christopher was at school and she had taken Laura down to Sue as soon as she knew the welfare officer was coming. Kathy was sitting in front of the fire in an attitude of complete despair.

'She seems very efficient,' Clare observed, coming in and closing the door. 'I suppose they're used to problems like this.'

Kathy turned her head. '*She* might be, but *I'm* not. Clare, did you hear what she said? They're going to send a signal to Brian's captain. He's going to know – probably today. Everyone on the ship's going to know.'

'No, they won't. Not everyone. They're not going to put out an announcement about it.'

'The captain will know. The radio officer will know. The whole mess will know. You can't keep things like that secret. And if they bring him home, everyone else is going to know. Mum and Dad – the whole family. Everyone.' She covered her face with her hands. 'Clare, I can't face it, I *can't*.'

'You can. You've got to.'

'Nobody will want to know me,' Kathy said, beginning to weep. 'Nobody will be my friend any more.' Her voice began to rise, her sobs to sound shrill.

'*Kathy!*' Clare gripped her shoulders and shook her as she might have shaken a child. 'Kathy, stop it. *I* know, don't I? And I'm still your friend. I still want to know you. So will everyone else. And if they don't, they're not worth bothering about. They're not real friends.'

'That's easy to say. I'd still rather have them than not. I don't want to be deserted, Clare. I don't want to be all on my own with this.'

'You're not on your own. You've got me. And you've got your mum and dad and the rest of your family, and all your friends. You'll still have them. I'm sure you will.'

'And what about Brian? Will I still have him?'

Clare looked at her. 'Do you still want him, Kathy?'

Kathy turned away and said in a muffled voice, 'Don't ask me that,

Clare. But I'm married to him. I've hurt him enough already, and this is going to make it a hundred times worse. But if I *can* make it up to him – if there's any chance at all of making our marriage work – I've got to try. He deserves that. It's the least I can do.'

Chapter Twenty-Six

Brian was home within a week. He had been flown home and arrived late one night, tired and in need of a shave. Kathy, waiting nervously in the pale, tidy lounge, stood up when she heard the taxi but didn't go to the door. She was still there, standing in the middle of the shaggy rug, twisting her hands together, when he came in.

'Hello, Brian.'

He didn't answer. He stood in the doorway, looking bigger than ever. His uniform had always made him look smart and in command, but now it also made him look threatening. She shrank back. 'Brian . . .'

'Well?' he said at last. 'Brian *what*? Just what have you got to say to me, Kathy?'

'I'm sorry,' she whispered. 'I'm really sorry.'

'*Sorry*?' He came a step towards her and she shrank away further. 'You're *sorry*? And is that supposed to make it better? Is it? Is that supposed to make everything all right?'

She shook her head. The tears fell from her eyes straight on to the rug, and she tried, ineffectually, to staunch them with the back of her hand. 'It can't. Nothing can make it all right, I know that. But I *am* sorry.' She looked up at him and the tears ran down her cheeks and neck and into the collar of her blouse. 'What else can I say?'

'Well, you're going to have to say something,' he said grimly. 'You're going to have to say a hell of a lot. I didn't come all this way just to hear you say *sorry*.'

He turned away from her and then back again, thrusting his clenched hands into his pockets as if only there could they be safe. Kathy cringed as he loomed over her. His brows were drawn together in a heavy frown,

287

his mouth set in an angry line, and the muscles of his cheeks were clenched as tightly as his fists. He's going to hit me, she thought. I know he's going to hit me. And I deserve it.

'Have you got any idea what it's been like for me?' he burst out suddenly. 'Have you got any idea at all? Being sent for to go to the commander, the commander of the whole ship – being told what you'd done? Having to hear *him* tell me what my wife's been doing while my back's been turned? Have you got any idea how that feels?'

Kathy shook her head. 'I'm *sorry*.'

'Sorry! So am I sorry. Sorry you ever met that bastard Terry Carter, sorry you couldn't stay away from him. How long's it been going on, eh? Ever since we were married? Ever since you sent me that first "Dear John"? Didn't you ever stop shagging him, not even in the beginning? Was it always him and me, whether I was home or not? In the same *day*, sometimes?'

'No! No, it wasn't like that. You know it wasn't. I never made love with Terry before we were married, never. You were the first. You know that.' Her eyes were wide, piteous, begging him to believe her. 'I didn't mean it to start again. I thought we could just be friends, and then . . .' Her voice died away. 'I never meant it to happen,' she finished in a whisper.

'But it did, didn't it? It did happen. And now you've got yourself into a real mess.' He glanced around, as if realising for the first time that he was in his own home. 'Well, haven't you even got a drink to offer me? I've had a bloody long journey, in case you hadn't realised it.'

'I'm sorry. What would you like? I'll make some tea. Or some coffee.' She scuttled past him, like a kitten afraid of a slap. 'I've got some Ovaltine—'

'*Ovaltine?* My God, what do you think I am? A kid, waiting to be put to bed? And I don't want tea or coffee either. I want a proper drink. A beer. Wait a minute – didn't we have a bottle of whisky in the cupboard?' He made for the mahogany cabinet in the corner. 'Or have you given it all to your boyfriend?'

'Brian, don't! Of course I haven't given it to – to anyone. Anyway, Terry never came here. We never—' She couldn't finish. Scarlet, she watched as Brian took out the bottle of whisky and a glass. 'Do you think you ought to have all that much?' she asked timidly as he almost filled the glass.

'Now look,' Brian said warningly, 'don't you start telling *me* what I should and shouldn't do. Don't you start trying to sit in judgement on *me*. Not in *your* condition.'

Kathy was silent. He raised the glass to his lips and drained half the contents. For the first time in her life, Kathy thought she might like a drink too, but she'd been told that alcohol was bad for a pregnant woman. Bad for the baby.

Once again, she felt the shock of appalled dismay at the realisation that she was pregnant, and her hands went involuntarily to cover her stomach.

Brian saw the movement and his face darkened. 'My God,' he said, as though it had only just hit him too, 'you really are, aren't you? You really are carrying that bastard's . . . *bastard*.'

'Brian! Don't call it that.'

'Why not? What else is it?' He took a step towards her. 'It's not mine, is it? It's his. It's a bastard. That's not swearing. It's the proper word for it. *Bastard*.'

'Brian!'

'I told you, Kathy,' he said, and she knew that he really was close to striking her now, 'I'll not have you taking me to task, not over my drinking or my language, nor over anything else. You haven't got the right.'

Kathy sat down suddenly. She did not know what to do or say next. Ever since she had known that Brian was coming home, she had dreaded their meeting. She had tried to imagine it, tried to think of something to say, but her mind had blanked it out. And now that it was happening, she still had no more idea how to handle it.

He's right, she thought. I don't have any rights at all, any more. I've given them up by what I've done. I don't even deserve to be allowed to stay in my own home.

She looked up at him. They'd have to talk in the end, of course. As Brian said, he'd come a long way over this and he'd be expected to go back with something settled. She could see he was too tired to talk that night, after the long journey – the first time he'd flown – and that huge whisky he was drinking. Sure enough, after a few minutes he began to slur his words and stumble, and it was easy enough then for Kathy to persuade him to go to bed.

Once there, he was asleep almost at once. She looked at him doubtfully. Did she have the right to get into bed beside him? Did he want her to? And what would he think – what would he *do* – when he woke to find her there?

She found a spare blanket and went downstairs again, to sleep on the sofa.

*

Brian woke her next morning. Light was just beginning to filter through the curtains, and she blinked at him uncertainly. 'What time is it?'

'Seven o'clock. What are you doing down here? Don't you even want to sleep with me now? After dragging me all this way, are you telling me I'm not good enough to share your bed? Your own husband – only you seem to have forgotten that.'

Kathy struggled to sit up. 'I didn't know what you'd want. I thought you might –'

'Listen,' he said, shooting out a big hand to grab her shoulder, 'I'm your *husband*. Remember? I've got rights. Now, come up to bed.'

Kathy stared at him and felt a shiver run over her body. 'Brian, we've got to talk.'

'I know that, but first, we'll just make sure you know exactly whose wife you are. Who you belong to.' He jerked her to her feet.

Kathy stumbled and fell against him. 'Brian, please don't.'

'Don't say that to me,' he hissed. 'Don't you ever dare say that to me. There's nothing you can tell me not to do, understand? *Nothing*. You've been unfaithful to me. You've been with another bloke, and you're carrying his baby. There isn't a thing you can tell me to do or not to do. And now you're coming to bed with me.'

He hauled her up the stairs. Kathy stumbled after him and let him throw her down over the bed. She lay there, her hands once again protecting her stomach, and gazed up at him beseechingly.

He stood for a moment staring down, and then dropped himself heavily on top of her. 'You're mine, Kathy. Mine. All mine. And don't you ever dare to forget it again.'

It was over very quickly. Afterwards, Kathy lay still and silent, staring at the ceiling. She felt used and broken, as if she'd been a rag doll, twisted and turned this way and that and then finally tossed aside in disgust. There had been a kind of contempt in Brian's usage of her, a furious disdain, a vindictiveness that was nothing to do with love. He hates me, she thought. He hates me, yet he won't let me go.

She lay for about an hour while Brian slept, and then he stirred and reached for her again. This time, though, he merely pulled her close and kept his arm around her, stroking her bare shoulder.

'I'm sorry, Kath,' he mumbled into her hair. 'I didn't mean it to be like that. I reckon I was still a bit stoned. I'm sorry if I hurt you.'

Kathy listened in amazement. '*You're* sorry? But I thought you were so angry with me. I thought you were never going to forgive me.'

She felt him sigh. 'Angry? I suppose I am. I know I *was* – I was bloody livid. And I'd like to kill that bastard Carter, but – hell, Kath, you're my wife, we're married. We've got to work it out somehow, haven't we? We've got to decide what to do.'

'Yes,' she whispered, 'we have.'

'The commander told me that,' he said. 'After he'd told me about the signal – when he told me they were sending me home. He said we'd got to work something out. I had to know what was going to happen before I go back. The padre told me that too. So I guess that's what we've got to do. Talk about it, work something out. And *then* I'll kill Terry Carter!'

Kathy looked at him doubtfully, unsure about whether he was joking. It didn't seem a subject to make jokes about, but Brian was like that sometimes, making jokes about things that weren't funny. A lot of his naval friends were.

'Would you like a cup of tea?' she asked, sliding away from him. 'I'll make one and bring it back to bed.'

'That's right,' he said, lying back. 'Bring your old man a cup of tea. Let's start the way we mean to go on, shall we?'

Kathy went down to the kitchen. She felt confused and uncertain. Brian's lovemaking – if it could be called that – had been rough and perfunctory, concerned only with his own physical release. There had been no emotion in it, unless you counted his undoubted fury. He hadn't set out deliberately to hurt her, but he hadn't been gentle either. She could only hope that he hadn't hurt the baby.

The baby . . . Whatever he said, whether or not he was really sorry for the way he'd treated her, he wouldn't be able to forget the baby for long. Even now, she thought, he was deciding what to say next. What to do. What to tell her.

She carried the cups upstairs. Brian was lying in the same position as when she'd left him, on his back, his arms behind his head. His eyes watched her as she came round to his side of the bed and put his cup on the little table, then went back to her own side and hesitated.

'Well? Come on, get in. Or are you too disgusted?'

'I'm not disgusted,' she said, getting quickly back between the sheets. Immediately, his arm came round her, clasping her against him. 'I'm just sorry.'

'You said that last night.'

'Well, I am,' she said. 'I'm sorry I've got us into this mess. I'm sorry I've let you down and hurt you.'

'Oh,' he said, 'I'm getting used to that.'

Kathy flinched. 'I suppose I deserve that sort of thing.'

'I don't know what you deserve,' Brian said. 'In olden days, they'd have put you in the stocks and thrown rotten eggs at you. Or whipped you through the town. There doesn't seem to be anything like that now. The worst I could do is divorce you, and then I suppose you'd go straight back to that sickly bastard and marry him. So that wouldn't be much of a punishment, would it? Since he's the one you obviously prefer.'

'Brian, I haven't said—'

'You don't have to,' he said. 'It's bloody obvious.' And, when she didn't reply, 'Well, isn't it?'

I can't tell him it's true, she thought. I've hurt him enough already. I can't make it even worse. 'No. It's not obvious.' She closed her eyes. 'It's you I love, Brian. It's you I'm married to.'

'Huh!' he said bitterly. 'Pity you didn't remember that when you were shagging him.'

There was another long silence. Brian sat up, removed his arm from around her, and started to drink his tea. Kathy sat up too. The liquid was hot and sweet, and she realised how much she had needed it. She waited, silently, for Brian to speak again.

'Well?' he said at last. 'So what are you going to do about all this?'

Kathy turned her head to look at him. 'What do you want me to do?'

He shrugged. 'Does that matter? I thought I was the last person to have any sort of say in this. You seem to live your life without any reference to me – why should I have any choice? What about Carter? What's *he* going to do about it? It's his kid, after all.'

Kathy swallowed. 'He doesn't know.'

Brian sat very still. 'Doesn't *know*?'

'No. He's gone to London.'

'Why in hell's name has he gone to London?'

'He's working there. He got promotion.'

'Got *promotion*? Well, jammy sod. It's nice to hear *someone's* life's going well.' Brian slammed his cup back on the table. 'And he doesn't even know? He doesn't know you've got a bun in the oven?'

'Brian, don't talk like that. Please. It's a baby.'

'And you don't bloody have to tell me that!' he shouted. 'I *know* it's a fucking baby, don't I! That's why I'm here now. It's *his* baby. I've been dragged back halfway round the world because you're expecting his baby, and he doesn't even fucking *know* about it! And don't tell me not to swear. I'll swear all I like. I'm *entitled* to swear.'

Kathy said nothing. She was trembling violently. This was what she'd been dreading – the eruption of Brian's temper. And he was right, she thought, he *was* entitled to be angry. He was entitled to shout and swear. He was entitled to throw her out of the house, if that's what he felt like doing.

He turned to her. He grasped her shoulders in both hands and twisted her to face him. 'You asked me what I want you to do? It's too late to do what you ought to have done, the minute you thought this might have happened. It's too late to get rid of the bloody thing, but that's what you'll do, Kathy. You'll get rid of it, see? I've got to go back to the ship next week, and I'll be home again in April. And if there's a baby in this house then, I tell you this for certain: either it goes or I do. That's all there is to say about it.'

Kathy stared at him. 'Brian, what are you saying? I can't – it's against the law, I'd go to prison. It's *murder*!'

'I'm not telling you to get it taken away now. I said, it's too late for that. Too many people know about it, for a start, and the doctor's one of them, more's the pity. But you can get rid of it when it's born. Have it adopted, and make sure it's all over by the time I come home.'

'But I can't be sure it'll be born before—'

Brian looked at her. 'I'm not coming home until it's over, Kath.'

'Brian, it's my *baby*.'

'It's *his* baby. Give it to him. I don't care what you do with it, only *get rid of it*.' He stopped and took a deep breath, then said in a dangerously quiet tone, 'It's either the baby or me, Kath. You can't have both.'

He slid out of bed and walked out of the room. Kathy heard him go into the bathroom, heard him turn on the shower. She sat very still, listening, for a few minutes, and then she twisted round in the bed and flung herself face down on the pillow.

She did not know how long she wept, but Brian didn't come back into the room, and eventually, after a very long time, she dragged herself out of bed and went downstairs to find the house empty.

Chapter Twenty-Seven

Clare took the children to her parents for Christmas and saw Kathy at the same time. Her friend's pregnancy was advancing and she was beginning to show. Her parents knew there was a baby coming, and had reacted just as Kathy had predicted. 'Just like Victorians,' she said bitterly. 'Never darken this doorstep again! Honestly, Clare, they talk about the swinging sixties and free love, but there's not much sign of it round here. Love costs a hell of a lot more than you think.'

'Surely they'll come round. They can't shut you out for ever.'

'Dad could. Mum will probably be all right, once she's got over the shock. And once the baby's gone.'

Clare shook her head, feeling Kathy's pain in her own heart. She knew that Brian had decreed that the baby must be adopted, and she could not understand how Kathy would be able to bear to do it. She thought of giving away one of her own children and shuddered.

'You know you can always come down to me, don't you?' she said. 'Any time you want to.'

Kathy smiled. 'Thanks, Clare. I may just do that. It'll be a relief to be with someone who doesn't think I'm a scarlet woman.'

It was not long after Christmas when Winston Churchill died. He was ninety years old and had been ill for some time; some people said he was senile at the end and hardly knew who he was, let alone the things that he had done.

Clare found such a thought tragic. She had been born right at the beginning of the war and had grown up with his mellifluous voice in her ears, using words she didn't understand, but somehow, with his very

294

tone, instilling hope and comfort into his listeners. Even as a small child, she had noticed that backs straightened when he spoke, and other voices took on a new strength of their own. And as she grew older he became one of her heroes, a bulldog of a man with a wit as sharp as her mother's carving knife.

She watched the funeral on television one cold January morning. Alex was with her. He had come up the lane and asked if he could watch, saying that Veronica didn't want to see it, it would make her cry.

'It's making me cry,' Clare said, putting some large potatoes into the Rayburn to bake for lunch, 'but you can stay if you like, so long as you don't mind me sniffing.'

'I shan't mind at all. I'll sniff with you.' He glanced around the warm kitchen. Clare had brought the television out from the other room and left the children in there to play. 'It must be hard, having to cope with everything by yourself.'

Clare shrugged. 'I've got used to it. I won't say I'd rather not have to, but there's nothing to be done about it.'

'But Martyn seems to be away more than he's at home. He's hardly ever had more than a few weeks here ever since I first knew you.'

'Oh, we had nearly eighteen months together before we came to Devon, and I'm hoping his next draft will be a shore draft. It ought to be.'

The funeral had begun. They sat quietly together, watching the grey, sombre scene: the crowds of people lining the route, the gun carriage draped in the Union Jack, the escort of soldiers and sailors marching solemnly beside and behind. Three hundred thousand people had gone to the lying-in-state and three thousand people were crowded into Westminster Abbey, where the Queen waited to bid her final farewell.

'He was a great man,' Alex said quietly.

Clare nodded. 'I know.' She shook her head sadly. 'He seems always to have been there. Either Prime Minister or Leader of the Opposition. Making pronouncements. Getting us through the war. We've got so much to thank him for.' She sighed. 'Alex, why is it that all the good people seem to die at once? President Kennedy, and now Winston Churchill. Oh, I know he hadn't been doing much for the past few years, he was so old – but he was still in Parliament till quite recently. It seems to be such a loss. He was *there*, and now he's not any more.'

'I know, but there'll be other good people, Clare. There already are – look at Martin Luther King, he's been given the Nobel Peace Prize. That's good news. And the new President, Lyndon Johnson, he seems a good sort. There'll be others, people we haven't heard of yet. The gaps will be filled.'

'I don't know,' Clare said, watching as the gun carriage was greeted at Tower Bridge by a seventeen-gun salute before the coffin was taken to its final resting-place at Bladon. The slow dipping of the dockside cranes, like huge, solemn obeisances, filled her eyes with tears. 'People like Winston Churchill leave too big a gap. I don't think there'll be anyone who can quite fill that.'

The potatoes were beginning to fill the air with their savoury aroma. Clare could hear the voices of the children coming from the other room, singing 'Puff, The Magic Dragon'. Christopher had learned a lot of new songs at school and he was teaching them to Laura. There won't be anything left for her to learn when she goes, Clare thought. She caught Alex's eye and smiled, rubbing away the tears with the back of her hand. 'They don't understand.'

'Of course they don't. Why should they? Did you understand, when you were their age?'

Clare considered. 'Well, the war was on when I was a baby and a little girl, so it was different. I knew about air raids and bombs and Germans – but now I come to think of it, I suppose I didn't really *understand*. It was normal life to me. Children think whatever life they have is normal life, don't they?'

'I suppose so,' Alex said quietly. 'I don't really know much about them.'

Clare laughed at him. 'Alex! You're a *teacher* – how can you say you don't know about children?'

'Not about small ones. Oh, I see yours and Sue's and the kids some of our other friends have – but that's not the same as living with them. Going to them if they cry in the night, feeding them, giving them a bath – that sort of thing. That's how you get to know your children.' He gave her a rueful glance. 'But you know all about that, don't you? How does Martyn manage when he comes home after a year away? It must be difficult to adjust.'

'Yes, it is.' Clare thought of the first time Martyn had come home after a year away, when Chris had been just approaching his first birthday. She had been so determined that he would feel a part of this new little family that she'd overdone it, and Martyn had ended up by snapping at her. She had been hurt but accepted that he needed her time and attention, and that perhaps he didn't really want to share so much in Christopher's daily needs. Well, men were like that, she'd thought, and maybe she'd been foolish to think Martyn was different.

'They're different every time he comes home,' she said. 'It's like getting to know different children each time. He does help with them, of course he does, but mostly he thinks it's best if I look after them.'

Alex looked at her. 'If it were me, you'd hardly get a look in!'

Clare laughed again, but she felt slightly uneasy. Alex seemed to be telling her something about himself and his own marriage. Does he really want children? she wondered. Veronica wasn't keen, she knew that. What would happen if Alex really longed for a family and Veronica went on refusing?

'Did you have a good Christmas?' she asked, changing the subject. 'I've hardly seen you since.'

'Yes, very good. We went to Veronica's parents, over near Ashburton. They always make a big thing of Christmas, and of course Ronnie gets showered with presents.' He sighed a little. 'Her father's not so well, though. He's been having heart problems. The doctor's told him to ease off a bit, but he's one of those people who's always on the go – gardening, playing golf, sitting on various committees. Can't accept that he's getting older and ought to slow down – says he enjoys it all so why give up? And she's just as bad – between them, they have a pretty active social life.'

'Well, they can pass some of that on to me if they like,' Clare said wryly.

Alex smiled. 'Your social life not too active?'

'It's almost invisible,' she retorted. 'Did Veronica tell you I started evening classes last September? I thought I'd try something useful and do lampshade making. We'd got a standard lamp with no shade, so I got the frame and the materials, and got a babysitter once a week, and what d'you think I ended up with? A lampshade that cost more than if I'd bought it in the shops and looks very homemade indeed!' She shook her head. 'That's the extent of my social life. I have more fun with the kids, and seeing people like Veronica and Sue during the day.'

Alex stared at her. 'Don't you ever do anything more than that?'

'How can I? I can't afford babysitters too often, and where would I go on my own? The pictures are no fun by yourself and I can't go into pubs, even if I wanted to. Things like the WI are mostly in the evenings, and if they're in the afternoons I couldn't take the children anyway. I can't keep on asking other people to look after them.'

'But you must get so fed up,' Alex said. 'Everyone needs a bit of social life.'

Clare shrugged. 'I can't complain. I chose not to live on a married quarter estate, where there'd be lots of other wives in the same boat.' She smiled. 'That's a joke, but not a very good one. What I mean is, I decided I wanted privacy more, and that's what I've got.'

'Well, look,' Alex said, 'I wouldn't mind coming up to babysit sometimes if that's any help. And if there's anything you need doing around the place – jobs you can't cope with – just let me know. It's too much for one person, looking after children and a house all on their own.'

'Plenty do it,' Clare said. 'We know the score before we start. Nobody forces us.'

'Do you? Do you really know what it's going to be like? Do you really understand it?' He got up. 'You can't really have known what it would be like to be on your own for months on end, with two kids and no husband.'

The funeral was over. Sir Winston Churchill had passed from life. Clare switched off the televison. 'No,' she said quietly, 'I suppose I didn't. I suppose nobody really knows what their life is going to be like, do they, when they make their choices? We only find out afterwards.' She looked up at him. 'But once we've made them, we have to stick to them. We have to make the best of it. That's what I think, anyway.'

Their eyes met. A message passed between them, a message that was too subtle to be grasped just at that moment. Later, Clare thought, she might understand, but for now it would have to be slipped into a drawer in her mind, to be taken out and studied when Alex had gone.

'Yes,' he said at last, a little sadly, 'that's what I think too. We make our choices and we have to stick with them.'

The kitchen door burst open. Christopher and Laura had been long enough alone and wanted company. They hurled themselves at Alex, squealing with delight, and he laughed and opened his arms to them both.

It does seem sad that Veronica won't have children, Clare thought, watching them. He really would make the most marvellous father.

Alex went back down the hill, feeling as if he had left warmth and comfort behind and was now walking into a colder climate. Which was odd, he thought, because Dale View was never as warm as his own house. The kitchen was cosy and the living-room warm enough when the fire was lit, but the rest of the house was chilly without central heating, while his own home was warm right through. He sometimes suggested that the heating could be turned down in the bedrooms during the day, but Veronica shivered and shook her head. 'You know I hate being cold. I like it to be warm wherever I go. And it only makes the rest of the house draughty, when you open doors into rooms that aren't heated.'

Yet somehow there was still a feeling of starkness in his house, as if something was missing, something that would bring life and colour and a warmth that didn't come from radiators and electric fires.

Children, he thought, pushing open the front door. That's what's missing. He paused in the hallway, imagining a couple of small bodies hurling themselves at him, wrapping their arms about his knees, begging to be lifted up, to be hugged and kissed.

Instead, a door opened upstairs and Veronica's voice called down, a little querulously. 'Where on earth have you been? I've been waiting for hours.'

Alex glanced up. She was on the landing, wrapped in a pale blue housecoat, her long fair hair draped on her shoulders. She looked pale, almost ethereal, her mouth as full and pouting as a child's.

'I've been watching the funeral. I told you.'

'Watching the *funeral*? Oh, that's so morbid. I shall be thankful when it's all over and we don't have to see any more of it. The last few days have been so dismal. All that lying-in-state and people going past . . . It's gruesome.'

'They were just paying their respects,' Alex said quietly. 'We owe him a lot, Ronnie.'

'Well, maybe we do, but that doesn't mean we all want to see him lying there *dead*.' Veronica came down the stairs and stood on the bottom step so that she was on a level with him. 'What shall we do now, darling?'

He looked at her. 'Have some lunch, I suppose? And then maybe go out for a walk this afternoon?'

'In this cold?' She shuddered, drawing the housecoat more closely round her. 'It's *bitter* out there. Like Siberia. No, let's stay in. Let's light a fire in the drawing-room and toast crumpets and make love on the rug, by firelight. Let's pretend we're snowed in and no one can disturb us.' She laid her hand on his sleeve and looked up at him through her lashes. 'Let's be just us.'

299

Alex smiled. 'And how do we make sure no one disturbs us? We aren't really snowed up – anyone could come and knock on the door.'

'We won't answer it.' She came a little closer. 'Nobody has to know we're in.'

Alex gazed down into her eyes. They were wide and blue as Dutch china, her skin as flawless as porcelain. Clare's skin was good too, but she had more colour from taking the children out every day, and her eyes were a dark brown, like an otter's fur. There were other differences too, things that weren't just physical: a childlike quality in Veronica that Clare didn't have, a depth in Clare that was absent from Veronica.

Clare wouldn't have been still in her dressing gown at lunchtime, or suggested spending all afternoon by the fire, making love. She couldn't have done. The children were about all the time, filling the air with their voices, wanting drinks and biscuits and cuddles. The house seemed full of them, full of the warmth of family life.

This house, he thought, seemed cold despite its enveloping centrally heated warmth. In this house, there were no sounds of play or squabbling, no cheeping toddlers, no childish laughter. There was nothing to stop him and Veronica from making love in any room in the house, at any time of the day.

'Let's have lunch,' he said, moving away a little, 'and then I really would like a walk. I haven't had nearly enough exercise this week . . .' He caught her disappointed eye and felt a stab of remorse. 'And then we'll light the fire, I promise.'

He would find it easy enough to make love to Veronica. She was his wife and he loved her. He didn't really want anyone else in his life at all. But he did wonder, sometimes, just fleetingly, if it would be any different making love to her if she had borne him a child. If there would be an added depth to it, a richness, an even closer bond.

He wondered if he would ever know.

At Dale View, too, they toasted crumpets by the fire that afternoon. They had been out for their normal walk that afternoon, after their baked-potato lunch, panting up the hill to the Pimple in the bitter cold. At the little triangular building on its knoll, they had stared out towards the mast of North Hessary Tor, feeling the wind like ice in their faces, and then they'd turned and run almost all the way back. The fire, stoked up before they went out, was burning with a cheerful glow and Clare was glad to draw the curtains early and have tea on the rug, lit only by the flames.

'It's nice here,' Christopher said contentedly. 'Nice and warm.'

'We'll play a game after tea,' Clare told him. 'Happy Families. You like that, don't you?'

'We're a happy family,' Christopher said, his chin dripping with melted butter. 'You, me and Laura.'

'What about Daddy?' Clare asked. 'Isn't he a happy family too?'

'Only sometimes,' he said. 'Only people here can be a happy family.'

Clare looked at him, feeling suddenly depressed. How could she explain to a child about the Navy, and how being away didn't prevent their father from being part of the family? But perhaps he was right – perhaps you did have to be present. After all, Martyn had been absent for most of Laura's life so far, and she would have little memory, if any, of those first months when he had been at home.

'I shan't go in the Navy when I'm a man,' Christopher observed. 'You have to be away from your children too much. I shall have a job at home, like Uncle Alex.'

'Well, it would certainly be very nice if Daddy could be home all the time,' Clare said, thinking of the few months they had spent in Gosport with Martyn coming home for midday lunch as well as every night. Lucky Veronica, having that for the rest of her life! And yet sometimes Veronica didn't look as if she thought she was lucky. She looked discontented, dissatisfied, as if something was missing. As if she was bored and restless.

'It's not as easy as that, though,' Clare said, trying to explain to the children. 'You see, when I met Daddy he was already in the Navy. And if we hadn't got married, we couldn't have had you two, could we? But Daddy can't come out of the Navy for a few years yet, so we have to put up with him being away, you see?'

Christopher nodded. He seemed to have lost interest. 'I've finished my crumpets,' he said, pushing away his plate. 'Can we play Happy Families now?'

They had just finished their game when the telephone rang. Clare went out to the kitchen to answer it, thinking that it was probably her mother. Instead, she heard Kathy's voice on the line.

'Clare? Clare, I've got to talk to you.'

'Kathy! How are you? Are you all right? The baby's not—?'

'I'm all right,' Kathy cut in. 'As far as that goes, anyway. The doctor says he wishes all his patients could be as healthy as me.' Kathy sounded almost bitter, as if she wished it were otherwise. 'Clare, have you heard about the ship?'

'The ship?' Clare's heart seemed to turn to ice. 'No – I haven't heard a word. I haven't had the radio or the television on since this morning. What's happened? What's wrong?'

'Nothing. Nothing's happened. It's just that – well, it's coming home early. They'll be back at the end of March. Clare, they're coming home *six weeks* early.'

'Early? But why? How d'you know?'

'Brian told me. Everyone will hear soon, but he was allowed to send me a special message. The welfare officer came to see me this afternoon.' Kathy's voice shook, and Clare realised suddenly that she was close to tears. 'Clare, you know what this means? He'll be home before the baby's born. I'm getting bigger all the time – I'll be the size of a house when he comes back. Clare, I can't bear him to see me like that – he'll never stand it. I don't know what he'll do. I don't know what *I* can do.' The trembling voice rose higher and higher and finally broke on a sob. 'Clare, please help me. Let me come and stay with you. Just until the baby's born – *please*.'

Clare listened in dismay. Kathy's sobs sounded in her ears, tearing at her heart, but before she could reply, she became aware of other sobs and screams.

'Kathy, I'm sorry, I'll have to go. It sounds as though the kids are killing each other in the other room. I'll ring you back—'

She dropped the receiver and ran into the living-room, visions in her head of burning coals setting fire to the rug. I know I put the guard back, she thought, I know I did. I'm *sure* I did . . .

She opened the door. The guard was in front of the fire and no coals had fallen out. Laura was lying on her back on the rug, with Christopher astride her, shaking her by the shoulders. Her mouth was wide open and she was screaming her head off.

'*Christopher!* Stop it at once! What on *earth* do you think you're doing?'

He stopped and turned. His face was red with fury. He glared at his mother and tried to shake her off as she lifted him away from his sister's recumbent body.

'Why are you shaking Laura like that? Can't I trust you for a single minute on your own? Whatever is it all about?'

She could barely hear his reply over the sound of Laura's continuing howls. Impatiently, Clare pushed her son aside and lifted the smaller child, giving her a swift examination. 'You're all right. He hasn't hurt you, so stop that yelling. Now, Chris, tell me just what you thought you were doing.'

He stood before her, scarlet and sobbing. His shoulders heaved and trembled; his voice almost choked on the words. 'She wouldn't play with me. She wanted all the cards herself. She wouldn't play properly.' He took a deep, shuddering breath, and roared the last few words. *'All I wanted to do was play Happy Families!'*

Chapter Twenty-Eight

Martyn was appalled when Brian returned to the ship after his unexpected leave with the news that Kathy was pregnant.

'She's *what*?' he said incredulously. The two men were leaning over the rail on a quiet part of the deck. Brian had been back for over a day, his face like thunder, refusing to answer any of the questions put to him by the other men in the mess, but now they were alone and he'd spat the words out as though they were poison.

'You heard. In the club. Up the spout. Got a bun in the oven. Hell and *damnation*!' He had taken a bar of chocolate from his pocket and started to unwrap it. Now he hurled it from him and watched as it sailed through the air and landed with a small splash amongst the waves. 'Wouldn't you have thought she could have waited a while? It's as if the minute my back's turned she's off with that bloke Carter. Can't keep away from him. Why? What does she see in him – can you tell me that, for God's sake? What's he bloody got that I haven't got?' He turned and paced restlessly along the steel deck, than came back to stare into Martyn's face. 'What's the bloody *matter* with her? She's like a flaming bitch on heat, can't leave it alone.'

'Kathy?' Martyn said, thinking of the small, slight girl with her short, fair hair. 'Brian, I'd never have thought – I mean, she just doesn't seem the type. I can't believe it.'

'Oh, you'd better believe it,' Brian said bitterly. 'It's true enough. She doesn't deny it – she can't. It's in there all right.'

Martyn shook his head. 'And you're sure it's Terry Carter? Did she tell you that?'

'Oh, yes. Came right out with it, the bitch.' Brian paced again. 'And – believe this one as well – she only wants to keep it! Says it's *her baby*.'

He mimicked her voice sneeringly. 'It's his bloody baby too, she doesn't seem to think of that. How am I supposed to feel, seeing another bloke's kid in my house? Am I supposed to offer congratulations? Let it call me Daddy? In a pig's ear!'

'So what's going to happen?'

Brian sagged against the rail. 'God knows. I told her she's got to get rid of it as soon as it's born. Get it adopted. I told her I'm not going back till it's over and gone.'

'And is she going to?'

Brian lifted both hands. 'Martyn, it's no good asking me what Kathy's going to do. I would never have thought she'd send me a "Dear John", but she did. I'd never have thought she'd do this, but she has. How the hell am I to know what she'll do now? All I know is, I told her and then I walked out and left her to think about it, and the next day I came back here. And if you ask me, I might as well not have gone for all the bloody good it did.'

Martyn was silent for a moment or two. Then he said, 'God, I'm sorry, Bri. It's a hell of a mess.'

'You can say that again,' Brian grunted.

'Look. You know if there's anything I can do, you've only got to say. Anything. We've been mates a long time, Brian. I'll stand by you in this.'

'Yeah, I know.' Brian gave him a twisted grin. 'But I don't reckon there's much anyone can do about this. Well – maybe there's one thing.'

'What?'

'Tell your Clare not to have Kathy down at your place,' Brian said. 'You know what those two are like, thick as thieves, and before we know where we are they'll be ganging up together. Kathy'll be running down there the first minute she can, crying on Clare's shoulder, and I don't reckon she deserves it. She's got to see it through herself.'

'Well, I don't know,' Martyn said doubtfully. 'I've never been one to lay down the law at home. And when I'm not there—'

'You said you'd do anything.' Brian looked at him. 'This is all I'm asking, Mart. Just this one thing. Okay?'

Martyn sighed. He was shocked by Kathy's behaviour, and angry on his friend's behalf. He could imagine just how he'd feel if Clare had done this to him. He wouldn't want her running to his best friend's wife for comfort either.

'All right,' he said. 'I'll write and tell her.'

'You can't have Kathy staying with you,' Martyn wrote. 'Not while

I'm there, anyway. Brian's my oppo. I can't have his wife in my house while she has some other bloke's kid.'

Clare stared at the letter. She screwed it up in her hand, then smoothed it out again, looking at it as if she thought the words might have been wiped out. They were still there, black and uncompromising.

'He's telling you to turn me out, isn't he?' Kathy said, watching her across the breakfast table.

'He knows I won't do that.'

'He's telling you to do it, all the same.' Kathy shook her head. 'It's all right, Clare, I knew he'd do that. It stands to reason, he won't let me stay here once he comes home. He and Brian have been friends for years. It's natural he'll take his side.' She sighed. 'He's in the right, after all.'

'Kathy . . .'

'Clare, face the facts. I've been unfaithful to Brian. I've let him down. I'm carrying another man's baby – every time he looks at me, he'll remember it. He'll end up hating me – if he doesn't already.' Kathy bit her lip and stared at the table. Her voice shaking, she added, 'I don't think we've got much chance of making a go of it, Clare. It doesn't matter what I do, he'll never be able to forgive me.'

'Oh, Kathy,' Clare said helplessly. 'I'm sure that if you just give him time . . .'

'Time!' Kathy echoed scornfully. 'That's just what we haven't got, isn't it? Time to get ourselves sorted out, time to get to know each other properly, time to make a marriage work.' She lifted her head and gave Clare a bitter look. 'None of us naval wives gets time, you know that. We just get started on a marriage and our husbands are whipped away to the other side of the world for a year, and when they come back we've got to start all over again. Only we haven't just gone back where we started last time, we've gone two steps *further* back than that. Our men have changed. They've been all over the world, they've had runs ashore in places like Hong Kong, and Singapore, and Malta. And what d'you suppose there is to do in those places? They don't go off on nice little coach trips to see the local sights, you know. They go to pubs and nightclubs and – and *worse* than that. They have the local trollops crawling all over them, and don't tell me that after weeks at sea they don't like it. And take advantage of it.'

'Kathy! You mustn't talk like that. You mustn't even think it. Not about Martyn and Brian. They're decent men. They *wouldn't*.'

Kathy curled her lips. 'Don't you believe it, Clare. They're *normal* men. They would.'

306

Clare started to move things aimlessly about on the table. She picked up the marmalade and put it down again. She put the used plates together and took them out to the scullery, where she stood staring into the sink. She felt upset, sickened. She didn't want to go on with this conversation.

Kathy came out and stood in the doorway behind her. 'I'm sorry, Clare. I shouldn't have said all that. It's just that I don't think we get any help. You know that welfare officer who came to see me here? And the one I saw in Portsmouth? Have you noticed them coming round again, to see how things are? Have they picked up the phone and rung up? Have they written a letter?'

'They did get Brian brought home on compassionate leave,' Clare pointed out.

'Yes, they did, and that's where their responsibility stops. They told me that, Clare. After he'd gone, I rang them up to try to find out what I should do next, and they told me that he'd been brought home and it was up to him now. It was his business, not theirs.'

'Well, I suppose it is, really.'

'And if he refuses to have anything to do with it? To do with *me*? It's not my fault he's on the other side of the world. How *can* we sort it out on our own, when he's not even here?' Kathy turned away in despair. 'Naval marriages don't have a chance. We don't even know that they'll work when the men do come out of the Navy. We'll have been through so much separately, we won't be the same people. How are they going to settle down? How are *we* going to settle down – will we really like them once they're home every night? Will they like us?'

Clare didn't turn round. She stared out of the window, at the little grassy bank and the arching branches of the rowan tree. There were a few snowdrops clustered in the grass at its foot and Liquorice was investigating them curiously. 'We have to hope so, don't we? We have to believe it. We have to work at it.'

'Yes,' Kathy said, 'and it seems to me it's us wives who have to do all the working.'

Kathy went back into the kitchen. She had been here for two weeks now, long enough for Clare to write and tell Martyn and receive his reply. That was another thing that made this kind of marriage so difficult: any discussion had to take place at long distance, and you couldn't always wait for a reply. Sometimes you had to make your own decision. Kathy had known that Martyn wouldn't like the idea that she was at Dale View, and she'd known that he would not want her there when he came home.

'It's all right,' she said. 'I shan't be a nuisance to you. I'll leave before he comes home. I don't want to make things difficult.'

'But where will you go? If you won't go home—'

'Not won't,' Kathy said. 'Can't.'

'So where will you go?'

'I don't know.' Kathy sat down heavily and leaned her arms on the table. 'I just don't know.'

'What about your mum and dad?'

'I've told you, they won't have anything to do with me. At least, Dad won't. Mum'll come round eventually, but she won't be able to do anything to help. He won't let her.'

Clare sat down too and gazed at her friend. 'I don't know what to suggest.'

'I thought I might try for a job somewhere,' Kathy said. 'A live-in job, as a sort of housekeeper. Where they wouldn't mind a baby.'

Clare stared at her. 'But I thought Brian said you had to – to—'

'Get rid of it,' Kathy said quietly. 'Have it adopted. I know. But I don't think I'm going to be able to.'

'You mean you want to *keep* it? But how can you? How can you look after it? What will you do? What will *Brian* do?' The questions came tumbling out as Clare grappled with this new idea. 'Kathy, I don't see how you can.'

'Nor do I.' Kathy's hands rested over her stomach. She was big now, so big she'd wondered if she might be expecting twins. 'But I don't think I can give it up, either. It's my *baby*, Clare. My son, or my daughter. How can I give it away to strangers? I just can't.'

'And Brian?' Clare's voice came out in a whisper. 'What will happen about Brian?'

'I shouldn't think,' Kathy said deliberately, 'that he'll ever want to see me again. I suppose he'll probably divorce me.'

Divorce. The word hung in the air. It was an enormity, a terrible thing to think about. It carried a stigma. And when there was an illegitimate child as well . . .

'He won't give me money, you see,' Kathy went on. 'He won't give me money for the baby. And why should he? He says it's either the baby or him.' Her steady voice wavered and then cracked again into tears. 'I don't want to lose him, Clare, but I *can't* give up my baby. I just *can't*.'

That afternoon, Kathy took Laura down to meet Christopher from school. She had made herself useful during the time she'd been with Clare – cooking meals, playing with the children – and they were all going to miss her company. Clare, making scones in the warm kitchen, wondered what she would do. Would Brian really turn her out of the house and divorce her? It seemed so cruel.

Kathy's always been in a muddle over those two, she thought. When Brian's around, she can't resist him, yet as soon as he's away she turns back to Terry. Which is really the right man for her? Perhaps neither was.

There were still six weeks to go before the *Dramatic* returned. No need for Kathy to go back to Fareham until she wanted to. At the same time, she had to make some decision about where she was going to go and what she was going to do after the baby was born. And it was so lonely for her, Clare thought, stamping out the scones and putting them on a baking tray. With Brian so far away, and so angry with her, and the baby due at just the same time as he came home, how could poor Kathy be expected to make any decisions at all?

'What about Terry?' she asked that night, after the children had been put to bed. 'Does he know about all this?'

Kathy shook her head. 'What's the point of telling him? He's gone now.' She started to cry. 'I've messed everything up, Clare. I had two men who loved me and I've spoilt it all. What sort of a mother am I going to be? What use am I to *anyone*?'

'Kathy, you mustn't talk like that! And you'll be a lovely mother – look how Chris and Laura love you.' Clare stopped and bit her lip. 'D'you really think you should keep this baby, Kathy? If you did what Brian wanted, there'd be others. You could put all this behind you and start again.'

Kathy stared at her. The mound of her stomach seemed bigger than ever. She laid her hands across it, lacing her fingers together. '*This* is my baby, Clare. This one is going to be born. How do I know there'll be others? It might be the only one I ever have.' She sighed and looked into the fire. 'And how do I know Brian will want me, even if I do give it away? I told you, I don't think we've got much chance. What's the point of giving away my baby if I'm going to lose him anyway? What's the point of losing both of them?'

They went to bed soon after that. Clare lay staring out of the window at the bright stars. She did not know how she could help her friend. She could not see further ahead than the day, so soon approaching, when the ship would return and Brian would face his wife once more. And the date, so close to that day, when Kathy's baby was due to be born.

If only Brian and Martyn were not such close friends. She was sure Martyn wouldn't have objected to Kathy's presence if she had been anyone else. Surely even now, if she could only make him realise how desperate Kathy was . . .

I'll write to him again in the morning, she thought, turning over to try to get to sleep. I'll tell him I can't turn Kathy out. She's my friend as much as Brian's his. We've got to look after her.

Kathy too was lying awake. She had drawn her curtains to shut out the night and kept her bedside lamp turned on. Things seemed even worse in the dark, as if her thoughts themselves turned black, and the shadow that weighed upon her during the day became a thick, suffocating blanket of despair.

Her hands moved slowly over her stomach. She could feel the baby now, a bundle of knobbly knees and elbows and a hard, round ball which must be its head. For the moment, it was quiet, but it was often active, squirming and kicking against the walls of its little prison. A living human being inside her, a son or a daughter who owed its existence to the love she and Terry had felt for each other . . . And I've got to give it away, she thought. I can't do it. I can't.

If only she could look forward to the birth with joy, planning as Clare had planned for her babies. Talking about prams and cots, knitting little matinee jackets – why were they called matinee jackets, when nobody would dream of taking a tiny baby to an afternoon theatre performance? – and decorating its bedroom. Choosing names. Kevin or Stephen were popular now for a boy, Sharon or Julie for a girl. Or something more unusual – Kathy had recently read a book in which the heroine was called Bethany, and she knew of someone else who had called their son Damian.

If Brian had his way, she would know none of these joys. Worse still, she would never experience the deep pleasure of holding her own baby in her arms, never feel him nuzzle at her breast, or see his first smile. The pains of giving birth would be nothing to the anguish of giving him up.

I can't, she thought. I *can't*.

She turned out the light and the darkness pressed in upon her, like a hard, iron band tightening about her head and body, crushing her in a grip that had no mercy. The tears began to slide out of the corners of her eyes, slipping down her face and into her ears before dripping on to the pillow.

She made no sound. She simply lay there, her face and pillow wet with the salt of her misery, until finally she fell asleep.

*

The iron band was still there in the morning.

At first, when Kathy woke, she was aware only of the deep unhappiness which had continued through her dreams and stayed with her when she awoke. She lay for a moment in the still-dark room, hearing the children's voices as they ran in and out of the bathroom, Clare hurrying them to come down for breakfast. It was always a rush in the mornings, with Christopher having to be taken down the lane to catch the bus for school. Sometimes Kathy got up then too, but more often lately she had stayed in bed and got up after Clare and Christopher had gone out. Laura would come up and snuggle into bed with her then, and Kathy would revel in the warmth of the small, soft body and make believe, just for a while, that this was her own baby, cuddled close in her arms.

This morning, when Clare popped her head round the door to see if she was awake, Kathy struggled to sit up and gave a sudden grimace of pain.

'What is it?' Clare set down the cup of tea she was carrying. 'What's the matter?'

Kathy lay propped on one elbow, one hand on her side. 'I don't know. I feel funny.' The iron band that had gripped her the previous night returned, squeezing her abdomen so tightly that she cried out. 'Clare! Clare, what's happening to me?'

'I think you're in labour.' Clare stared at her with frightened eyes. 'How long have you been getting pains?'

'I don't know. I've only just woken up. They can't have been going on while I was asleep.' The pain faded and Kathy relaxed, only to start up again, her face screwed up in agony. 'It's happening again! Oh, *Clare!*'

'I'll call a doctor.' Clare fled down the stairs. Although she had had two babies of her own, she had no idea what to do if Kathy were suddenly to give birth. Could it really happen so quickly? And so early? Her fingers shook as she lifted the telephone and dialled 999. An ambulance first, then her own doctor. What about the hospital? Kathy hadn't been booked in, since she'd intended going back to Fareham to have the baby. There was a maternity home just along the road, but surely you had to book in there early. Would they take an emergency? The voice cut in almost before the last 9 had been dialled and she asked for an ambulance. 'There's a woman here going into premature labour.'

She rang her own doctor's surgery but it was too early for the receptionist to be there and she was put through to the home of the duty doctor. 'My friend's staying with me – she's expecting a baby and I think it's coming early. I've sent for an ambulance – I'll have to go, she's calling me.' She was just about to put down the receiver when the doctor's calm voice asked for her name and address. 'Perry,' she said hastily. 'Dale View. I must go . . .' She dropped the instrument and ran up the stairs.

The children were hard on her heels. 'Is Kathy poorly? Why is the doctor coming?' Christopher asked anxiously. 'Will they take Kathy to hospital?'

Clare turned at the bedroom door and snapped at them to go downstairs again. 'No, don't do that. Go into my bedroom and watch out of the window. You can tell me when they arrive.' She ran into Kathy's room, pushing the door shut behind her. 'How are you? Are they still coming?'

Kathy was half out of the bed, as near doubled up as she could be with her bulk. She looked up at Clare, her face white and beaded with sweat. 'Clare, it's awful. It hurts so much . . .' A groan tore its way past her lips. 'I can't . . . I can't . . .'

'I know.' Clare knelt beside her. 'Here, hold my hand. As tight as you like. I've called the doctor, and an ambulance. They'll be here soon. Don't worry. Everything will be all right.'

'I'm scared,' Kathy whispered. 'It shouldn't be happening yet. It shouldn't be coming for another five weeks. Six. Clare, suppose it dies, suppose my baby dies.'

'It won't die. It's not that early.' Clare tried to remember what she had heard of premature births. 'There was a girl in the same ward as me when Laura was born, her baby was two months early. She was fine. She only had to stay in until she weighed five pounds and then they let her go home. There wasn't a thing wrong with her.' She felt Kathy's hand tighten on her own, crushing her fingers so that her wedding ring bit into the flesh and she wondered if the bones would break. 'Is it really bad?' she whispered, thinking even as she spoke what a ridiculous question that was.

'I'll die,' Kathy moaned. 'You can't hurt like this and not die . . . This is a judgement on me, Clare, it's a punishment. I'll die and so will my baby, my poor, poor baby . . .' The contraction gripped her again and she closed her eyes and groaned.

'You won't. You won't die, and nor will your baby. You're just giving birth, Kathy, and this is what it's like.' Clare spoke firmly, almost angrily. 'I won't *let* you die.' Where on earth was the ambulance? 'In a few hours you'll have a lovely little baby, and both of you are going to be perfectly all right. Just hold on tightly. They'll be here soon.' Had she

312

given the address properly? she wondered. Were they driving up and down Whitchurch Road now, searching for Dale View? She heard the door open and looked up to see Christopher peeping in.

'Mummy, I'll miss the bus to school . . .' His eyes widened as he saw Kathy twisting on the bed.

'It's all right. It won't matter if we miss the bus this morning. I'll explain to Miss King. Is the ambulance coming yet? I expect they'll ring their bell. Go and look out of the window again, there's a good boy.'

'The bell's ringing now. I can hear them coming up the lane.'

'Oh, thank goodness. Go and let the men in, Chris. Tell them to come upstairs. Laura, you get into Mummy's bed and stay there. No, don't start crying, *just do as you're told*.'

'It's coming again,' Kathy said through gritted teeth.

'Hold on. Hold on tight.' Clare could hear Christopher clattering down the stairs. Would he be able to open the door? There was a bolt at the top which she always fastened before going to bed. Had she opened it this morning? Yes – she'd taken in the milk. She could hear him now, explaining to the men, hear them answering him with blessedly deep voices. She heard their footsteps, heavy on the stairs, and as Kathy's pain faded again and the pressure on her hand relaxed, Clare stood up, more relieved to see them than she had ever felt in her entire life.

'All right, love,' they said, taking in the situation at a glance. 'All right. The doctor's coming too – followed us up the lane, she did. You'll be all right now. Everything will be all right now . . .'

Miraculously, it seemed to Clare, everything *was* all right. Once the doctor and ambulance men were there Kathy's panic seemed to subside and her own fears were allayed. The baby, it seemed, was coming quickly but not disastrously so. There was time to get Kathy into the ambulance and along the road to the maternity home, and there, only two hours later, her baby son was born. Clare went in that evening and found Kathy lying rather pale and tired in bed.

'I've got a little boy.' Kathy looked bemused, as though somehow she'd never really expected it to happen. 'I've got a little boy of my own.'

'I know. He's lovely.'

'Have you seen him?'

'The nurse showed me as I went past the nursery. He's in an incubator.'

Kathy giggled weakly. 'Sounds like a baby chick! He weighs four pounds seven ounces. That's not bad for seven and a half months. No wonder I was so big. They said if I'd gone full term I'd have been like a barrage balloon.'

'Well, it's over now and he's going to be all right.' Clare hesitated. 'What will happen now?'

Kathy looked at her. 'What do you mean, what will happen?'

'Will they keep you here till he's put on weight? Or will you come back to Dale View? You can, you know. For a while, at least.'

'You mean, till Martyn comes home. Well, I don't really know what else I can do. I'll have to think of something, though, won't I? Brian won't let me go back to Fareham, sure as God made little chickens.'

Clare felt sorry she had spoken. Kathy looked so exhausted, and this should be a time for celebration, not more worry and anxiety. 'Don't think about it now,' she said hastily. 'Look, have you let your parents know? They'll want to come and see you. And we ought to send a message to Brian.'

Kathy turned her head away. 'I suppose we should. Though I don't imagine he'll care.'

'Kathy! Of course he'll care. He loves you. I'm sure he does.'

'No,' Kathy answered, shaking her head, 'he doesn't. Not any more. That's over, Clare.' She hesitated, then said thoughtfully, 'I'm not sure he ever did, really. He wanted me – but as a sort of possession. He wanted me to be his..Like a – a car or a watch, or something. That isn't love. And if I'm really honest,' she added, 'I'm not sure I ever really loved him either. You know, I couldn't believe my luck when he first asked me out. I didn't think I'd ever get a boyfriend like him – good-looking, exciting to be with. It was like being taken out by a film star. I was completely dazzled.'

'You were in love with him. You were both in love.'

'Yes,' Kathy said, 'but that isn't the same as *loving*.' She was silent for a moment, then said in a low voice, 'It's Terry I really love. I know that now. Brian and I – we both made a mistake. He couldn't let go when I first tried to break away – and I thought I had to be loyal, just because he was first. We were both wrong.'

Clare gazed at her and tried to understand. She had never doubted her love for Martyn, or his for her. She could not imagine waking up one morning, knowing that it had all been a dreadful mistake. She could not imagine the tragedy of loving a man, and bearing his baby, while still married to someone else.

'But what are you going to do?' she asked at last.

'I can tell you what I'm not going to do,' Kathy said, her voice

314

suddenly stronger. 'I'm not giving up my son. Never. He's mine, and he's staying mine.'

There was a new determination in Kathy's voice. Even though she looked so weak and exhausted, lying there in the white hospital sheets, there was no mistaking that tone, that look in her eye. Kathy's mind had been made up at last.

It's going to be so hard for her, Clare thought as she walked back along the road. Harder than it's ever been before.

For a woman alone with a baby that was not her husband's, life could be very cruel.

Chapter Twenty-Nine

Her heart trembling, Kathy drove up to the garage door and stopped the car. She sat for a moment gazing at the house. It looked very little different from when she had left it, save that there were daffodils coming up in the front garden and a pink dusting of blossom beginning to show on the little cherry tree she and Brian had planted last year. The curtains were still half drawn across the windows; they gazed back at her, blankly, as if telling her that they no longer recognised her, that this was no longer her home.

But it is, she thought, opening the car door and getting out, and I haven't got anywhere else to go.

She unlocked the front door and stepped inside. The air was slightly stale, but the central heating, left on low, prevented it from feeling chilly. She walked from room to room, trying to capture the feeling of familiarity, of being at home in her own surroundings, but it evaded her and she sensed an inimicality in the very walls, the furnishings and possessions that she had chosen and enjoyed so much.

A wailing sound from outside sent her hurrying back to the car. Timothy was awake in his carrycot on the back seat, screwing up his face ready to start screaming. She bent over him, lifting him out, nuzzling into his neck.

'Ssh. Ssh. It's all right, Mummy's here. There's a good boy. There's my lovely little boy. Stop crying now. We're home.' She held him against her, staring up at the blank-faced house, and repeated it as if to convince the building itself. 'We're *home*.'

It did seem a little more like home later on, when she had brought in all their luggage and made up the bed. Her mother had come in a day or two earlier and made sure there was milk in the fridge, and bread in the bin, and Kathy found some cheese and eggs and a few vegetables as well. Tomorrow she would need to go shopping, but for tonight there was enough, and all Timothy needed was her breast.

She sat before the electric fire, feeding him and thinking over the events of the past few weeks. Once the panic of his birth was over, she had been able to rest for the first time since she had known of her pregnancy, lying in the bed looking out of the window over the valley of Crowndale and feeling oddly at peace. It was as if she had been given a breathing space. Nothing mattered but the baby, and there was nothing for her to do but regain her strength and get to know him.

Timothy. From the first moment of his birth, when she had heard his thin, wailing cry and held him in her arms, she had known that there was no possibility whatsoever of giving him away. His eyes had been open, the dark, slaty blue of all newborn babies' eyes, and she had looked into them and felt a thrill of recognition. For a moment or two they had regarded each other, a long, grave look that was like an introduction. For the rest of my life, you will be there, Kathy had thought, a part of me that no one can take away. Whatever happens, you and I will belong to each other in a way that nobody else can belong. You are my son.

Early though he'd been, he was from the start a healthy and strong little boy, putting on weight almost at once. He had had to stay in the maternity home until he was three weeks old but, as Clare had said, as soon as he reached five pounds Kathy was allowed to take him home. Home being, at that time, Dale View where Clare and the children had been waiting impatiently to receive them.

Christopher, proud and protective, had appointed himself the baby's guardian, settling himself near the carrycot whenever he could, tiptoeing about when Timothy was asleep and frowning heavily at Laura when she made a noise. He went to school reluctantly and made straight for the cot when he came home, as if to check on his charge's wellbeing.

Laura, who had him to herself all day, was fascinated. She watched spellbound when Kathy bathed the baby, examining his tiny toes and fingers, gently stroking the minute shells of his ears. When Kathy fed him, she curled up beside her on the sofa, absorbed by this novel manner of feeding, and found it difficult to believe that she had ever done the same.

'Timothy's going to live with us always,' Laura announced, drawing her old blanket around her.

'What do you mean, always?' Clare asked, startled. 'Timothy can't live here always. He'll have to go home one day.'

Laura stared at her. Her mouth turned down at the corners. 'This is home. Timothy's home now.'

'No. Timothy lives in Fareham, with his mummy and – and daddy,' she finished uncertainly. There had been no decision about that yet, as far as she knew. Brian hadn't written since he'd been notified that Timothy had been born, and Martyn too had maintained a stony silence on the subject. When Martyn came home Kathy and Timothy would have to leave, but she couldn't say that to Laura. She didn't know what to say.

'Daddy won't mind,' Laura said confidently. 'He'll like Timothy. Anyway, he's hardly ever home.'

Her words struck at Clare's heart. How could it be right for a child to speak of her father in such an offhand tone, as if his wants mattered no more than those of the most casual visitor? But perhaps that was how he seemed to a child Laura's age, who could barely remember him being at home for more than two or three weeks at a time. As a visitor, important to them in some vague, barely understood way, but with no real say in how the household was run.

'And isn't that just what he is?' Kathy said when Clare told her this. 'That's how he seems to the children because that's what they see. Laura's right. We're just pretending at being married.'

'You sound so bitter,' Clare said sadly. '*I* feel properly married. I feel we're a family.'

'But your children don't,' Kathy said. 'Your children see life as it really is, without trying to convince themselves it's something else.'

She thought of that now, sitting before the electric fire with her son in her arms. Had she been right, or was Clare really keeping a family life as it should be, with her open fires and her homemade scones and walks on the moor? Just how easy would it be for Martyn to settle into the life that Clare had created and developed?

They do come home different people, she thought. How can they help it? And we've changed too.

And in a few days, Brian himself would be home.

Kathy turned her mind deliberately away from that thought. She had trained herself not to think troubling thoughts while feeding the baby. He seemed to sense her feelings and would stop sucking, or if he finished feeding he would vomit later, or cry with stomach pains. Instead, she gazed down at his face, marvelling yet again at the petal softness of the skin, the fan of dark lashes spread on his cheek, the tiny oyster-shell ears. One hand was spread on her breast, each finger perfect, each nail a minute scrap of mother-of-pearl. He smelled of baby soap and talcum powder.

She had thought and talked endlessly about what she was to do next. There had been no word at all from Brian, or any hint in Martyn's letters to Clare as to what he was thinking, what he meant to do. Clare had tried to reassure her, telling her of a woman she had met on the train once, coming down to Plymouth to meet the ship Martyn was serving aboard then. 'She'd found out he was having an affair and she hadn't written to him for months – but she was still coming to meet him. And I saw them together the next day, looking like newlyweds.' Perhaps when she met Brian again, he would feel some of his old love for her again, and even be able to accept Timothy.

At least I can try, she thought. I've got to try, for all our sakes. Even though we don't love each other the way we thought we did, there could still be something. And if there is, I have to make it up to him for all I've done.

Timothy had finished feeding and fallen asleep. Gently, she lifted him and carried him up to the bedroom to lay him in his cot. She hesitated for a moment, wondering whether to put the cot into the spare bedroom. It was going to be difficult enough, even if Brian did agree to accept the baby, and it would surely be easier if Timothy slept in another room. But he had never done so before, and in these strange surroundings he would surely need his mother's presence. She decided to keep him there at least until Brian came home.

She went downstairs to make herself some supper. Life seemed to have been a series of difficult decisions lately: whether to meet Brian in Plymouth, going into Devonport dockyard with the other naval wives as the ship came in; whether to stay at Dale View; whether to do as she had finally done, and come home to wait for him.

'I can't go into the dockyard with a baby in my arms,' she said, 'and I can't meet Brian without him. He's got to decide for himself – it's either both of us or neither of us. But I can't force him to make a decision like that in front of everyone else.'

She couldn't stay at Dale View either. That would have been unfair to Clare and to Martyn. So in the end, it seemed that there was nothing for it but to return home and wait until Brian came, as eventually he must.

In their own home, they would have time and space to talk. In their own home, she might be able to show Brian that their marriage could still, if they both tried hard enough, be made to work.

*

Brian too was in a state of turmoil over his homecoming.

Martyn had told him that Kathy was staying with Clare and he'd received the signal telling him about the baby's birth. He'd stared bitterly at the message, thinking how different it would have been if the baby had been his own. How he'd have gone racing down to the mess, feeling ten times his normal size, waving the piece of paper and announcing drinks all round the first possible minute, to wet the baby's head. How his mates would have clapped him on the back and made all manner of bawdy jokes. How he would have looked forward to the first photograph of his baby son.

Instead, he had nothing to boast about, only something to feel ashamed of. Jokes there could be, yes, but not the sort of jokes he could laugh at. And, anyway, the only oppo he would be telling was Martyn. Nobody else was going to know of his humiliation.

'She's had it,' he said, as if imparting news of a death rather than a birth. 'Came early, apparently. A flaming boy.'

'Well, it had to be one or the other,' Martyn observed, and then, feeling he had perhaps been a bit heartless, added, 'I'm sorry, Bri. It's a mess. What are you going to do?'

'How the hell do I know? It doesn't seem to be up to us how our wives run our lives, does it? You tell your Clare she can't have Kath to stay and she doesn't take a blind bit of notice, and my Kath has another bloke's kid and I'm supposed to say hooray, here's some money for a pram . . . They seem to think because we're away we don't matter. We're just money machines.'

'Come on, Bri. It's not really like that.'

'Isn't it? You tell me what it is like, then.' Brian scowled at the scrap of paper in his hand. 'What do *we* get out of it? We know what they get – a nice house, furniture, all the trimmings, and the freedom to live like single girls. But what is there in it for us?'

'Clare doesn't live like a single girl. She brings up the children – looks after the house. She looks after me when I'm home—'

'And how often is that? Meanwhile, all your pay goes to keep them and the house, and you can hardly afford a jar when we do get ashore. And you're one of the lucky ones! All I get is the knowledge that while I'm away she's having it off with some other bloke, and getting herself in the family way. And *I* have to pretend it's my family! Where's the joy in that?'

'I thought you'd told her to get the baby adopted?'

'Oh, I did, I told her in no uncertain terms. But she's not going to do it, is she? It's *her* baby – as if that was something special! I'll tell you the real reason, Mart – it's because it's *his* baby too. She won't give it up because it reminds her of him. Well, it'll remind me of him too, won't it? And suppose it even *looks* like him. Neither of us is ever going to forget.'

'So, if she won't give it up?' Martyn said after a pause.

'She'll have to get out, won't she?' Brian's voice was savage, but after a moment he shook his head and brushed his hand across his forehead. 'Oh, I dunno, Mart. I just dunno. The way I feel right now, if I walk into the house and see that kid there, I reckon I'll go mad. I won't be able to help it. And yet, when I see Kath, I know my knees'll go weak the way they always do and I'll just want to get her into bed . . . I tell you what, it's just tearing me to bits. One minute I feel I could kill her and the next I just want none of it ever to have happened, so we could be as we were and I'd know she was really mine. And what I'll feel like when I actually *see* her – I just haven't got the foggiest bloody idea!'

Martyn sat in the radar office and brooded. Soon he would be a chief petty officer, and once again he'd been asked to consider taking the steps necessary to go through from the ratings' mess to the officers' wardroom. He knew he could do it, and part of him wanted to. The other part wanted to be at home.

Ever since he was small boy, going into the Navy had been his ambition. He could remember being taken on a trip on the river Dart, not long after the war, and seeing Dartmouth College on the hill overlooking the little town. He'd made up his mind then and there that he'd be a sailor, in the Royal Navy, and sail all over the world.

He hadn't gone to Dartmouth after all – that was where officers did their training, and boys from ordinary families, educated at ordinary grammar schools, didn't often qualify for entrance there. However, he'd been happy enough to sign on as an apprentice and go to Collingwood. Most of the lads there came from similar backgrounds – officers were a different class and Martyn soon realised that he would have felt out of place amongst them.

These days, however, class and background were not necessarily a guide to ability. The grammar school Martyn had attended had given him a good start, and developed his quick intelligence. He had passed his apprenticeship with flying colours and knew that he could do an officer's job. He thought of rising to the dizzy heights of lieutenant commander. He thought of the security of knowing that he was guaranteed a good position, with excellent pay, until he was forty or fifty years old, and against that he considered the alternative of leaving at thirty and finding work in the competitive area of Civvy Street. And never going to sea again.

There was a third choice – he could stay on in the Navy as a CPO. It was a good job, with reasonable pay and plenty of responsibility, but it seemed daft, somehow, to commit himself to a further ten or fifteen years' service without going as far as he could.

If I were still single, he thought, it would be easy. There'd be no contest. But I'm not single. I'm a married man, with a wife and children. It makes a lot of difference.

However, he couldn't keep putting off the decision for ever. And that meant discussing it with Clare. Martyn didn't look forward to such a discussion. And he knew that this was because his own mind was already more than half made up.

Kathy did not know how long she would have to wait for Brian to come home. Normally, half the ship's company went on leave immediately on return, and the other half when they came back. Brian had always favoured first leave, but Kathy had no idea whether that was what he had chosen this time. Sometimes there wasn't a choice; it depended on seniority and what others in the section wanted.

She spent the time cleaning the house and getting in provisions. On the second day, her mother came to see her. She stood awkwardly on the doorstep, disapproving yet longing to see her new grandson. Kathy let her in and she walked over to the carrycot, perched across two chairs, and peeped inside.

'Kathy, he's beautiful.' Her face softened and she touched his cheek with one fingertip. 'Oh, he's gorgeous . . .'

'I know.' Kathy came to stand beside her mother and they looked down together at the sleeping baby. 'I couldn't give him away, Mum. I just couldn't.'

'No. Of course you couldn't.' Kathy's mother shook her head and a tear slid down her cheek. 'If only it could have been different . . . It shouldn't have been like this, Kathy.'

To her immense surprise, Kathy felt her throat ache with tears. Unable to control them, she drew in a deep, shuddering breath and began to sob. 'I know. I know. Oh, Mum, it's all such a mess, and I don't know what to do.' She turned and her mother took her into her arms as if she were a child, and held her, murmuring soft words of comfort. 'I don't know what Brian's going to say.'

'Oh, Kathy. My poor, poor Kathy. My poor baby . . .' They wept together, their arms about each other, while Timothy slept beside them. 'Hasn't he written at all?'

Kathy shook her head. 'I haven't heard a word since the baby was born. I wondered if the welfare people might bring him home again, or arrange a shore draft, but they said, no, he didn't want to come, and it was up to him and me to sort it out. They don't really care, Mum. They told me – the *commander* told me – that Brian's like an expensive piece of machinery: he's cost a lot to train, and he's got to go where he's told. He belongs to the Navy, not to me.'

'That's cruel,' her mother said. 'It's inhuman.'

'It's the Navy,' Kathy said.

They made a pot of tea together and sat drinking it, waiting for the baby to wake. Kathy told her mother how she had decided to come home and wait for Brian to return. 'Clare's going to ring me and tell me which leave he's got, so at least I'll know when to expect him. The ship comes in tomorrow morning.' She shivered. 'I feel so scared . . .'

'He'll never turn you out, surely,' her mother said.

Kathy gave her a wry look. 'Won't he?' She paused for a moment. 'What would Dad do if I turned up on the doorstep with Timothy in my arms? Would he let me in?'

Her mother bit her lip and looked at the floor. 'You know your father. He's got very strong opinions. He'll come round, I'm sure.'

'I wonder,' Kathy said. 'I bet he doesn't know you're here today, does he? I bet he's told you not to come.'

'I do have a mind of my own, Kathy.'

'He *has* told you, though, hasn't he?' Kathy said. 'And I don't suppose you'll tell him you've been.' She shook her head. 'Men – they're still living in the Victorian age. Masters in their own homes. Head of the family. Going off for a year at a time and expecting everything to be done just as *they* want it. While we're the ones who have to do all the work, manage the money, look after the house, bring up the family—' She stopped abruptly. 'Well, you know what it's like, Mum – you had years of it when Dad was in the Navy.'

'Yes, I do know what it's like,' her mother said, a little sharply, 'but we were different from you girls today. We didn't sit about moaning, we just got on with it. And at least all my children were your father's.'

There was a dead silence. Kathy stared at her mother and then turned away, her eyes filling with tears.

At once, Mrs Stubbs got up from her chair and came over, putting her arms around Kathy's shoulders. 'I'm sorry, Kathy. I'm sorry. I shouldn't have said that. I don't know why I said it.'

'It doesn't matter,' Kathy said drearily. 'It's true. And it's how you really feel, isn't it? You think I've let Brian down, and you're right. I have. I've let Brian down and I've let you and Dad down, and all the family. I've let everyone down.' She looked over towards the carrycot. 'I've even let my baby down. Maybe I should have given him away, to a family who would all love him, to a mother and a father who really wanted him.'

'Kathy . . .'

'Don't try to make it right, Mum. You can't. Nobody can, because it *isn't* right, is it? Nothing – nobody – can make something like this right.'

Mrs Stubbs was silent for a moment, then she said, 'We can't change anything, Kathy. All we can do is make the best of it. You've got a lovely baby, and that's a start. Whatever happens next, whatever Brian decides, nobody's going to take your baby away from you. And I'll stand by you – whatever your father says.'

Kathy turned back and gave her a watery smile. 'Thanks, Mum. It's nice to know I've got you. And Clare – she's been a real friend. It's good to know that not everybody hates me.'

'Nobody hates you, Kathy!'

'No?' Kathy said, with a lift of her eyebrows. 'A father who won't let me over the doorstep? A husband who's probably going to kick me out of the house? Well, if they don't hate me, I hope nobody ever really does! Anyway, let's stop talking about it now. It's time for Timothy's feed and I don't like upsetting him.'

The baby was beginning to stir and utter faint murmuring cries. Kathy lifted him from the cot and gave him to her mother to hold while she unbuttoned her blouse. Mrs Stubbs gazed down at him, her face once more softened, and then lifted him against her cheek.

'Poor little scrap,' she said. 'He's done nothing wrong. None of this is his fault. It's not fair of anyone to make his life more difficult.' She handed him to Kathy and her expression tightened. 'I'll tell your father I've been here today and I'll tell him what a fine grandson he's got. We'll not let him down, and we'll not let you down either. You can turn to us any time you need, Kathy.'

Brian had chosen first leave, Clare told Kathy over the phone. *Dramatic* had docked and Martyn was at home again. She had seen Brian briefly before leaving the ship, but she didn't know just when he would arrive in Fareham.

'They start leave on Friday. He could be there by the evening – unless he goes to Bristol first, to see his family.'

Kathy didn't think that was likely. Brian had never got on well with his stepfather, or even his mother. Bristol was probably the last place he would go.

'Did – did he ask about me?'

Clare sighed. 'I didn't really have time to talk to him properly, Kathy.'

'So he didn't,' Kathy said flatly. 'He'd have made time for that, if he really wanted to know.'

'Kathy, I don't know what to say,' Clare said miserably. 'I've asked Martyn and he won't tell me. If I ask him how Brian is, or what he wants to do, he just says, "What do you think"? It doesn't sound very hopeful, I'm afraid.'

'I never thought it would be,' Kathy said, 'but I have to try. If he doesn't want me any more, there's nothing I can do about it, but I have to give it a chance. I owe him that at least.'

She rang off, leaving Clare to her reunion. Perhaps she and Martyn had got it right and their own marriage wouldn't be harmed by the continual separations. Kathy hoped so.

Meanwhile, she must prepare for Brian's arrival. His favourite meal – roast chicken, roast potatoes, vegetables and gravy – must be cooking so that he smelt it as he came through the door. There must be a pudding too. An apple pie, smelling of cloves. And a few bottles of beer and a bottle of wine. Finally, she prayed that Timothy would be asleep and not crying as Brian came home.

She rang the railway station to find out the train times. There was one arriving at seven in the evening and another at nine thirty. He could be on either of those. There were others in between, slow trains and trains he could catch by changing at different stations, but he wasn't likely to do that. He had no patience with long, slow journeys.

Kathy went to the shops for the chicken and vegetables. She made the apple pie and got all the other preparations done in the morning. The house was clean and tidy, the windows sparkling. Timothy's cot had been moved into the spare bedroom and she hoped she would hear him if he woke in the night. She put all his toys and clothes in there too, so that there was no sign of him in her and Brian's bedroom. If it is still 'our' bedroom, she thought with a tremor.

At six o'clock, she put the chicken in the oven. She fed Timothy and bathed him so that he smelled sweet, and put him into his best nightgown. She held him against her and he cuddled into her neck. When she laid him in his cot he gave her a beaming smile.

'Oh, Timmy,' she said, feeling the ache of tears in her throat, 'he's got to love you, he's got to. I won't be able to stand it if he doesn't.'

The baby murmured and kicked for a while, then fell asleep. Kathy checked the oven and put the potatoes in to roast. She sat in a chair by the window, staring along the road, then wondered what Brian would do if he came round the corner and saw her there. He might turn round and walk away. She moved further back into the room and stared at the fireplace.

It was dark by now and she would have to put the light on, she couldn't sit there in the dark. She debated whether to draw the curtains. Brian would see the light, but would he stop to look through an uncurtained window and turn away? If they were drawn, would he be more likely to come in? She drew them, opened them again, drew them back. The people across the road will think I'm signalling to them, she thought with a nervous giggle.

In the end, she kept them drawn. It wasn't only. Brian who would be able to see in if they were left open – anyone else walking along the street would be able to observe their meeting, and she couldn't bear the thought of that. She sat down again, feeling shut in. Now she would have no idea when Brian turned the corner and came along the road.

He might come and see the light on and just go away, she thought, and I'll never know he's been.

She basted the chicken and potatoes. Should she put the carrots on to boil or would it be best to wait until Brian came in? If he came on the later train, they'd be cooked well before time. Best to leave those and the Brussels sprouts till later, perhaps, and turn on the heat when she heard his key in the door.

The table was laid, with their wedding-present dinner service, glasses and cutlery. Kathy went over and stared at it, wondering if she could do anything to improve it. She wished she'd thought of putting a candle in the middle, or a small vase of flowers. Too late now. She shifted the knives and forks slightly, picked one up and examined it to see if that was a tiny spot that could be polished off. No. Nothing there. A trick of the light, that was all. She gave the tablecloth a tweak and moved away.

Should she switch on an extra bar on the electric fire? It was still chilly in the evenings and Brian would be returning from the tropics. She flicked the switch down and sat in an armchair, leaning back as if to relax but unable to stop her hands gripping the arms as if she were about to be tipped out.

Timothy cried out and she jumped up and ran upstairs. He didn't seem to have woken. She smoothed the covers over him and stroked his face, settling him down again. It wouldn't be long before he needed a feed, and one thing she really didn't want was to be feeding him when Brian walked in. Perhaps she should wake him now and get it over with. But suppose Brian had arrived on the seven-o'clock train and stopped for a drink before coming home. How could she know just when he was likely to walk in?

At eight o'clock she looked at the chicken again. It was just coming to perfection and the potatoes were a golden brown. The smell was mouthwatering. She gazed at it for a minute or two, wondering what to do. If Brian had caught the earlier train, he would be just walking in at the door now, hungry and ready for a meal. But perhaps he had decided to eat in Fareham – he wouldn't have been expecting her to be here with a meal ready, after all. She took the chicken and potatoes from the oven and put them on dishes, covering them to keep them warm. There was certainly no point in cooking anything else until he arrived.

Nine o'clock came and went. Nine thirty, when the second train was due to arrive. Kathy woke Timothy and fed him. Ten o'clock came, when Brian might be reasonably expected to walk through the door, then ten thirty – perhaps he'd stopped for a drink at a pub.

She made herself a cup of cocoa, and at eleven, she went upstairs and changed into her nightdress – the long white one that Brian liked best. She pulled a dressing-gown over it and went downstairs to sit beside the electric fire a little longer.

At midnight, she went to bed.

He's not coming, she thought, turning out the light at last. He's not coming back.

Chapter Thirty

It was noon next day when Brian walked through the door.

Kathy was in the kitchen, drearily fishing nappies from the spin-dryer. She had a pile of them in a bucket on the kitchen table, waiting to be hung out, and another bucket full of baby clothes, washed separately. Fretful little noises from Timothy's carrycot, in the lounge, indicated that his next feed was almost due.

When she heard Brian's key in the lock, Kathy lifted her head. Her heart jerked and she felt suddenly sick. 'Brian . . .' she whispered, and turned her head to look along the passage to the front door.

Brian came in, looking as usual slightly too big for a normal house. He was wearing civilian clothes and carrying his canvas bag. He set it down in the hall, turned to pull the door closed, then looked along the passage and met Kathy's eyes. 'What in hell's name,' he said slowly, and with a hard edge of anger in his voice, 'are *you* doing here?'

'I *live* here. I'm your *wife*.'

He took a step towards her and she backed away, suddenly afraid. 'Not any more. I thought I'd made that clear. You keep that kid, I said, and it's out you go.' His eyes travelled swiftly over the scene in the kitchen. 'Unless you're going to tell me you've started taking in washing?'

'Brian, please, listen to me. Give me a chance.' She looked up at him, pleading with her eyes, her voice, her uplifted hands. 'You can't throw me out.'

'I can. I will.' He loomed over her. 'I've got right on my side, Kathy. You've been unfaithful to me. You've committed adultery. I can divorce you for that. You've had another bloke's bastard and you've brought it back to my house to flaunt at me. No judge in the country's

328

going to tell me I can't throw you out. I gave you your chance, Kathy, but you're like all the rest: give you an inch and you'll take a mile. Well, you've tried it on me once too often. Get out.'

'*Brian!*'

'I said, get out. You and your bastard. Now. This minute. Before I get really angry.'

Kathy shook her head, more in disbelief than refusal. 'You can't mean it. I can't go just like that. We've got to talk—'

'Talk?' he said. 'What is there to talk about?'

'About – about us. We've got to try to sort things out.' From the other room, she heard the baby begin to whimper and her heart sank. Brian turned his head.

'Is that it? Is that Carter's kid?'

'It's my baby, Brian. Mine. I can't give him up just like that. You don't understand—'

'And do you understand me?' he demanded. 'Have you ever even tried? From the very first – from the day you sent me that first "Dear John" – have you ever given a moment's thought to what it was like for me? Stuck out at sea for weeks on end, away for a year at a time, not knowing what's going on at home, not knowing whether you were telling me lies in all those letters you sent? Not knowing whether you were sleeping around with every Tom, Dick or Harry who happened to come your way?'

'Brian! You know I'm not like that.'

'How do I know?' he asked. 'How do I know what you're like? You can't wait for me to get out to sea before you've got your knickers off with this Carter bloke. How do I know he's the only one? There could be hundreds of 'em for all I know. Well, you've got caught and serve you right, and now you'll have to take the consequences. But you don't take me for any more rides, Kathy Bennett. This is the end of the line for you and me.'

Timothy was crying in earnest now. The raised voices had upset him, Kathy thought frantically, and the fact that he was hungry . . .

She stared helplessly at Brian. 'Please let's talk,' she whispered. 'Please.' She took a step towards him and laid her hand tentatively on his arm. 'I thought you'd be home last night. I cooked your favourite meal. Roast chicken. It still in the fridge, look.' She opened the door of the fridge so that he could see the chicken on its plate. 'Let's have a nice lunch together when I've fed Timothy, and talk about it. Please.'

Brian stared at her. He looked into the fridge and saw the chicken there, the cold roast potatoes, the vegetables that had been prepared and not cooked, the bottles of wine and beer. His lip curled. 'Think it's bloody Christmas, do you? And just what else were you going to offer me out of your stocking?'

Kathy flinched. 'Don't be crude.'

'Crude? *Crude?* You think you've got a right to tell me off for being *crude?* My Christ, Kathy, you just about take the biscuit, you do. After all you've done, you've got the brass neck to stand there and tell me what words I must and mustn't use. Well, there are a few short words I've already used this morning, Kath, and I'll use 'em again, and I'll go on using them until you bloody take notice. Get out. Out of my house. *Out.'*

He took a step towards her. As he lifted his hand to strike, the baby cried out again, a shriek of rage and hunger and fear at being left alone, at the sound of fury in the deep, strange voice of the man who was so emphatically not his father.

Kathy, desperate, ducked under Brian's arm and ran into the other room. 'It's all right, my love, it's all right. Nobody's going to hurt you. Oh, my precious, my sweetheart, don't cry, it's all right, everything's all right. Mummy's here . . .' She lifted him into her arms and held him against her, patting his back and murmuring in his ear. As his sobs diminished, she turned and saw Brian standing in the doorway.

He stared at her. His eyes rested on the baby and she saw them darken, saw the flush rise in his cheeks. Suddenly afraid, she stepped back, her arms holding the baby protectively against her.

Brian reached out and took Timothy from her arms. He handled the baby awkwardly, unaccustomed to the shape and fragility. Her heart in her mouth, Kathy watched. 'Brian, don't hurt him. None of this is his fault.'

Brian turned a scathing look upon her. 'Just what do you think I am, Kathy? I know it's not his fault, poor little bugger. I'm not going to take it out on him – he's got enough trouble in front of him.' He laid the baby in his cot and stared down at him for a moment, then turned back to her. His eyes were black.

'That should've been *our* kid, Kathy,' he said quietly. 'That should've been *my* son. But you've ruined all that, haven't you? You've wrecked everything. You've mucked up all our lives.'

The temper which Kathy knew he had been keeping barely under control ever since he had walked into the house, erupted at last. His face suffused with fury, he lunged forward, and before she could twist away he had her by one shoulder. With the other hand he slapped her face and head, once, twice, three times, again and again. She cried out and lifted her hands, trying to ward off the blows, but he was in a frenzy now and could not stop. When she fell to the floor, he went with her, kneeling to deliver his slaps, and then he clenched his fist and punched her hard in the stomach.

'Pick the bones out of that,' he said, standing up as she lay gasping and moaning at his feet. 'And now I'm going out. I'll be back tonight, and I want you and that *bastard* out of this house when I come home. And don't ever come here again, Kathy. Don't you ever dare come here again.'

Kathy lay on the floor, gasping. Her head rang and her stomach throbbed with pain. She heard the front door slam and his footsteps march rapidly away up the street. She knew that he meant what he had said.

They had come to the end of the road.

Her face was swollen and bruised, her head aching and her stomach sore, but she dared not linger. Driven by the need to feed the screaming baby, Kathy dragged herself to her feet. While he sucked, she thought of what she must do. The pile of damp nappies must be put into a bag or a pillowcase, the clothes and necessities packed. She could take the car – Brian had left on foot – but where to go? She could not go back to Clare, or to her own parents. In every house, it seemed that there was a man who would not let her in.

There was only one person who could help her. Terry.

Kathy knew that his mother must have his address. Her hand shaking, she picked up the telephone and dialled the number. Her voice was little more than a whisper.

'Who wants to know?' Mrs Benson's voice asked suspiciously.

'Kathy. Kathy Bennett. I used to be Kathy Stubbs. We – we used to go out together.'

'Oh. Yes, *I* remember.' It didn't sound as if she had any fond memories, Kathy thought miserably. Was there anyone left who would take her side? 'I hope you're not going to bring him any more trouble.'

If only you knew, Kathy thought, but she was too desperate to care about lies now. And for all she knew, Terry might be in love with her still, and glad to welcome her back . . . Not that I could ask him that, she thought. I just need some help, and it's his baby . . . 'I just want to contact him,' she said to his mother. 'It's quite important.'

'Well, I don't know . . .' The voice was doubtful. 'I suppose it won't do any harm.' She gave an address in Notting Hill. 'Don't you go unsettling him now,' she warned. 'He's doing well in his job, just got himself a nice little flat and everything.'

He'd got himself a nice little flat in Gosport, Kathy thought, hanging up, but that didn't stop him moving away. She thought sadly of the flat overlooking the harbour. She'd helped Terry choose that, and it had seemed like home to her. She wondered whether his new flat was as nice, and whether that too could seem like home.

Packing up again didn't take long. She settled Timothy in his carrycot in the back of the car, scurrying back and forth with her luggage, desperate now to get away before Brian came home, praying that there would be nobody about to see her and remark on her bruised face. However, most of the neighbours were young couples who were out at work all day, and the street was empty as Kathy, with tears streaming down her sore and aching face, started the engine and drove away up the street.

'What are we going to do, Timmy?' she asked the sleeping baby behind her. 'Whatever are we going to do?'

Martyn had also chosen to have first leave. He came home, carrying the same sort of canvas grip as Brian, and changed into civvies, hanging his uniform up with care. You had to look smart when you were a PO, but it was good to relax in grey slacks and an old pullover. He roamed around the house, getting used to the feel of all the space.

'You've been on a huge aircraft carrier all these months,' Clare said, amused. 'Dale View's tiny in comparison.'

'But Dale View's all mine,' he explained. 'On *Dramatic* I had about two square feet to call my own. Here, there's just you and the kids and two cats, not a thousand other men.'

'Well, I can see that would make a difference,' she said with a grin. 'And which do you prefer?'

'Just at the moment,' he said, pulling her close, 'I never want to see another ship.'

He felt a twinge of guilt as he spoke. It was true enough at that moment, but he knew it wouldn't last. After a few weeks, the space of Dale View would begin to contract, to seem constricting, and he would start to hanker after the space of the ocean. Clare's company, much as he loved her, did not fill the gap left by the raw camaraderie of his shipmates. The more easygoing life at home would seem frustrating in comparison with the tight, efficient routine of the Navy.

Even the responsibilities were different. On board, it was easy – there was a rule for every circumstance, and a book of regulations to refer to if you were ever in doubt. Everything was cut and dried. In Civvy Street there were a hundred decisions to be made – where you were going to live, how you were going to organise it, what furniture you wanted, how the children were to be treated. It seemed endless, a continual stream of decisions from the small and pettifogging to the major. Martyn found himself irritated by them, wondering how anyone ever got any work done with all these fiddling little things to do as well.

Sometimes it just seemed safer, and somehow easier, to stay in the Navy. All you had to do was sign a form, and life would go on as it already did, in the way that you knew and understood. But when Martyn thought of this, he also thought of Brian and other men he knew whose home lives hadn't been able to stand the strain. It was frightening to realise how badly things could go wrong at home when you were away for long periods.

That won't happen to me and Clare, though, he thought. Clare's strong and she loves me – we love each other. Nothing like that could ever happen to us.

Clare too knew that what he'd said wasn't really true. However glad Martyn was to get home, he would soon be hankering to go back to sea again. What the attraction was, she couldn't understand – conditions could be almost squalid, with all those men crammed into tiny spaces, living together for months on end. Martyn's ship was a fighting vessel, and the machinery for getting it around the world and accommodating aircraft had taken priority. The men came last, squeezing into odd corners here and there. The officers' mess was better, of course – that probably had figured on the original plans, Martyn had once said, a little cynically – but the ratings and sailors had to take what they could get. Often it was no more than a corridor with hammocks slung along the sides.

'I'd go mad if I had to live here,' Clare had said when she saw it. 'There must be some powerful attraction.' But what it was, Martyn could never quite explain. A combination, it seemed, of the camaraderie of a ship's company, bound together by the constrictions of their life, the excitement of arriving in a foreign port, the sense of freedom from the rest of the world as the ship ploughed through the waves, a world of its own with its own rules and laws and customs.

'I'd go mad if I had to do a shore job, going to an office every day,' Martyn said.

Clare looked at him in shock. 'But you've always said you'd come out at thirty!'

He glanced away. 'Well, yes, I know that's what I *said*, but I've been thinking. I'll get my Chief's buttons soon. That's as high as I can get if I stay below decks. But I could go through for officer. I could get sub-lieutenant's rings. And then I could get higher. I could go for lieutenant and maybe even lieutenant-commander. I'd get a good screw then, and a good pension when I come out. It's worth thinking about.'

'So when would you come out?'

'Oh, I dunno – forty, forty-five. The longer you stay in, the better the money.'

'It works the same way if you come out at thirty,' she said. 'You could get a good job; you've got a good trade, and you could work your way up that ladder just as well.'

He shook his head. 'I don't know that I could. And we'd have to move anyway. You have to go where the work is.'

Clare didn't see why the work couldn't be in Plymouth, perhaps in Devonport dockyard itself, working on the ships. She went upstairs to get the children out of the bath, where they had been splashing for the last ten minutes. She had hoped that Martyn would share this job, but after the first time, when he'd stood awkwardly at the door watching, he hadn't seemed keen.

'I'm all crinkly,' Laura said, holding up her hands. 'Why am I all crinkly?'

'You always go like that in the bath.' Clare lifted her out and wrapped her in a towel. 'You've been in a bit too long.'

Laura shook her head. 'No. I stay longer.'

'It's time to come out now. Tea's ready.' On Sundays, the children had their baths before tea and then came down in their dressing-gowns to have tea by the fire. Clare had made a batch of rock cakes and a jam sponge and bought some crumpets to toast. Usually, there was a good serial on television to watch. It was *Treasure Island* now, with a sinister, soft-spoken Long John Silver, and she thought Martyn would enjoy that too.

Later, when the children were in bed, she returned to the subject of the Navy.

'I honestly thought you'd want to come out at thirty. You always said so.'

Martyn looked irritated. 'Well, I've changed my mind. I'm entitled to, aren't I? It's my life.'

Clare bit her lip. 'It's ours too. Mine and the children's. We've hardly seen you over the past few years – well, really ever since we were married. I think we're entitled to some consideration too.'

'For God's sake,' he exclaimed. 'I *am* considering you, aren't I? I'm trying to earn more money, so that we can afford a decent standard of living. You know what it's like now; we've just about got enough to scrape by, and that's all. What with a mortgage and two kids, and you not earning anything, I've hardly got enough money for a decent run ashore sometimes. Can't you see that? Or maybe you'd rather I didn't go ashore, just stayed on board all the time.'

'Don't be silly. Of course I don't want you to do that. You need to get off the ship, but does it have to be so expensive?' Unwillingly, Clare remembered the remarks Kathy had made about shore runs. 'What do you do when you go ashore? How do you spend the – the time?'

'How do I spend the money, you mean,' he said, disgruntled. 'How do you think? You've seen blokes in Pompey, and in Guz.' Guz was the naval name for Plymouth. 'We go and have a few drinks, of course. What else is there to do?'

'I don't know. I suppose I always thought you'd go and look at – at the sights. Whatever there is to see. Like people when they go on holiday.'

'Holiday!' he snorted. 'It's not a flaming holiday, Clare. It's work, and damned hard work too, when we're at sea. We're not on a flaming cruise. We don't want to go sightseeing, we just want to feel the land under our feet and relax a bit with a pint in our hands, that's all.'

'So why are you so keen to stay in?' she asked. 'If you come out, you can do the same sort of job and come home every night. Isn't that what you want?'

'Look, the Navy's my life,' he said as if trying to explain to a child. 'It's what I know. It's what I'm good at. I know the routine, I know the ropes. The longer I stay in, the better I'll get, and if I go for an officer it'll be better still. I might not even go to sea as much then. I could get a shore draft and be at home. And we'd live better. The money's good. Why chuck all that up when I don't have to?'

Clare sat gazing into the fire, still troubled. She thought of the long, lonely months, the years she had spent alone already, bringing up the children by herself, managing the finances, making decisions about the house. The burst pipes she'd had to cope with alone last winter, the snow when she'd been unable to get down to the shops, the leak in the roof, the day part of the ceiling had fallen in on the landing. Martyn had been away on all of these occasions, too far away even to consult. She'd had to do it all alone.

And there were the children, growing up without their father. 'Daddy', a mysterious figure seen only in photographs, their only contact with him letters and postcards. Clare told them as much as possible, but there was often little in his letters that they could understand, and it was only in the past few months that Christopher had been able to scrawl a few childish words at the bottom of her own. To Laura, Martyn was almost a stranger.

'They'll need you even more as they get older,' she said. 'Chris needs a daddy to play football with him and fly kites and all that sort of thing. And Laura will only just have got used to you when you'll be away again.'

'Well, that's the way it's going to be for the next five years anyway,' he said. 'They'll be all right, Clare. Plenty of kids have had to grow up like that, hardly seeing their fathers. It doesn't do them any harm.'

It doesn't give them any family life either, she thought, but Martyn was sounding impatient and she thought perhaps it was best to change the subject now, for a while anyway. They'd need to talk about it a ain, but she didn't want anything to spoil these first few days together. She reached forward to put another log on the fire, and thought of Kathy.

'What do you think Brian's going to do?' she asked. 'I mean, I know he must be upset but he can't go on ignoring the situation. He and Kathy are going to have to talk it over.'

Martyn's face closed up and she knew she'd said the wrong thing. 'There's nothing to talk about. She's got another bloke's kid. She can't expect Brian to take that on.'

Clare looked at him. 'You mean he won't have anything to do with her?'

'Not while she's keeping the kid, no. Why should he?'

'But she's his wife! They've got to talk about it.'

'Look, the Navy brought him home as soon as she went to the welfare. He told her then. Get rid of the kid and he'd talk, but if she was set on keeping it, it was all over. She knew the score.'

'She can't give Timmy up, Martyn. He's her baby. It would be like me giving up Chris or Laura.'

'No, it wouldn't, because Chris and Laura are mine as well. This kid isn't Brian's and he can't be expected to support it and pretend it's his – it's just not on. Stroll on, Clare, every time he looks at the kid he's going to remember Terry Carter and what she did with him. You just can't expect a bloke to put up with that. Can't you see it from his point of view?'

'Well, yes, I can,' she admitted, 'but I can see it from Kathy's as well. I can see the the baby won't mean anything to Brian – but he does to Kathy. He's part of her. She's carried him in her body for nine months and given birth to him. It *is* like Chris or Laura as far as she's concerned. A mother loves her babies, Martyn, no matter who the father is. She can't help it. It would tear Kathy apart to give him up now.'

Martyn pursed his lips. 'Well, I can see it's hard for her, but she did get herself into this mess, Clare. Brian didn't. The way I see it, she just can't have them both. If she really wanted to save her marriage, she ought to have given the baby up the minute it was born.'

Clare shook her head. She knew that in theory Martyn was right but in practice it was almost impossible. Perhaps it would never be possible to explain this to him, though; perhaps men could never quite understand the power of the bond between mother and child. If they did, she thought, they'd never be able to go away and leave their own children.

'So what will Brian do?' she asked in a small voice. 'What will he do when he arrives home and finds her there with Timothy?'

Martyn looked at her. 'Is that what she's done? Gone home?'

'Yes. She went just before the ship came in. She was going to get the house ready, have a meal waiting for him when he arrived – all that sort of thing.'

'Well, I should think she's got a shock coming to her, then,' Martyn said. 'Brian was going home yesterday – catching the morning train. I reckon he would have got home just about dinnertime. I just hope she had a good dinner waiting for him, that's all, because the way he was looking he was going to need caviar off a golden plate to bring him round to having some other bloke's bastard foisted on him, and even then it'd be a pretty thin chance. I wouldn't be surprised if he chucked her out the minute he walked in.'

Clare stared at him in dismay. 'He wouldn't! He couldn't do that. They need to talk – to discuss things. He couldn't just throw her out.'

'I tell you,' Martyn said, 'the way old Bri's been the past few weeks, she'll be lucky if that's *all* he does. Kathy's not the only one who's been torn to pieces over this.'

'But where will she go? What will she do?' Clare got up. 'I'll have to find out. I'll ring her – she can come back here. If Brian's really turned her out—'

'No.' Martyn reached out and caught her by the wrist. 'No, Clare. You're not to ask her back here.'

They stared at each other, Clare disbelieving, Martyn implacable. She tried to pull away but he gripped her tightly. Her face paled. 'Martyn, let me go. You're hurting me.'

'You're not to ring her up,' he said. 'You're not to invite her back here. Brian's my oppo, and I'll not have Kathy here, not after all she's done to him.'

Clare's eyes were fixed on him as if she could not believe her ears. She shook her head a little. 'Are you really telling me I can't have my friend here? My best friend, when she's in trouble?'

'You've helped her enough,' he said. 'It's my turn now to help *my* best friend. I've seen what it's done to him, Clare. I've seen what things like this have done to other blokes. It destroys them. I'm not going to lift a finger to help Kathy. She's made her bed – she'd better lie on it, either by herself or maybe with Carter, since she can't seem to keep away from him.'

'All right,' Clare said shakily, 'I can understand you don't want her here while you're here, but once you've gone away again—'

'No,' he said. 'Not while I'm home – and not after I've gone away again, either. This is my house and I'll say what goes on in it *all the time*. Not just when I'm here. I'm not a flaming visitor, Clare.'

'No,' she said, 'but you behave like one while it suits you. You're happy enough to go off and leave everything to me. And now it seems as if you're going to do that for the next twenty years, instead of just the next five. Where do you think that's going to get us?'

Her dismay at his earlier pronouncements, coupled with his attitude towards Kathy, welled up together. 'You want it all, Martyn, you want it all on a plate. You're all the same, you naval men – you think you can leave us at home to cope with everything, and yet you still want to have the final say. Well, I can tell you this – you don't tell me who my friends should be and whether I can help them or not when they're in trouble. And I'll tell you something else, too.'

She paused. She knew that she wasn't making idle threats; this was a feeling that had been growing deep inside her for months, perhaps for years, and had been trying to surface ever since he had begun to talk about staying in the Navy. 'All this separation is driving us apart,' she said quietly, 'If you stay in another ten or fifteen years, I don't think we'll still be together at the end of them. The longer you're in, the further apart we're going to grow.'

Chapter Thirty-One

By the time Kathy had found Terry's address, it was almost dark. She stopped in the narrow road, looking at the row of houses. They were nice houses, she thought, probably built in Regency or Georgian times, the sort of houses Georgette Heyer's characters might have lived in. They had steps leading up to their smartly painted front doors, and steps leading down to basements with tiny courtyards. Probably quite a lot of them had now been converted to flats.

She found the number and checked that Timothy was still asleep before getting out of the car. Thank goodness she had been able to stop at a quiet spot to feed him, and he wouldn't need any more attention for a couple of hours. She looked up at the house and felt suddenly nervous. Suppose Terry wasn't at home?

There was a light in the window on the first floor. She climbed the steps and looked at the row of bells with names beside them. Terry Carter. Flat 2. Would that be the one with the light? She stared at the bell for a moment, then gathered together all her courage and pressed.

It seemed an eternity before she heard sounds from inside. And then, less than a split second before the door opened and Terry stood before her.

There was a long silence.

'Kathy,' he said at last. '*Kathy . . .*'

'Hello, Terry,' she said with a nervous little laugh, and then stopped, unable to think of another word.

'Kathy,' he repeated in a bemused tone. 'What on earth are you doing here? How did you know my address?'

'I asked your mum.' She stared at him, not knowing what to say. 'Terry, I've got to talk to you.'

'Why?' He took in the state of her face. '*Kathy!* What on earth's happened to you?'

What hasn't happened? she thought ruefully. She looked past him, into the passage. It was quite bare, carpeted with what looked like coconut matting, and there were stairs leading up to the flats. She looked at Terry again.

'Could – could I come in?'

He looked doubtful. 'I suppose you can, but wouldn't it be better if you just told me what you want? It's not really very convenient . . .'

Not convenient, she thought, her heart sinking. He doesn't want me here. He doesn't want to know. She half turned towards the car and then looked back at him. 'There's someone else with me, Terry. Someone you ought to meet.'

He stared past her. 'I can't see anyone.'

'No, well, he's rather small, you see.' She gave him a desperate glance, begging for help. 'It's – it's a baby.'

'A *baby*?'

'It's *our* baby, Terry. Yours and mine.' She saw the shock on his face, the involuntary glance around to see if anyone else was within earshot. 'I'm sorry, I didn't mean to blurt it out on the doorstep. Please, can't we come in?'

'Oh, my God,' he said. 'Oh, my God.'

'*Please.*'

He gathered himself together. 'Yes. Yes, all right, but you can't stay.' He looked at her, shock and dismay and confusion chasing each other across his face. 'I'm sorry, Kathy, but you really can't stay.'

She stared at him. 'Not at all? Not even for a few minutes?'

He gestured helplessly. 'Kathy, what can I say? You can come in for a few minutes, yes. I mean, I'll give you a cup of tea, whatever you need. But you can't stay long. I mean, you can't stay the night – it's awkward . . .' He looked at her again, and suddenly she knew.

'You're married, aren't you.'

'No,' he said, 'no, I'm not married. But I'm engaged.'

'Oh, *Terry* . . .'

'Well, what was I supposed to do?' he demanded, suddenly defensive. 'You didn't want me any more, you'd made that clear. You didn't want me messing up your marriage. There was nothing for me to wait for. And when I moved to London . . .'

Kathy nodded dumbly. Her throat felt as if it had a huge, burning lump in it. 'Is it – is she – someone you've met here?'

'She's in the same office,' he said reluctantly.

340

'And how long have you been engaged?'

'Two months.'

She looked past him into the corridor. 'Is she here now? I'm surprised she hasn't come to see who's at the door.' She began to back down the steps. 'I'd better go. It won't do you any good to have a baby turning up on the doorstep.'

Terry shook his head. 'We're not living together, Kathy, it's nothing like that. And anyway, she's gone away for a few days to see her mother. But you still can't stay,' he added swiftly. 'You must realise—'

'Oh, yes, I can see that.' She felt dead inside, as if her last hope had been snatched from under her nose. She looked up at him and burst out suddenly. 'Why didn't your mother tell me? When I asked for your address, why didn't she *tell* me?'

Terry looked uncomfortable. 'She doesn't know. Look, when I left Gosport I decided I had to cut all my old ties. You know I never got on well at home. I gave her my address, obviously I had to do that, and I sent her a Christmas card and that sort of thing, but she's not really bothered about me. She was glad to see the back of me. So why tell her when I got engaged? I'll tell her next time I send her a card, and that'll be soon enough for her.'

A thin wailing sounded from the car. Kathy turned automatically and then glanced back at Terry. He was staring in the direction of the cry, and when he looked back at Kathy she saw his brow crease.

'You said it's our baby. Is that really true?'

'Of course it is. Why else would I come to see you?'

He flinched and she cursed herself. 'Obviously not because you decided you loved me after all,' he said bitterly. 'That's what I thought for a moment when I saw you on the doorstep. I should have known better.'

'And what if I had come to say that?' she asked quietly. 'What would you have done then?'

Terry sighed. 'I'm not sure I know anything any more.' He passed one hand across his brow. 'Can I see the baby? Did you say it's a boy?'

'Yes. His name's Timothy.' She hesitated. 'Shall I bring him in?'

'Yes. Yes, you'd better. It's too cold to stand here.' He waited while she went down the steps to the car and reached in for the carrycot. She brought it out and locked the car door, and then came up the steps. Terry made no offer to help carry the cot. He led the way indoors and she followed him, closing the front door behind her.

'It's up these stairs.'

Kathy found herself in a large room with a high ceiling and a wide bay window. It was furnished with a fitted carpet in deep red and the same sofa and chairs that Terry had owned in Gosport. She looked at them, feeling a lump of sorrow in her throat, and set the cot down gently on the sofa.

Terry came slowly across the room and looked inside. 'Timothy, did you say?'

'Yes. He looks like you. A bit.'

Terry stared at the baby. He was awake now, waving his fists in the air, his dark eyes wide open. Slowly, Terry put down his hand, one finger extended, and the baby gripped the finger and immediately brought it to his mouth and began to chew. Terry made an odd sort of choking noise, somewhere between a laugh and a sob. 'Oh, Kath . . . Why didn't you tell me? Why didn't you let me know?'

'I don't know,' she whispered. 'I couldn't think straight. I didn't think you'd want to know. All I could think of was what Brian would do.'

'And what has he done? Or can I guess?' He looked at her face again. 'Oh, God, He did that, didn't he? He hit you.'

She nodded. 'He's turned me out. He doesn't want me any more, and he doesn't want . . .' She indicated the baby. 'He wanted me to give him away – have him adopted. I couldn't, Terry. I just couldn't. I hoped he'd come round, but he came home today and he just told me to go. I think he'll probably divorce me.' She twisted her mouth wryly. 'He won't have any trouble getting evidence.'

'And I suppose I'll be cited, won't I?' Terry said. 'I'll be cited as co-respondent.'

Kathy's eyes widened. 'I suppose you will. Oh, Terry, I'd never thought of that! Oh, how awful. And your fiancée – will she have to know?'

'I guess it'll be difficult to keep it a secret.' He looked down at the baby again. 'What a mess. What a bloody awful mess.'

'I know,' she said. 'I'm really sorry.'

They were both silent for a few minutes, then Terry said, 'Could I hold him for a minute?'

'Of course.' Kathy lifted Timothy from the cot and handed him over. His father took him, not awkwardly, as Brian had done, but with his arms curved to the shape of the baby, as if he were accustomed to handling him. Timothy lay comfortably against his chest, gazing up into his face, and to Kathy it was as if this had always been meant to happen, as if not only she but Timothy as well had come home.

'Oh, Terry,' she said, a wave of misery breaking over her, 'I'm so sorry. I really am so terribly, terribly sorry.'

In the end, she did stay the night. There was nowhere else to go. She took the car away and parked it further down the street, in the hope that none of the neighbours would notice, but Terry said he'd have to tell his fiancée anyway. 'It'd be much worse if she found out from someone else.'

'Will she be very upset?' Kathy asked inadequately, and he gave her a sardonic look.

'Well, what do *you* think? We've only been engaged a few weeks. I told her a bit about you, but not everything. Now it's all going to have to come out.'

'It shouldn't make any difference. It all happened before you knew her.'

'A baby on the doorstep and you think it won't make any difference? Being cited in a divorce?' He turned away and paced across the room. 'Kathy, what is it about you? You're an ordinary girl, you don't set out to seduce every man you set eyes on, but you're trouble all the same. Or is it just me?'

It's just you, she wanted to say. It's because I love you. But she couldn't say that now. Terry was engaged to someone else, and maybe she loved him too, maybe he loved her. Kathy couldn't walk in and disrupt his life all over again.

'Brian would probably say the same,' she said with a small laugh.

'Yes, I suppose he would.' Terry stopped by the cot and looked down at the baby, now fast asleep. Kathy had fed him half an hour ago, sitting in one of the armchairs, while Terry discreetly busied himself in the little kitchen. He had come back while she was changing Timothy's nappy, and sat in the other chair, watching, then he brought in a tray with two plates of scrambled egg on toast and a pot of tea.

'If only I'd known,' he said now, touching the baby's cheek gently with one fingertip. 'You ought to have told me, Kath.'

'I didn't think you'd want to know. I didn't know what to do. Brian had to know, and it was all so awful, having to think about giving him away. There didn't seem any point in telling you.' She looked at him. 'Would it really have made any difference?'

He sighed. 'I suppose it would have depended on what you wanted to do . . . How can I tell? You let me down, Kath, you let me down twice. How could I know you wouldn't do it again?'

'Brian said that too,' she said quietly. 'I don't blame either of you.

343

You're right, Terry. I'm nothing but trouble.' She got up and came over to the cot and stood beside Terry, looking down at their son. 'But I won't be trouble for him. I'm going to look after him. I'm going to make sure he has a good life.'

'Are you?' Terry's voice was edged with unaccustomed sarcasm. 'And how are you going to do that, Kathy? Where are you going to live – in your car? What are you going to do for money? I suppose you've left your job. Just how are you going to make sure this baby has a good life?'

Kathy stared at him and sank into one of the armchairs, her face white. She realised that she hadn't thought a minute further than this. When Brian had turned her out, there had been no one to turn to but Terry. She couldn't go to Clare and she knew that her father would not let her in the house, there was very little else that her mother could do to help her and she had no other friends close enough to help in such an emergency. Terry had been the only one.

'Terry, what am I going to do?' she asked, her voice shaking.

He sighed and sat down opposite her. 'If only you'd told me sooner. If only you'd told me at the beginning.' He got up again and paced the room, anger once more edging his voice. 'If only you could have made up your bloody *mind*. We could have been a family. We *ought* to be a family.' He stopped and stared into the cot again. 'This is my son, and I can't be a proper father to him. How do you think that makes me feel?'

She shook her head. She'd thought it would help, coming to Terry, and instead the agony was even worse. She had never considered what it would mean to him, never even tried to see into his mind. I'm just a useless, selfish bitch, she thought miserably, I'm not fit to be a mother.

She looked at Terry's face, seeing the tenderness that softened it as he gazed down at his son, the gentleness with which he touched the baby's cheek. He's right, she thought, we ought to be a family.

'I shouldn't have come. I shouldn't ever have told you.'

Terry shrugged and sat down again. 'What's the use of talking like this?' he said wearily. 'What's the use of going over it all? You're here now, and we've got to sort something out. We've got to decide what we do next.'

'We?' she said in a small voice.

'Yes, we. I'm involved now, like it or not. I can't turn you out into the night, like Brian did. Timothy's my son and I've got to take responsibility for him.'

344

Despite her guilt, Kathy felt a small surge of hope. 'But what about . . .?' She gestured with one hand. 'I don't know her name. Your fiancée.'

'Sheila. Her name's Sheila.' He sighed. 'I don't know. I don't know what she'll do. Obviously she's going to be upset. Who wouldn't be?' He gave Kathy a very straight look. 'I thought we could have a good life together, Sheila and me. Maybe we still can – if she can get over this.'

'Yes.' Kathy glanced away. 'I didn't mean I wanted you to . . . I didn't want to come between you. I honestly didn't know you were engaged, Terry. I wouldn't have come if I had.'

'I know,' he said. 'I know.'

After a short silence Kathy, her voice breaking, said, 'Terry, it's been so awful. Not knowing what to do. Not knowing what Brian would do. And when he came home and – and hit me, I was afraid he'd go for the baby too. I can't ever go back.' She touched her face. 'Even if I didn't have Timothy, I could never go back.' Her voice broke completely and she covered her face with her hands. 'I don't know what to do next! I just don't know what to do . . .'

Terry got up and went to sit on the arm of her chair. He put one arm around her shoulders and held her, and she turned her head and leaned against his side, weeping. He waited a few minutes, until the storm had subsided a little, and then said gently, 'You're worn out. You can't make any decisions tonight and you can't go anywhere else. Look, you'd better go to bed. I'll sleep here on the sofa.' He gave her shoulders a gentle squeeze, then let go and stood up. He left the room, returning a few minutes later with an armful of bedding.

Kathy found a handkerchief and wiped away some of her tears. She looked up at him with a tremulous smile. 'What will the neighbours say?'

'We hardly know them yet, so it won't matter. Nobody notices what anyone else does around here anyway. Come on and I'll show you the bedroom.' He picked up Timothy's cot and took her through the adjoining door. The bedroom was small and plain, and Kathy felt the tears come to her eyes again as she recognised the bed where they had made such tender love in the flat overlooking Portsmouth harbour. 'There. You know where the bathroom is, and the kitchen. Just get yourself anything you need and I'll see you in the morning.' He looked at her for a moment, then reached out and touched her swollen cheek, as gently and tenderly as he had touched the baby. 'Oh, Kathy, Kathy . . .' Then he stepped back a little and gave her an odd, formal little nod and turned away.

'Goodnight, Terry,' Kathy whispered, watching him go. As the door closed, she turned and looked down into the cot, at the sleeping face of her son. Her son – and Terry's. 'Goodnight . . .'

It was eleven o'clock next morning before Clare was able to telephone Kathy's number in Fareham. All night, as she lay beside Martyn in bed, she had been worrying about her friend and determined to contact her as soon as possible. Although she knew that she could not invite her to come back – at least until Martyn had gone away again – she had no intention of obeying her husband's command, and abandoning Kathy. If she could do nothing else, at least she could talk to her.

'I need to do some shopping,' she said after breakfast. 'Do you mind staying with the children?'

'Shopping? On a Sunday?'

'Yes, the Drake Stores will be open. We need some – some toilet paper.' She wondered whether that was one of the things you could legally buy on a Sunday. The laws were so muddled. You could buy newspapers but not a Bible, milk but not bread – or was it the other way around? Anyway, she was sure you could buy toilet paper and she just hoped that Martyn wouldn't check the cupboard where she normally kept a few spare rolls. If he did, she would simply say she'd forgotten they were there.

I'm starting to tell lies now, she thought guiltily. It's the first time I've ever lied to Martyn. Where is it all going to end?

A lie about toilet paper didn't seem so very serious, but it was the bigger lie that was important. Not telling him that she was going to telephone Kathy was the real lie, and it was one he'd take very seriously. I can't help it, she thought, getting out the old bike she seldom had a chance to use these days. He shouldn't have told me not to ring her. He ought to know I don't abandon my friends, any more than he wants to abandon his.

It was a fine morning, with a real touch of spring in the air. As she cycled along Whitchurch Road, Clare could see the bulbs flowering in the gardens. The snowdrops were over, and crocuses freckled the grass with purple and gold. A few daffodils and narcissi blew golden trumpets in the soft breeze, and as she dropped down into Tavistock she could see the leaves beginning to tinge the branches of the rowan trees and the silver birches with a faint, shimmering green.

Clare cycled down Pixon Lane and went through the gate into the Meadows. She got off her bike and pushed it along beside the river and out through the gate on to Plymouth Road, close to Drake's statue. The river was running swiftly over its rocks, the trees over-head touched with that faint shadow of green from the buds that were about to unfurl.

The little shop was busy as usual on a Sunday morning. Clare bought a toilet roll, and then made for the telephone box.

The phone was answered on the third ring. She pressed button A, her heart beating fast. 'Kathy?'

There was a brief silence. 'Who's that?'

Oh, no, she thought. It's Brian. 'It's Clare here, I – I wondered if I could speak to Kathy.'

He gave a short laugh. 'You'll have a job. She's not here.'

'Not there?' Clare's mind whirled. 'Where's she gone? What's happened?'

'I've chucked her out, that's what's happened. As to where she's gone, I don't know and I don't care. To London to find lover-boy, I wouldn't wonder, unless she's on her way down to you. And if she does turn up on the doorstep, you know what you can tell her, don't you? Get rid of the kid. And then – and *only* then – I might think about having her back.'

Clare listened in horror. She had never heard anyone speak so brutally. And he sounded drunk, too. Whatever had been going on?

'You've turned her out?' she whispered. 'And the baby?'

'Well, you don't suppose I asked her to leave him behind, do you?' Brian snorted. 'Another bloke's by-blow? No, Kathy's gone too far this time. I tell you, I've had enough. And you can tell her that too, if she comes to you.'

'Oh, Brian—' Clare began, but the telephone clicked in her ear and she knew he had hung up. Slowly, she replaced the receiver and walked out of the kiosk.

As she cycled back up the hill to Dale View, she knew that she would, after all, have to tell Martyn about the phone call. This was something she couldn't keep secret. She was too upset. And too desperately worried about her friend.

While Clare was making her call to Brian, Terry also was using the phone. Like Clare, he had been awake most of the night, acutely aware of Kathy in the next room, thinking about the baby, thinking about his wife-to-be. He had told Kathy the truth when he'd said he hoped to make a good life with Sheila, yet he could not deny there was some very strong bond between himself and Kathy. She was first in my heart, he thought, and I suppose she always will be. But I can't break my engagement for her. I can't hurt Sheila, and I'd never really know if she'd stay with me.

He hadn't been enough for Kathy before. Why should it be any different now, even though they had a baby?

Timothy. His baby. His son. Sheila had said she didn't want children yet, not for a few years. He had been looking forward to having them sooner than that – but Timothy was there *now*. His son was in the next room, and so was Kathy. They were, in a bizarre way, a family.

I mustn't think this way, he told himself, turning over for the hundredth time. I've got to think how to help them – and how to get them out of my life. I can't afford to have Kathy mess me up again.

There was only one person he could think of who could, or would, help, and that was Clare.

'I can't go to Clare,' Kathy had told him. 'I've been there for weeks, but Martyn's home now and he's Brian's friend. I can't go back – at least until he's gone. I wouldn't be surprised,' she finished miserably, 'if he tells Clare she's got to have no more to do with me.'

Terry wouldn't be surprised either, but he wasn't convinced that Clare would obey such an order. Being a naval wife made women very independent, he'd noticed. They had to cope with everything while their husbands were away, and it made them less inclined to knuckle under and take orders when they came home. And he couldn't see Clare as the sort to walk out on her friends when they were in trouble.

At least I can ring her up, he thought, and tell her Kathy's here. Someone ought to know, after all. And so, after he had made toast and coffee for Kathy and himself and left her in the living-room to feed Timothy, he went down to the front hall and picked up the phone to dial Clare's number.

Martyn answered. His voice grew cold as Terry said who he was. 'You've got a nerve, ringing here.'

'Never mind that,' Terry said. 'Can I speak to Clare?'

'No,' Martyn said tersely. 'You can't. She's gone out.'

'When will she be back? Can I ring her later?'

'No, you bloody well can't. Don't you think you've caused enough trouble? You've already buggered up my oppo's marriage. You're not going to start having a go at mine.'

'For God's sake, Martyn, you know that's not what I want to do. Look, I just want to talk to Clare. Kathy's here and—'

'Kathy's *there*? With *you*? Well, if that don't take the biscuit! That didn't take her long, did it?'

'Martyn, listen. It's not like that. She came here because Brian threw her out and she had nowhere else to go. He's beaten her up. She's desperate. I just thought someone ought to know where she was. I thought Clare might know somewhere she could go until she gets herself sorted out. She can't stay here.'

'Oh, can't she? Don't want her yourself now, is that it? If you want my opinion, you and Kathy *deserve* each other.'

My God, Terry thought, how did it all come to this? All we did was love each other. If she'd only stuck by me the first time . . . If she'd only not been engaged, so that we could have felt free and happy about it all . . .

Aloud, he said, 'Just tell Clare I called, will you, Martyn? And tell her Kathy's with me.' He put down the phone.

A small sound made him glance up to see Kathy standing at the top of the stairs, pale beneath her yellowing bruises, holding the baby in her arms. She was dressed as if ready to leave. 'It's no use,' she said flatly. 'Clare won't be able to have me back. There's nowhere for me to go, Terry.' She looked down at the baby and gave a deep, shuddering sigh. 'I'll have to give him up. You're right – I can't give him any sort of a life. I'll have to give him away . . .'

Chapter Thirty-Two

C lare unlatched the gate on to the moor and ushered the children through. She started to walk up the hill towards the Pimple, the children running on ahead.

Her heart was still racing with anger. She hadn't said anything to Martyn about her phone call until after lunch, not wanting an argument in front of Christopher and Laura, but as soon as the meal was over and they were washing up together in the scullery, she'd told him.

He had stared at her, his eyes darkening. 'You rang Brian? Without telling me?'

'I was ringing Kathy,' she said. 'I didn't tell you I was going to because I knew you'd make a fuss. But I don't see why I shouldn't speak to my friend, especially when she's in trouble.'

'And who got her into trouble?' he retorted. 'You know what I think about that, Clare.'

'Yes, I do, and I also know what *I* think about it.' She faced him squarely. 'I've got a mind of my own, Martyn, and I'm entitled to my feelings. I won't let my friend down.'

'I told you, you're not having her here.'

'Not while you're here, no – it would be too awkward, because you'd make it awkward. But when you're away I shall have her here whenever I like. She's my *friend*, Martyn.'

'And I'm your husband.' He laid down his tea-towel and glowered at her. 'You'll do as I say over this, Clare.'

They stared at each other, and Clare felt a sudden quickening of panic. They had argued before, even quarrelled, but never quite like this. This, she knew, was a moment as critical as that one a night or two ago, when she had told Martyn that if he insisted on staying in the Navy she was afraid it would drive them apart.

'Martyn,' she said, 'don't let's argue over this. The important thing is that Kathy isn't there any more. He's turned her out. Martyn, Brian's turned Kathy out of the house.'

'I know,' he said, picking up the tea-towel again.

Clare stared at him. 'You *know*? You mean he's rung *you*? This morning?'

'No, though I wouldn't be surprised if he does. And maybe I'll give him a buzz myself.' He gave her an odd look. 'You shouldn't have gone out this morning, Clare. You missed the excitement.'

'What do you mean? What are you talking about? What's happened?'

He lifted his eyebrows slightly, teasing her. Clare felt her anger rise and she dropped the dish she had been holding back into the water and grasped his arms. '*Tell* me, Martyn.'

He flinched away. 'Hey, your hands are wet! Look, all that happened was that I had a phone call too. From Terry Carter.'

'*Terry?*'

'Yes, *Terry*. I told him he'd got a nerve, ringing here. He wanted to talk to you, but you were out, weren't you, making your own secret phone calls?'

'What did he say? Why did he ring?' She shook him by the arms. 'Martyn, stop being so stupid and *tell* me.'

'For God's sake, Clare, stop grabbing me like that . . .' He twisted himself away. 'He wanted to tell you his paramour's there with him, that's all. In London. So you can stop worrying, all right? And maybe you'd like to ring Brian again and tell him. Someone ought to tell him where his wife is, I should think.'

'I don't want to ring Brian. I want to talk to Kathy. Did you get Terry's number?' She shook his arms again. '*Tell* me, Martyn. Kathy's my friend – she needs help—'

'*No!*' he snapped, losing his temper. He swung his arms up suddenly, forcing her away from him. 'And stop shaking me like that. I've told you – you're not speaking to her, and that's an end to it.'

Clare let go of his arms and reached for the towel that hung behind the door. She dried her trembling hands and walked out of the scullery, leaving the dishes in the sink.

Martyn followed her. 'Where are you going now? What are you doing?'

'I'm going out,' Clare said coldly. 'I'm going for a walk. And please don't come with me. I need to be on my own. I need time to think.'

She strode up the hill, still quivering with suppressed rage. We've never quarrelled like this before, she thought, and it seems crazy to quarrel over someone else, even though Brian and Kathy are friends. But it's more than that. It's shown me a side of Martyn I never knew existed.

Somehow, she knew she would have to come to terms with it. She and Martyn were married and wanted to stay married. It was something she must learn to accept, just as she must learn to accept his change of heart over the Navy, just as she must learn to accept another ten or fifteen years of loneliness.

There was an even more urgent problem to be considered – that of what Kathy was going to do next. Was she going to stay with Terry? Clare knew nothing of his life now: he had sent a card at Christmas with a scribbled note inside giving her his new address, but that was all. She had copied the address into her diary, and had sent him a card in return, but they'd had no other contact. She had no idea whether he would want to take Kathy back. She was a married woman. Even in London, there would surely be a stigma attached to a young man living with a married woman.

A voice interrupted her thoughts, and she turned to see Alex loping up the hill behind her.

'Clare! How are you? Where's Martyn? I thought he was coming home this week.'

'He did,' Clare said shortly, turning back and continuing up the hill. Alex fell into step beside her and she felt him glance quizzically at her face. 'He's decided to stay in this afternoon,' she added lamely.

'On a marvellous afternoon like this?' Alex waved his arms as if to encompass the whole of Dartmoor. The sky above was a pale, tender blue, scuffed by a few smudges of thin white cloud; the grass, dull after the winter, was already turning green, the bracken beginning to push tight-clenched fists through the ground. A few sheep were grazing close to the cricket ring, some of them with lambs not long born.

Clare said nothing and Alex looked at her a little more closely. 'Is everything all right? You look upset.'

'Yes, of course.' She stopped. 'No, it's not. We've had a row.'

'Oh.' He looked nonplussed. 'I'm sorry. Look, I'll leave you alone. You don't want me hanging around.'

'No. It's all right. Please, don't go.' She looked up into his face and knew suddenly that she could talk to Alex, that she had always been able to talk to Alex. 'It's Kathy,' she said in a rush. 'Oh, Alex, she's in terrible trouble.'

'Kathy? Your friend – the one with the baby?' Alex and Veronica had met Kathy several times while she was staying at Dale View, although they didn't know her true story. 'What's wrong? The baby's not ill, is he? Hasn't her husband come home as well?'

'Yes.' Clare stopped and looked at the ground. The children were now at the top of the Pimple, chasing each other around the little triangular building. 'I suppose that's part of the trouble,' she said unhappily. 'You see, he's not the baby's father.' She looked up and met Alex's eyes.

'Not the baby's . . . oh, *lord,*' Alex said comprehensively.

'Yes. You see why she's in trouble. The Navy brought Brian home when she first found out, and he told her she must give the baby up for adoption. But she couldn't. She just couldn't part with him. She went home to Fareham to wait for Brian, and when he came he – he threw her out.'

'So where is she now?'

'She's gone to London. She's with Timothy's father, but I don't know what's going to happen. Terry rang up this morning while I was out and spoke to Martyn, but Martyn wouldn't listen to him and he won't let me ring her. I shall, all the same – Kathy's my friend – but I just had to come out to think it through, first.' She looked up at him. 'You see why I'm upset.'

'You're worried about her,' he said, and she nodded.

'It's not only that, though. Martyn and I have never quarrelled like this before. I can understand Brian being angry, and I know Martyn's his friend just as I'm Kathy's, but she's a human being, Alex, and she's in trouble, and all she wants is to be able to keep her baby. I can't turn my back on her, and Martyn shouldn't expect me to.'

'No,' he said quietly, 'of course you can't, and I'm sure he'll realise that. He's probably upset too. It must be worrying for him to see what's happened to his friend. He probably worries about it happening to him too.'

Clare stared at him. 'But I'd never—'

'No, of course not, but it must seem like a possibility to him.'

'So why is he talking about staying in the Navy for another fifteen years?' Clare asked bitterly. 'The children will be almost grown up by the time he comes home to stay. Our lives will be almost over – that part of them, anyway.'

Alex sighed and laid his arm across her shoulder. 'I don't know, Clare. I know the Navy can have a very strong pull on some men. My own father – and Veronica's. It was seeing that as a child that made me determined not to join up, but on some boys it has quite the opposite effect.'

'Christopher says he's not going into the Navy,' Clare said, and Alex smiled slightly.

'Well, he's got plenty of time to make up his mind. But your friend Kathy hasn't, and it's her we ought to be thinking about now.'

Clare nodded and they walked on together. 'I don't know what she wants to do – perhaps she'll stay with Terry now. Perhaps things will turn out all right after all.'

'Well, I suppose that's why she went to him,' Alex said, but Clare shook her head.

'I think she just didn't know where else to turn. And he's the baby's father, after all.' Her mouth twisted ruefully. 'He didn't even know she was expecting it, you know. It's going to be a bit of a shock.'

'It certainly is,' Alex said. 'I can't imagine how I'd feel if a woman from my past turned up on my doorstep carrying a little white bundle.'

'It isn't funny,' Clare said. 'And anyway, Timothy had a blue blanket.' She caught his eye and laughed a little, reluctantly. 'But, really, it *isn't* funny. I don't know what she'll do if he turns her away too.'

'Has she ever thought about it? She must have known Brian wasn't likely to agree to keep the baby.'

'Oh, yes, she did, but she didn't seem to be able to get any clear idea. I think she's been too upset and frightened to think clearly at all. The only suggestion she ever came up with was to get some sort of living-in job, where they wouldn't object to the baby. You know, a sort of housekeeper like Veronica's parents have.'

Alex stopped. 'But that's the answer!'

Clare looked at him, surprised. 'What d'you mean? What's the answer?'

'Veronica's parents. The woman they had has left – didn't suit them or they didn't suit her, I'm not sure which. They're desperate for someone else. I'm sure they'd give Kathy a chance.'

'Veronica's parents? Near Ashburton?'

'Well, she's only got the one set as far as I know,' Alex said, smiling.

'And you really think they might be willing to take her on? If she still needs a job?'

'I'm sure they would. I'd recommend her, Clare. I've seen her enough times, I've seen her with the children and with you. She's helped you round the house quite a bit, hasn't she?'

'Yes, but . . .'

'Well, you don't seem to be living in squalor,' he pointed out. 'And if that's the kind of work she wants and you think she'd do it well . . .'

'Oh, she would! She's very houseproud – the house she and Brian bought is like a little palace.' Clare stared at him, feeling the first flicker of hope that she'd known for days. 'Oh, Alex, if only they would! It would be perfect.'

'Well, look,' he said, 'let's finish our walk now and then we'll both go home and I'll ring the folks while you try to get in touch with Kathy. Martyn won't actually stop you, will he? Would you rather I ring her?'

'No, I'll do it.'

'Right, then, you find out if she still needs somewhere to go and then ring me, and we'll take it from there.' He stopped and took her hands, looking into her eyes, as pleased as if Kathy were his own friend and he as anxious as Clare herself. 'How does that sound?'

'It sounds wonderful!' Heedless of where they were and who might see them, Clare flung her arms around his neck and kissed him. 'Oh, Alex, it's wonderful, and *you're* wonderful! What would I do without you?'

'Well, you might behave a bit more discreetly when you're out on the moor,' he said, smiling, and removed her arms from around his neck. She blushed and laughed, catching his eye, and then they both stood still for a moment, their gaze locked.

'Alex . . .' Clare said uncertainly, and he put one finger on her lips.

'It's all right. We're friends. It's what friends do – help each other. That's all.'

'Yes,' she said, feeling oddly shaken. 'I know. That's all.'

Martyn had lit the fire when she arrived home. He had filled the coal scuttle and brought in some logs, and he had laid a tray for tea. The kettle was simmering on the Rayburn.

Clare took it all in at one glance and knew that it was meant as an olive branch. She kissed him and stood within his arms for a moment, then gently freed herself.

'I just want to make a phone call.'

His face darkened at once. 'You're going to ring her?'

'Yes, of course I am. She's my friend, Martyn.'

'Despite what I told you?' he went on, as if she hadn't spoken. 'Despite the fact that I've expressly told you not to have any more to do with her?'

Clare turned and faced him. 'I told you, Martyn, she's my friend and I won't desert her. I also told you that you can't tell me what to do as if you were some Victorian patriarch. This is 1965. Women don't go down mines any more, and we've got the vote, just in case you haven't noticed. You choose to leave me at home in charge of everything so you've got to accept the fact that I can make up my own mind. Now, I'm going to ring my friend, so give me that number, and then we'll have tea by the fire.'

Martyn stared at her. She stood very still, facing him, and then, with a furious snort, he tore a scrap of paper from his pocket and flung it on the table between them. Then he turned and marched out of the kitchen, leaving her alone.

Clare sat down by the telephone. She discovered that she was shaking, and it took her a moment or two to gather her strength before she smoothed out the scrap of paper and dialled.

The telephone rang several times. She's not there, she thought with a sinking heart. I've left it too late and she's gone. Or Brian's found her—

The ringing stopped abruptly. A small, wary voice said, 'Hello,' and Clare felt weak with relief.

'Kathy? Kathy, is that you?'

'Oh, *Clare*!' Kathy's voice sounded in her ear; she was obviously crying. 'Oh, Clare, I don't know what I'm going to do. I've been such an *idiot* – I've ruined everything. Brian's thrown me out – he won't have me back and I've nowhere to go.' She drew in a great, shuddering breath. 'I'm going to have to give in, Clare. There's nothing else I can do.'

'Kathy, wait. Tell me what happened. What did Brian say to you? What did he do?'

'He threw me out,' Kathy said. 'He told me to go and never dare come back. He means it, Clare. He won't have me back and I don't want to go . . . I can't go back to him, Clare.'

'No, of course not.' Clare closed her eyes. 'What about Terry, what does he say?'

'He says he'll give me some money,' Kathy said dully. 'He says he'll help with Timothy. But there's nothing else I can do.' She paused for a moment. 'He's engaged.'

'Oh.' Clare felt blank. 'Oh, I see.'

'Her name's *Sheila*,' Kathy went on, as if this made a difference. 'She's away at the moment. I can't stay here, she's coming back next week . . . Clare, I can't mess up his life all over again. What am I going to do?'

'That's what I want to talk to you about,' Clare said, trying to sound calm. 'What do you want to do?'

'I want none of it ever to have happened,' Kathy said miserably. 'No, I don't – I don't want Timothy never to have been born. He's all I've got. But I can't keep him, Clare.' Her voice began to rise again. 'I'm going to have to give him away. I've got no other *choice*.'

'Yes, you have. Listen to me, Kathy. Try to stop crying, and listen. You do have a choice. *Listen*. You remember Alex? Alex and Veronica?' Quickly, Clare told her what she and Alex had been discussing that afternoon. 'He's going to telephone them this afternoon. He's going to ring me soon and tell me what they say, but he's sure they'll agree to see you, at least. And I'll ring you and tell you as soon as he does. Now, what do you think? Would you like to go to them?'

'They won't have me,' Kathy said dolefully. 'They won't want anyone like me. They'll want someone decent and respectable, they'll never—'

'Kathy, you *are* decent and respectable. You've just been in a muddle and had some bad luck, that's all. Alex understands that. I'm sure Veronica will too, and her parents. He wouldn't have suggested it if he hadn't been sure.'

'Oh,' Kathy said. 'Oh, if only they would . . .'

'I'll ring you back as soon as he rings me,' Clare promised. 'Now, I'll ring off so that he can get through, but don't go away, Kathy, and don't think any more about giving Timothy away. You're not going to have to do that.'

She put down the telephone and turned to find Martyn standing in the doorway. They looked at each other silently.

'Well, you've been busy, haven't you?' he said at last. 'Consorting with Alex Challoner when you were supposed to be going for a walk. Fixing up a nice cushy little number for Kathy. Going against my wishes.'

'I told you,' Clare said, feeling her cheeks flush but keeping her voice steady, 'Kathy's my friend and I want to help her. I *will* help her. And I haven't been consorting with Alex – we met each other by chance. And if Veronica's parents are willing to give Kathy a job as their housekeeper, I don't see that it has anything at all to do with you.'

Martyn stared at her. Clare met his eyes, but her heart was sinking and she felt sick with misery. Looking into Martyn's eyes then was like looking at a stranger. Fearing that he would see her tears and take them as a sign of weakness, she turned away.

The telephone rang and she snatched it up. It was Alex, telling her that Veronica's parents were very interested in the idea of having

Kathy, and were asking if she could go down to them immediately, so that they could have a talk.

'I'm sure she will,' Clare said, feeling a great surge of relief. 'Thank you, Alex. Thank you very, very much.'

She put down the telephone and then picked it up again to ring Kathy. Throughout both calls, she was aware of Martyn standing in the doorway and watching her.

When she finally replaced the receiver again, she turned and looked him in the eye. 'Don't say anything,' she told him. 'Don't say a word. I don't want to discuss Kathy with you again – ever.'

Chapter Thirty-Three

Alex also had some explanations to make when he'd finished his telephoning. He went into the big living-room, where Veronica was lying amongst a pile of cushions on the sofa, reading a magazine. It was warm and comfortable, with a fire burning in the grate. Veronica had lit a couple of table lamps which gave the walls a mellow glow, contrasting with the greyness of the gathering dusk outside. Alex sat down by the window, gazing out across the valley.

Veronica laid down her magazine. 'Tell me again. You met Clare up on the moor and she told you her friend Kathy had been turned out of her home and needs a living-in job where she can have her baby with her. And you thought Mummy and Daddy would take her as their housekeeper.'

'Well, they'll give her a chance. A month's approval on either side. It seems fair, and it gives poor Kathy a breathing-space.'

'What I don't understand,' Veronica said, 'is why she needs it at all. She's got a husband, hasn't she, and a home of her own? What's gone wrong with that?'

Alex sighed. 'It's not a very happy story, Ronnie. Apparently the baby's not her husband's. There was another boyfriend – she broke her engagement once because of him, but Brian came home and persuaded her to go back to him. Then, when he went away, she met the other man again and, well, things obviously went too far.'

'And Brian won't accept the baby. Well, you can hardly blame him. Why didn't she just give it up for adoption, then? That seems the most sensible thing.'

Alex looked at her. Veronica was swathed in soft, creamy wool – a skirt that fell in soft folds around her ankles, and a loose jumper with a big rolled collar. She looked like a small animal, peeping bright-eyed from its nest.

'That's what he wanted her to do, but she couldn't. It was her baby – she couldn't part with it.'

'Well, I'm not surprised he turned her out,' Veronica remarked, picking up her magazine again. 'You can't expect a man to take on someone else's baby. It seems to me she made her choice and now she'll have to live with it.'

'Yes,' Alex said quietly, 'I think that's what she's trying to do.'

Veronica glanced at him across her magazine. 'I hope you're not going to get too involved, Alex. I don't really know why you've had to drag Mummy and Daddy into it. She's not our friend, after all – we don't know anything about her. She might turn out to be awful.'

'She's Clare's friend,' he pointed out. 'And we met her several times while she was staying there. She seems a decent sort, and the baby's a little smasher.'

'Is he?' Veronica said indifferently. 'Can't say I took much notice of him.'

'Oh, Ronnie, you must have! He's a great little chap.'

'I told you, I didn't take much notice. If you want to know the truth, I didn't much care for Kathy – I always thought there was something a bit odd about the way she stayed all that time with Clare. I thought Brian was worth ten of her – funny, scrappy little thing she is, with that short hair.'

'He's a good-looking chap, I suppose,' Alex acknowledged, 'but that doesn't mean much. He doesn't seem to care a lot about his wife.'

'Why should he? Did she care about him when she went off with someone else?'

Alex's brows drew together in a look that was half reproach, half disbelief. 'Ronnie, don't be so hard. She's made a mistake, but she's paying for it – she'll pay for the rest of her life. We all fall by the wayside at some point in our lives. And there's the baby to think of – none of it's his fault.'

'And that's another thing,' Veronica said. 'Why should Mummy and Daddy have to have a squalling baby foisted on them? I'm amazed they agreed to it, if you want to know the truth.'

'They sounded quite excited, as a matter of fact. Your mother told me she was really looking forward to having a baby about the place.'

Veronica's small, pretty face tightened. 'Is that meant to be a dig at me?'

'Of course it isn't! All the same . . .' he hesitated ' . . . I think she'd like to be a grandmother. She has a look in her eyes sometimes—'

'Oh, yes, I've seen it! As soon as we arrive – eyeing me up and down to see if I'm showing signs of being pregnant. As if I were a brood mare! Well, she can stop wondering because I've decided I don't want to have babies. Ever.' Veronica picked up her magazine again and riffled it open.

The room was very quiet. The fire hissed softly as a piece of coal shifted position. Outside, the view had almost disappeared in the darkness. Alex sat very still, his hands gripping the arms of his chair. 'What did you say, Ronnie?'

Veronica glanced up, as if startled. 'What? What do you mean?'

'What did you say about babies? About you not having babies?'

'Well, just that, I suppose. You know I've never been keen, darling.'

'No,' he said, 'I knew you weren't keen to have babies *yet*. I've been hoping lately that you'd soon be ready – especially after seeing little Timothy. But this is the first I've heard about any decision not to have them *ever*.'

'Well, I didn't think it was worth mentioning,' she said casually. 'I mean, we haven't actually discussed it for ages, have we? I thought you felt more or less the same.'

'We haven't discussed it for ages because I didn't want to put pressure on you. And I don't feel the same, not in any way. I want a family, Veronica, and I don't want to wait·much longer.'

'Well, I'm sorry,' she said, keeping her eyes on her magazine, 'but I've just told you what I've decided. I think we're happy enough as we are.'

'*You* think?' he exploded, coming out of his chair so suddenly that she gave a little squeal of surprise and dropped her magazine. '*You've* decided? Don't you think this affects us both? Don't you think it's something we ought to discuss *together*?'

'No, not really.' She had recovered herself and gazed up at him defiantly. 'I'm the one who'd have to have them and look after them. I'm the one who'd have to go through all the misery and discomfort, and losing my figure, and all the *pain*. And the cleaning and washing and feeding afterwards, and then having to take them to school – it never ends, Alex, I've seen it in other people. Look at Clare, she's never got any money to enjoy herself and she's tied to those children morning, noon and night. What sort of a life is that? I tell you, I'd rather go on enjoying life as we do now. We're all right as we are, Alex. We have a good time. Why spoil it?'

'We're just playing at life,' he said. 'All right, we can do as we please, but I happen to think having children is important, and why shouldn't we enjoy that too? If you want to know, I envy Clare her kids. I'd love a couple like Christopher and Laura.'

'Well, I'm sorry,' Veronica said, 'but I'm not going to give them to you. I don't want them, Alex, and that's all there is to it.' She picked up her magazine and spread it open on her lap.

Alex gazed at her, baffled. There seemed to be nothing he could say. Veronica had quite clearly made up her mind and saw no reason or purpose in discussing the matter further. However, the subject was by no means closed to him. He had a hundred things to say.

He stood nonplussed for a moment or two, then walked out of the room. He went into the kitchen and stood in the darkness, staring out into the shadowy garden. He felt a tumult of emotions: dismay, hurt, disappointment, betrayal. She's let me down, he thought. She's condemning me to a life without any children of my own – a life I never wanted, never even considered. And she hasn't even done me the courtesy of talking it over with me.

Veronica was right – she was the one who would have to bear the children. But by getting married at all, hadn't she tacitly agreed to have them? Wasn't that part of the marriage contract, part of the vows they'd made?

With a sudden, swift movement, he went out to the hall and grabbed his jacket from a hook. Shrugging it on, he pulled open the front door and strode rapidly up the path to the main road, then turned and walked aimlessly along it, not knowing where he wanted to go, not knowing what he wanted to do.

The house lay behind him, its rooms softly lit, warm and enticing. When he came home, he knew that Veronica would welcome him, gentle and pretty as a kitten, waiting to be caressed, to be stroked and cuddled and made love to. Waiting for everything to be all right between them – as long as she got her way.

That's what their marriage had been from the start, he thought as he strode along. Everything arranged for comfort, for convenience, for enjoyment and pleasure . . . *as long as Veronica got her way*.

Now, for the first time, Alex wasn't prepared to give it to her. He wanted his own way.

Terry found his emotions veering between relief and sadness at the solution to Kathy's problem. 'It sounds as if it could be the best thing all round,' he said. 'Even if you decide not to stay there, it'll give you time. And Brian may come round after a while.'

'I'll never go back to Brian,' Kathy said. 'Not after what he did to me. I'd always be afraid he'd do it again – and I'd never take Timothy anywhere near him.'

Terry nodded. He looked down into the carrycot as Kathy lifted it, ready to take it out to the car, and said, 'I'm sorry things didn't turn out differently for us, Kathy. I'm sorry we can't be a proper family.' He touched the baby's cheek gently, letting his palm rest for a moment against the downy skin. 'It all seems such a waste, but I can't go back to how we were – not now.'

'No.' Kathy looked up into his eyes. 'You really do love her, don't you?'

Terry sighed. 'Oh, Kathy, I'm not sure this is the right time to ask me that. I feel as if I've been turned upside down and shaken. I thought I did, yet you were always there, like a shadow in the background. And when I saw you on the doorstep on Saturday night – well, I couldn't believe it. I thought for a minute I was dreaming, that none of it had happened. But I'm engaged to Sheila And she . . .' He gave Kathy a half regretful, half reproachful glance. 'She loves me enough to marry me, you see.'

'And I didn't.' Kathy nodded. She felt numb, although she knew there was pain there, waiting to stab her. 'Well, I hope it all goes well, Terry. I hope she'll understand about me and Timothy.'

She knew there was no doubt that Terry would tell Sheila. He had already told Kathy that he would send money each month towards the baby's upkeep. Sheila would have to know that, and it would be a test of her understanding. A test a lot of girls would fail.

'Well,' she said through the ache in her throat, 'I'd better be going.' She looked at him again and they stood awkwardly for a moment, unsure how to part. A kiss seemed inappropriate and anything else worse. In the end, she simply turned away and walked down the steps to the car.

'Keep in touch,' Terry said. 'Let me know how things go – and don't go anywhere else without letting me have your address.'

'I won't.' She opened the car door and laid the carrycot on the back seat, then got into her own seat. Without looking up, she started the engine, slipped the car into gear and took off the brake. The car moved slowly forwards.

'Kathy,' he said suddenly, urgently.

Kathy put her foot on the accelerator. She looked straight ahead. 'Goodbye Terry,' she said under her breath. 'Goodbye . . .'

The tears were already running down her cheeks as she turned the corner, catching one last glimpse of him in her mirror, standing at the top of his steps watching her out of sight.

Keith and Elizabeth Curtis awaited Kathy's arrival with some apprehension.

'I hope we're doing the right thing,' Elizabeth said. 'It sounds a sad story. Goodness knows, she shouldn't have done what she did, but how many lonely young naval wives have gone down the same path? It's hard to blame the husband either – it can't be easy to come home and find your wife with another man's child. But according to Alex she just hasn't anywhere else to go.'

'He says she's a decent enough young woman really,' Keith agreed. 'Well, they'll have to sort it out between them. Anyway, we'll have a talk with her and if she does stay we'll still have a month to decide – if she doesn't suit us, she'll have time to find somewhere else.' He smiled. 'It might even be fun to have a baby about the place. So long as she can still take a lot of the work off your shoulders.'

Kathy's job, if she stayed, was officially defined as 'housekeeper', but in fact Elizabeth intended to use her just as much as a kind of secretary. The cleaners who came in for a few days each week saw to most of the housework, and Kathy would be expected to oversee them and take on some of the cooking. Elizabeth also wanted someone to help her with the business of the various village activities with which she was concerned.

'Obviously, she'll need time to look after the baby,' she said, 'but he'll sleep a lot to begin with – I hope. It'll be practice for when we have a grandchild.' She sighed a little. 'Though it doesn't look as if Veronica's in any hurry in that department.'

Keith nodded. He was as disappointed as Elizabeth that Veronica and Alex didn't seem to want to start a family yet. On the other hand, he wasn't sure that Veronica was ready to be a mother. She's still such a child herself, he thought, like a little girl playing at house. Which is all very well, but you can't play at being mothers and fathers when you've got a real live baby to look after. It's not a doll.

'Well, perhaps when she sees this young Kathy with her baby, it'll spur her on a bit,' Elizabeth suggested. 'Make her go broody.'

'I hope so. I'd like to hold my grandchild in my arms before I die.'

Elizabeth looked at her husband in consternation. 'That's no way to talk, Keith! You've got years ahead of you.'

'Have I?' Keith sighed and shook his head. 'I don't know, Beth. I feel so tired sometimes, and I have an idea the doctor knows more than he's telling me. That's one reason why I'd like to get settled with someone who can get to know our ways, so that—'

'No!' she said sharply. 'You mustn't say such things. I won't listen to them. Anyway, I don't believe for a moment that the doctor's holding out on us. He would tell you to stop doing so much if he thought for a moment that – that – well, I won't even countenance it. Don't say another word.'

Keith smiled. In fact, the doctor had told him quite emphatically that he should cut down on his activities, but he hadn't told his wife that. What was the point of retiring to a quiet, dull life, when all he wanted to do was enjoy the kind of life they'd both been looking forward to for years while he'd been in the Navy?

'Well, I'm sure having Kathy here will help a lot,' he said. 'And as you say, seeing the baby about the place might give Ronnie ideas. Now, she ought to be here soon – I'll just go and open the gates.'

Kathy drove through the gates half an hour later. It was mid-afternoon when she arrived, having stopped near Exeter for a sandwich and to feed Timothy. Following the directions she had been given, she drove slowly through the narrow, twisting lanes between their high banks and found the house quite easily. She paused at the entrance to the drive, gazing around her.

It was like arriving in heaven, she thought. The broad lawns, stretching away from the high walls, with two or three great cedars and a variety of smaller trees and shrubs dotted about to break up the expanse. The grass like an emperor's robe, a rich velvet swathe of gold and purple and white crocuses; drifts of daffodils like patches of fallen sunshine, and thick cushions of primroses. And the house itself, long and low, built of mellow local stone, its mullioned windows curtained with the thick vines of creepers and scrambling roses, still bare as yet but promising a riot of colour to come.

It can't be true, she thought, I can't be going to live here. Not after all that's happened. Life isn't like that. I don't deserve it.

As she sat there, lost in wonder, she saw the front door open. A man and a woman appeared and stood there, waving. They came out on to the drive and beckoned her closer.

Well, she thought, here we go. I've got a second chance – let's hope I don't make a mess of this one!

The remainder of Martyn's leave passed with an uncomfortable sense of tension. Aware as always of time slipping by, Clare tried hard to regain her usual delight at having him home, living what she still thought of as a 'normal' way of life, but she knew that things were not the same. Martyn's attitude over Kathy had hurt her and, worse, changed her view of him, and she needed time to come to terms with it.

Kathy had telephoned to tell her that she was now at Ashburton, but when Clare tried to share her relief with Martyn he shrugged it aside.

'You said you didn't want to discuss her with me again. Suits me.' And he walked out of the room.

She went after him. 'Martyn, I didn't mean it. I was upset. Of course I want to talk to you about things.'

He stopped and faced her and, to her dismay, she saw the hardness back in his eyes. 'Well, I don't want to hear about her. You know how I feel, Clare. She's caused my best oppo a hell of a lot of grief. He's seeing a solicitor about divorce, you know.'

'Oh, no,' Clare said. 'Oh, how awful. Poor Kathy.'

'Poor Brian, you mean. What did he ever do to deserve all this? Anyway, I'm sick of hearing about it all, ruining my leave. We're supposed to be enjoying ourselves, remember?'

'I know. I'm sorry, Martyn. I do want to enjoy your leave – it's lovely having you home.' But the words sounded lame and uncertain in her own ears, and she knew he heard it too. He snorted and went out into the garden, and Clare turned away sadly. Somehow everything seemed to be going wrong between her and Martyn, and somehow she had to put things right before he went away. She couldn't let him go back to the ship with bad feeling between them.

Still, at least Kathy seemed to be settling happily. Clare had seen Alex the day before, when she'd been having coffee with Veronica, and she'd asked if they'd seen her friend.

'Yes, she's fine,' Alex had said. 'Got the house running like clockwork and seems to have taken on the job of general secretary as well. Veronica's parents are thrilled with her, aren't they, Ronnie?'

'She certainly seems to have got her feet under the table,' Veronica said and, when Clare looked at her in some surprise, added a little grudgingly, 'Yes, I suppose she's doing a good job.'

'And Timothy's all right? She can cope with the house as well as him?'

'That's what she's there for,' Veronica observed, and Clare saw Alex give his wife a warning glance.

'Timothy's as good as gold. Veronica's mother's completely besotted with him.'

'It'll be different once he starts to crawl and run around,' Veronica said, and added defensively as Alex started to speak, 'Well, it will be, won't it? A small baby in a pram is one thing, but a toddler's another – they get into everything.'

'You make him sound like a nest of ants,' Clare said, trying to lighten the atmosphere and wondering if there really was a tension or whether she was imagining it. It's me, she thought, I'm so upset about Martyn I see friction everywhere.

'Well, I think it's silly, if you want to know the truth,' Veronica said bluntly. 'It can't work – two elderly people and a baby. It's not as if he was their own family. Personally, I don't think you should ever have suggested Kathy going there.'

Clare stared at her, shocked. 'I'm sure it'll work out,' she said, 'and if there are any problems, all they have to do is tell her.'

'They won't. They're too soft. And Mummy's mad about babies, always has been. You know what it is, don't you? They're hoping I'll take the hint and start producing babies of my own. Well, I've told Alex, they'll have to wait a long time – we've decided not to have a family. Haven't we, darling?'

Clare, deeply embarrassed, looked at the kitchen table. There was a short silence and then Alex said, very quietly, 'No, Veronica. We haven't decided. *You've* decided. And that's a very different matter.' He got up. 'Sorry about this, Clare. It's probably better if I'm not here. I'll say cheerio.' He closed the door behind him.

There was another short, uneasy silence, then Veronica gave a little, tinkling laugh. 'Oh, dear! The lord and master *is* feeling the huff, isn't he? They really do take themselves seriously, don't they, these men?'

'Maybe he thinks it's a serious matter,' Clare said. 'Do you really not want any children, Veronica?'

'No, I don't.' The china blue eyes were defiant. 'And quite honestly, I don't really know what all the fuss is about. It surely ought to be the woman's choice – she's the one who has to go through all the misery. And do all the work afterwards.'

'It's not all work and misery,' Clare said. 'It's fun. And they give you such a lovely, warm feeling. I wouldn't be without mine, and I don't suppose Sue would be without hers. Nor anyone else we know. As a matter of fact, I think it's just about the most worthwhile job in the world – bringing up children.' She hesitated, wondering whether Veronica was frightened of the birth itself. 'I know actually having them isn't much fun, but it's soon over, and with gas and air—'

'Don't!' Veronica jumped up and snatched up the coffee-cups, banging them down by the sink. 'Don't talk about it! I don't want to hear. It's horrible. Anyway, it's not just that, it's everything to do with children. I simply don't want any.'

'But you like Christopher and Laura, don't you?' Clare asked, bewildered. 'You always seem to, anyway. You don't mind having them here – you look after them for me. And they love you. You'd make a wonderful mother, Veronica.'

'Looking after them for a couple of hours is an entirely different thing,' Veronica said. 'I didn't have to give birth to them and I don't have to get up to them in the night. I don't have to change their nappies or potty-train them or do their washing. I don't have to be tied to them. I like my life the way it is, Clare. I like to be able to go about and meet my friends and have a lovely home. And that's another thing – Alex is always grumbling about how much I spend, saying we can't afford this house on his salary and all that kind of thing, which is ridiculous because Mummy and Daddy never mind helping out, but what does he suppose babies cost? Nobody I know who's got babies has got any money at all. It all goes on special foods and talcum powder and prams – it's neverending.'

Clare said nothing. There was nothing, she thought, to be said. Veronica had clearly made up her mind.

As she walked up the lane on her way home, with Christopher and Laura stumping along beside her, she felt disturbed, as if the world were turning upside down around her. Nobody seemed to be the same as they were a few months ago, she thought sadly. Everything seemed to be changing, and not much of it for the better. As fast as one person got sorted out, another one seemed to be in trouble.

Veronica seemed to think that once she had made her feelings plain, the matter of babies would be forgotten, but Clare had seen the look in Alex's eyes when he played with her own children, and she'd heard the tone in his voice when he had left the kitchen. She knew it would not be forgotten.

Chapter Thirty-Four

Martyn's leave was over, and therefore Brian's as well. Both were, for different reasons, glad to get back on board. Martyn was miserable, knowing that none of the issues between himself and Clare had been resolved, and Brian was still angry, hurt and disappointed over Kathy.

He would not admit to the hurt and the disappointment, however. He would express his anger only to Martyn and his other shipmates. All of them knew by now that he and Kathy had parted, and those who knew the story were loud in their sympathy. They took him ashore in the evenings and trawled the pubs of Union Street and tried to persuade him to pick up girls.

Brian wasn't interested. He sat in the bars, nursing rum and chasers, trying to blot out his misery. He'd tried women while he'd been in Fareham, after Kathy had left, and had found it a bitter experience. It was all right until the last moment and then he'd look down into the unfamiliar face and feel a sick horror at what was happening. He'd think of Kathy and the last time he'd seen her – the way he'd lashed out at her, the feeling of her flesh bruising under his fist – and the anger and the shame were transmitted to the girl who lay beneath him then. He wanted to crush her, to squeeze the life out of her, yet at the same time he loathed himself for his savage desire. Appalled by his feelings, his potency had abruptly left him and each time he rolled away, unable to complete the act, disgusted with both himself and his partner.

Drink was the only other substitute, the only way to oblivion. He'd spent the rest of his leave either getting drunk or recovering, hating both Kathy and himself. Returning to the ship was a relief, bringing him back to a routine he understood, but he knew that drunkenness would only bring him more problems and that somehow he would have to find a way through without its dubious aid.

Dramatic was still in port while the second wave of its crew went on leave, and would then be in refit for a few months. We'll have a chance to live a normal life for a while, Clare thought, waving Martyn off on the first morning with a sense of relief. He'll never be able to come home at lunchtime like when he was at Collingwood, but at least we can be together in the evenings and at weekends. That's what most people have, after all.

She took Christopher to school. Laura was impatient to start too, but the best Clare could do for her was have other children in to play once or twice during the week and let her go to their homes in turn.

She had made friends with several more young mothers by now, and one of them suggested setting up a playgroup. After some discussion, they decided to take one morning each to have all the children. Clare had them on Tuesday mornings, so on Mondays she got her washing done while Laura was at Peggy's house, and when the children arrived on Tuesdays the unfurnished front room was ready for them, with a pile of paper to draw on, a box of crayons and a selection of games and puzzles.

On her spare mornings, she whipped quickly through the housework and then settled down to some serious painting and drawing. Her cartoons for the weekly newspaper were still doing well and she had begun to send a few out to other newspapers and magazines. To her delight, she'd had several accepted and she was hoping to get a commission with one of the women's magazines for a regular slot.

'They pay well too,' she said to Veronica, meeting her for a cup of coffee in Perraton's café, on Bedford Square. Veronica had suggested the Bedford Hotel, but Clare wasn't accustomed to going into hotels for coffee – or indeed for anything else. Her only experience of a hotel had been on her honeymoon. They sat at a table overlooking the square, and chose a cake each. 'It's marvellous to be able to earn a bit of money – without having to go out to work, too! And the playgroup's a terrific help. The children love it.'

'That's one of the things that puts me off having children,' Veronica observed, putting two teaspoonfuls of brown sugar into her cup and stirring. 'No sooner do people have them than they're looking for ways to get rid of them. Babysitters, child-minders, school – anything will do, just to get them off your hands for a while.'

'That's not true!' Clare protested, uncomfortably aware that she felt a sense of release every morning when she delivered Laura to someone else's house for a couple of hours. 'We love our children, but having them twenty-four hours a day does get tiring. It's nice to have some time to ourselves. Anyway, it's not just that, it's good for them to have other children to play with. Laura's a different child now that she's got playmates every day.'

'Well, I'm not going to fall into the trap,' Veronica declared. 'Alex is still sulking about it, of course, but he'll come round. And I'm making sure there'll be no mistakes – I'm going to start taking that new pill.'

Clare stared at her. 'You're not. It isn't safe, you know. People have died.'

'Oh, pooh,' Veronica scoffed. 'Only a few, and who's to say they wouldn't have died anyway? I'm not going to get – what is it? – thrombosis. It's the best way, Clare. You just pop one in your mouth each morning and that's it. You don't have to worry about a thing.' She winked and added in a low, wicked tone, 'And no more rubber overcoats.'

'Veronica!' But Clare couldn't help laughing. It was what Martyn had always said, that making love with a sheath was like wearing a rubber overcoat. 'Anyway, there's another new thing coming out now – a coil, they call it. You have it fitted inside you and it just stays there. That sounds much better.'

Veronica made a face. 'And have someone messing about with my insides? No thanks. Mind you, either one of them ought to save a few babies being born that shouldn't be – like your friend Kathy, for instance.'

Clare's smile faded. 'How is she, Veronica? She rang me up a couple of weeks ago but Martyn answered and cut her off. Now that he's back on the ship, I could ring her, but I don't like to do it during the day and he's home again in the evenings.'

Veronica shrugged. 'She seems okay. We went over at the weekend but we didn't see all that much of her – kept herself out of the way. She cooked Sunday lunch and Daddy wanted her to eat with us, but she stayed in the kitchen. At least she knows her place.'

Clare was silent. She didn't like to think of Kathy being treated as a servant, but she supposed that was what she was. 'What about the baby?'

'Didn't see it. Alex did – she was out in the garden and he went and looked in the pram and talked to her, but I didn't bother. Mummy seems to like having it about, but I don't know how she'll feel when it starts crawling. They've got some nice pieces of china, you know, quite valuable, and she won't want it messing about with them.'

'The baby's a little boy,' Clare said gently. 'A *he*, not an *it*. And his name's Timothy.'

'Well, I know that,' Veronica said, looking astonished. 'I'd have a job not to. Alex raved about it all the way home.'

'Weren't you at all interested? I mean, it's not the baby's fault, and he really is lovely.'

'If you want to know the truth,' Veronica said, 'it's Brian I feel sorry for. It's not his fault, either. He can't help having to go away, and she knew he'd have to before she married him. Just like you and Martyn. But *you* don't go off with other men the minute his back's turned.'

'I know.' Clare found it difficult to understand herself sometimes. She had been shocked and upset by Kathy's behaviour, yet at the same time, she could understand it. She knew what the loneliness was like, and how desperately you could long for company, for friendship and laughter. And love. 'But I can't take sides like that. Kathy's my friend.'

'And Brian's Martyn's friend. I liked him, you know. He seemed a really nice chap. I don't know what she was thinking of – I wouldn't have looked at anyone else, if I'd been his wife.'

Clare frowned a little. She had only managed to speak to Kathy briefly a couple of times, and she was sure there was something her friend wasn't telling her. Also, Martyn had told her that now both leave sessions were over he meant to bring Brian home occasionally for supper, and to stay the night. Clare had replied that this was unfair: if she couldn't have Kathy there, or even speak to her on the phone, she didn't see why Martyn should bring Brian. That's easy, Martyn had said, Brian was the injured party, and Kathy would find out just what that meant when the divorce went through. And meanwhile he'd bring Brian home whenever he wanted, and Clare could either like it or lump it.

Clare had said no more, bitterly hurt as much by his tone as by his words, and had simply nodded when he'd told her this morning he would be bringing Brian home with him that evening. There was no point in letting the situation spoil their own relationship, and she just had to push aside her own feelings and get used to it.

'He's coming home with Martyn tonight,' she said. 'Well, it'd be more accurate to say Martyn's coming home with him – Brian's got the car back from Kathy now. He's staying overnight and they'll go back in the car in the morning. I dare say they'll go out for a drink after supper.'

'What, leaving you at home? That doesn't seem fair.' Veronica paused. 'I'll come and babysit if you like, so that you can go too.'

'Oh, no. I couldn't ask you to do that.'

'Why not? I shan't mind. Alex is out tonight anyway, he's got a boring parents' evening at school. Tell you what, I'll come up anyway, and if you don't want to go we can have a natter while the boys go out and enjoy themselves.' Veronica glanced at her watch. 'What time did you say you have to collect Laura?'

'Oh, my goodness! I'd forgotten.' Clare scrambled to her feet. 'I'll just catch the bus. Honestly, Veronica, you don't need to come up tonight – they won't want me along.'

She almost ran from the café, and scurried across the road and beside the church wall to the bus stop. Almost before she had settled in her seat on the bus, the conversation had been forgotten.

Veronica did not forget, however. She finished her coffee and then strolled out and along West Street, glancing in the shop windows as she passed. She hovered for a while outside the big windows of Sweets, with their displays of fashionable clothes, and then made up her mind and went inside.

Veronica was wearing a new jumper and skirt when she arrived at the back door of Dale View that evening. The jumper was a pale, misty blue that set off her blue eyes and long fair hair, and the mini skirt swirled about her legs. Her lips and eyes were made up in the latest colours and her nails gleamed with polish. She did not look like a babysitter.

Clare opened the door and gave her a look that was half pleased, half exasperated. 'I told you not to bother—'

'Go on, you know you'd like to go out for a drink with the boys.' Veronica came into the kitchen where they had just finished eating supper. Martyn and Brian were still at the table, and Christopher and Laura were scooping the last of their pudding from yellow bowls. They waved their spoons at Veronica.

'Bread and butter pudding! It's lucky Alex isn't here, he's mad about bread and butter pudding.'

'Clare's a smashing little cook,' Brian said, eyeing Veronica with appreciation. 'We've met before, haven't we?'

'Mm, that's right.' She gave him a warm, sympathetic look. 'I'm so sorry to hear of all your troubles. You've had a rotten time.'

Clare glanced uneasily at Martyn, not sure whether he'd told Brian that Kathy was working for Veronica's parents. Whether he had or not, Brian didn't seem to be worried about it. He shrugged and said to Veronica, 'Part of the risks a sailor takes. Some women can take the separation, some can't.'

'Well, I think you're very brave,' Veronica said. 'A lot of men would have been devastated.'

'No use letting it get you down,' he said, and then turned to Martyn. 'Do we really want to go out to the pub? Why don't we just have a nice cosy evening at home with the girls? That's what I miss, to tell you the truth – we can go to pubs any time.'

Martyn looked slightly startled. 'Well, I suppose we could. Clare's lit the fire in the other room – we could watch the box, or have a game of Scrabble. We've got a few beers in, haven't we, Clare?'

'Yes.' Clare was as surprised as he was to hear Brian suggest an evening at home, but perhaps it really was what he missed. He must have been lonely in that house in Fareham, after he'd sent Kathy away – though no lonelier, she reminded herself sternly, than Kathy had been for all those months.

'Okay, that's what we'll do, then. We'll do the washing-up while you get the kids to bed, and then we'll get the Scrabble set out. Come on, Bri.'

'I can play Scrabble too,' Christopher said, relinquishing his bowl. 'Mummy lets me play.'

'Don't be daft,' his father said. 'Of course you can't play Scrabble. It's much too hard. You can't even read properly yet.'

'I can. I can read my Noddy book. And I can read all the words on the cornflake box.'

'He can, too,' Clare said. 'He can read really well. He finds quite a lot of words in Scrabble.'

'Well, he's not playing Scrabble tonight,' Martyn said. 'Scrabble's a game for four, and there are already four of us. You can count to four, can't you, Chris?'

His mouth set sulkily, Christopher nodded.

Veronica reached over and rumpled his hair. 'Come on, Chris. We'll go in the other room and get the set out while Mummy puts Laura to bed, and then you can get into your pyjamas and watch us play Scrabble till it's your time. You can help me with my words.'

Christopher's sulk disappeared instantly and he gave her a wide smile and tugged at her hand. 'Come on. We can make some words ourselves. I know lots of words, *lots*.'

Veronica turned her head and gave Brian a wink. 'There you are,' she said. 'He's just like all the rest of you men. Let him think he's having his own way, and he's a little angel.'

'Not all of us,' Brian said, giving her a level look. 'Some of us are devils when we get our own way.'

Clare, lifting Laura from her highchair, glanced from one to the other. And wished, suddenly, that she hadn't told Veronica that Brian was coming to Dale View that evening.

The evening passed quickly. They had two games of Scrabble and then Veronica stretched herself like a cat and said she really ought to go. 'Alex will be home soon, expecting his cocoa and slippers.' She gave Brian a wicked glance. 'You see, I'm the perfect little wife.'

'I bet you are,' he said, and uncoiled himself from his chair. 'I'll walk down the lane with you.'

'Oh, there's no need,' she protested, but he stopped her with the lift of one hand.

'Of course there is. It's pitch dark out there. You don't know who might be about.'

'In Whitchurch?' she laughed, but made no further protest, and a few minutes later they set off together down the garden path. Clare watched them go, then returned to the living-room, feeling unaccountably uneasy.

'Well, that was all right, wasn't it?' Martyn remarked, getting up to help her clear away the glasses. 'Old Bri seemed to get on well with Veronica, even if she is a commander's daughter.'

'You know Veronica doesn't let that make any difference.' Clare packed away the Scrabble. 'Martyn, does he realise that Kathy's staying with Veronica's parents?'

'Not *staying with*,' he corrected her. '*Working for*. There's quite a difference.'

Clare brushed that aside. 'Does he?'

'I don't know, do I?' he said irritably. 'He knows her address, I suppose, but I don't see any reason why he should know they're anything to do with Veronica. *I've* never told him, if that's what you're asking.'

'I wonder if we should. Tell him, I mean.'

'Why? What difference will it make?' Martyn took the Scrabble and put it on a high shelf, out of the children's reach. 'Look, just leave well alone, Clare, will you? Brian's got enough on his plate. He's started seeing a solicitor down here now – it seems more sense than in Fareham, when he's hardly ever there. I mean, he's not going to bother going to that house at weekends just to rattle about on his own, is he?'

'No, I suppose not. What will happen to it? What will happen to all their furniture and stuff – all those wedding presents?'

'How should I know? They'll have to sell up, I suppose, and share it

375

out between them, though I don't know what Brian will do with his share, he'll have nowhere to put it. Maybe he'll keep the house and let it furnished. Could be a better bet. Anyway, he can't do anything about it for a while – these divorces take years to go through.'

Clare thought of Brian and Kathy trying to share out the furniture – the three-piece suite, the dining-table and chairs, the beds and wardrobes and chests of drawers. The wedding presents and, worse still, the more personal, intimate things: books and records, pictures, ornaments. And the photograph albums. The fat white one with all their wedding pictures in, and the one they'd filled with honeymoon snaps.

It'll break Kathy's heart, she thought. I don't know how she'll ever be able to bear it.

Everything was cleared away and washed up, and Clare was more than ready to go to bed before Martyn glanced at the kitchen clock and said, 'Brian's taking a hell of a time. I bet he's gone skiving off down to the Cattle Market for a last pint. Think I'll wander down and see if he's okay.'

Clare looked at him. 'He wouldn't have done that, surely. He'd have come back and asked you to go too.'

'Not if he'd got it into his head to have a swift half. The trouble is, Brian's swift halves tend to stretch a bit . . . I'd better go and have a look. Send out the search party, you know.' He reached for his jacket, but at that moment they heard the back door open and close, and a moment later Brian came in through the scullery, grinning a little sheepishly.

'Hi. Hope you weren't getting worried about me.' He went on quickly, giving them no time to speak. 'Alex wasn't back yet, so Ronnie invited me in for a coffee and we got talking.' He shrugged off his coat and turned away to hang it on the hook. 'Nice place they've got there.'

'Yes, it is,' Clare said, glancing at Martyn and then away again. 'Well, I think I'll go to bed. You won't be long, Martyn, will you? We've all got to get up early in the morning.'

She went up the stairs, leaving the two men to lock up. Coffee, she thought. And calling her Ronnie. I don't like it.

There was nothing she could do about it, however. Nothing, other than make sure Martyn didn't invite Brian home too often and that, when he did, she didn't let Veronica know in advance.

By the time Kathy had been a few weeks at the Grange, she felt almost as if she had always lived there.

The first month had passed without any comment being made as to whether she suited the Curtises or not. She wondered whether she ought to say something herself, but was afraid to seem too pushy. They would tell her quickly enough if she didn't suit them, she thought, and went on with her daily tasks, grateful for every minute that passed.

Keith Curtis came upon her in the garden, hanging out washing. He stood for a few minutes in the dappling shadows of a silver birch tree, watching quietly, then stepped forward, smiling, as she picked up the empty basket. 'A nice domestic sight.'

'Oh!' Kathy turned quickly. 'I didn't realise you were there.'

'I'm sorry. I didn't mean to spy on you. It just struck me as very pleasant to watch a young woman hanging out her baby's washing.' He glanced at the row of white terry-towelling nappies blowing in the breeze. 'All on a May morning – it's like something from a nursery rhyme.'

'I'd better look out for blackbirds, then,' Kathy said with a grin. 'I don't want one flying down and pecking off my nose!'

'No, indeed. Are you busy, or is that a silly question? Let's sit down for a few minutes and have a chat.'

Kathy glanced at him with a touch of alarm. 'Is there anything wrong? Something I should have done – or shouldn't?' Or my marching orders, she thought with a thump of her heart. Please don't give me my marching orders.

'No, not at all. Everything's very right, as far as we're concerned.' He led her to a garden seat at the edge of the lawn and they sat down together. At the far side of the lawn was a thicket of shrubs and trees, some showing a froth of pink and white blossom, others breaking into fresh green leaf. Beyond them the fields sloped up to the moor, already clothed in golden gorse and touched with the purple of early heather. The sky was an upturned bowl of blue, misted by a gauze of feathery cloud.

Keith Curtis turned towards Kathy and studied her face. She looked back at him, feeling her heart quicken. He was a handsome man, she thought, with his thick white hair and dark eyebrows and keen blue eyes. He had firm lips too, and he hadn't run to fat as so many men of his age did. He must have been a real heartbreaker when he was young.

'You're looking a lot better,' he said suddenly, and she blushed. 'Elizabeth and I were appalled when we first saw you. All those bruises and that thin, frightened little face. You seemed to need as much care and love as that little boy of yours.'

Kathy shook her head. 'It looked worse than it was. Brian didn't really beat me. He just lost his temper for a minute or two. I don't blame him.'

'I'm afraid I beg to differ. No man should treat his wife like that – whatever she's done.'

'I think a lot of men would agree with Brian rather than you,' Kathy said quietly.

'More's the pity, then. I'm not dismissing what you did, Kathy, my dear – we all know that you made a bad mistake – but Elizabeth and I know all too well the pressures young naval wives face, and we've seen these tragedies before. Separation is a dreadful thing when you're young.'

'I probably shouldn't ever have married Brian in the first place,' Kathy said, staring at the grass beneath her feet. 'I broke off our engagement once, you know – sent him a "Dear John". I felt terribly guilty, but it seemed the right thing to do at the time. I just wasn't sure . . . And then I met Terry and we started to go out together, and it all seemed to be so right – until Brian came home and decided he wanted me back.' She sighed. 'I shouldn't have let him persuade me. It wasn't his fault – he was entitled to fight for what he wanted. But it wasn't really right for either of us, only we just didn't know.'

'It certainly sounds as if you were rather confused,' Keith Curtis said. 'But it's all in the past now – there's nothing you can do to change it. What you have to do now is decide what you want to do next, and how you are going to bring up young Timothy.'

Kathy lifted her head and looked at him, fear gripping her heart. 'I hoped I might stay here, for as long as you want me. But if you think it's not going to work out—'

'I didn't say that,' he said, putting his hand over hers. 'No, Elizabeth and I are very happy to have you here, and the baby's no trouble at all. You do all the jobs that we hoped you'd do, and you've taken on more besides. And we like your company. We'd like you to stay, but you have to look to the future as well, for Timothy's sake. You may feel you want to go back to your own career.'

Kathy shook her head. 'No. Not for years, anyway. I want to bring up my baby myself, not send him to a nursery every day. And I love it here.' She hesitated, then added in a low voice, 'It's like a haven. I can't believe my luck.'

Keith smiled. 'Then that's settled. I can't tell you how pleased I am.' He too paused, before going on, 'You see, there's something else that perhaps you ought to know, and I know you'll keep it to yourself. It's about Elizabeth.'

Kathy looked at him. His tone was solemn, and she felt a quick beat of apprehension.

He met her eyes, then turned away, gazing far away at the gold and purple moor. 'I saw my doctor yesterday. You know I've been having a few heart problems. Well, the news isn't good. There's an operation that could possibly help, but it's a new procedure and the consultant's not sure I'm suitable for it.' He shrugged and smiled faintly. 'It looks rather as though I've got to start putting my affairs in order, as they say.'

Kathy stared at him, appalled. 'That's awful.'

'Yes. It's bad news – we were hoping to enjoy many years of retirement here. And you know how much Elizabeth enjoys her village activities – she virtually runs the place.' He smiled a little. 'She's always been a bossy sort! So at least she'll still have that.' He glanced at Kathy. 'But I can't pretend it's going to be easy for her. She'll need a good deal of support, the sort of support you're already giving her.'

'I'm so terribly sorry,' Kathy said after a moment. 'You know I'll do all I can to help. I'll take as much work as possible off her shoulders. She lets me do quite a lot of the secretarial work now, but if there's anything else . . .'

'I'll tell you straight away,' he said, and squeezed her hand. 'Thank you, Kathy. I think you must have been sent to us, do you know that? You came along at just the right time.'

'The right time for me, too,' she said, and then asked, 'What about Veronica? Have you told her?'

Commander Curtis's face seemed to close up. 'No, and I don't think we will. I don't think Veronica would take such news very well. She's still very much a child, and it's probably best that she doesn't know. We'll tell Alex, of course. He's coming over later this week, on his own. There are a few matters we want to discuss with him, but we've asked him not to mention his visit to Veronica, and we'll ask him not to tell her about this either.'

'I see.' They sat for a few more minutes in the morning sunshine, before Keith got up, saying he was going to take advantage of the fine weather to do a little gardening. Kathy watched him go, feeling sad, and then returned to the kitchen where Timothy was beginning to stir in his pram, ready for his mid-morning feed.

It doesn't matter who you are, she thought, life just isn't fair. She stood for a moment, looking down at her baby son as he stretched and rubbed his eyes with fists like curled flowers, and wondered how it would treat him.

I won't be able to protect you always, she thought, lifting him and holding him against her heart, but I'll give you as good a childhood as I can, my love. Maybe that's as much as anyone in this world can do.

Chapter Thirty-Five

Alex had a free period on Thursday afternoons, and could leave school early if he wanted to. Usually, he stayed in the staffroom, correcting homework or preparing for the next day's lessons, but on this Thursday he had driven over to the Grange and spent an hour or so with his parents-in-law.

It was the first time he had ever done such a thing. Visits were invariably family occasions, with Veronica taking the leading role. She was their daughter, and he just 'came with' her. It had never occurred to him that the Curtises saw him as a special person in his own right.

Their news struck him dumb. His father-in-law had always seemed such a strong man, both physically and mentally, the kind of man anyone might take their troubles to. Of course, he'd gained a great deal of wisdom during his years in the Navy, but he had an inner strength too. The way he was taking this blow illustrated it perfectly, Alex thought: no whining, no self-pity, just a pragmatic shouldering of the job of making life as easy as possible for his widow when his time came.

'I've no intention of giving up anything until I have to,' Keith told him. 'I'll be sensible, of course – I'll put my feet up whenever possible and I'll rest more – but just sitting about all day doing nothing would drive me quite mad, and I won't do it.' He smiled at his wife. 'Beth understands. She knows I'd be quite impossible to live with.'

'I'm really sorry,' Alex said, 'and you know Veronica and I will do everything we can.' He mentally gave up the whole summer's surfing. Veronica would want to be over here the whole time.

Keith shook his head. 'We don't want you to tell Veronica. She wouldn't be able to cope with it. The last thing we need is for her to be upset. We just want things to go on as normally as possible.'

Alex imagined Veronica's reaction – a hysterical one, he thought, a refusal to believe at first and then a frantic need to be with her father, fussing over him the whole time, weeping, begging him not to do this, to give up that . . . No, he could quite see why they didn't want Veronica told, but at the same time it didn't seem right, somehow. Veronica was a grown woman; she *ought* to be able to cope with such a situation.

They've always over-protected her, he thought, and now they're doing it again, although it's to protect themselves as much as her. Perhaps it always has been. But how will she ever grow up if we keep her cocooned?

'Does Kathy know?' he asked, and they nodded.

'Yes. She's a sensible young woman, and a great help to Elizabeth. She takes a lot of work from her shoulders, and we like having her about. And the baby, of course.'

Elizabeth Curtis smiled. 'Oh, yes. He's a dear. It's a joy to see her with him out in the garden. They're almost family – though it's not quite like having my own grandchild, of course.' Her face was sad for a moment and Alex felt a twinge of guilt.

'You know I'd like to start a family,' he began, 'but Veronica doesn't feel ready yet. There's nothing I'd like more.'

'Oh, she'll come round,' Elizabeth assured him, 'in her own time . . .' But although she said no more, the inference was plain. It might be in Veronica's time, but not in Keith's. It was that, more than anything, that persuaded Alex that Keith's time was indeed short.

Shaken, he went out into the garden and found Kathy sitting there, writing letters on a seat while Timothy lay in his pram under the silver birch, talking to the leaves that hung over his head. She looked up and smiled.

Alex sat down beside her. 'They've just told me,' he said. 'I feel a bit knocked out.'

'I know. It's a shock. And it's so hard to believe, when you look at him. But I know he's been feeling quite unwell at times, and they've done all the tests. There doesn't seem to be much doubt.'

'It's going to hit Veronica so hard,' he said. 'They don't want me to tell her, but she's going to have to know . . . some time. And how am I going to tell her that I knew and never mentioned it? It doesn't seem right. She's their daughter – she ought to be told.'

'I suppose they have their reasons,' Kathy said diplomatically.

Alex sighed. He looked at her bent head, at the shining cap of wheaten hair. She was so small, like a little elf perched there on the seat in her green slacks and tunic. She didn't look any stronger or tougher than Veronica, yet she'd been through a hard time, a lot of loneliness and emotional upheaval, and she'd survived. And now, even though her own future was by no means certain, she was lifting the burden from his mother-in-law's shoulders and giving her support – doing what Veronica herself ought to be doing.

She had even brought a baby into Elizabeth's life.

If I could only persuade Ronnie to have a baby, he thought. It would bring them closer together. It would make Ronnie grow up. It might even keep Keith alive, just waiting to see it born . . .

Veronica was in no mood that evening to talk about starting a family. 'Where have you been?' she demanded as Alex walked in through the door. 'I thought you'd be home. I rang the school and they said you'd left early. What on earth have you been doing?'

'I'm sorry. I didn't expect you to be home yourself. You were supposed to be in Dartmouth with the Ashleys.'

'They had to cancel,' she said impatiently. 'I came straight back after tea with Jessica . . . Alex, I've been *frantic*. I've phoned *everyone*. Nobody had any idea where you were.'

He sighed. He'd hoped not to have to tell her, but he couldn't lie. 'I've been over at the Grange to see your parents.'

Veronica stared at him. 'To see Mummy and Daddy? But what on earth for? We were over there only a week or two ago. Anyway, you never go over there on your own, never.'

'Well, I did this time. Your father wanted . . .' Alex cast about in his mind. 'He wanted a bit of help in the garden.'

'In the *garden*? You don't look as if you've been gardening.' Veronica stared at him, her eyes narrowing. 'You're not telling me the truth, Alex.'

'Ring them and ask,' he said, hoping she wouldn't, but knowing they'd back him up if she did.

'Well, when was this arranged? You never mentioned it this morning. Did Daddy ring you up at school?' They both knew this was unlikely, especially for something as trivial as a bit of help in the garden. 'What are you hiding from me, Alex?'

Alex's heart sank. He had known it was going to be difficult, keeping the truth from Veronica. He wished deeply that he could tell her, but Keith and Elizabeth had impressed upon him their desire that she should not know, at least for a while. He couldn't break his promise only a few hours after it had been made.

'Your father asked me a few days ago. I forgot to mention it. It went clean out of my mind till this afternoon.' He was telling lie after lie, making them up as he went along, horribly aware that he was overdoing it. He'd seen it in boys at school, caught out in some mischief and embellishing their lies when the first one would probably have been enough to save them. He stopped and folded his lips tightly together as if to prevent his tongue from giving him away any further.

Veronica stared at him. Her face was hard. Clearly, she didn't believe him, but to his surprise and relief she said no more, simply turned away with a shrug.

'Well, if you're determined not to tell me the truth, I suppose I can't make you. I don't think they keep thumbscrews in Bakers' shop. Anyway, I hope that whatever you were doing there, they gave you some supper, because there isn't any here. I've had an egg.'

'I don't want anything.' Alex looked at her unhappily. 'Ronnie, don't be upset. There's nothing sinister in it.' Another lie. 'There isn't any reason why I shouldn't go and visit your parents, is there? You weren't going to be here, I had a bit of free time – where's the harm in it?'

'There isn't any harm in it at all. At least, I hope there's not.' She turned and faced him again. 'But it does seem very strange that you should take it into your head to go and visit them on your own *for the first time ever*, not long after that Kathy person has taken up residence there. Very strange indeed.'

She walked out of the room, leaving Alex to sink into an armchair and bury his head in his hands. In trying to protect Veronica from a painful truth, he seemed to have exposed her to an equally hurtful misunderstanding.

True to his word, Martyn brought Brian home with him at least one evening a week, and suggested that he should come at weekends as well.

'And suppose I ask Kathy over?' Clare asked. 'I honestly don't see why I can't have her here, if you're going to keep bringing Brian. She needs me – I'm her only friend in Devon.' She finished the washing up and began to dry the dishes, while Martyn leaned against the door-jamb watching her.

'There's a difference, isn't there? Kathy's let Brian down badly. He hasn't done anything to her.'

Clare looked at him in frustration. 'Please, Martyn. You know I can't go and see her. If we had a car—'

'If we had a car,' he pointed out, 'I'd be using it to get to Devonport every day instead of having to flog all the way across Tavistock to catch the train.'

'It's not my fault Dr Beeching axed the Whitchurch line.'

'You're the one who wanted to live here. You're the one who couldn't be satisfied with married quarters. It takes me an hour to get in every morning and an hour to get back at night, and when it's raining I get bloody soaked walking all that way. The buses never seem to coincide with the trains and if I catch the Plymouth bus at the bottom of the lane I've got just as much of a walk at the other end. If we had to live fifteen miles from the dockyard, we could at least have lived a bit nearer the station.'

'We did! We didn't know the line was going to be closed! Oh, what's the point of going on like this? We were talking about Brian and Kathy, not trains.'

All their arguments seemed to end up like this lately, first going off at a tangent and then round in a circle, and nearly always ending up with Martyn's dissatisfaction with some aspect of their life.

Clare gazed at him despairingly. 'Martyn, what's the matter with you lately? I thought it would be so nice having you home while the ship's in refit, yet all we seem to do is bicker. We never used to be like this.' She picked up a dinner-plate and rubbed it distractedly. There was a tiny spot of cabbage still stuck to the pattern and she scraped it off with her fingernail and wiped the plate again.

He shrugged. 'It's not what's the matter with me, it's what's the matter with you. You don't seem to have time for me any more. You're always busy with the kids and when there is a bit of spare time you go off walking by yourself on the moor. I don't seem to matter.'

'Martyn, of course you matter! You matter more than anything, you're my *life*.' She put her hands on his shoulders, willing him to believe her. 'I only go out for about half an hour when you come home. It's not too much to ask, is it? Just that little bit of space is all I need – it does me so much good, just to get out by myself.' She slotted the plate into the wooden rack above the sink. 'Do you really want me not to do it any more?'

He turned away. 'Oh, do what you like. It doesn't matter what I want, does it? You won't move nearer the dockyard, you won't let me bring my friends home, you can't be bothered to spend your time with me when I do get back . . . I'm just a pay-packet round here. What I want doesn't come into it.'

Clare stared at him. She had had no idea he felt like this. She had known for a long time that things weren't the same between them, but she'd thought it was just one of those awkward patches that all marriages went through from time to time. It was just such a nuisance that it had to be during one of the short times they had together – but, then, they could hardly have an awkward patch when they were apart! It was just another of the difficulties of naval life . . . But if Martyn was feeling truly unhappy, something must be done about it.

At the same time, she felt that not all his remarks were fair, and she tried to make him see this.

'Martyn, none of that's true. We decided *together* where we wanted to live. You were as pleased with Dale View as I was. And you do bring your friends home. You bring Brian whenever you please – I just don't want him here at weekends, that's all. It's you who won't let me bring *my* friends here – I've asked time and time again if I can invite Kathy over. And I do spend my time with you – I'm here all the time. It's just that one half-hour . . .'

'And what's so important about that particular half-hour?' he demanded. 'Is it really just a walk all on your own you're so keen on – or are you meeting someone else?'

Clare caught her breath. 'What are you suggesting?'

'Oh, I'm not suggesting anything,' he said, turning away. 'I'm sorry, Clare, I shouldn't have said that. I'm just feeling a bit fed up with things lately, that's all.'

Clare said nothing for a moment. Then she shrugged and said, 'All right. If it matters to you so much, Martyn, I won't do it any more, I won't go for a walk. But it's not as if I'm out of the door the minute you walk through it. We always have a cup of tea together first. I thought you liked having the children to yourself.'

'Look,' he said, 'by the time I get home in the evening I've had just about enough. Have you got any idea what it's like on board a ship in refit? The noise goes on and on – drills, hammers, saws screeching, you've never heard anything like it. By the time I've walked over to the station in the morning and got to the ship, and spent all day in that din trying to do my own job, and then come back on the train and walked all the way from the other side of town, all I want is a bit of peace and quiet. I don't want to be left with two screaming kids on my hands while my wife goes off for a nice quiet walk.'

Clare leaned both hands against the edge of the sink. She was shaking all over. Martyn had been irritable lately, he'd lost his temper once or twice over things she had thought were trivial, but he had never spoken to her like that before. He had never referred to Christopher and Laura as 'two screaming kids'.

'Oh, Martyn,' she said, 'is it really that bad? You've never said anything like that before.'

'Well, what's the point of moaning? It's the way things are, isn't it? You don't want to hear me beefing about the ship when I get home. But I do need a bit of rest, Clare, honestly I do. Otherwise I'm just going to crack up.'

Clare turned and looked at him. He does look tired, she thought with sudden perception. And it sounds awful, the way he puts it – that long journey every day and all that noise and dirt and inconvenience. It sounds horrible.

'So why are you so keen to stay in the Navy?' she asked quietly. 'That's what this is all about, isn't it? Nothing's been the same between us since you started to think about becoming an officer.' She took a deep breath. 'Would you feel better about things if I agreed? Is that what you really want, Martyn? Is it?'

The discussion went on all through the evening and into the night. When they went to bed, it had still not been resolved. Try as they might to see each other's point of view, it always came back to the same thing – Martyn wanted to stay in the Navy, whether as a rating or an officer, and Clare wanted him to leave at thirty. Yet, paradoxically, neither was completely sure. Martyn knew how much he missed the family while he was at sea, he knew how the continual separations could jeopardise a marriage – and Clare knew that if he did come out at her behest, he might never forgive her for it, and this in itself might drive them apart.

We've lost faith in ourselves, she thought, lying in the darkness as they tried to go to sleep. We used to think nothing could come between us, and now we're both afraid that something will.

'It's because of Brian and Kathy too, isn't it?' she said at last, knowing he was still awake. 'That's scaring you too. You think I might stop loving you and go off with someone else.'

'Clare, I never said that—'

'But you can't help thinking it. Martyn, you used to trust me – we trusted each other. What's happened to it all?'

'I don't think anything's happened to it, not really,' he said slowly, 'but when you see your oppos getting "Dear Johns", and when you see them coming home to find their wives playing around with other blokes, well, you can't help thinking it could happen to you. I don't want to end up like Brian, coming home and finding I've lost you. You don't know what it's been doing to him, Clare. He's nearly gone round the bend with it all. I mean, I know he's got a temper, he always has had, but I thought he'd learned to keep it under control – I'd never have thought he'd actually *hit* her. I don't want to—'

Clare felt her blood turn to ice. She sat up and snapped on the light, staring at him. '*What* did you say? Brian hit Kathy?' Her mind whirled. So this was what she'd sensed in Kathy's voice on the few occasions they'd managed to speak. This what what Kathy hadn't told her. 'When? When did this happen?'

'Well, when d'you think? When he came home and found her with the baby, of course. He just saw red. She was lucky it was no worse.'

'No *worse*? How bad was it, for heaven's sake?'

'I don't know. She wasn't badly hurt, Clare, she didn't have to go to the doctor or anything. Anyway, he never really saw what it was like: he went out and she was gone by the time he came back.'

'Poor Kathy. Oh, how awful.' Clare drew her knees up under the blankets and rested her forehead on them. 'No wonder she ran away.'

'Well, it was pretty bad for him too,' Martyn pointed out. 'He feels like a thug, and at the same time he thinks she deserved it—'

'*Deserved* it?'

'She's pushed him pretty far,' Martyn said quietly. 'You know what he's like now, Clare. He's a mess.'

'He doesn't seem like it when he comes here. He seems to be quite enjoying the single life – flirting with Veronica, going out drinking during the week . . .'

'You only see the front he puts up. He's as miserable as hell underneath it all. There's only one thing that'll make him feel better, and that's another woman. One who'll really love him and make him feel good again.' Martyn reached up one hand and drew his finger down Clare's bare arm. 'Clare, let's stop talking about all this now and try to get to sleep. Lie down and cuddle up against me. Please.'

Clare turned and looked down into his face. He looked younger in bed, younger and more vulnerable. She felt her heart ache suddenly with love for him. He was right, she thought. Nothing had happened to their love, not really. It was still there, underneath all their worries.

It had to be.

Chapter Thirty-Six

The children's voices sounded from the room they shared. It was time to get up. As it was half-term at school, there was no need to rush, and Laura wouldn't be going to the playgroup. Clare decided to walk down to see Veronica.

'You look a bit washed out,' Veronica said, setting the mugs on the kitchen table. 'Is everything all right?'

Clare settled the children in the big, square hallway with a game of snakes and ladders and came back to the kitchen. She pulled a chair up to the round table. For a moment or two, she was strongly tempted to confide in Veronica, but a glance at the pretty, flower-like face decided her against it. Veronica had no experience of unhappiness: she wouldn't know what to do or say.

'I'm worried about Kathy,' she said. 'She's been at your parents' house for weeks now, and I haven't even been over to see her. Brian's got the car back, so she can't get over to see me either.' She looked at Veronica. 'I wondered if you or Alex would take me over some time.'

Veronica's face tightened. 'Oh, I'm sure Alex would be delighted. He's always looking for an excuse.' The back door opened and she turned her head. 'Here he is now, why not ask him yourself?'

'Ask him what?' Alex enquired. He was looking tired too, Clare thought, and rather drawn, and there was an obvious tension between him and Veronica, whose voice had iced over like a freezing pool when she spoke to him. Perhaps she'd been wrong when she'd thought that Veronica was a stranger to unhappiness.

Clare sighed. Life seemed to be going wrong for everyone at the moment. 'I want to get over to Ashburton to see Kathy, but there isn't any way. I wondered if you might be going some time – I don't want to be a nuisance, but I feel so guilty, not seeing her, and I'm worried about her . . .' She looked up at him. 'I don't want you to make a special journey.'

'No, we were intending to go one day this week. We can squeeze you into the car as well, can't we, Ronnie? Kathy'll be thrilled to see you.'

'Are you sure you don't mind?' Clare looked at Veronica, feeling sure she did mind, but Veronica shook her head so that the fair hair flew around it like a cloud.

'Of course not. It'll be nice to have you along, and Kathy can take you out for a picnic somewhere. I must admit, it'll be rather nice to see my own parents without a stranger hanging about.'

'Ronnie!' Alex said sharply. 'You know they don't look on Kathy as a stranger – she's like one of the family.'

'But she isn't one of the family, is she?' Veronica pointed out. 'And she may not be a stranger to them – or even to you, darling – but she is to me. I never saw much of her even when she was staying with Clare.'

Alex opened his mouth, but before he could speak the hall door opened. Laura trundled in, carrying the snakes and ladder board under her arm, and Christopher came and leaned against him.

'Hello, bunnies,' Alex said, cuddling them against him. 'Are you coming over with Veronica and me to see Kathy one day this week?'

The two children gazed at him. 'See Auntie Kathy? In your big house?'

'Not my big house. Veronica's mummy's and daddy's big house.'

'Oh, *yes*,' Laura breathed. 'And we'll see Timothy as well, won't we? Mummy, we're going to see Auntie Kathy and Timothy. D'you want to come too? I 'spect you can.'

'Yes,' Clare said, smiling. 'Yes, I'm coming too.' She looked at the little tableau before her and her voice caught suddenly in her throat. They looked so right, the three of them, she thought – Alex and the two children, clustered together like a little family. This is what he needs. This is the kind of life he craves. Why can't Veronica see it?

She turned her head and looked at her friend. Veronica too was watching her husband and the two children. Clare realised that Veronica could indeed see it, and that something inside her recoiled from the whole idea.

Kathy was waiting at the door when the car came up the drive. She'd been diffident, volunteering to stay in her own room or in the kitchen, where Clare could come with the children to find her, but the Curtises had been shocked at the idea.

'You're not a servant, to be pushed into the staff quarters. You're – well, I'm not sure really *what* you are,' Elizabeth Curtis said, and her husband smiled.

'Perhaps *dogsbody* would be a good description.'

'Indeed it wouldn't! I hope not, anyway. Kathy may be our housekeeper but she's also my personal assistant and friend. That's how I feel, anyway,' she said to Kathy. 'You're part of the family.'

'I'm glad, but I won't interfere with your family day. Clare and I will take the children for a walk and a picnic.'

She was thankful, when the others arrived, that she had decided to do so. Veronica, first out of the car, was decidedly cool, raising her eyebrows when she saw Kathy and deliberately ignoring her while she greeted her parents effusively. Alex followed, turning back to help Clare get the children out of the back seat. He also greeted the Curtises first, shaking hands with Keith and kissing his mother-in-law, before greeting Kathy with a warm smile, and laying his hand for an instant against Timothy's cheek.

'This chap's growing fast. And what a grin!'

'I know. I sometimes think he'll split his face.' Kathy turned to Clare and they hugged each other. 'Oh, it's so *good* to see you again. And the children. My, haven't they grown? And you've had Laura's hair cut.' She introduced her friend to the Curtises. 'They're so good to me. I'm hardly allowed to lift a finger.'

'She does *all* the work about the place,' Elizabeth contradicted. 'She's a jewel and we can't thank you enough, Alex, for suggesting her.'

'Oh,' Veronica said acidly, 'Alex is always full of good ideas.'

There was a tiny silence. Clare glanced swiftly at Veronica and saw the bright, hard smile pinned to her face. Why, she's really jealous of Kathy, she thought in surprise.

They all went indoors. Kathy had laid tea-things in the big conservatory and Elizabeth invited Clare and the children to join them, but Kathy had already prepared a picnic and they went through to the kitchen, leaving the family alone. The children ran out into the garden while Kathy made a cup of coffee and they settled at the kitchen table to relax.

'It's so good to see you,' Clare said. 'It's been awful knowing you were only just across the moor and I couldn't get here. I wish we had a car.'

'I could have come over at the beginning, while I still had ours,' Kathy said, 'but I didn't like to, with Martyn still home. I didn't know how he felt about me.'

'Not very good, I'm afraid,' Clare said ruefully. 'We had a bit of a row about it, actually.' She paused. 'Kathy, is it true that Brian hit you?'

Kathy looked down at her coffee-mug and twisted it between her fingers. 'Yes. Yes, it is.'

Clare stretched her hand across the table and laid it on Kathy's arm. 'I'm really sorry. How – was it bad?'

'Bad enough. Oh, nothing was broken, but I had some nasty bruises. It was sore for a while.' She gave Clare a twisted grin. 'I wasn't looking very beautiful when I arrived here. That's another reason why I didn't come over – I hated being seen like that.'

'I wish you'd told me. I'd have come, somehow. Was it the night he threw you out?'

'Yes. It was horrible. He was like a stranger. I was frightened – and I was frightened for Timmy, too.'

'He wouldn't have hurt the baby! Surely?'

'No, I don't think he would, not really, but I wasn't in any state to know that. I just wanted to get out.' Kathy shivered. 'I didn't know what to do, or where to go. I couldn't come down here because of Martyn, and I knew my father wouldn't have me at home. He's always been so against anything like that. Even if he had taken me in, he'd have gone on and on at me about my marriage vows – I couldn't take it. There didn't seem to be anyone, except Terry. He's Timmy's father, so – well, so that's where I went.'

'And you found he was engaged.'

'Yes. I don't blame him, mind. I'd already let him down twice and he had no reason to know I would ever go back to him again. He didn't know anything about Timothy. He just wanted to start life afresh. But when I saw him with Timmy, it all seemed such a waste.'

'Do you still love him?' Clare asked quietly.

Kathy gave her a look of such tragic despair that she gasped. 'Yes, I do. I always did. It was just that Brian always seemed to be able to override me somehow. It was as if I never had any will of my own when I was with him. And Terry's not like that. He waits for you to make up your own mind. Anyway, there's not much point in thinking about it now, is there? I've lost him and that's all there is to it.'

She got up and took the coffee-mugs over to the sink, swilling them under the tap. Her voice was still breaking but she was so clearly determined not to give way that Clare could think of nothing to say. 'Let's take these kids out for their picnic, Clare. There's a lovely spot not far away, down by the river – there's a pool just right for them to paddle in, and little waterfalls, it's really pretty. We can take Timmy most of the way in his pram, we'll just have to carry him the last bit.'

They gathered up the children and Kathy rested a shopping basket on the end of Timothy's pram. They set off through the garden and out of the gate on to the lane. Clare looked around her with interest. Being without a car meant that she could only go where trains or buses would take her, and although there were plenty of places to visit in this way, it was a special delight to come somewhere that she could not otherwise have reached. She had enjoyed the ride across the moor too, shuddering at the grim grey prison buildings at Princetown and exclaiming with pleasure at the little bridge at Dartmeet and the steep, rolling moors and hidden valleys of the river Dart.

The lane was quiet, bordered by high banks still studded with primroses the size of half-crowns. After a while, they turned off along a track leading into a wood. Here, fresh young leaves laced the branches with green and the ground beneath the trees was beginning to mist with bluebells. The children scampered on ahead, playing hide and seek amongst the bushes, and Timothy chortled as his pram bumped along the rutted track.

'It's lovely through here,' Kathy said. 'So peaceful . . . Clare, has Alex told you anything about Commander Curtis?'

'Only that he was in the Navy, Why, what should he have told me?'

'He's ill,' Kathy said quietly. She stopped suddenly and turned a stricken face to her friend. 'Clare, he's going to *die* . . .'

Clare stared at her. The tears were pouring down Kathy's face. She held out her arms and Kathy fell into them, sobbing like a child. Appalled, Clare held her closely, patting her shoulder. I should say something, she thought helplessly, but what do you say? You can't say *It's all right, it's all right* because it's not all right . . . 'Kathy, that's terrible,' she heard herself say. 'How do you know? Whatever's the matter with him?'

'It's his heart,' Kathy said, recovering herself a little.

Clare looked along the track. Laura and Christopher were coming back round a bend and she waved at them cheerfully. They stared for a minute and then turned and ran off again. Relieved, she turned her attention back to Kathy.

'There doesn't seem to be anything they can do. He's got tablets and he's all right so long as he doesn't do too much, but one day they think he'll have an attack and—' Her sobs broke out again.

'I'm really sorry,' Clare said. 'But why hasn't Veronica said anything? She's never said a word – nor has Alex.'

Kathy shook her head. 'Veronica doesn't know and they don't want to tell her – not yet, anyway. Alex knows. He asked me to tell you. He thought one of her friends should know, and he said you were the best one.'

'I'm not Veronica's best friend,' Clare said, bewildered. 'She's got heaps of friends she goes about with, people she's known much longer than me.'

'He thought you'd be the best friend when she needed help,' Kathy said. 'She will, you know. Whether they tell her before anything happens, or not, she's going to take it very badly. She thinks the world of her father.'

'I know. Oh, poor Veronica. And poor Mrs Curtis too.' Clare stood for a moment, trying to absorb this latest piece of news. 'Everything seems to be happening at once. You're just trying to pick yourself up after one blow and another knocks you flying. Is it always going to be like this, Kathy?'

'I don't know. It isn't for everyone, is it? Some people seem to live peaceful, happy lives – but maybe they've had troubles we don't know about, or maybe they've still got some to come. Who knows?' Kathy pulled herself together. 'I suppose all we can do is struggle through and hope for the best.'

It seemed a faint sort of a hope at the moment, Clare thought as they began to walk on along the track. Herself and Martyn seriously at odds, a tension between Veronica and Alex, Kathy facing the world alone with her baby, and now this dreadful news about Commander Curtis . . . It didn't seem likely that all these things could come right.

'Mummy! *Mummy*! We've found the lake. Can we paddle in it, can we?' Christopher was tearing back along the track, hopping up and down with excitement. 'Laura's taking her shoes and socks off but I told her we'd got to ask you first. Can we, Mum, can we, can we paddle?'

'Lake?' Clare said. 'I didn't know we were coming to a lake.'

Kathy laughed. 'We aren't. It's just a little pool in the river. It's quite safe. Wait till we get there,' she said to Christopher. 'You can take off your shoes and socks, but wait till we get there before you go into the water.' She turned back to Clare. 'Let's try to forget it all for an hour or two. Let's just enjoy being with the children. There's nothing we can do about anything now, and I've been looking forward so much to seeing you again.'

Clare nodded. The track had led them to a stile, where they left the pram and gathered everything, including Timothy, into their arms to walk the last hundred yards or so. When they reached the bank of the little river, they found a wide grassy patch leading down to a shallow beach, covered with fine shingle. They spread blankets on the grass and Kathy laid her baby down to lie on his back and kick his legs.

'I come here a lot,' she said. 'It's so peaceful, and so lovely. I can almost forget all the things that have gone wrong, and just be glad that I'm alive. And do you know what?' She turned her head towards Clare. 'I'm even more glad that I've got Timmy. I know it's caused an awful lot of trouble, but he really is the best thing that ever happened to me.'

'Yes,' Clare said, watching her own children splash into the shallow water, and thinking of Veronica. 'Babies are like that.'

Chapter Thirty-Seven

Martyn had still not finally decided what to do about his career in the Navy. After their last long talk, he'd begun to feel that Clare was coming round to the idea of his staying in the Service. He knew she didn't like it, but she could see the advantages and perhaps was more willing to put up with the disadvantages. Most importantly, she could see how much it meant to him.

'I always wanted to be a sailor,' he'd said to her. 'That first time I came to tea at your house, I told you then that I had ideas about getting to be an officer. Clare, you know I hate being away from you – but it's what I always wanted to do.'

'I know.' It was hard for her to accept, but men saw these things differently. Through all the ages, men had gone away while wives stayed at home and brought up the children. Even in the 1960s, it still wasn't so very different.

'Let's leave it a bit longer,' she said. 'You don't have to make up your mind yet. Let's wait a bit and see how we feel then.'

Brian was also thinking of trying for promotion to the upper deck. He'd started divorce proceedings now and decided to make a new start. He kept away from the Union Street pubs and seemed to have made up his mind to enjoy life again.

'If I'm going to be a single bloke, I may as well enjoy it,' he told Martyn. 'Get myself a nice willing girl and have fun. But I'm not getting tied down again – I've had enough of that for a game of soldiers!'

He found himself an attractive, red-headed Wren and they went about together during their spare time. Then there was a brunette who worked in the dockyard stores, and then a blonde he met at a dance. None of them lasted long. Brian had meant it when he'd said he just wanted to have fun. Otherwise, he was going to concentrate on his career.

'We could get to be in the same wardroom,' he said to Martyn. 'That'd be a lark, wouldn't it?'

'We'll never get the same ship together again,' Martyn said, but the idea of them both becoming officers was an attractive one. Ever since they were boys, they'd followed the same path, and it was good to think they might continue to do so.

I think I really will do it, Martyn thought. I'll let it rest for a few weeks, like Clare says, and then I'll tell her I definitely want to go for it. She'll have come round to the idea by then. I'm sure she will.

Alex was making regular visits to the Grange now, helping Keith to sort out his affairs. Usually, he went after school, sometimes taking Veronica with him and sometimes Clare. It was better that Veronica didn't always come, he told Clare, for she would be certain to wonder why he spent so much time shut up in the study with her father. She was already beginning to wonder why he went so often.

'Why do you need to keep going over to the Grange?' she demanded. 'And why does it always seem to be when I've arranged to meet someone for lunch or a round of golf? *I* like to see Mummy and Daddy too.'

'Why do you always have these other arrangements?' Alex retorted, guiltily aware that he only made his own arrangements after consulting her diary. 'Anyway, you wouldn't be interested. We're just sorting through old papers and things.'

Veronica stared at him. 'Old papers? What on earth for? Anyway, that doesn't matter, I'd spend the time with Mummy.'

'Your mother's hardly ever there. She seems to be out most of the time, running the village.'

'There's no need to be sarcastic,' Veronica said coldly. 'My mother's very well respected in the village.' She gave him a narrow stare. 'I suppose that Kathy's there, though, with her baby.'

'Most of the time, yes. She looks after the house, after all. And does a lot of secretarial work for your mother.'

'And for Daddy? Does *she* come and help sort through old papers as well?'

Alex sighed. 'Veronica, don't start being silly.'

'That's what you men always say,' she said crossly. 'As soon as the conversation starts to get uncomfortable, you tell us not to be *silly*. Well, I may not have all the experience that your friend Kathy has had, but I don't think you can call me silly. At least I haven't betrayed my husband and got a baby to prove it!'

'That's a rather nasty thing to say,' Alex said quietly.

Veronica shrugged. 'The truth often is nasty, I'm beginning to realise. Honestly, Alex, I don't know why you all make so much fuss over that woman. She's nothing but a common little tart, and I don't like the way she's wormed her way into the Grange. She's got Mummy and Daddy wound round her little finger. What do we know about her, after all?'

'She's Clare's friend,' Alex pointed out.

'Yes, well, that's the only reason I haven't said anything before. I like Clare. But that doesn't mean her friends are going to be all they're cracked up to be. I never did take to that Kathy, and I don't like her being at the Grange, getting into Mummy and Daddy's affections. She's out for what she can get, you mark my words.'

'And now you *are* being silly,' Alex said. 'Kathy's a nice girl who's made a mistake and will spend the rest of her life paying for it. She deserves some sympathy and some help.'

'Well, she's certainly getting that,' Veronica said. She narrowed her eyes suddenly and stared at Alex. 'She's getting more than her share of sympathy from you. Maybe that's what the attraction is. Maybe that's why you keep going over there – to see poor dear Kathy.'

'Veronica! Don't be ridiculous—'

'Oh, yes,' she interrupted, 'that's the next stage, isn't it? *Silly* for when things get uncomfortable – *ridiculous* when they start getting too near the truth. Oh, don't bother, Alex, I haven't got time to stand here arguing with you, I'm meeting Jessica for lunch at the Bedford. Give Mummy and Daddy my love, and tell them I'll come over as soon as you can spare the time to take me with you.'

She snatched up her handbag and walked out. Alex watched her go up the path to the Whitchurch road, her white dress fluttering around her knees. Veronica could have cancelled her date quite easily, he thought, but in truth she preferred to go out with her own friends, visiting the Grange only for Sunday lunch or when there was going to be a gathering there at which she could glitter and shine. An ordinary day, with her father busy in his study and her mother dashing to this meeting or that, and little attention being paid to Veronica, wasn't at all her cup of tea.

He didn't pay too much attention to her wild half-accusations over Kathy. She didn't really believe them herself; they were just ways of expressing her own annoyance. And why was she annoyed? Because he

398

was doing something without consulting her, he thought, and because she considered him to be encroaching on her territory.

Alex sighed, wishing that Veronica's parents would lift their embargo on her being told of her father's illness. She'll never grow up if we all go on treating her like a child, he thought, yet we all know that if we do tell her the truth she'll go into hysterics and make everything even more difficult. Meanwhile, she's beginning to sense there's something going on, and of course she's jumping to the wrong conclusions and now she'll start upsetting herself over them . . .

However, there was no time to worry about that now. He wondered if Clare would like to go over to the Grange with him. He rang her up to ask.

'I'd love to,' she said, 'but Chris is at school and Laura's supposed to be going to Natalie's. Why have you got a day off?'

'My school's closed – plumbing repairs. We'll be back in time to meet Christopher and we could take Laura with us. Kathy would be thrilled to see you, I know.'

'Yes, I'll come,' she decided. 'I'll just give Sue a ring to tell her Laura won't be coming, and we'll meet you at the bottom of the lane. Are you sure the Curtises won't mind?'

'They'll be delighted,' he declared, and rang off feeling suddenly light-hearted. He seldom saw Clare alone these days. Their walks on the moor had never been more than chance meetings – although he was guiltily aware that he often engineered that chance, and sometimes suspected that Clare might be doing the same – and since he'd been spending more time at Ashburton he'd had less time for walks. A drive across the moor, with no company other than Laura in the back seat, was like a bright ray of sunshine in a day that had started out in gloom.

Veronica arrived at the Bedford Hotel early for her lunch date. She sauntered across the road towards the church. It was too sunny and warm to go indoors yet, and she would see Jessica arrive from here. She sat on the wall beneath a flowering cherry tree and lifted her face to the sun.

'Now that's what I call a pretty sight,' an approving voice remarked, making her jump. 'You look just like part of the blossom.'

Veronica opened her eyes. Brian Bennett was standing before her, his hair so black and gleaming it looked polished, his dark blue eyes crinkling at her in a disarming grin. She stared at him and felt herself blush. 'Whatever are you doing here?'

'Oh, I had a make and mend,' he answered easily. 'Thought I'd come and take a look round Tavistock – might saunter up and see Clare later on. I could always change my mind, of course,' he added. 'Take another pretty girl for a drive instead.'

'I'm meeting a friend for lunch,' Veronica told him a little regretfully, 'but you could come up and have a cup of tea later on if you like. Alex has gone over to my parents'.'

'I've got a better idea. Why don't I take you out to tea? It's a wonderful day for driving over the moor. What time d'you think you'll have finished your lunch?'

'Oh, about two, two thirty.' Veronica looked at him, feeling her heart kick a little with sudden excitement. Going out with Brian Bennett had a curious illicit attraction, combined with innocence. Nobody could complain about her going out to tea, and yet she knew she shouldn't be doing it. Anyway, she thought, it'll teach Alex a lesson – he's going over to see Kathy, after all. Not that she had any intention of telling Alex.

'Yes, all right,' she said, tilting her head to smile up at him. 'I'll come. Where shall we meet? I walked down.'

'Tell you what,' He grinned conspiratorially. 'You walk through the Meadows to Pixon Lane and I'll meet you there, by the gate. Then we won't start any gossip!'

Veronica spotted Jessica, walking towards the door of the Bedford Hotel. She slid off the wall, and gave him a quick, smiling nod. 'Yes. I'll see you there – say two thirty.' She ran across the road and caught up with her friend on the hotel steps, feeling a giggle of excitement bubble up inside her. There was no harm in it – no harm at all – but it gave her a huge sense of satisfaction to think that she was doing something that Alex wouldn't know about and wouldn't particularly like if he did. I'll show him, she thought. I'll show him he's not the only one who can have secrets.

'You're looking very pleased with yourself,' Jessica commented as they walked into the restaurant. 'Got something special to tell me?'

'No, I haven't,' Veronica retorted, knowing exactly what was in her friend's mind. 'And you needn't start looking at my waistline like that either. I'm *not* pregnant – and I'm never going to be!'

The drive across the moors was every bit as pleasant as Clare had expected it to be.

Clare sat beside Alex, the window wide open to let in the warm air. Summer had really arrived, she thought, feeling the breeze blow her hair around her face. In the back, Laura kept up a constant flow of chatter, but she didn't seem to notice whether anyone listened to her or not, and Alex and Clare were free to carry on their own conversation.

'It's like having a babbling brook in the car with us,' Alex commented with a grin.

'I know. Her tongue starts moving the minute she wakes up. Sometimes she even talks in her sleep. She doesn't seem to require too many answers, though, so you can still think your own thoughts most of the time.'

'It's what they call stream of consciousness,' Alex said. 'We get kids like that at school – can be very distracting to the others, but they don't even seem to know they're doing it. They grow out of it eventually, or else have it knocked out of them by the others.'

'I can't see anyone knocking it out of Laura. She's not the sort to let herself be bullied.' Clare was silent for a few minutes, then asked, 'How is Commander Curtis now? Is he any worse?'

Alex shrugged. 'Difficult to tell. He keeps so much of it to himself. I think he does rest a bit more, but he's so anxious to get all the finances sorted out, he seems to spend all his time doing accounts. He has an enormous amount of investments made over the years, and they're all in a bit of a muddle. He needs an accountant to sort it out really, but that might prove too expensive to be worthwhile, so we're struggling through together.'

'It seems a shame he's got to do all that,' Clare said. 'He ought to be enjoying himself, doing whatever he fancies. I'm sure Mrs Curtis would prefer it.'

'They both want to go on as usual. They're living the way they've always wanted to live, and they don't intend to change it. Once he's got all this business sorted out, he'll be able to relax more, but he'd never feel easy if he knew she'd have a muddle to cope with after – well, if anything happened to him.'

'What a nice husband he is,' Clare said with a wry smile, and Alex gave her a quick look.

'That sounds a bit wistful.' He hesitated, then said, 'Is everything all right, Clare? You seem a bit subdued lately.'

She gave a little laugh. 'Oh, you know how it is. Everyone has their ups and downs. Martyn and I went through a sticky patch a little while ago. It sort of shakes you up a bit.'

'I see. I'm sorry.' He gave her a sympathetic glance. 'Shame it had to be when he was at home.'

'Well, it's not so easy to have them when he's away – though there have been a few times when we've got at cross-purposes through letters.

It's horrible quarrelling by post: people misread what you write and take offence at things you never meant that way. I try not to let it happen, but when you're apart for months at a time . . .' She sighed. 'And that means that I have to keep all the things to myself that most wives would grumble about as a matter of course, without any harm coming of it, and if I do it when he's at home it just spoils the time we do have together. In the end, you're not having a normal marriage at all.'

'Sometimes I wonder just what a normal marriage is,' Alex observed. 'It's not necessarily easier just because you're together all the time.'

Clare didn't speak for a minute or two, then said quietly, 'I've noticed things aren't so easy between you and Veronica lately. It's to do with babies, isn't it?' She added hastily, 'Tell me to mind my own business – I shouldn't have said anything.' She turned to look out of the window, her face burning with embarrassment.

They were just coming down the steep hill to Dartmeet. As usual, a number of cars were parked by the old packhorse bridge, with people picnicking by the river or going to the Badger's Holt for coffee or lunch. Alex negotiated the narrow bridge carefully and didn't speak until they were climbing out of the valley on the other side.

'It's all right, Clare. It's good to have someone to talk to about it. It's not something I can discuss with her parents – it seems so disloyal, though I know they want grandchildren as much as I want my own kids. But in the end it's up to Ronnie and she seems dead set against it.'

'I know, and yet I think she'd make a lovely mother. She's so good with children.'

'It's not so much the children. She pretends it is and talks a lot about the house being untidy and the furniture knocked about, but it isn't really that that bothers her. It's the whole process of having them – the pregnancy and the birth. She's really terrified of it, Clare, and I can't persuade her into something she's so frightened of.'

'Well, I didn't much enjoy being pregnant,' Clare confessed, 'but I'm glad I went through it. It does come to an end, after all, and it's all worth it when you've got your baby in your arms.' She gave him a sympathetic glance. 'I'm sure she'll come round eventually. And at least you really love each other.'

Alex said nothing, and she wondered what he was thinking. You needed to love someone very much indeed if they were going to deprive you of something you badly wanted – something that would affect your whole life. Perhaps he was beginning to wonder if he really did love Veronica that much.

She leaned back in her seat and Alex glanced at her again and smiled. 'You look more relaxed than I've seen you in weeks.'

'I feel it,' Clare said. 'It's like being on holiday. It's so lovely to come out like this, to be going to see my best friend . . .' She glanced at him shyly. 'It's lovely to be with you, too. I don't have to watch my words. I feel I can say anything I like and you'll understand.'

Alex looked straight ahead. He seemed to be thinking deeply, to be choosing his own words. In the end, he said quite simply, 'That's the way I feel too, Clare, when I'm with you.'

Veronica slipped into the front seat of Brian's car and smiled at him. She had had no difficulty in keeping her meeting a secret from Jessica, saying that she was going to walk home through the Meadows. She had sauntered down Plymouth Road and through the gate opposite the primary school, crossing the canal and the river to emerge in Pixon Lane where Brian was waiting. Within a few minutes, they were driving up Down Road towards the moor.

'Where are we going?'

'I thought we'd go out to Dartmeet,' he said. 'There's a place there that does the most fantastic cream teas. It's a pretty spot too – we might go for a walk along the river.'

'Sounds gorgeous.' She stretched herself like a cat. 'Oh, this is fun! Alex and I haven't been out like this for ages. We're always doing something serious these days. He's getting very solemn.'

'It doesn't do to be too solemn,' Brian said. 'Life's for living and enjoying. I've made up my mind not to get tied down again – not for a long while, anyway.'

'Well, I can't blame you, but don't you think you'll want a home of your own again someday?'

'Someday, perhaps, but not yet.' He grinned at her. 'Blokes that aren't tied down have a lot more fun than those who are.'

'Go on, I bet you're all the same when you're away from home. I've heard all about sailors on shore runs – my father was in the Navy, you know.'

'He was an officer though, wasn't he? He'd have been in the wardroom.'

'He still knew what sailors got up to in foreign ports.' She slanted a look up at him, thinking what a handsome profile he had. 'So, you're going to have fun now, are you?'

He glanced sideways and caught her eye. 'Well now, that depends, doesn't it?'

'Does it?' she asked, her heart thumping a little. 'What does it depend on?'

'On whether anyone's prepared to have fun with me,' he said. 'It takes two, you know.'

Veronica caught her breath. She turned away and looked out of the window at the rounded hills with their craggy tors piled on top. For a moment, she felt vulnerable and a little scared, driving off into the middle of Dartmoor with this breezy sailor. Then the delicious feeling of doing something rather daring and secret washed over her again, and she turned back and gave him a teasing smile.

'Well, I'll have to see if I can find someone who'd like to have fun with you,' she said. 'I'm sure there's somebody.'

'I'm sure there is too,' he said with another of his sidelong looks. 'And someone not too far away either, I reckon. Don't you?'

They arrived at Dartmeet and turned left to park the car. A coach full of tourists was just pulling out and it was quiet by the ancient bridge. They wandered along to where the two branches of the Dart met to become one river, and then on along the valley beside the tumbling water. There was nobody about; the few early visitors who had arrived had stayed around the bridge and the teashop. After a while, they came to a patch of soft grass on the bank, and Brian suggested sitting down to rest.

'What a lovely spot,' Veronica said, settling down beside him, 'and what a lovely afternoon this is turning into. You know, the day didn't start out all that well – Alex and I had quite a little squabble this morning.'

'Did you? What about – or don't you want to tell me?' Brian lay on his back, gazing up at her.

Veronica shrugged. 'Oh, it was nothing secret. He keeps on going to see my parents, that's all. It seems so peculiar – he never used to go without me, but now he makes his own arrangements. I mean, they're *my* parents – I ought to be the one arranging our visits. But he seems to have taken them over.'

'Seems queer,' Brian said, his eyes half-closed. He grinned suddenly. 'You're sure it's your parents he goes to see? He hasn't got some little girlfriend tucked away over there, has he?'

Veronica turned and looked down at him. 'I've begun to wonder,' she said. 'I've begun to wonder if that's really the answer. He's getting very friendly with your Kathy—'

Brian's eyes snapped open. He stared at her. 'My Kathy? What on earth are you talking about?'

'Well, she's living there, isn't she? As a sort of housekeeper or secretary or something. You knew that, didn't you?'

'No,' he said, sitting up. 'No, I didn't know that. Do your parents live at the Grange?'

'Yes, of course they do. Brian, you must have known . . .' But even as she said it, she realised that there was no reason why he should have known. Since the evening when he had walked down the lane with her and come in for coffee, they hadn't seen each other at all. He probably hadn't given her a thought, and unless Martyn had told him that Kathy was with her parents, there was no way he would have discovered it. 'I'm sorry,' she said. 'It just didn't occur to me that you wouldn't know that.'

Brian said nothing for a moment, then he shrugged and said, 'Well, it doesn't really matter, does it? Not to me, anyway. But I'd watch that husband of yours, Veronica. Kathy's a bitch, there's no two ways about that, and she'll be looking out for another man now she's lost me. And that Terry Carter doesn't seem to be too keen to take her on.'

'Alex wouldn't,' Veronica said, her voice quivering a little. 'He's not the sort – he'd never . . .'

Brian looked at her and slipped his arm around her shoulders. 'That's not what you were saying a few minutes ago. Look, Ronnie, men are men. They take their chances when they can, and Alex isn't any different from the rest of us. If Kathy sets her cap at him, he'll have a job to put her off. And if he's making excuses to go over there without you, I'd say it was suspicious.'

'Yes,' she said in a small voice. 'Yes, it is.' She looked up at him, her eyes filling with tears. 'What am I going to do? Suppose it's true. Whatever can I do about it?'

Brian looked down into her face. Her eyes looked huge, like violets in the rain, and her lips were trembling. He held her with one arm and used the other hand to stroke her hair. She was soft and pliant against him, and he could feel the beat of her heart through his shirt.

'Don't look like that, Ronnie,' he said gently. 'I don't suppose anything will happen. Not if Alex has got any sense – not while he's got you to come home to. But if you're at all worried – if you need anyone to talk to – just remember, you've got me. Just give me a call and I'll come running!'

He bent and kissed her on the lips. For a brief moment, Veronica froze and he thought she was going to resist, but then she sighed a little, caught her breath on a tiny sob, and relaxed against him. He released her lips and she leaned her head against his shoulder.

Brian held her for a moment more, then, slowly, he held her away from him. He looked down at her woebegone face and shook his head.

'The man's mad,' he said. 'Any bloke who's got a jewel like you and doesn't know how to keep it polished is utterly mad. I'd know how to look after you, if you were mine . . .' He held her eyes for a few seconds and then said, 'We'd better go back to civilisation. Let's go and see what those cream teas are like, shall we?'

Chapter Thirty-Eight

Dramatic's refit was due to end in July. The new ship's company joined throughout June and after a few weeks commenced their leave. There was a recommissioning service and then she would be back at sea.

Martyn felt his accustomed excitement at the thought of going to sea again. The start of a commission was like the opening of a new book, with new characters and a different setting. The captain and commander were different, most of the men had just left other ships – the entire company was fresh and raw, waiting to bond together, to become a cohesive and efficient whole. Over the next weeks and months, they would go through a subtle struggle for supremacy, like hens in a run establishing their pecking order. The hierarchy was established already, of course, by rank and seniority, but there were a multitude of more intricate, hidden relationships, and on these depended the 'feel' of the ship and its crew, and ultimately its success.

Clare saw his anticipation and willed herself not to feel hurt by it. He was a sailor, and being a sailor wasn't like an ordinary job. She'd known it from the start and it was crazy and unfair of her to object because he wanted to go on being the man she'd fallen in love with.

During those last few weeks, she made every effort to behave as if she didn't mind – at least, not too much.

'Are we going to go and stay with Mum and Dad during your leave?' she asked. 'I wondered if we could hire a car for the week. It's so much easier than the train, with the kids.'

'Don't see why not. We could drop in and see my folks as well on the way. Let's stay a night there, and then go on to Gosport. I'll see about getting a car – an 1100 would do, they're not too pricy to hire.'

They set off a fortnight later, in holiday mood. Martyn's parents made a fuss of the children and said they wished they could stay longer, and what about calling in again on the way back? Clare, who had anticipated this, agreed at once. She knew that Martyn's parents were as fond of the children as her own were, and Christopher and Laura enjoyed having a fuss made of them. She grinned ruefully at Martyn as they drove away.

'Your mum always goes to so much trouble, she makes me feel guilty. All those cakes she made – we were never going to be able to eat them all. And when Laura turned her nose up at that apple pie, I thought I'd die.'

'Shouldn't worry about it. She ought to know by now what kids'll eat. Give 'em a bar of chocolate for their afters and they'll love you for life.'

They were out of Ivybridge now and heading towards Buckfast. Clare saw the abbey on their left. We ought to go and look at it some time, she thought. The children are getting old enough now to do that sort of thing. As always, however, there was the problem of transport: you just couldn't get anywhere that didn't have a bus or train service, and even then it was often a long and tortuous journey.

'I wish we had a car,' she said.

'Well, I'll get my Chief's buttons soon,' Martyn said. 'Not that there's much point in us having a car when I'm away most of the time.'

'There'd be a point for me,' Clare said. 'I could learn to drive. It'd make all the difference in the world to me, to be able to get about with the children, without having to wait in the rain for buses or walk all the way across Tavistock to catch the train.'

'Oh, I see, it's different for you having to walk across Tavistock, is it?' he said, without rancour. 'Doesn't matter when it's me footslogging over twice a day.'

'Well, it is different. You don't have two children with you. It's hard work, Martyn. A car would help a lot.'

'Well, I don't know that I'm all that keen on my wife driving all over the countryside while I'm away,' he said. 'Women aren't good drivers anyway. Better wait till next time I'm home for a while.'

Clare said nothing. She didn't want to upset the happy mood in which they'd left home. All the same, she felt resentful at Martyn's attitude. Why shouldn't she go about when he was away, and why shouldn't she learn to drive? Who said women were worse drivers anyway? Men, that's who!

She told her sister Valerie about it when they went over to

Portsmouth. Valerie and Maurice had recently acquired another car, and the two men were examining it, staring under the bonnet at the engine and lying on their backs to look at its underparts. Christopher and his cousin Johnny were out there too, squatting on the pavement. The two sisters went into the back garden with Stephanie and Laura and left them to it.

'I'm going to learn to drive,' Valerie said. 'I'm having two proper lessons a week and Maurice is going to take me out for practice the rest of the time. He isn't going to take the car into work, he's going to use his moped just like now, so that I can have the car.' She looked at Clare. 'Martyn doesn't really mean he wouldn't want you to learn to drive, would he? That's positively Victorian.'

Clare shrugged. 'There are plenty of men who still do think that way. And you know what they all say about women drivers; they're a joke. But it's stupid, Val, when I've got the two children to take about. It would be daft to have a car in the garage and not be able to drive it. Not that we look like having one at all,' she added gloomily, 'not for years, anyway. We just never seem to have enough money.'

'What about your drawing?' Valerie asked. 'You're doing quite well with your cartoons, aren't you? Couldn't you do something else in that line? Laura will be going to school next year, so you'll have more time to yourself. If you could earn a bit extra, you could buy a car yourself.'

'It's an idea,' Clare said thoughtfully. 'I'm pretty sure that women's magazine is going to commission a few. I've sent them a series of sketches with the children in them – rolling down the Pimple, playing in the snow, that sort of thing. They seem to like them and I'm trying to work them up into a strip cartoon. I thought I'd call it Kiffer – you know, that's what Chris used to call himself when he was tiny.'

'Well, there you are, then,' Valerie said. 'You'll be famous in no time, and then you'll be able to buy a car for you and one for Martyn as well!'

Clare laughed. 'What on earth would we want two cars for? But you're right, Val, I could try to earn a bit more with my drawing. I've done some little paintings of the moor as well – maybe I could sell them. I thought I'd ask the little teashop in Tavistock to put them on their walls so people could see them,'

She and Martyn went back to her parents' house, driving round the top of the harbour on the road that went along the top of Portsdown Hill. From there, they could see the harbour spread out beneath them, filled with ships and boats of all sizes, from tiny rowing boats to tall-masted yachts, from warships to submarines. Beyond the harbour the Isle of Wight nestled between the wide-stretched arms of the Solent.

Clare's fingers itched suddenly for a pencil and sketchbook, and then she thought of the nights when she and Martyn had driven out to Stokes Bay on his motorbike, just to look at the lights of Ryde and kiss in the dark before he took her home. It seemed a long time ago and she wondered if he remembered it too. Probably not, she thought sadly. Men didn't seem to have memories like that.

Martyn turned in his seat and grinned at her. 'I was just thinking,' he said. 'Why don't we slip out later on this evening and sneak out to the bay for a look at the lights? It'll be like old times.' He winked. 'We could even pretend we're not married . . .'

Brian was on leave too. He went to Fareham to see to the sale of the house and sort out the last of the furniture. On their solicitors' advice, he and Kathy had each made a list of what they wanted, and after a bit of quibbling agreed to share it out. Brian's share was going to be stacked in a friend's garage and Kathy's had already been taken down to Devon.

Once that had been done, there was nothing to keep him there. He took the keys to the local estate agent dealing with the sale, and drove back to Plymouth. He had decided he might as well stay on the ship during his leave, making use of the accommodation, and come ashore each day.

When he arrived, he went to a telephone box and dialled Veronica's number. 'I'm back.'

'Oh, Brian. Was it awful?'

'Not really. I'm glad to have that part of it done with, anyway. Now I just have to wait for the divorce to come through and I'm a free man. At least it won't be hard to prove adultery, and Kathy's not defending it.' He paused. 'When can I see you?'

'I don't know. Any time. Alex doesn't start his holidays till next week. What about tomorrow?'

'Tonight would be even better,' he said, adding quickly, 'That's just a joke. I know you can't . . . I'll pick you up soon after nine, all right? The usual place?'

'Yes,' Veronica said. She hesitated. 'I've missed you, Brian.'

'Never mind,' he said, smiling into the telephone. 'We'll make up for it tomorrow.'

They went down to Whitsand Bay. The tide was low and the beach stretched below the cliffs, wide and white. Here and there, the cliffs jutted out to make a little cove, sheltered by jagged rocks.

There were a few families already on the sands nearest the cliff path coming down from the road, but as Brian and Veronica strolled further along the beach they found quiet spots with only one or two families in occupation, and finally they came to one that was completely isolated.

'Let's stop here,' Brian said, swinging the picnic basket down on a flat rock. 'We'll have it all to ourselves. Our own private beach.' He took out a tartan blanket and spread it on the sand.

'It's beautiful.' Veronica stood with her arms outstretched, as if trying to draw the whole great vista of sea and sky and sand into her embrace. She turned slowly on the spot, her short skirt fluttering about her legs, her head thrown back so that her hair streamed down her back like a shimmering cascade of sunlight. As she turned to face Brian, she caught his eye and gave him a wide, dazzling smile.

'You're beautiful,' he said huskily. 'Veronica . . .'

He caught her in his arms and she melted against him, parting her lips for his kiss. For a few moments they stood together, locked close, and then he drew her down on to the blanket.

Veronica giggled and pushed him away. 'Let's swim. Are we going to swim?' She jumped up again and slipped out of her skirt and blouse. Underneath, she was already clad in a skimpy scarlet bikini and her body was tanned a light, golden brown, gleaming as if she had been lovingly polished. She pulled her hair back from her face and tied it in a ponytail, and Brian stared at her, caught by a sudden odd sensation. He turned away quickly.

'The tide's too far out.' He glanced at the rippling waves, a wide lacy border on the sands, edging the rocks. 'It's on the turn. We'll swim later on.' He reached for her again. 'Ronnie—'

'Let's have coffee, then.' Her voice was high. She collapsed, relaxed as a kitten, on to the blanket beside him, pulled the picnic basket to her and took out a Thermos flask and two mugs. 'We've brought lots of food, enough to last us all day.' She glimmered a smile at him. 'We've got all day, Brian. Let's just relax. There's no hurry for anything.' She poured the coffee and handed him one of the mugs, then lay back on the sand and stretched herself out like a cat. 'Oh, this is *so* lovely.'

Brian sat beside her, sipping his coffee, glancing down sideways at her supine body. He had never seen her so nearly naked; their outings had all been to places where people might see them, never anywhere as private as this. They had kissed and caressed, had daringly fondled, but never any more. Now, on this secluded beach surrounded like a fortress by rocks, invisible from the cliffs above, they were as hidden as if they'd been in a bedroom, and he could feel the heat of desire spreading through his body.

He leaned over and ran his fingertip lightly down her stomach, from the point between her breasts to the top of her bikini pants.

Veronica gave a little squeal and opened her eyes. 'Don't,' she said, giggling.

'I can't help it,' he said. 'You look so tempting. Like a kitten, rolling over so its tummy can be rubbed.'

'Well, I don't want my tummy rubbed,' she said unconvincingly. She sat up and picked up her coffee-mug. 'Honestly, Brian, if you're going to be naughty I shall have to get dressed again.'

'Don't do that. It would be such a waste. You look gorgeous with no clothes on. Well, nearly no clothes.' He eyed the bikini appreciatively. 'You'd look even better with none at all.'

'Brian! I'm warning you.' She gave him a severe look. 'We've had all this out before. I'm a married woman and I love my husband. You and I are just friends, all right?'

'Pretty loving friends,' he murmured, and she blushed a little. The blush spread down her neck and coloured the fine, silky skin of her breasts.

'Yes, all right, loving friends. And you're a naughty boy. But that's as far as it goes. Now drink your coffee before it goes cold.'

They sat side by side, gazing out at the sea. There were no ships to be seen, and no sound save that of the soft, sibilant whisper of the waves and the mewing cries of the seagulls.

'We could be alone on a desert island,' Veronica said softly. 'We could be the only people in the world.'

'I wish we were,' he said. 'I'd like to be the only man in the world, if you were the only girl.'

Veronica giggled. 'You'll break into song next!'

'I could, too. I could sing to you all day.' He touched her bare shoulder, making tiny circles with his fingertip. 'I could sing you love songs.'

'I shan't warn you again . . .'

'Good,' he said, pulling her closer. 'I was hoping you'd say that.'

'Brian!' She pulled away. 'Honestly, you're *incorrigible*.'

'My,' he said, 'that's a big word for a little girl. All right, I'll be good. For a while, anyway. Can't promise more than that.'

Veronica gave him a suspicious glance, but there was a spark of mischief lurking deep in her own eyes. He knew that she enjoyed these games as much as he did, but he was determined that the game was going to get serious. It was just a matter of timing.

412

They finished their coffee and lay side by side on the blanket. Brian stripped down to his swimming trunks and caught Veronica eyeing him covertly. He was lean and brown, his skin a deeper tone than hers, and his muscles were firm from exercising with the weights and chest expanders he used every day.

He turned on his side. Veronica was stretched like a cat beside him. The odd sensation he had experienced earlier came back and he reached out and touched her face, suddenly aware of a resemblance to Kathy. He wondered how he had never noticed it before. Her smallness, her blonde hair – longer and thicker than Kathy's but, drawn back in a ponytail as it was now, just as close to her small head.

Kathy.

That was why he wanted her, he realised, because she was small and pretty and blonde, and as near to Kathy as he could get these days. *Kathy* . . .

He wanted to throw himself on her, to take her there and then, to vent on her all the miserable, angry disappointment that had been simmering inside him all this time. Kathy . . .

No. This was not Kathy. This was Veronica, who was small and sweet and desirable in her own right.

He forced a grin to his lips. 'The tide's coming in. Let's have a swim.'

'Oh, yes.' She scrambled up, her face alight with excitement. 'Look at the waves! Oh, I love it when it's rough!'

Do you indeed? Brian thought, watching her run down the sand. I'll bear that in mind for later . . .

He followed her, feeling the exhilaration of the salt breeze, the crumble of the sand beneath his feet, the sudden chill of the water as he ran beside Veronica into the water. He heard her gasp and caught her hand, laughing and dragging her with him. She squealed and tried to resist, but he only held her the more firmly, and pulled her into deeper water until, clutching each other and yelping with laughter, they were both swept off their feet and tumbled beneath the waves.

'Oh,' Veronica gasped, coming to the surface and shaking her head. She coughed and choked, giggling and wiping her long, streaming hair from her face. 'Oh, look out, here comes another one . . .' He held her as the wave broke over them, and then drew her further out. 'Not too far. Not out of my depth.'

'It's all right.' He scooped her into his arms and held her like a baby, cradled against him. 'I'll look after you.' He stood firm, legs apart, rocked by the next wave but not letting her go, and looked down into her face. His excitement rose. 'Ronnie . . .'

Veronica stared up at him. 'Brian, I don't—'

He bent his head and kissed her. Her lips tasted of salt, mingled with the sweetness of her own moisture. He felt her quiver in his embrace and tightened his arms about her. She slipped her arms up and around his neck, perhaps only to hold herself steady, but the movement pressed her breasts against his bare chest, and the thin fabric of her bikini, soaked and softened, might as well not have been there. His heart leaped.

A second wave broke over them, splashing foam into Veronica's face, and she spluttered and then giggled again. 'Put me down, Brian. You'll drown me!'

He let her go and instantly she swam away from him, ducking her head through the breaking waves. Brian pursued her and reached out his hands, but she was like a fish, twisting this way and that, always just out of reach and laughing at him. At last he caught her ankle and gripped it firmly, pulling her back towards him and back into his arms.

'You're like a mermaid.' Her hair, soaked to a darker shade of blonde, streamed about her shoulders and floated on the glittering azure water. 'I didn't know you could swim like that.'

'We were in Malta when I was little. Everyone learns to swim there.' She laughed up at him. 'I'll race you to those rocks.'

'All right.' He let her go and they ploughed towards the crags. Veronica swam like a seal, barely breaking the surface to breathe, and although Brian's strength gave him greater power they arrived simultaneously at the rocks and clung there together, breathless and laughing.

'You're fantastic. You're marvellous. I've never known a girl like you.'

'Of course you haven't – I'm unique.'

As he reached for her again, she ducked beneath the surging water and was off again, streaking through the waves. He watched the slender tanned shape of her body, glimmering beneath the restless surface, the golden hair spreading out behind her, and felt his desire rise again, more powerfully than ever.

They played together in the water for almost an hour. Veronica was like quicksilver, shimmering through the waves, elusive and uncatchable. She taunted and teased him, drifting as relaxed and loose as a rag doll tantalisingly out of reach, and then, just as he thought he had her in his grasp, came to sinewy life and twisted from his clutching fingers, dived through the crest of a wave and then laughed at him from the smooth glassy trough beyond.

'Just you wait till I catch you,' he threatened, shaking a fist so that droplets flew glittering through the air. 'I'll give you something you won't forget in a hurry!'

'Oooh!' she squealed in mock terror. 'Oh, Brian, what will it be?'

'You'll see,' he grunted, ducking beneath the water in an effort to catch her from underwater, and the words repeated themselves in his head. 'You'll see . . .'

Veronica's legs wafted before him, blurred and greenish-white in the diffused light. He stretched out a hand and missed, tried again and gripped her ankle. She kicked and struggled, but he refused to let go, and as he came to the surface beside her his hand slid up her calf and the full roundness of her thigh.

They stared into each other's eyes.

'Brian,' she whispered. 'Brian, don't . . .'

He kept his hand where it was, moving gently but firmly, stroking and shaping. He saw the change in her eyes, the widening and darkening; he saw the parting of her lips.

'*Brian* . . .'

Brian swept his free arm through the water and caught her hard against him in a kiss. She wriggled in his hands and he felt the desire flame through his body. He released his hold for a moment to drag at her bikini pants, but in the moment that his hands ceased to grip her she kicked herself away and swam for the shore. In a second, he was after her, but she stayed clear and they arrived on the sand together, pulling themselves to their feet in the lacy edges of the tide.

Veronica gave him a wild, frightened glance. 'You shouldn't have. You know I don't want—'

He caught her hand. 'I'm sorry. I didn't mean to scare you. It was just fun.'

'Fun!'

'It wasn't any different to anything we've done before,' he said quietly. 'I've touched you there before.'

'Yes. Yes, I know.' She looked down at her toes, sinking into the wet sand. 'It just seemed different. I didn't think you were going to stop.'

Brian looked at her for a moment. He thought of a film he had seen once with Burt Lancaster and – who was it, Deborah Kerr? – making love at the edge of the sea, rolling in the waves. He'd felt his excitement rise when he'd watched it, and as soon as they'd arrived on the beach today, he had pictured that scene in his mind, with himself and Veronica taking the parts played by the two film stars. The idea had been there even earlier, when he'd first suggested coming to Whitsand; perhaps even before that.

There was nothing Brian wanted so much at that moment than to throw Veronica down in the surf and make passionate love to her. He wanted it so badly that he quivered with it, but he held back. The time will come, he told himself, and it'll come before we leave this beach today. For the moment, he would wait. But not much longer.

'Ronnie,' he said gently, touching her shoulder, 'you're not scared of me, are you? You don't really think I'd do anything to hurt you. Or anything you didn't want me to do. You don't really think that.'

She gazed at him uncertainly. Her body shivered under his touch. He moved his palm on her shoulder, very softly.

'No,' she said at last, 'no, of course I don't. I'm sorry, Brian. I shouldn't have—' She shivered again and wrapped her arms around herself. 'I'm getting cold. Let's go in.'

They made their way back to the blanket. Veronica was shuddering now, and Brian picked up her big, fluffy towel and wrapped it around her. He pulled her close, held her enveloped in the towel, and then began to dry her, very gently, patting her arms and back and waist. After a moment, he stood back and let her finish the job herself.

'Better?'

She nodded, not looking at him. He regarded her for a moment and then picked up his own towel and rubbed himself briskly. 'The sun'll do the rest. What you need is a hot drink and something to eat.'

'There's another flask of coffee. And some sandwiches.' She sat down on the blanket, her knees drawn up, while he poured the coffee. Her hair was still very wet, and he used his own towel to squeeze it dry.

'You're a silly girl, Ronnie. You know I'd never do anything to upset you. We were just having fun. It was fun, wasn't it?'

She nodded. 'Yes, it was. I'm sorry, Brian. I spoilt it.'

'No, you didn't. Anyway, it was probably just as well. I expect I did get a bit carried away. You're so lovely, and – well, I should think every bloke who's ever set eyes on you must have fallen a bit in love with you, so why should I be any different?'

Veronica stayed very still. Then, slowly, she turned her head until her eyes met his. 'Did you say what I think you said?'

He grinned. 'I wouldn't be at all surprised! Come on, Ronnie, you must have known.'

'No. I didn't know. I thought – well, there's Kathy.'

'But that's all over,' he said in a tone of surprise. 'That's been over for months. To tell you the truth, I didn't think I'd ever want to love any woman again – till I met you.'

She was quiet for a few moments, then she said carefully, 'But I'm married.'

'I'm afraid that doesn't stop other blokes falling in love with you.'

'Well, no.'

'I've told you,' he said seriously, 'nothing is going to happen that you don't want, Ronnie. Nothing at all, that you don't want.'

Veronica stared into his eyes. Her pupils were wide and black. She moved, almost imperceptibly, closer. He felt her breath on his cheek. 'Brian, I thought I was imagining it. I couldn't believe – I've thought about you so much lately. I've been so muddled. Wanting you to kiss me and – and touch me, and yet not wanting to be unfaithful to Alex. You see, I love him too and—'

'I know you do,' he said.

'I didn't know it was possible to love two people at once,' she whispered, and laid her head on his shoulder. 'Oh, Brian, what are we going to do?'

'We're not going to do anything,' he said quietly. 'We're just going to eat our lunch like two civilised people. Maybe after a while we'll have another swim, and then we'll take you home – before the tide comes in and completely cuts us off.'

Veronica looked round and gave a little cry. 'It would, too! Oh, we mustn't be too long, Brian. Alex'll be home by half past four. We mustn't get cut off!'

They ate their lunch. Veronica relaxed somewhat, but he could see that she was still tense, her voice higher than usual, her mannerisms and gestures a little artificial. She was very aware of him: when their hands brushed, she almost jerked away, turning her head aside so that he wouldn't see her colour rise.

When they had finished their picnic, he lay back on the blanket. The sun beat down on them and Veronica glanced down at her tanned body.

'We'll burn if we stay here much longer. Perhaps we ought to go.'

'Not yet,' he murmured as if already half asleep. 'Let's put the towels over us. They'll be dry by now.' He sat up and reached for his towel, spreading it over himself from neck to toes. 'There. Let me do yours for you.'

Veronica lay down and he draped the big towel over her, smoothing it gently over her body. His hands caressed her from waist to breast, lingering over the soft curves. Veronica jumped a little and then lay still, quivering.

Brian leaned over her, then lowered himself slowly to kiss her, his body brushing against hers. 'Veronica. I love you. I adore you. Let me love you,' he murmured against her skin. 'Let me love you properly. Just once. Just so that I'll know what it feels like. Veronica, please . . .'

'I can't, Brian . . .'

'Please,' he repeated, his hands slipping beneath the towel and finding her breasts again. 'You're so lovely. Ronnie, I want you so much. Just once. That's all I ask. Just this once, to make this day perfect. Ronnie, I love you, I love you. I *love* you . . .'

Veronica lay beneath him. She could hear nothing but the whisper of the sea, and the plaintive cry of the seagulls. And it seemed that the surging of her blood matched the urgent rhythm of the waves, and the cry of her heart echoed the call of the birds above, and the pulsing, yearning ache of her body blended with the compelling desire she could feel in Brian's hands and mouth. Just once. Only once . . .

It wasn't quite as it had been in the film, a tumult of surf and sand and wild wetness, but it came nearer to Brian's dream than anything had ever done before.

Chapter Thirty-Nine

Once all the ship's company was in place after their various leaves and courses were over, HMS *Dramatic* sailed for a short voyage across the Bay of Biscay to ports in France and Spain. This was a trial run, to make sure that the refit had been successful, and after a fortnight in Devonport for fine-tuning, the ship would visit various home ports before Christmas and then set out on one of the long voyages to which Clare had come to resign herself.

Another ten or fifteen years of this, she thought, taking Christopher to school on the first morning of term. I honestly don't think I can face it.

She was glad to have other matters to occupy her mind. She had completed her 'Kiffer' cartoons and sent them off to the magazine, and now she was concentrating on some water colours of local views. The autumn colours cried out for oils, but Clare had used up most of her last Christmas present and couldn't afford more just yet. She took Laura up to the Pimple and sat on the bench sketching the view of the tors. Soon she would have enough to take to the local teashop.

Her parents were coming down soon for their usual three weeks. Clare moved into the smallest bedroom so that they could have the double bed, and cleaned the house from top to bottom. She made sure the gardening tools were in good condition too, knowing that Bill would want to spend as much time as possible out of doors.

'I'll dig that vegetable patch over and get some potatoes in,' he said almost before he'd humped the suitcases indoors. 'And we could put in a few strawberries too, if you like. You need a bit of good manure – d'you know anyone with horses? And those shrubs want pruning right back or they'll be going wild.'

'I wondered if we could decorate the hallway and stairs,' Clare suggested. 'I can't manage it on my own.'

'We'll need ladders. I'd have put a couple in my bags if you'd told me. Your mother seems to have packed almost everything else. Here, give me that bootcase.'

Clare looked at the luggage, wondering which was packed with boots, before she caught his eye and realised he was up to his old tricks again, playing with words. She rolled up her eyes and handed him the suitcase. 'That's not a proper spoonerism, Dad.'

'Spoonerism?' he said. 'Who's talking about spoonerisms? That's a Whitingism. I don't see why I shouldn't be famous as well.'

Clare laughed. She had been saving a few jokes of her own for when her parents came, but she couldn't equal the ones her father had brought. At supper that night, he regaled her with an interminable account of a 'friend' of his (Bill's stories always happened to mythical friends) who had had to go all the way to Japan to get special parts for his new car. On the way home, the captain had announced problems with the aircraft and everyone had had to throw out all their luggage as they flew over a desert. The 'friend' had very reluctantly thrown out his bag of precious spare parts, which had split in mid-air, whereupon a passing Arab far below had flung up his hands and cried, 'Allah be praised! It's raining Datsun cogs!'

'Get it?' Bill asked. 'Datsun cogs – cats and dogs. There's a Japanese car called a—'

'Yes, all right, Dad, I get it,' Clare said. 'Actually, it's quite clever, it's just that it took so long to get there. And don't tell me the one about the Indian who could remember everything in the world, you've already told that one twice.'

'Oh, you mean when he was asked what he'd had for breakfast last Wednesday and he said eggs, and then ten years later the same bloke met him and said "How", and he said poached,' Bill said rapidly, before anyone could stop him. 'No, all right, I won't tell that one.'

He settled down into a routine exactly as if he was at home, getting up in the morning and putting on old clothes to go out into the garden, while Clare and her mother took Christopher to school and walked back across Whitchurch Down or did some shopping in Tavistock. The housework was quickly done between the two of them and in the afternoons they would go for a walk before meeting Christopher again, or sit in the garden in the autumn sunshine.

The woods across the valley seemed to have been draped with a blanket of red and gold, misted with the haze of September. On the moors, the bracken was crisp and brown, and down on the main road the horse chestnut trees were thick with conkers. Christopher collected pocketfuls every day and brought them home to bake in the Rayburn, and he and his grandfather had ferocious conker fights outside the back door.

'He does love to play with his grandad,' Iris said, watching them as she peeled potatoes for supper. 'He must miss his daddy so much.'

'Yes,' Clare said, trimming a large cabbage. 'And he's not the only one.'

Something in her voice made her mother look up quickly. 'Is everything all right, Clare?'

Clare rested her hands on the edge of the draining board. 'Oh, you know, just a bit fed up. When the ship sails after Christmas it's going to be the third time since we were married that Martyn's been away for a whole year, and he's had goodness knows how many months away on shorter commissions. I'm just about sick of it, to tell you the truth. And now he's talking about signing on again—'

'Signing on?' Iris broke in. 'I thought he'd made up his mind to come out at thirty.'

'So did I, but now he's got it into his head he wants to go through for an officer, and that means another ten years and probably fifteen.' Clare looked at her mother, her eyes filling with tears. 'I don't think I can stand any more, Mum, honestly. I could put up with it all the time I thought he'd be out at thirty and we could settle down to a normal life, but now – now it's never going to be like that. The children will be grown up by the time he comes out of the Navy and we'll never have had an ordinary family life, with us all at home all the time. They'll never have had their father here. It's not fair to them, Mum, and it's not fair to me.'

'But surely you've talked about it?'

'Not like you and Dad talk about things,' Clare said wearily. 'Not discussing all the pros and cons and deciding together what to do. Martyn makes up his own mind and then tells me, and I'm supposed to agree with him. He doesn't want to hear anything against his ideas.'

'Well, I suppose it is his life. He's got a secure future, with good pay, and if he did become an officer he'd get even more. I can understand the way he thinks, Clare. He wants to do the best for you and the children.'

'But is it the best? Look at Chris now. He needs his father to play football and conkers with him, and teach him the things boys want to know. And Laura misses him terribly. And what about my life? I can't do anything, Mum. I can't go anywhere without thinking about the children and having to be back for them. Valerie suggested I could get a job, but I can't because Martyn's never here to give me a hand with things. And he'd have a fit if I had to go out to work when he's on leave. He thinks we all ought to be around to keep him company, but he doesn't give a thought to what it's like for us without him.'

Iris gazed at her in consternation. 'Honestly, Clare, you've got to discuss it with him. He can't go off for another year leaving you feeling like this.'

'Why not?' Clare said bitterly. 'It's what he did last time.'

Her mother sighed and peeled another potato. 'Yes, but you're getting more and more upset all the time. It's not going to get better, is it? After another year of being resentful you're going to feel even worse. You're fed up now, and by then you'll be really angry, which isn't going to do anyone any good.'

'Try telling Martyn that,' Clare said. 'He'll just say what they all say: if you can't take a joke, you shouldn't have joined. He'll say I knew what I was getting into when I married him, but I didn't, Mum. Nobody knows what it's going to be like till they've done it, and then it's too late.' She threw down the stalk she had been trimming until it wasn't much bigger than a pea. 'I've never complained before, I've never made a fuss. Even when he went away the very night before Chris was born, when I was actually in labour, I never whined. I did know it was going to happen and I knew I had to put up with it, and I was *glad* to, because otherwise I wouldn't have had Martyn at all. But that was when I thought I could see an end to it. Now, I can't. He's gone back on our agreement, Mum, that's the top and bottom of it, and that's what I don't like. If we'd changed our minds together, it would have been different, but we didn't, and I feel really let down.'

She gathered up the trimmings and put them into the bucket that Bill had insisted be kept for compost. He had started a heap in the far corner of the garden, behind some shrubs. It would be good mulch in a year or so, he said, but Clare couldn't look ahead that far. In a year or so Martyn would be starting whatever training he had to do for his transfer to the wardroom, and she didn't want to think about it.

Iris was worried and upset by Clare's outburst, but there wasn't much she could do about it. It was between her and Martyn, she said to Bill when they went to bed that night, and they had to sort it out themselves.

'I sometimes wonder if we should have let her get married so young. She's managed very well, but she's had a lot to put up with. She's been on her own a lot more than we thought she'd be.'

'It's the branch Martyn's in,' Bill observed. 'Radar and radio and all that – it's all still pretty new and there's just not enough of them so they're always at sea. And a lot of chaps do come out at thirty, and that makes it harder still.'

'They don't seem to give any thought to the wives and families. Clare told me that when Kathy was here that time, she got the welfare people to come out, and they said the men are looked on as pieces of equipment, like machines. They're supposed to keep their private lives private. It doesn't seem right, Bill, not when they've got so many separations. It's bound to cause problems.'

'Well, young Kathy certainly had a few,' Bill agreed, getting into his pyjamas. 'But our Clare won't go that way – getting off with other men, I mean. She's not that sort – we've brought her up properly.'

'Kathy's mum and dad are decent people too,' Iris reminded him a little sharply. 'And he was in the Navy himself – they know what it's like. Not that they've given Kathy much sympathy, though I did hear her mum's hoping to come down and see her.'

'Well, like you say, there's nothing we can do.' Bill got into bed. 'I mean, we'll help all we can, of course, but we can't tell 'em what to do. Clare might have got married young, but she's twenty-five now and she's been in charge of her own life since she was nineteen. She's got to make up her own mind.'

Iris got in beside him. I wouldn't mind so much if she could do that, she thought, but the trouble is that Martyn's made it up for her and she doesn't seem to have a choice. That's what's making it so hard.

'Well, I suppose we all go through rough patches,' she said, lying down beside her husband and switching off the light. 'We've been through one or two ourselves, and we've managed all right in the end.'

She turned over and was asleep within seconds. Bill, startled by her last remark, lay awake a little longer, puzzling over when the rough patches had been in his own long marriage. For the life of him, he couldn't remember.

'We'll take Laura down to Plymouth today,' Iris said at breakfast. 'It'll be nice on the Hoe and we can walk down to the Barbican and see the fishing trawlers. It'll give you a bit of time to yourself, too.'

They set off to catch the bus at the Honour Oak tree, and Clare decided to take the opportunity to walk further than usual and do a new painting. She was just gathering her things together when the postman arrived and gave her a letter.

'From London?' Clare said, turning it over in her hand. 'I wonder who—? Oh! Perhaps it's the magazine. The contract!'

Her fingers trembling with excitement, she ripped it open and scanned the closely typed page. At first, the words made no sense. She read them again, and slowly the meaning became clear.

'It's from a *publisher*,' she said to Bartholomew, who was licking his paws on a kitchen chair. 'At least, someone who's starting up as a publisher. He says he knows the magazine editor and she showed him some of my Kiffers – and he wants to talk to me about illustrating some children's books!' She sat down suddenly. '*Me* – doing pictures for children's books! Can you believe it?'

Bartholomew stopped licking and regarded her with large orange eyes.

'Yes,' she said, 'they could well be pictures of cats. Pictures of *you*, Bartholomew. Why, you could be as famous as Orlando the Marmalade Cat!'

Bartholomew closed his eyes disdainfully. Fame, he seemed to imply, was not dignified, but his excited mistress didn't care about that. She was reading the letter again and wishing that there was someone here to tell, to share her excitement.

'I'll go and tell Veronica,' she decided. 'She'll be pleased for me. I'd tell Sue, but she's away on holiday. Come on, Barty, you can go out in the garden for a while, it's a lovely morning. And don't catch too many birds!'

Veronica was in her kitchen when Clare arrived. She bustled about, making coffee and chattering, but her voice was high and tense and when she set the mugs on the table Clare saw that she looked pale and red-eyed. She put aside her own news and looked at her friend with concern.

'What's the matter? You look upset.'

'Oh, nothing. Everything's fine, honestly.' Veronica looked away. 'How are your parents – are they enjoying themselves? It's been lovely weather for them, hasn't it? I expect your dad's getting some gardening done. He always keeps himself busy, doesn't he, helping you about the place? My father's keen on gardening too, have I ever told you that? Oh, but you've been over there, haven't you, to see – to see—' To Clare's consternation, her voice wavered and then broke completely, and she burst into tears.

'Veronica! Whatever is it? What's the matter?' Clare jumped up and went round the table to her friend, putting her arms about Veronica's shoulders. 'What's happened? Is it Alex? Are you ill? Tell me, Ronnie.'

'Oh, Clare,' Veronica sobbed, her face buried in her hands. Tears trickled through her fingers and dripped on to the table. 'Clare, it's awful, *awful*! You can't imagine . . . And there's no one I can tell. No one. People will *hate* me . . .'

'Veronica, don't be silly. Of course people won't hate you. It can't be that bad. Tell me about it. Tell me what's happened.'

'You won't want to know. You'll hate me too.'

'I won't. I promise I won't.' Clare dragged her chair round the table and sat down, her arm still around Veronica's shoulder. 'Have you got a hanky? Wipe your eyes and blow your nose, and then tell me all about it. Come on, now.'

Veronica raised her head and gave her a doubtful look, then she found a handkerchief and did as she was told, giving her nose a good blow. She looked very young and woebegone.

'Better now?' Clare asked, and Veronica nodded. 'So what's the matter? What's happened?'

'Well,' Veronica said with the air of someone about to jump from a high diving-board, 'to start with, I'm pregnant.'

Clare stared at her. 'But that's not bad news! That's wonderful. It really is. Veronica, I know you're scared of having a baby, but honestly it's not as bad as all that – and anyway, even if it is, it's soon over and then you've got a lovely baby to look after. And even if you feel sick now—'

'You don't understand,' Veronica interrupted. 'It's not Alex's baby.'

There was a short, appalled silence.

'Not . . . *Alex's* baby?' Clare managed to say at last, faintly.

'No. It's Brian Bennett's.'

'Brian's?'

'Yes. He – well, we went out together a few times. There wasn't anything in it. Not at first. I just felt sorry for him. And I was upset about Alex too, going over to see Kathy so much.' She looked at Clare defiantly. 'He was messing about and leaving me on my own, and I didn't see why I shouldn't have a bit of fun too. But that's all it was, I swear. I never meant this to happen,' she finished miserably.

'I don't suppose you did.' Clare tried to sort out the welter of information. 'But what do you mean, Alex was going to see Kathy? You surely didn't think that he and she—'

'Well, what else was I to think?' Veronica demanded. 'He never used to go over there on his own, and it always seemed to be when I had something else planned. What other reason could he have? It only started after she'd arrived there. It's been going on all summer, Clare. It's obvious what he's been doing.'

Clare gazed at her helplessly. Perhaps I ought to tell her, she thought. Perhaps I ought to say that Alex hasn't been going to see Kathy at all, but to help your father sort his affairs out because he thinks he's going to die . . . But how could you say something like that to a girl who was already frantic with terror over her own situation? It wasn't up to Clare to break news like that. Oh, what a mess, what a dreadful mess.

'So, because you thought Alex was having an affair with Kathy, you decided to start an affair with Kathy's husband. Ronnie, that's—'

'No!' Veronica interrupted. 'I told you, it wasn't like that. I met Brian here a couple of times and I felt sorry for him, that's all. And then I ran into him in Tavistock one day and we went for a drive – it was that day you went over to the Grange with Alex – and we went to Dartmeet and had tea. He told me what Kathy was like and that I ought to keep an eye on Alex, and after that – well, he used to ring me up quite often, just to talk, and sometimes we'd meet and go for a walk or something like that. It was all perfectly *innocent*.' She looked down at her fingers, twisting themselves together on the table. 'I suppose we got sort of fond of each other, but it was all just fun, there was nothing serious in it, and it was nice having someone to – to kiss,' she said in a small voice. 'But I never meant it to go any further than that, honestly I didn't.'

'Oh, *Veronica*,' Clare said. 'How could you have thought it wouldn't? With a man like Brian?'

'Well, I thought he was safe,' she said in an injured tone. 'I wasn't to know he'd go too far.'

Clare looked at her and sighed. You should have been made to grow up years ago, she thought. You've been protected and sheltered all your life and you've stayed a child and been glad to, because that way you didn't have to take any responsibility. Unfortunately your body didn't see things the same way . . .

'So what happened in the end, or can I guess?' she asked.

'We went down to Whitsand for the day, just before Alex started his summer holiday. We walked along the beach till we found a little cove all to ourselves and we swam and sunbathed . . . I think he meant to do it all along,' she added drearily. 'He kept touching me when we were in the water. I liked it – it was fun – but in the end he just wouldn't stop, and we – we – well, you know.'

'Did you try to stop him? Did he force you?'

Veronica hesitated. 'I asked him not to. Several times. I did, honestly, but—'

'Just asking wasn't enough,' Clare said, and Veronica shook her head. 'So you let him. You let him make love to you.'

'Yes.' The word came out as a whisper, and Veronica's head hung so that her long fair hair fell around her face in a curtain. Tears began to drip on to the table again.

Clare gazed at her in despair. She could imagine just how it had happened. Veronica, the child, flirting and teasing, with no idea of what her coquettish ways could do to a man. They'd obviously indulged in some kind of kissing and petting before, and no doubt Veronica had persuaded herself that it didn't matter, that so long as they didn't actually go 'all the way' it didn't count. It would have counted all right if she'd caught Alex doing the same with Kathy, Clare thought wryly, but it was amazing how you could justify your own actions and not other people's. Not that any of that mattered now. The important thing was that Veronica was pregnant.

'Was that the only time?' she asked.

'Yes. I wouldn't go out with him again. I felt awful, Clare. I cried all the way home. I'd never meant to be unfaithful to Alex: it was only because I knew he was going to see Kathy—'

'Wait a minute,' Clare broke in. 'Did you really and truly, in your heart of hearts, think he was having an affair with Kathy? Did you? Or were you just using that as an excuse for your own behaviour?'

Veronica stared at her, shocked. 'Clare! That's horrible! I thought you were my friend. I thought you'd promised to help me.'

'I did. I am. I just want you to be sure what you were doing. You can't honestly believe he was playing about with Kathy. In your own parents' house? Do you think they would have just sat there and let that happen?'

Veronica looked away, biting her lip, her fingers twined tightly together. 'Well, what else could it have been?'

'I think you should ask him,' Clare said quietly. 'You're going to have to talk to him, you know.'

Veronica looked down at her lap. 'I know. I thought of trying to pretend it was his baby, but he'd know it wasn't – he's always been so careful. I've been talking about going on that pill, you know, but he wasn't keen, he thinks it isn't natural, so we've just kept on as usual. Except that just lately we haven't – not much, anyway. He'd know it wasn't his.'

'It wouldn't work,' Clare said, dismayed by the idea. 'You'd be telling a lie every day, pretending the baby was his all through its life. And suppose it looked like Brian?'

'I know. Oh, Clare, what am I going to do? He'll divorce me, I know he will, just like Brian's divorcing Kathy. What will I do then? My parents will be so upset. Everyone's going to hate me.' Her voice was rising again. 'They are. They're going to *hate* me.'

'They're not. They're not. No one's going to hate you.' Clare tightened her arm around Veronica's shoulders. 'Stop it, Ronnie. Stop it. Crying isn't going to do any good. We've got to *think* about this.'

'I've thought,' Veronica sobbed. 'I've thought and thought and *thought*. I haven't thought about anything else. It's no *use*: there's no way out. I don't know what to do, I don't know what to *do*!'

Neither did Clare. She went on holding her friend, appalled by what had happened. It was so easy, she thought. You only needed to be just that bit more unhappy or discontented, or even merely bored. Or lonely . . . It was so easy to persuade yourself, as Veronica had done, that you had justification.

She thought of her own friendship with Alex. Their innocent walks on the moor together. The January morning when they'd watched Churchill's funeral on television. The day they'd gone to the Grange together. Their easy companionship, their confidential talks. It could all so easily have led to something more . . . And that, she realised suddenly, was the day when Veronica and Brian had gone to Dartmeet for tea. They must have been there as Alex and Clare drove past on their way home . . .

'Have you told Brian?' she asked. 'Does he know?'

Veronica shook her head. 'No. I told you, I haven't seen him since. He rang me a few times. He wanted me to go out with him again, but I knew what would happen. He thought once we'd done it we'd go on. I didn't want to. I didn't want to do it at all, but we were on our own and I was frightened.'

'*Frightened?* But I thought you said he didn't force you.'

'He didn't, but I was afraid that if I didn't let him . . . There was no one else about, and I knew about him hitting Kathy. I told you, he meant to do it all along and he's so *big* . . .'

'Well, you'll have to tell him,' Clare said, digesting this. 'He ought to know. It's his responsibility.'

Veronica gave her a bitter look. 'And d'you think he's going to accept it? D'you think he'll even admit it? It's my word against his – I can't prove what happened.'

'Aren't there blood tests they can do, or something?' Clare asked doubtfully. 'I'm sure I've heard of paternity cases.'

'Clare, *don't*. That's horrible. They can't do anything till the baby's born, anyway. I've got to do something before then. It's two months already – Alex is bound to notice something soon.'

'I know, but I still think Brian ought to know. Would you like me to tell him? Would that help?'

'He's at sea,' Veronica said flatly. 'He won't be home till the end of the month and then they're going away again. What can he do about it, anyway?'

'I just think he should know. It isn't right that men can do this and then just sail out of trouble. And after the way he treated Kathy . . .'

'Yes,' Veronica said. 'I'm no better than her, am I? And after all I've said about her.'

'None of us knows what we'd do in any situation till we've been there,' Clare said. She looked at Veronica. 'Alex loves you. Don't you think he'll forgive you? Don't you think he'll help?'

'I don't know what he'll do. I just don't want him to know. I don't want him to stop loving me – I don't want him to know what I'm really like.'

'Oh, come on,' Clare said, 'you can't be married to someone and not know what the other's like. You can't hide your real self from someone you're living with.'

'I don't even know who my real self is,' Veronica said hopelessly. 'I don't seem to know anything any more.'

Clare got up and made some more coffee. The situation seemed really to be as hopeless as Veronica thought it, and yet she knew that something must happen. Life did not stand still. Veronica's pregnancy would become obvious, and Alex would have to come to terms with whatever feelings he had – betrayal, she supposed, anger, bitter disappointment. She wondered if he would want someone to talk to about it all, and knew that this could be another danger point.

'As I see it,' she said, sounding like her own father, 'there's only one thing you can do, and that's tell Alex. He's got to know, Veronica. And if you don't tell Brian, I'm sure *he* will!'

'Yes, I suppose he will. Clare, you don't think he'll do anything silly – he won't go after him or anything like that?'

Clare tried to imagine Alex 'going after' Brian, squaring up to him and knocking him down, but the picture refused to come. All the same, she thought, you never knew. Even gentle Alex might turn to violence when he discovered the truth.

'I just don't know,' she said helplessly. 'I really don't know . . . Look, Veronica, let's just think about it a bit longer, shall we? I'll come down and see you again soon. And I promise you I'll do whatever I can to help. All you have to do is call me.'

She walked back up the lane, having said nothing about the letter.

Veronica's problem filled her mind for the rest of the day, turning over and over in her head as she went back home, ate a snack lunch in the garden, and then walked down to the town. She collected Christopher, still deep in thought, and they took their favourite route home, through the Meadows, up Pixon Lane and along Down Road to the little path that led to the edge of Whitchurch Down. When they arrived home, she found Bill and Iris and Laura already there, in a state of high excitement.

'Daddy!' Laura shouted as soon as she saw her mother. 'Daddy's coming home! Daddy's coming home *tonight*!'

'Daddy? What on earth are you talking about?' Clare looked at her parents. 'Whatever has she got into her head now?'

'It's true, it's true,' Laura insisted. 'We've seen his ship. We saw it coming in the water.'

'She's right,' Iris confirmed, smiling all over her face. 'We were up on the Hoe and we saw *Dramatic* coming through the Sound. She must have hit a snag and they've brought her back into port.'

'*Dramatic*?' Clare felt a mixture of joy and dismay. 'Are you sure? Are you sure it wasn't some other carrier?'

'I hope,' her father said in a tone of mock affront, 'that after a lifetime in Pompey dockyard I can tell one aircraft carrier from another. It was *Dramatic* all right. You'd better fill the katted calf, Clare. Martyn will be home for supper tonight, or I'm a Dutchman.'

Chapter Forty

E ven more startling than *Dramatic*'s sudden return was the fact
that Martyn brought Brian home with him.

'Why?' Clare hissed at him out in the kitchen. 'Why did you
have to bring him? He can't stop the night, you know, he'll have to go
back. I don't even know where *you're* going to sleep! Mum and Dad are
in our room, and I'm in the little one, and—'

'Stop panicking.' Martyn gave her a smacking kiss, the sort he
indulged in when he was being a breezy, every-nice-girl-loves-a sailor.
'It's all fixed up. We're sailing early tomorrow morning, and if Bri hadn't
got his car garaged in Devonport we couldn't have come home at all. He
won't mind dossing down on the settee. You'd rather I came back than
stayed on board, wouldn't you? We can manage in the single bed.'

'Yes. Yes, of course.' Clare picked up the chicken she'd roasted for
supper. At least there was enough food for them all . . . 'It's just that I
wish you hadn't had to bring him as well, Martyn.' After hearing
Veronica's revelation Brian was the last person she wanted to see, and
she certainly didn't feel like breaking her own good news. She sighed
irritably.

'But I've just *told* you—' Martyn broke off and looked at her more
closely. 'There's something else, isn't there? Some other reason? What's
up, Clare? Come on, spit it out.'

'No. I can't. Not now.' Not at all, if I can help it, she thought
frantically. It only needed Martyn to blunder in where angels feared to
tread and the cat really would be set among the pigeons. I'm getting as
bad as Dad, she thought, and indicated the vegetables with a movement
of her head. 'Bring those in, Martyn, will you? Everything will be
getting cold.'

Brian was going down well with Bill and Iris. They knew about his and Kathy's history, of course, but they'd never been told all the details, and they'd only met Brian once or twice before. He was exerting all his charm now, telling them stories of the exotic places he'd been to, and when Martyn and Clare entered the room they were all laughing heartily.

'He's a star turn, that Brian,' Iris said as she and Clare washed up later. 'Kept us in stitches, he has. It does seem sad that Kathy couldn't stay faithful to him, like you and Martyn have.'

'I don't think it's as simple as that, Mum. Brian isn't always the life and soul of the party.'

'No, I don't suppose he is, but we've all got our other sides. We just have to learn to rub along with each other. You don't imagine your dad's always been the easiest of people to live with, do you?'

'Well, naval life doesn't give you much chance to learn to rub along,' Clare said tersely. She badly wanted time to herself, to assimilate all that Veronica had told her that morning, and her mother's companionable chatter was beginning to grate on her. Also, she wondered what this sudden homecoming would mean. Martyn had told her that although the ship was sailing again early next morning, it would only be for a few days and she would then return for up to a week. Brian would be in Devonport, at a loose end.

I must warn Veronica, she thought. I must let her know as soon as possible.

Warning Veronica wasn't so easy, though. Although Martyn and Brian were gone before six thirty next morning, leaving her virtually alone until her parents and the children were awake, she couldn't possibly ring her friend until after nine, when Alex would have left for school.

Clare decided to see Veronica on the way back from taking Chris down, but it was a lovely morning and Iris insisted on coming too. They walked back together along the main road, passing Veronica's house. Clare tried desperately to think of an excuse to call in without taking her mother too, but none came to mind, and when they arrived at Dale View, Bill announced that he was taking them out for the day.

'We're going to catch the train and go to Exeter. We can be back in time for Christopher. I'm taking you out for lunch.'

'For lunch? What's brought this on, then? Won the football pools, have you?'

'Saved up my pocket-money,' Bill said. 'I'll have you know I've gone without Mars bars for six months to pay for this little treat.'

'Well, there's a sacrifice,' Iris observed sardonically. 'I never even knew you liked Mars bars!'

Bill grinned at Clare and dropped one eyelid in a wink. 'Amazing, isn't it, how little a wife can know about her husband. Have I eaten one whole Mars bar every evening of our marriage, or have I not?'

'You have not,' Iris said smartly. 'For one thing, you wouldn't have had enough ration coupons during the war. And for another, you can't stand Mars bars. You always used to give yours to the children.' Iris shook his arm fondly, and they smiled at each other. She turned to Clare. 'That's why he bought them – so that he could give them to you and Val and Ian. If he'd got something he did like, you'd never have had a chance!'

Clare shook her head and rubbed her eyes. 'Why are we standing here talking about Mars bars? Look, there's something I need to do—'

'Nothing that can't wait till tomorrow,' her father said briskly. 'Go and get titivated up, the two of you, and put that granddaughter of mine into a pretty frock. I want to take my three favourite girls out for the day and I want everyone to admire them as much as I do!'

'I didn't even get a chance to make a phone call,' Clare said to Veronica next morning. This time, Iris hadn't insisted on accompanying her to school with Christopher, and Bill seemed· content to spend the entire day in the garden. Clare had been knocking on Veronica's door by twenty past nine, and had broken the news of *Dramatic*'s return alَ.ost as soon as she was across the doorstep. 'There seemed to be someone looking over my shoulder the whole time, and when we got back, it was too late – Alex would have been home from school.'

Veronica nodded dully. 'He was back early, too,' she said, as if that made a difference. 'Clare, he suspects something, I'm sure he does. He's been looking at me in a peculiar way. As if there's something he wants to say to me but can't quite find the words . . . Either that, or he wants to tell me about Kathy.'

'About *Kathy*?'

'Yes. *You* know. I told you how he keeps going over to the Grange to see her, and—'

'Veronica,' Clare broke in, 'Alex isn't going to the Grange to see Kathy. He *isn't*.'

'How do you know? How do you know what he's going there for?' Veronica stared at her. 'I know there's something going on, I know it. And if it isn't Kathy . . .' Her face paled. 'It's you, isn't it? It's you . . .

You've always been friendly. You went with him one day . . . How do I know he's going there at all?'

'No. Veronica, stop it. It's *nothing* like that, nothing, I *promise* you. Look, you've got to ask Alex, you've got to make him tell you.' And that's going to help a lot, she thought, finding out her father's seriously ill . . . She struggled to get the conversation back on an even keel. 'Look, let's deal with one thing at a time, shall we?'

'Yes. Brian. So when's the ship coming back again?' Veronica sounded flat and hopeless, as if discussion were useless but might help to pass the time. 'Thursday?'

'I think so. What are you going to do if Brian rings you up?'

'Oh, I don't suppose he will. I told you, I said I didn't want to go out with him again. I told him.'

'Brian doesn't necessarily take no for an answer,' Clare said grimly, remembering how he had won back Kathy after the 'Dear John'. 'You'll have to tell him, you know.'

'What's the point? He'll only deny it. He'll say I can't possibly know who the father is—' She broke off, colouring, and Clare seized on the point.

'Can you? You really are sure? There couldn't be some mistake?'

'No. None at all. Alex is always so careful. He uses a sheath every time. And anyway, we didn't make love that week, not once. Not for over ten days.'

'Well,' Clare said, 'they're both going to have to know. And you've got to ask Alex about the Grange too.' She looked at her friend sadly. 'I really am sorry, Ronnie. None of it's going to be easy for you. But you know I'll do whatever I can to help, don't you? I'll do anything.'

'Thanks.' Veronica gave her a wry, shaky smile. 'I may hold you to that. I'll probably turn up on your doorstep one night with a suitcase . . . You're making quite a speciality of this, aren't you, Clare? Are you sure you won't get fed up with helping us fallen women?'

Clare's eyes filled with tears. 'Don't be so silly, Ronnie. You're not a fallen woman, and I don't think for a minute that you're going to be appearing on my doorstep with a suitcase. Alex would never turn you out.'

I hope I'm right, she thought later, walking slowly up the lane. I hope to goodness I'm right.

Dramatic was back in Devonport on Thursday evening. And on Friday, just as Clare had feared, Brian turned up on Veronica's doorstep.

434

'I told you I didn't want to see you again. How did you manage to get time off, anyway?'

'Make and mend,' he said cheerfully. 'We all got them, to give us a long weekend. I brought Martyn up in the car but I got the impression I wasn't flavour of the month with Clare, so I thought I'd take the opportunity of coming to see my favourite girlfriend. Take her for a drive somewhere – stop in some quiet spot, you know?'

'Please,' Veronica said, 'please go away.'

Brian's eyes narrowed. 'Now, you don't mean that, Ronnie. You're thrilled to see me really. I bet you've been lying awake every night, wishing we were down at Whitsand together again. It was fun, wasn't it?' He stepped a little nearer and touched her cheek with his finger. 'Aren't you even going to give me a little kiss?'

'Brian,' Veronica said faintly, her eyes closed.

'Come here,' he murmured, sliding his arms around her. 'We've been apart too long. I've missed you, Ronnie.'

'Brian, *please*. Not here on the doorstep.'

'Where, then?' His eyes glinted wickedly. 'Indoors? In bed?'

'No. *No*. Look, I'll come out with you. For a drive. But nothing else. And I must be back by five. Alex will be home then and wondering where I am.'

'We'll be back in plenty of time for you to titivate yourself up for Alex. Come on, and we'll find a nice quiet spot where you can tell me just how much you've been missing me.'

Feeling like a prisoner being led to her doom, Veronica followed him to the car. She glanced uneasily from right to left, wondering how many of the neighbours were watching from behind their curtains, and slipped into the front passenger seat. Not that it'll matter soon, she thought, when Alex knows. Nothing will matter then.

Brian drove fast out of Tavistock. He took the Gunnislake road, twisting round the hairpin bends and down to the bridge over the river Tamar. Veronica looked at him in bewilderment. 'Where are we going?'

'Where d'you think? A trip down Memory Lane. It worked pretty well last time, after all.' He took his eyes off the road to grin at her. 'I thought this time we'd go the pretty way.'

Veronica screwed her hands tightly together and lifted them towards her chest. 'Brian, I don't want to go down to Whitsand. Please. There isn't time. And besides, I told you – it's over. I should never have let you do what you did. It's not going to happen again.'

'We'll see about that.' There was something vicious in the way Brian was driving, and she felt a tingling of fear. 'I'm getting a little tired of women saying no to me, Veronica.'

Veronica was silent. She stared out of the window at the steep woods and rocks of Morwellham, and wished she had never agreed to come with him. It had only been to avoid a scene on the doorstep, she thought, and would that really have mattered so much? And how did she know that Brian really would take her home by five? He didn't seem to be in the kind of mood to think of Alex.

'Brian, you know I'm married.'

'Of course I do,' he said lightly. 'That's what makes it all such fun.'

'Not for me,' she said. 'I don't find it fun at all. I'm sorry we ever started it. I never meant it to go so far. Brian, please take me home.'

'No,' he said, 'you didn't mean it to go so far, did you? There's a name for girls like you, you know that? Know what it is? It's *cock-teaser*. Well, this is one cock that doesn't take at all kindly to being teased. As you are shortly to find out.'

Veronica drew in her breath sharply. She gave a quick look at his profile, set and angry, white about the lips, and with a small muscle twitching in his cheek, and then turned her head and stared out of the window again. Her eyes filled with tears.

'Brian,' she said in a trembling voice, 'you've got to take me home. Now. Please. *Please*.'

Brian said nothing. He kept his eyes on the road and increased his speed. They passed through the village of St Germans with its big church, and along the river. Crafthole. Portwrinkle . . . They were at the top of the cliff, where the road ran close to the edge. Brian pulled the car in and stopped the engine. It was high tide. Below them the foam surged over the rocks, as delicate as lace, as dangerous as darkness.

Veronica sat very still. She watched as he turned to her. Her head was already shaking. 'Brian. *No*.'

'That's not what you said down on the sands that day. Well,' He grinned. 'You did say no, but you didn't mean it, did you? No more than you mean it now.'

'I did. And I mean it now.' She held him off with her palms pressed flat against his chest. 'Brian, there's something I've got to tell you.'

'What's that? Alex getting suspicious? Don't worry, Ronnie, he can't prove a thing. Nobody has ever seen—'

'It's not that.' She drew in a deep breath and faced him. 'I'm pregnant.'

Through the silence, she could hear the thunder of the waves on the rocks below. Or was it the thunder of her own heart, the roar of her own blood, sounding in her ears? She stared at him, seeing the narrowing of his eyes, the hard compression of his lips. Fear gripped her suddenly, and she was horribly aware of how far they were from home, of the fact that nobody knew where they were, that Brian was strong as well as angry.

'What did you say?' he said at last in a low, hard voice.

'I'm pregnant. I – I'm expecting a baby, Brian.' She swallowed. 'Your baby.'

'No,' he said. 'No. No. *Your* baby, Veronica.'

'Brian, it's yours – it is. I swear it is.' Her voice was rising hysterically. She beat softly on his chest with her clenched fists, then lifted them to her cheeks. 'It's *your baby*!'

His hands shot out and gripped her wrists. His grasp was hard and cruel, twisting the delicate skin so that it burned. He stared into her eyes. 'You can't prove that. You're a married woman, as you were pleased to remind me a few minutes ago. Nobody would believe it was mine.'

'They would. Alex would. He'll *know*, Brian. He will. Oh, what am I going to *do*?'

'What thousands of women before you have done, I imagine,' he said coldly. 'Brazen it out. He wants kids, doesn't he? Well, he's going to have one. He doesn't have to know, Veronica. You don't have to tell him. You don't have to tell him what date it's due – fiddle it about a bit. Bloody hell, if you'd had any sense you'd have made *sure* it could be his that same night!'

'I didn't know. I never thought—'

'For crying out loud, Veronica, how old are you? You know the facts of life by now, for Christ's sake. Look, I don't know what you're making such a fuss about. So you're up the spout? It doesn't matter, dammit. You're safe. *We're* safe.' He relaxed his grip and stroked her cheek, smiling suddenly. 'We can have a bit of fun without worrying.'

'Fun?' she echoed blankly. 'What do you mean, fun?'

'Well, we can't make the same mistake twice, can we?' he said unconcernedly. 'Can't put another little beggar in, the situation's been filled.'

'That's a filthy thing to say,' Veronica said after a moment.

'If you say so.' His hand had moved round to the back of her head. He stroked her hair, then slid his fingers down into the neck of her blouse. 'Come on, Ronnie, don't let's waste our time. Here we are where it all began – the least we can do is seal it with a kiss. I'll be going away again soon – we may not get another chance.'

Veronica felt a great surge of anger rise up in her. She lifted her arm and struck his hand away. 'Leave me alone! I'm not going to kiss you, I'm not going to do anything with you. I wish I'd never let you touch me in the first place – I must have been mad. I want to go home. Take me home.'

Brian laughed, and her skin crept at the sound. 'Oh, no, little Ronnie, we're not going home. Not just yet. You owe me something for all those times you refused to speak to me. I told you, I don't take kindly to being teased and given the cold shoulder. I've had a bit too much of that. I swore when Kathy did it to me that I'd never let another woman get away with it, and I don't mean to go back on that.'

'Kathy . . .' she whispered. 'Kathy got pregnant and you hated her for it . . . And now you've done the same thing, you've made me do the same thing to Alex . . .'

'I didn't make you do anything,' he said, 'but I will now, if you don't give in nicely.'

'No!' she panted, thoroughly terrified now. 'No! You won't – you can't—'

'I can. I will.'

'*No*! Please, Brian, please take me home, *please* . . .'

'Afterwards,' he said, and drew her into his arms. 'Afterwards.'

Veronica screamed. She pummelled his chest, turned her head aside from his seeking mouth, squirmed desperately in his arms. He was pulling at her clothes, dragging her blouse aside to reveal her breasts, already swelling with her pregnancy. He bent his head, sucking and biting greedily. Veronica screamed again and managed to get one of her hands free. She grabbed a handful of his hair and yanked.

Brian's head jerked back. 'You little *bitch*.'

Veronica reached behind her and grappled with the door-handle. It moved under her hand and the door fell open. She tumbled backwards, away from his reaching hands, and rolled into the road. Brian swore and reached again, ripping her skirt. Veronica scrambled to her feet and began to run along the road.

Behind her, she heard the car start up. Choking with fear, she scuttled along the cliff edge. There was nowhere to go, other than down the twisting little path into the cove, or on along the road. There was nobody else about.

'Alex,' she sobbed. 'Oh, Alex, Alex . . . I'm so sorry, Alex, I'm so *sorry*.'

The car was close. She knew just what Brian would do. He would open the door as he drew level and grab her, forcing her back into the

438

car. Or he would jump out and throw her down in the grass on the top of the cliff and rape her there and then. She glanced wildly about and then ducked through the wire fence and slid over the edge, on to the little path. There was no escape that way, she knew it, but there was nothing else she could do. She had to try.

The car's wheels skidded above her. She looked up, expecting to see it stop, expecting to see Brian leap down the cliff towards her.

Instead, she saw the car break through the fence. The front wheel teetered on the edge, earth and grass and stones breaking away from beneath it. As she watched, appalled, it crept into space and hung there for a brief moment of time, a moment that seemed an eternity. Then, so slowly that she could not understand why Brian did nothing to stop it, the whole car toppled over and surged forward to somersault down the face of the cliff and on to the black, tide-washed rocks below. She just had time, as it passed her, to see Brian's horrified face, his mouth wide open in sheer terror.

Chapter Forty-One

Veronica lay looking up at Alex in silence. His face was grave. She could not tell if he was angry or simply sad, but she thought he must be angry. Any man would be angry.

'Oh, Alex,' she said, and turned her head on the hospital pillow as tears came flooding from her eyes and trickled into a wet patch.

'I know.' He sat down on the chair beside the bed and took her hand. 'I know.'

'It was all my fault,' she said miserably. 'I was being so silly. It was all my fault.'

'No,' he said. 'No, it wasn't all your fault. I don't think it was your fault at all.'

'It was.' Suddenly she felt angry herself, as if something that was hers was being taken away from her. 'Alex, it *was* my fault. I shouldn't have gone with him. I shouldn't ever have let it happen. You can't say it wasn't my fault. It was.'

'It was his fault too.'

She turned her head back and looked at him. 'He's dead, isn't he?'

'Yes.'

'And there'll be an inquest and all that.' She shivered. 'Everyone's going to know.'

'I've been asking about that. You may not have to go.'

'Of course I'll have to go,' she said sharply, and then turned away again, the tears beginning once more. 'I've had a miscarriage, Alex.'

'I know,' he said, and gripped her hand more tightly. 'Did you realise you were pregnant? It was very early.'

'Yes. Yes, I knew I was pregnant.' Again, her head rolled on the pillow and she looked directly into his eyes. 'Alex—'

'It was his, wasn't it?' he said quietly. 'It was his baby.'

'Yes,' she whispered, and kept hold of his hand.

'Do you want to tell me about it?' he asked after a moment, his voice seeming to come with difficulty, and then, with sudden desperation, 'Veronica, were you going to leave me?'

'No. *No*. Oh, Alex, it was so awful.' She began to cry in earnest so that he had to strain to catch her words. 'I never meant it to happen. I was just being silly. It was fun, at first, having someone to talk to on the phone and then we met by accident in Tavistock – it really was by accident. You'd gone over to the Grange and we went out to tea – and it all seemed to start from there. There didn't seem to be any harm in it – I thought we were just friends, only we flirted a bit, you know. Then when he kissed me he said it was just a friendly kiss, it never meant anything else – and I was lonely and upset. I thought you and Kathy – or you and Clare . . . I didn't know *what* to think. It all seemed so strange, the way you kept going over to the Grange and you didn't want me with you. It made me angry, it made me want to get back at you – so I let him kiss me, and it seemed to make me feel better. But I never meant it to be any more than that.'

She paused for breath, and reached blindly for a handkerchief. Alex took his from his pocket and handed it to her. She wiped her face and blew her nose and then went on, her words jerking through her sobs. 'We went down to Whitsand – not this time, it was weeks ago at the beginning of the holidays – and we swam and sunbathed and – and it just seemed to happen. I didn't really want it to, but I didn't know how to stop him. I don't think I could have stopped him,' she finished miserably, and blew her nose again.

Alex stared at her. His face was like stone. 'Did he force you?'

Veronica shook her head. 'No. Not really. I don't know. I wanted to stop him, but there was a part of me that wanted it too. I think he would have forced me, but he didn't. Not then.'

'So when did he?'

'The last time,' she whispered. 'On Friday. I didn't want to go with him at all – he came to the house. I hadn't seen him since that other time. I wouldn't go out with him again, I was so ashamed, and then I found out about the baby and I was frantic. Clare said I ought to tell him—'

'Clare knew about it?'

'She knew about the baby. She didn't know about me and Brian, not before that. She said I'd have to tell you both. Then he came to see me on Friday afternoon. He said he didn't like being told no, and I knew

441

he'd make a scene if I didn't go with him – and I knew I had to tell him. I didn't know he was going to go to Whitsand. There wasn't anything I could do about it once we were in the car.'

'And when you got there?'

'I told him about the baby.' She looked at him, her eyes brimming once more. 'He said I couldn't prove it was his, he said I could tell you it was yours and you'd believe me. He said – he said we could have some fun now, because it wouldn't matter any more what we did.'

Alex muttered something under his breath. Veronica looked at his face and felt a tremor of fear. She had never seen him look so angry.

'And he tried to force you then?'

'Yes. I didn't want to. I managed to get out of the car and ran along the road and he drove after me. I got through the fence and tried to get down the cliff – I knew I couldn't get away from him, but I had to try – but he came too close and the car just went over the edge. It seemed to take for ever.'

She closed her eyes, shuddering, seeing it all again: the slowly toppling car; the look on Brian's face; the cliff breaking away as the car plunged into the sea; the huge mountain of spray and foam. She heard again the crash, the clatter of metal and the splashing as the broken pieces flew into the air and landed on rocks and then in the water. She heard a wild, frantic screaming that went on and on until she realised it was her own voice, and managed to reduce it to a despairing wail.

'Don't talk about it any more. Don't think about it.' Alex held her hand in both of his. He leaned over her and freed one hand so that he could put his arm around her shoulders. He laid his face beside hers on the pillow. 'It's all over and you're safe. Oh, Ronnie, my darling, darling Ronnie . . . You're safe, you're with me, that's all that matters.'

'But the baby . . .' she whispered.

'There'll be other babies, if you want them, but not until you're ready. You're the important one, Ronnie – you're the most important person in the world to me.'

'No. I didn't mean that. I meant . . . Alex, I was *pregnant*, and it wasn't your baby. You'll never be able to forgive me – I'll never be able to forgive myself.'

'You will,' he said steadily, 'because I already have forgiven you. I know what happened. It's just as you said: you were silly and it went further than you meant. It wasn't your fault.'

'It *was*!' Veronica cried. 'Alex, for God's sake, *stop treating me like a child*.'

There was a shocked silence. Alex lifted his head and stared at her.

442

Veronica stared back, frightened but defiant. He opened his mouth to speak but she forestalled him.

'I'm sorry, Alex, but you've got to stop protecting me. I'm not a child. I'm a grown woman. I've got to take responsibility for my own actions. I can't go on hiding behind other people. I can't go on behaving like someone who's never been allowed to grow up. Can't you see that?' She took a deep breath. 'Since I've been in here, I've had time to think. I've been behaving like a little girl, wanting my own way, wanting life to be easy and pleasant and fun, and always feeling dissatisfied, as if there was something missing. Well, there was. I wanted to be grown up, like Sue and Clare and – and Kathy, but I was frightened of it. Well, I'm not frightened of it any more.' She added in a subdued tone, 'I don't know how I ever could have been.'

'You're right,' Alex said at last. 'We have been protecting you – all of us. You seemed to need it somehow, as if you really were still a child. Just lately I've been wondering whether we should. I could see that you needed to grow up, but I couldn't see what to do about it.'

'I suppose it started with Mummy and Daddy,' she said. 'They always kept me in a cocoon, as if I were something precious.'

'And so you were. So you are – to all of us.'

'Nobody,' she said, 'ought to be that precious.'

They were silent again, and then Alex said, 'There's something I have to tell you, Veronica.'

'What?' For a moment, her eyes held the kind of fear that had always made him want to protect her from unpleasant truths. 'What's happened?'

'I'm sorry,' he said. 'This is just about the worst time to have to tell you this . . . Your father's not very well, Ronnie. He—'

'Daddy? Not well? What's the matter with him?' She struggled to sit up.

'He's had a slight heart attack,' Alex said carefully. 'It's not a serious one, but it's a warning. He's in the Springfield Hospital.' He took a breath and then said, 'That's why I've been going to the Grange. His doctor told him a little while ago that his heart was failing. It could give out at any time. He wanted to set everything in order, and he asked me—'

'Daddy's heart could fail at any time and you *never told me*?' Veronica was scrambling out of bed, feeling for her slippers. 'I've got to go to him.'

'Ronnie—'

'That is just the sort of thing I mean,' she blazed, dragging on her dressing-gown. 'Protecting me – not telling me things. He could have *died* – do you realise that? And I'd never have had the chance of being with him, of telling him . . . And what would you have done then, the lot of you? Pretended it hadn't happened? Pretended he'd gone away on holiday? Oh, for heaven's sake, surely I never seemed to be *that* much of a child!'

'Ronnie, what are you doing?'

'I'm coming home, of course,' she snapped. 'I don't need to be in here being mollycoddled. I'm perfectly all right. I want to go over to Springfield and I want to go *now*.'

'Ronnie, you've got no clothes here.'

'Then I'll come out in my dressing-gown,' she said, standing before him, and to his astonishment she looked suddenly taller, stronger, a different Veronica. 'Go and tell the nurse, Alex, while I collect my things together. I'll leave those flowers and chocolates – they can have them. And then bring the car round. We'll go home and pack whatever we need, and then we're going to his hospital. I want to be with my father and mother.'

Brian's death had been reported in all the newspapers and on television as well. There were pictures of the car, smashed on the rocks at the foot of the cliff, and a photograph they had got from somewhere of Veronica and Alex on their wedding day. There was no mention of Veronica's miscarriage, and although people could have drawn their own conclusions, she and Brian were referred to simply as 'friends'.

Clare and Martyn read the reports together. They sat on the sofa, holding hands, the newspaper spread across their laps. Clare turned her face into Martyn's shoulder, tears running down her cheeks.

'It's so awful, Martyn. Poor Veronica. And poor Brian, too. Whatever they'd done – whatever he'd done – he didn't deserve that.'

'D'you think it really was his baby?' Martyn asked. 'I mean, could she know for certain?'

'She seemed pretty sure. Yes, I think it was. Oh, I know she was silly, Martyn, but he shouldn't have taken advantage of her like that, and especially after Kathy. You wouldn't have thought he'd want to do the same thing to another man.'

'I don't know,' Martyn said. 'Brian was in a funny mood these past few months. He took the business with Kathy pretty hard, you know. He talked about not wanting to be tied down, just having fun – but I don't think it was fun, not really. I don't think he ever really got over her.'

'I know you think she treated him badly,' Clare said, 'but it wasn't really her fault, you know. Brian seemed to sweep her away, and she didn't know any different to begin with. When she met Terry, she did what she thought was the only thing possible – wrote and told Brian their engagement was over. If he'd accepted that . . . Oh, what's the use of going over it again?'

'I know, but you're right really. There isn't any reason why a girl shouldn't be allowed to break off an engagement if she really thinks it's a mistake.' Martyn looked at her. 'The trouble with Brian was that he could never take no for an answer. He was my oppo, Clare, and I tried to stick up for him, and I even persuaded myself he was right, but just lately – well, I could see that he ought to have given way. He thought he could own her, and he couldn't. Nobody can own another person.'

Clare was silent for a while, then she said softly, 'There was a time when I was scared about us too, Martyn. But we're all right now. Aren't we?'

'Yes,' he said. 'Yes, we're all right now.'

They sat quietly for a few minutes and then Clare said, 'I'd like to go and see Kathy. Could we hire a car for a day and go over to the Grange?'

'D'you think we should? I mean, you told me about Commander Curtis being ill, and Alex and Veronica will be over there. They won't want us.'

'They don't have to have us. It's Kathy·I want to see. Brian was still her husband. I know it was all over, but they were still married and she's the one who'll have to make arrangements. She needs her friends with her, Martyn. We can leave the children with Mum and Dad.'

'Yes,' he said. 'Yes, we'll hire a car. We'll go today.' He put his arms around her and drew her close. 'Oh, Clare, I've been so miserable lately. Things just haven't seemed to be going right for us. And ever since I started to think about staying on in the Navy, you seemed to get further and further away from me.'

'I didn't want you to stay in,' she said honestly. 'I felt let down. I felt as if the Navy was more important than me.'

'It isn't.' He kissed her lips. 'Nothing's more important to me than you and the kids, Clare. And all this . . .' He nodded towards the newspaper on their laps. 'All this has made me realise what's really important. I'm not staying in the Navy. I'm coming out at thirty.' He gave her a rueful grin. 'You know, I think I was just scared of coming out. The Navy's a world of its own: it looks after you and takes the responsibility off your shoulders. And you were right when you said the wives took all the burden, they do, but from now on, *I'm* taking responsibility. I know I'll still be away a lot in the next few years, but I'll give you all the help I can while I'm here, and after that we'll settle down in Civvy Street and have a proper family life.'

'Oh, Martyn,' she said, and gave him a hug. For a moment they held each other close and then she drew away and gave him a rueful smile. 'But you know, you don't have to do that. You see, I've been thinking too – about people trying to own each other. We're very close – we always have been – but that doesn't give either of us the right to make big decisions about the other's life. And ever since I've started to make something of my drawing, well, I've realised just what it's like to be able to do something that means a lot to you. Drawing's my thing, it's a part of me and it's an important part, and I've got something else to tell you about that, in a minute – something good. And the Navy's an important part of you.'

'But if it's making you unhappy—' Martyn began.

Clare shook her head. 'It was me that was making myself unhappy,' she said honestly. 'To begin with, I accepted the fact that you'd have to be away a lot. I knew it from the start and I didn't see any reason to complain. It was better than not having you at all! But lately, well, I know everyone gets a bit fed up, but I let it get on top of me somehow. I forgot how important the life is to you. I forgot that you always did say you wanted to stay in.' She put her arms round him again. 'We can manage, the children and I, and there will be times when we can be together for long periods. The main thing is that we both know what's really important to us, and that we don't ever forget it.'

Martyn sat without speaking for a few moments. Then he rested his cheek against hers and said huskily, 'Nothing else will ever be as important to me as you are, Clare. No matter how far apart we are.'

'And nothing,' she answered softly, 'will ever be as important to me as you.'

Kathy was given the news of Brian's death by a policeman who drove up to the Grange and told her, in the kitchen. She sat there, white-faced, listening as he gave her the details in a brogue as rich as Devonshire cream, and then he put the kettle on and made her a cup of tea.

'Is there anyone who can be with you, my dear? Your mum and dad, be they around?'

Kathy shook her head. 'I work here. I'm the housekeeper.'

'Your employers, then? Should I call someone?'

'They're not here,' she said dully. 'Commander Curtis was taken ill this morning. He's in hospital having tests and Mrs Curtis is in there, waiting. I ought to be with her . . .'

'Don't they have a daughter?' The policeman was from the next village and knew the Curtises slightly and by repute. 'I'm sure I've heard tell—'

'Yes. She lives in Tavistock. Her name's Mrs Challoner – Veronica Challoner.'

'Veronica Challoner?' He stared at her, then rubbed his face. 'I didn't realise . . .' He shook his head, looked at her again, and then said quietly, 'There was a Mrs Veronica Challoner in the car just before it happened. She fell down the cliff. She'm not killed,' he said quickly as Kathy gave a cry and started to her feet. 'She'm in hospital – she'll be all right.'

'Oh, how dreadful. How awful. Poor Alex. Poor Mrs Curtis. And Commander Curtis – he's ill himself.' The numbness that had spread over her as he gave her the news was transforming itself to an ache, as if cold limbs were beginning to feel the pain of returning life. She dragged her mind back to Brian. 'What do I have to do now?'

'Well, there'll be an inquest, see, and then you can arrange the funeral. You and your husband –' he looked embarrassed '– you were separated, like, is that right?'

'Yes, but I was still next of kin.'

'I'm afraid you'll have to deal with all the arrangements, then. The undertaker will help you. There'll be a death certificate . . .' He looked at her. 'I'm sorry, maid. 'Twould be best if you could find someone to help you. A friend, like . . .'

'Yes.' There was only Alex, Kathy thought, and he would be occupied with Veronica and the Curtises. Clare would help, but there was no way for her to get to the Grange, and Martyn had been Brian's friend. She dragged her mouth into a smile for the policeman's sake. 'I'll manage. Thank you for coming to tell me.'

'All part of the job.' He stood up and picked up his helmet. He was a middle-aged man, probably not far off retirement. He had probably told scores of people their nearest and dearest had met with accidents and died, Kathy thought, even in this quiet part of Devon. 'All part of the job. Not a very pleasant part, but it has to be done. You sure you'm all right now, my dear?'

'Yes.' She stood up, found her smile again. 'Yes. Thank you.'

He went, doubtfully, as if it didn't seem right to be leaving her alone, and Kathy sat down again, staring in front of her. The tea stood untouched. The house was very quiet.

Brian, dead. It was impossible to take in. Brian couldn't be dead. He wasn't old enough. He was too healthy, too strong. He wasn't ready.

He hadn't even finished divorcing her.

Brian, dead.

Kathy tried to picture it. The policeman hadn't known much. Brian and Veronica had evidently quarrelled and she'd been running away from him, trying to climb down the cliff, when the car had gone over. What had they been doing? Why had Veronica been with him, and why had she been running away? Kathy could imagine only too well. She felt bitterly sorry for Veronica, and at the same time angry with her. When a girl had a man like Alex for a husband, what was she doing messing about with someone else?

She was aware, too, of another emotion, an emotion that was slowly overwhelming all the others. It made her think of Brian as he had been: bright and breezy, free and easy, the typical sailor, like a gale of fresh sea air blowing into her life and sweeping her away on the current of his personality. Scooping her into his arms, smothering her with kisses, refusing to take no for an answer; making her laugh, making her love him, making her say yes, yes, yes . . .

It made her want to cry.

She thought of their first engagement, her proud delight in showing him off to her friends. And then the separation, the loneliness, as if the tide had gone out, leaving her high and dry on a solitary beach. Her growing friendship with Terry, the ease she had felt in his company, the disturbing knowledge that she shouldn't be engaged to Brian – 'didn't deserve' to be, as she'd said to Clare, as if she were somehow unworthy of his love.

The 'Dear John'. And Brian's return, once again refusing to take no for an answer. His determination to win her back, a determination so intense that it had convinced her, as if she'd no longer had a will of her own, as if Brian had taken over all her senses.

Perhaps he had. And perhaps that was what he'd done to Veronica.

But he didn't deserve to *die* for it, she thought passionately. He didn't have to be punished that much.

She bowed her head and rested it on her arms on the table, and began to cry. And recognised the emotion she felt for what it truly was.

Grief.

Veronica was still pale when she arrived at the hospital, but she was composed and quiet. She tiptoed into the room where her father was, and went up to his bed. She bore a huge sheaf of flowers and a golfing magazine, which she laid on the table, and then looked at him.

'And just what do you think you're doing, frightening us all like that?'

Keith Curtis raised his eyebrows. He was sitting up and there didn't seem to be much wrong with him, but he had an oxygen cylinder and mask by his bed.

Veronica noticed them and bit her lip. She looked at him again, drawing her brows together in a frown. 'I've been really worried and you look as fit as a flea.'

'I am,' he said. 'There's nothing wrong with me at all. They're keeping me prisoner.'

'Oh, Daddy.' Veronica dropped on her knees by the bed, the teasing note gone from her voice. 'Daddy, do you realise what you did to me? You could have died and I wouldn't have known till it was too late. Why didn't you tell me you were ill?'

'I wasn't. It was just a warning.'

'Don't make excuses!' There was real anger in her voice, and he blinked in surprise. 'Alex and Mummy have told me everything. You were trying to protect me, but I don't want to be protected. I want to be grown up – a woman – I want to be useful. Not a child. Not a doll. A real, useful woman.' She took his face between her hands and kissed it fervently. 'Now, you are not to keep anything from me again, and you are to let me help. I'm going to stay at the Grange while you're in here, and for as long as you want when you come out. Is that understood?'

'Message received and understood,' he said solemnly, 'but don't do too much. You're not fit yourself.' His face softened. 'My poor Ronnie – what's been happening to you?'

'Nothing that doesn't happen to thousands of silly young women,' she said soberly, 'but the end was rather worse than it usually is . . . I've been very stupid, Daddy, and I've been very lucky. It's made me see a lot of things more clearly.' She took a deep breath. 'I know what the doctors have told you, but there's something I want to tell you too. As soon as my doctor says it's all right, Alex and I are going to have a baby. Probably lots. And they'll need two grandfathers. One simply isn't enough.' She stood up and looked down at him. 'Stay alive, Daddy, please. Stay alive, for all of us.'

As Clare had expected, Kathy was almost pathetically grateful and pleased to see them. She fell into Clare's arms, sobbing, and Martyn made more tea while they sat at the kitchen table and went through the whole story. He was shocked and sobered by Kathy's grief: for some reason, he had not expected it. She and Brian had parted, were divorcing – he hadn't thought of her as still having feelings for her husband. They didn't evaporate just like that, she told him. And whatever you felt – or didn't feel – for someone, it was tragic that their life should end in such a way.

'So what happens next?' Clare asked.

Kathy shrugged. 'There'll be an inquest. I suppose they'll call it accidental death – what else could it be? Then we can have the funeral. The welfare officer's been to see me – now that he's dead, they're taking an interest again.' Her voice was bitter. 'They're being quite helpful, actually, taking a lot of it off my shoulders. I can have his ashes scattered at sea if I like.'

'He'd have liked that,' Martyn said. 'That's what he would have wanted.'

'Yes. That's what I thought. And then there's just the financial situation to sort out. Everything's mine now. There'll be some money to come from the house – not much, but it'll help – and I get a widow's allowance from the Navy, and an allowance for Timothy.' She looked at them with sudden anguish. 'I said no, it didn't seem right, but we were still married, and as far as they're concerned Timothy's . . .' She took a deep, shuddering breath. 'It's for him, so I suppose I'll take it.'

They were silent for a few minutes. Clare glanced at Martyn and said, 'What will you do when it's all over? You know you'll be welcome to come and stay with us for a while.'

Kathy shook her head. 'I'll stay here for a while. The Curtises need me. And Mum's rung up: she says they want me to go home and see them – and take Timmy. It seems a shame, doesn't it, that it takes something like this to make Dad want to see his grandson . . . But as long as the Commander and Mrs Curtis want me here, I'll stay. I've got to earn a living somehow, after all.'

After a while, she and Clare cooked a meal while Martyn took Timothy for a walk in the garden. The two girls talked quietly together, reminiscing about the early days of their courtships and marriages, sometimes weeping a little, sometimes finding laughter. They ate together, with Timothy in his highchair at the end of the table, banging his spoon and opening his mouth wide for helpings of mashed carrot.

As dusk fell and Kathy put on the lights, Clare said that they must go. 'I'll come again,' she said, hugging Kathy. 'I'll come again as soon as I can.'

They drove away. In a week, Martyn would be away again, but she hoped that this would be their last separation for a while. She hoped they would be able to stay in Tavistock, but she was prepared now to accept a change, provided they could be together.

As they pulled out of the drive, another car turned in. For a moment, Clare thought it was Alex and Veronica, coming home from the hospital, but then she realised that the car was an unfamiliar one.

She turned her head, and then stared at Martyn. 'Do you know who that was?'

'No. Didn't notice. Was it someone we know?'

'Yes,' she said, turning her head to gaze after the disappearing car. 'Yes, it was. It was Terry . . .'

Terry came into the kitchen and took Kathy into his arms immediately. Kathy, too bewildered to protest, laid her head against his shoulder and burst into tears.

'Oh, Kathy,' he said. 'My poor, poor Kathy. My poor darling.'

They stood for a long time until her sobs began to diminish, then he led her to a chair and sat her down, keeping his arms about her as he used one foot to drag another chair close. He kissed her face and stroked her hair, and used a tea-towel to mop up the tears. She wept again, and he waited patiently and then repeated the process.

At last, she lifted her head and gave him a shaky smile. 'What are you doing here?'

'Repairing flood damage, it seems,' he said. 'Kathy, I had to come. I saw it in the papers. I had to come to you.'

'But Sheila?'

'I told Sheila about you from the beginning,' he said quietly. 'She knew when you came to London that time. We talked about you. She said I must come.'

'Oh. I see. So you've got to go back to her? You've only come—'

'No,' he said. 'I've come because I want you back. We should be together, Kathy. We belong together – you, and me, and Timothy. Sheila knows that. She knew from the beginning that I still loved you.'

'But you told me—'

'I was trying to convince myself,' he said ruefully. 'I tried hard to believe it, but it was always you, Kathy. It's always, always been you.'

Kathy was silent. She thought of all that had happened, all the pain and unhappiness and sadness that had been caused. And now, it seemed, there was happiness after all to be found, but at what a cost.

'I don't know, Terry,' she said. 'It's too soon . . . I can't even begin to think of anything else yet.'

'I know,' he answered. 'I don't want you to be upset, Kathy. Just remember that I'm here. As a friend. As Timothy's father. As whatever you want me to be.'

Kathy looked at him, at his lean, quiet face, at the dark eyes that could be so intent, so passionate, so deeply loving. She put out her hand and covered his with her own. 'I will,' she said. 'It was always you for me as well, Terry. I'll remember.'

And although none of them knew it, it was at that same instant that Veronica and Alex, leaving the hospital, turned to each other and kissed. And Martyn, driving back across the moor, stopped the car and took Clare in his arms.

'We'll be all right now. We've got each other. We're so, so lucky . . .'